Escape and Honor

The Legacy of Afreean Book 1

Lilly Grace Nichols

Lilly Grace Nichols

Book Cover and Maps by Lilly Grace Nichols

Edited by Logan Pyron

ISBN: 979-8-9920851-0-5

First edition—2024

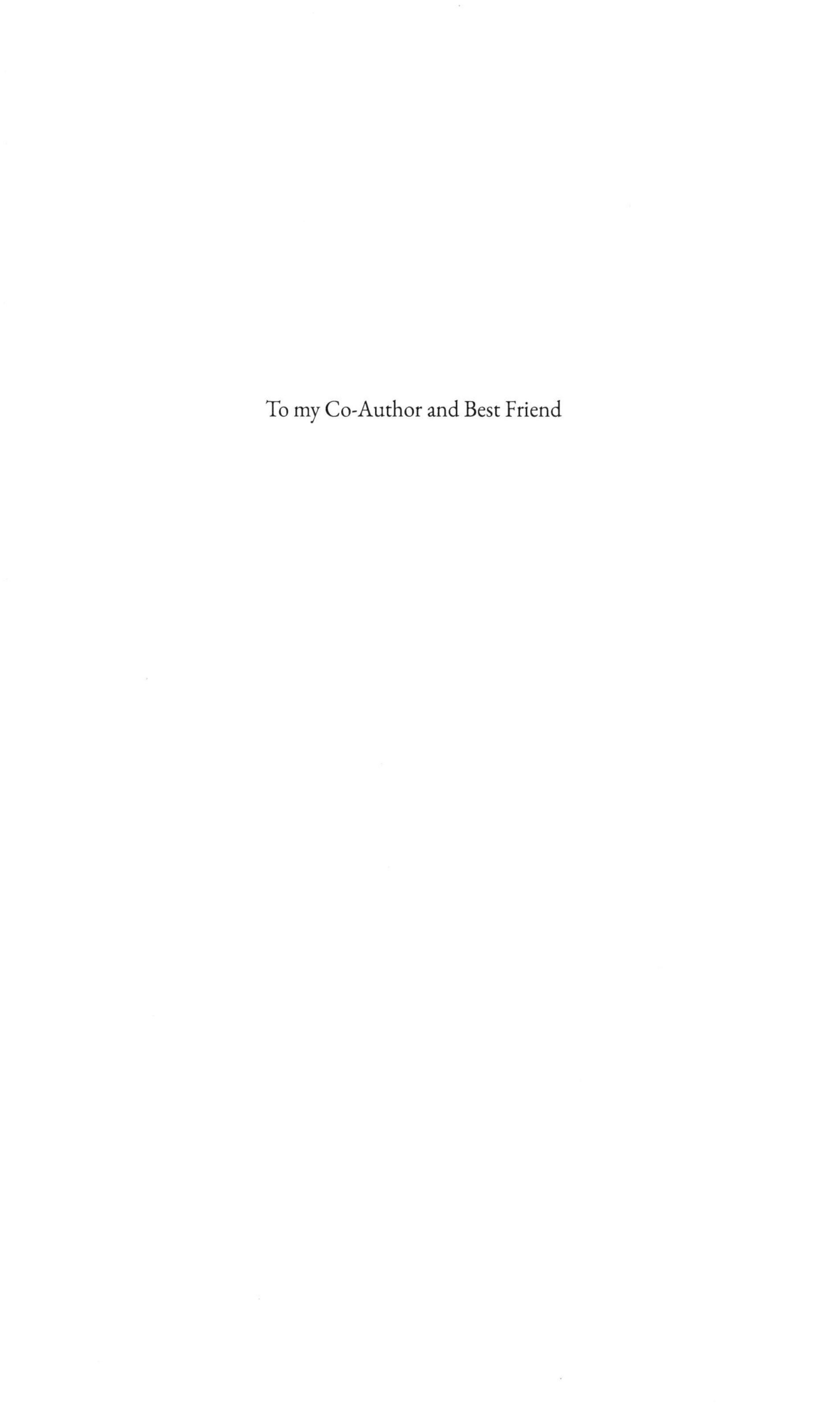

To my Co-Author and Best Friend

The Deltide Chain
Xich
Trivsau
Quazesig
Verlim
Pon-Yelum
Urbselva
Entransen Mts
Entransen Lake
Silvas
Averi
To Igrium
The Continent Of Caloi
To Frigac

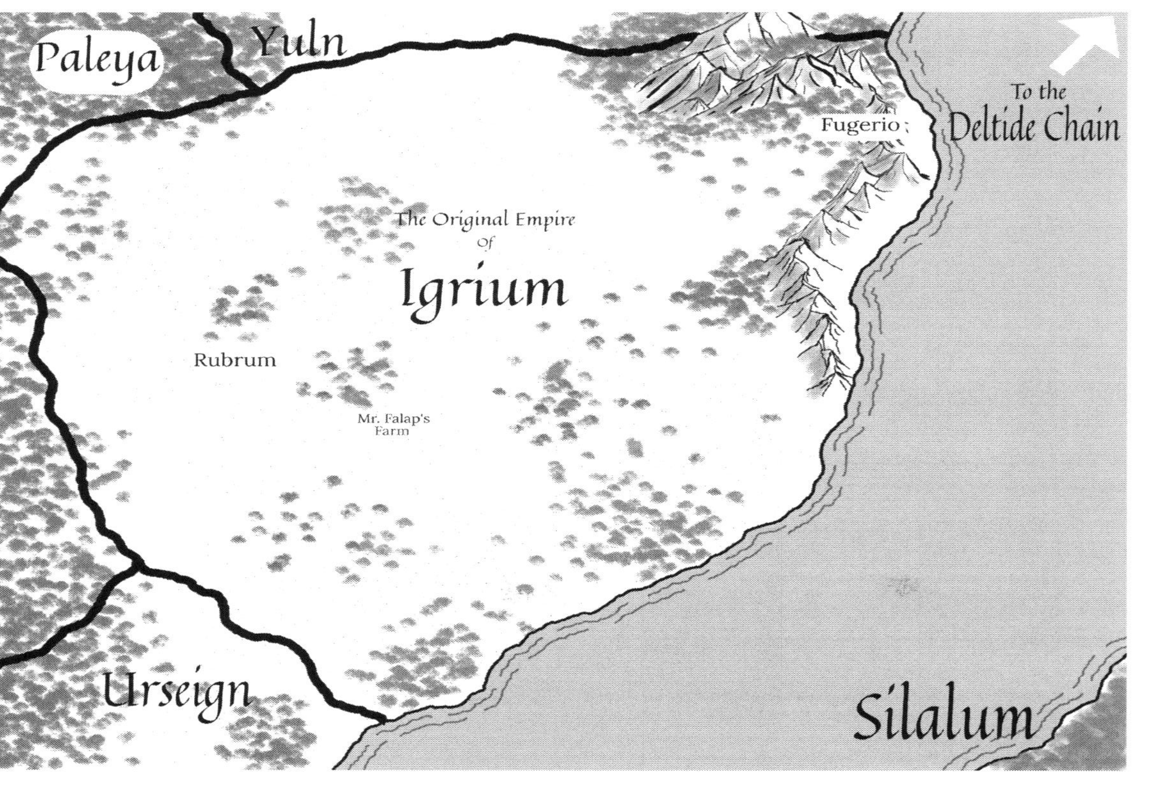
Paleya
Yuln
To the
Deltide Chain
Fugerio
The Original Empire
Of
Igrium
Rubrum
Mr. Falap's
Farm
Urseign
Silalum

Chapter One

The robotic android stared at Tetra Cairn with its large, semi-human eyes. There was no depth to its violet gaze, but that didn't make the choice of her next actions any easier.

She wiped the raindrops from her forehead as she stepped forward out of her platoon's uniform line. Second Lieutenant Tarson watched Tetra through narrowed eyes as she held out a throwing ax for her trainee to take. Tetra stopped in front of the tall woman and gripped the ax's leather-wrapped handle with her left hand.

As quick, and as powerful, as a griffin, Lieutenant Tarson grabbed her wrist and squeezed it. Tetra's heart jumped with fear, but she didn't let it show as her commanding officer lowered to meet her eyes.

"Don't try me today, Cairn." Tarson spat, her eyes glittering dangerously. "I'm not in the mood for any of your games. Hit that android clean in the chest like I know you can."

Letting the silent threat stir the air between them, Tarson let go of Tetra's wrist and stepped back. Tetra watched her commanding officer for a few moments, wiping pesky raindrops from her eyes, then turned to face her target.

The stone-still android continued to stare at Tetra from across the training yard. She met its soulless, violet gaze and moved into position, raising the single-headed ax above and behind her head.

One hit; that's all it would take. Tetra eyed the android's armored chest. She inhaled deeply, then exhaled. She could do this. She had hit targets from further distances than this, even moving ones. Yet her skills with a throwing ax were not the problem in this moment.

The *segione* tally scars covering her right arm tingled as if invisible bugs crawled underneath her skin. She met the android's eyes again, and a tremor went through her upraised arm. Despite her knowing the training-droid was only a robot, it was still made to look like a Silvanian soldier—from the hated enemy kingdom of Silvas—with its dark olive-toned, silicone skin; dark hair; and green-tinged armor. She had already dealt a killing blow to a Silvanian look-alike just yesterday in training, so she should be able to do it now. But as she stabbed the other training droid in the chest, she had felt herself becoming more numb to the action—just like everyone at Norland Military Academy wanted all of their soldiers to feel.

The android ahead of her lifted the longsword it held in both its hands and burst into a sprint with inhuman speed. In those few heartbeats, Tetra made her decision. She threw the ax and watched it spin towards the oncoming android. The ax's blade hit the android's arm, and the longsword fell out of its grip with a clatter upon the concrete ground. The robot stopped suddenly and bent down to pick up its misplaced weapon.

Tetra was there before it could reach it. She slammed her shoulder into its metal chest and knocked it down. As it moved to get up, she grabbed the android's own sword with both her hands, lifted it, and pressed the sharp side of the blade into the now-sitting robot's throat. She locked eyes with the droid, and it gave her a slight nod—the sign that she had defeated it.

"*CAIRN!*" Tarson's yell rose above the steady rain.

Tetra cringed and slowly turned around—longsword still in her hands—to face her commanding officer's rage. Lieutenant Tarson marched towards her, a glower reddening her narrow face. Tetra forced herself to keep her gaze lowered and away from the daggers in Tarson's eyes. She tightened her grip on the longsword's hilt and wondered, for a moment, what might happen if she used it to defend herself.

The thought fled as Lieutenant Tarson stopped a couple steps away from her. "Put the weapon down," she growled.

Tetra half-turned back to the android that was still sitting on the ground and handed the longsword back to it. Even if she did try using it for defense, it would only bury her deeper into the trouble she had brought upon herself.

When she turned back to her original position, Lieutenant Tarson continued, "What was that?"

Tetra stayed silent. Anything she said now would only make the Second Lieutenant angrier.

"I thought I told you to hit that android clean in the chest, not to disarm it!" Her commanding officer took another step forward and grabbed the collar of Tetra's shirt, jerking her forward. "What are you trying to do to me, Cairn? Are you trying to thwart my authority again?"

Tetra's heart skipped a beat, but she continued to keep her gaze away from Lieutenant Tarson's. She had no ill will towards her commanding officer's authority; she just didn't respect the way she seemed to get it.

Lieutenant Tarson snarled and raised her hand. Tetra's head jerked back at the stinging slap. She sucked in a sharp breath through her teeth and squeezed her eyes shut so her commanding officer wouldn't see the glare in her eyes. The steady rainfall concealed most other noises in the training yard, but Tetra knew her platoon well enough to know they were whispering jeers and holding in laughter at the sight. She blinked open her eyes and hoped it looked like she was blinking rainwater out of them and not trying to push back the hot tears trying to escape.

She turned her face forward again and couldn't help but cringe at the sharp sound of a blade being drawn from its sheath. Lieutenant Tarson held the serrated, segione dagger with one hand and grabbed Tetra's right wrist with the other. Shame slid into Tetra's stomach like slime as she looked down at the tally marks that scarred her right arm.

Were they even worth it? A part of her wondered...but she pushed the thought aside before it could go any further. Being a brainwashed killer wasn't who she was—no matter how much dishonor was heaped upon her and her family name for rejecting it.

She gritted her teeth to keep from crying out as Lieutenant Tarson twisted her arm sharply to find an empty space. After years of disobedience, there was almost no clear skin on that arm; not even on her dark, bumpy birthmark that covered the inside of her elbow and matched the others covering her skin.

Tetra squeezed her eyes shut and clenched her jaw as the dagger's serrated teeth carved into her arm. Just as quick, Lieutenant Tarson lifted the weapon and let go of her wrist. Tetra breathed in a shaky breath and opened her eyes. Blood slowly bubbled out of the small wound.

Her commanding officer leaned down, inches away from her nose. "Don't expect the mercy of a tally scar the next time you do something like this."

Because the public humiliation of a segione scar is ***merciful****,* she thought bitterly.

Tarson continued, "You're running out of room for any more of those; and I hate that someone from my platoon might end up with one—" Lieutenant Tarson paused for a moment, as if whatever thought she was about to speak next was too horrible to say. Yet she did, "—but if this continues, I won't hesitate to give you a *malscar*."

Tetra's heart dropped into her tightening stomach. She couldn't help the flash of horror that swept across her face before she regained composure. Lieutenant Tarson must've seen it because she smiled wickedly.

"So don't get to that point, Cairn." Her smile faded back into its usual sneer. "Be thankful I've warned you ahead of time."

Dread, not thankfulness, continued to tighten itself around her stomach like a noose. She continued to say nothing as Lieutenant Tarson took a step back and turned partway to address the rest of her watching platoon.

In a voice that rose above the rain, she said, "The rest of you will continue this exercise with Lieutenant Grahm." Then she turned back to face Tetra. Tetra lifted her eyes for a moment and her heartbeat quickened at the fiery danger looming in her commanding officer's gaze. "While you and I are going to have a little chat."

LIKE THE REST OF Lieutenant Tarson's "chats", Tetra was forcibly led to Norland's "correction room" and given the school's mandated punishment for a fifth-year student's disobedience to a commanding officer: five lashes.

Another slash of searing pain whipped across Tetra's back and the back of her arm. She dug her nails into her palms as a small cry escaped her lungs. The manacles keeping her chained to the wall dug into her wrists as she slumped down to her knees.

"We're done. Here—" Something landed softly on the floor next to Tetra, but she didn't move. "I sent for a medbot to come and take care of this. Once it's finished, come to my office."

Between her pained, quick breaths, Tetra replied, "Yes...ma'am."

Lieutenant Tarson stepped closer with heavy footfalls and unlocked the manacles. Tetra's arms fell as if weights were tied to her wrists. She hissed as the muscles in her back screamed at the sudden movement, and she lowered herself to the floor in a pitiful heap to ease the pain.

"I wish I could say I hope you'll learn from this, but I have no hope for you anymore." Tarson's footsteps receded. "You're a disgrace to the Cairn name, trainee. Don't expect the emperor to show mercy to you this time around once I've reported all of this."

Tetra cringed at the comment and the pain throbbing through her torn back. The correction room's door opened and closed behind her with a hydraulic hiss, leaving her alone in the quiet pain.

She heaved in a deep breath but let it out in a grunt as the back of her ribs pressed into her torn back muscles. Even in the small breaths there was no relief—just like what always happened when she received this punishment.

Tetra slowly shook her head at herself with a shaky sigh. Hadn't she thought it would be easier this time? Why was that always her thought process before doing something disobedient? Why did she think like that? Why did she keep doing this to herself? No one except for her seemed to be affected by her actions; no mindsets seemed to change, and the opinions of others didn't seem to differ from their usual. The only thing she seemed capable of doing was dragging her family's name through the mud and hurting herself and the one person she had befriended.

The unpleasant memories from that experience brought forth the sludgy pile of guilt cemented in the back of her mind. She gritted her teeth as nausea bubbled upwards from her stomach. These thoughts only ever seemed to come when the physical pain was too much to turn her focus on.

Will I ever be free of these? Tetra rolled her eyes at herself. *No, because straudwin cowards don't get to be free of their guilt.* Her gaze moved to her segione scars and, with careful movements, she twisted her arm to see the newest one. It was still bleeding, but the sting had left (or it was just overshadowed by the new, throbbing pain in her back).

More nausea filled her stomach, and Tetra pulled her legs up to her chest as much as she could without stretching her back muscles. Lieutenant Tarson's threat came back to her mind and circled threateningly like a griffin from the Clan of Scavengers would around a carcass it was about to consume. If she did anything else, she would get a *malscar*. The skin of her face tingled at the thought. She was already ridiculed for her arm of segione tallies and her birthmarks...how much worse would it be if she received the greatest shame the army had to offer? (Besides dishonorable discharge, of course—her parents' honorary will specifically stated she had to serve Igrium in some way, and Emperor Ignis was keen on keeping all of their wishes as much as he could.)

Could she continue her stand against Igrium's hatred for all things that didn't succumb to its fearmongering authority with that threat hanging over her head?

Just as she had the thought, another one struck her: what would Emperor Ignis have to say when he read Lieutenant Tarson's newest report about his dishonorable legal charge? A trickle of fear sent a shiver through her taut muscles.

Before she could think on it further, however, the door to the correction room opened. Tetra turned herself over on the floor as a pear-shaped medbot floated into the room. It fixed its single eye lens upon Tetra and stopped in the air next to her.

"I was sent with orders by Lieutenant Tarson to help," it said in as much emotion as its robotic interface could allow.

Help. Tetra had a feeling her commanding officer hadn't used that specific word, but she nodded towards the robot.

"Thanks."

"Please sit up and I will take a look at the wounds."

Gritting her teeth, Tetra moved herself up onto her elbows. She used the wall to help get herself the rest of the way up and then leaned her shoulder against it. With even more difficulty, she took the shreds of a t-shirt she had been wearing and dropped it to the floor.

"Is that...good?" She asked between breaths.

"Yes."

The robot hovered over to Tetra and moved behind her back. Like all the other times, the medbot inspected her wounds, cleaned them with one of its antiseptic-filled appendages, then took a roll of bandages from one of the compartments built into its body and wrapped those around her torso. It also took care of her bleeding tally mark. Due to the nature of the punishment, Tetra was given no painkiller, per protocol.

"I am done." The robot moved to face Tetra; its long, spindly arms folding back into hidden compartments in its body. "Is there anything else I can do for you?"

Tetra opened her mouth to reply with a "no", but then she stopped herself. She bit her lip and flicked her gaze from the medbot to the floor, then back to the medbot. Should she mention the strange pains that had been wracking her body for the past month? She had been too afraid to go talk to any of the rotating doctors at Norland's infirmary because of their attitudes towards her. Yet this was only a medbot...

"Actually, I do have a question," she finally said.

The medbot's eye lens rotated slightly. "I will try to answer as best I can."

"I've been feeling these...strange pains for the past month."

"Where?"

"Um—everywhere."

At first, she only felt the fiery pains in random muscles, but they had steadily grown worse. As Tetra tried going to sleep even last night, the pains slowly came over her entire body. It felt like someone lit a fire inside her organs and burned every part of her—bones, muscles, nerves—from the inside out until even her skin was awash in the burning flames.

"What kind of pain is it?" The medbot asked with another rotation of its lens.

Tetra rubbed her thumb across her segione tallies. "It's—it's like a sharp, burning pain."

The medbot didn't reply immediately, although Tetra could tell it was processing her answers by the slow spinning of its eye lens. Finally, it stopped moving its lens and focused it on Tetra.

"I am sorry, Trainee Cairn, but I do not know what could be causing your pain," it replied. "My sensors say nothing is wrong with you besides your wounds, so I would suggest going to the infirmary for a more in-depth scan. They will be able to help you better than me."

That wasn't what Tetra wanted to do. She could already see the looks the doctors were going to give her in her mind's eye.

She held in a frustrated sigh and said, "I'm not sure I'll be doing that, but thanks anyway."

The robot nodded its box-like head. "I strongly advise going to the infirmary, but that is your decision to make. Good day, Trainee Cairn."

With that, it turned and floated out of the correction room. The door slid shut behind its retreating form. Before any unwanted thoughts could flood her brain again in the quiet atmosphere, Tetra turned her focus to the new white shirt lying in a heap where Lieutenant Tarson had thrown it. With careful movements that wouldn't upset the injuries on her back, she managed to get the shirt over her wrapped torso—just in time, too. The door opened again with a hydraulic hiss, and Tetra jerked her head in its direction. Her heart stuttered as Lieutenant Tarson's glowering countenance stepped into the dim room.

"Get up, *Cairn,*" the second lieutenant spat. "I was just given new orders: His Imperial Majesty wishes to speak with you."

Tetra's heart sank below her stomach. What would her legal guardian have to say about her disobedience now?

With shaky movements (from both pain and growing fear), Tetra used the wall to lift herself up from the ground and stepped forward to follow Lieutenant Tarson towards the office of Emperor Ignis himself.

Chapter Two

Aabir blocked Tycho Rissis' sword with his shield. He lunged with his own blade. Metal clashed against metal as his short sword slid off his opponent's armored shoulder. He rammed his shield into Tycho's and stabbed his blade into his opponent's stomach. Thunder rumbled as if the rainy sky itself was watching their sparring match, roaring approval for Aabir's winning blow.

Tycho grunted and pressed his sword-hand to his middle. "Straudwin!" He cursed.

Aabir removed his sword to his side, grinning triumphantly. He could not help the boast that escaped his lips. "I win."

Tycho's eyes blazed for a moment underneath his helmet. However, it quickly dissipated with his own matching grin. "Ah, you just got lucky." He waved Aabir's comment away. "If it wasn't raining, I'd be winning every one of these rounds."

"So, you are saying your skills depend on the weather?" Aabir raised his brow and gave his friend a pointed look.

"I guess." Tycho shrugged, then locked eyes with Aabir. "Again?"

Aabir opened his mouth to reply "yes", but their commanding officer, Second Lieutenant Denir, shouted above the hard rain before he could. "Trainees! Fall in!"

"Next time," Aabir told Tycho as he sheathed his sword.

They, along with the thirty-eight other teenage boys in their platoon, moved towards their commanding officer. With practiced precision, they all lined up in two rows, at attention, in front of Lieutenant Denir's intimidating presence. The lieutenant's dark eyes studied each one of them as he slowly paced down the line.

"If you all want to pass the exams coming up, I need to see better performance—especially from you, Jazeston." Lieutenant Denir stopped in front of Brutus Jazeston's bulky figure, "I've seen gelatscies quicker than you! And you, Warlin—" He turned his neck and locked eyes with Aquilo Warlin's fixed gaze, "What would your parents think if they saw that sloppy footwork I just witnessed from you?"

Aabir gulped and glanced out of the corner of his eye at his friend's set jaw. He knew it must be killing Aquilo to not be able to speak out against their commanding officer's verbal abuse. Thankfully, he had learned *some* self-control throughout his years at Norland and held his tongue.

Lieutenant Denir moved further down the line, calling out others and telling them what they had done wrong. With each name, Aabir mentally steeled himself for the verbal onslaught coming his way. He had seen the lieutenant observing him and Tycho's fight and knew there would be something said about the few mistakes he knew he had made.

"Rissis, I never knew *rain* would be your demise." Lieutenant Denir stopped in front of Tycho and stared him down. "Are you allergic to water? Is that what's wrong with you?"

Tycho, wisely, did not answer.

Water droplets flew off Lieutenant Denir's head as he shook it and gestured towards Aabir. "Sorrel beat you every single time, Rissis! I've never seen you do so badly, and I never want to see it again! Do I make myself clear?"

"Yes sir!" Tycho lifted his right fist to his chest in a salute.

Lieutenant Denir nodded sharply then turned his head towards Aabir. Aabir moved his gaze forward as the lieutenant stepped in front of him. Lieutenant Denir stared at him for a few tense, silent moments before stepping back and turning his attention to the entire platoon.

He raised his voice and said, "Sorrel, here, was the only one who actually did anything halfway correct today!"

Aabir blinked in surprise. Was that a public compliment? From Lieutenant Denir? This must be some crazy dream because nobody received compliments from the second lieutenant.

"I'm ashamed to call you all my platoon." Lieutenant Denir continued to pace, "All of you—full-blooded Igrians—beaten in our own game by someone of Silvanian descent? It's dishonoring, is what it is."

Aabir gritted his teeth at the jab. He could feel the stares of his surrounding platoon-mates but chose to keep his eyes forward. The safest thing to do was act as if his commanding officer's comment had not irked him.

"I better see some improvement by the time we get to Trivsau next week." Lieutenant Denir stopped his pacing, his eyes roving over them all. "Firstdein morning—o' five-hundred hours. Be at the train station on time or be punished. That's all for today. You're dismissed."

All forty trainees saluted him in precise unison, then dispersed towards the double doors leading out of the walled training yard. Aabir trailed behind Tycho as the group moved through the bare corridors that led to other outdoor training yards and into their platoon's specific armory/locker room. When Aabir finished taking his armor off and put his academy uniform on, he left with Tycho and Aquilo to head up to their dorm.

"I can't believe Lieutenant Denir said that!" Tycho exclaimed as the locker room door swung shut behind him. "*Allergic to water*? Ha! I'd like to see him try to fight in a downpour..."

"At least he didn't threaten you with your parents." Aquilo put his hands in his pockets with a side-glare aimed at Tycho. "I know I made some mistakes out there, but I didn't think my footwork was *that* bad." He lowered his chin with a frustrated sigh and added in a lowered voice, "Even if I was the 'star trainee' in the platoon they'd still find some fault with me, I'm sure."

Aabir glanced at him out of the corner of his eye then turned his neck in the opposite direction to face Tycho. "I'm sorry for bringing that down on you, Tycho."

He wanted nothing better than to complain with them both about what their commanding officer had commented, but he figured it would be best to remain silent on the subject. His friends—even if they did not see Aabir as Silvanian—shared similar views with Lieutenant Denir when it came to Silvas and the other kingdoms aligned with it. Yet that did not stop the comment from replaying in his head. Had he not proved himself enough to put an end to those comments?

"Eh, that wasn't your fault." Tycho shrugged as a grin split apart his frown. "Ya can't help it that you're his 'golden trainee'."

"Excuse me?"

Tycho nodded knowingly. "Yeah...you don't do anything wrong, you don't break the rules, you're the best swordsman in our platoon..." He shrugged again and elbowed Aabir in the ribs good-naturedly. "How couldn't that be the case?"

Aabir slapped his friend's arm away and rubbed his side. "Um...because I've never seen him show favoritism towards me—or anyone else for that matter?" Aabir glanced over at Aquilo again, "And if anyone was the favorite, wouldn't it be Aquilo?"

Aquilo snorted. "Definitely not." He raised his voice and looked over at Tycho pointedly, "Lieutenant Denir has *no* favorites."

"See?" Aabir turned to look back at Tycho and gestured with his thumb towards Aquilo. "Even Aquilo says it's not true, and he's smarter than both of us combined."

Tycho rolled his eyes and shook his head. "Well, if you all won't listen to me then I'll just stop talking."

"Oh? I've never seen a miracle before," Aquilo said.

Aabir tried to hold in a laugh, and it came out more as a snort. Tycho sent them both glares and opened his mouth to make some remark—proving Aquilo's point—but then they stepped into Norland's huge entrance hall and all their attentions were turned towards Lieutenant Tarson and the girl with the short, auburn hair and huge birthmarks being dragged along beside her.

Aabir could feel Aquilo tense up beside him. *Don't do it, don't do it, don't*—Aquilo's raised voice broke through his thoughts, "Traitor!"

The tall, arched ceilings echoed the word so all the other trainees and commanding officers milling about turned to stare at them for a moment. Aabir cringed and turned towards Aquilo just as Lieutenant Tarson barked out, "Shut up, Warlin!"

Aabir glanced back over at the second lieutenant, and he ended up locking eyes with Tetra Cairn. It only lasted a moment before Tetra looked away, but it was long enough to bring back the regretful memories and accusations he wished would stay locked up.

Lieutenant Tarson and Tetra both continued on their way out the entrance doors. To turn his focus onto something else other than the guilt and shame churning his stomach, Aabir looked over at Aquilo's glowering countenance.

"Why couldn't you keep your mouth shut?" He asked.

Aquilo shot him a withering glare and crossed his arms. "I have the right to talk to that traitor any way I like, even if she is my cousin." He turned his glare to the spot where Tetra had just been. "If she can go and drag the Cairn name through the mud, then I'm allowed to call her out on it. I may not share her family name, but everyone knows we're related—and the last thing my parents and I need is her dragging our reputation down along with her own."

Without waiting for a reply, he headed towards the back of the entrance hall. Aabir glanced over at Tycho and they both shared a "what are we to do" look, then followed after him among the others filling the grand hall. They walked underneath the balcony that spanned the length of the back and side walls and entered a smaller hallway.

Aabir glanced over at the infirmary's open entryway, then his gaze trailed to the hydraulic-closed door next to it. A shiver went down his spine as they passed the correction room, and he turned his gaze forward. *Don't think about that time. Don't think about that time. Don't think about it...*

"I wonder what she did this time." Tycho's voice, thankfully, brought Aabir's focus back to the present.

"What?" Aabir looked over at him.

"I said, 'I wonder what she did this time.'" Tycho raised his brow. "Are you alright?"

"I'm fine." Aabir scratched the back of his neck. "Just thinking."

Well, he was trying not to think of certain things.

"Does it by any chance have to do with a certain someone I just asked about?" A mischievous glint entered Tycho's eyes.

Aabir returned the look with a glare. "Not in the way you are thinking."

"OK, OK." Tycho nodded his head slowly, as if he did not believe Aabir but would let it slide. "Anyway, are you ready to go to Trivsau?"

Aabir silently thanked Deleyon for the subject change as they headed towards the stairway at the end of the hall.

"I guess." He said as they began ascending the stairs. "I haven't really thought about it."

"Well, I hear it's gonna be hot."

"I would assume so... it *is* a desert."

They ascended the rest of the stairs, and Aabir stepped up into a new corridor. A few other male trainees were moving up and down the hall, while the muffled sounds of talking and laughter came from behind some of the closed dorms. Aabir's heart almost leapt out of his ribcage as a huge ***BOOM*** resounded behind one of the doors. It was immediately followed by laughter and jeers. He rolled his eyes at himself and quickened his pace to keep up with Tycho.

"I've heard the food's pretty good, too." Tycho continued, unfazed by the possible sound of someone being pushed out of their bunk. "I wonder if we'll even get to eat it."

"Uh—maybe." Aabir replied, "We were able to eat the food in Magnae and Paleya, so..."

Honestly, he had not thought another thing about their upcoming trip to the capital city of Xich since Lieutenant Denir made the announcement last week. He knew they were going (he was not going to face the wrath of Lieutenant Denir ever again by forgetting), but it was just a thought in the back of his mind. The three fifth-year platoons took quarterly trips to different fortresses or centers of Igrian military power to get a glimpse of what they would all be doing after they graduated. Aabir always found them interesting, but their presence only reminded him of what he would be doing for the next four years of his life: fighting for an empire whose morals he did not even agree with.

Tycho nodded. "I hope you're right." They slowed to a stop, and he opened their dorm's door. "I'd like to get the full experience, y'know."

"Mm-hmm. I'm sure your stomach will not suffer."

They stepped into the dorm. Aabir moved over to his bunk and flopped down on it with a sigh.

"My stomach might not, but I know I will. Can you imagine what wearing armor there is going to feel like? My guts are gonna melt." He could hear the frown in Tycho's voice, "I hate the heat."

"You both talking about Trivsau?" Aquilo's voice came from the direction of their dorm's desk.

"Mm-hmm." Aabir grunted upward with his legs hanging off the bunk, and looked in his direction.

Aquilo did not look up from the open chardex on the desk; the device's holographic interface mirroring the pages of an open book. "I can't wait to go."

"A break from your parents?" Tycho pried.

Aquilo lifted his head and turned to face him. "Why else would I wanna go?"

"Fair point."

As they both continued to speak, Aabir rifled through the clothes in his drawers underneath his bunk and stuffed them in a backpack he also kept in one of the drawers.

"Ya leaving us?" Tycho asked.

Aabir turned his neck and looked up at him. "I'm not wasting my weekend here."

"That's also a fair point."

"Are you all staying?"

"Ha!" Tycho shook his head with a smirk. "Not in a million years."

"I would, but my parents told me I've gotta come home before we go to Xich." Aquilo frowned, his gaze focused on the stylus he was turning over in his fingers.

Tycho went over and put his hand on Aquilo's shoulder. "I hope you survive." His face was grave, but his eyes held a spark of humor.

Aquilo glared up at him. "Don't mock me, Rissis."

"I'm not!" Tycho put his hands up in surrender, and a smile finally broke across his face. "Well, I'm only halfway-joking. Honestly, Aquilo, your parents scare me. I truly hope you do survive whatever fate they have planned for you."

Aquilo's frown deepened but he did not reply. His silence told Aabir he agreed with Tycho.

There was a lull in the conversation and Aabir went back to finish packing. Right as he zipped his backpack up, a buzzing sensation went through his wrist. He stood up from his bunk and tapped the flat top of the tiny, oval device strapped around it. A small, semi-translucent screen appeared in the air above the rounded plate. He pinched the holographic screen with his fingers and made it wider by separating them. Then, he swiped his finger across "incoming call".

"Hey, Matha." He said as the screen changed and showed his mother's smiling face.

"Hello, Aabir." Her arched eyebrows lowered. "Are you in your dorm?"

"Hi, Mrs. Sorrel!"

Aabir jumped back at the sudden, loud noise and clinched his fist, almost punching Tycho in the face. He stopped himself when he realized who it was and shot his friend a glare before turning his attention back to the screen.

"Hello, Tycho." Matha said wryly.

Tycho pressed his face into the holonode's camera range. "Have you made any pomen pie?"

"No, I have not. They aren't in season yet, but I probably will in the next few weeks." Matha's eyes flicked between both their faces and a knowing smirk twisted one corner of her mouth. "But I'm sure that when I do Aabir will let you know."

Tycho grinned with a thumbs-up and stepped out of Aabir's personal bubble. "That's all I needed to know." Aabir watched as he climbed up into his own bunk. "I'll leave you alone now."

Aabir rolled his eyes with a smirk. "Anyway..." he locked eyes with Matha across the screen, "Did you need me for something?"

"I just wanted to ask if you could stop by the store on your way home to get some arla spice and Paleyan bread."

"Sure. I'm actually about to leave now."

"Good. I will go on and transfer some money to your account." She let out a weary sigh. "We will see you soon, then."

Aabir narrowed his eyes and studied her face. Now that he was looking, he could see the dark circles under her large, violet eyes—the same shade as his.

"Are you OK, Matha?" He asked.

"Yes..." She gave him a strange look.

"You just look tired."

Matha stared at him quietly for a few moments, and that is when Aabir noticed a glimpse of worry shadowing her soft features before she hid it with a shake of her head.

"Your sister has been keeping me on my feet all day." She gave a breathless laugh and Aabir could hear the fake lilt in her voice. She was hiding something; whether from him or from someone that might be listening in on their holocall. It did not matter. When Aabir got home, he would get to the bottom of it.

"Well then. In that case, I'll be home soon," he said.

Matha shot him a grateful glance. "Thank you, Aabir. We will see you soon. Love you."

"Love you, too. Bye."

He ended the call, turned the holonode off, and rolled his sleeve back over the device. He bent down and picked up his backpack by its straps before swinging it over his shoulders.

"I guess we'll be seeing you on Firstdein morning." Tycho broke the silence.

"Yeah." Aabir said distractedly, his thoughts converging on why his mother would be worried. "I'll see you all later."

"See ya, Aabir." Aquilo replied.

He headed towards the door, opened it, and exited his dorm. The door clicked shut behind him and he marched down the hall. One of his platoonmates—Septimus Boll—nodded towards him as they passed each other. Aabir nodded back, but he did not stop to talk like he normally would.

There were only a few times in his life that he remembered his matha ever being worried, and none of those times had been minor. There had been the time after his grandparents (her parents) died; the times when Igrian patrolmen raided their house on "surprise inspections" to make sure they were not secretly Silvanian spies; the moment when he told his parents about secretly taking the application test to join Norland (and being accepted into the school) to outwardly show that his family members were not loyal, Silvanian spies; and the time when he and Tetra Cairn were caught trying to escape Norland.

Aabir grabbed the wooden railing as he descended the flight of stairs. More trainees from his platoon passed by him, but he paid them little attention.

If Matha was sending him to get groceries, then that probably meant no one's life was in danger. Still, the fact that she seemed to be worried about someone overhearing them meant it might have something to do with their Silvanian background. Aabir himself was born and raised in the capital city of the Igrium Empire, Rubrum, but his parents moved here from Silvas with their families when they were both teenagers. So ever since Emperor Ignis declared war on Silvas and any other kingdom or empire that went against Igrium, those who descended from any of the Alliance Nations to the third generation were looked down upon in suspicion and contempt by most Igrians.

And yet... Aabir gritted his teeth as Second Lieutenant Denir's comment ran through his head again. He passed underneath the arched entryway into the entrance hall. He thought that by now his commanding officer—and everyone else at Norland—would no longer see him in a bad light. The last time he received a segione scar was months ago (and that was for being late to his first period class five times in a row). By all accounts, Aabir should have been the "golden trainee" like Tycho said.

No matter what their orders were during training exercises or what they were forced to learn in class, he did it. He had come to realize that his personal convictions did not matter when it came time to protect him and his family from the suspicions of Igrian authorities. It was not ideal by any means, but it was safe. No matter how much he wished he could, he would not do what Tetra Cairn did—throw caution to the wind and put himself in dangerous situations as blatant disobedience to Igrium's moral system.

Aabir blew a long sigh through his nose and acted as if he was ignoring the two guards stationed on either side of the academy's towering entrance doors. He pushed one of the heavy wooden doors barely open and slipped out between them onto the veranda spanning across the white building's front. Rain fell in sheets beyond the veranda's flat roof, blocking the view of even the towering everpines that covered Norland's walled grounds.

Aabir breathed out another sigh and shifted the straps of his backpack to a more comfortable position. He was not going to let a little rain stop him. Not caring about the other guards stationed on the veranda, he jumped down the stairs and ran like a wild man through the pouring rain. Nothing was going to stop him from figuring out, and trying to fix, the newest problem facing his family.

Chapter Three

"OH, TETRA..." EMPEROR IGNIS' eyes were closed as he rubbed his temples, "Why didn't you just hit that droid in the chest?"

Tetra pressed her lips into a thin line and glanced down at the small puddle of water forming around her wet boots. Despite the towel she had been given to dry off before entering the emperor's private office, her hair and clothes were still soaking wet. Surrounded by opulent furniture and real canvas paintings hanging on the walls in gilded frames, she looked like a half-dead scurrus without its bushy tail. It didn't help that the emperor himself was sitting at his beautiful, dark cherry wooden desk in all the imperial authority one could have when their empire stretched over an entire continent.

He sighed, and Tetra lifted her head, trying to avoid the emperor's gaze. Emperor Ignis's glare locked onto her eyes, sinister frost sparking deep within their dark blue depths. Nope, forget the scurrus. She was more akin to an annoying speck of dust caught in his eye.

"All you had to do was obey Second Lieutenant Tarson," he continued. "What was so hard about doing that? I've seen you throw an ax, Tetra—that would've been a simple thing for you to do." He put his clasped hands atop his desk and leaned forward, "So why didn't you?"

Tetra swallowed and did everything in her power to not meet his frightening eyes. "I—I don't know, Your Imperial Majesty."

"Don't lie to me." The edge of a sharpened blade lined the tone of his voice.

"I..." *Don't want to end up a mindless killing machine*, "I figured it'd be more of a challenge if...I didn't...y'know..."

Her voice faltered. By the sharpened look on the emperor's already-sharp features, he still didn't believe her answer. Granted, neither did she.

Tetra inhaled as deeply as she could without causing more pain to her throbbing back muscles and finally said, "I couldn't do it."

Emperor Ignis was silent for a moment. Tetra's heart rate began to speed up as her mind blanked, like the calm before a rolling thunderstorm.

"You're a disgrace."

She flinched at the aloof way he spoke the insult. She already knew it, but to hear it come out of someone else's mouth always made the knowledge of it that much more concrete.

"You're eighteen, Tetra. I shouldn't have to be dealing with your disobedience anymore." He narrowed his eyes. "You've done nothing these past ten years except dishonor your parents', your family name, and *me*." His voice lowered, "And I will not stand for it any longer."

A chill went up Tetra's aching spine. Going against all the protocol she had ever been taught, she lifted her head and met the emperor's gaze. The destructive frost that glistened in his eyes before had been overtaken by shadows that darkened his entire countenance. She had seen this look on his face only a few times before, and it always preceded a punishment that made the five lashes she had just received look like small cuts in comparison.

"Tetra Cairn, I believe it's time for you to be reassigned." His face was like stone. "I'm always in need of new personal guards, and—because of your insubordination—you've just signed yourself up for the task."

Tetra's heart dropped as tremors of fear ran through her limbs. Forgetting all her convictions—and her pride—in the onslaught of fear, she fell to her knees and bowed low towards Emperor Ignis. The wounds on her back cried out for her to stop, but she stayed on the ground. The pain was only temporary, and she would do anything to not receive this punishment.

"Please, Your Imperial Majesty..." her voice shook as she tried to form the words in her head before she spoke them, "I promise I won't do anything else to dishonor you. But please—don't turn me into a personal guard."

"And why shouldn't I?" He asked, "You've made promises like this to me before, and I've yet to see you keep any of them."

Tetra had also been waiting for *him* to fulfill all the promises he had made to *her* for the past ten years, instead of the lies and half-truths he only seemed capable of giving.

She pushed the unhelpful thought to the side as she tried to form a reply, "Because...because losing my—my memories again isn't what I want." Which was a nicer way of saying she didn't want to become one of the many brainwashed zombies that protected Emperor Ignis with undying loyalty. "I can't—I can't lose them..."

The emperor said nothing for a few moments, but Tetra could feel his gaze ever on her bowing form. Warm blood seeped into the bandages wrapped around her torso. She wondered for a moment if the blood was staining the white shirt she wore, but her focus moved away as Emperor Ignis finally spoke.

"I wish I didn't have to do this, Tetra—" Some of the sharpness in his tone dulled, "—but you've left me no choice. I, nor your parents, would've wanted this to happen, but your actions must be answered in the only way that will leave them with any honor."

"*As if the two most infamous Igrian generals of their day had so little honor that my actions would've somehow even made a dent in it*" was what she always wanted to say when someone told her what a dishonor she was to the Cairn name. Yet she knew, deep down, how disgraceful she truly was—and it hurt.

Being Marin and Aries Cairns' only child meant she carried all the honor and respect their lives' achievements brought. Everyone expected her to hold the weight of that mountain well and with no complaints. But she didn't want to carry it, nor could she just let it down. Despite her amnesia having taken away all memories of her parents, there was a small part of her that still wanted to make them proud; to know that they were looking down on her from the Warriors' Hall with satisfaction instead of disappointment.

If only there were other ways to do so instead of following in their blood-stained footsteps.

"Let me prove it to you," she said.

"Prove what?"

"Prove my—my loyalty, Your Imperial Majesty." The one good thing about having her face to the floor was the fact he couldn't see her grimace. "Just give me a—a few more days to show that I—I can change. I'll show you that I can be trusted again, and that I—I won't have to become a personal guard to do so."

"Hmm..."

Blood pounded in Tetra's ears. Had she really just said that? Was it really worth doing everything she was told to do? Yes, one half of her said, because then her brain wouldn't be completely wiped and replaced with a loyal cabbage-brained zombie. But, the other half countered, she would end up becoming a loyal soldier anyway if she did everything asked of her, and it could be considered worse since she would be in her right mind doing it.

Oh, why did she let her fear speak for her? Why hadn't she thought this through? There must've been something else she could've said to get out of this whole mess without signing a deal with Malackin.

Get out of this mess... Tetra latched onto the thought. There was a way—only one that was possible, that is—for her to get out of this mess with her mind intact. She could try to escape again. Her mind began racing at the thought.

"Stand, Tetra."

None of the emperor's words had ever sounded sweeter than those. Tetra obeyed, but sucked in a sharp breath through her teeth at the stinging pain raking across her back. Ignis watched her in silence as she struggled to a standing position.

When she was finally standing straight, and all emotion and pain she was feeling were wiped from her features, Emperor Ignis said, "I've heard your proposal, and I accept."

"Really?" Tetra blinked in shock. He was showing *mercy* towards her?

"Yes." He raised a brow. "I'll let you go on the trip to Xich with your platoon, and if you obey every single order given to you then I'll renounce your punishment. However, if you disobey even *one* order, your new assignment will begin when you return." This time he locked eyes with her. "Do you understand?"

"Yes, Your Imperial Majesty."

"Then I will send word to your commanding officer, and—" A knock on one of the office's double doors broke through his words. A spark of annoyance entered his gaze before being hidden by his cool and collected demeanor. "What is it?" He called past Tetra.

"Crown Prince Ryder asks for an audience, Your Imperial Majesty." One of the personal guards called back from out in the hall.

A slight frown pulled the corners of his lips down. Tetra wondered if that was the look her parents wore in the Warriors' Hall every time she did something they wouldn't approve of.

"Send him in." Emperor Ignis finally said.

It took all of Tetra's willpower not to turn around as she heard both the heavy doors open then close as a pair of soft, loping footsteps entered the large room.

"Ryder—" The emperor's gaze was set on the crown prince coming up behind Tetra, "—I'll be with you in a moment."

The crown prince's cracking voice replied, "Yes, Patre." The fabric of his clothes rustled as he sat on one of the leather couches sitting against the wall.

The full force of Emperor Ignis' gaze once again landed back on Tetra. Despite his mercy towards her, she still couldn't help the shiver that ran down her spine.

"I will send word to your commanding officer about this, and will be in contact with her the entire time that you're gone." His eyes narrowed on her. "Don't make me regret this, Tetra."

"Yes, Your Imperial Majesty." Tetra put her right fist over her heart and bowed on one knee. "Thank you for the second chance."

"Go."

Tetra gritted her teeth as she forced herself back into a stand. Without another word, she spun on her heel and headed towards the office doors. She spotted Crown Prince Ryder out of the corner of her eye and noticed his wide eyes watching her movements.

With his brown curls, round face, and pointed nose, he looked more like his Paleyan matha, Empress Rillunia, than Emperor Ignis, but the shape and color of his eyes were definitely the emperor's. Tetra slowed and nodded towards him once before continuing out of the office. She had never officially met the crown prince, but with his father being her legal guardian, they had run into each other a few times.

She glanced back at the emperor's office and saw Prince Ryder standing from the couch, still staring at her retreating form. But as he stood, two of their personal guards closed the doors. Poor guy. Tetra already hated having Emperor Ignis as her legal guardian, but at least he wasn't her father. She had overheard some of the things the emperor had said about his son, and they sounded almost as bad as the things Tetra had been called by Lieutenant Tarson and the other trainees at Norland.

Two more of the emperor's personal guards stepped over to Tetra to escort her back to Norland. She followed between them as they led her through the towering, grand corridors that connected all the rooms and opulent assembly halls in the governmental section of the emperor's vast fortress. Rain pattered against the curved, glass ceilings and high windows. Lightning illuminated the hallway for a moment and was quickly followed by a peal of thunder.

Neither of the guards spoke or even looked at Tetra as they marched on either side of her. She glanced at one of them out of the corner of her eye and gulped as she imagined her face with the same blank look she saw in his eyes. A shiver went through her and raised chill bumps along her arms. The thought was horrifying, and yet it would probably become her reality by the next week if she didn't at least try to escape.

One of the guards grabbed her arm and shoved her into a new hallway, which sent a shock through the wounds on her back. Tetra seethed and shot him a glare as he let go. The guard didn't notice, of course. Only the usual blankness of having one's brain turned to mush showed upon his face. Tetra had been through this portion of the fortress many times and could easily find her way back to Norland's grounds without an escort, but her three escape attempts kept that from happening.

Speaking of escape attempts... Tetra went over the emperor's deal in her head again. Neither option was good. She would end up brainwashed one way or another, and that's what she had been trying to prevent for years. Yet how was she supposed to escape when Xich was occupied by Igrium and the Silvanian Alliance?

The last time she had been to the desert nation was before Silvas had helped defend over half its territory. She had seen on the news recently that the capital city of Trivsau, where all Norland's fifth-year platoons would be staying, was split in two by a fence Igrian forces erected during the last battle fought there. Now both sides of the war were tensely waiting for the other side to make a move. Which, if Tetra was going to escape, left her with two options: take her chances by trying to escape on Igrium's side or try to make it over the fence onto the Alliance's.

That led her to another question: if she did successfully escape, where would she go? Staying in any of the kingdoms that were part of the Igrium Empire as a fugitive didn't sound appealing. The continental empire of Frigac was too far away; plus, she had heard their border security was the best in the known world. And the continent of Silalum, with its tales of hallucinations and wild animal attacks, was only ever used as a death-sentence. This left her with only the other Alliance nations that populated the continent of Caloi.

That thought didn't sit too well, either. How would Silvas react to the Igrian daughter of the Cairns'? Her parents had created and led the Fire Raids that burned down almost half of Silvas' cities, killed millions of innocent people, and finally destroyed Igrium's once-prosperous alliance with the kingdom. Tetra figured they wouldn't be too keen on having her in their borders, and the rest of their allies would most likely have the same views...but what if they didn't?

Tetra was so consumed with her thoughts she didn't notice the grandly decorated corridors had been replaced with walls covered only in holoframes displaying pictures of past battles and legendary Igrian generals. They had entered the military portion of the fortress. Armored guards of the military's honorguard corps stood as sentries along the walls and beside the doors leading to the offices and council rooms of Igrium's highest military personnel. They weren't brainwashed with the C.B.M like the emperor's personal guards—where they were forced into the tube-like machine that was able to block whatever memories the emperor wanted—but the intense training they went through conditioned them to the point that they never questioned any order.

An invisible weight pressed upon Tetra's shoulders as they turned a corner down a new corridor. A few doors ran down each side of it, but there were two in particular that always grabbed her attention. As they passed, Tetra's eyes turned to the two doors that—no longer labeled—she had been told used to be her parents' two separate offices.

As if to commemorate the two Cairn generals, a holoframe with their portrait was hanging on the wall between their two office doors. In it, they both wore similarly stern, stoic expressions, and Tetra again wondered how she could've come from them. Both sets of their brown eyes seemed to judge her as she passed, and she jerked her gaze to the floor. Even if it wasn't visible in the picture, she could almost feel the condemnation coming from them.

Despite that, Tetra still mumbled the common Igrian phrase of "May you both find honor and glory in the Warriors' Hall" as she was forced to continue forward. Maybe if she said it enough times it would actually prove true.

The invisible weight lifted as the guards led her into another hallway lined with windows. Dark skies devoid of Soll's bright light poured rain upon the view of everpine trees. Even though she couldn't see it from where they were, Tetra knew that Norland's white-bricked walls were proudly standing in the middle of the small pine forest. The fortress had been built around the old military academy's grounds many years ago, making it a part of the huge complex Emperor Ignis called "home".

The all-too-familiar doors that led out into the towering trees were up ahead. One of the guards gave Tetra another shove as her pace slowed. She really didn't want to go back—not yet, if at all. She could already hear the degrading remarks and curses of her roommates and everyone else she passed in the halls. Word traveled fast when the Cairns' disobedient daughter caused more trouble.

The same guard shoved her shoulder again, and Tetra—unwillingly—found herself in front of the doors. She took a step towards them while glancing over her shoulder at the two guards. They watched her with blank eyes, but she knew they wouldn't move until she walked through them.

Sighing, she pushed open the door and stepped into the downpour. Chill bumps rose along her arms as the cold rain soaked into her already damp clothes. She moved as fast as she could, without hurting her back, along one of the side paths between the trees. The sweeping boughs of the everpines helped to shield her from some of the rain, but she still looked like a sopping wet mess by the time she ascended Norland's steps and moved underneath the veranda. The honor guards stationed outside the school's entrance doors looked as if they were trying hard not to smile as their eyes followed her movements towards the entryway.

Here goes nothing. Tetra pushed one of the old, heavy entrance doors open with a grunt. A wave of heat washed over her as she stepped between the doors and into the empty entrance hall. She glanced around at the lack of people before she realized: it was the weekend, so most of the trainees had gone home.

Pressing a relieved smile back, Tetra moved towards the grand staircase leading up to the hall's second-floor balcony, her footfalls echoing in the vast space. A couple teachers sent disapproving looks her way as they passed, but neither said anything—to Tetra's relief. She slowed and stepped up onto the first stair with a wince as her pulse pounded through her back.

"Miss Cairn?"

She jerked around at the sudden voice, and sucked in a sharp breath of regret. She squeezed her eyes shut and leaned against the stair's banister, willing the sharp pain to dissipate again. Hurried footsteps came towards her and were soon followed by the same, familiar voice.

"I'm so sorry, Tetra."

A few moments passed, and when Tetra could breathe without hurting herself, she opened her eyes and locked them with the Head of Norland's janitorial services. "It's OK, Rasiela." She slowly straightened and lowered her arms off the banister. "It's not your fault."

Rasiela Reese pursed her full lips. "Honestly, Miss Cairn—one day you're not going to be able to use that back of yours anymore, and then what will you do?" She shook her head and, without waiting for a reply, asked, "What did you do this time?"

Tetra rubbed the inside of her segione-covered elbow with her thumb. "I...might've willfully disobeyed Lieutenant Tarson..."

Rasiela's plum-colored eyes flicked between Tetra's face, up to the second story balcony, then back to Tetra. "Is that who you are going to see now?"

Tetra nodded.

Like a mother with her mud-covered child, Rasiela's lips twisted into a frown. "Well you can't go looking like that." She gestured with her arm for Tetra to come with her. "I have some towels in my office you can use."

"Um—thanks, Rasiela, but I probably shouldn't keep Lieutenant Tarson waiting—"

"—She probably doesn't even know you are here." Rasiela's soft voice reassured her, "And if she does and you do get in trouble, I will take the full blame."

Tetra turned her neck and glanced up at the balcony, then slowly nodded. Now that she was in the dry air, she felt even more soaked than she did outside. And now that she was here, she realized she wasn't quite yet ready to face the rest of her C.O.'s fury.

"Fine." She stepped back down. "Thank you."

Rasiela nodded once then turned around and headed towards one of the arched entryways lined on the right side of the hall. Tetra followed at a slower pace, but always kept the woman in sight as they moved through the classroom corridors before finally stopping at a door marked "*Janitorial Services*".

"After you," Rasiela opened the door and gestured for Tetra to go through.

She did so with a nod. The sharp smell of chemical cleaners hit her in the face as she walked into the closet masquerading as an office. She glanced at the walls of shelves covered in cleaning products, the industrial-sized washer and dryer taking up half the wall, then the workshop table stuffed in the back corner with a dark blue tool chest sitting on top of it.

"Is that a new tool chest?" Tetra half-turned to watch Rasiela as the cleaning lady went over to the washer and dryer.

"Yes, it is." Rasiela bent down and picked up a couple towels sitting in a laundry basket.

"I like the color."

"Me too." She walked back towards Tetra and gave her one of the two towels. "And it doesn't have that pesky drawer that sticks every time I try to close it."

Tetra thanked her, unfolded the towel, and wrung out her waterlogged hair in it; cringing as certain movements made her back singe with pain. Rasiela was quiet while she did so, but when she lifted her head their eyes locked—where she finally noticed the questioning look in the other woman's gaze.

"Do you need to ask me something?" Tetra scrunched the front of her shirt in the towel.

Usually when Rasiela brought her to her office, it was because she wanted to talk with Tetra about matters that didn't need to be overheard by prying ears. The cleaning lady was from Silvas and still held on to the kingdom's moral code, like Aabir Sorrel and his family. Since Tetra held similar beliefs, Rasiela Reese had become the only person in Norland who was actually kind to her—and the only one she could trust.

"I assume you just came back from a talk with Emperor Ignis?"

Tetra sighed. "Yeah."

"And?"

"And..." Tetra glanced at the floor, "he almost had me turned into a personal guard."

Rasiela said nothing for a moment. Then she let out a simple, "Oh."

"Yeah..."

"But he decided not to?"

Tetra wrung the towel in her hands. "Not exactly." She sighed and looked up into Rasiela's eyes. "I—I told him I'd do...that I'd do anything he asked if he would reconsider. So, I've been given the chance to go to Xich. If I obey all of the orders given to me, then I'll be free to have my brain intact. But if I do end up disobeying even one order then—well..." she shrugged.

"I see..." Rasiela crossed her arms, her brow scrunching in thought. "What are you going to do?"

"I—I thought about...um—trying to escape. Again..."

Rasiela slowly nodded. "I agree."

Tetra blinked in surprise. "You do?"

"Well, it sounds better than just giving up on your convictions. And if you do end up disobeying some order given to you, you will not need to worry about being punished for trying to escape. You will end up with the same punishment either way."

A small spark of hope lit inside Tetra's chest. "That's what I was thinking, too."

"Which city are they sending you all to?"

"Trivsau."

A light entered Rasiela's eyes. "Well, that should work in your favor, then."

Tetra narrowed her eyes. "How?" Out of the few possible options, she couldn't see how any of them could.

"If you're able to get over the fence, then you will be out of Igrium's borders."

"And in Silvas'. How is that any better?"

Rasiela tilted her head slightly. "If you are captured on Silvas' side, I would hope they would be smart enough to tell from your record that you disapprove of Igrium's moral code, and would not imprison you."

"But I'm a *Cairn.*"

"That could be a problem..." The cleaning lady scratched the side of her neck thoughtfully, the light in her purple eyes taken over by an undecipherable mix of emotions.

Tetra slumped her shoulders. There went that bit of hope. She dropped the soaked towel in her hands and grabbed the other one Rasiela was holding.

"Unless..."

Tetra's heart skipped a nervous beat at the strange tone of Rasiela's voice. The cleaning lady glanced furtively over her shoulder towards the open door before locking eyes with Tetra again. Tetra watched her warily as she leaned in closer. What was she doing? She had never acted this secretive before.

"Miss Cairn, do you trust me?"

Tetra blinked and scrunched her nose. What kind of a question was that?

"Um—yes..." She replied slowly, "I do."

"Good." Rasiela nodded once. "Then I need you to trust me when I tell you to take your chances going over the fence onto Silvas' side."

"But—"

"—Just trust me, Tetra." She could detect Rasiela's Silvanian accent coming through more, "I have...connections in Silvas that can help you. All you must do is get over that fence. I will do everything I can to make sure you are not thrown into prison because of your parentage."

Something in Rasiela's stern expression rekindled Tetra's hope. There might be a way now... A way that could lead to the freedom she had never had in her remembered life.

But what sort of connections did Norland's cleaning lady have?

"Are you sure?" She asked.

"Yes." Rasiela's gaze softened for a moment. "I hate to see you go, but I would hate it even more if you were to come back." The softness left her eyes, replaced with a hard determination. "Igrium does not need any more brainwashed soldiers in its ranks. So, promise me that you will try everything in your power to not come back here."

Tetra gave her a sharp nod. "Yes ma'am. I promise."

"Good." She straightened and took a step back. "Well, I'd say that is as dry as you are going to get for now." Her Silvanian accent was now only a hint in the first few vowel sounds. "Goodbye, Tetra. I hope we do not see each other in this place again."

A sense of finality settled upon Tetra. Even if she did come back to Igrium, it would only be as a mindless personal guard. She probably wouldn't even recognize Rasiela if she ever saw her again.

"Thank—thank you, Rasiela," she began, "for everything. I'm glad this school had you here to clean it." She let a small grin escape her lips.

A ghost of a smile flickered across Rasiela's features. "I am too, Miss Cairn," she replied, "and do not worry about Silvas. I will try to take care of it all. You have my word."

"Thank you." Tetra held out the second wet towel. She wished there was more she could say to express her gratitude for the many acts of kindness Rasiela had shown her over the years, but her brain seemed incapable of coming up with anything in the moment.

Rasiela took it with a nod and picked up the other one off the floor. "Go on now. You don't want to keep Lieutenant Tarson waiting."

A shiver went through Tetra, her back muscles growing sore at the mention of Tarson's name. "No, I don't."

She moved around Rasiela and, with one last nod towards the cleaning lady, exited the office without looking back. With each step, her heart raced in hopeful anticipation. Now that she knew where she would be if her escape attempt was successful, all she had to figure out was getting there...

The wheels turned in Tetra's mind as she headed down the classroom hallways towards Lieutenant Tarson's office, and not even the thought of that unpleasant visit could douse the growing enthusiasm the thought of freedom brought her.

Chapter Four

THE HOVERTAXI CAME TO a stop in front of the familiar red brick, two-story garage. Aabir opened the curved door and stepped out into the rain. He pulled the grocery bag out, then slung his backpack over his shoulder before slamming the car door shut. The android driver's wave could barely be seen through the dark glass as it began to drive down the puddle-marked street.

The ear-splitting screech of metal scraping against metal turned Aabir's attention back to the only open garage door of the three. He ran up the sloped driveway and slowed to a stop once he was under the building's roof.

"Aabir? Is that you?"

He turned in the direction the familiar voice was coming from as Patre stepped out from behind a black hovercar. A smile came over his father's weathered face, and Aabir could not help but smile back. He had been expecting gloom and doom from his whole family when he arrived, but this was normal. Maybe that meant whatever Matha was worried about was not as bad as he had been expecting it to be.

Patre came over and they embraced. A whiff of the familiar oil and sharp, metallic odors that clung to his father's uniform drifted past Aabir's nose, and a pang of sadness came over him. Not for the first time, he wished he had never chosen to go to Norland. They let go and the feeling only grew as his gaze landed on his brother, standing behind Patre. Zeke wiped his hands on the pants of his matching blue uniform as he walked over to them, a grin forming on his soot-covered face.

"Did you lose a fight with the rain today?" He asked.

Aabir raised his brow and folded his arms. "I could ask you the same."

Zeke glanced upwards at the singed tips of his curly hair. "Well..."

"He just did, actually," Patre shook his head with a sigh. "And that's why you do not mix two flammable liquids together."

"I read the labels wrong." Zeke scratched the back of his neck with a sheepish grin. "Yeah, my face kinda hurts now... Is that normal?"

Aabir shared an eye roll with their father. Patre put his hand on Zeke's shoulder and turned him in the direction of the back door. "It has happened to me before and I lived," he said. "But go wash off and have your matha look at it."

Zeke nodded, shot another grin at Aabir (albeit this one more pained), then ran off to the door. As he moved through the open doorway, Patre called out, "And don't blame me this time!"

Aabir breathed out a laugh as the door squeaked closed. Patre turned back to face him, harsh shadows deepening the lines in his face. The smile left Aabir's own as their eyes met. Even the very atmosphere that had been light when Zeke was there grew heavier without his younger brother's grinning presence.

"So... Matha called me earlier," Aabir lifted the bag of groceries, "and she seemed...worried. I asked her what was wrong, but she wouldn't tell me."

Patre exhaled deeply through his nose. He crossed his arms and worked his jaw, as if he was trying to figure out the right words to say. "They've started raiding our house again."

A shock of cold went down Aabir's spine. "What? When?"

"Two nights ago. They even trampled your matha's garden and killed some of her tomeplants—which she was not too happy about."

Aabir curled his free hand into a fist. "Did you tell them I was a trainee?"

"We did, and after they looked it up to make sure we were not lying they left our house only partially destroyed. So, we did get off better than we have in the past. Only a chair's leg was broken—and your matha's tomeplants."

Aabir remembered the many times his family's house was raided—before he joined Norland. Clothing, dishes, and other loose items would always be strewn on the floor; furniture would be scattered and broken; and some of the patrolmen snooping through their house would leave a hole or two in the walls or floors.

"Still..." An ember of anger lit up inside his chest. Him being a trainee was supposed to keep all of that from happening. Yet here they were again—the cycle starting all over no matter what he had done to try and stop it. He lowered his glare to the concrete floor.

A weight landed on his shoulder, and he jerked his head back up. Patre gave his shoulder a squeeze.

"It's not your fault, Aabir." Their eyes locked again. "Your joining Norland has helped us for five years. But with the way the war is going right now, I'm not surprised this happened."

"But that should not be the case!" Thunder rumbled outside, as if to accentuate his words. "None of this should be happening! My being at Norland should have kept us safe from scrutiny for the rest of our lives, yet *they* are dishonoring *us*! Does the emperor really think the family that would send their child to Norland would be in league with Silvas?" Patre gave him a pointed look and Aabir only then realized what he had said. One corner of his mouth turned upward into a sheepish grin. "Well, the family they think sent their child to Norland."

Patre nodded once, the corners of his mouth turning upwards into a smile it looked like he was trying to suppress. It quickly disappeared, though, as he said, "Yes, well when the Alliance is actually winning in the war—maybe not the emperor himself, but—someone higher up thinks that we in Igrium might have something to do with it."

"I guess."

Yet even with that logical answer, it still did not sit well with Aabir. Especially when he had already given years of his life to protect his family, only for his efforts to be pounded into dust.

A strange look came over Patre's features. "Aabir...I hate to ask this, but your matha and I have been wondering if the war is not the only thing to blame."

A thread of guilt wormed its way into his heart. He kept his eyes on Patre's as he replied with as much conviction as he could muster, "I haven't done anything that would put suspicion on us. The only segione scar I have gotten this year is for being late. Everything they tell me to do, I—I do it. I do it all."

He could no longer hold his father's gaze and looked back down at the floor. The things he had done to keep his family safe...to keep *himself* safe... He gulped down the bile that tried to rise in his throat. The accusations creeping in the back of his mind came forward into the light. "*You coward,*" they said, *"you Straudwin coward."*

"Aabir, don't go there." Patre's voice broke through the accusing thoughts, "I can see it on your face. Stop doing that to yourself. Remember, you do have a choice. Your Matha and I don't expect you to do anything else. We are thankful for everything you have done to protect us, but that was never your job in the first place."

Yes, he might have had a choice before joining Norland, but now there was no going back. He was stuck, and not even an attempt at escape could free him.

"But I had to do something." He did not lift his head. "I couldn't just let our personal lives continue to be burst into every time someone in power grew suspicious, or when any of us said anything good about Silvas."

"I know. But protecting this family is not your job. It's mine."

"Yes sir." Aabir sighed through his nose. "I know all of that, but—like I've said before—I just...I just wanted to help."

"And you have done so," Patre replied, "more than your matha and I have ever asked. We do appreciate it, of course, but you need to stop if you are only doing it to win our approval. You are our son, and no matter what you do—or don't do—that will never change."

Aabir had already heard his parents tell him that many times before; but instead of saying so, he only replied with a simple, "Yes sir.", and then found himself in the crushing embrace of Patre's strong arms.

"We love you, Aabir."

Through the crushing of his ribs, Aabir coughed out a "Love you, too". Patre let him go and he sucked in a deep breath of the lightened atmosphere.

Immediately, Patre's holonode began to buzz. The small screen appeared between them as he lifted his arm and swiped his finger across its surface.

"Hello, Elnim." Aabir smiled as the familiar drawl of their family friend, Mister Falap, came from the holonode. "I hope I'm not bothering you, but I just had a question I needed to ask."

Patre nodded with a smile. "Of course. Aabir and I were just talking."

Mister Falap's sun worn features brightened and he moved his neck as if trying to spot Aabir in the holonode's limited camera. "Is he still with you?"

Aabir stepped up beside his patre, and Mister Falap grinned as their eyes locked. "Hey, Aabir."

"Hey, Mister Falap," Aabir replied. "How are you doing?"

"I'm doing well. Just getting things ready for the growing season." His blue eyes flicked down for a moment before returning to Aabir's face. "Did you just come home from school?"

Aabir glanced down at his gray uniform. "Yes sir."

"How is that going?"

If it had been anyone else, he would have lied about how "great" it was, but he had known Mister Falap his whole life and the elderly man already knew the reasoning behind Aabir joining Norland. So he replied, "About the same."

Mister Falap's grin lessened with an understanding nod. "I see." He paused. "But at least you're still learning to swordfight, right?"

"Yes sir."

"And how's that going?"

Tycho's "golden trainee" comment from earlier popped into Aabir's head. "Not bad." He shrugged nonchalantly. "I beat my friend in every sparring match today, so..."

Mister Falap's grin returned. "Well, I'm glad to hear you're enjoying some part of it. I think a lot about you being there, and what all you might be learning..." He cleared his throat with a shake of his head. "But anyway, that's not why I called."

"You had a question you needed to ask me?" Patre said.

"Yes—I wanted to know the next time y'all were going to come visit. I forgot to write it down when you told me, and now I've completely forgotten what you said." He sighed with a shake of his head. "It seems like I have to write everything down in order to remember it nowadays." His smile returned. "But I guess that's just what happens when you're eighty."

Patre nodded with a knowing smile. "I think we should be coming in three weeks." He paused a moment, uncertainty beginning to etch a line in his brow. "But I will ask Zerah when I finish up here to make sure that's right, and I can have her message the dates to you if you would like me to.

"That sounds fine to me." Mister Falap smiled. "Then I won't hold y'all up any longer. I just wanted to make sure y'all were coming."

"We wouldn't miss it." Something that almost sounded like longing laced Patre's tone.

Aabir sent him a questioning look but had no time to express it as Mister Falap replied, "Goodbye, then. I will see y'all—hopefully—in three weeks."

Aabir turned his head to face the screen again. "Bye, Mister Falap."

Patre repeated the phrase. With one last nod from Mister Falap, the call ended and Patre lowered his arm as the screen blinked out of existence. Aabir lifted his gaze back to his patre's dark violet eyes, a question rising to the surface of his thoughts.

"Does he know about what's going on?" He asked.

Patre shook his head with a sigh. "No, he doesn't." He rubbed his hand over his face, his eyes moving to a distant point behind Aabir. "Your matha and I would rather wait and tell him when we visit."

"Why? Why not just tell him and get it over with?"

"Because this is something that needs to be discussed in person." Patre's look grew pointed. "A holocall or message would not do it justice."

It only took Aabir a moment to realize what he was saying as he remembered the strange way Matha had spoken to him earlier when she called—as if she were afraid their call was being monitored. And if that was the case, then he agreed that waiting was the best option. Mister Falap was a full-blooded Igrian, but his opinions on the war and Emperor Ignis opposed what was seen as "good" to the rest of surrounding culture. So, if he ended up saying something blasphemous, then Aabir and his family might end up paying for it.

A small ember of anger lit up inside Aabir at the fact that they even had to think about these things, but he gave no voice to it as he nodded. "OK."

Patre gave a sharp nod, then turned towards the hovercar he was working on. "How about you go on up to the house?" He said, "I have a few more things to finish here, so you can tell your matha that I will be done in about an hour."

"Yes sir."

Aabir spun on his heel then walked out of the garage through the back door. Immediately, he turned to his left and rushed up the metal stairs that led to his home as the rain continued to drench him like it did the plants filling Matha's garden on his right. He slowed only a little as he stepped up onto the landing, opened the door, and rushed inside. The door slammed shut behind him.

His younger sister, Nevaze, lifted her head up from where she was lying on the couch. "Aabir?" Her eyes widened. "You look half-drowned."

"Thanks." He put the grocery bag down and leaned against the wall to take his boots off. His eyes scanned the living room for anything amiss, but whatever the patrolmen destroyed during their raid had been fixed and put back in its rightful place. "Where is Matha?"

"In the kitchen." She gestured with the holovision remote towards the open entryway that led to that room, her eyes turning back to the screen floating against the wall opposite her. "She's taking care of Zeke's face."

Aabir could not help the grin that escaped his lips. "Did you see him?"

Nevaze only nodded slowly, her eyes fixed on the screen as she flipped through the channels. "Mm-hmm."

Seeing as he was not going to get any more of a reaction from her, he dropped his second boot next to the other along the wall with all the other shoes of his family, picked up the grocery bag, and headed towards the kitchen. He stopped, however, as a highlight reel of a fight in the Constantia Tourney appeared on the screen. Aabir's stomach clenched as one of the two competitors stabbed the other with their trident before pushing them into the water.

"Aabir, you're blocking the screen! I can't see!" Nevaze complained at the exact same time Matha's voice rose from the kitchen, "That better not be the Constantia Tourney I hear, Nevaze!"

"Aabir is in my way, and I can't change it!

Aabir blinked out of his stupor and snatched the remote from Nevaze's hand to change the channel. Once a cooking channel appeared, he handed it back to her.

"Sorry, Nevaze," he said.

She took the remote back with a glare that quickly disappeared as he moved out of the way.

"It was my fault, Matha." He said as he stepped into the warm light of the yellow room. He immediately spotted her pulling small bottles and bandage wraps out of the medicine cabinet. "I'm sorry."

"It's alright, Aabir." She shook her head as she set a roll of bandages on the counter. "I guess I should be used to it by now—the sports channels have always started talking about them this early—I just hate for you all to be exposed to what they've become."

Aabir nodded slowly. The Constantia Tourney sporting events his parents had grown up with before Igrium attacked the kingdom of Yuln and the war started were a far cry from the bloodbath they had become.

Pushing those thoughts to the side, he gestured with the grocery bag and said, "I got what you told me to."

She finally looked over at him with a weary smile. "Thank you." Then, she turned back to the cabinet. "Just set it right there and I will take care of it."

Aabir placed the bag on the table, then leaned against the counter with arms crossed. "So...is that for Zeke?"

"Mm-hmm." Matha rolled her eyes. "I don't know what I'm going to do with him."

"He is accident prone..."

She looked at Aabir out of the corner of her eye. "If he would actually take the time to look around, there would be a lot less *accidents*."

"True." He shrugged, then Zeke himself stepped into the kitchen with a clean face.

"Are you all talking about me?" He gestured dramatically to himself.

"Yes, and your accumulation of accidents." Matha picked up a small lotion bottle and turned around to face him. "Here—" She handed him the bottle, "—put this on your face. It will help with the burns."

"They aren't that bad." Zeke took the bottle, an annoyed look on his reddened face.

Matha put her hands on her hips. "Put it on."

Aabir's heart jumped at her sharp tone, and he tried to hide a grin at Zeke's squirming. "You better do what she says, Zee."

Zeke shot him a glare before turning back into the hall, moaning over his shoulder, "But it smells horrible..."

With a roll of her eyes, Matha turned back around and began putting everything on the counter back up in the cabinet.

"Did you have a good week?" She asked.

"Eh. It was OK." Aabir shrugged. "How about yours?"

"Well...I found a new tea shop that sells tea almost as good as those in—" she abruptly stopped herself with a quick glance around before continuing on with a completely new thought, "—and—and the pomens are growing. Like I told Tycho on the holonode, I should be able to start baking pies in—"

"—What's wrong, Matha?" He cut in, visibly uneasy about her strange behavior. He had a horrible suspicion of what it could be.

"Oh, nothing out of the ordinary..." She gave Aabir a pointed look and mouthed, "*We think they put cameras in our house again.*"

His eyebrows shot up and he mouthed back, "*What?*"

Matha only nodded slowly in reply. She finished putting up the medicines and slammed the cabinet closed.

A worm of dread wriggled into Aabir's stomach. Chill bumps rose along his arms. Before he joined Norland, their home was being visited on a weekly basis by Igrium's patrolmen officers for questioning and raids. Patre and Matha soon figured out it was because secret, microscopic cameras had been hidden in their home. So, every time they said anything referring to Silvas in a good light, or anything that might be considered code, they were soon paid a visit by Igrian law enforcement.

During that time, Aabir had overheard his parents' multiple talks about how it was getting harder to defend themselves. The officers who did the questioning were great at twisting the family's words to make whatever they had said seem worse than it actually was, which helped in his decision to join Norland.

He had also heard stories from other kids from other Alliance nations at his old school where one, or both, of their parents were put in prison because they had said something that sounded "traitorous" to the Igrium authorities. That thought had scared him into taking Norland's entrance exam, and then forging his parents' signatures and lying about their agreement for him to go. Once he was accepted, only then did they find out—and it had taken him years to build back their trust.

Now, the old fear had reemerged. He opened his mouth to ask the questions popping into his mind, but then snapped it shut in realization.

This was ridiculous! He should be allowed to talk as freely as he wanted to in his own home! He shot a glare at the yellow walls and silently cursed whoever had come up with the idea to plant secret cameras in people's houses.

Matha picked up the grocery bag and pulled out the bread and bottle of arla spice. "If this rain ever stops, I will need your help in gathering more tomeplants and budded potatoes," she said. "We can check on the pomens, too."

Aabir scrunched his nose and sent her a questioning look. Then realization dawned on him and he nodded. "Yes ma'am."

His parents also figured out during those years that Matha's garden was big enough to talk quietly in without any cameras picking up on their words. She and Patre, and even Aabir a couple of times, had had many discussions out there disguised as vegetable picking.

"Matha? Is supper almost ready?" They both turned around as Aabir's middle sister, Ereliev, stepped into the kitchen; her back bent low to hold Yahel, their youngest sister, by the hand. Ereliev's eyes landed on Aabir, and she said, "Oh. When did you get home?" as Yahel cried out, "Aabir!" with a wide smile.

"A few minutes ago." Aabir turned his gaze from Ereliev down to Yahel's bouncing form and smiled. "Hey, Yahel!"

Yahel's tight curls bounced as she skipped over to Aabir with wide eyes. "I—I went to school today, too!"

"Yeah?"

He heard Matha replying to Ereliev, but could not make out her words as Yahel said, "Yep! And guess what I did?"

"What?"

"I drew a griffin!" Yahel puckered her lips in a pout. "I—I was going to bring it—bring it home, but my teacher—she not let me."

"Well, maybe you can bring it home in a few days," Aabir replied. "She probably just wanted to project it in a holoframe so everyone else can see it."

Yahel's face brightened. "Yeah! She—she did that with my tree picture before."

"Aabir?" Matha cut in.

He straightened and turned to lock eyes with her. "Yes ma'am?"

"Did your patre tell you when he was going to be coming up here?"

Aabir blinked. "Oh, yeah! Sorry I forgot to tell you—he said in about an hour."

Matha nodded and turned her head back in Ereliev's direction. "Then we have enough time to bake the corafish before your patre gets here. Can you slice the bread while I start that?"

Ereliev shrugged. "Sure."

"And Aabir—" Matha turned back to him, "—can you go make sure your brother is actually putting that medicine on his face?"

Aabir grinned. "Yes ma'am."

"And if he hasn't, please act like you are eighteen and not five. I don't want to hear any yelling or arguments." She put her hands on her hips and eyed him as if she could read his thoughts.

"I won't!" Try as he might, Aabir could not keep the grin off his face. He put his hands up in mock surrender and side-stepped towards the open entryway leading into the hall. "I promise. I'll just tell him you told him to."

She nodded sharply. "Good. Thank you."

He reached down and mussed Yahel's short hair before striding out of the kitchen. Light spilled from the ajar door leading to he and Zeke's bedroom as he headed towards it. Soft footsteps sounded behind him, but he did not turn his head. Yahel liked to try and sneak up on him whenever she thought she could catch him off guard, so he let her. Sometimes.

"Zeke?" He slowed to a stop and pushed the door open; acting oblivious to his second shadow. "Are you in here?"

Zeke stared at him from the desk chair situated on the opposite wall, below the room's single window. Pale splotches covered his face, concealing his burns.

Aabir grinned. "What happened to your face?"

"Shut up." Zeke frowned as he bent down and picked up a sock from the floor and threw it at Aabir.

It hit Aabir's arm. Quick as a griffin, he caught it before it fell completely, and—keeping his eyes on Zeke's smirking face—flung the smelly sock back at his brother. Zeke's smirk fell as the soft projectile hit him in the chest. "Hey—!"

"—Boo!"

Aabir jerked his leg away from the slight touch and spun around. "What the—?" His gaze lowered to Yahel's bouncing form.

She beamed. "I got ya, Aabir!"

He twisted his lips into a frown. "Yeah, you did!" He had completely forgotten about her. "You're as sneaky as a peryton."

Zeke clapped, and Aabir turned a glare towards his smirking brother. "Good job, Yahel."

His attention was diverted by a growl that sounded as fierce as a forest kitten's. "I'm the sneakiest peryton!" Yahel curled her hands in an imitation of talons like those of the famous predators'. "And if—if you steal my treasure, I'll come and—and scare you again!"

Aabir held his hands up in feigned surrender. "I promise I will never try to steal your treasure, oh fearless peryton."

From down the hall, Ereliev's voice called out, "Yahel! Come here!"

"I think someone's trying to steal your treasure!" Aabir said with feigned surprise.

Yahel glanced over her shoulder with another growl. Then a cross between a squeal and a giggle came out of her mouth before she hugged Aabir's leg and ran down the hall back towards the kitchen. Aabir shook his head with a grin and stepped through the doorway to his bed. He dropped his backpack onto the floor and sat on the edge of the mattress.

"How did it feel for the big, bad trainee to be scared by a three-year-old?" Zeke crossed his arms and leaned back in the spinning chair.

"Shut up." Aabir shot him another glare and, for a moment, wished trainees were allowed to bring their weapons off the school premises. Not to do any harm to pesky brothers, but just to scare them.

Zeke snorted. "I mean—I've never seen anyone jump when she tries to scare them; not even Nevaze—"

A pillow to the face cut off his words. Aabir gave a sharp nod. "I told you to shut your mouth."

Zeke grabbed the pillow in both hands and hurled it back. Aabir, however, was ready and caught it. He then flung it back onto his bed and, with a raised brow, turned back to face Zeke with arms crossed.

"You're going to have to do better than that if you want to surprise *me,*" he said.

Zeke rolled his eyes. "Because you're just *so* smart and *so* tough."

"Well...yeah." Aabir shrugged with a smirk. "And, you know, training and all that stuff helped, too."

"I didn't know the army used pillows in modern warfare."

Aabir opened his mouth to make another remark, but his mind went blank. A scowl grew on his face, but he tilted his head towards Zeke anyway. "I'll give you that one."

His brother puffed out his chest. "You might be fast with a blade, but my wit is ten times faster."

"You mean your smart aleck-ness?"

"Takes one to know one."

Aabir scoffed, and Zeke raised his brow as if to say, *I told you so.* Aabir only rolled his eyes. He would not give his brother the joy of winning—even if he had.

A few moments of quiet followed, broken only by the sound of the chair's squeaking as Zeke spun around in a slow circle. "Speaking of blades..." he began slowly, "could you teach me some more moves tomorrow?"

Aabir raised a brow. The last time Zeke had asked him for sword fighting tips, it had been to impress a girl—and then he got into a fight with someone else over the same girl and came home with a broken arm.

"I'm not teaching you anything else to try and impress another girl."

"No, it's not for a girl this time." Zeke stopped spinning in the chair to face Aabir. An unusual somberness had taken away his cheerful demeanor.

Aabir found himself struck by the moment. Worry wormed its way into his head. "What's wrong, Zee?"

Zeke gave a breathless laugh. "Well—that." His hand flopped in Aabir's direction before falling back in his lap.

"Uh—what?" He lowered his brow and stared quizzically at his brother.

"Even after living in this empire our whole lives and being surrounded by other Igrians, we still somehow don't sound like them."

Was Zeke complaining about...dialects? Aabir scrunched his nose. "Are you saying we sound Silvanian?"

Of course, Matha and Patre had Silvanian accents, but ever since the war started when he was seven, they began forcing themselves to speak with more of an Igrian one to sound less suspicious—even ordering him and Zeke to call them "Matha" and "Patre" instead of the Silvanian terms of "Emra" and "Appa". So, he and his siblings had grown up hearing them speak with a weird mixture of both dialects, but he never thought he sounded much like them.

"That's what I hear all the time at school." Zeke shrugged and turned his face down towards the dirty clothes strewn all over the floor. "That and other colorful remarks about how I look like a straudwin Silvanian."

Aabir remembered Zeke telling him of a few fights he had gotten into at school because some of the students decided to choose him as their residential punching bag, but he also knew his brother had been the one to start a couple of them, too.

"I'm not going to teach you anything so you can attack people for calling you names—again." Aabir shook his head. "Matha and Patre would blame me for your stupid actions, then we would both be in trouble."

"I promise I will only use it in self-defense!" Zeke pleaded with wide eyes.

"But how would learning to sword fight help? You aren't allowed to bring weapons to school."

"That hasn't stopped others." Zeke frowned then shook his head, "No, never mind. Could you teach me something else, then? I know they teach you more than how to use weapons at Norland! You tell us all the time about the new things you've learned in training. I know you know how to fight without weapons."

Aabir knew he walked right into that one. He blew out an exasperated breath and almost told his brother "no"; but when he met Zeke's dark violet eyes, he noticed the shadowed look turning them almost black with fear. It took him aback. He tilted his head slightly and kept his gaze locked on Zeke's, unwilling to let it go.

"What's really going on, Zeke?" He asked.

His younger brother blinked, and a few emotions flashed across his face, but the fear continued to stay in his darkened eyes. "It's about school." He scratched the side of his face, just like Patre always did when he was in deep contemplation or worried about something. "I assume Patre told you about the raids?"

Aabir nodded, so Zeke continued, "Well, at school there's now a group of patrol officers who...who pick all of us of Alliance descent out randomly to question us." Zeke licked his lips. "I think they do it because they know our parents' aren't there to help us answer any of their questions or take the blame for something we might say."

His heart began to pound as Zeke's voice shook, "And I—I almost messed up yesterday, Aabir." He put his head between his hands and slowly shook it. "They picked me out as I was walking in, and—and led me into this empty classroom. I thought I was prepared for it because a few of my friends who also got picked told me what had happened to them, and because of what has been happening here." He gestured with one hand to the room around them. "But I—I wasn't."

Aabir clenched his hands into fists. "What happened?"

"They...they asked me my name. I told them, and I also mentioned I had a brother who was training at Norland. They all laughed except for this one guy—I guess he was their commander or something. He was the one asking the questions. Anyway—" Zeke paused for a moment and lifted his head to lock eyes with Aabir again, "—he...well, he pulled out a dagger and—and put it to my throat. He said if I was lying then...well, there would be an—an accident."

"He threatened to kill you?" Aabir widened his eyes in disbelief.

Zeke slowly nodded and looked away. "Yeah. Yeah, he did."

"But that's illegal!"

"I guess not anymore." Zeke shrugged helplessly. "Anyway, they finally looked it up to see if I was lying—I wasn't, obviously—and they all finally shut up about it. But the questions..." He sighed. "Aabir, some of them made absolutely no sense. I tried to answer them all as honestly as I could, but some of them I really didn't have an answer for. They were about...politics and other things I don't know or care about.

"But whenever I said, 'I don't know', I could see the commander—or whatever he was—grabbing the hilt of his dagger and then I would tell them I didn't watch the news or pay attention to politics and that kind of stuff." He shrugged again. "I know I didn't give them the answers they wanted, but I think they finally used some comm—"

He immediately shut his mouth with a quick glance around the room. Aabir's heart skipped a nervous beat and his gaze followed Zeke's over the olive-painted walls. That was too close.

They both locked eyes again as Zeke finished, "—they realized I'm a teenage boy, and 'why would I have evil plans to overthrow the empire?'."

"So, then they just let you go?"

Zeke grimaced. "Yeah. Thank Deleyon."

"What did Matha and Patre say about it?"

The chair squeaked as Zeke shifted in it. He bit his lip again and averted his gaze. "I...I haven't told them."

Aabir's eyes widened. "*What?*" He said in a lowered voice, "Why not?"

"They already have to deal with worrying over what happens here." Zeke did not lift his head. "I just—I can't go and join Norland like you did, but I can keep them from worrying every time I go to school."

Aabir glanced down at his clenched fists. That sounded like something he would do—actually, something he had already done. His mind went back to the talk he had just had with Patre, and guilt pricked at his conscience.

Despite that, he finally said, "Fine. I won't tell them, either. But don't expect them to be happy when they finally find out—because they will." A shiver went down his spine. "Trust me. I know."

"Thank you." Zeke shot him a relieved grin.

Aabir shook his head but did not reply. Why was he encouraging this? He looked up over his brow at his brother and a thought hit him. What else was Zeke hiding? And were Ereliev and Nevaze having the same problem at school, too?

"Do you know if they've questioned Ereliev?" She and Zeke both went to the same high school.

Zeke shook his head and shrugged. "Not that I know of. Although it could have happened, and she just didn't tell me—but then she probably would have told Matha and Patre and they *definitely* would have said something to me. So..."

Aabir nodded. "And what about Nevaze?"

"All she has said is that a couple new patrolmen guard her school now." Zeke's lips twisted into a knowing frown. "But I know Nevaze, and if they ever questioned her, she would come home crying, and would tell Matha and Patre everything."

"Yeah, she would."

They both shared an eye roll.

"Which leads me back to my original question: can you teach me something? I would like to know I can at least try and defend myself if that ever happens again. Even if I only live a few more seconds, at least I can say I tried instead of just sitting there."

Aabir looked back down at his fists. He had learned many different forms of self-defense in training, and if he could use that knowledge for something good—like protecting his brother from possibly dying—then that seemed to outweigh the con of possibly teaching his brother how to knock someone out over a girl and getting himself expelled.

"Okay, I will." He lifted his head and saw the excitement on Zeke's face, so he held up his hand and continued, "On one condition: you only use what I teach you to defend yourself—nothing more. I don't want to come home next week and find out you knocked someone out because of a petty disagreement. Deal?"

"Deal."

Aabir nodded once and fell back on his bed with a sigh. "I can teach you some stuff tomorrow if it's not raining."

"OK. Sounds good." Zeke stood from the chair and, in a posh, nasally accent, added, "Now then—I believe Matha baked some cookies the other day, and Ereliev hid them from me. So, if you will excuse me, I believe I must find them before they're all gone."

Aabir lifted his head. "What kind are they?"

Zeke glanced down at him as he strutted out of the room. "Her vanilla-mint ones."

His mouth watered at the mention of his favorite cookie, and he shot up out of bed to follow his brother. "I think I should come and help you look for them."

"Only if I get the biggest ones."

"Fine."

Worries abated for the time being, they both went off into the hall in search of the delicious treasures.

Chapter Five

THE TORRENTIAL RAINS STOPPED overnight, so Aabir took Zeke out into the garden before lunch to show him a few self-defense moves. He stepped in a huge puddle on the stone path that cut through the rows of growing plants and groaned as the muddy water soaked into his running shoes.

"What?" Zeke, who was a few steps ahead, glanced over his shoulder.

Aabir gritted his teeth and waved the question away. "Nothing."

He turned his gaze away from his dirty shoes and looked around at the short rows of leafy vegetable plants and tendrils of vines growing along the ground and creeping up trellises. He inhaled the smells of wet earth and flowering plants as he followed Zeke to the back of the garden where their pomen tree stood proudly with its blue-tinged leaves reaching up towards the cloudy sky; its topmost ones barely reaching past the brick buildings that enclosed the garden. Round, green fruit speckled with dark purple spots hung from its branches in pairs. Aabir's mouth watered at the sight of them, his thoughts turning to the buttery taste of Matha's pomen pie.

"How about right here?" Zeke asked as he slowed to a stop and stepped off the path into the shadows underneath the tree's boughs, his shoes squelching along the muddy ground. Aabir, again, sent a begrudging glance down at his wet shoes before joining his brother.

"A little mud won't hurt you, oh fearless warrior." Zeke crossed his arms with a smirk.

Aabir sent him a scowl. "They're my favorite shoes!" He replied, "*And* my socks are wet. Do you know how awful wet socks are?"

"Then don't wear them when it's muddy outside."

"I only have two pairs of shoes, Zeke, and the other I can't get dirty." If he got to the train station on Firstdein morning with mud-spattered boots, Lieutenant Denir would have a fit—and Aabir would be punished accordingly.

"Whatever." His brother rolled his eyes before changing the subject, "So what are you going to show me first?"

Aabir pushed the thoughts of his shoes away to focus on the present matter. He motioned for Zeke to come close. "Come here so I can show you what to do."

Zeke eyed him warily. "You're not going to hurt me, are you?"

"I'll do it slowly so that I don't." He rolled his eyes and gestured towards the ground in front of him again. "Now come here."

With tentative steps, Zeke did so until he was only about a foot away. Aabir met his brother's gaze, and a flash of envy went through him at the fact that, from this close, he could tell Zeke was a little bit taller than him.

"Now," he pushed the thought away to focus, "try to attack me."

Without hesitation, Zeke sent a fist flying towards Aabir's face. Aabir moved back, blocked his brother's arm with his own, and sent his own fist hammering down towards Zeke's face. Zeke squeezed his eyes shut as Aabir stopped his fist in midair.

"And that's how you block," he said.

Zeke opened one eye, then the other, as Aabir moved his fist away and stepped back. He let out a relieved sigh.

"I really thought you were going to hit me there for a second."

Aabir shrugged, the hint of a grin forming. "I could say the same for you."

"Yeah..." Zeke sent him a sheepish smile. "You did tell me to attack you, so..."

"True." He nodded. "Well—now I want you to try doing what I did. I'll go slow for you—*and* I want you to do it slowly, too."

Zeke nodded and stepped back. "All right. I'm ready."

Aabir slowly went to attack him, and Zeke's arm came up at the same speed to block his strike; his other fist coming down towards Aabir's face as if moving through molasses. He stopped short and locked eyes with Aabir expectantly.

"How was that?"

Aabir nodded. "Not bad. Now let's see if you can still do it at a normal speed."

Over the next few minutes, they went over the same move until Zeke got the hang of it. Then Aabir showed him a couple more moves that he could use in many different scenarios. When Zeke got the hang of those, Aabir already had the next move in mind.

"Now if someone comes at you with a dagger, distance is going to be your best option." He stared his brother down and put as much authority as he could in his voice, "Don't try to be a tough guy and get yourself stabbed. If you can, run away."

Zeke stared at him with wide eyes. "But I don't want to be a Straudwin—"

"Running away to defend yourself from an attack is the wiser option." The familiar guilt churned Aabir's stomach, but he tried to ignore it. "You only defend yourself if there is no possible way for you to gain that distance. Understand?"

"Sure..."

Aabir raised an eyebrow. "I can show you what it feels like to not run away if you would rather take the 'tough guy' approach."

"All right!" Zeke frowned and shot him a glare. "I'll take the coward's option if I ever have too."

Aabir shook his head and was about to rebuke his brother, but the squeak of the front door grabbed his attention. Nevaze stepped onto the landing with a basket in her hand. Ereliev, Matha, and Yahel followed out behind her, and the three sisters tromped down the metal staircase as loud as a group of perytons. Matha closed the door behind her and followed them. A large basket, like the one Nevaze had, hung from the crook of her arm.

"What are you two doing?" Nevaze called out as she stepped off the last stair and started running towards them.

"None of your business." Zeke replied in a sharp tone.

Ereliev made it to the ground and finished helping steady Yahel as the youngest Sorrel practically jumped down the last few steps. "We heard some yelling," she added in her matter-of-fact way.

"Like I said, Ereliev, it's none of your business."

Even across the garden, Aabir could feel Matha's burning glare. "Do not be rude to your sisters, Zeke!"

He sighed a breath of relief and glanced behind his shoulder at Zeke's reddening face.

"Yes ma'am," his brother said through gritted teeth.

Nevaze made it over to them and slowed to a stop, panting. Her large eyes landed on Aabir and she asked, "So what were you doing, Aabir?"

He turned his gaze back to Zeke. His brother gave him a "if you tell them what I told you, I will murder you in your sleep" look.

"I was just teaching Zeke a few moves," he replied with a shrug, turning his gaze back on Nevaze's short form.

She tilted her head and stared at him quizzically for a moment, her light purple eyes flicking between him and Zeke.

"All right." She blinked, then lifted the basket towards him with both her hands. "Matha wants us all to pick tomeplants. Are you coming?"

Aabir lifted his head and looked over at Matha. She met his gaze for a moment as she walked towards the tomeplant trellises, and her words from last night popped into his head.

"I'll be right there," he said and looked back down at Nevaze.

She nodded and skipped back over to Matha. Mud squelched underneath his shoes as he turned around and faced Zeke. They locked eyes, and Aabir said, "I need to speak with Matha, Zee. We can practice later."

Zeke looked like he wanted to argue, but understanding dawned in his expression and he nodded once. "Sure. I'll go see if Patre needs any help."

"OK."

With that, Zeke strode down the path towards the house and garage, and Aabir headed over to the fruit side of the garden. Nevaze was already helping Matha pick purple and yellow tomeplants from their dark green vines. Ereliev was crouched next to Yahel and trying to help her pick a few of the tart fruits amidst the broken vines and pointed leaves of the ones that were trampled by the patrolmen.

"Come here, Aabir." Matha waved him forward. He jogged the last few steps to get to where she was. "See if there are any good ones over here."

Aabir stepped over into the mud next to the plant she was pointing at. She gave him an almost imperceptible nod and turned back to the one she and Nevaze were working on.

"We believe they put cameras in nearly every single room of the house," Matha said in a lowered voice as she worked, "We've had conversations in almost all of them that patrolmen later reiterated back to us during their questioning."

Aabir picked off a fat, yellow fruit and bent to place it in Matha's large basket. "Are there some in the garage?" He asked.

"We're not sure, but just to be safe we always talk out here about these sorts of...things." She sighed, and a hard edge entered her tone. "Even though we shouldn't even have to do this—but it is the world we live in."

A ball of anger hardened in Aabir's chest. "That shouldn't be the case, though, Matha." He picked off another large fruit and thought about hurling it across the garden to cool his anger. But instead, he placed it in the basket. No point in having Matha angry at him, too.

"I know."

He stooped lower to get a better look at the half-hidden tomeplants. "Just because you and Patre were born in Silvas doesn't mean the emperor has a right to do all of this!"

Matha stopped working for a moment to give him a pointed look. "*I know,* Aabir, but there is nothing we can do about it." She went back to picking her precious plants. "If we could leave Igrium, your Patre and I would, but for right now, that is just not the case."

Wait. Did she say "leave Igrium"? He stopped working and looked over at her. "Did you just say what I think you said?"

"What do you mean?" Matha flicked a loose strand of curly hair away from her eyes and stared at him quizzically.

"Did you say—" He sent a furtive glance around the quiet garden, despite the fact no camera's microphone would be able to pick up their conversation, before locking eyes with Matha, "—'leave Igrium'?"

Ereliev jerked her head up. "You said that, Matha?" Her eyes flicked between both of their faces.

"Yes, I did," Matha replied.

Ereliev opened and closed her mouth a couple times in wide-eyed silence. Aabir could not blame her; he felt the same surprise that was showing on her face. All this time, he thought the idea of leaving the empire put a bad taste in his parents' mouths.

"You mean...you and Patre have—you both actually talked about that before?" He asked.

Matha nodded slowly. "Yes..."

"But I thought...well, I figured that my—well..." Aabir lifted his arm and rubbed the back of his neck with a sheepish smile.

"—That your past actions would have kept your Patre and I from ever thinking anything good about leaving?" Matha raised a brow.

Guilt tried to claw its way to the forefront of his mind, but he kept it at bay by focusing back on Matha. "Yeah..."

"Well, it didn't." She dropped two small tomeplants in their shared basket. "In the last year we...we have mentioned it more than normal, but now with the raids happening again it has become more evident that—if it were ever to become a possibility—we would leave and never come back."

She paused for a moment, then added with a sigh, "Igrium is no longer the place of prosperity and freedom it used to be."

Aabir could barely remember a time when the empire he always called "home" had been the utopia his parents' spoke of in their reminiscences. He had only been seven-years-old when Igrium declared war on Silvas and everything began to go downhill for those of Silvanian descent living in the empire.

"But..." Ereliev helped Yahel pick a bright purple tomeplant off its vine, "where would we go if we did end up leaving?"

"You don't need to be concerned about that, Ereliev," Matha replied firmly. "We are not leaving. It is impossible."

Aabir began, "But if it did become possible—"

"—No more, Aabir." Matha turned her head back in his direction. "I do not want to hear another word about it from either of you. I should have never said anything in the first place."

"Yes ma'am." Both of them replied begrudgingly.

An unsettled quiet came over them as they continued picking tomeplants. Matha soon stood and moved over to the patch of budded potatoes growing opposite them and began pulling up the red vegetables by the bright orange flowers growing from the tops of them.

Aabir tried looking for good tomeplants, but his thoughts soon took him away from the garden. What would happen if the borders opened back up again? Just as the question entered his thoughts, another, more devastating, one rose up to counter it: if they did then that would mean Igrium had won the war and the kingdom of Silvas would no longer exist.

And if that happened, would he, his family, and every other Igrian citizen of Alliance descent have their freedoms back? Or would Emperor Ignis come up with some reason to continue keeping them all under surveillance?

A shiver went down his spine at the thought and he tried returning his focus back to the fruits at hand. But as he did so, he picked up the sounds of many pairs of harsh footsteps echoing from somewhere outside their home. Aabir lifted his head at the strange noise, and his heart quickened as he heard loud voices coming from Patre's garage. He leaped up from the ground, his heart now racing. Something was wrong, and he could—

"Aabir!" Matha's yells stopped him in his tracks. "Wait!"

He turned partway and gave her a dubious look. "What—"

The garage's side door burst open, and he jerked his head forward again. His heart pounded a sporadic rhythm as six patrol officers marched into the garden. The dark blue undertones of their metallic armor were dull in the dreary light, yet the sight of it shot a spike of fear in Aabir's chest as unbidden memories resurfaced:

Being pushed into a corner with his crying siblings as Matha and Patre tried to create a protective barrier between them and the patrolmen mercilessly tearing through their house; the courage he tried to have during his first questioning that was buried underneath an avalanche of anxiety over him saying the wrong things and losing his parents; and the heart-thudding terror of being chased by similar groups of armed honorguards, then getting caught by them and dragged to the office of the emperor himself...

His mind would have continued to race through the horrible memories, but the sound of a sword being pulled from its sheath brought him back to the present.

The sharp eyes of the lead patrolmen took a cursory glance around the garden before landing on him. "Are you Aabir Sorrel?" He asked.

Aabir tried to erase any of the haunting emotions from his face. No longer was he a scared little boy or disobedient third-year trainee. He was a fifth-year, fully capable of taking care of himself.

"Yes sir." His voice sounded cool to his ears, even with the roiling turmoil inside of him.

The lead patrolman nodded sharply. "We need to speak with you."

"About?"

"In private." His tone left no room for argument.

Aabir opened his mouth to reply, but Matha stepped up beside him and said, "You may all speak out here if you wish. The rest of us will go inside while you talk."

"Um..." Aabir glanced over at her, but Matha kept her eyes on the group of patrolmen, her soft features set in stone.

"No." The lead patrolmen replied and gestured towards the stairs. "*You'll* stay out here and *we'll* talk inside."

Matha did not seem taken aback by him ordering her around in her own home. "Very well, then. If that is what you wish." Aabir finally caught her gaze as she turned to look at him. "We will stay out here."

What was going on? He stared hard into his matha's face, hoping he could gauge some answer from her hardened features. She slightly nodded towards him and turned around again, but not before sending him one final hopeless look that the officers could not see.

Confusion and fear warred in Aabir's churning stomach as he found himself leading four of the patrolmen up the stairs and into his house, while the other two stayed down in the garden with their swords drawn.

"In there." The lead guardsman gestured towards the kitchen.

Aabir focused on taking deep breaths to calm his insides as he stepped through the kitchen's entryway and was told to sit at the kitchen table's corner seat. A chill went down his spine and any "heroic" thoughts from before dissipated as he realized his back was to the wall with the four guardsmen surrounding him.

"We hate to do this, Trainee Sorrel," the lead guard took the seat opposite his', "but due to a new proclamation signed by the Emperor Himself, we must."

If that was supposed to calm Aabir down, it did quite the opposite. But he kept his voice steady as he replied, "What are you meaning to do?"

The lead officer leaned forward and overlapped his arms upon the table. "We have a few questions to ask you." A look of dissatisfaction came over his face. "I would rather not question a trainee with as little marks on his record as you, but the emperor's word is law and all those of Alliance descent—be they soldier, trainee, or other honorable roles—must go through the same questions as everyone else."

Aabir curled his shaking hands into fists underneath the table. "Yes sir. I understand," he said, although he still did not.

Was the emperor so paranoid over the possibility of Alliance spies that he would question even those signed into honorable military service?

"Good." A falsely warm smile spread across the officer's face. "I hope we can keep this as civil as possible."

And with that totally nonthreatening statement, he began, "How did your parents' come up with the idea for your joining Norland?"

Aabir's heart dropped into his roiling stomach. Where did they come up with a question like this? Who would... Then he remembered the cameras, and how he had said something yesterday to Patre about Igrian authorities only thinking his parents had let him join Norland. *Great.*

He glanced between all four distrusting faces of the patrolmen. Their probing eyes were all trained on him, and he knew from past experiences that they would analyze every word he said—looking for any lies that would automatically *prove* to them that he was a Silvanian spy.

Despite his wariness at revealing any of the truth, there would be no way to hide it. Not if they had listened to his and Patre's conversation, anyway.

Taking a deep breath, Aabir locked eyes with the lead patrolman and said, "They didn't, sir. I was the one to do so."

The officer's features hardened into an emotionless mask. "Then how did *you* come up with the idea?"

"One of the teachers I had at my old school was telling us about how we were all the right age to be able to join any of Igrium's military academies. I thought learning how to sword fight for a school subject was cool, so she let me take the test to see if I was smart enough to join."

Sword fighting was, of course, not the main reason for him choosing to join Norland, but it had been the one thing he tried to use to psyche himself up for going to a military school.

He inhaled deeply before continuing, "I didn't tell my parents about it, and they only found out later when they were invited to a meeting with Norland's Headmaster. At first, they weren't happy, but then they went to the meeting and said I could join afterwards."

"What changed their minds?" The head patrolman asked.

Aabir tried to look nonchalant and shrugged. "Honor."

They had actually felt pressured to let him join because of how honorable being chosen as a trainee was in Igrium's culture, and they knew with all the scrutiny against them at the time that if they declined his only chance of going there, it would seem like their self-proclaimed loyalty was wavering. So, they told him he was going to Norland—and then he spent almost his entire Growth Season break grounded.

The hardened officer looked unfazed. "And what do you think of the school now that you are approaching graduation?"

"Well, I still think sword fighting is the best part." At least he could be completely honest with that answer. "But I've also made good friends there."

"Do you have any special plans for when you join the army after you graduate?"

"No sir. I figured I would just join and make my way up the ranks—if it's even possible."

"I would think with your record and training that you would strive for more than just the basics."

Aabir locked his fingers together to keep himself from moving them. "Well, my friend, Aquilo Warlin, he has grand plans for rising up quickly in the ranks—but he's a great strategist and comes from a highly-honored military family. And since I'm not that great of a strategist, nor my family name important, I just always assumed I would have to be like everyone else who joins."

"With those plans, it seems you either do not realize your talents, or you don't care about joining in the first place." The lead officer raised a brow. "Which is it, Trainee Sorrel?"

His heart skipped a frantic beat. "My—my talents, sir?" He tried to fake confusion as he scrunched his nose and redirected the conversation away from the latter part of the patrolman's statement. "I didn't think the ability to sword fight was something that could help me rise in the ranks."

"There are some circumstances where it can—but you didn't answer my question."

Great. His hands shook even more as he silently prayed to Deleyon for an answer that would not get him or his family imprisoned.

"Well, sir—I guess a little of both," he said. "If what you are saying is true, even if I did rise in the ranks—how far would I actually go? And for me not caring—well... I know how it's a great honor, but my thirteen-year-old self didn't even realize if I joined Norland that I would immediately join the army right after I graduated. That wasn't on my radar, and I still don't even think about it much." He shrugged again, hoping that answer did not label him as anything more than an uncaring teenager.

"Hmm... you're not letting cowardly thoughts get the better of you, Trainee Sorrel, are you?"

Aabir straightened. "Excuse me?"

The head patrolman put up his hands in surrender. "I didn't mean to hurt your honor, but I felt I must ask that—especially with a certain incident your record claims you committed a couple years ago." His eyes locked on Aabir's and would not let them go.

Aabir's tongue stuck to the roof of his mouth. The shame he had kept at bay leapt forth into the forefront of his thoughts and bombarded him with the dark memories of his biggest, most humiliating failure.

"I learned from that mistake, sir." He tried to put as much conviction into his voice to win over the patrolmen and the accusing whispers in his head. "Believe me, I will never try anything that stupid again. It was the biggest mistake I ever made in my life. I wish I could go back and change it."

"And the one you tried to escape with—Tetra Cairn—have you had any interactions with her since?"

"No sir. I cut all ties with her after that."

"All right, then."

The officer continued shooting him questions about Norland, his family, and his loyalty—even having him repeat a few Igrian pledges to show it. Aabir answered them all as honestly as he could without revealing the deeper reasons for certain decisions. It was the easiest questioning he had ever been forced through, and he knew the only reason for it was because he was a trainee. The patrolmen did not want to dishonor him any more than they had to. Even if it was the Emperor Himself who enacted the legislation, questioning a trainee with Aabir's impeccable record on the grounds of being a possible spy could be considered dishonorable by some—and the patrolmen would want to put off as much of it as they could.

The tense session soon ended, and all the patrolmen filed out the front door, slamming it behind them. Aabir stayed seated as the quiet of the house settled around him. He inhaled deeply, then exhaled to calm his racing heart.

Despite how easy he seemed to have gotten off, it still left him uneasy. What if he came back next weekend and said something else that could raise suspicions? Would he get off as easily with another questioning session? Or would it only get progressively worse with each one he was put through?

He propped his elbows on the table and put his head between his hands. There was no way he could ensure his family's safety by being at Norland anymore. Patre told him it was not his job to protect them, but Aabir needed to do something. He could not go back to Norland and act as if everything was fine and normal while his house was being raided and his family questioned. No, something had to be done. But what?

Matha's words from the garden came back to him. The only thing that ensured their absolute safety was if they left the empire for good. But even as he had the thought, he knew it was impossible—just like Matha had said. All the borders were closed off, and no one would let a family of Silvanian descent go through them. That would raise too many red flags.

There was also the fact that he could not escape Norland or the army, when he joined in the coming months, without showing himself to be a Straudwin coward of the worst order. *That* would make their predicament so much worse.

Was there any way of escaping this empire?

Nope. Aabir sighed as he answered his own question. *Nothing can be done.* They would just forever be surveilled and questioned until someone won this war—and at the rate it was going, that could be another ten years.

He let out another sigh as he stood from the chair, then headed back outside and into the garden. When the door closed behind him, he heard Matha shout, "Aabir? Is that you?"

"Yes ma'am," he called back while descending down the stairs.

Matha came over to him, worry shining in her eyes. She grasped his shoulders and pulled him into a hug.

"I'm so sorry for letting that happen," she said, "but I didn't know what else to do. Trying to dissuade them only causes more problems."

He squeezed her back. "I know, Matha," he replied in her ear. "But it went better than I thought it would."

She let go and looked him in the eyes. "Well, I guess that's better than anything else that has happened."

He thought to himself, *that should not be the case.* "Why must it seem so hopeless?"

"That's just the world we live in." Matha shrugged, her lips falling into a frown. "And only Deleyon can help us now. We can at least hope in Him."

Aabir nodded sullenly, turning his gaze to the ground. At least they were not completely in the dark, even though it felt like it in that moment.

Matha put her hand on his arm. He lifted his head and locked eyes with her again. "One day we will think of something, Aabir." She gave him a small smile that fought against the heaviness in her eyes, "But for now we must continue on as we have. Your patre still has his garage—and customers, we own a hovercar, I have this garden... We are much better off than many of Alliance descent are."

"You're right," he replied, "but I still wish there was a way out."

"I do too, but I also know how important it is to look at the positives while we are in this situation. I know my earlier comment might have said otherwise, and I'm not oblivious to the dangers of our situation, but the only way any of us will be able to truly live through this is if we hold onto the hopes that we have..." She sighed before adding, "No matter how small they are."

"I'm sorry we have to face this again, Matha." It felt like it was the only thing he could say.

She gave his arm a small squeeze. "I am, too." There was a pause between them, and in it another small smile came over her features as she lowered her arm. "Well, how about we go check on one of those little blessings I just mentioned?"

He sent her a questioning look as she turned and headed along the garden's central path, sending him a bigger smile over her shoulder. "Let's go see how our pomens are doing."

Chapter Six

SOLL BEAT DOWN ITS bright heat upon Tetra, and all those in her platoon, as they marched through the streets of Trivsau in full metal armor. She blinked back drops of sweat that fell into her eyes and swiped her gauntleted hand across her forehead to dispel them. She had forgotten just how hot the desert kingdom could be and sent a jealous glance around at the few Xichians walking purposefully in the street in their light, flowing clothes. Yet that pang of jealousy quickly passed and was replaced by guilt as Tetra's gaze landed on a small boy sitting among the wreckage of a destroyed building.

This wasn't the first time she had been to the desert kingdom's capital, but it had changed dramatically since her last visit. Crumbling walls and missing windows were the lightest marks left after the previous battle fought in its streets. Tetra stepped over a chunk of sandstone wall sitting in the street and glanced over at the closest pile of rubble where it had come from.

The famous city—once known for its beautiful, spiraling skyscrapers—now looked like a pod of blue sky-whales had fallen from the sky and landed atop it, leveling most of the buildings and leaving them in crumbling ruins. Tetra barely kept her eyes forward as Second Lieutenant Tarson led the platoon further down the street. A few merchants were trying to sell their merchandise in what was left of their storefronts, yet the few citizens that walked past continued on without stopping. If they had been selling food, Tetra had a feeling they would have more business.

The faces of the people had also changed. When Tetra visited for the first time during her Resting Season break only three months ago, Igrium had only taken over part of Xich and was slowly making its way towards Trivsau, so the people she saw had the countenances of those in any bustling city. But now, she could tell that every person her platoon passed was trying very hard to ignore the Igrian trainees. She even noticed a few sneers or glares that quickly disappeared once they realized she was looking at them—and they weren't the only ones doing so. A pair of Silvanian guards glared daggers at the trainee platoon through the wire links of the dividing fence as they passed.

Tetra stared up at the barbed wire atop the towering, chain-link fence with narrowed eyes, thoughts of escape coming back to mind. Most of the barrier was being fortified with thick, furrum-metal plating, but there were still some sections—like this one—that had yet to be dealt with; and the weaker portions seemed the best option for her escape.

How hard would it be to climb it? Yes, the barbed wire could be a problem, but not if she wore her armor. But if she wore her armor, she would lose her stealth.

She lowered her head and looked out the corner of her eye at the other obstacle she would need to face. More Silvanian soldiers in their dark, green-tinged metallic armor and Frigian soldiers in dark leather armor marched in small units or stood as guards on the other side of the fence, like Tetra's platoon was doing. She locked eyes with another of the Silvanian soldiers and turned away from the hostility cemented on his face.

It seemed everyone but Igrium itself hated anything to do with the empire. Tetra couldn't blame them, though. She would be angry, too, if the city she lived in and loved had been brought to ruin.

Ever since they began the sweltering march next to the capital city's dividing fence—to gain more field experience for what everyone else would be doing after graduating into the military, Tetra had wondered how much she could really trust Rasiela's words. She had never felt so much hostile tension in her entire life until now as both sides faced each other with only a puny fence to keep them apart. It was like a dark calm before a windstorm—and Tetra needed to jump right into it.

"Hey!" Lieutenant Tarson yelled as someone on a hoverbike wound past her with a beep of their horn.

A couple of her platoonmates murmured curses at the driver going past. Tetra tracked the hoverbike with her eyes until it disappeared around a corner. Besides walking, hoverbikes seemed to be the main source of transportation in the thin streets. She spotted another out of the corner of her eye and wondered how fast they could go.

No, that won't work, she mentally chided herself for the idea. This escape plan had to be successful. She couldn't jeopardize it by trying to learn how to drive a hoverbike when she had never driven any sort of vehicle before. Walking would just have to do.

Up ahead, the row of blocky buildings ended, along with the fence. Tetra's heart skipped a beat as the street turned into a stone bridge as dusty as the streets. As they marched onto it, their platoon was pushed to the bridge's protective barrier to make room for a unit of Igrian soldiers driving on hoverbikes past them. The armor on Tetra's arm gave a small screech as she rubbed up against the thick stones, tempting her gaze to glance over the barrier at the dizzying drop into pitch-black darkness. Her stomach flipped at the sight, and she immediately averted her gaze.

"Don't get too close there, Cairn." One of her platoon mates, Mabel Frauss, chided in a low voice behind her, "We wouldn't want the dishonorable coward to get in an *unfortunate* accident."

A couple others around them heard the comment and snickered. Tetra was thankful her helmet hid her burning face. Everyone in the platoon knew she hated heights and used that knowledge accordingly.

At least Mabel was only threatening her with empty words this time instead of using her sharp daggers.

They finally made it to the other side of the bridge, and she let out a quiet sigh of relief as the buildings and the fence took up both sides of the street as if there hadn't just been a huge split between them. Thankfully, she wasn't planning on living in Xich if she escaped. Living in a kingdom where the ground was made entirely out of flat, towering rock outcroppings that descended into inky darkness was not an ideal location for her to live in.

Without a dizzying drop to worry about, Tetra continued scanning her surroundings and keeping track of the mental street map she was creating. So far, she had been doing everything she was told to do and was being the good little trainee she told Emperor Ignis she would be—on the outside, of course. Her thoughts were an entirely different matter. They were full of forming escape plans and ideas that screamed "dishonorable trainee" and caused her to silently apologize repeatedly to her parents' spirits.

She pushed the disheartening thought to the side and fixed her gaze on a short stretch of brightly colored buildings that didn't look like they had been damaged in the previous battle. As she peered at two Igrian soldiers chatting on the flat roof of one of the buildings (who were probably supposed to be on guard duty), the tips of her fingers and toes began to tingle. Worry filled her heart; it was a sensation that had become a more normal occurrence the past couple months. She flicked her gaze around wildly as her heart began to pound.

No, no, no! This can't be happening! Not now.

One of the guards on top of the roof shouted, and Lieutenant Tarson stopped the whole platoon. Tetra tripped to a stop before bumping into the person in front of her. More shouts came from those around her, but she couldn't discern what they were saying as her thoughts converged in a wild panic upon the tingling slowly taking over her fingers and toes. How long would it take this time for the sweeping, invisible flames to wrack through her body?

Yet as the shouts continued, and her comrades surged around her towards a singular point, the tingling didn't move any further. As the thought settled in her head like a shield against the swarm of arrows dipped in pools of fear, she began to think more clearly again—and immediately chided herself for getting into such a panic. What if she found herself in a battle and was injured? Was that any way to act in that situation?

A scream cut off her mental scolding, and she blinked out of her stupor. She caught sight of something falling from the fence before it landed amidst Lieutenant Tarson and her platoon.

Tetra took a step forward, but then stopped. Should she try to escape right now? She glanced around and noticed more Igrian soldiers running, or zipping on hoverbikes, towards the ruckus, then turned her head forward again as the group of trainees began moving back from the center of their circle.

No. Now was not the right time. There was no room for mistakes this go 'round, and running off without a plan was a big one.

Her curiosity piqued now that she didn't have to worry about escaping right then, she took a few steps towards the spot where Lieutenant Tarson's raised voice was coming from. Her commanding officer was arguing with someone as Tetra caught the words, "—stays on this side."

She slowed to a stop and pushed herself between two of her platoonmates to get a better look. Lieutenant Tarson faced a few Silvanian soldiers who stood on the other side of the fence. Her heart skipped a beat as she noticed the shaking heap of fabric curled up at the second lieutenant's feet. Even from a distance, she could see tears falling down the bronzed face of the Xichian, teenage girl.

It all clicked together in Tetra's head. The girl must have tried climbing the fence while the guards weren't looking; but then they clearly saw her, yelled, and scared her enough to where she lost her hold and fell.

"—know her parents, and they are on this side," one of the Silvanian soldiers gestured towards one of her comrades as she spoke. "If you will—"

"—I will not have some Straudwin spy get over on my watch." Lieutenant Tarson cut her off, then turned her face towards the girl and barked, "Get up!"

The girl pushed her long, dark hair back from her face and looked up at Lieutenant Tarson. "*Weli Va*! I—I no spy. I—only want—family," she replied in broken Alenguan." *Weli Va*—please!"

"Get up!" Lieutenant Tarson barked again.

"What's going on here?"

Tetra turned her head as Igrian soldiers broke through the trainees' circle. The man who spoke had the insignia of a sergeant etched into his shoulder plate.

Lieutenant Tarson turned her hard stare upon the man. "This sniveling wretch was trying to climb the fence."

The sergeant stepped forward. "Well, thank you for catching her, but you can leave this in our hands now, Second Lieutenant," he said with a respectful nod and a salute towards her.

"And I would under normal circumstances, Sergeant," Tarson returned the nod, "but I have orders that say otherwise."

"I mean no disrespect, but you are no longer a sanctioned commander in these types of situations. I was told you were only patrolling the routine guard posts—not administering punishments."

"And if these weren't orders from the Emperor Himself then I would let you do the administering."

Lieutenant Tarson pulled her holonode out of a small pocket compartment in her arm's armor and turned it on. Tetra's heart skipped another nervous beat. The only reason Emperor Ignis would get involved with something like this is if it involved her.

The sergeant raised a dubious brow. "The emperor?"

Lieutenant Tarson gave him a sharp nod and showed him the message she had just pulled up. He was silent for a few moments as he read the message with Emperor Ignis' signature at the end of it. Then, he looked back at the second lieutenant's face and gave her a slow nod.

"I see." He waved his hand towards the Xichian girl still lying on the ground and stepped back. "Do what you need to, Second Lieutenant."

"Thank you, Sergeant." Lieutenant Tarson's eyes locked onto Tetra's. "Cairn! Come here."

Tetra's heart dropped, but she marched forward with robotic movements as her platoonmates' indistinguishable whispers flitted past her ears. This must be a test the emperor designed to see if she would actually do what she said she promised.

Dread sent shivers through her muscles as she glanced down and locked eyes with the Xichian girl. The fear she saw in their teal depths couldn't have been faked.

She peeled her gaze away and immediately erased the frown from her own face. This did sound like something Emperor Ignis would do—either create a situation to test her loyalty, or twist any that came up to serve that same purpose.

"Yes ma'am?" She asked as she stopped in front of Lieutenant Tarson.

The sergeant turned his gaze on her. "Did you say 'Cairn'?" He asked, "As in Generals Aries and Marin Cairn?"

"Yes," Lieutenant Tarson sneered, "but don't let that fool you. This one's the worst excuse for a Straudwin coward you could find. She has more tallies than anyone you've seen."

The man blinked in surprise and gave Tetra a guarded look but said nothing else.

"I told you to get up!" Tarson looked back down at the Xichian girl.

The girl finally pushed herself up onto her knees, then got up into a standing position. She stared with wide eyes, hunched over and trembling like a leaf, as her gaze moved between Lieutenant Tarson, Tetra, and the sergeant.

Sweat beaded Tetra's brow as Lieutenant Tarson's gaze locked on her again. Metal rang, and her commanding officer held out her segione. She couldn't help but cringe slightly as her eyes landed on the serrated blade. Phantom pains throbbed through her right arm and she forced herself to keep both arms still.

"Mark this spy, Cairn," a challenging gleam entered Lieutenant Tarson's gaze, "and show His Imperial Majesty your loyalty and what little honor you have left."

"I not a spy!" The girl cried out in her heavy accent.

Her gaze whirled around in a panic, but she must've realized her hopeless predicament with the circle of trainees and soldiers surrounding her because her shoulders soon slumped even further. Tetra felt a flash of pity for her, but it immediately turned into self-pity as Tarson inched the segione closer.

"Take it, Cairn." Her C.O. growled.

She finally took the dagger's hilt in her shaky, tingling hand. Once her hands were free, Tarson immediately grabbed the sides of the girl's tear-streaked face. Tetra locked eyes with the girl again and gulped. She had learned in both history class and training that anyone caught breaking second-degree laws in Igrium, like pickpockets, were given a cut across the forehead. And in special circumstances, like times of war, it could also be used as a warning; a way to spread fear to those of other kingdoms. Like now.

Tetra had to pull her gaze away from the girl's and locked it onto the middle of her bronzed forehead. She tightened her grip on the segione's hilt. If she made a mistake now, she might not get any chance to escape. She *had* to do this. There was no choice.

She lifted the segione. One little mark. That's it. That's all it would take. She would make it as painless as possible, and the mark as small as possible. It would be better for the girl's sake if Tetra did it rather than anyone else.

"She is not a spy!" The Silvanian soldier's accented voice broke through Tetra's concentration, and she shot a glance at the daggers the woman was glaring at them all.

"Quiet!" The sergeant barked as he turned to face the Silvanian soldiers. "You know our laws, you Straudwin, and the girl will pay fairly for breaking them." He turned back and nodded towards Tetra. "Proceed, Trainee Cairn."

"We don't have all day," Lieutenant Tarson added with a frown.

Tetra took a deep breath and lifted the dagger again. She tried to keep her eyes on her target, but they flickered back down to the hopeless fear shining in the girl's eyes. And just like with all the other times where she had disobeyed, she realized she did have a choice.

She knew her superiors were only being cautious about letting possible, important information loose into their enemies' hands, yet that didn't give them the right to permanently mark someone who was obviously not a spy. The girl had most likely been separated from her parents during the battle and ended up on the wrong side of the fence.

Could Tetra truly mark her when her gut said she was innocent? When she herself had been marked by this same segione for only trying to do what she thought was right? How could she administer the same dishonor to this girl that she wasn't even willing to receive herself?

"Cairn..." Lieutenant Tarson's tone held a sharp edge, "I'm losing my patience."

A sharp, needle-like pain stabbed Tetra's fingertip, and a jolt of new dread went through her. She would've dwelt on it further, but her commanding officer's gaze held a spark of danger that seemed even worse at that moment. So, she promptly ignored the pain as she lowered the segione and looked away.

"I—I can't—" Her words were cut off by a snarl.

"You Straudwin coward!"

She jerked her head up just as Lieutenant Tarson let the Xichian girl go and grabbed her instead. Blood pounded in Tetra's ears as she stared into the fiery depths of Tarson's eyes.

"I've had it with you, Cairn!" Spittle flew into Tetra's face as her C.O. spoke, "You're a dishonor to me! You're a dishonor to your family name! And you're a dishonor to this entire empire!" Her voice lowered as she added, "And I'm glad that the emperor is finally seeing fit to put you in your place. But first—"

She pried the segione from Tetra's aching hand and raised it up. In a higher voice that made Tetra's ears ring, she called out, "—it's time to finally mark this traitor for what she's worth!"

Tetra stared up at her commanding officer with wide eyes. She took an involuntary step back but bumped into someone. She jerked her head around and looked up into the disapproving expression of the sergeant. He locked eyes with her and frowned before grabbing both her shoulders in an iron grip. Without any words, he lifted his eyes and nodded towards Tarson.

Jeers and curses from her platoonmates and a few of the Igrian soldiers filled the air around her. Nothing like the prospect of spilled blood to get their hardened consciences excited. Her stomach churned and her head began to pound with all the noise.

"The emperor has kept this from happening for too long, but now that your fate is sealed, I see no reason to not continue." Fear sent shivers through Tetra's muscles as Tarson spoke in a much calmer and collected voice, "I have a feeling he will find it easy to forgive me for doing this. You wouldn't be the first of his personal guards to have a malscar anyway."

And with that calm finished, the windstorm hit. Lieutenant Tarson grabbed the side of Tetra's helmet and jerked her face forward. Tetra gulped at the dark ferocity in her commanding officer's expression. What monster from Malackin's Pit had she awakened?

A sharp pain stung her neck as her helmet was yanked off. Then, her commanding officer grabbed the side of her head to keep her still. She winced as the metal from the gauntlet dug into her skin.

"Hold still, or your eye may have an unfortunate accident." Tarson leaned her head forward with a grim smile. "And we wouldn't want that, would we?"

A cold wave washed over Tetra despite the dry heat, and she stood as still as she could while shaking uncontrollably. That would just be her luck; getting a malscar *and* losing an eye at the same time.

More invisible needles began to stab at her fingers and toes, as if whatever caused the pains felt her distress and wanted to add more to it. She gritted her teeth and squeezed her eyes shut.

Small, sharp teeth dug into her cheek. She sucked in a sharp breath through her nose. The teeth dug in deeper. She clamped her mouth shut before a scream could come out as one of the metal points hit her cheekbone. With meticulously slow, agonizing movements, Lieutenant Tarson carved the first line down Tetra's cheek, only stopping when she reached her chin.

Tears fell from Tetra's eyes. The salt from them stung her new cut, but she couldn't stop them. It was either cry or scream, and screaming would only add to the humiliation. Not everyone could see her tears, but they would most definitely be able to hear her screams.

The sharp teeth dug into the bridge of her nose, and the slow, agonizing process continued horizontally. The new, painful line dug its way to her ear before it stopped.

"And now you look like the Straudwin coward you really are," Tarson said.

Tetra opened her eyes a crack, then blinked the blurriness away. Her face stung with the stings of syrup bees, while the invisible needles continued lengthening their attack to the rest of her feet and hands. She met Tarson's gaze with her own, and her pounding heart dropped into her stomach at the malicious pleasure she found in her commanding officer's eyes.

"It's a shame, Cairn," Tarson shook her head in mock sadness. "You could've been just like your parents. You could've had all the honor and fame a person could ever want, yet now you'll forever be the lowest of the low. And the only thing you would've had to do was this—!"

Tarson spun and slashed the segione across the Xichian girl's forehead. The girl cried out and fell onto her knees, covering her head with her hands. Tarson nodded sharply and looked back over at Tetra.

"Hmm." A thoughtful look came over her face, "Now you two match."

Despite the needles stabbing her hands, Tetra curled them into fists as a spark of anger lit in her chest. The thoughtful expression disappeared from Tarson's face as their eyes locked. Her voice dipped down dangerously as she asked, "Are you angry, Cairn?"

Tetra didn't reply. Her C.O. eyed her for a moment, then struck out with her metal-encased fist and punched her new malscar. Tetra couldn't hold back a cry as her head jerked away with the burst of pain. Fresh tears fell as the lieutenant clamped a hand around her chin and yanked her face upwards until they were eye-to-eye.

"Because I sure am." After a painful moment, Tarson grimaced and jerked Tetra's face away before letting go. In a louder voice she yelled, "Trainees! Get in formation! We're heading back to the palace!"

Tetra felt the sergeant move away from her. So, she immediately put her aching hands up to her face to stanch the bleeding, and to cover the dishonorable wound from the leering eyes around her.

The needle-like pain in her hands and feet slowly moved into her wrists and ankles. Its unstoppable movement only added a new panic to the swirl of emotions she was already drowning in.

The gods were punishing her, weren't they? Maybe they had finally had enough of her, or maybe her parents sent in a special request to torment their failure of a daughter who just dragged their name through the mud with a malscar.

Shame boiled in her already-churning stomach, relieving her mind of its panic for a moment. *I have a malscar...*

Lieutenant Tarson's earlier remarks hit her crumbling mental defenses like bolts, causing the pulsing pain of her new wound to worsen. She was marked like Straudwin himself, the most infamous coward in Igrium's history; and would forever be counted as even less than she already was because of it.

She heard low voices and sent a wary glance over towards her C.O. and the sergeant. The sharp glare Tarson shot towards her sent her heartbeat racing even more. So, she lowered her head and began shuffling towards her platoonmates to get as far from the furious woman as possible.

"Not you, Cairn," Tarson barked. "You're staying with me."

Her stomach churned again as she met the fury burning on the Second Lieutenant's face. Tetra almost lost her lunch right then—to top the whole humiliating experience off—but she was able to keep it down as she stayed right where she was until her platoonmates moved into their respective formation. Lieutenant Tarson and the sergeant both shared a nod, then her C.O. stepped over and grabbed her arm.

"Move, trainees!" Tarson ordered.

A sharp cry rang behind them. Tetra jerked her head to look back over her shoulder as she was dragged away. A couple soldiers had pulled the girl off the ground and shoved her away from the fence. Their eyes locked for a moment, and guilt clawed at her heart at the blood she saw dripping down the girl's ashen face. Tarson jerked her forward, and she turned her face away.

Blood ran between the fingers of her gauntlet and down her arm. Her face stung with the sporadic pounding of her heart, and she wondered if it looked as bad as the girl's had.

No, it looks worse. She gritted her teeth as a sharper, internal pain stabbed the middle of her palm. *Because it's a malscar, you Straudwin.*

As Lieutenant Tarson dragged Tetra back along the way they had come from the Xichian Palace of Commons, the sharper pains—now more like the tips of daggers instead of needles—poked the insides of her feet with each step until she was stumbling along the sandy streets instead of walking. Tarson only jerked her arm forward, which sent a shock of pain through her bones. It seemed to give permission for the invisible needles to continue their march through her insides, but at a much faster pace.

What sort of curse had the gods put on her? Torture by invisible needles?

She quickly wished that was the case, as the needles that coursed through her body turned into fiery daggers like the ones stabbing her feet. They cut into her muscles, etched their burning pains along her bones, diced her organs, and stabbed her nerves. Even her eyeballs felt as if someone was stabbing them through her skull, and she squeezed them shut to try and block out the pain.

Her knees hit the ground, followed by the rest of her body. Somewhere far away, Tetra could hear her C.O. yelling, but she couldn't make out the words through the sharp ringing in her ears.

Sharp. Everything was sharp. Too sharp.

That's why when the darkness began to overtake the corners of her mind, she let it. It soon covered her thoughts like a cool blanket and led her off into blissful peace.

Chapter Seven

MUFFLED VOICES SPOKE OUT of the darkness. Fog covered Tetra's brain, but she still tried to turn her focus towards the conversation. The more she tried, the clearer they became until she was able to make out Tarson's rough voice as she was saying, "...with her?"

"All of our scans said there was nothing wrong." Another voice, this one masculine, spoke up, "She must've blacked out either from shock or the heat."

"What about the fever? That doesn't sound like shock to me."

There was a pause. "The best answer I can surmise is that it was caused by the heat."

"But she's not sick?"

"No, she's not. Like I said, there's absolutely nothing wrong with her."

Tarson snorted, "Nothing wrong with her health-wise, that is."

"Yes. Well, whatever you do, if you want her to travel back to Rubrum as quickly as possible, make sure she gets rest."

"Alright, doctor. Thank you for the help."

A pair of footsteps walked away at a clipped pace. The fog had loosened its hold on Tetra's mind while they spoke, but she still had to run through what was said a couple times before their words finally sunk in: she was being sent back to Rubrum.

She snapped her eyes open and glanced around, but then immediately squeezed them shut with a moan as the movement of her eyeball sent a throbbing pain through the right side of her face. Without opening her eyes, she lifted her hand. Her fingertips barely touched the wound's bumpy surface with a sting, and she pulled it away.

Shame rushed to the forefront of her mind alongside the blur of memories, so she opened her eyes to turn her focus away from the onslaught of guilt. Where was she? Her heart pounded as she pushed herself up into a sitting position. This wasn't the room she and her roommates were supposed to be staying in during the trip...

"You're awake, I see."

Tetra jerked her head around and immediately hissed with a wince as a sharp pain rushed through her face's new wound. After a few moments, the pounding of blood through her cheek dulled somewhat and she opened her eyes again. Lieutenant Tarson's stone countenance stared at her coldly from across the small room. Tetra scrunched the blanket lying atop the cot she was sitting on in her fists.

"Yes ma'am." She said, keeping her gaze low.

"I messaged His Imperial Majesty, and he's sending an escort to take you back to Rubrum," Lieutenant Tarson said without any emotion. "Their hovertrain is scheduled to be here tomorrow morning. Until then, you are staying here—and *resting*." The last word was marked with a sneer.

"Yes ma'am." She nodded, keeping her expression emotionless.

Tarson took a couple steps towards the door. "Oh, and don't expect anything for dinner."

With that, she opened the door and stepped out of the room, slamming it shut behind her. As her marching footfalls faded, Tetra breathed in a shaky breath of the silent atmosphere. She lifted her head and slowly turned it from side to side to keep her eyes as still as possible while getting a good look at her surroundings.

There were no windows in the dim room. A single lightbulb on a string hung from the ceiling, illuminating the sink and mirror in the corner. The door Tarson left through seemed to be the only way in or out. A small vent was in the ceiling above the door—too small for Tetra to squeeze through, even without her armor.

Her armor... At the thought, she realized she wasn't wearing it anymore. She glanced down. Someone must've taken it off when she had fainted. Now all she was left in were her gray military fatigues.

She exhaled deeply through her nose. At least they were dark. So, if she did somehow escape this tiny room and it was night, she would have stealth on her side. But still, she had really needed her armor to help shield her body against the barbed wire when she made it to the fence. *If* she made it to the fence, that is.

But first things first... She turned her neck around and got another look at the room. What a mess she had gotten herself into. If she even made it out of this place, she would have to figure out where it was even located in the city. She shook her head at herself. What a mess.

A few moments passed as she picked apart her escape she had been planning before the malscar incident. As she sat there contemplating the different plans in the silent room, she came to the realization that none of them would work unless she actually knew where she was. She let out a frustrated sigh, then regretted it as the pounding of her blood stung through her face.

Well, sitting here wasn't helping. She slowly got up from the cot and stretched out her sore muscles. The doctor was right. There was no pain anywhere (other than her face, of course). Whatever had been wrong with her, at least it didn't have any lasting effects. She slowly shook her head before stepping over to the door. She might as well see if it was open...

Tetra grabbed the handle and tried to turn it. It wouldn't budge. *Well, at least I tried,* she thought.

Done with her quick investigation, she spun on her heel to go back to the cot, but then a muffled voice sounded from the other side of the door. She slowly turned back around as another voice joined the first. Were those...guards?

She took a quiet step back to the door and pressed the uninjured side of her face against it. She closed her eyes and focused her breaths to be as quiet as possible.

"...here."

There. The corner of her mouth lifted, and it sent a sting through her face. She ignored it and strained her ears to listen.

"...least we're not out in the sun," she could barely make out the other voice's reply.

There was a snort. "You always have to look on the bright side of things, don't you?"

"It's the only way I can work with you."

There was something familiar about their voices, but she couldn't place it. Pushing the thought to the side, Tetra continued to listen for any information as to where she might be. Their argument quickly petered out, though, and a sliver of frustration entered her heart. That had been a waste of—

But then, one of the guards started talking again, starting another conversation.

Tetra was confused. For guards, they sure did talk quite a bit. Granted, the only guards Tetra had ever seen personally were the emperor's personal guards and Igrium's honorguard corps—the brainwashed ones, and the ones trained to the point of brainwashing. Maybe what she was hearing was just normal behavior.

Well, she at least knew there were two guards outside. That was a start. She stayed pressed against the door for a few more minutes but found out nothing from their conversation that pertained to where she was.

However, she did find out why the voices sounded so familiar when they both said each other's names at two different points in the conversation: Brutus Jazeton and Rexsan Loir. They were both trainees, not real guards—which explained all the talking they were doing, and they were part of Second Lieutenant Dcnir's platoon. She could only guess as to why trainees were guarding her—possibly to spare the army from giving any *real* soldiers to the task—but it gave her a sliver of hope. She might be able to work with this. As long as her horrid cousin Aquilo didn't become one of her guards, there was hope of pulling something off.

An inkling of a plan entered her mind, and she let it come. Then a few ideas followed, and the more she thought upon them the more they multiplied. She began to pace in circles around the small room as she thought.

If the other trainee platoons were guarding her, then it was very likely she was in the Palace of Commons—the government building where Xich's president resided until Igrium came and took it over. It was the biggest building in Trivsau; a maze of pastel-painted halls, spiraling towers, and gardens that spanned over three large outcroppings the previous battle barely touched—despite the devastation done to the rest of the city. She knew a little bit of the building's layout, but she mentally prepared herself for the possibility of getting lost in the maze if she had to take another way she didn't know.

Then there was the fact that the Palace was at least a mile from the fence—and it would be a walk full of dodging patrols amidst the ruins of the city while trying to act natural to the citizens that might spot her. She lifted her hand to her face but didn't touch the malscar. Was there even anything natural about her appearance anymore? She stopped pacing and, despite the encroaching shame, walked over to the mirror to finally see the damage.

Her eyes widened as she met them in the mirror, and she swallowed back the bile rising in her throat. Shame filled her stomach with nausea. The malscar ran right below her right eye down to her jaw and from the bridge of her nose across to her right ear in large, puffy lines. Black stitches bound the wounds. It was so much worse than she thought it would be—and it was forever embedded into her skin for all to see, exclaiming that she was a dishonorable coward. The lowest of the low. Worth less than dust.

Tears welled in her eyes but she blinked them back. This was not the time for self-pity. She needed to plan now, or she would have no more opportunities to do so. She curled her hands into fists and turned away from the mirror to continue pacing. She turned her focus back to her ideas and the half-formed plans filling her head, yet the shame continued to lurk in the corners of her mind.

Tetra didn't know how long she paced in that room—going over all of her ideas and putting many of them together like an intricate puzzle—but she finally made a plan. She even began to feel a little confidence in its success; a rare thing when it came to her escape plans.

Taking in a deep breath, she turned to face the door. Now was the time.

She stepped over to the door and knocked. The muffled voices that had been constant background noise for the past who-knew-how-long immediately stopped. Tetra knocked again and, in a weak voice, asked, "Hello? Is anyone there?"

Silence met her words. She called out again, "Hello? Please, is anyone there?" She added a whine to the last word and hoped it sounded as pitiful to them as it did her.

"What do you want, traitor?" Brutus' voice called back.

"I—I need some help." Tetra gave a dry cough. "I don't—I don't feel so great."

Hurried whispers sounded outside. She pressed her ear to the metal door and caught a few snippets of the low conversation.

"...not sure what..."

"Might be..."

"...do we do?"

"...don't know..."

"...go get..."

Tetra glanced down at the floor. She gritted her teeth at the knowledge of the pain she was about to feel in her face, then collapsed on the ground. Her arms cushioned her head's fall, but a sharp dagger-like pain still ripped through her face at the jarring impact. She didn't have to fake the moan that escaped her lips.

"Please..." It wasn't hard to fake the whimper this time, "I think I'm sick..."

There was a pause. Then the sound of a lock clicking, and the door handle turned. Tetra looked up at Brutus and Rexsan's panicky faces through narrowed eyes.

"What's wrong with you?" Rexsan fiddled with his sheathed sword's pommel. He glanced behind his shoulder as if he was waiting for someone.

"I don't—I don't feel great." Tetra moaned and coughed a couple times. She gritted her teeth at the smartness of pain the movements caused her face. "I think—I think I'm sick. Call a—call a doctor—or something."

Despite the panic still evident on his face, Brutus narrowed his eyes with a nod. He turned his head towards Rexsan and said in a much deeper voice, "Go find Lieutenant Denir and tell him what's happening. I'll stay here and watch her."

Rexsan jerked his head in a nod and turned to go, but then he looked back and asked, "Should I tell one of the others to help you?"

Brutus' gaze glanced over Tetra's pitiful form. "Nah, I got it."

Without another word, Rexsan bolted down the hall. Tetra kept her gaze on the floor. Once Rexsan's echoing footsteps faded, Brutus stepped into the room and crouched down next to her.

"You look horrible," he said.

If Tetra wasn't trying to act sick, she would punch him right then. Be that as it may, she needed to wait a few more seconds for Rexsan to truly be gone. The fewer opponents she had, the better.

She lay there coughing for a few more moments that felt like hours before she "tried" to lift herself up with her hands. Brutus gave a snort at her pitiful attempt.

"Help—me up." Her throat was starting to hurt from all this fake-coughing. "On—onto the cot, please."

Brutus rolled his eyes but grabbed her hand. "If you get me sick, I'll kill you."

Sorry Brutus, but Emperor Ignis has first dibs on my fate, she thought.

She coughed into her elbow and said, "I—I'll try not to."

He helped pull her up. Their eyes locked and he sneered. "I can't believe I'm actually—"

Tetra rammed her palm against his face before he could finish the sentence. Brutus moaned as blood spilled out of his nose. Before he could do anything, she kicked him in the knee. As he fell, she kneed him in the head. He crumpled in an unconscious, armored heap with a *CLANG.*

Blood pounded in her ears as she reached down and removed his belt and swords from his waist. Both his sword sheaths clanged together as she stood and put the belt around herself.

Brutus was one of the few at Norland who preferred dual swords over a single one and shield. She had never really trained with them and felt better with only one in her hands, but it was nice to know she had another as a shield replacement.

After strapping them on, she glanced down to make sure Brutus was still alive. Her eyes caught the rise and fall of his chest, and a breeze of relief blew through her.

Even though he was annoying, she didn't think that was a good enough reason to kill a person. Nor did she think her conscience could handle it.

She glanced back over at her reflection in the mirror to make sure the belt and swords were on correctly, and couldn't help as her eyes trailed back up to the wound on the right side of her face. Another bout of shame clogged her throat as she let her gaze trail the two crisscrossed lines on her cheek before she forced herself to look away.

Turning her focus back onto her escape plan, she stepped over Brutus and poked her head out of the room. Both sides of the corridor were empty. The side on her left slowly curved downwards, while a set of metal doors stood centennial to the right.

Tetra stepped out of the room and shut the door behind her. She locked it and took a few quiet, loping steps towards the doors; the sword sheaths bouncing lightly against her legs. She stopped next to the door and pressed her ear against it. Blood, aided by her rising adrenaline, pounded in her ears. Between that and the thick doors, she couldn't hear a thing.

She unsheathed one of the swords and, after taking a steadying breath, knocked on one of the doors. There was a heart-thudding moment of nothing, then it cracked open. Tetra pressed herself into the corner as it opened wider, concealing her.

"Uh..."

"What is it?"

Tetra's stomach tightened. She recognized the owner of the second voice as Mabel Frauss.

The other voice cursed, and Tetra knew it to be another of her platoon mates: Accaly Lavrai. "I think those idiots are playing a prank on us."

"I don't think—" Mabel paused, "—wait—yeah, they would."

"That's probably why Rexsan didn't tell us anything."

"I'll have their heads if they jeopardize this for us!" Tetra could practically feel the anger undoubtedly reddening Mabel's face as the girl spoke, "Don't they realize this isn't just some training exercise?"

Tetra shifted on her feet as Accaly raised her voice, "Brutus! We know you're up to something! And it isn't—"

Her words were cut off as Tetra jumped out from behind the door and swung the sword into her knee. Accaly fell with a cry. Tetra knocked her out with the sword's pommel and barely lifted the weapon's blade up in time to defend herself from Mabel.

They locked eyes and Mabel cursed. "I should've known it was *you*." She spat.

Tetra pushed against the girl's weapon to give herself time to move back. She lifted the sword and blocked Mabel's next strike. Then, she attacked with her own. They both traded blows around Accaly's crumpled form.

Mabel landed a small cut on Tetra's arm. Tetra gritted her teeth against the small sting and countered with a lunge. The tip of her sword slid against Mabel's breastplate with a screech. Mabel smiled grimly at Tetra's disadvantage and sliced another cut along Tetra's other arm.

This needed to end. Tetra swung her sword in a low arc with all the force she could muster. The blade hit Mabel's armored thigh and unsteadied her. Taking the advantage, Tetra hit Mabel's wrist and she let go of her sword. It clanged to the floor as Tetra lunged forward and pressed the tip of her blade against Mabel's throat.

Despite her peril, Mabel sent Tetra a knowing smirk. "Go ahead, Cairn. Kill me," anger blazed in her eyes, "and show everyone how much of an Alliance Straudwin you really are."

Instead of giving into the bait, Tetra unsheathed her other sword and slammed its hilt against Mabel's head. She stepped back as the girl's limp form crumpled to the floor.

No, I won't kill you, Mabel, a small grimace turned the corners of her lips down, *no matter how much you might deserve it.*

Without dwelling on it further, she sheathed one of the dual swords and ran through the doorway into a new hall that curved to the right.

Tetra slowed to a stop at a sharp corner that ended the hall. Just as she was about to make sure no one was coming up the hallway, she heard the echo of heavy footsteps coming towards her direction. Her heart skipped a beat as she gripped the sword tighter in her left hand, her right hand fluttering down to the pommel of the other sword.

The footsteps continued to come closer. Tetra tightened her grip on the sword's hilt. When they were almost right upon her, she stepped out from behind the wall—sword raised—and found herself face-to-face with Aabir Sorrel.

Chapter Eight

THE ELDERLY XICHIAN MAN met Aabir's eyes. Aabir immediately looked away from the dismayed expression covering the man's wrinkled features; guilt knotting in his stomach as his imagination showed him a picture of that same look on Mister Falap's face. Ever since he and his platoon had arrived in Trivsau that morning, he had been bombarded by the harsh realities of the war—and continually reminded of how horrible the empire he was a part of could be. So far, it was becoming one of the toughest trips he had ever taken.

The man finished pouring water into Aabir's cup and turned away to do the same at the table behind theirs. Aabir glanced over his shoulder at the stooped man and wondered if he had already been a worker in the Palace of Commons, or if he was forced into the role after Igrium took over this side of the city. The thought did nothing to help his mood, so he turned his head forward and stared down at his plate of half-eaten food.

"You all right, Aabir?" Tycho asked before stuffing a piece of naan into his mouth.

"Yeah." Aabir shrugged and finished off his third stuffed leaf-wrap. He wasn't, but he had never confided in his family's past problems to his friends before, and he did not think it wise to do so now—especially with the sour look Aquilo had been wearing all afternoon.

"OK," Tycho said between bites, "You've just been quiet, is all."

"There's just nothing to talk about." Out loud, that is.

Aquilo—who was sitting across from them—snorted. "Even if there isn't anything to talk about, you somehow find a way to bring up *something*."

"I'm fine." Aabir rolled his eyes and tried to feign ignorance. "It's just been a long day and I'm tired, that's all."

Aabir knew he had not been himself all day. Ever since he left his house in the early morning hours, a weight had pressed upon his shoulders—a burden made up of his worries over his family and his half-formed ideas on how to help them. Needless to say, he had been too distracted to keep up with all the conversations going on at the tables around him.

"Mm–hmm." A smirk grew across Tycho's thin features. "I'm sure Tetra Cairn's little mishap has nothing to do with it."

Aabir blinked and turned to look at his friend. "I can't believe I'm saying this, Tycho, but you're actually right for once." And he was...mostly.

"Even though I'd rather not dispute that, I have a feeling it's wrong."

Aabir twisted his lips into a frown and tapped the table with his fingers. He did one stupid thing years ago and it seemed like it would forever taint him.

"Nope, it's not."

"Lay off him, Tycho." Aquilo broke through the budding argument.

Aabir looked over at Aquilo in surprise. He usually never said anything to dissuade Tycho's joking jabs. It sometimes made him wonder if some part of his uptight friend actually believed them to be true.

"What?" Tycho asked, "Do you actually believe him?"

Aquilo's serious gaze flicked between them both. "No one—especially not Aabir—would ever be worried about what happened today."

Although Aabir had a feeling he knew where Aquilo was going, he still asked, "What do you mean?"

"What I mean is that no one should be worried over Tetra because she got what's been coming to her; and no one with as good a record as you, Aabir, should be worried about the same thing happening to them."

Maybe not normally, but with the traitorous thoughts he had been having recently, any of his commanding officers would find him *worthy* of a malscar—which only added to the mixture of worries and emotions he was trying to suppress. He wished he could be as fearless as Tetra, but whenever he had that thought he was immediately reminded of his family and pushed it to the far corners of his mind.

"That's what I thought," Aabir replied, then took a bite of rice. Spicy flames erupted in his mouth, and he washed them down with some water.

"Sorrel."

Aabir jumped in his skin at Second Lieutenant Denir's voice. Mouth still on fire, he twisted around on the bench and stood with a salute.

"Second Lieutenant, sir," he said with a swallow.

Denir gave him a sharp nod. "I have an assignment for you."

"Yes sir?"

"I need you to take the place of Rexsan Loir in guarding Cairn." He raised a challenging brow. "Can you do that?"

Aabir tried to keep his expression neutral. "Yes sir."

"She's being kept in the old diplomatic prison tunnel. If Brutus Jazeston asks, tell him I'm sending his replacement right after you."

Aabir saluted him again as he left. Once he was gone, he turned around and inhaled the rest of his water as Aquilo and Tycho watched him amusingly.

"I told you not to get it," Aquilo said.

Aabir put the cup down with a bang. "I didn't think it was going to be that spicy!" He said between breaths.

"Well, are you better now?"

Aabir nodded and straightened. "Yeah, I think so." He picked up his tray and glanced between the both of them. "I guess I'll be seeing you both later."

"I'm so glad he didn't choose me." Tycho shook his head with a look of disgust. "Guard duty. Worse than a tally."

With a roll of his eyes, Aabir turned around and left the dining hall. Despite Tycho's complaints, he thought it was one of the best assignments given. Usually there was nothing wrong with guarding someone or something. Usually.

A small worm of guilt slithered through his conscience. Was it truly right to guard someone who was a prisoner because they acted on many of the same views that he believed in?

As he marched through the Palace of Commons (and got lost once in all the twisting corridors), he tried pushing the guilt to the side with thoughts that circled between wondering if his family was alright at that moment, fantastical ideas on how they could all escape Igrium, what Tetra could have possibly done to earn herself a malscar, and then back to his family. He soon made it to the empty, low-ceilinged hall the Xichian servant he had asked directions from told him about. His footsteps echoed against the claustrophobic stone walls.

Ahead of him, the hall turned into a sharp corner—something he had rarely seen since entering the curving, sloping Palace of Commons. He picked up his pace as the servant's detailed words were confirmed with each new step. The prison doors should be right—

Tetra Cairn popped out from behind the corner and Aabir found the tip of a sword at his throat. His heartbeat grew in tempo as adrenaline filled his veins. He widened his eyes and took an involuntary step back, but the sword moved with him.

"Tetra!"

He put his hands up in surrender and met her eyes—and that was when he saw it. The malscar. He could not help but cringe at the sight of the fabled punishment marring his past friend's face.

Something flashed across Tetra's hard features, but it immediately disappeared as she pressed the tip a little deeper into his neck, slightly breaking the skin. "What are you doing here, Aabir?" He blinked in surprise at the dagger-like edge in her tone.

"I...Lieutenant Denir sent me here to—to guard you." He licked his lips.

She tilted her head slightly. "Well, I think you're a little late..."

"Um..." He gulped, but it only pressed the sharp point a tiny bit deeper into his skin. "I think he would say otherwise..."

Her eyes narrowed. "Aabir, I can't stay here any longer. I need you to let me go."

"I—I wish I could, but you know I can't. Things are—things are hard enough right now for me and my family without me letting you go to top it all off! That...I can't do that, Tetra." Then a horrible thought hit him, "Who knows if we're even being filmed right now!"

Tetra said nothing, only staying still as she stared at him. He stared back, but now he could see a new emotion filling her gaze: worry.

"Why did you choose now of all times to escape?" He asked.

Something new darkened her fair features. Despite the firmness of her hold on the sword, her voice warbled slightly as she replied, "If I don't leave now, I'll be taken back to Igrium and turned into a personal guard."

"Wait—really?" Aabir remembered Emperor Ignis threatening Tetra with that before (back when they were still friends), but he had not thought another thing about it.

He scrunched his brow as he tried to imagine her as a blank-faced personal guard, and the thought sent a shiver down his spine.

Tetra nodded. "That's why I need to go. Now." Her stoicism melted away with a look of fear. "Please, Aabir. I know—I know I messed up last time..." Guilt flashed across her scarred face for a moment, "But this is my last chance to try. If I stay or if I get caught, I'm going to end up the same either way. Please...don't make me hurt you. I don't want to do that."

Aabir gave a dry laugh and glanced down at the sword between them. "I also would rather you not." He frowned slightly. "But I don't see how that could be possible. I can't do anything to risk my family right now, Tetra...but I don't want you to become a personal guard, either. I don't—I don't know what to do."

Tetra blinked in surprise, and a stab of shame stung Aabir. Did she seriously think he would have been fine with her becoming a personal guard? He knew when he severed all connections with her that it must have hurt her, but he had not realized she would ever think he hated her. That had never been the case. He gave the sword between them a hard look. Too bad it was too late to try and fix it now.

"I think I have an idea." Tetra gave him a strange look. "But you're not going to like it."

"Well, if it involves you removing your sword from my throat, I'm all for it." He gave her a grin, but her serious demeanor did not change so it fell. "What is it?"

"If I knock you out, then if you're questioned you can just tell them that you couldn't stop me because you were unconscious. And they'll also see it if there are any cameras."

"Uh...can you think of anything else?" He had been knocked out before, and it was not a pleasant experience.

"No."

He met her eyes and saw a desperation there he had only seen once. She really did see no other good options except this one. His lips twisted into a frown as he thought. It would only be one hit on the head...and it was Tetra.

Despite his distancing from her, Aabir knew he could trust her as much as his parents or his closest friends. She was a horrible liar, and they both knew it. He remembered her telling him once that whenever she tried to lie or tell a half-truth to Emperor Ignis, he would immediately catch it. So, she stopped doing it since all it did was get her into more trouble.

An ember of anger lit in his chest, and he curled his hands into fists. It was not at Tetra, but at the fact that he had to be thinking about this—that they were even having this conversation in the first place. He hated that the empire they were a part of was so twisted that they found themselves in this situation with only one possible way out of it—and it involved him getting knocked upside the head with the possibility that Tetra (or both of them) could still get caught.

"All right." He exhaled a frustrated sigh through his mouth. "But to make it work, we'll need to stage a fight to make it as authentic as possible, and you can knock me out as fast as you can in it. Deal?"

Tetra gave a sharp nod. "Deal." Despite the lack of warmth in her face, he could hear the sincerity in her words as she added, "Thank you, Aabir."

He gave her a small smile. "I hope you make it."

"Me too."

"Oh, and could you please not take my sword? I'd rather not lose it."

"I won't."

With that, he immediately stepped back and unsheathed his sword. Tetra lunged forward, and he lifted his blade to block it. Their swords rang as they hit, and Aabir used his heavier weight to push her back. He noticed her eyes widen slightly as she stumbled back and he retaliated with his own strike.

A worm of guilt wriggled through him as their blades struck again, and he tried to send her a reassuring look as their eyes locked for a moment. It's not that he wanted to fight her, but if he had just let her attack him without doing anything, then those who watched the security footage—especially Lieutenant Denir—would be able to tell that something was off.

Something in her expression softened for a moment, then it disappeared as her sword slid off his and she swung towards his legs. He blocked the strike, and—forcing himself not to take the opportunity to attack her open side—swung for her shoulder.

Just like he hoped, she jerked out of the way and lunged towards him again. He shifted on his feet to dodge the blade, noticing once again how she left herself open to attack on the side.

If this had been a normal fight, he would have used that to win. Instead, he once again swung for a spot he knew she would be able to counter.

She did, and they continued in their semi-fake fight until Aabir thought it was long enough to appease any suspicion.

Their blades struck again. Aabir's slid off hers and he went to swing at her legs in a slow arc. She easily evaded the swing and leapt forward. Aabir raised his sword and their eyes locked for a moment right before she hit him in the side. He winced and leaned forward, moving his hand to touch the spot to act as if he was in a lot more pain than he was.

Tetra took the opportunity; and before he could dwell on what was about to happen, a sharp pain rammed into his head and darkness took over his mind.

Chapter Nine

Once Aabir's unconscious form fell to the floor, Tetra took a few deep breaths to calm her racing heart before sheathing her sword and continuing her run down the hall. As she turned the corner into a new hallway with taller ceilings, she realized she should've asked Aabir where they were in the Palace of Commons. She shook her head at herself for the stupid mistake.

Just because it was the first time that they had spoken to each other in over two years was not a good enough reason for her to lose her head.

She always told herself that she didn't need any friends; that they were a luxury her dishonor would not allow her to have. And yet...if she hadn't been pressed for time, Tetra would've wanted their conversation to continue.

She rolled her eyes at herself as she slowed to a stop before checking the newest straight hallway for any signs of others. There was no one. So, she turned into it and picked back up into a sprint.

Amidst the rush of adrenaline and buzzing thoughts telling her to hurry and be aware of her surroundings, she could feel the usual hollow loneliness burrowing itself back into her soul. It was a normal feeling she could usually ignore—and in this moment she needed to—but it didn't seem to want to be ignored, no matter how hard she tried to push it out of her mind. The more she pushed, the bigger it grew.

Gritting her teeth, Tetra tried a new tactic as she turned a sharp corner: focusing on something else. And the newest hall she had entered was able to do just that. Huge, round windows lined one of the lavender-painted walls. It slowly curved inward, and Tetra could feel a slight ascent in the floor as she ran.

Bright moonslight spilled onto a small garden outside the windows. She caught a glimpse of Afreean's biggest moon, Luura, shining like a huge ember in the night sky between two towers. Worry wriggled into her thoughts at the sight of it. Hopefully none of the other three moons were full, either. Luura's light would already make being stealthy hard enough to deal with once she reached Trivsau's streets. She didn't need any of the other moons stealing her dwindling chances of stealth with their added luminance.

At the end of the hall, two arched entryways were cut into both opposing sides. Tetra slowed to a stop near the right one and peered around the corner. This one led into a lavender corridor lined with doors on both sides.

She glanced to her left and saw another hallway clothed in shadows. She peered into its darkness but could not see any light coming from any point further down its length. From the fluorescent light in the hall she stood in, she could see that lights were built into its ceiling, but—either from wanting to save power or that they just didn't work—it was obvious no one had been in that part of the palace for quite some time. So, she turned into the next lavender corridor and continued her run.

It only took her a few more minutes of running through more colorful, but empty, halls before she finally ran into some life—well, almost ran into it. Voices bounced along the unadorned walls of a new hallway, sending her rushing heart leaping into her throat. She came to a sudden stop, glancing back over her shoulder at the corridor she had just left. She might be able to hide in one of the rooms back there...

"—only a few hours left." One of the voices was saying in a refined, nasally Tulin accent.

Tetra scrunched her brow but didn't move from her spot. Why was someone from the kingdom of Tulphire here? She thought all their forces were helping Igrium in the Deltide Chain.

"Shh! Your voice is still too loud!" The other voice, this one with a halting Xichian accent, replied in a low voice. "Anyone could overhear us, and then what? What would I say in our defense?"

Tetra sent a quick glance around as a question came to mind: why would anyone, besides her, be worried about getting caught? Curiosity bubbled up amidst her fear, diminishing it somewhat. The voices didn't seem to be coming any closer, so—with another furtive glance over her shoulder—she took a few, quiet steps towards the rounded corner next to the entryway and pressed herself against it.

Even with her new position, she had to strain her ears to hear the Tulin voice's whispered reply, "Sorry."

"Thank you."

"Anyway, as I was saying: Phallum messaged and said once the networks are off, then we spread the word."

What were they talking about? What networks? Then it hit her: was Igrium about to unleash a surprise attack on Silvas?

Another rush of adrenaline went through her, and she gripped the hilt of one of Brutus' swords. Well, that only gave her another reason to get out of there as quickly as possible.

An image of the girl from the fence flashed through her mind, and another wriggle of worry wormed its way into her stomach. She might end up fine, but what about all those unsuspecting people?

The Tulin man continued speaking, but Tetra's thoughts kept her focus away from what he was saying. Maybe...maybe if she made it over the fence, she could tell someone in charge what she had just overheard...

You traitor! Tetra squeezed her eyes shut with a grimace at the intruding thoughts, *Already helping the enemy side. Tarson was right. Straudwin, coward, traitor—they're all good words to describe you.*

Her malscar began to throb, and she gritted her teeth. Or...maybe she should wait to see if Rasiela's promise worked. If it didn't, then she could use this knowledge as leverage to show her trustworthiness by selling out Igrium.

Oh, they both sounded horrible! Why did this always have to be so hard? Why couldn't she just decide without having the expectations of Igrium and her guilty conscience fighting for her attention?

The sounds of footsteps coming closer snapped her out of her thoughts. She pressed herself as far back as she could into the corner. Her heart pounded a steady rhythm in her ears as they came to a stop by the entryway.

The Xichian voice said, "Good. I cannot wait for this to be over. My people will finally be free of these *Draufvix* powers."

"Yes. Now, I have orders to go back to the fence. Either I or Toir will send you word when we are ready to move."

Tetra's heart skipped a beat, and she leaned her head a bit closer to the entryway at the word "fence".

"I will be waiting, then. *Falader.*"

"*Falader pir ju.*"

Both pairs of footsteps went off in different directions. Tetra peeked out from behind the entryway. Someone in the flowing, blue-hued garb of Xich was moving down the hall one way, while someone else in Igrian armor strode down the other. She waited until they both went into separate halls before bolting after the Tulin soldier. If he was going to the fence, then she needed to follow him—at least through the Palace. Once she was out in the streets, she would know where to go. Hopefully.

Tetra followed the heavy, metallic footfalls through more corridors and halls. As she did, she found herself having to hide in random rooms and in shadowed corners as she encountered more people walking through them. It made the process much slower, and she soon lost track of her unknowing Tulin guide.

She frowned as another servant passed through the corridor outside the small bedroom she hid in. Once the footsteps faded, she opened the door and stepped out on silent feet and continued down the curved hall; making sure not to jostle Brutus' dual swords with her legs.

The corridor soon split off into two separate ones, and Tetra stepped into the one with windows. She looked out the first and was greeted with the topmost view of a garden. Beyond the highest branches of the short pomen trees, she could see some of the moonslit ruins of Trivsau—and the dark chasm that lay between them and the Palace.

Her heart gave a small jump at the deep darkness made even more so by the night, yet she couldn't dwell on that fear for long as the closeness of the city brought on a growing hope. At this height, she could possibly scale the stone walls if she found a balcony, and then she would be able to use the cover of the trees as she looked for a way off the Palace's outcroppings.

She flicked her gaze about the rest of the view. A small smile escaped her lips as she spotted some balconies along a tower to her left, the topmost branches of pomen trees growing up against them. Though the thought of climbing down one of those trees reawakened her old fears, she knew it would be better to do that than risk scaling the wall.

So, with a silent "thank-you" to whoever planted those trees, she took a step back towards the hall she had just left, but voices coming from its direction stopped her. She looked around wildly for any hiding places, but only windows built into the flat walls filled the hallway she stood in. She sent a furtive glance over her shoulder towards the other end of the hallway; but if she ran down it, she would be going in the opposite direction of the balconies...

"They said she just came down here." A jolt of fear stabbed Tetra's pounding heart at the words coming from the gruff voice.

"Well, do they know which way she went now?" A higher-pitched, feminine voice asked.

There was a pause. "None of the cameras are positioned in that direction. Our guess is as good as theirs."

The woman gave a huff. "Stupid Xichians."

"Maybe she's hiding in one of these rooms."

"I doubt it, but I'll let Irven know to look through them when his team gets here."

Oh great. *More* people were looking for her. Tetra glanced down at the sheathed dual swords as the hurried footsteps drew nearer to the fork. She couldn't fight them, and she didn't want to run in the opposite direction, only to end up getting chased down and caught.

Her eyes flicked back over to the view of the balconies. She had to get to them, or else she would probably get caught trying to find another way out of this maze.

She grimaced as her only option became perfectly clear.

Oh, this is so stupid... With a steadying breath, she unsheathed one of the short swords and ran back out into the hall in the direction of the balconies.

"Wha—hey!" The man called behind her.

Tetra didn't stop or look back. She kept her gaze forward and clutched the sword's hilt tighter. Pounding footsteps followed her, and the woman said something in an authoritative voice about "all patrols, rendezvous to section—", but she didn't listen to the rest. Her heart beat a rhythm of blood and fear as adrenaline buzzed through her veins.

Despite the horrifying circumstances, the hall curved in the direction of the tower and split off into two corridors: one angling downward, and the other upwards. She headed for the one going down and slowed her pace only a fraction so she wouldn't run into the wall on the sloped floor. The pair of footsteps followed.

The first door came upon Tetra, and she only slowed long enough to open it, the footsteps drawing closer. Blood pounded in her ears as she slammed the door. Her fingers shook as she tried—twice—to lock it. It clicked and she ran through the furnished bedroom to the glass doors leading out onto a balcony.

"Hey!" The man hollered and pounded against the door. "Open this door!"

No thanks. Tetra turned the latch of the balcony's door, and a shiver went through her as she stepped into the cool night air. Luura and the smaller, blueish moon, Ilya, shone brightly in the starry sky. The other two moons only looked like fingernails. At least she would be able to see a little while climbing, even if the light didn't help with stealth.

Without waiting for her pursuers to break down the door, she stepped over to the balcony's ornate balustrade and looked down, her stomach churning slightly at the sight of her distance from the ground. The pomen tree's topmost branches brushed against the wall and grew wedged between the balustrades.

If she didn't think the gods hated her, she would have thought this was a gift from them. Oh well. Gift or not, she would take it.

Ignoring her fear of falling, she sheathed the sword and lifted one leg over the railing and touched down on the thin edge. She glanced down at the drop and immediately looked up as her heart fell into her stomach; memories of another, much taller, tree coming back to taunt her.

It's not that far, it's not that far, it's not that far... she continued to tell herself as she moved her other leg over and touched that foot down. She gripped the railing with both hands and breathed out a sigh of relief.

A crash sounded in the bedroom. Tetra's heart almost burst and she jerked her head to look over her shoulder. Her eyes caught sight of some thicker branches that might be able to hold her weight, but she would have to jump.

The balcony doors burst open. "Stop—!"

She jumped into the leaves. For a moment, she felt her life leaving her. Then, her hand touched a branch and she was back. Leaves and twigs slapped her in the face as she groped for any handhold. Tears slipped down her cheeks as pain stabbed her malscar. She finally latched onto a branch with trembling fingers and held on for dear life. She glanced down but couldn't see the ground through the tree's thick clusters of leaves.

"I need a patrol in sector fourteen to come to the garden now."

Tetra glanced up through the leaves at the sound of the woman's voice. She could see both Igrian soldiers standing on the balcony where she had just been, but they didn't move to follow her into the trees' thick leaves.

She breathed out a shaky breath. *That was close*—but she wasn't through just yet.

Not wanting to wait for the patrol to get there, she began inching her way along the branch towards the tree's trunk. Warm blood trickled down her stinging cheek. She hoped it was just a small cut, but common sense (and the pain in her face) told her at least one of her stitches had come out. That thought wasn't enough to dishearten her, however. Because just as it came, she was able to step onto a thicker bough next to the trunk. She grabbed hold of another branch and began her descent down the tree.

When she finally got to the bottommost boughs, she hugged the trunk and made her way down it like a scurrus. A rush of relief swept through her adrenaline-wracked muscles as her feet touched the ground. She let go of the trunk and took a couple unsteady steps back before getting her bearings and dashing off through the pomen trees towards the chasm.

The balcony door slammed shut behind her. Thank goodness she had lost a few pursuers for the moment. She immediately discarded the thought as the sounds of voices and rushing footsteps echoed along the towering walls behind her.

Not again! She groaned but kept to her course. All she needed to do was find a bridge and cross the chasm. She knew of the Palace's heavily guarded entrance bridge, and she had even seen a couple more, less ornate ones from walking around the huge complex. She hadn't seen one from the window, but her view had been limited... hopefully there might be one nearby.

Another—closer—shout sounded behind her. Tetra gritted her teeth and pushed herself to run faster through the scattered pomen trees and flower bushes. Her heart pounded against her ribcage, and her lungs screamed for air, for rest. Even all the miles she had run in training weren't going to be enough to keep her going much longer.

Come on, come on, come on! One bridge. I just need one bridge! Tetra thought as the pounding sets of footfalls drew closer. The trees and foliage thinned enough for her to see the gaping chasm ahead of her. Pieces of a ruined wall were stacked and scattered along it. Tetra's gaze swept over the fragmented structure and landed on the most wonderful sight she had seen thus far: a bridge.

Despite the pitiful barricade that was supposed to prohibit anyone from going on it, as well as the crumbling state of the bridge that would deter anyone in their right mind from doing so anyway, she ran toward it. Her fears screamed at her to run away, to find another bridge that didn't look like it was about to fall into the abyss, but her aching legs and heart told her she couldn't go any longer. The footsteps and voices drawing ever closer behind her also told her that this was going to be her only chance.

She soon made it out of the shadows of the trees into the bright moonslight. She forced herself to slow down as she came to the bridge's wooden barrier and jumped over its small height. The stone she landed on slightly shifted at her weight and she stumbled to a stop. Her eyes landed on a black fissure near her feet, and she gulped. Her exhausted heart pumped blood everywhere from her ringing ears to her shaking limbs. More fissures, some bigger than her, cracked through the bridge's walkway.

"Here she is!"

Tetra jerked her head and looked over her shoulder at the shadowed figures coming towards her from the trees. Forgetting her fear of falling, she picked back up into her wild run along the precarious bridge. A few of the huge stones shifted underneath her as her feet pounded atop them. She jumped over a fissure that ran along the width of the bridge, and her heart jumped into her throat as her foot slipped on the edge before she righted herself.

Focus. No fear. Not now. Not this close. She zig-zagged through the obstacle course of abysmal death and, finally, leapt over the other pitiful barrier and landed in the street.

Yes! Tetra couldn't help but smile as a cool wave of relief washed over her. It quickly passed at the sounds of her pursuers who were trying their luck at passing over the unsteady bridge. She pushed her legs into a run again and rushed down the street. A contingent of soldiers on hoverbikes were a little way ahead, so she took a sharp turn onto another street with ruined buildings on both sides. Maybe she could find somewhere to lay low and rest for a bit in the dilapidated houses.

Shouts and the hum of hoverbikes reverberated through the ghostly ruins. Tetra looked around for somewhere to hide. She caught sight of a few people sitting or sleeping amidst the crumbling stones and broken furniture. A few of them turned to look at her as she ran, but they all immediately looked away or went back to acting like they were asleep; as if they were trying to protect themselves from any more of the invading army's drama. More relief swept through her, though it came with a tinge of guilt at the reasoning for their obvious avoidance.

She tripped and accidentally kicked a singed doll with her foot amidst the trash and debris littering the street. It flew and hit the side of what looked to have been a market but was now an empty storefront. Someone shot up from the wreckage and stared at Tetra as she ran past. She glanced over her shoulder and noticed the shadowed figure following her movements, but then she looked forward again and turned onto another street. Then another, and another as her pace decreased with every step.

When she found herself only going at a jog, she turned into an alley and slowed to a stop at the ruins of what was once a lime green building. With heavy panting, Tetra carefully moved through broken pieces of wall, wood, and fabric to try and find a hiding place.

One of the corners of the house was still standing, with a large beam of some unknown material leaned up against it. She gulped in a deep draught of air and stepped towards the structure.

A small den cloaked in shadows lay underneath the beam. She eyed it warily and pressed herself against its plastic-like surface to see how sturdy it was. It didn't budge. She tried shaking it out of its position, but it still wouldn't move.

Satisfied, but exhausted, Tetra got onto her hands and knees and crawled into the cramped space. Echoes of shouts and the sharp hum of hoverbikes echoed along the streets, but she couldn't see anything other than the green building's debris. Her pounding heart began to slow its rhythm as she lay there in wait, wiping the blood off her face with the front of her shirt. It had stopped bleeding, but she was still careful not to open it again as she dabbed it.

Despite the fact she wasn't even out of her predicament yet, elation filled her. She had escaped the Palace! Now all she needed to do was wait for the soldiers to go to a different sector of Trivsau, then she could make her way to the fence and find a way to get over it.

As the minutes passed, exhaustion warred with elation still keeping her awake. And without meaning too, Tetra found herself dozing off in the tiny corner. The first time it happened, she blinked awake and pushed up onto her elbows to keep herself from doing it again. Her eyelids drooped and the muscles in her arms slackened as she dozed off.

No! Her head shot up and she bumped it against the beam above her. She hissed through clenched teeth as the pain seemed to wrack through her wounded face muscles, but she tried to console herself with the hope that the pain would keep her up. It didn't work.

Once its throbbing stings died away, she dozed back off. Off and on she fought against her tired body's will to sleep until she finally couldn't take it anymore. Reasoning that some sleep would be beneficial in helping her escape, she let herself succumb to a longer rest.

When she awoke next, she could tell she hadn't slept for long, but there was something different in the atmosphere that sent a prickle down her spine. She blinked her eyes open and found herself staring at the small, shadowy figure of a girl.

Chapter Ten

TETRA TRIED TO SCRAMBLE to her feet, but she hit her head on the beam again instead. She gritted her teeth and pressed her hand against the tender spot, never letting her gaze move from the new figure. Despite the moonslight illuminating everything else, the only thing Tetra could make out about the girl was her long, wavy hair that covered part of her soft facial features

"It is you!" The girl spoke in broken Alenguan. "When—when I saw you—um—running, I saw face and I—I knew it be you!"

"Who are you?" Tetra growled. The new girl didn't sound threatening, but that didn't mean she could trust her. Emperor Ignis wasn't always threatening, but he had still become the biggest threat of this century.

"Oh! I—I sorry. I did not mean to scare you." She shifted into a different sitting position and Tetra caught a glimpse of a cut in the moonslight. "My—my name is Stellinga. You not—know me, but I know you."

"Let me see your face."

She pushed back her dark hair and moved more into the light. Tetra widened her eyes in surprise as she recognized the Xichian girl from that afternoon. The girl's large, teal eyes met Tetra's. Her bronze skin had an almost ethereal glow in the orangish-blue moonslight, and Tetra could also see that someone had given her wound a few stitches, as well.

"You..." Tetra cleared her throat and tried again, "I remember you, too..."

Stellinga pushed a loose strand of hair back behind her ear. "When I—see you running, I just knew it was you. I—I saw your—your..." She pursed her lips in thought. "Um...I cannot remember word...uh—you know—" She gestured to the cut across her forehead.

Tetra lifted her hand and pointed to her malscar. "Wound?"

"Yes!" Stellinga's face lit up for a moment. "Yes, that word. *Wound...*" She spoke the word a few more times underneath her breath before continuing, "So, I left where I staying to try and find you. I—I ask around and some told me they saw you come here. So, I found you." She shrugged as if it was no big deal, but the pleased smile that flashed across her features said otherwise.

Tetra, however, was not pleased. Worry churned her empty stomach as she met Stellinga's eyes and asked in a hard voice, "Who told you? And have they told anyone else?"

Stellinga's smile died as she shook her head with wide eyes. "Those around here." She circled her arm to gesture towards the ruined buildings around theirs. "And you do not need to worry. We—we do not like Igrium, and no one will help them if we not have too."

Tetra narrowed her eyes. "And yet you're talking to me...an Igrian."

"You different." Stellinga looked down. "You—you not hurt me."

"Yeah, well it didn't do much good." Tetra shook her head and glared at the ground near Stellinga. "For either of us."

There was a moment of silence broken only by the echoing hums of hoverbikes that sounded in the distance. Tetra rolled her shoulders and looked back up at Stellinga's face. "Do you know where the Igrian soldiers are now?"

Stellinga stared at her as if she was processing the question. Then understanding lit up her gaze. "They pass through already." She gestured with her thumb to the area where the alleyway met the street. "I think they further down in the *Chuxat* place."

Tetra had no idea where that was, but as long as it was far enough away from here...

"Scoot back."

Stellinga rose from her sitting position and stepped back around the rubble as Tetra emerged with stiff, popping joints from her hiding spot. She lifted her arms and stretched with a relieved sigh. Then, she lowered and picked up her stolen sword belt and put it back on. She lifted her head and caught the wary look Stellinga was giving her.

"I'll only use them if anyone tries to attack us," she said with as much sincerity as she could muster. Then she realized what she had said: *"us"*.

Stellinga glanced down at the swords again, then back up at her. "OK." She nodded and sat down on a huge chunk of brick.

Tetra stared at the teenage girl strangely. Was there some sort of air about her that screamed 'trustworthy'? Or did Stellinga just have zero trust issues? She sent the girl another confused look before choosing a chunk of stone to sit on as well.

Once she did sit, Stellinga asked, "Why you run from them?"

Tetra glanced around to make sure that there was truly no one near them, then she replied in a low voice, "The same reason I have this," she pointed to her wounded face again. "I don't agree with everything my fellow countrymen do, and to keep myself from becoming a brainwashed zombie I've made a nuisance of myself to Emperor Ignis. So, I was—I'm *trying* to escape."

Stellinga scrunched her brow as she processed Tetra's words. Then she asked, "So you...like me? Like my people?" An eagerness brightened her gaze. "You dislike Igrium, too?"

She disliked most of it, but mentioning the small number of things she didn't mind about her native empire wasn't going to help her in this situation, so she shrugged with a simple "yeah".

"And you trying to escape? Like I did?"

"Yep."

"*Fre'yop!*" She exclaimed with a clap that bounced off the quiet ruins.

Tetra stiffened at the noise and jerked her head around. When it was silent for a couple minutes, she let out a quiet sigh of relief and sent a glare towards Stellinga. The girl met her hard stare with wide, apologetic eyes.

"Sorry." She whispered with a sheepish small smile. "I just excited because I want to escape."

"Still?" Tetra blinked at her in surprise, then peered deeper into the girl's eyes. She was being serious. "Even after getting punished?"

Stellinga nodded. "Mm-hmm."

That sounded like something she would do... Tetra lifted her hand and cupped her chin as she continued to stare thoughtfully at Stellinga, ideas swirling in her head. She wouldn't have expected this courageous tenacity from the small, timid-looking girl, but maybe they could both help each other...

"Stellinga..." Tetra began, "do you know anything about hoverbikes?"

"*Mene*! Yes, my *Opie* teach me how."

This was getting better and better.

"And would you by chance know how long they can hover in midair after a jump?"

Stellinga pursed her lips while twirling a strand of hair between her fingers. "Um—I think my friend did it for a few seconds once..." She shrugged. "I sorry. I not know. Most not jump them in the city—streets too small—and I never been to no bike trails before. I just know how to drive."

"Oh." Tetra twisted her lips into a frown and lowered her gaze to the ground as she thought.

She had watched a couple videos of professional hover-bikers doing flips and long jumps, and from those she figured Stellinga's guess was correct. If they weren't close to the magnetic streets that caused them to hover then gravity would eventually pull them down like everything else.

"Why you ask?" Stellinga's question pulled her back to the present, where she lifted her gaze to the alley beyond the green building's ruins.

"Because I need to know for my escape plan."

"Well, I not sure you be able to find someone who knows tonight."

"I figured." Tetra shrugged and lowered her gaze, looking down at Stellinga. "So, I guess I'm gonna have to figure it out myself."

Because even if she was caught, what did she have to lose?

Stellinga nodded, determination sharpening her features despite the worry creeping into her gaze. "And I find out, too."

"All right, then." Tetra stood up off the rock. "Do you know of a hoverbike we could use?"

SHADOWS BRUSHED OVER TETRA and Stellinga as they drove underneath a towering suchwriy plant that hadn't been torn down in the battle. Tetra clung tighter to Stellinga's waist as the teenage girl picked up speed. She closed her eyes against the sting of the cold, desert air—the only area of her face the borrowed helmet didn't cover. Stellinga slowed down again as she turned the hoverbike onto a new side street, then went back to their usual speed.

Tetra glanced down at the sandstones blurring past their feet by only a few inches. She didn't think being on a hoverbike would be bad, but now that she was actually riding one, she realized how much she disliked the experience. She would take riding in a closed-in hovercar any day over the openness of a hoverbike—and still, she was planning on riding it a couple stories into the air.

She shook her head at herself but didn't give into the worries niggling at the back of her mind. This was her last chance—and she wasn't going to waste it by worrying.

"We close." A shock of thrill went through her as she barely caught Stellinga's accented words above the hoverbike's thrumming generators.

"Remember: take us to the place where we were today," she replied.

Stellinga's sleek hoverbike helmet bobbed a couple times in answer.

Another wave of uneasiness cooled the thrilling sensation and churned Tetra's already-turned stomach as she returned to going over the plan again. There might be nothing for her to lose, but she found herself wondering—again—what might happen to her newfound acquaintance if her plan didn't work.

If they were caught, Tetra had a feeling that whatever she said in defense of Stellinga wouldn't help the other girl since they were both riding a stolen Igrian hoverbike; and the few pieces of armor Tetra now wore would tell anyone where they had gotten it. Though she had been the one to actually knock the Igrian private out while Stellinga hid in an alley, she didn't think their captors would see it as all her fault. Plus, there was also the fact that they were both about to try and jump over the city's dividing fence onto the enemy's side.

Needless to say, they would both be in trouble.

The hoverbike lurched to the right. Tetra tightened her hold around Stellinga's waist, teeth gritted, as they finished the sharp curve and straightened back up again. She loosened her hold with a grimace, the waves in her empty stomach splashing with guilt and tension.

There would be no more hoverbike rides after this—at least not with the little amount of armor she was wearing.

The only things she had been able to put on was the polyanium-mail shirt that would usually be worn under her armor, the helmet, and she had barely had time to put on the private's gauntlets before they had to escape the sight of a group of soldiers headed their way. She looked ridiculous and was glad no one from Norland could see her in that moment—unless they got caught, then her platoon might get to see. She pushed that thought aside as she flicked her gaze ahead.

The street ahead of them, thankfully, stretched out like a long snake curving slowly inward. There would be no tight turns for at least a minute. Just as she had that thought, Stellinga turned the hoverbike sharply into the ruins of a tall building. Tetra's heart jumped into her throat at the jerking movement.

"Stellinga!" She hissed once the shadows of the crumbling walls draped over them. "What—"

Stellinga jerked her neck around, fear shining in her widened eyes through the open-faced helmet's visor.

"Soldiers!" She whispered back, powering down the hoverbike.

The blue glow of the bike's electromagnetic generator-rings dissipated into the harsh shadows, and a jolt went through Tetra as her feet hit the ground. The bike wobbled as she got off and held it steady for Stellinga to do the same. When the teenage girl did so, she flipped the kickstand down with her foot and they both rushed into the building's corner to hide.

"You go first." Tetra kept her eyes on the moonslit street as the frantic sounds of scrabbling went on behind her. She pulled one of her swords out and glanced over her shoulder before joining Stellinga's crouched form in the cramped corner.

Keeping her face turned towards the gaping hole between the crumbling walls, Tetra asked in a whisper, "Where did you see them?"

"When we—turn—I saw—one turn in front—of us." Heavy pants broke Stellinga's broken Alenguan even more. "I not—think they—see us."

"Were they further down the street?"

Stellinga nodded, her lips a thin line.

Only a few tense moments later, a group of hoverbikes zipped past the building. Tetra's muscles tensed as she tightened her grip on her sword's hilt until the whir of the last bike dissipated into the unusually quiet city.

"Alright," she stood and looked down at Stellinga, "I think we're in the clear now."

Stellinga nodded. Tetra stepped towards the hoverbike so the other girl could get out. She kept the sword in hand until Stellinga started the hoverbike, then sheathed it and got on behind her. Stellinga backed out of what was left of the building and continued on their course.

Their path led mostly straight with—thankfully—only a few curves, and the intensity of the floodlights that illuminated the fence soon filled the night air ahead of them. Stellinga made a slow turn around a corner and came to a stop in the sharp shadows.

And there it was: the one obstacle they still needed to face.

Stellinga powered the hoverbike down and kicked the kickstand out. Tetra glanced upwards at the short, spiraling buildings still standing around them. This was the place. She recognized the bright orange and dark-red buildings from that afternoon. And if she remembered correctly, they were only a few buildings down from the flat-roofed guard tower.

She got off the bike and immediately unsheathed both swords, flicking her gaze around their surroundings as Stellinga pulled her helmet off and got off the bike as well.

"Are you sure this'll work, Stellinga?" The drone of hoverbikes and the marching of footsteps surrounding the chain link fence drowned out her question.

At least we don't have to worry about being too loud here, she thought. In a louder voice, she asked the same question.

Stellinga turned around. "Yes. Be—before I tried escape—escaping the first time, I told Silvanian soldier my name. She—she know my parents. They let Silvanian soldiers stay in our house. And she said she take me to them if I get over fence."

Tetra doubted the Silvanian soldier would still be there now, but as long as Stellinga warned those on Silvas' side what they were about to do then there wouldn't be as much chaos once they made it over there. It hadn't been a part of her original plan, but Stellinga had been insistent on doing it. She had told Tetra that if the Silvanians were aware ahead of time of what they were about to do, there might be a chance of them helping to soften their landing.

It sounded better than breaking half the bones in their bodies, so Tetra figured it couldn't hurt. But now that she could see, and hear, how busy it still was, she began to wonder if this was a wise move.

"Be careful," she finally said.

"You no need to worry." Stellinga lifted her arm and placed her hand on Tetra's shoulder. Tetra stiffened and met her steady gaze. "I be safe."

With a small smile, Stellinga removed her hand. She took the shawl from around her shoulders and put it over her head, perfectly covering the stitched-up wound on her forehead. With silent footsteps, she turned and moved towards the fence in the shadow of the building. Tetra ground her teeth as she watched Stellinga step into the bright, fluorescent light coating the street; her heart pounding in sync with each of the girl's quick steps.

A group of heavy footsteps came towards the alley's opening, and Tetra moved closer to the building with wary steps until her back pressed against the stone wall. The Igrian soldiers soon passed without so much as a glance in her direction. She let out a small sigh of relief, yet it did little to stop the racing of her heart.

She turned her attention back onto Stellinga's blue-clothed form. The teenage girl had joined two young men wearing Xichian garb, and Tetra could see they were talking. A few moments passed, and she also noticed all three of them were slowly walking towards the fence as they spoke. If she hadn't known better, she would've thought they were just having a conversation while taking a stroll. Yet, if she was a trained soldier with orders to guard the fence, it might look suspicious.

Just as the thought came to her mind, a pair of Igrian soldiers stepped towards the group. She tapped her fingers against her sword hilts as she watched the trio split up in opposite directions, then sighed in relief through her nose as the soldiers continued on their way with only brief looks towards them.

Stellinga turned and headed towards Tetra as the two men walked out of sight, but instead of walking back into their alley, she continued right past it. Tetra opened her mouth to get her attention, but then closed it with a confused frown. What was she—?

A yell sliced through the air. Her heart skipped a beat and she pressed her back further against the wall. Stellinga and the Igrian soldiers in the street all jerked around in the direction the Xichian men went.

Stellinga put her hand up to her mouth as soldiers rushed past her. Tetra stepped a little closer to the lit street without leaving the shadows as hard Alenguan and rushed Xinxan words filled the night air. What was happening?

Out of the corner of her eye, she saw Stellinga bolt towards the fence. She jerked her head in the girl's direction and scrunched her brow.

A small smile lifted the corners of her lips as the Xichian girl slowed to a stop along the fence where a group of Silvanian soldiers were gathering. Her hands flew in quick gestures as she spoke to them.

Admiration filled Tetra as she watched. What a smart move.

As quick as she had done it, Stellinga spun around and walked back towards the alley's direction. Not even the shawl covering her face could hide the girl's bright smile.

When she finally stepped back into the shadows of the alley, Tetra met her glimmering eyes and sent her a smile. "What'd you do?" She asked.

"They brothers who used to go to school with me, so I told them what we trying to do and they said they help." Stellinga's smile somehow grew bigger as she spoke, "They fake a fight with each other to—to..." She paused, a look of hard concentration taking over her features. "*Werv'wei tiroe...*"

"Distract?"

Stellinga pursed her lips. "What that word mean?"

"What those two people just did to help us."

"Oh!" Stellinga's smile returned, "*Fleora!* Er—thank you. Yes, they *distract* with fight so I able to go to fence. The Silvanians I speak with told me they help us. I—I not tell them you Igrian, though..."

"That's OK." Tetra shrugged and gestured towards the hoverbike. "Did you by chance see the guards on the roof?"

Stellinga nodded. "Yes. They also...*distracted*."

"Good." Tetra could still hear the sounds of the fight in the street, which meant this was the best time to get on the roof. "Are your friends going to be OK?"

"They be fine." Stellinga rolled her eyes. "They fight a lot at school. This not new."

"Then, we need to go."

Tetra spun on her heel and rushed back over to the hoverbike. Stellinga's footsteps followed close behind, and she was soon putting her bike helmet back on. The bike's hover-rings lit up in a soft blue as she turned it on, and she kept her hands on the handlebars to keep it steady as it rose into the air a few inches.

Without saying anything more, Tetra led Stellinga and the hoverbike around to the back of the building where the guards were stationed. In the glow of the hoverbike, they were able to find the stone staircase that led up to the roof.

Tetra looked over her shoulder and mouthed, "*Slowly.*"

Stellinga only nodded in reply.

They both ascended the stairs with careful movements, using the blue glow of the hoverbike between them as their only light source. Two voices spoke above them: the sounds of the ongoing fight in the street below acting as a backdrop to their conversation.

Tetra's heart raced faster with each step until she thought it would burst out of her chest. She squeezed the sword hilts in her hands a little tighter.

Whatever it took, she and Stellinga would both be getting out of here. They would escape—and she wouldn't let the uneasy thoughts gnawing at her subconscious keep her from accomplishing that.

She gestured for Stellinga to stop once they made it only a few steps away from the top, but then continued alone. She peeked her head over the low stone wall that wrapped around the roof and spotted the guards. Their backs were to her as they talked to each other, the crossbows they both held bobbing slightly as they spoke. The fluorescent lighting shone sharply against their dark-gray armor and gave her a good view of the short swords strapped to each of their belts, solidifying in her mind the only chance she had at winning: surprise.

Her eyes scanned the rest of the mostly empty rooftop and landed on a large, mounted crossbow positioned in the corner of the roof. At least she didn't have to worry about them using *that* to try and stop her on the enclosed space. Though if she didn't take both guards out, it might become a problem during the jump.

When she finished her inspection, she lowered her head and locked eyes with Stellinga. "*I'm going. Be ready,*" she mouthed.

"*I am,*" Stellinga mouthed back.

Without waiting for any fear to talk her out of it, Tetra snuck as quietly as she could onto the rooftop. She stepped up behind them, and just as the female guard turned her head to look over her shoulder, Tetra slammed her sword's blade against the side of her knee. She fell forward with a grunt, and her partner spun around—crossbow at the ready.

Tetra arced the sword in an upward stroke and the crossbow flew out of his hands. She only stopped once the sword tip reached his throat. Their eyes met, and she forced her expression to stay neutral at the look of surprised disgust on the man's face.

"A straudwin—?"

She knocked the flat of her other blade against his head. He stumbled under the blow and she used the hilt of the first sword to knock him out.

"Tetra!" Stellinga's voice cried out.

She spun around in time to block the other guard's lunge.

"A malscar?" The woman sneered and pushed harder against Tetra's crossed swords.

Tetra gritted her teeth and pushed the woman's sword to the side. Their blades slid off each other with metallic shrieks that would notify anyone in the street below that something was wrong. Her heart skipped a fearful beat, but she still thrust a sword towards a gap in her opponent's armored side while blocking with the other. The sword hit resistance and the guard gasped sharply. Tetra pulled the blade away and the woman leaned over as blood pooled around the new hole in her armor.

Their eyes met. She moved forward just as the woman cried out "Intruder!", then knocked her unconscious as well.

"They coming!" Panic tinged Stellinga's voice.

"Come on, then!"

Tetra wiped the blood off her sword as best she could against her armor while Stellinga brought the hovering bike up to the roof. She sheathed both swords then joined the other girl in getting the bike onto the short wall. Once it was up, she held the hoverbike steady as Stellinga climbed onto the barrier with shaky movements then sat on the bike.

When she was seated, Tetra followed; though she paused for a moment at the sounds of footsteps and raised voices coming up the stairs. Dread crept into her muscles. She stood up straight and forced herself not to look over the edge as she sat on the seat behind Stellinga.

The first soldiers stepped onto the roof.

"Go!" Tetra yelled.

Stellinga slammed on the pedal and Tetra's heart leapt into her throat as she was almost thrown off the back at the burst of speed. She shut her eyes and wrapped her arms around Stellinga's torso.

Oh, please let us make it. Please let us make it...

Stellinga's body jerked up, and Tetra clung even tighter, as the hoverbike's front lifted upward. The Xichian girl let loose a bloodcurdling scream as the cold air streamed into their faces. Tetra's eyes snapped open, and she immediately turned her gaze forward as all the Igrian soldiers in the street sailed by below them. The fence's barbed-wired top seemed to come closer in slow-motion as the hoverbike lost altitude. It began to turn sideways as it fell.

"Jump!" Tetra ordered.

At her command, they both pushed off the hoverbike towards the oncoming fence. She kept her hold on Stellinga as time seemed to slow even more. She tried to turn them in midair so her mail-coated backside could protect the screaming girl as much as possible.

Something scraped against Tetra's leg then immediately dug into it with sharp teeth. She caught sight of a hovertruck below before she squeezed her eyes shut. The teeth tore through her flesh, ripping a scream out of her throat. She was jerked back, and her body hit the fence, yet the fiery teeth stayed where they were in her leg.

More pain erupted in her hip and along her side, and Tetra's hold on Stellinga loosened. She opened her eyes just as the girl fell, still screaming, from her arms before landing amid a group of Alliance soldiers standing in the open back of the hovertruck. Her relief at the sight was quickly swept away by another wave of excruciating pain in her left side.

Nausea filled her stomach. Loud, chaotic voices with different accents sounded below her and seemed to fill her swimming head with their cacophony. Her heart beat a sporadic rhythm that pounded throughout her whole body.

And for the second time that day, Tetra welcomed the calming darkness that reached its tendrils through her mind and enveloped her conscience until there was nothing.

Chapter Eleven

"So... you talked to her?" Second Lieutenant Denir raised his brow and stared Aabir down with his hooded gaze.

"Yes sir." Aabir lowered his eyes to the lieutenant's chin. "I figured if I talked to her then I'd be able to win her trust and it would give me time to surprise attack her; but...I guess she figured out what I was doing. She did tell me she was trying to escape, though, and I would have told you that, sir, but...well, she knocked me out."

Denir shook his head and mumbled something under his breath. Then he lifted his chin. Aabir could not help the shiver of fear that went down his spine as their eyes met.

"So, you failed?"

Aabir gulped but nodded once. "Yes sir. I'm sorry, sir. I—"

"No excuses, Sorrel!" Lieutenant Denir moved his face closer to Aabir's. "You had a job to do, and you failed. The emperor himself has been breathing threats down our necks because of Cairn's loss, and I *hate* having my honor looked down upon." A dangerous glint entered his eyes. "And you, Jazeston, and Loir have done just that. So..."

Metal rang as he pulled out the segione sheathed on his belt. Aabir's eyes flicked down to the small weapon as his heart rate quickened.

"Give me your arm." Denir's tone sounded like the calm before a windstorm.

Aabir lifted his shaky left arm and pulled back his sleeve where a few white tally scars stood out against his brown skin. Without waiting, Lieutenant Denir sliced through his forearm. He gritted his teeth at the sudden sting but made no move to defend himself. Blood pounded in his ears as Denir removed the segione and began to clean it.

"No one fails me and gets away with it, Sorrel." Denir sheathed the dagger and met Aabir's eyes. "Don't let it happen again."

"Yes sir." Aabir pressed his hand against the new tally before his blood dripped onto the floor.

"Get that cleaned up then continue on with today's duties." The second lieutenant spun around and headed towards his temporary desk in the Palace of Commons. "I have *your* mess to sort out."

Aabir saluted him as best he could without getting blood on his uniform, then spun on his heel and marched out of the room. He shut the door behind him and breathed out a sigh through his nose, shooting a glance down at his hand covering the wound. Thank Deleyon he got away with only a tally, *and* that Xich seemed to lack better security. If the cameras had had sound, then he definitely would not have gotten away with only that.

He headed down the curved corridor that housed his platoon. At least Tetra had made it. Despite their encounter that could have ended up turning out horribly, he was glad it ended with her finally accomplishing what they both considered almost impossible. Since he had woken up from getting hit on the head and heard she had made it over the fence onto Silvas' side, a tiny seed of hope had been planted inside him—a seed that said if Tetra could make it out of Igrium, then maybe he and his family could, too.

He stopped at the door of his temporary room and opened it.

"—is horrible," Aquilo's moan reached out into the hall.

"What is?" Aabir asked as he stepped into the room and shut the door behind him.

Aquilo and Tycho both turned their heads in his direction. A grin spread across Tycho's face.

"He has awakened!" He said with a dramatic gesture from his top bunk.

"Finally." Aquilo stood from his own bunk and stepped towards Aabir, a look of urgency on his face. "What happened? What did Lieutenant Denir say?"

"Um...well..." Aabir lifted his hand away from the bleeding tally mark.

Aquilo sucked in a sharp breath and their eyes locked. "So, she's gone, isn't she?"

"Yeah. Sorry, Aquilo."

"What happened?" His friend's reddening face was a mixture of hopelessness and anger.

He pressed his hand back against his arm and stepped over to the small bathroom as he elaborated, "I was walking down the hall, about to turn the corner, when she jumped out and put a sword to my throat. I tried to talk her out of doing anything stupid and tried to bide my time, but she must've seen what I was doing. So, she was ready when I tried to surprise her, and she knocked me upside the head."

He turned the bathroom sink's faucet on and put his arm under the rush of cool water. It soon numbed the sting.

"I guess that's why you only got a tally. You weren't technically on 'guard-duty' yet," Tycho said. "I heard Lieutenant Denir gave Rexsan and Brutus both ten lashes."

Aabir winced and, again, silently thanked Deleyon that he had gotten lost before officially taking Brutus' place. "I didn't realize that happened to them."

He turned the water off and grabbed a clean washcloth to dry his arm. Then, throwing it to the side, he turned around and stepped back into the room.

Aquilo shook his head and glared down at the floor. "And it shouldn't have happened in the first place," he said through gritted teeth, "They should've known she might try something like this!"

He muttered a few curses under his breath as Aabir went over to his bunk and pulled out the military-issued first-aid kit from his bag. Just as he sat down on the side of the thin mattress, a holonode rang.

"It's mine," Aquilo said with a huff as he tapped his wrist device.

Aabir glanced up as his friend sighed heavily through his nose. A curdle of fear—not for him, but for Aquilo—formed in the pit of his stomach as he read the caller's ID on the seemingly-floating screen. The room's atmosphere thickened as Aquilo sent them both an apologetic look before accepting the call.

"Hello?" He said.

"Aquilo." A woman's disapproving face appeared on the holographic screen. "I assume you heard about your cousin..."

"It wasn't my fault, Matha! I swear I had nothing to do with it." Aquilo's voice rose as he defended himself, "Lieutenant Denir put me on the schedule to guard her this morning before she left."

Aabir acted ignorant of the conversation as he continued cleaning his newest tally to keep it from infecting. He noticed Tycho scrolling through what looked like a list of returning Constantia Tourney competitors on his holonode in an act of ignorance, too.

"Yes, and you better be on your knees thanking the gods that was the case, Aquilo Warlin," Missus Impera Warlin said in a harsh tone, "because if it had been you, your patre and I would've likely disowned you for such an idiotic act."

The threat was not even aimed towards him, but Aabir still felt a chill go down his spine. This was not the first conversation he had overheard between the Warlins, but he wished it might be the last. The calls all sounded about the same to him, and it always made him wonder why Aquilo did not start acting like Tetra did. If Aabir was in his boots and had parents who seemed to hate him so much, he would probably be doing the same things as her. Yet Aquilo avoided trouble just as much as Aabir.

"I know, Matha." Aquilo sighed. "Was there something else you needed to tell me?"

"Reports are coming in from Trivsau that a battle is on the horizon. They say Alliance forces are evacuating all citizens on their side to a safe camp a few miles out of the city. Your patre thinks the battle will happen in the next couple of days—and I agree with him."

More fear curdled in Aabir's stomach as he pulled a large bandage out of the first-aid box. He lifted his eyes and met Tycho's eager gaze.

"Really?" A note of excitement entered Aquilo's tone.

"Yes," his matha replied, "though I have a feeling your commanding officers will schedule you all to leave before it ever begins. Your patre just sent two battalions to Xich—and he is not the only one doing so—so there will be plenty of hovertrains coming in to take you all home. However, if you do somehow find yourself in the battle: remember the name you carry, and don't let us down."

Aquilo straightened. "Yes ma'am."

"I will see you when you get back. Goodbye."

Her face blinked off the screen, and the air in the room lightened significantly. Aabir breathed in deeply through his mouth and exhaled through his nose.

"A battle..." Excitement tinged Tycho's words, "Man, I hope we do get to fight in it. I'd like to show those Alliance upstarts what it means to be victorious."

"I hope so, too." Despite the foul mood one of his parents' calls usually put him in, Aquilo's eyes sparked with contained excitement as wistfulness entered his voice, "I'd be able to gain back the honor Tetra's traitorous run took from our family."

Aabir stuck the bandage on his forearm. Though his friends were enthusiastic, he hoped they would leave before the battle ever began. Even knowing the fate he would face after graduating, he still did not know what he would do when put into a battle against Alliance soldiers; against the nations that held his family's values. Hopefully the rule that trainees could not fight in battles—unless dire circumstances dictated it—would save him from having to face that decision for just a little bit longer.

He frowned and closed the first-aid kit. These cowardly thoughts were not helping his roiling stomach.

"How about we go train?" Tycho straddled the side of his bunk before landing on his feet with a thud. He turned and faced Aabir and Aquilo with a grin. "I want to be ready in case we do find ourselves in a battle."

Aabir's stomach began tying itself in a knot.

"I'm in." Aquilo stood again and grabbed his sheathed sword lying against the side of his bunk. "What about you, Aabir?" Their eyes met, and he hoped his friend could not see the worry he felt. "We don't have any orders until afternoon patrol along the fence, and I'm sure Lieutenant Denir wouldn't say 'no' to you training."

He glanced over at his sheathed sword leaning up against his own bunk. The idea did sound nice... And it would help give him a reprieve from the awful worry knotting his insides.

"Alright." He stood and grabbed his sword before looping it onto his gray uniform's belt.

Tycho continued to talk about his hopes for the coming battle as they exited their room and started down the hall. Aquilo added a few comments about what he also hoped for as they went down a tower of spiral stairs. Aabir said nothing, which even he knew was unusual for him to do, but neither of his friends seemed to notice as they continued on through the curving, twisting halls and corridors of sandstone.

"Do you know where we're going, Aquilo?" He finally asked as they passed through a sol-lit hallway lined with tall windows on one side, a garden of pomen trees taking up their outdoor view. He did not remember going this way yesterday when they went to the Palace's training yards.

"Yes, I do," Aquilo replied from a few steps ahead. "The training yard we went to should be down this hall."

The conversation ceased for a few moments as they continued marching down the hallway in search of the entry leading to the yard. A low ***boom*** resounded outside.

"Stop." Aabir held up his hands as Tycho and Aquilo both turned questioning looks towards him.

Another, much louder boom shook the stone floor underneath them.

"What was that?" Tycho asked.

Aabir's heart thudded against his ribcage. *Please, Deleyon, please let that be an earthquake...*

Heavy, metal footsteps rushed towards them from the direction they were headed. Aabir unsheathed his sword as Tycho and Aquilo spun to face whoever was coming. An Igrian soldier clad in dark gray armor slowed to a stop in front of them, placing his hands on his knees as he panted.

"What's going on?" Aquilo asked in a demanding tone.

Another boom shook the ground. The soldier—Aabir could see he was a private by the insignia etched onto his armor's pauldron—straightened with a heaving breath. "Silvas—Silvas hacked into our—our telecommunications database and—locked us out. So—Captain Havlaw sent us—to warn all the district generals. The Alliance is attacking!"

And with that, he rushed off. Aabir's pulse quickened as he watched the man disappear down the hall.

"The battle started?" He flicked his gaze between Aquilo and Tycho's excited expressions. "Now?"

"That must be what's shaking the floor!" Tycho's smile widened. "We're going to get to be in a real battle!"

"We need to tell Lieutenant Denir." Aquilo wore a stoic look on his face, but Aabir could see eagerness shining in his eyes.

"The quicker, the better!" Tycho said, then raced off in the same direction they had just come from.

Aquilo slapped Aabir's shoulder. "Let's go!" And then he was off, too.

Aabir glanced out the window at the trees as their branches shook in the wind. He lifted his gaze and spotted a few black dots hovering over the city in the bright blue sky.

Hovercraft, he thought with a gulp, then he glanced over his shoulder at the direction Aquilo just went. He really was about to face a battle. They all were.

Oh Deleyon, what am I supposed to do? He waited for any kind of answer, but then another resounding boom shook the Palace of Commons and he forced his feet to move down the hall after his friends. Another boom sounded, its deep rumblings shaking the floor for longer.

Adrenaline began to buzz through his veins as his stomach knotted itself even tighter with fear. "Whatever happens," he prayed under his breath, "please let my platoon and I make it."

With that prayer, he picked up his pace and ran back the way his friends had gone; the resounding rumbles outside continuing to announce the beginning of a new battle.

Chapter Twelve

SCREAMS TORE THROUGH THE air around Aabir as he and those of all three trainee platoons followed their commanding officers through the masses of Xichian citizens scrambling around them for safety. He kept his eyes on Buren Rodrich's armored back to keep himself, and those following *him*, from getting lost in the chaos. The Palace of Commons' grand entrance was full of those trying to get to safety from the battle happening in the streets. Aabir kept one hand gripped on his sword's pommel, and the other on one of his backpack's straps to keep his irrational fear of losing either in the rushing mob at bay.

Blood pounded in his ears, in rhythm with his hurried steps. Panicked faces blurred past. More rumblings shook the ground. Harsh Alenguan yells and rushed Xinxan voices filled the air. He gripped his sword's pommel tighter. It was all too much...

Heat washed over Aabir as he followed Buren outside into the Palace's main courtyard. The distant rumblings of battle reverberated off the lofty white walls. People continued streaming around them, but he found it easier to keep closer to Buren as there was more space in the protected area.

Slow shadows spilled over the courtyard, stealing the hot sollight away. Aabir glanced up at the dark underside of an Igrian hovercraft, and a wave of dread swept through his torso. He turned his gaze forward and pushed aside all the thoughts clamoring for his attention. All he needed to focus on was following Buren to safety. Everything else could be figured out once they all made it to the hovertrain station and were headed home.

A Xichian family—the matha carrying a crying baby in her arms, and the patre holding the hands of two little boys—almost ran into him as they tried to enter the Palace. He locked eyes with the matha for a moment as they rushed past him. He shook his head, then continued on his course. There was nothing he could do for them, no matter how much his guilty conscience showed him that could be his family.

More moments of focused running passed, and he slowed as Buren did in front of him. Aabir was about to ask why, but then he came to the realization as the rushing crowds pushed him, and his platoonmates in front of him, against the metal side of the entrance bridge.

"This is ridiculous," Tycho said with a curse. He had been in a bad mood ever since Lieutenant Denir told them all the trainee platoons had orders to leave immediately.

Aabir wanted to say something, but Buren picked up the pace and his focus was turned back to the task at hand. A couple minutes passed, and they made it off the bridge. He found himself slowing for a moment as his eyes locked onto the sights before him. Huge hovercraft—airships with rows of mounted crossbows the size of train cars atop their long, flat decks—filled the blue sky like oversized sky-whales as they shot huge, fiery crossbow bolts at each other and the ground. Screams echoed as one of the bolts was shot into a still-standing building in the distance with an explosive ***BOOM.*** Aabir watched in horror as it crumpled in a cloud of dust.

"My platoon!" He blinked out of his stupor as Lieutenant Denir yelled above the cacophony, "Get in three lines and follow me—"

The lieutenant spun around as his words were cut off by a resounding, mechanical groan. Aabir fixed his gaze on the hovercraft making the noise. It hovered in the air a few blocks from their position, a crossbow bolt as long as a train car lodged perfectly in the middle of the Igrian emblem painted on its metal side.

More groans filled the overstuffed air as the craft's nose tilted forward.

"Take cover!" Denir yelled.

Aabir, his platoonmates, and the citizens around him did not need to be told twice. He followed Buren and Septimus over to a thick, crumbling wall lining the street. The groans turned to a high-pitched whine that made his ears ring even when he covered them. He pushed himself against the wall's side next to Septimus as Tycho, a few more of his platoonmates, and even a few Xichians squished themselves against the protective barrier.

Heart-pounding seconds passed. Right as he wondered if the hovercraft had somehow been able to keep itself in the air, there was a deafening explosion and the earth below him quaked. He pressed himself further against the wall and gritted his teeth as people cried out around him. Dust and sand billowed above and around their huddled group. Somewhere in the city, sirens began to blare.

A few moments passed, then Buren's voice spoke close to Aabir's ear, "Do you think it's safe?"

"I don't know..."

Septimus pushed himself up into a crouch. "I'll look."

Everyone, including Aabir, turned their eyes on the trainee as he poked his head over the top of the wall to assess the situation. Septimus coughed then lowered himself completely behind the wall.

"There's a lotta dust, but from what I could see it looks like Lieutenant Denir's warning worked," he said with another cough. "No one seems to be hurt."

A couple of the Xichians in their huddle heard his words and immediately got up and rushed off in the direction of the Palace's entry bridge. Their departure caused the rest to follow them, leaving Aabir and his platoonmates behind the wall.

"Well then..." Buren said when they all left.

"We need to find Lieutenant Denir." Septimus stood and held out his hand for Aabir.

Aabir grabbed his wrist and was helped to his feet. "Thanks."

The taller trainee gave him a sharp nod before turning to help Buren up. Aabir did the same for Tycho.

"Thanks." Tycho rubbed his hand across his buzzed head, flinging dust particles off. "I'm glad we missed that."

"Yeah." Aabir turned his neck as he looked around at the dust-clouded street. He hoped there were not any Xichians near the explosion...

"There he is!" Septimus pointed in a direction beyond the crumbling wall.

Aabir narrowed his eyes and spotted their commanding officer moving through the throngs of citizens and rubble littering the wide street. Lieutenant Tarson and Lieutenant Grahm were with him, as were a growing crowd of trainees from all three platoons.

"Let's go." Septimus took the lead as they all walked across the large street to their platoons amidst the rushing Igrian soldiers heading towards the battle and scrambling Xichians still running for safety. "Lieutenant Denir, sir!"

Lieutenant Denir swiveled his head in their direction. Their appearance did nothing to the stoic concentration plastered across his hard features. He only sent a sharp nod towards them, then turned to the other commanding officers. Aabir could see his lips moving, but he could not make out the lieutenant's words over the ringing in his ears and the cacophony of other noises filling the street.

A group of Igrian soldiers and a pair of medbots joined their gathering circle. Aabir, and the others around him, stepped out of the way so they could get to their commanding officers.

As he did so, his gaze trailed to a smoke cloud billowing ominously only a few city blocks ahead of them. An image of dead bodies scattered everywhere appeared in his mind's eye. His stomach grew nauseous at the thought, so he turned his gaze back to Lieutenant Denir's rigid, yet calm, demeanor. Heaving up the rest of breakfast would only add to the unthinkable havoc surrounding him.

"Trainees!" Lieutenant Tarson's harsh voice turned everyone's attention towards her intimidating countenance. "Everyone is accounted for. We still have our orders to get you all to safety, so if anyone is hurt, a medbot will care for you once we reach the trucks. And if anyone decides they'd rather fight in this battle then obey these orders, you will either die a dishonorable death in it or you will come back a dishonorable straudwin. Now let's move!"

With those rousing words, Aabir and his platoon formed their respectable ranks alongside the other two groups, and they were soon making their way along the street towards the guarded lot where Igrium kept many of its vehicles. Amidst the settling dust clouds, he could see the Igrian soldiers from before marching along with them, weapons drawn. He gulped and looked ahead again. He hoped that did not mean the battle was that close to their position, but the uneasiness churning his stomach said otherwise.

After a couple minutes, they made it to a large, sandy lot full of Igrian military hovertrucks. Each second lieutenant barked orders at their specific platoon in a rush to fill ten of the armored vehicles, so Aabir followed his specified group of platoonmates into the back of one of them. He had no idea how fast his heart was racing until he finally sat on one of the seats lining the truck's inner side and found himself breathing in deep draughts of air to calm himself.

The sensation of rising went through his stomach for a moment as the truck's electromagnetic generators hummed to life. He turned his neck to watch their departure through the opening in the back and counted four hovertrucks following behind them as they made their way onto the streets.

"Aabir? Are you OK?"

He blinked himself out of his stupor and fixed his eyes on Tycho's questioning look. "Uh—yeah. Yeah, I am."

Physically, he was. Mentally? He was not so sure. They were only on the outskirts of a battle, and he was already wondering how he might be able to live through four years of fighting in the midst of them.

I really am a Straudwin coward.

"Aabir?" Tycho's voice broke through his self-pitying thoughts. "Are you sure you didn't get hit on the head or somethin'?"

"Not that I know of." Aabir shook his head and forced a smile. "Really, I'm fine. Just tired."

"I can't wait to graduate." Brutus Jazeston said from the seat across from them. A scowl darkened his already-bruised face. "I hate this. I feel like a coward for leaving."

Though he had a feeling the comment came out of Brutus' anger towards Tetra's escape and the pain his back was definitely in because of it, he dared to ask, "Even if it's the more honorable route?"

Brutus' glare turned towards him. "There should be nothing honorable about not fighting those Alliance straudwins who would dare sneak an attack on *us*."

"We're only trainees, Brutus..."

"So? I probably know more about war than half those who are fighting right now."

"That's probably true, but none of us have the experience they do."

"That's why we should be able to fight right now to get that—"

A squeal broke off his words. Chillbumps rose on Aabir's arms as he pressed his palms against his ears. He had heard that sound in his patre's garage, and experience told him something was disrupting the truck's electromagnetic pulse. Which meant...

He lowered his hands despite the grating noise and gripped the front side of the bench seat as the hovertruck fell to the ground. Everyone, except for Aabir, jolted out of their seats then landed back on them as it lifted again.

"Hold on!" He called out.

Everyone copied him as the truck fell and skidded along the ground. Again and again, it continued the motion as the squealing grew louder. Aabir gritted his teeth and wondered if his ears would end up bleeding. The truck jolted again. This was the worst he had ever heard the noise. It almost sounded like that one hovercar that had blown up in their driveway before patre could even get a look at it.

Oh no... His eyes widened and he looked around frantically at his jostled platoonmates. "I think it's gonna blow!" He tried to yell over the incessant screech.

Almost everyone turned their eyes on him just as the truck hit the ground again and skidded over every imaginable bump in Xich. Aabir gritted his rattling teeth as it continued to skid and silently prayed they would make it to the hovertrain station before the generator gave out. The western station was only a twenty-minute walking distance from the Palace of Commons. Surely, they were almost there...

BOOM!

Aabir cried out as he was thrown from his seat. There was another ***BOOM***. He slammed against Brutus as they both hit the other side of the truck. The air rushed out of his lungs with a gasp. Someone landed on his legs, and he could feel another body against his back. Spots danced in his vision. The ringing in his ears that had dissipated came back with a higher pitch.

More explosions sounded above the ringing. A sharp, metallic odor filled the air. He lay there, gasping for breath until his lungs no longer hurt, before trying to sit up. The spots had disappeared, but dust filtered into the back of the truck and blurred his vision. A few others from his platoon were also moving around.

Aabir blinked a few more times until what he was seeing finally registered in his brain.

The truck had landed on its side. He turned his head, his gaze roving over the mass of armored trainees he found himself in the middle of. The person on his legs let out a groan and he jerked his neck in their direction. Tycho lifted his head and their eyes locked.

His friend blinked bleary, unfocused eyes up at him. "What...what happened?"

"It—it sounded like the—like the electromagnetic generator blew up."

"Great..."

Tycho moved his hands underneath him and pushed himself up into a sitting position. Aabir pulled his legs towards himself, out from underneath the weight of his platoonmates, and carefully stood up. He helped Tycho and a few others, including Brutus, do the same.

"Oh no..." Tycho's voice died off.

Aabir spun around to face him, his heart hammering against his ribcage. "What?"

"Look."

He lifted his arm and pointed out the open back. Aabir's eyes followed in the same direction. "Oh."

Smoke mingled with the dust above the toppled body of the hovertruck behind them. Aabir strained his neck to see about the fate of the others, and he thought he saw another trail of smoke rising a little behind it. Resolve calmed the frantic waves crashing in his stomach.

"We need to make sure everyone is OK."

A weight fell on his shoulder, and he turned to see Tycho's hand there. "I'll go with you."

He nodded and began to make his way out of the toppled vehicle on shaky legs, Tycho right behind him.

Buren stepped towards them as they passed. "I'll come, too."

"Thanks." Aabir sent him a nod and stopped to help another of his platoonmates stand up.

Brutus joined their growing group. "I'll go with you guys."

Aabir opened his mouth to reply, but heavy sets of footsteps coming from outside stopped him. He jerked his head in the direction of the open back. Hopefully that was Lieutenant Denir coming with help.

A distinctly accented voice sliced that hope in half. "Halt!"

The atmosphere in the back of their toppled hovertruck grew tense. Aabir grabbed the hilt of his sword in a tight grip as the rings of other weapons being drawn out of their sheaths surrounded him. *Oh Deleyon, no...*

Seven armed Silvanian soldiers rushed in front of the truck's open back, and two Frigian soldiers clad in brown, leathery armor joined them. His heart jumped into his throat. He could see more Alliance soldiers running to the other trucks behind theirs.

This is bad.

One of the Silvanian soldiers stepped forward. "No one move. We have this truck," he gestured with his short sword to the dead hovertrucks behind them, "and the rest of your convoy surrounded."

Two swords rang out and Brutus stepped up beside Aabir. Out of the corner of his eye, he could see a pained sneer on the trainee's face.

"By whose authority?" He spat.

Aabir gritted his teeth but continued to keep his gaze on the bristling soldiers. *Way to go, Brutus.*

"By the authority of the Rulers of the Allied Nations." The same Silvanian man replied, "We do not wish to do you harm—no one wants to see trainees killed—but we will if you do not all drop your weapons *right now*."

There was an unmoving pause. Then Septimus stepped up beside Brutus and spat a wad of spit at the soldier's feet. "Over my dead body."

Oh, Deleyon. Deleyon, why? Why did his platoonmates have to be so idiotic now of all times?

One of the Frigian soldiers spoke in the deep, rough *Ivachku* tongue and stepped towards them, brandishing a Frigian *Owry* ax-spear in her hand. In heavily accented Alenguan, she added, "That can be arranged."

Aabir only blinked once, and the woman had the tip of her long Owry pressed into Brutus' throat.

"Move, and he dies." Her eyes glittered dangerously between the slit of her helmet and visor.

The Silvanian soldier from before stepped into the truck. "Drop your weapons, or she'll do as she says."

Aabir clenched his hands into fists. They were only trainees! They were given orders not to fight! He flicked his gaze to the owry's spear tip, and the fear now evident in Brutus' sharpened features.

"Please, don't kill him!" His heart pounded wildly against his ribcage as he spoke, "We're only trainees, and—and we were given orders to get to the hovertrain station to go back to Igrium. None of us are allowed to fight in the battle! Please, forgive his brash comments and let us go peacefully. We won't cause any trouble."

One of the Silvanian soldiers snorted and also stepped into the truck. "You may only be trainees, but we're not stupid enough to let three platoons of perfectly trained, future soldiers go free."

"Drop your weapons!" The Frigian woman barked.

Brutus, despite death being only a hair's breadth from his throat, continued to hold both his swords. Aabir ground his teeth to keep himself from cursing. Of course retreating just had to be dishonorable in this situation. He wanted to lash out at his stubborn platoon and the Alliance soldiers, but that would only get him killed.

Red rimmed his vision at the unfairness of the situation. Blood beat a steady rhythm in his ears. He did not want to oppose the kingdoms that he morally agreed with, but no one was going to hurt his friends—no matter how moronic they were being. He moved his hand as nonchalantly as he could and grabbed the hilt of his sheathed sword.

"Fine, then." The Silvanian man who stepped into the truck first waved to the rest of his comrades to come forward. "Deynla, do it."

As he spoke, Aabir unsheathed his sword and barely had time to block the woman's killing blow. The owry nicked Brutus' neck as Aabir pushed it up and away with the flat of his blade. Then he sliced sideways and up. The tip of his sword stopped at the Frigian woman's neck where the pieces of her thick, leather armor converged to create a small opening.

"Drop your weapon." Aabir ordered at the sound of rushing feet. "Come any closer and she dies!"

He could feel the presence of his friends and platoonmates moving around him. Out of the corner of his eyes, he noticed soft light glinting off their raised weapons. His chest heaved as he sucked in shaky breaths. The stray thought that this might end in a bloodbath tightened a chain of guilt around his pounding heart. Oh Deleyon, he hoped not...

"*Tri-shuw*!"

The woman locked eyes with him, and Aabir could see burning hatred intermingled with fear in her gaze. For a moment, he wondered if she would try attacking him, but—with eyes still burning holes into his head—she dropped her owry.

"And your shield."

He could barely hear a few Ivachku words being mumbled under her breath as she dropped her round shield. It fell with a loud ***clang*** that reverberated in Aabir's ears.

"Now," he said, "you'll let us all go so this doesn't have to get messy."

"What? Aabir—"

"—No." Aabir cut off Tycho's complaint without turning to look at his friend. He continued addressing the Alliance soldiers, "I promise we will leave you all alone. Drop your weapons, move to that side—" he jerked his head to the right, "—and keep silent."

Tense silence met his words, releasing some of the tightness in his chest. If they were being quiet, than this might just actually work...

"This is ridiculous." Brutus' mutter broke through his mental celebration.

Before Aabir could reply, the bulky trainee shoved him aside and stabbed one of his swords through a crack in the woman's armored abdomen. Ice rushed through Aabir's veins as the woman screamed. Brutus pulled out his bloodied blade and shoved her away. She fell in a crumpled heap.

"No!" Aabir shouted and turned his glare on Brutus.

Brutus shot him one back. "I'm no coward, Aabir. Nor should you be."

Anger kindled in his chest. His knuckles whitened as he gripped the hilt of his sword. "I gave her my word! She was defenseless! How is *that* the honorable thing to do?"

"It's not."

Aabir jerked his head in the direction of the new voice. Lieutenant Denir stood there, a team of Igrian soldiers with him. Aabir noticed the drops of blood that covered his armor, shield, and sword as he strode into the overturned vehicle.

The Alliance soldiers glanced around. Their wary silence immediately roared into a battle cry, and they surged forward to attack the newcomers. Aabir watched the fight unfold in wide-eyed, horrified silence. The truck's quarters were cramped, and with the Alliance soldiers surrounded, they had nowhere to move and were all quickly killed.

Aabir stared at the dead bodies, horror choking him. This was not supposed to happen. They were supposed to leave Xich without being part of the battle!

All his anger was doused in a tidal wave of guilt. The leather grooves of his sword's hilt brushed against his gauntleted fingers, and he gripped it before it could fall on the bloody ground. Oh Deleyon, he had done this...

"Let's move, trainees!" Lieutenant Denir stood from wiping his sword on the other Frigian soldier's leather armor. "We don't have much time. The Alliance is trying to take over the hovertrain station. Our orders still stand, though—there's a train waiting for us. Get your packs and move!"

Aabir blinked and tried to push his swirling thoughts to the side by turning his focus onto sheathing his sword, then looking for his pack amidst the scrambling trainees around him. When he found it, he joined the others who were following Lieutenant Denir out of the truck.

A cough escaped his throat as he breathed in the smoke-tainted air. More of his platoonmates shuffled out of the truck and followed behind him. The dust in the air seemed to come over his mind as he followed Tycho. His muscles shook as if he had been training for hours. He was vaguely aware of more people joining their group, and the increase of Igrian soldiers around them. Metal rang against metal. Screams and battle cries echoed through the streets.

Through the dust, the hovertrain station rose before them like a jumble of crumbling rounded skyscrapers. Hover rails came out of their sides at different intervals on arched bridges that spanned through the air as if going over water. Multiple hovercraft shot flaming bolts at each other in the air space above.

Ranks of Igrian soldiers lined the entry bridge and stairs leading into the station. Aabir's eyes locked onto a medbot floating down the stairs. He blinked and realized there were more of the small, boxy robots moving through the crowds around him. And that was when he noticed soldiers carrying gurneys through the station's open entrance. An image of the woman Brutus killed flashed through his mind, and Aabir's chest tightened under the weight of the guilty reminder.

He barely processed ascending the stairs as the memories swept through his mind repeatedly, carried along on the winds of accusations battering at his mental walls. Hundreds of echoing voices accosted his ears as he stepped into the hovertrain station. The sharp smells of chemicals and blood filled his nostrils, bringing him back to the present for the moment.

Makeshift hospital beds took up most of the floorspace in the opulent entrance hall. Field doctors and medbots bustled around blood-soaked gurneys and moaning bodies. A thunderous boom shook the large chandeliers hanging from the towering, rounded ceilings.

The sights sent a chill through Aabir. He decided to keep his gaze on the tiled floor as he and the other three platoons were led through the frantic activity. Only when they made it to their hovertrain did he lift his head. They all filed into three train cars on a long passenger hovertrain. Aabir glanced at the other cars and saw medbots pushing gurneys into them.

More guilt pressed in on him at the available space the trainees were taking up. No matter how much he did not want to fight in the battle (any more than he had already been pushed into), those who were mortally wounded needed to get out of the city before he did. Yet he tried to push it aside by telling himself he was not the one who had given the orders for all the trainees to leave. As Lieutenant Denir had told his disgruntled platoon earlier, Igrium had more than enough reinforcements coming in to fight in the battle without wasting the army's possible future leaders.

Aabir filed onto the train and found an empty window seat. He took his pack off and sat down with a sigh. Tycho soon joined the seat beside him. They were both uncharacteristically silent as the rest of the trainees filed into the train cars.

The familiar humming of the electromagnetic generator began. He clenched his stomach at the noise and turned his face towards the window. *It won't explode*, he told himself. No one would even think to stop a hovertrain moving the wounded to a safer area...right?

The view of the station outside the window began to move. Aabir kept his gaze forward as the hovertrain picked up speed and practically flew out of the station and into the dusty sollight outside. The ruins of Trivsau passed by until the view became an indistinguishable blur. It gave his mind a great backdrop to think through the images he had just witnessed, and the guilt that continued to press upon him.

What would he tell his family when he got home? That he had almost killed someone? If the Frigian soldier had not dropped her weapon, would he have done what he threatened? Even if it would have been in defense of his friend, could he still have killed someone?

Aabir closed his eyes and leaned his head back against the seat. His adrenaline rush had left him exhausted, and he soon found himself falling under sleep's embrace—only to be met with nightmares filled with battles and screams.

Chapter Thirteen

Muffled, accented voices penetrated the soothing darkness over Tetra's mind. Sharp heat tore through her leg, and she groaned. The voices stopped for a moment. Her pulse pounded through her head and her leg. What was happening...?

"I'm sorry," a clearer voice spoke close to her, "but this is going to hurt."

Tetra couldn't open her eyes or lift her heavy tongue to reply. A piercing pain dug into her already-burning leg and she let out a scream. The calm nothingness from before swooped back and she welcomed its numbing embrace.

"Tetra..." The familiar voice seemed to speak from a great distance, "You need to wake up now."

Fog filled Tetra's head. She took in a deep breath and caught a delicious whiff of something spicy. An empty pit yawned open in her stomach at the smell. She opened her dry mouth and tried to speak, but only a moan came out.

She went to move, but a sharp pain spiked up her leg. Another moan escaped her lips.

"I—I bring medicine to—to help."

Tetra gritted her teeth until the throbbing pain dissipated. Once it was gone, the fog was lifted a little and she blinked her bleary eyes open. A faceless blob filled her vision, and she continued to blink until it came into focus.

A stripe of sollight touched Stellinga's smiling, but weary, features. "I bring my *ahni's* soup, too."

Tetra lowered her gaze to a steaming bowl in the girl's hands, and her stomach growled as loud as a peryton.

"Here—" Stellinga put the bowl of stew down, "—I help you up."

Under different circumstances, Tetra would have rejected the offer, but she could barely lift her own head. So, with a sigh, she let Stellinga help her to a sitting position. The piercing pain stabbed through her leg as she sat up, and she gritted her teeth against a cry.

Stellinga stopped moving her halfway. "I sorry, Tetra."

"Keep...going." Tetra hissed between breaths.

Stellinga did so. With more shuffling and dagger-like pains, she helped Tetra lean against what felt like a pole. Tetra focused on her breathing as she waited for the pain to die off again. As she did so, the thought occurred to her that this was a different kind of pain than the fiery, needle-like type she had felt before. Which brought up another question: what happened to her?

She finally opened her eyes and caught the worry etched across Stellinga's stitched brow.

"I'm OK." She tried to smile, but it only caused Stellinga's brow to scrunch down even more. Forgoing the feigned happiness, she lowered her gaze to the stoneware bowl on the ground. "Is that for me?"

"Oh! Yes..." Stellinga straightened and picked the bowl up before handing it to her. "Here."

"Thanks."

Tetra could already feel some energy returning as the spicy aroma reached her nose again. Stellinga set the bowl on her blanket-covered lap. Purple and green vegetables, rice, and pieces of beef floated in the broth. She picked up the metal spoon from the bowl's lip with only a slight tremor in her hand and lifted it to her lips. Warm, delicious spiciness exploded in her mouth, and she was soon gobbling up the rest of it.

Neither said anything as she ate, which was fine with Tetra. The fog was still lifting from her head, but she could feel her flow of thoughts returning to normal.

As she took another spoonful of soup, she finally registered their surroundings. A thin blanket covered the lower half of her body and the puffy pallet underneath her. Another, larger pallet lay on the sandy ground next to hers. Xinxan speech and footsteps filtered in from outside her dim surroundings as shadows of people passed by. Tetra noticed two people's unmoving shadows on both tent's sides, and uneasiness settled in her stomach.

As her thoughts became clearer, she was reminded of what had transpired during her hoverbike escape. Knocking Aabir out, running through the Palace of Commons, meeting Stellinga, stealing the hoverbike, fighting the guards, and leaping over the fence all came back to her.

She placed the spoon in the now-empty bowl and set it to the side. "Stellinga..." The Xichian girl turned her face towards her and met her eyes. "Where are we?"

"A...a camp." Stellinga turned her gaze to the floor and fooled with the hem of her tunic. "Outside Trivsau."

"So, did we make it over the fence?"

She nodded, then looked back up at Tetra with watery eyes. "Yes, but you—you almost not."

The sharp memory of those heart-pounding moments before Tetra blacked out came to the forefront of her mind. She looked down and pulled the blanket off her legs. Her breath hitched as her eyes landed on the white cocoon of bandages wrapped around her right leg.

So that explained where the pain was coming from...

"How did we get here?" She lifted her head and noticed shadows had come over Stellinga's countenance. "I remember making it over the fence...but what else has happened? Why...why are we in a camp? I don't—I don't remember there being a camp on either side of Trivsau."

"It...new." Stellinga wouldn't meet her gaze as she continued, "You—you sleep over two days."

"What?" Tetra's jaw dropped. Two days? No wonder she felt so...off.

"Yes. Two days." Stellinga nodded matter-of-factly, completely oblivious to the shock her words brought. "We—we jump over fence, and—and you save me from hitting sharp wire." She sniffed. "I—I not say details, but you—you got...stuck. The hoverbike not get high enough."

A shiver went down Tetra's spine despite the fact she had blacked out through most of it.

"Silvanian soldiers catch me, then they got you down. Igrium—no, *Igrian* soldiers say—they say bad things at you." A tear spilled down Stellinga's cheek as she lifted her gaze and met Tetra's. "They make life hard for us in Xich, but I not know how mean Igrians really be to their own until that day. I—I glad you not hear what they said."

Tetra clenched her hands into fists in her lap as heat crept up her neck. At least she had been out for the whole humiliating experience...

"I'm sorry you had to hear it, Stellinga."

Stellinga shrugged. "It not your fault. I just—I just so happy you save me from hitting wire." More tears spilled down her cheeks and she wiped them away with her hands. "Anyway, after you get down, the *much nicer* Silvanian soldiers took us both to hospital. As they took care of you, they ask me questions about what we doing, why I with you, who my family is, stuff like that. I tell them all I know, and then—and then my parents came!" The shadows on Stellinga's face dissipated in the beams of her smile.

"They did?" Tetra couldn't help smiling back.

"Yes!" More tears spilled down her cheeks, but her eyes were shining. "I tell story over again to them, and they stay with me at hospital while I wait for you. We got news you had been taken care of, and we go to see you. My *opie* went back to our home to get clean clothes for us, but—but before we see you or he come back, fighting begin."

Wait...she had slept through a *battle*?

Before she could ask, Stellinga barreled on, "Me and my ahni tell soldiers there that we take you with us. They refuse, but my ahni talked with them and she get permission to keep you with us as long as—oh, what that word...?—I not know it, but I think you say it before. They outside tent now."

Tetra glanced at the unmoving shadows on either side of the tent. So, she had guards. Alliance guards. Growing uneasiness tightened her stomach, but she said nothing so Stellinga could finish.

"All this side of city was already leaving by time we did. We all made it—even my Opie, but he caught in...I think word is '*explode*'..."

"'*Explosion*'?"

"Ah, yes. That sound right." Stellinga nodded and began playing with the hem of her tunic again. "He caught in *explosion*, but he in medic tent now. I think he OK, but I not see him since morning of yesterday."

Tetra didn't really know what to say to all this, so all she said was, "Oh. But you know he's OK?"

"Mm-hmm. Medbots give me or Ahni word twice a day. We just not able to enter medic tent because there not enough space for visitors."

"Oh—good."

"So, that what happen." Stellinga shrugged again, still fooling with her tunic's hem.

Tetra still had so many questions. "When did the battle happen? Did—did the Alliance win?"

"Morning after we escape, and it end only yesterday. And yes, Alliance win." She lifted her eyes to the tent's ceiling and said, "*Fle-Rova*."

Tetra leaned her head back against the tent pole. They had actually won. Trivsau would be free. And if the predictions she had heard back at Norland were true, then Xich might join the Alliance's war efforts against Igrium soon. She wanted to ask a bunch of questions about the logistics of the battle, but Stellinga probably wouldn't know anything about them, so she kept those thoughts to herself. She would just have to figure it out later.

She sighed through her nose and put the blanket back over her legs. Another sharp pain sliced through her leg at the sudden movement, and she sucked in a sharp breath as it left as quickly as it had come.

Stupid leg.

"Oh, I forgot!" Stellinga turned and picked up a small cup and held it out to Tetra. "Your medicine."

"Thank you."

Tetra took the cup with a grateful nod. Purple-tinged liquid sloshed around in the plastic cup. She pinched her nose with one hand and, after a couple breaths through her mouth, downed the medicine. It had a fake fruit taste that could've been worse, but it still left an undesirable film on her tongue. She handed the cup back to Stellinga with a grimace.

"I can get water to help if you like." Stellinga took the cup in both her hands.

Tetra nodded with a dry cough. "That'd be great."

"I be right back.

She shot up and stepped over to the tent's entry flap. Sollight poured into the dim tent as she did so, and Tetra shielded her eyes from the brightness. Yet through her fingers, she noticed the gleam of green-tinted armor before the flap fell closed.

A shiver wracked through her muscles as she put her hand down. Hopefully Rasiela had gotten word to the Alliance person she was in contact with, and Tetra wouldn't be in this situation for long. Despite the thought, seeds of fear fell into her mind, and they immediately sprung with doubtful thoughts of the cleaning lady's assurances.

"Where are you going, *Mra Stellinga*?" Tetra's heart skipped a beat, and she jerked her head in the direction of the entrance at the sound of the heavy, Silvanian-accented voice.

"I go get water for Tetra," Stellinga replied.

"So, she's awake?"

"*Mene.*"

"All right. Go on, then."

"*Fleora.*"

Tetra heard Stellinga's footsteps fade away as the tent flap cracked open, and had to squint her eyes as the light came in. She noticed the shadowed face of the guard peeking in before letting the flap close again. Another shiver went through her despite the dry heat. Was there something she needed to do...?

The same Silvanian voice spoke again. Tetra tried to make out the words, but they were too low for her to catch. She guessed they must be calling someone, because she heard another, deeper voice—this one more muffled than the first—replying when the first voice stopped. Maybe they were reporting to their commanding officer about her finally being awake.

Oh Rasiela, Tetra put her head in her hands with a heavy sigh, t*hese better be some strong connections you have.*

The guard's conversation soon ceased, and less than a minute later Stellinga returned with a bigger cup of water. Tetra lifted her head and accepted it.

"Thanks."

Stellinga stayed standing, her brow pinched in worry. "You good, Tetra?"

She took a swig of water to wash away the film still coating her mouth. "Yeah, I'm—" She stopped the lie before it fully formed.

Maybe Stellinga could calm some of her uneasiness... She turned her neck in both guards' directions to make sure they looked the same as before. Satisfied with their stillness, she lifted her head and locked eyes with the younger girl.

"Stellinga," she began in a low voice, "do you know what my position might be right now?"

Stellinga scratched her creased forehead, right above her stitches. "Um...I think I understand," she finally said. "You mean if you...er—what that word...ah! If you prisoner?"

Fear tightened her stomach. "Yeah."

"I not think so." Even with her heavy accent, Tetra could hear the uncertainty in her voice, "They not say you prisoner, but my ahni not able to tell guards to leave. One outside there—" she gestured with her hand towards the guard she had spoken too, "—told me to tell him when you wake. He say something about person in charge needing to know."

So, her suspicions were true. Tetra lowered her gaze and put a hand on her nauseous stomach. "Thanks for telling me."

There was a moment of silence. Fabric rustled as Stellinga lowered, and Tetra jerked her head up at a touch on her shoulder. The girl's steady, teal gaze met hers. Now that they were—uncomfortably—close, she could see the dark circles underneath Stellinga's red-rimmed eyes, and it caused her fears to calm for a moment.

Here Stellinga was—living in a refugee camp outside the decimated city she once called home, waiting for her father to be healed and possibly for word from other family members and friends caught up in the battle—yet she was taking care of *Tetra*, of all people. Tetra might have worries of her own, but she wasn't facing the levels of uncertainty and fear Stellinga must be.

"You not need worry, Tetra," she said in a firm voice. "I tell them how you not hurt me and how we escape, and soldier who see you not hurt me even agree with me. I not think anyone try hurt you. I—I not understand all talked about when you in hospital, but I know they talk of your scars and they not seem angry like—like Igrians about them."

Tetra lightly touched her malscar's stitches. Rasiela's words about her record came to the forefront of her mind, and she glanced down at the tallies covering her arm. Could the dishonorable scars actually prove to be useful?

"Thanks, Stellinga." She lowered her hand with a steadying sigh. "That...that helps."

Stellinga's smile returned, and she let go of Tetra's shoulder before scooting back a little on her knees. "Good."

Fear had loosened its grip on her chest, but she couldn't completely quell it. There were still little niggling thoughts in the back of her mind whispering "what if's" to keep the chains of fear alive, but she tried to ignore them. "Where is your ahni, Stellinga? Is she OK?"

"She good." Stellinga's smile faded as a calm seriousness overtook her features. "Well, she say she good. She been helping cook at food tent to keep herself...*rytuk sov*...um—oh! Busy. Keep herself *busy*..." She began to twirl a strand of her long, brown hair. "She do that when she not want to think. She—she been worried ever since first battle and I stuck on other side of—of fence, and now...now we here."

Tetra didn't know what to say to that, so she let a thick silence stretch between them until the words came to mind. "I'm sorry for everything that's happened, Stellinga." She kept her gaze lowered to her fingers as she twiddled the blanket with them. "And I'm sorry that you all have had me—an Igrian—to deal with on top of it all. I'm...I'm grateful for all you've done to help me, but if it's too much I'm sure I can leave."

"No! You not need do that, Tetra. You no trouble; not at all. We happy to help—you did save me, and we want return kindness."

"But I didn't save you." Tetra lifted her head and set her gaze on Stellinga's sincere, almost offended, expression. "If it weren't for you, I don't think my plan would've worked. I don't even know how to drive a hoverbike—let alone jump it off a building!"

"But you not give me this," Stellinga pointed to her stitches. "And you one who come up with plan in first place. I never would have think that one up!" She chuckled. "Even if I did, I be too scared to try. You got hoverbike, and you protect us from guards. I never be able to do that! So, I say it *mostly* you."

She crossed her arms with a knowing smile, daring Tetra to argue.

Tetra had never saved anyone in her life, nor would she have been able to save herself during her escape attempt without help. So, despite Stellinga's uncompromising appearance, she opened her mouth to argue, "Stellinga—"

But someone called outside their tent, "*Mra* Stellinga? May I come in?"

They both turned their heads in the direction of the new shadows. Tetra caught the wary glance Stellinga shot her; and though her heart thumped wildly in her chest, she sent the girl a nod. There would be no point in trying to stop this conversation from happening. It was best to just get it over with.

"*Mene*," Stellinga said.

The tent flap lifted. Sollight shone against polished, dark greenish-gray armor as two Silvanian soldiers stepped into the small space. Fear again tightened its hold on Tetra as her eyes flicked between their faces. The first, a heavyset man with two daggers sheathed at his sides and the hilt of a longsword poking out over his shoulder, ducked his head so as not to hit it on the tent's sloped roof. He set his probing, violet gaze upon her, and she immediately looked away as her anxiety pulled her imagination into its dreadful grasp. Despite the tent being too cramped for him to use the longsword, it wouldn't be too hard for him to crush her with his bare hands.

Recognition pushed that scary thought to the side as the rounded face of the woman who had tried defending Stellinga at the fence stepped in after him. She met Tetra's eyes and blinked before looking away in Stellinga's direction.

"Thank you, *Mra* Stellinga," The man nodded his head in the girl's direction as he undid the scabbard around his chest. "I hate to ask, but could you please wait outside while we talk to Miss Cairn?"

"Oh, *meneva yestl vahj*—um, of course." She scrambled up and grabbed the empty bowl from the ground, "I just...go put this away." Tetra met her eyes and Stellinga gave her a reassuring small smile. "Then I wait outside until you done."

She rushed out of the tent in a swirl of billowing fabric. The space's atmosphere grew ten times more tense as the man pulled the sheathed longsword off his back and sat down on the ground opposite Tetra, laying the sword on his lap. The woman stayed standing next to the tent's entrance, her hand resting on the pommel of the sword hanging from her belt.

"Miss Cairn..." Tetra forced herself to look up at the man's face as he spoke, "I am Captain Keane Ulanc of the Silvanian fourth infantry regiment. You and Miss Stellinga fell into our district the other night."

Tetra only nodded to tell him she was listening. He continued, "So I have been ordered to ask you some questions."

An interrogation... of course.

He leaned forward slightly. "Private Glaslir here has already told me about what happened for you to receive that malscar, and I know they are only given to those Igrium's army deems the lowest of the low. So, I would like to know why the daughter of the Cairns' has one."

For a moment, she wondered how he knew who she was, but then she remembered she had been in a hospital occupied by the Alliance where a DNA test was surely done. They probably knew more about her than she did.

"Because...I pushed my commanding officer to her breaking point." Tetra flinched as the memory of the burning hatred in Lieutenant Tarson's eyes flashed through her mind. "She'd already told me back in Igrium that if I did anything else she'd give me one. I told myself to just obey her when the time came—since I might've ended up being one of the emperor's personal guards with no memory of it anyway—but I...I just couldn't do it."

"Hurt Stellinga?"

"Yes sir."

She lifted her hand and rubbed the rough segione tallies on the inside of her elbow at the pause that stretched between them.

"Your record says that you have...quite a few misdemeanors." One corner of his mouth lowered in a slight frown. "And by the amount of segione tallies you have, I see it was not lying. Is there a reason why you decided to stand against your commanding officers by doing these things? Why would you risk your well-being by disobeying Emperor Ignis?"

"Um...I—I don't necessarily stand for everything Igrium does."

"Explain."

She breathed out deeply through her nose. What should she say? Her gaze became fixed on some sand covering her palette as she lowered her brow in thought.

Why did she have such a strong conviction for standing up against the cruelty her native empire was so well-known for during the war? What started it? The answer slowly came to her as the quiet moments ticked by.

"When I...when I was first forced into Norland, I was immediately thrown into a world full of older kids always picking on me for being ugly; and commanding officers and teachers who only saw my parents' when they looked at me—and expected just as much."

Those first few years were absolute torture. She was the youngest trainee at the time; was suffering from not knowing the first eight years of her life; and the large, puffy burn scar on her head was easily seen for over a year until some of her hair finally grew back to cover it. The knowledge that she wouldn't be able to leave—due to her parents' honorary will—only made everything worse.

"When I was around ten or eleven, I finally got tired of everything and outright refused one of my teachers when he gave me a homework assignment to do." Her lips twisted to the side. "And he could easily see it was out of rebellion, so I got my first segione tally. Despite the pain and that I was dishonoring my parents' memory, I began to disobey or cause problems with the other trainees. I didn't care at that point. So that's when Emperor Ignis began asking to see me and issuing punishments himself. I even tried escaping Norland twice, but I was caught both times."

A freezing chill swept through her as the horrible memories resurfaced, and her gaze locked onto her segione tallies. The second time she had tried to escape, she fell from one of the everpine trees outside Norland and almost died at the impact. She remembered laying in a hospital bed as a twelve-year-old wishing the fall had just killed her.

"I...I was lonely, and I thought everything in the world was horrible and against me. Then in my first official year as a trainee, I—I made a friend." Her first, and only, one. "His name was Aabir, and his parents were Silvanian. He liked to talk a lot, so I got to know all about his family, his beliefs, his favorite foods, and other random things that'd come up in our conversations.

"And, I'm not sure when it happened, but that's when I started to see things differently." She took a deep breath before continuing, "I'd never known another perspective other than my own, so I clung to everything he said. He always seemed to be happy no matter what happened, and I wanted that. So, my attitudes started changing and I actually found myself caring for other people and not just me.

"And as I learned more about the world outside Norland's walls and saw all the things Igrium was doing, the injustice Aabir told me about 'stabbed me in the face', and I wanted to do something to stop it. So that's when I started getting these—" she gestured to her arm, "—for disobeying or trying to find loopholes in my commanding officers' orders that I didn't think were right."

Colonel Ulanc was silent for a moment. "And this friend of yours', Aabir, did he follow your lead?"

"Not really." A pang stabbed Tetra's heart. "He was much quieter about his dislike of Igrium's morals, but he had to be. He told me he joined to protect his family, and going against his commanding officer's orders was a good way to put them in a bad light. So, the only thing we did was try to escape Norland." She gripped the blanket in her fists as the guilt-ridden memories resurfaced. "It didn't work."

"I see. And yet there is one thing I am not hearing in all of this, Miss *Cairn*," his accent grew deeper with the emphasis put on her family name. "I may not be Igrian, but I do know a little about how important honoring one's family is to you all. So did you just not care about your family's honor?"

"No sir." Tetra shook her head and met his eyes. "I did care—I just never realized how much until Aabir talked about his parents and how he was taught to respect them. It was...a bit different than how I was taught, but I liked it. He told me I could honor my parents by doing good and setting that example." She gave a mirthless laugh. "No one at Norland, or even Emperor Ignis, believed that was the case, but I did for a while."

She had finally grown out of that fantasy after her and Aabir's failed escape attempt. She knew, deep down, that Aries and Marin Cairn were looking down on their dishonorable excuse for a daughter with more disgust than any other parents ever had.

"And what about now?"

Tetra picked up on the added layer in the colonel's question and thought through her answer before replying, "I know their spirits hate me right now and I...I wish they didn't, but I've done too much already to try to fix it. And even if I could, I don't think I'd be able to."

Just like she hadn't been able to hurt Stellinga even with the threat of becoming a personal guard hanging over her head.

She noticed the colonel and Private Glaslir sharing a look before Colonel Ulanc asked her another question, "What is your opinion on your parents' 'fire raids'?"

Tetra's heart skipped a beat at the cool tone of his voice. It gave her the impression of a sharp, gritanium blade lying in wait for someone to do, or say, something horrible in order to use it.

"I think attacking innocent civilians under the guise of 'protecting one's empire' is horrible and I wish I didn't carry the family name that created those raids in the first place."

Colonel Ulanc's stonelike expression didn't change at her answer, but she didn't feel like she had given him provocation to use the metaphorical sharp dagger. A sliver of relief calmed her racing heart a little. Thank goodness her eyes revealed practically everything she was thinking about and made her a horrible liar.

Colonel Ulanc asked her a few more questions about her parents, being a trainee, and about her and Stellinga's escape. Tetra answered them all as honestly as she could (some of the questions about her parents' she couldn't answer because of her amnesia), but Colonel Ulanc seemed satisfied with what she had to say. His squarish face proved impossible to read and she clung to the fact that she couldn't sense any hostility coming from him as the basis for his feelings towards her.

Tetra stifled a yawn as she finished answering another question. She began to wonder how much longer this questioning would last when the colonel finally said, "Thank you, Miss Cairn, for your cooperation." He abruptly stood and strapped his longsword back on. "I'll send your answers to my commanding officer and continue on from there. Until then, we will leave you to rest."

He barely looked her way as Private Glaslir lifted the tent flap and he exited. She sent Tetra one last look before also making her exit.

Tetra breathed in a shaky breath as the peaceful quiet of the tent enveloped her. Well, it seemed like everything went fine... Hopefully no one thought she was an Igrian spy.

The tent flap moved and she jerked her head in its direction as Stellinga stepped into the tent. With a nervous look, the other girl asked, "So how it go? I not hear much outside with people walking and talking."

"I think it went fine." Tetra's last word ended in a yawn she couldn't hold back. A weariness had set itself in her bones, and she found herself wanting to obey its will.

"Good." Stellinga grinned and lifted the entry flap again. "I can go see if Ahni need help in food tent so you sleep. I bring more food and medicine when you wake. *Falader.*"

She left, and Tetra scooted back down into a lying position upon her palette. The pain meds must've kicked in because only a low throb went through her leg as she moved it. She closed her eyes and let the thoughts of amazing Xichian food and the muffled noises out in the camp lull her into sleep.

Chapter Fourteen

THE IMAGE OF BRUTUS stabbing the Frigian woman, Deynla, echoed through Aabir's mind. He shook his head, trying to remove the thought, and then focused his gaze on the clear, holographic board set in front of the history classroom. Mr. Grahan droned on about when Igrium ravaged the kingdom of Yuln and started the war as he wrote down another date, but it was all background noise to Aabir—despite how much he wished he could focus on it. Even with his dislike of history—and this particular event—it was better than remembering.

Three days had passed since the battle, and his thoughts continued to circle back to that moment like a griffin from the scavenger clan circling around a piece of roadkill. He played with the corner of a page of light in his chardex. That woman's death was his own fault, he knew. It might as well have been his own sword plunging into her. He should have never tried to go for diplomacy with all his blood-thirsty platoonmates surrounding him.

The only consolation he had from the entire ordeal was that Lieutenant Denir agreed with him on Brutus' actions and did not see Aabir as a coward for not killing her. Their orders had been to avoid the battle, and since he had followed them as much as he could, his C.O. was not dishonored by it—but almost everyone else in his platoon seemed to be. Only Tycho and Aquilo had spoken more than ten words to him that did not include the words "coward", "straudwin", "fool", and a few other, more colorful, terms that would make his parents regret letting him go to Norland even more than they already did.

Mr. Grahan turned around to face the class, his sharp eyes roving over each of his students. "I want you all to look through the last five chapters of '*The History of Yuln*" tonight. If you have any questions about the essay that I did not address, do not hesitate to contact me."

He looked down at the holonode attached to his wrist a moment before the bell rang. "You're dismissed."

Aabir closed his chardex as he stood from his desk. Grabbing it in one hand, he joined the flow of people leaving the classroom. The low chatter in the room was engulfed in a multitude of voices as he stepped out into the hall.

"Aabir!"

"Hmm?" He turned around as Aquilo joined him.

"I'm going to the library real quick, so if you need any last-minute chemistry answers, I'll be there."

"Thanks." Aabir replied, "but I think I actually got the ones I need this time."

And thank Deleyon he had, because what he really wanted to do during break was call his parents, not sit in a library going over more schoolwork.

Aquilo shrugged. "OK. See you in chemistry, then." He patted Aabir's shoulder and joined the river of trainees again.

With a sigh, Aabir glanced around the busy hall, searching for a private place to call them without walking to his dorm on the other side of Norland.

He joined the flowing streams of trainees until they broke off into two different sets of corridors, then turned into the one that would lead him to the dining hall. Some trainees used the huge area as another study hall during breaks, but he hoped there would not be anyone in there right now.

The cafeteria's wide, double doors came up on his right. He slowed, exited the flow of traffic, and pushed one of the doors open a crack. Peeking through, he frowned at the sight of two small groups of third and fourth years chatting and doing homework at the tables.

He huffed a breath. *Well, there went that idea.*

He deferred to going outside and turned to enter the sea of packed teenagers. His gaze landed on the door opposite the dining hall entrance. A small sign above it read "*Janitorial Services*".

Hoping the janitor was not in there right now, he started moving towards the door.

Aabir made a short path through the walking trainees onto the opposite side. He sent a furtive glance around, but no one was paying attention to him. With a deep breath, he turned the door's knob and opened it enough to peek his head through. Darkness greeted his eyes, and he could not help but smile.

He reached his hand out and felt along the wall for a light sensor. His hand passed over a smooth patch of the wall and bright, fluorescent lighting illuminated the room. He entered and shut the door behind him. Shelves full of cleaning supplies lined two of the walls, and a workbench with a dismantled cleaning bot atop it leaned up against the other.

Aabir pulled his sleeve away from his holonode and turned the device on with a flick of his wrist. The holographic screen appeared in the air above it. He tapped on his "contacts" app and called Matha. It only dialed a couple times before her face filled the screen.

Her eyebrows lowered. "Are you all right, Aabir? You look tired."

He glanced over his shoulder at the closed door then back to her. "I'm fine, Matha. I just wanted to know how everything was."

She pursed her lips and looked as if she did not believe him, but she only answered his question. "We're fine. Nothing has happened today."

"Good."

Aabir had called his parents a few times since coming back from Xich, but he had not told them any of the details about their early departure. All they knew was that the trainees were forced to come back because of the battle.

"You are getting enough sleep, yes?" Matha raised her brow.

He shrugged and looked anywhere but at her knowing gaze. "Well...not as much as I normally do."

"Why not?"

He closed his eyes with a huff, then opened them again. "Why does it matter?"

"Because I'm your matha and I care for you. I might even be able to help." The camera angle tilted as—he assumed—she stood, and the living room's background soon turned into the kitchen. "I think I still have some of those sleeping supplements your patre used to take..."

Aabir frowned and glanced down at his boots. Would they be strong enough to pull him into a dreamless sleep, though?

The sound of a cabinet closing came from the holonode. "I found them." He lifted his gaze back to Matha's worried countenance. "I can give them to you when you come home tonight, but I would like to know: is it only because you're having trouble falling asleep? Or is it something else?"

"Um...no ma'am. It's not that." He lifted his free hand and rubbed the back of his neck without meeting her eyes. "I...I uh..."

Oh, why was this so embarrassing? It was only Matha! It is not like he had to tell her what the nightmares were about.

"I've been having nightmares." He shrugged as if it was no big deal, but the memories of the warped images from the last three nights rushed into his head and sent a shiver down his spine. "It's nothing. I just can't seem to fall asleep after I wake from them." Because his brain would not stop replaying them *and* his actual memories.

"Hmm. What are you not telling me, Aabir? Did something happen in Xich?"

"No—"

"—And don't lie to me, Aabir Sorrel." Sharpness edged Matha's words.

He sighed through his nose. "Fine. Something—something did happen..." He shut his eyes as if it would shut the memories out. "Our escape convoy was attacked by Alliance soldiers. Brutus said something stupid, and they went to kill him but I...I stopped them."

The words continued to come forth, "I didn't kill anyone, Matha—I promise. I only threatened to. I—I don't believe I would have been able to, anyway... But I told them to drop their weapons, and one of them did. Then, I promised we wouldn't harm them, but they had to let us go. But before that could happen, Brutus...he...he killed the woman who was unarmed. Then Lieutenant Denir and some other soldiers came and killed the rest of them."

He finally opened his eyes. The judgmental horror he feared might be on Matha's face was not there, only a soft sadness.

"Oh Aabir..."

"I know—I know I wasn't the one to deal the killing blow, Matha, but—but I was the reason she had no weapons—no shield—to defend herself with." He breathed another sigh. "I don't know how I'll survive the next four years..." *If I even do survive*, he added to himself.

Now that the confession was over, he felt a tiny bit better. Yet it still did nothing to relieve the guilt pressing in on his chest.

"It wasn't your fault," Matha said. "I know you might think so, but you did everything in your power to keep it from happening. There was no way you could have known it would happen. Even *I* know it's dishonorable to kill an unarmed person."

"Still..."

"Don't beat yourself up, Aabir." Matha paused for a moment. "And don't worry about the next four years. You *will* survive. Your patre and I will make sure of it."

Aabir's heart jumped at the strange phrase, and he sent her a questioning look. "What?"

Matha's face drew closer to the screen. "We don't know how exactly," he could tell she was whispering, but his holonode automatically turned the volume up so he could hear her at a normal volume, "but we are trying to come up with ideas. Just please—don't worry, Aabir. Deleyon will open a way, I'm sure of it. Your patre and I have not lost hope. We know there must be some way to get out of...*here*."

Ah. Escape. Despite the hope Matha's words were supposed to bring, it only brought on a new gale of worry that Aabir had not thought of until now as the Silvanian soldier's words floated through his head.

"But—but will we even be allowed in?" He asked, hoping Matha understood the hidden meaning. "I don't believe they like trainees...no matter who I'm descended from."

Matha scrunched her brow as a worried thoughtfulness entered her dark purple eyes. "Your patre and I never thought of that, but I can see what you're saying..." Her voice trailed off into a pause. She blinked and the worry disappeared from her features. "But I don't want you to worry about any of this, Aabir. We will figure out something."

Just then, in the background Yahel's young voice cried out, "Matha!"

The camera angle jerked as Matha turned. A small smile lit her face as she looked back at Aabir through the screen. "I need to go, Aabir. I will call you later, though. Love you."

"Love you, too."

The call ended, and he let out a sigh. He tapped his holonode off and pressed his fingers against his temples as the fuller truth of his reality continued to load his shoulders.

Here was just another disadvantage that came with his choice to join Norland. If his family did somehow find a way to escape, could his being a trainee keep them from getting into any of the Alliance nations?

"Can I help you?"

Aabir spun around, heart hammering in his chest, and locked eyes with Norland's janitor. "Um...I'm sorry. I—I was just trying to—to find a private place..." His voice trailed off at the hard look in the woman's eyes. "I'm sorry. I was just leaving."

"You are Silvanian, aren't you?" She asked.

He blinked at the random question, then twisted his lips into a frown. "Um...I was born here in Rubrum..." Not that it was any of her business.

"Look—I know that was a strange question, kid, but I overheard your conversation."

Oh no. "You...you were eavesdropping?" He glared to keep the fear from showing on his face.

"You're in *my* office." Her plum-colored eyes peered into him. "I have a right to know why a trainee would want to hide in here—and now I do."

Oh no, oh no, oh no.

She glanced at the open door behind her, then leaned in closer to him. "You were Tetra Cairn's friend, yes?" She whispered.

Aabir knew he should keep his mouth shut, but the knowing look on the woman's face told him she already knew he and his family were plotting something. "Yes ma'am..."

She nodded once. "Then meet me outside in the everpine trees later this afternoon before you leave for the weekend. I might be able to help you."

"And how do I know this isn't some sort of trap?"

"Tetra trusted me." She shrugged and crossed her arms. "I'm not asking you to come, but I might have a solution that could help you and your family leave Igrium—if that's what you were hinting at."

Was it that obvious? Aabir sent a silent prayer to Deleyon that whoever was behind the hidden cameras in their house had not picked up on Matha's words.

She moved to the side so he could leave the room. "If you decide to come, I'll be waiting."

He blinked in surprise as a familiar, slight accent crept into her words. He took another assessment of her features and mentally slapped himself. She had purplish eyes, and only those of Silvanian descent could have that eye color—like *his* eye color. How had he never noticed before?

"You best get going, trainee," the woman said. "Your break ends in a few minutes," her accent becoming more obvious to him now.

Aabir took a wide step past her and sent one last glance in her direction. She met his eyes and blinked, then shut the door on his back.

Heart still hammering, Aabir began walking down the hall with quick steps. He barely registered his surroundings as the images of what just happened replayed in his head.

Fear joined the guilt tightening around his chest. Someone knew about his family's possible escape plan. Someone knew the treason they were planning to commit—and she was most likely of Silvanian descent. That should have made him feel better, but there was too much fear flooding his head that no reasonable facts could counter.

Aabir turned down a new corridor towards the chemistry lab, the woman's proposition replaying in his head. He did not want to meet up with her for any reason; but despite the fear, his curiosity was piqued.

What did she mean about having a solution to help them? How could Norland's janitor, of all people, be able to do anything for them?

Maybe he should go…just to make sure that he and his family were not in any danger. His grip tightened on his chardex. And if this woman did pose a threat to them, he would know and could act accordingly—in whatever possible way he could.

A few of Aabir's platoon were heading into the lab up ahead. He made sure to fix an expressionless mask upon his features as he moved closer towards them. Hopefully none of them would be able to sense that something was wrong, because he was not in the mood to be insulted.

He swallowed a grimace. That would be the last time he tried to protect any one of them.

Just as the thought came, he knew it was not true. No matter how much they jeered at him now, he also knew from prior experience that it would soon disappear, and they would all be back to their normal camaraderie.

Aabir stepped through the doorway into the chemistry lab and headed over to the empty seat next to Tycho. He met his friend's gaze, and Tycho waved him over with a grin.

That was when another thought hit him: if he and his family did leave Igrium, he would lose his friends. Despite everything he disliked about Norland, all his closest friends were here and the thought of leaving them carved a strange, hollow feeling into his stomach.

"What's wrong with you?" Tycho asked as Aabir sat down.

So many things. "Chemistry."

"I feel you." Tycho nodded with an understanding frown. "But at least you did all your work. I had to suffer through one of Aquilo's science lectures during break to get any answers out of him."

Aabir smirked, his swirling thoughts focusing on the present for the moment. "Well, you could've done it instead of watching streams for five hours..."

"Those shows will help me more in life than any of this—"

The bell rang, cutting off the rest of his answer. Their chemistry teacher, Mr. Faull, stood from his desk at the front of the lab. "Alright. Today we're going to continue going through chapter seventeen. Open your chardexes to where we left off on page one-hundred and eighty-seven..."

Aabir withheld a sigh and did as they were asked. As Mr. Faull began to go over the information, his mind began to wander back to all the worries and memories from before, and to what he might be able to do should the woman prove untrustworthy.

The only thing keeping him grounded was the small bit of hope the woman's proposition kindled in him. It might be a trap, but it also might be the answer to his prayers. Either he would be helping his family more than he ever had before, or he could be putting them into more danger.

With a silent prayer to Deleyon, he finally decided to fully cling to the hope of the mysterious offer—and he had no intentions of listening to his fear and letting go of it.

Chapter Fifteen

"I'm sorry to interrupt, *Axei Rabetta,*" Captain Ulanc stepped into the tent as Tetra, Stellinga, and the girl's matha were eating supper, "but I have orders for Miss Cairn."

Only a few minutes ago, Tetra had woken up to the smell of paprika and cumin and the sounds of her adopted caretakers' footsteps crunching on loose sand as they came into the tent. When Stellinga helped her sit up, Rabetta had squashed her in a fierce hug that she figured only ended abruptly because it brought slices of pain through her leg. In a mixture of Xinxan and Alenguan, the older woman thanked her multiple times through tears for "rescuing Stellinga" and "not hurting her like evil Igrians wanted".

As with Stellinga, Tetra tried to push the praise aside to tell her it had not only been because of her that they escaped in the first place, but Rabetta was even more immovable in it than her daughter. So, Tetra accepted it all without rebuttal, just as she readily accepted her pain medication and the plate of black rice mixed with vegetables.

Stellinga and Rabetta sat down with her in a triangle surrounding the tent's single lantern with their own plates before they all began to eat. Tetra said nothing as she ate, but she did listen to—and tried to figure out—what Stellinga and Rabetta's Xinxan conversation consisted of as they ate. It was nice to eat with them. She figured this was like having a normal family (even if she had no idea what they were saying). A warm feeling entered her chest at the thought, and she basked in the warmth of the moment—until Captain Ulanc's towering presence came in and spoiled it.

The hairs on Tetra's arm rose. Had Rasiela's word not been enough? Was she being sent back to Rubrum? "What is it, sir?"

"My commanding officer listened to all your answers from earlier today, and we both agreed you were not lying."

Her heart hammered in her chest despite the supposed good news. "I'm glad."

"And I want you to know that he has decided not to send you back to Igrium."

Tears pricked her eyes at the news, but she blinked them away before she made a fool of herself. She would have thanked all of Igrium's gods who were listening in that moment, but she knew none of them had anything to do with this. So instead, she said "Thank you, sir," to Captain Ulanc.

He dipped his chin. "But he sent me with another question for you. Last night, he received a request for you to be returned to Igrium's forces—and there was a high monetary reward attached."

Who in Igrium would spend money to get *her* back?

"Although he did not accept their offer, we want to know why your return would be so highly valued."

Why, indeed? Tetra licked her lips. "I'm not sure, sir. I...I didn't think I was worth anything to Igrium." She paused as a possible answer came to her, "Maybe...maybe it's because I'm a Cairn, and my coming back to Igrium to be an imperial personal guard is the more honorable option compared to staying in Alliance territory."

"That's what we thought as well. We just wanted to make sure there were no other options, since it was a hefty sum." He cleared his throat. "But onto the other news: around the same time last night, my CO was also sent orders to have you brought to Urbselva to meet with one of our leaders."

Her pounding heart skipped a beat. "Who?"

Ulanc's cool expression didn't change. "Chief Advisor Baene Ruzek."

A sliver of fear pricked her heart. Her parents had killed the former Silvanian steward's fiancée in the Fire Raids. Only one reason came to her mind as to why he would want to speak with her: revenge.

Yet knowing this, she still asked, "Why—why would he want anything to do with me?"

"I wasn't told. All I know are my orders, and those are to get you on the next hovertrain leaving for Urbselva tomorrow."

"T—tomorrow?" Tetra looked down at her empty plate, fear hammering away inside her chest.

"Yes," Colonel Ulanc replied, "you will be sent to the medic tent for a final checkup before leaving at thirteen-hundred hours for Urbselva."

Something fell onto one of Tetra's shoulders. She jerked her head up and saw Rabetta's stone expression, then the woman's hand lightly gripping her shoulder. Not wanting to offend the kind woman, Tetra stayed still. Stiff, but still.

"She must go?" Rabetta's usually sweet tone took on a hard, dagger-like edge. "Why can Tetra not stay? We take care of her."

An unusual warmth filled her chest at the words. The tightness in her muscles slightly loosened, and she turned her neck back in Captain Ulanc's direction to hear his reply.

"And your efforts are appreciated, *Axei Rabetta*. But when you took her in, you were told that she would not be in your care long." The lines under his eyes softened. "Your family has done well, but Chief Baene's orders outweigh ours."

Rabetta's grip loosened on Tetra's shoulder, and she sighed. Her voice went back to its normal pitch as she replied, "*Ti-ye*. I—understand."

Ulanc bowed his head in Rabetta's direction. "Thank you for your cooperation." He lifted his head and locked eyes with Tetra again. "I will see you tomorrow, Miss Cairn. Good evening."

He then spun on his heel and left the tent. A heavy silence filled the small space as the entrance flap fell back into place. Tetra turned her head as Stellinga reached over and gave her wrist a squeeze.

"I sorry, Tetra." Stellinga's head and shoulders slumped, her large eyes watering. "I—I wish you able to stay."

"It's alright, Stellinga." Tetra swallowed the bile rising in her throat. "At least...I'm not going back to Rubrum."

But being sent to Silvas for possible revenge wasn't a great option, either.

Stellinga only shrugged her shoulders. Rabetta removed her hand and scooted closer to Tetra.

"I wish you stay longer," she smiled sadly, "but I not able to do anything else. Forgive me, Tetra, but I not have authority in this situation."

"I know." Tetra sighed. "Thank you for supper, Rabetta, and—and for letting me stay with you." She flicked her eyes to meet both their sad gazes, "I owe you both."

Rabetta's eyes widened, and a fierceness settled into her expression. "You owe nothing. You save Stellinga, and you always welcome stay with us." Something must've changed in Tetra's expression, because she added sternly, "And no argue with me."

A smile peeked through the corners of Tetra's mouth. "Yes ma'am." She turned her gaze back over to Stellinga, "But I will say: your daughter is amazing at driving hoverbikes."

Stellinga sniffed and smiled as Rabetta replied in a proud voice, "Just like her *opie*."

"Thank you." A blush darkened Stellinga's cheeks.

Tetra's smile widened, but it soon disappeared as her thoughts turned back to the day ahead of her. "I know it's early, but I think I'm gonna try to get rest." Then she wouldn't have to think about it for a few hours.

"You do that." Rabetta nodded and piled up their few dishes. "I go take these back to kitchens and help them clean, but I be back. It be later, though."

"OK."

Stellinga nodded and hugged her matha. "I go get ready and try sleep, too."

Rabetta squeezed her back and said something in Xinxan. Tetra turned her focus on getting back into bed as they continued speaking to each other in the foreign language. The pain medicine hadn't fully kicked in, but she was able to creep carefully under the blanket without too much discomfort.

Once their long embrace ended, Rabetta picked up the stack of dishes and left the tent, Stellinga following behind. As their footsteps disappeared into the camp, hot tears pricked at Tetra's eyes. She pressed both fists against them and breathed out through her teeth to quell the flood.

She didn't know what was worse: going back to Rubrum to be brainwashed or being sent to the enemy kingdom's vengeful advisor. She tried to tell herself that there must be another reason, but she and her fear couldn't think of anything else.

She reached her arm out and turned the lantern off, then moved into the most comfortable position she could and pulled the blanket up to her chin. There was nothing like a little bit of comfort in the night to welcome the oncoming army of spiraling thoughts. Memories of past punishments mixed in with new, imaginary scenarios of her arrival in Silvas. There were ones where Chief Baene used her as a punching bag, where she found herself locked up in solitary confinement, and a gruesome image of her execution on live holovision to punish her for all her parents' actions.

Round and round they went—growing worse the longer Tetra lay there dwelling on them. She knew most of the thoughts she was coming up with were outright ridiculous, yet she couldn't seem to stop the flow of fear. It had locked her up in her own mind-prison and wouldn't give her the keys to escape.

She turned her head from side to side as the minutes ticked by. Her flow of thoughts soon slowed, and she could feel herself on the blissful cusp of sleep—until a small, tingling sensation sparked in her side.

Oh no, no, no... She gritted her teeth as the horribly familiar tingling of pain lengthened its reach along more of her side. Then the tiny, invisible needles began to poke at it. Maybe it was because she was lying down, but it seemed the tingling, needle-like pain was growing much quicker through the rest of her body than it ever had before.

With each heartbeat, each needle of pain grew into a knife. Then, invisible flames came right behind them and began to burn through every part of her aching body. Spikes stabbed her lungs with each painful breath as if an army of phantom ants were biting into every inch of her skin.

Tears escaped her closed eyelids, but they did nothing to quench the fire burning her face. She groaned and tried to pull both her legs into the fetal position, but her injured leg decided to add more pain to the whole experience when she tried to move it, so she left it straight.

Why, why, why was this happening? Was this more punishment the gods were heaping upon her? Hadn't she suffered enough without her body trying to tear itself apart bit by bit?

She kept herself as still as possible as the hour-long minutes dragged on. Above the ringing in her ears, she heard the tent flap move. Her mind was able to register that Stellinga was back, but that's all she seemed able to comprehend other than pain. She tried opening her mouth to tell Stellinga to get help, but it stayed clamped shut.

Cold fear sent an icy chill through the heat consuming her. What more could be wrong with her? She tried to open her eyes, but the tiny, phantom needles kept them shut. Again, she tried to open her mouth. When nothing happened, she tried moving her fingers, her toes. Any attempt at movement was met by a fresh wave of agony.

Oh no. Could she—was this some sort of paralysis? Is this what the gods and her parents had cooked up for her? "*Oh, you're going to stay in Silvas?*" She imagined them saying, "*All right then, you just won't be able to do anything to dishonor our family name no matter what you try to do. Have fun in utter misery!*"

If she could, she would have laughed at the absurd thought just out of sheer exhaustion, then another wave of burning pain shut off all humor. Thankfully, even with the inferno burning her organs, she found herself dozing off. She would always wake up to the slicing rhythms of pain, but then would fall back asleep for a few minutes—or however long it was. Time meant nothing through the fiery pain.

Yet as it continued, she found herself dozing off less and less until—finally—she fell into a light, but restful, sleep.

Chapter Sixteen

Someone shook Tetra's shoulder. She blinked her eyes open without any needle-like pain to keep them shut and exhaled a relieved sigh. A small sliver of soft sollight ran along one of the tent walls, and she stared at it as the sleep lifted from her mind. She would never take the simple act of opening her eyes for granted again.

"Tetra?" Rabetta's soft voice sounded close to her ear.

As she turned her neck to focus her gaze on the kind woman's face, she also made a mental note to never take hearing for granted, either. "Hmm?"

"I sorry to wake you, but there are soldiers outside waiting to take you to medic tent."

"OK." She could speak! "Thanks for waking me."

Not even the lurking fear of her upcoming confrontation with Chief Baene could keep the warm happiness away.

Rabetta nodded, a sad smile playing on her lips. "I wake Stellinga to say bye, OK?"

A hollow shadow chased away some of the warmth as she registered those words. "Yeah, sure."

The older woman moved out of Tetra's line of sight, and a moment later low Xinxan words reached her ears. She lay there a few moments more, blinking and wiggling her stiff fingers and toes to make sure she could move fully before getting herself into a sitting position. Sharp tendrils of pain rode up her leg, sending shoots of fear through her, but they immediately died away as she reminded herself that her leg was injured and she hadn't had painkillers yet.

She shook her head at herself and finished the struggle of sitting up. Thankfully, she could tell the pain in her leg wasn't as bad as it had been yesterday. Either the painkillers from last night were still working (*on just my leg*, she thought with a frown), or the wounds were healing quicker than she thought they would.

"You are leaving, Tetra?"

Tetra lifted her head and realized Stellinga was also sitting up; her long hair frizzing around her face as she blinked away the sleep. Their eyes locked.

"I guess so," she replied with a shrug.

Stellinga nodded slowly, her eyes losing focus as she processed the words. After a few moments, she pulled the covers off her legs and stretched. "You able to eat with us, though?"

"*Yon*, Stellinga." Rabetta looked over at her daughter with a shake of her head.

Stellinga's countenance fell. "Oh."

Tetra lowered her gaze to the ground, then folded her arms and rubbed them as silence filled the tent. She didn't want Stellinga and her family to have to take care of her, but she also didn't want to leave their kindness. The only families she had heard of or seen were Aabir's and the ones on holovision, and being here gave her a little more inside information as to why her former friend loved his family so much.

"You ready?" Rabetta asked.

Tetra looked up and nodded. "Yes ma'am."

"Here—" a small smile came over her face, "—we help. Stellinga!"

As Rabetta helped put Tetra's boot on her uninjured foot, Stellinga stood and stepped over to them. With both their help, Tetra was able to stand. She wrapped her arms around their shoulders for stability. They then helped her hobble out of the tent. Warm sollight touched her face as the tent flap fell behind them, and she blinked her eyes until they got used to the brightness.

Tents of all sizes and colors surrounded them. The fragrant smells of spices and cooked meat tinged the air, while the sounds of shuffling and low voices came from some of the tents around them. The dawn sky was tinged with soft purples and pinks as Soll made his entrance into the new day. The only thing inhabiting the clear air at that moment was a mass of small, black dots—most likely a school of fish—floating high in the air.

She had never realized how pretty the sky could be.

"Are you ready, Miss Cairn?"

She lowered her gaze and met the eyes of the Silvanian soldier who was on guard duty outside the tent. *No, I'm not.*

"Yes sir."

Though his brow rose in a dubious expression, he nodded. "Hold on for a moment." In a louder voice, that probably woke up everyone sleeping around them, he called, "Isa! It's time."

A moment later, another Silvanian soldier marched out from behind their tent. Tetra met her eyes, and the woman sent her a pursed look before turning her face towards her partner.

"Then let's get on with it," she said.

"Here," the first guard turned his gaze on the two Xichian women, "let us take her, *Axei* Rabetta. That way you can go on about your day."

Claws squeezed Tetra's heart, and she looked between Stellinga and Rabetta's faces. So, this was it, then...

"We not have anything to do, *Huxk,*" Stellinga replied. "It no trouble to help."

"Thank you, but—"

"—Sir, if I may," Tetra cut in, "If they don't mind doing it, I'd rather they help me." She lifted her hands from their shoulders in a quick gesture, "It's more comfortable with them both being more my height."

The guard looked like he was going to argue, but then he shrugged. "If *Axei* Rabetta is fine with it, I will not argue."

She bit her lip and glanced over at Rabetta. The woman's bronzed features glowed as she sent Tetra a smile. "Like Stellinga said, we not have anything to do." She turned her head in the guard's direction. "We take her."

"Alright. Then follow me."

With the first soldier in the front and Private Isa trailing behind them, they began making their way through the rows of tents.

Tetra glanced at Rabetta out of the corner of her eye and said in a low voice, "Thank you, *Axei* Rabetta."

"It no trouble, Tetra."

They both shared a smile, then a thought hit her. "Maybe...they'll even let you see your husband."

At that, Rabetta's eyes watered. "I hope you right."

"I hope so, too." She glanced over at Stellinga's words and noticed the tear trailing down the teenage girl's cheek as she gave Tetra a smile.

Tetra smiled back before turning her head forward. They walked—well, she hobbled—in companionable silence through the wakening camp. Most weren't out yet, but she caught a stronger whiff of the savory scent she had smelled earlier as they passed a huge, white tent surrounded by Alliance soldiers. She glanced over and saw a short line of people waiting outside it for food. They all looked tired or sad to some degree, and she looked away as claws pricked her heart again.

Her gaze landed on a small boy walking in the long shadows of the tents—a stuffed leos cat in one hand, and an older-looking girl leading him with the other. Their wide eyes watched the small group pass, but Tetra averted her gaze at the wary fear she had seen on their dirt-streaked faces.

As they continued to walk, more and more people began to fill the pathways and makeshift bridges connecting the outcroppings. The first time they walked across one of these rubber-like bridges, Tetra couldn't help but send a wary glance down at it.

Stellinga must've caught the look on her face, because she said, "You not need worry, Tetra. Our people been making *suchwriy* bridges for thousands of years. They sturdy."

Even so, her heartbeat didn't slow down until they stepped off of it. She lifted her gaze at the welcome feeling of hard, sturdy ground under her boot and ended up locking eyes with an elderly, Xichian man for a moment. She looked away from his hopeless, red-rimmed eyes as hollowness filled her stomach. They passed more people, and Tetra continued to notice all had similar expressions of hopelessness, fear, grief, and even anger covering their countenances. She finally had to lower her gaze to the desert sand under their feet and kept it there as guilt clawed at her hollow insides.

Her people had done this. Emperor Ignis and his hunger for power had destroyed Trivsau; killed thousands of people—both those fighting and civilians; and misplaced the millions of others who called the capital city their home. A small spark of anger lit inside her chest to accompany the slimy guilt.

Before she could dwell on it further and fan its tiny flame, the Silvanian soldier ahead said, "We're almost there."

Tetra barely lifted her gaze and spotted the biggest tent she had seen. They soon made it and were given access inside by one of the Alliance soldiers guarding the entrance. When she stepped past the white entrance flap, the strong smells of blood and antiseptic accosted her nose.

A medbot hovered over to their group and, after receiving instructions from the Silvanian soldier, led them through rows of beds, more medbots, and field doctors. Her gaze flicked over the people on each of the hospital beds they passed. Most were asleep, but she spotted a few who were awake. There was a young woman sitting up and feeding her baby, her arm in a sling. An elderly woman lay shivering with multiple blankets atop her; and a small boy—about five or six—was sitting up in bed with bandages wrapped around his shoulder where his arm used to be.

He met Tetra's eyes for a moment, but she looked away as remorse fanned the flame of her anger. She glanced down at her bandaged leg and silently thanked any other deities there were, besides Igrium's vengeful host, that she still had it.

Stellinga gasped.

"What?" Tetra looked over at her.

"You see your *opie*?" Rabetta added.

Stellinga shook her head, but wonder lit her eyes. "No," she pointed with her free hand, "but look."

Tetra followed the direction with her gaze. Her eyes widened for a moment, before understanding dawned on her. She couldn't help but smile at the sight of the large griffin. "I'm glad they're here to help."

The intelligent being was standing only a couple bed rows ahead of them. Its curved beak opened and closed as it spoke with one of the Silvanian doctors; and its large, brown tufted ears twitched as the doctor replied. Large bags hung from its mane of dappled, brown and sandy feathers. It clutched another bag in one of its front talons.

"How you know it helping?" Stellinga asked.

"They're neutral in the war, but they don't want enmity with either side, so the closest clans usually help both armies after each battle with gathering supplies and finding those missing on the battlefields."

Stellinga's gaze stayed locked on the winged being. "Wow. I—I know there some clan nests close to—to Trivsau, but I never see real one before. Have you, Ahni?"

"Only from a distance." Rabetta replied, and Tetra could see out of the corner of her eye that the woman's gaze was fixed on the griffin, too.

"I don't think they like big human cities," Tetra added.

This was the closest she had ever been to one before. There were a couple clans that lived in Igrium, but they mostly stayed away from Rubrum.

Something zipped past their heads.

"Another!" Stellinga jerked her head to watch the small, flat-faced griffin stop in the air above them with flapping wingbeats.

Its head turned impossibly on its still, small shoulders as it looked around the tent with eyes that took over most of its face. It was much smaller than the first griffin and didn't have a mane of feathers like the other did.

"It cute."

The griffin's eyes narrowed as the words left Stellinga's mouth, but it continued whatever it was doing without so much as a glance in their direction.

"This is the spot." The medbot's voice broke through Tetra's griffin-bound stupor. "I have notified a doctor; he will be with you all shortly."

She blinked and lowered her gaze to her empty bed. One of the beds beside it was also empty, while an older man wearing an eyepatch slept atop the other. The lead guard thanked the bot as Rabetta and Stellinga helped Tetra to the bed. She sat down with a sigh as the pressure left her uninjured leg. Rabetta helped get her cocoon of a limb onto the bed then propped it up with pillows from the empty one beside hers'. Stellinga, meanwhile, scanned the room in every direction, her brow lowered in concentration.

Tetra almost asked what she was doing before she remembered the girl's patre was somewhere in here, and she found herself looking for the man as if she knew what he looked like, too.

Stellinga gasped and whispered, "Opie?"

Rabetta's head jerked up and she turned to face her daughter. Tetra's heart skipped a beat as she saw the tears spilling down Stellinga's face, then she looked in the direction the girl gestured to. Rabetta said something in Xinxan and both of them immediately rushed down the aisle.

Private Isa started to say, "Hey—!" but her words died as the mother and daughter stopped near a bed at the very end of the aisle. Tetra couldn't help but smile as she watched Rabetta wake the bearded man, then their hug as he realized who she was. Stellinga joined the group hug.

Warmth fluttered in Tetra's chest. At least she got to see that before leaving Xich.

Yet as she watched, a strange thought came to her head: had her parents ever hugged her like that? She wasn't much for touch, and by the pictures and all the things she knew about her successful parents, she couldn't see them showing that kind of affection either, but it still made her wonder. She hated that her brain couldn't remember the answer.

"Miss Cairn—" she jerked her head in the direction of a Silvanian doctor standing next to her bed, "—my name is Doctor Hite. I was one of the doctors who took care of you after your...leap over the fence."

Tetra nodded towards him, her gaze flicking back to the teary reunion. Doctor Hite's head turned in the same direction and a small smile cracked through his professional demeanor for a moment. Then he returned to business and began telling her what they had done to help her leg while he took the bandages off. She tried to listen, but her focus kept returning to the reunion; so, all she got from the doctor's long explanation was that they had used muscle regeneration technology to help speed up the healing process of her leg, something about it taking longer, and a few other random tidbits of information that didn't stay in her head long.

Only when he had taken all the bandages off did her attention turn from the Xichian family. Her eyes bulged at the deep, ugly wounds mutilating her reddened flesh, making it easy to see where the barbed wire had wrapped around her leg. Nausea churned her stomach as her imagination showed her what she must've looked like hanging from the fence that night, and she forced her gaze back onto the reunion.

Doctor Hite put new bandages around her leg and reassured her that the cells in her muscles would continue to regenerate at their quickened pace, but that if she wanted them to continue at that speed, she would need to see a regeneration specialist in another week. He told her a few more things that would keep her from hurting her leg even further, gave her a pair of crutches, and then left.

Private Isa had to break up the happy reunion now that their reason for being in the medic tent was over, and all three women came back over to Tetra's bed. Tetra fitted the crutches underneath her arms and stepped onto the ground with her good leg. She met Stellinga's teary eyes, then Rabetta's. She opened her mouth to apologize for cutting their meeting short, but both women beat her to it by squashing her in a hug.

"*Fleora, fleora, fleora,* Tetra!" Stellinga said through tears while Rabetta added her own Xinxan thanks.

"Um...you're welcome," Tetra replied.

It was the most warming, yet uncomfortable, experience she had had in her remembered life.

They soon let her go and the guards led them back out of the tent and into the hot sollight. Again, Tetra looked upon the haggard faces of the Xichians inside the camp, but then she turned her gaze over to Stellinga and Rabetta's relieved countenances. She met Stellinga's eyes, and the girl mouthed "*Fleora*" with a smile. Tetra smiled back with a nod.

As they traveled back through the camp, her eyes roved over the sadness and distress surrounding them. The warmth of elation in her chest hardened to a resolve as hard as gritanium metal. She gripped the handles of her crutches tighter as she made a promise to herself.

If she survived the meeting with Chief Baene today, she would look for ways to help stop the sufferings of those affected by the war—like Stellinga and Rabetta. She didn't know what that would look like for the Igrian daughter of the Cairns' who was now in Alliance territory, but she would try whatever she could. And by doing so, she would show her parents, the gods, and the entire Igrium Empire that she could bring honor to her family name by doing something other than following the fiery, bloodied legacy she had been left with.

That invigorating thought helped to keep the whispering fears at bay as she continued limping along after the soldiers towards the hovertrain station—and then onto Silvas.

Chapter Seventeen

SOMETHING MOVED IN THE everpine trees towering above Aabir. He jerked his head around, heart hammering, and turned in a full circle.

What was that—? The thought barely entered his head before he spotted a chittering scurrus scrambling up one of the thick tree trunks, its thick plume of a tail disappearing into the needle-covered branches. He sighed in relief and pressed his fingertips against his temples.

This was so stupid. If someone were to see him standing out here, they would immediately know something was going on. No one went out into these trees by themselves unless they were planning on breaking a rule—and that was the last thing Aabir needed people to think at the moment.

He blew out a frustrated sigh and continued peering through the trees. The janitor had said to meet her out here...yet there was no sign of her. The fear he had been trying to suppress trickled forth to the forefront of his mind. Was he being fooled? Was this some sort of trick to keep him occupied while she went and told the authorities everything she had overheard?

Aabir gritted his teeth and curled his hands into fists at the thought. He spun on his heel in the direction of one of the side paths leading to Norland and took a few steps forward, his pack bouncing against his back. If that was the case, he would need to get back to his family before—

"—Kid!"

He jumped at the sharp whisper and reached to grab his sword, but then remembered it was still in his dorm.

"Who are you?" He seemingly asked the trees around him.

Norland's janitor stepped out from behind one of them. Aabir turned to fully face her, not bothering to hide his glare. "Oh."

She crossed her arms and raised one arched eyebrow. "Do not give me that look, Trainee Sorrel," she said in a Silvanian accent. "I'm the one who is risking herself to try and help you."

"And why would you do that?" He knew it was not smart to deflect against possible help, but he was too angry, too scared, to accept it yet.

The woman's cool demeanor seemed unaffected by his obvious feelings towards her. "Because I know how much harder it has become to live in this empire with Silvanian blood flowing through your veins." Her already-deep voice lowered even more, "I've been dealing with the raids, too, and I almost lost my job here when Igrium lost Trivsau."

He narrowed his eyes and copied her stance with crossed arms. "Well, if you're dealing with the same things we are, then how can you help us out of them?"

"I'm only dealing with them because my job dictates that I stay until it truly becomes a life-and-death situation."

Now it was his turn to raise a brow. "Being a *janitor* is keeping you here?"

"No."

Aabir was quiet as he waited for her to elaborate. She only stared back at him with her hooded gaze.

"OK..." He finally said, wondering if this woman might be crazy. "Could you elaborate...?"

She twisted her lips to the side for a moment. "You and Tetra Cairn tried to escape Norland a couple years ago, yes?"

His adrenaline kicked in as memories pushed past the mental barriers he tried so hard to keep around them. Images of lightning and exhausting sprinting flashed through his head. He dug his nubby fingernails into his arms.

"Yeah, we did," he said through gritted teeth. "Why are you asking? Can't you just answer *my* questions without asking your own?"

"The only way I can possibly answer your question safely is if you answer all of mine. I'm already risking much just by talking with you, *Trainee* Sorrel," he winced at the sharp reminder, "so don't go ruining it."

Shame churned his stomach as his and Matha's conversation came back to him. He worked his jaw as he settled his facial features into stone before replying, "Fine."

"And after your failed attempt, why did you stop communicating with her?"

Aabir turned his gaze down to his boots. "When the team of patrolmen pounded on my parents' door in the middle of the night to interrogate them for my actions, they told me as soon as they could that I wasn't allowed to hang around Tetra anymore. They said she was a bad influence and had put us all in danger." His back throbbed with phantom pains. "And at that point, I agreed with them."

"So that's why—according to your record—you stopped questioning your commanding officers and did everything asked of you?"

Aabir lifted his wide-eyed gaze and met her eyes. "You looked through my record?"

She nodded once. "I had to learn as much about you as I could before this meeting."

"But—but how did you get access?"

"I have my ways."

Her cool expression stopped him from asking what she meant by *that*, and instead he said, "OK then..." Though an uneasy shiver went down his spine despite the words. What else did she know about him?

"I also learned of your newest misdemeanor." Her head barely tipped to the side. "It said you failed in stopping Tetra from escaping."

"Yeah." Aabir glanced down at his newest segione scar.

"Is that what actually happened?"

He opened his mouth to say it was, but he stopped when he saw the look in her eyes. "You think something else did?" He ventured to ask.

"I do."

Oh Deleyon, help me get this right... He lifted his arm and scratched the back of his neck. He could just lie about it, but would that ruin the small chance he might have of getting help?

Loud, excitable voices echoed through the trees, and they both jerked their heads in the direction of the cobbled path not far from their meeting place. Aabir's heart began its marathon sprint again as he noticed the forms of trainees through the trees as they walked away from Norland along the path. Even with the thick tree trunks and low hanging boughs keeping him and the woman hidden, he stayed silent and kept watch until they were out of sight.

Only when their voices ceased did he finally turn back to face the woman. She also turned and met his eyes.

She raised her brow and asked, "Well?" in a hushed tone as if the possibility of them being spotted was not even a concern to her.

Aabir had to think through the last part of their interrupted conversation before he could finally answer in an equally low voice, "Well...you'd be right." He huffed a sigh. "I was on my way to guard her, when I found a sword point at my throat—and she was holding it. It wasn't too difficult for me to realize what she was doing, and she asked me to let her go. I said I couldn't, but then she said Emperor Ignis was finally going to turn her into a personal guard if she didn't escape."

He kept his gaze locked on hers as he continued, "I didn't want that to happen to Tetra—I wouldn't wish that fate on my worst enemy! —but my family is in danger again, and I knew that if I let her escape, I would only be sending us all to jail...or worse. So, I faked trying to attack her, and she knocked me out to get away."

"And what are your thoughts on her successful escape?"

"I'm glad she made it," he shrugged, "and if my family weren't still here, I would have joined her."

"Hmm..." She paused, her features softening for a moment before going back to their former hardness. "Tell me, Aabir Sorrel, if you had a chance to help the Alliance right now—without it hurting your family, of course—would you do it?"

Aabir blinked. That was not a question he was expecting.

"If you did, it would help all of you—especially you—with the problem of being accepted into any of the Alliance kingdoms without suspicion," she added.

"I—I don't know..." his voice died away and he shot a furtive glance back over at the cobbled path as the sound of more voices arose, but the trainees quickly passed and he forced himself to continue speaking even as anxiety told him their chances of being spotted were only growing the longer he did so, "I would have to know for sure that it wouldn't bring any danger, or even suspicion, to me or my family. And I...would need to know if what I was doing was going to end up killing anyone. I don't...I'd rather not do it if that were the case."

The woman pursed her lips thoughtfully. "I can promise you that what you will be asked to do is secretive and would not lead to any suspicions being pointed to any of you," she replied. "And about the killing...I can only promise that what you do could possibly help save millions of lives. But this is war, Mister Sorrel, and I can't promise that people will not die."

He frowned as the Frigian woman's face flashed through his head. "I know we're at war...and saving people sounds great, but...I'm not sure..."

Fear churned his stomach as his words died away. He was beginning to feel like he knew what she was asking him to do, and the thought terrified him.

"How about I let you think about it over the weekend?" She gave him an understanding nod. "Come to my office at this time Firstdein afternoon and you can tell me then."

Aabir nodded slowly. "OK... I can do that."

"And come up with a cleaning-related excuse to see me," she replied. "I don't want anyone to overhear and get suspicious. Do I have your word?"

"Yes." He met her eyes. "But how do I know I have yours', Miss...?"

"You can call me 'Rasiela'." She dipped her chin towards him. "And you will know you have my word when you go through this weekend and no patrolmen come pounding on your door to arrest you for treason."

Aabir's heart rate increased at her words, but he only nodded again with a glare. "That better not happen."

One corner of Rasiela's full lips lifted slightly, and she turned to go. "I'll see you then, Mister Sorrel—I promise. Good day."

She dipped her head towards him again then left in the direction of Norland. Aabir watched her go until she disappeared in the trees. When her crunching footsteps faded completely, he looked up into the huge pine boughs blocking most of the sollight high above his head.

"Deleyon..." he said in a low voice, "I don't know if you're even listening, but I need your help in this. My parents have told me all the stories about what you did for Silvas in the past, and I know this isn't as big as an entire kingdom, but I need you to help me just like you have Silvas. I need to know if this is the right thing. Please..."

Despite the rising and falling noise of more trainees leaving Norland, he waited a few minutes for an answer, for a sign of any kind, but all he heard were scurruses clambering around in the branches above. No beings appeared out of thin air. No wind blew the trees. Nothing.

He sighed. In some of the stories Matha and Patre told him about Deleyon, the god did not give an immediate answer, so maybe that was Aabir's case. With that in mind, he stepped in the direction of the main path leading out of Norland as his thoughts swirled with the conversation he just had.

Still mumbling prayers under his breath, he made his way through the trees and slipped onto the cobbled path when no one was around. Then, he made his way along it, through the fortress' halls, and into a parking garage where he found a taxi waiting silently for its next rider. He got into the vehicle and told the android driver his home address. The hovercar lifted off the ground as the android started it, and the parking garage's dark interior began to pass by Aabir's window.

He took in a deep breath of the taxi's leathery smell and exhaled as Rasiela's offer ran through his head again. It sounded like it should have been an easy "yes", but if his guess about what the offer could be was right, then he had his reservations. She said no suspicions would arise around him and his family, but could she really promise that? She seemed like she knew a lot—or had access to whatever knowledge she wanted, that is—and Aabir knew Tetra had trusted Norland's janitor a little by the few times he had seen them talking together in the halls. So, she had, at the very least, not lied about that, but there was still too much he did not know.

He leaned his head back against the seat and watched the window's changing view out of the corner of his eye. The dimness of the parking garage's stone walls was soon replaced by bright sollight reflecting off the many windows of Rubrum's towering skyscrapers. The android driver joined the slow flow of traffic in the direction of Aabir's home.

However, even with all the worries of what Rasiela's offer brought to his mind, there was one that stood out above the rest: if he accepted her offer, how would his parents react when they found out their son had become a Silvanian spy?

Chapter Eighteen

Tetra slept through most of the hovertrain ride to Urbselva. When she woke up, she had been given time to get ready in one of the train's bathrooms, and was given a new set of clothes—a dark green tunic and white pants—to look presentable in front of Chief Baene.

After doing so, she finally took a glance at herself in the sink mirror—and then wished she hadn't. The shower and clothes could do nothing to hide or soften the shameful malscar she now bore. She glanced down at her uncovered arms and wished she had been given something with long sleeves to wear. The uniforms she usually wore covered most of her tallies, but now the whole world would be able to see just how much of a dishonor she was to Igrium. It also didn't do anything to cover her large, splotchy birthmarks, either.

There was a knock on the bathroom door. "Miss Cairn," an accented voice said, "I don't mean to rush you, but we are here—and I would rather not keep Chief Baene waiting."

Her stomach flipped at the mention of the meeting. "I'm coming."

Replaying her new oath in her head, she opened the door and stepped out into the train car's claustrophobic hall on her new crutches. The Silvanian soldier—one of five who had been tasked with transporting her to the chief advisor—gave her a silent nod before turning around and heading down the hall back to the passenger car. Tetra followed as fast as she could. They soon joined the rest of the group of soldiers, then entered the line of other Alliance soldiers, and a few Xichians, who were in the train as well.

Tetra widened her eyes when she stepped off the hovertrain and into the mountainous boarding station. She tightened her grip on her crutches, heart racing, as she peered around the bustling place. It was the largest hovertrain station she had ever seen, and the size made her even more nervous than she already was about the meeting with the chief advisor.

Her escort moved into a small circle around her, blocking off most of her ground-level view. However, as they began to move, she noticed that she could still see some of the masses of people around them, nor did they block the cacophony of voices echoing along the towering ceiling height. Grand chandeliers hung from the rounded, stone ceiling high above the bustling crowds of people on the ground floor and the multiple levels of enclosed catwalks.

An accented voice on a loudspeaker broke in above the echoing noises, telling the whole station that a train was leaving in five minutes. Strange accents and different languages flitted by Tetra's ears. She turned her head in all directions to catch glimpses of those her huddle of guards passed.

Hovertrains sat upon the ends of their magnetic rail tracks—both on the ground and on elevated rails above—waiting for those filing inside their sleek bodies to hurry so they could begin their journeys into the lit tunnels pockmarking the wall to Tetra's right. She strained her neck to try and see over the shoulders of her guards, but they were all taller than her and kept her from seeing how long the station actually was. She frowned slightly and turned her attention back to the snippets she could catch of those around her.

Businessmen and women passed through the crowds with their briefcases, talking as if to thin air with auric-buds in their ears. Parents held their kids' hands as their teenagers tried to follow them from a distance. Men and women dressed in the dark, blue-tinged armor of the Silvanian Guardsmen Corps were stationed next to hovertrains and moved about in the masses. Tetra turned her neck up at the sound of a pair of heavy footfalls above them and noticed two more guardsmen marching along one of the many catwalks above.

It reminded her of Rubrum's station—only twice as big and with more languages other than alenguan spoken throughout.

Her entourage turned into a lane of people all heading towards the exit. Their pace slowed, but never fully stopped, as they waited. And as they slowly moved ahead, she noticed what looked like massive tree trunks outside the tall wall of windows they were approaching.

Ambulate trees. She immediately thought back to the things she had read and watched online about the Silvas Kingdom's infamous plant life, and the architecture it brought, as they drew ever closer to the grand exitway. From the little she could see, the pictures online did the giant trees' sizes no justice.

They finally made it to the end of the line. Guardsmen lined the wall of windows. One of the soldiers guarding Tetra gave their IDs to one of these same guards, and he let them pass through the open exit doors with a nod. They stepped out of the towering exitway and onto a huge terrace, but Tetra's eyes were glued only on the sight before her.

Trees taller and wider than any skyscraper she had seen spread out before her in a forested city. Metal, glass, and brick met the dark brown tree trunks in swirling lines and geometric patterns. Holographic billboards stretched across the tree-buildings' bark, thousands of bright ads moving and flashing along their faces.

Branches full of green leaves started halfway up most of the trees, while a maze of clear tubes stretched out below their thick boughs. Tetra noticed small figures moving inside these connecting tunnels from building to building. Hovertrams moved between the differing heights of the tubes, their rails attached to many of them for support. Down below, traffic clogged the magnetic roads nestled between the window-covered exposed roots of the trees.

It was all so big...

"This way, Miss Cairn," one of her guards said.

Tetra blinked out of her stupor and followed the lead guard down some stone steps leading off the veranda and onto a busy sidewalk. When they made it off the steps, she glanced back over her shoulder at the hovertrain station, her jaw still slack.

Sollight bounced off the wall of windows built into the mountain's base. Her gaze traveled upwards along the natural, rocky face until her view was obscured by the full-leafed, bottommost boughs of the ambulate tree-buildings. She had learned about Urbselva's mountainous border and how it made almost all attacks against the city nigh impossible, but she had never realized just how big they actually were. She had thought the mountains in Igrium were tall, yet they were anthills compared to these giants.

"Miss Cairn..." Impatience sharpened the guard's tone.

She blinked and turned her head forward again, sending him an apologetic nod. She hadn't realized she had been staring, but there was so much to see. "I'm coming."

They led her to a hovercar parked beside the sidewalk. An insignia with a detailed ambulate tree surrounded by the words "One kingdom, One government—united in Deleyon" was imprinted on the side. One guard opened the back door and motioned for Tetra to enter. She did so, and soon found herself squeezed in the back seat between two of the armored soldiers, her crutches laid awkwardly between all of them, as the other guards sat in the seats facing them. The android driver turned the hovercar on without any instructions and merged the vehicle into traffic.

As they inched through the city, she tuned out the soft chatter and traffic complaints of the guards and turned her head in both directions to look out the windows on either side. Her eyes drank in the greens and dark browns of the city—colors she would have never expected to see so abundant in any metropolis. Outdoor tea shops and markets were built into the bases of the tree-buildings and spilled out onto the busy sidewalks. Gardens and balconies wrapped around the trunks of some buildings at differing levels.

It was all so different from anything she had ever seen during her other travels that it was easy to distract herself from her fears. That is, until one of the guards said, "We should be at the Altelo in a few minutes."

His Silvanian accent deepened as he spoke the name of Silvas' royal palace, and the anxieties she had been able to evade during the ride came back to the forefront of her thoughts like a rolling storm cloud. She folded her arms and rubbed her hands up and down them as if cold.

Less than a minute later, the Altelo came into the front windshield's view and immediately took over it. Tetra's eyes widened and her jaw slackened at the size of the tree-building's two front exposed roots. They were bigger than any of the others she had already seen in the city; both of them curled into an almost perfect circle that looked as big as the Constantia Tourney stadium in Rubrum.

And the tree itself... The android turned onto another road, and Tetra turned her head to see out the tinted side window. Two Igrian stadiums could easily fit inside its wide trunk. Balconies wrapped around it at every level she could see—the small forms of guardsmen marching along some, and others overflowing with plants. Huge boulders were built into the bark of the roots; so small compared to the tree they reminded her of the cobblestone streets back in the historic sections of Igrium.

Everything about it screamed "powerful", "permanent", and "elegant"—similar to what Emperor Ignis' vast fortress proclaimed. Her anxiety latched onto those words and used them to paint a picture of her chat with Chief Baene, and the vengeful punishments he had at his disposal.

By the time the android driver stopped in front of the Altelo's grand entrance, Tetra's fear had already come up with multiple images of her excruciating death sentence that defied any logical thoughts she tried throwing at it.

"Come." The soldier, who had been the one to speak before, spoke again.

Tetra gulped as the guards began filing out the doors. She gripped her crutches with shaky hands and scooted across the seat to follow. The same guard who had spoken helped her out onto the bustling sidewalk, then slammed the door shut behind her.

"This way, Miss Cairn."

The five soldiers moved around her and led her through the opening between the converging front roots. As they walked, she lifted her gaze and was met with the Altelo's full glory. She couldn't even see the tree's bottommost branches because they were higher than those of the others surrounding it. More balconies continued up the tree until they, too, disappeared amongst the bluish-green leaves of the other branches. A cold shiver went down her spine despite the humidity.

Stone and bark came into her peripheral, and she lowered her gaze as they slowed to a stop before entering the enclosed area created by the roots. A row of armored guardsmen lined the opening. And just like in the train station, one of the soldiers in her escort showed a guard their IDs with his holonode, but then he showed Chief Baene's written orders for her appearance.

Tetra silently prayed to whatever deity that had been helping so far that the guardsmen wouldn't let them through. But a moment later, he stepped aside. Her heart pounded an anxious beat as one of her escorts put their hand on her shoulder and steered her forward. Two of the guardsmen observed her with wary gazes as she was led through a semi-translucent holographic screen; its pale blue light turning green before going back to blue as she stepped through.

The weight of their stares stayed upon her as she waited for the Silvanian soldiers to go through the same screen and to have their weapons checked; and only when they circled back around her and continued on their way did she let herself breathe.

She caught glimpses of pomen trees and bright flowers as they passed through the natural entrance and into, what she assumed to be, a courtyard, but her focus didn't stay on the landscaping as her anxious thoughts clamored for her attention. The hard looks on the faces of the guardsmen flashed through her mind, solidifying her fears as reasonable. If the people who were most likely trained to keep their emotions in check couldn't hide their displeasure at having a Cairn in their midst, then she could easily see any of the fearful images plaguing her mind coming true.

The muffled clamor of several voices drew her out of the dark sludge of her thoughts. She lifted her head as they passed through a tall, guarded doorway and into the Altelo. Her breath hitched as her eyes roved over the grandeur she had stepped into.

A huge, long hall stretched out along either side of them where, she guessed, the tree's two front roots were. Pale natural light filtered in from floor-to-ceiling windows along the wall behind them, shining against the gold and crystal chandeliers hanging from the rounded ceilings.

Ahead, two grand, spiraling staircases mirrored each other on the opposite wall. More guardsmen lined the walls and second-story balcony, while finely dressed people bustled around the marbled floors. Tetra hunched her shoulders and turned her face to the floor as a few of them sent questioning glances towards the group of Silvanian soldiers. She hoped her escort blocked her enough from the view of the civilians.

They passed under the balcony and slowed to a stop at a circle of elevators that reminded her of the glass tubes outside in the city. They waited for one of the elevators to open, then all six of them stepped inside the small space. As the doors closed, she noticed one of her guards swiping his finger across a touchscreen set into the wall, and she couldn't help the awe that mixed with her fear at the amount of floor numbers flying past his finger. He finally pressed the number "*112*" and the elevator began its ascent.

Her stomach dropped as their speed increased, the small screen above the doors skipping through the floor numbers. The elevator soon came to a stop, and the doors opened with a small ding that caused her heart to skip a frightful beat despite its chipper sound.

She found herself being ushered into a small, semi-circular room then through a set of double doors guarded by four guardsmen. Through the small gaps of her escort, she caught glimpses of the newest room. Green-tinged light spilled onto a set of lavish furniture situated near a curved wall of windows, leaves fluttering in the wind outside its view. A teakettle and wooden tea set sat atop a small counter near the sitting area.

On the opposite side of the room, a tall woman sat at a desk typing away on her holoputer's holographic keyboard. The one soldier who had taken the lead throughout Tetra's escort stepped over to the desk.

The lady raised an arched brow and asked in a thick accent, "Can I help you?"

"We were here on orders from Chief Baene," the soldier replied and pulled up the order on his holonode like he had done for the guardsmen below.

The woman was silent as she read the words. Then her chin tilted as she looked back up at the man's face. "Yes, Chief Baene has been expecting her. Give me a moment..." Her voice trailed away into a mumble.

Through the spaces between her escort, Tetra noticed she was speaking into a small microphone on her desk. After a few minutes, she finally lifted her head and said, "He says she can come in now."

The soldier dipped his head towards her and gestured for Tetra to come forward, and she did so. The woman's eyes widened in horror as their eyes met, and Tetra immediately remembered her malscar. She ducked her head as heat crept into her face.

If only she hadn't put her hair into a bun, then she could have at least hidden some of her hideous face behind it.

"Um...you are Miss Cairn?" The woman asked after an awkward pause.

"Yes ma'am," she replied through gritted teeth.

"Chief Baene will see you now, then."

Though she was feeling quite ungrateful for the whole ordeal, she said a quick "Thank you." so she wouldn't have to lift her head in an acknowledging nod. Only when she turned away did she barely lift it enough to be able to see over her brow as two guardsmen opened a set of wooden double doors next to the woman's desk. Inhaling a deep breath to try and steady the hammering of her heart, she took a few limping steps through the doorway and into the chief advisor's office.

Chapter Nineteen

THE DOORS SHUT BEHIND her with a sense of finality. She jerked her neck around at the noise, and that's when she noticed another, single guardsman standing in the corner between the doors and a wall.

A wall that was covered in daggers.

Tetra's heart skipped another frightened beat. She took an involuntary step away as her eyes roved over the sharp collection covering the wood panels. She would've thought it impressive if she didn't have the horrible feeling that they were about to be used on her.

"Miss Cairn."

She turned at the accented voice, blood pounding in her ears as anxiety-driven images blew through her head.

A tall, wiry man in a dark suit leaned against the side of a large desk. Tetra's memory immediately pieced the pictures of Chief Baene Ruzek she had seen online to the face of the man standing before her. His small eyes studied her, their light bluish-purplish color contrasting against his dark olive skin. The look reminded her of the calculating one Emperor Ignis always wore during their meetings.

The similarity didn't help with her fear.

"Yes sir?" Her voice hitched on the last syllable, and she cleared her throat.

"Did you have a nice trip here?" He spoke each word with careful and practiced delivery.

"Um...yes—yes sir."

He nodded sharply and gestured with his arm towards the other side of the room. "Good. Please have a seat."

Not wanting to lose focus on him for too long, she only spared a glance out of the corner of her eye and noticed two leather couches around a short table, illuminated by the soft light coming through another large curved wall of windows like the ones in the other room. She flicked her eyes back onto his still form and limped over to the sitting area, keeping her unwavering gaze upon him.

The ghost of a smile flashed across his long face. She narrowed her eyes at the fleeting look and sat down on the edge of a couch. She leaned her crutches against her lap, keeping a tight hold on them. Even if running wasn't a possibility for her, she wouldn't be caught unaware. She had trained with a cudgel before, and she would go down fighting before she let anything happen to her.

Chief Baene took a step forward, his arms folded. "Miss Cairn, I don't know what was told to you, but I didn't bring you all the way here to hurt you."

She narrowed her eyes and tried to keep the shadows of fear plaguing her mind from showing on her face. "You...didn't?"

He shook his head. "No, I didn't."

Hmm. That sounded like something Emperor Ignis would say before doing exactly the opposite. "Then why would you bring me here?"

"Because I have a few questions to ask of you."

Likely story. "Why not just have someone back in Xich do it?"

"Because *I* need to be the one to ask them—" her heart jumped into her throat as he spoke, and he put his hands up in surrender, "—but not because I aim to hurt you."

Her knuckles whitened as she tightened her grip on her crutches. Chief Baene's lips twisted into a slight frown, and he sighed.

"I see we need to clear the air here." His piercing eyes locked onto hers, and she was able to see the frustrated sincerity in his gaze. "Miss Cairn, I don't hold you accountable for the sins of your parents. Nor do I blame you for the battles they waged or the Fire Raids. And I most certainly do not blame you for Queen Orinna's death. You would have only been a child when those events happened. Why should I consider hurting *you* for what *they* did?"

Tetra couldn't meet his eyes any longer and lowered her gaze to his freshly-shined, black leather loafers. "Because...of how much they hurt you...and Silvas..."

"Because that's what Emperor Ignis has done ever since he started this war?"

"Yes sir."

Chief Baene sighed again. "I'm not like the emperor, Miss Cairn. I'm no longer a vengeful person and have not been for quite some time." He paused. "So may I now ask you some of those questions without being attacked by your crutches?"

She lifted her head and noticed a spark of amusement in his eyes, which sent a surprised jolt through her. Emperor Ignis never would've made a comment like that...

She studied him through narrowed eyes for a moment, but then finally replied with a simple, "Yes sir."

Though she still didn't fully trust him, at least she could tell he was being somewhat honest.

He stepped over to the sitting area and sat on the couch across from her. "So…" he leaned back, arms crossed, "Your profile says you have amnesia, and I remember you were not able to answer any of the questions asked of you regarding your parents because of it. So, tell me: is there anything at all you can tell me about them?"

A chill went down her spine. She had had a feeling Silvas knew more about her then she would've liked, but the fact that her personal profile had been dug through still surprised her.

"Only what I've been told, sir." A phantom pain throbbed through her skull where her burn scar lay covered by her hair. "I mean—there are a few fuzzy memories from before, but I couldn't tell you what's happening in them because *I* don't even know."

He nodded once. "I know this might seem like a strange question, Miss Cairn, but when you woke up after the fire, what could you do? Could you talk? Could you understand what things were? Or did you have to start all over with everything you would have learned while growing up as a younger child?"

Tetra blinked, her mind running through the earliest memories. She had been able to do practically everything an eight-year-old should be able to do even with all her memories and prior knowledge stolen by the amnesia. A strange feeling skittered through her thoughts. It had never bothered her before, but the way Chief Baene asked the question planted a tiny seed of doubt inside her.

"I…I was able to talk and do all those things…" She cleared her throat to remove all emotion from her voice, "Why do you ask?"

"Because it struck me as odd that your profile said you were found to have amnesia, then only a couple weeks later you were enrolled into Norland."

She silently processed his words for a few moments, and the seeds of doubt sprouted. What was he getting at? And why was it just now sounding so odd to her?

She opened her mouth to ask the first question, but then the office doors opened. She jerked her head in their direction as a young woman stepped into the room, the doors closing behind her. The woman's almond-shaped eyes landed on Tetra, and something about their brown depths looked familiar…

"Ah, you're just in time, Felicita." Chief Baene's voice brought Tetra's gaze back to him. He stood with a smile and gestured towards the woman, "Miss Cairn, this is Lady Felicita Eyrie, my assistant."

"Hello, Miss Cairn." Lady Felicita's eyes widened slightly as their gazes met, but then she looked away with a dip of her chin.

Embarrassed heat crept up Tetra's face, so she nodded to hide her malscar for a moment. "Lady Felicita."

When she lifted her head, she couldn't help but stare at the woman's beautiful, heart-shaped face. A flash of recognition came over her soft features, and another jolt of surprise went through Tetra.

Where had they seen each other before...? She tried to grab for anything in her mind that could answer that question, but everything seemed to be out of reach. Chief Baene had said her last name was "Eyrie", so maybe that's where Tetra's familiarity was from. She had learned about Silvas' former Army General Alistrade Eyrie and seen plenty of pictures of him, and even a few of his family, so maybe she had seen this woman in one of those before.

But that didn't explain the woman's recognition of Tetra...

"You made it just in time," Chief Baene said, "I only began asking Miss Cairn some of the questions I had for her a moment ago."

"Oh, good," Lady Felicita walked over to the sitting area, her long braids swinging around her shoulders. "I was hopin' I'd be able ta join you."

Tetra blinked in surprise at the woman's accent. It sounded like a cross between a Pon-Yelish one with a faint Igrian drawl.

Lady Felicita pressed her yellow dress down as she sat on the couch opposite Tetra. Chief Baene sat down on the couch's opposite end. Tetra's eyes, again, found Lady Felicita's, and she noticed another flash of recognition brighten the woman's eyes.

That small moment gave her the courage to ask, "Um...forgive me, my lady, but have we met before? I feel like I've seen you somewhere..."

"It's quite possible tha' you have." Lady Felicita smiled softly. "I'm at almost every council meeting and press conference Chief Baene goes to."

That didn't answer her question fully, yet she could feel Chief Baene's probing gaze upon her and didn't push the subject anymore. She would just have to try and get answers later.

"Lady Felicita has been my assistant for over a year, and—hopefully—will one day become an advisor herself." She returned her gaze to the Chief Advisor's calm countenance as he spoke, "So she will be staying during this time."

"Yes sir," Tetra replied.

She was fine with that. Despite her beginning to see that Chief Baene was not the Emperor Ignis clone she thought he would be, she had to admit it was a relief to have the young woman present.

"Now then," Chief Baene began, "where were we...?"

The doubt with her amnesia came back to mind, sending an icy chill down her spine. "You said you found it odd that I'd had amnesia and was able to do practically everything without having to relearn any of it," she said slowly. "So, if I may be so blunt, sir, what were you getting at?"

Something lit up in Chief Baene's face. He shared a quick glance with Lady Felicita before leaning forward and resting his elbows on his knees. His eyes locked onto Tetra's.

"I'm wondering if you even have amnesia in the first place."

"What?" Invisible bugs crawled along her burn scar as she gave him a dubious look. "No, I—I have amnesia. A chandelier fell on my head as my parents' house burned. The—the doctors took brain scans, and they confirmed that I have it."

"Do you remember the doctors who gave you this news?"

The memory came back to her as he spoke, and with it, a new doubt she had never known until now.

"Yes sir." Her voice came out low and she looked down at her hands, away from Chief Baene's piercing gaze. "It...it wasn't a doctor, sir. It was Emperor Ignis. But there was a doctor there—Doctor Bengha, I think—who confirmed his words."

"I see."

The possibility of what the chief advisor was proposing grew in the back of her mind, and she didn't like it.

"But...I have a burn scar." Her heart began to pound a fearful rhythm as she tried to pull out any logical facts that might show her amnesia was actually amnesia. "And I've seen the video of my parents' house burning down. I—I was even allowed to visit its ruins."

She pushed back a little of the auburn hair along her forehead, along with her embarrassment, to show the tip of her raised scar-tissue. "This is real and goes along the top of my head. I don't think the pain it caused me could have been faked."

Chief Baene nodded. "And I believe you—but I'm not saying you were not caught in a fire. What I am saying is that someone might have used your accident to try and hide something you might have known."

Dread coiled tightly in her chest.

"That was one of the main reasons I had for this meeting." Chief Baene continued, "It seemed strange to me that on the night your parents died, you supposedly woke up with amnesia and were put into the emperor's control as his legal ward."

"You're saying he killed my parents?" She asked.

Her parents' house wasn't the only one to burn down that night. Two of them were the homes of people who had been suspected of disloyalty to Igrium: Prince Joash Ignis and Advisor Aquila Tralp. Rumors spread that Emperor Ignis was the one who ordered their quarters in the fortress to be burned, but that rumor didn't make sense for the other five, loyal homes that had been destroyed as well.

Chief Baene shook his head. "No. I know for certain that your parents were completely loyal to Igrium, and it would be stupid of him to kill the two people responsible for many of his victories at the beginning of this war."

"Then what are you trying to say?"

"I want to know if the emperor is hiding anything." Chief Baene's voice was calm—the exact opposite of the inner turmoil his words stirred in Tetra. "Igrium has always used the C.B.M ever since the machine's creation, so I don't find it hard to believe that it could have been used on you."

The C.B.M... Of course that was it—the one machine every kingdom except for Igrium had outlawed due to the inhumane ways it could be, and was, used. The machine capable of turning any sane person into one of Emperor Ignis' brainwashed personal guards.

Tetra leaned her crutches against the couch and finally let go of them to put her head in her hands as the truth settled in. This was way too much. She hadn't come expecting Chief Baene to shine a light on the darkness of her amnesia's reality—or whatever she should call it now.

Someone had *stolen* her memories. And now that she was finally seeing through this new lens, it was becoming obvious that Emperor Ignis himself must have been the one to do it. No one besides him had the power in Igrium to use the C.B.M. on whomever they wanted. He had been the one to tell her she had amnesia, *and* he was the one who had orchestrated her life ever since.

"I'm sorry for putting this all on you, Miss Cairn."

She lifted her eyes and met the chief advisor's softened gaze. "No—um...thank you for telling me, sir. It—it makes a lot of sense." She sighed through her nose. "And I can't believe I haven't been able to see it until now."

"With the amount of work put into the whole charade, it would be easy for anyone to believe it—including myself," he said. "But, thank Deleyon, a few things did leave me with questions."

Tetra straightened as she tried to sort through the tumult of thoughts before asking, "So how are you planning to figure out what he might've hid? And why do you even want to know?"

What would be so special about something her eight-year-old self might know?

Chief Baene shared another glance with Lady Felicita, and the waves in Tetra's stomach churned more fiercely. She dug her nails into her palms. If they were planning on poking around through her mind, she wasn't going to just let it happen. She might be a Cairn in Silvas' borders, but that didn't give them the right to experiment for some random memory she wasn't even sure was there.

"I want to know for national security reasons." Chief Baene locked his gaze with Tetra's again. "Now I'm not saying you are your parents, but for someone to—like I said—go to so much trouble to erase the memories of Aries and

Marin Cairn's daughter, it leaves me wondering what was so important." He straightened. "Children pick up on a lot more than we give them credit for. You might have overheard a secret plan your parents were talking about and spoken of it to Emperor Ignis after the fire, or you might have memorized a secret code you weren't supposed to see."

Tetra nodded slowly and looked down at her clasped hands.

That only solidified Emperor Ignis' reasoning for erasing her memories instead of just killing her. It would be a major dishonor to kill the only child of two people so highly honored. Despite how twisted it was, she could see the emperor's logic behind it: erase her memories to cover up the problem and get a trained, loyal soldier out of it.

She couldn't help the small, grim smile that escaped her lips at the thought. She definitely ruined the latter part of those plans.

"So, I've asked Lady Felicita to help you find your memories again," Chief Baene said.

Tetra lifted her head and sent them a questioning look. "How?"

"The C.B.M. can't erase memories—it only blocks 'em." Lady Felicita replied, "There is a list o' questions we can ask you tha' were created ta help those with memory loss from the C.B.M. get them back."

"So..." She flicked her gaze over to the woman's familiar face. "You'll only be asking me a bunch of questions?"

Lady Felicita nodded with a small smile. "Yes."

"Nothing else?"

"No, Miss Cairn. Just questions."

"But before we get to your answer," Chief Baene cut in, "I have another reason for asking you here."

She turned her head back in his direction, wondering what other life-altering words he was about to say. "Yes sir?"

"Despite your...many misdemeanors at Norland, your profile said you had some of the best grades in the school, and you would have graduated early had you not caused your commanding officers, and the emperor, so many problems." He raised a brow and the skin around Tetra's malscar tingled. "However, I read through some of the reports of your misconduct, and I heard your answer from the questioning in Xich, so I know many of those tallies were earned out of a strong set of—what we in Silvas and the Alliance would say are—morally-right convictions."

Tetra lifted her hand and rubbed her fingers along the rough segione tallies there. The only person who had ever said anything close to that was Aabir, and then Tetra had destroyed their friendship and he never spoke to her again. Still, she didn't know quite what to make of the comment and kept silent so Chief Baene could continue.

"So, I'm here to make you an offer." He paused to take a breath. "Shortly before you leapt over the fence in Trivsau, I received a message from a trusted source telling me of your arrival. They also told me that if I let you leave to do whatever you wish, I would be wasting your potential. I don't want to keep you here as a prisoner—you have not broken any of our kingdom's laws and I would rather not see you locked up in a cell—but I do need you to stay in Urbselva until we can figure out why Emperor Ignis erased your memories; so instead of wasting the rest of your time, I'm extending you an offer to attend Duschel University."

The name rang a bell in her head. "I think I've heard of it before..."

"It's where I graduated," Lady Felicita said, "Chief Baene helped me get in there as well."

"Really?"

Chief Baene nodded once. "Lady Felicita is also from Igrium, Miss Cairn." Something akin to pride broke through his serious demeanor as he turned his head in Lady Felicita's direction.

"My matha and I fled Igrium after Emperor Ignis had my patre executed." A shadow passed over the woman's face as she spoke, "So we came over here ta Silvas because my patre knew Chief Baene."

"And I owed him a favor," Chief Baene added.

"He helped my matha and I get settled here, and he helped me get into good schools—including Duschel."

"And now you want to help *me*?" Tetra couldn't keep the dubious tone out of her voice, "The daughter of the Cairns?"

There was a pause. Then, "I know it seems hard ta believe, Miss Cairn," Lady Felicita implored her with wide eyes, "but I assure you that this offer is genuine. We only want ta help you regain your memories and have you do somethin' else worthwhile as we go through the process."

Tetra's mental defenses rose back up. These kinds of things didn't just happen to anyone—especially not her. "I don't mean to be rude, Chief Baene, but how am I supposed to believe that your offer is sincere? You never owed my parents' anything, and—I'm sorry, Lady Felicita, but—my last name isn't held in any high regard here in Silvas, either."

Lady Felicita gave her a sad smile as Chief Baene replied, "No, but you could make it so." He seemed to grow a bit taller, and his voice took on an authoritative tone, "You can refuse my offer, Miss Cairn, but I would still have to keep you here in Urbselva. You came under *my* jurisdiction when you jumped over that fence, and I'm giving you an offer many in Silvas would gladly take."

He paused. "This has nothing to do with your parentage or what they did against our kingdom. You could see this as a great way to honor your parents' by doing something truly worthwhile, and it might even lead to a greater legacy than theirs."

Tetra's vow popped into her head, and she straightened. *How had he known...?* She pushed the thought aside. There was no way he could have known about her silent vow, yet his last words struck her like a blow from Mabel Frauss' sword.

A small frown pulled the corners of Chief Baene's lips down. "Or I can have you locked up here in the Altelo and you can waste away. Your choice."

Her fear came back and tightened around her chest like a noose. Lady Felicita sent Chief Baene a disapproving look, and he sighed.

"I don't take my words back, Miss Cairn," he said, his eyes flicking over in Lady Felicita's direction, "but I truly don't want to see you lose your freedom. Please consider taking up my offer. You remind me a little of Lady Felicita, and if more people in our government were like her, Silvas would be in a much more prosperous position."

His serious, set gaze bore into her. "I'm not saying any of this flippantly, either. Ever since I received that first message, I have thought long and hard about this. So, believe me when I say my intentions are sincere and for the good of many."

Tetra could tell he was being truthful by the look in his eyes—despite the rest of his stone-like facial expression. It was a nice contrast against Emperor Ignis who always had the authoritative countenance of a wily peryton about to eat her.

"So, I can either go to Duschel or stay locked up here?" She finally asked.

He offered one sharp nod.

She sighed and went to scratch the side of her face but stopped herself as she remembered her malscar. "Where would I live?"

"In the dorms."

"And who would be paying for all of this? I don't have any money."

"If the questions work in bringing your memories back, and whatever information is hidden there, I will use that as a form of payment." He paused to lean forward. "I wouldn't do this if I didn't think the information hidden in your mind was valuable, but I do, Miss Cairn. So please—take up my offer. It will only come once."

He was giving her *free* education? She narrowed her eyes and scrutinized his daunting, but seemingly sincere, countenance. What sort of information did he think might be in her head?

She glanced over at Lady Felicita's hope-filled eyes, and the same twinge of familiarity struck again. Well, if she did stay, then she might be able to figure out why the young woman seemed more familiar than any picture off the Net ever would, and why she seemed to recognize Tetra as well.

The whole situation was strange and completely not what she had been expecting when she left Xich. Yet if Chief Baene's words could be trusted (and her gut was telling her "yes, he could"), then this might be the best way to complete her vow.

"Alright, sir." She locked eyes with Chief Baene and nodded sharply. "I'll accept your offer."

"Good." He nodded back. "I'll need to make a few calls and sort out a few favors I'm owed, but once that is done, we will take you to Duschel's campus." He sent her an almost grateful look. "Thank you for taking up this offer, Miss Cairn. I know it's not what you expected, but I promise it will be worth it. Though I can't say that I liked your parents, I don't want to see any legacy—not even their name—soaked in innocent blood. I look forward to seeing how you might change that."

Tetra nodded. She still didn't fully trust his motives, but the honesty in his eyes—and the threat of being locked up—kept her fears of accepting his offer at bay. Lady Felicita sent her an encouraging smile that loosened a few of the tight cords of anxiety inside her.

"Well, it looks like I'm going back to school."

Chapter Twenty

Aabir's weekend flew by in a whirl of mumbled prayers, worrisome thoughts, talks with his family, and pomen pies. Before he knew it, Seventhdein night had come and he was off in a taxi, headed back to Norland so he would not have to fight Firstdein morning traffic.

He had not told his parents about Rasiela's offer despite wanting to badly. The only thing holding him back from doing so was how much worry he had seen in their eyes. The entire atmosphere of their home had shifted so much that when Aabir first stepped through the front door on Fifthdein afternoon, he could almost feel a heaviness fall upon his shoulders that had not been there before.

His parents told him that patrolmen had come into their house that morning and ransacked the place while no one was there. Matha came home to flipped-over furniture, clothes and belongings strewn across the floor, the holovision's small projector broken, and her few pieces of expensive jewelry missing.

They also found out Tuovah and Neiva Ivington, a young couple who lived across the street from them (whose parents were Silvanian and Frigian, respectively), also found their townhome in similar disrepair around the same time. Him, Zeke, and Patre all went over to help Tuovah pick up furniture and put things back where they belonged since Neiva was pregnant and could not bend down to help.

Later, Zeke confided to him about one of Ereliev's friends telling him she had been questioned at school like he was. However, they could not tell him what actually happened during her questioning because they themselves did not know.

Aabir squeezed his eyes shut as the memory replayed in his mind again:

"Ereliev?" He knocked on her bedroom door.

A quiet moment passed. Then a muffled "What?" came from the other side.

"Can I come in?"

Another pause. "I guess."

He opened the squeaky door and stepped into his sister's bedroom. She was sitting at her desk, scribbling something down in a chardex.

"What are you doing?" Aabir asked.

"None of your business." Ereliev stopped writing and turned an annoyed glare up at him. "What do you want?"

He crossed his arms with a frown, ticked off by her attitude. She could be so annoying sometimes, and it always rubbed him the wrong way.

"I just came to ask if everything was OK."

Ereliev rolled her eyes and turned her head away from him, back to the chardex. "Sure, it is," she replied in a sarcastic tone, "Our house is being destroyed on a weekly basis; Patre's business is going down; one of my friend's parents just got put in prison because her grandparents were from Pon-Yelum and they said something good about the kingdom... Everything is so *great."*

Aabir snorted with an eye roll. "Thank you, Captain Obvious."

She shrugged, still not looking at him. "You asked the stupid question." Her hand moved in furious strokes as she began to write again.

He ground his teeth to bite back a retort and took a deep breath before coming out with the full truth, "Zeke told me one of your friends told him that you were questioned at school today."

She immediately stopped writing. There was a pause, then she spun around in her chair and glared up at him. "So?"

He blew out a frustrated breath. "I just wanted to know if you were OK."

A shadow passed over her sharpened features, but when it passed it only seemed to magnify her anger at him. She stood abruptly from her chair, fists at her sides.

"Brela had no right to tell Zeke that," she said, "and you have no right to ask me about it, either."

He narrowed his eyes. "I only want to help you, Ereliev."

"I don't need your help!" She barked, "And I don't need you telling Matha and Patre about it, either. You've kept Zeke's questioning from them, and I want you to do the same for me."

"You just said you didn't need my help."

"That would be helping them, not me." She crossed her arms, her gaze lowering to the floor for a moment. "I...I don't want to add anything else onto their shoulders right now." Her gaze sharpened again as she met his eyes, "So don't tell them anything, Aabir."

"I don't even know what happened!"

Now that she was this close, he could see an undeniable shadow of fear mixed in with the angry heat in his sister's periwinkle eyes. Forgetting all his earlier frustrations with her, a burst of fiery anger like he saw in her gaze blazed to life inside his chest. If anyone had hurt his sister...

"What happened, Ereliev?" His voice came out harsher than he meant it too, but it was not aimed at her.

She winced, but the moment of weakness gave way for a quiet like the calm before a windstorm. "Get out." Her voice was immovable—like Matha's when she was angry.

"Ereliev..."

"I said get out!" Ereliev shouted.

Aabir opened his mouth to reply just as Matha's voice rose from down the hall, "Ereliev? Who are you yelling at?"

"Aabir won't leave me alone, Matha!" Ereliev turned to look in the direction of the open doorway.

"Aabir, don't bother your sister." Matha's voice held a note of frustration. "I shouldn't even have to tell you this!"

"Sorry, Matha." Aabir called back, then turned his head at the satisfied look Ereliev was giving him. In a lower voice, he said, "I only want to help, Ereliev. I promise I won't tell Matha and Patre—just like I did for Zeke."

"You being the perfect child can't help me, Aabir." She crossed her arms and mimicked his unyielding pose. "Now leave."

He opened his mouth to ask her what that last comment meant, but he could see the determination in her eyes and realized it would be a hopeless battle. So, with one last helpless glare in her direction, he turned and left her room. She slammed the door behind him.

AABIR PUT HIS HEAD in his hands with a frustrated sigh. Rain hit the taxi's window, each raindrop reflecting the glow of the streetlights and flashing holographic billboards. In the distance, the lights of the Constantia Stadium illuminated the dark, cloudy sky. The sight of the huge, domed structure rising with the skyscrapers above the low buildings they passed only caused another knot to tighten in Aabir's insides.

He wished Deleyon would have given him an answer already because he was feeling the urge to accept Rasiela's offer with each pounding memory. If he could do something to keep any of these things from happening to anyone, he wanted to do it. Yet he also did not want to make a deal with Malackin by saying "yes." So, he resigned himself to waiting. Ever...so...impatiently.

"Could you turn up the radio?" He asked the android driver. Music was the perfect distraction he needed right now.

"Certainly." The android replied in its chipper, computerized voice.

Its silvery, human-like hand reached out and tapped the holographic screen a few times next to the steering wheel.

A news reporter's monotone voice amped up in the small space, **"—and in better news, the Tourney's Planners have released**

the list of veteran competitors coming back this year—"

Aabir clenched his fists as his stomach whirled. The last thing he needed to hear right now was anything about the Constantia Tourney. "Hey, could you—"

He stopped himself as the reporter continued, "**—new reports about the prisoner rounds. In light of the Alliance's win in Trivsau earlier this week, His Imperial Majesty has ordered that all prisoners-of-war from that battle not being used in any trade-off will be put in the Constantia Tourney this year."**

His heart rate increased, and he dug the nubs of his fingernails into his palms as he listened.

"In a press conference this afternoon, he stated," The reporter's voice was replaced with an audio clip of Emperor Ignis', "***'All enemies of our empire will be brought low in the face of our wrath—even if it takes the death of every prisoner-of-war to do it. My advisors and I are also looking into the release of rule number three-hundred and eighty-five, which will take care of all possible Alliance spies living in our grand empire.'***"

Aabir's stomach tightened as the reporter's voice came back on, **"Rule number three-hundred and eighty-five, also known as the 'Death to Deceit' rule, is being processed by the Emperor, his advisors, and the Tourney's Planners right now. This rule will give the Tourney access to any and all prisoners found in our borders who have been arrested for treason, and attempted treason. Although it is too late to implement it into this year's competition, they have high hopes that it will be put into the Tourney next year. So, for all—"**

"—Turn it off," Aabir ordered in a harsh tone.

The android did as it was told without a reply, and the blissful sound of pattering rain and blowing wind filled the tense atmosphere once again. Despite the reporter's nice usage of words, Aabir knew exactly what this newest rule was going to do—and it twisted his stomach even more with dread. He gritted his teeth and pressed his fists against his forehead.

They were going to put innocent people into the Constantia Tourney to be murdered on live holovision for all of Igrium's bloodthirsty, desensitized crowds to cheer over. He had had friends (back before he joined Norland) whose parents had been arrested for "attempted treason" because they were caught saying good things—on secret cameras—about the Alliance kingdoms they, or their parents, had lived in before coming to Igrium. And now there was the strong possibility that they would be put in the Tourney for doing so—if they were not already dead.

It made him want to punch Emperor Ignis in the face, but that truly would be a death sentence—for him and his family.

Another tangle of worry tightened around his thoughts. Though if things continued the way they did, he would not have to do something as drastic as that to Igrium's imperial ruler for them to all end up dying in the Tourney.

He lifted his gaze to the hovercar's ceiling. *Deleyon,* he thought, *I have to do something. This injustice is stupid, and I hate it all. I know I haven't heard your reply, but I think I need to accept Rasiela's offer.*

Silence met his quiet prayer, but he did not let it bother him as he recalled some of the stories his parents had told him about the heroes Silvas' sole deity used to save the kingdom's citizens—even when they were in different nations. He remembered one such story where some guy with a long name he could not remember had rescued a group of Silvanians who had been taken captive by one of the kingdoms that now made up Igrium's original empire. He had infiltrated the palace dungeons by pretending to be a servant and gained the trust of the guards to rescue those captured. The story ended with him doing so, and everyone sailing back to Silvas.

As Aabir's imagination played the story over in his head, a burst of sharp hope went through him. Matha and Patre never told him if the man ever heard from Deleyon before going on his mission, but they did say it was done by His hand. So maybe that was his own case. Maybe he really was supposed to do this to help save his family before any of them could end up in the Constantia Tourney. They were all Silvanian, so surely Deleyon would be with him to do this even if he had not heard a direct answer.

With this new Constantia rule, imprisonment and dishonorable death already loomed over him and his family. So, if he took Rasiela's offer, he would only be accepting the risk of what was already there. There would be nothing for him to lose—unless he declined.

Rasiela had said he might be able to help a lot of people if he took this job. What if she had him search for some piece of information that ended up saving a lot of Alliance people in Igrium from this new rule? Or what if it stopped another battle like the one in Trivsau from happening?

The image of the woman being stabbed and the countless others he had seen in Trivsau flashed through his mind's eye, bringing with them a mixture of guilt and resolve.

How could he pass up an opportunity like that and not hate himself daily for it?

Though that did not help to abate all his fears, he felt the cords of worry loosen their hold on him as he silently made his decision. With a deep exhale through his nose, he closed his eyes and leaned his head back against the taxi's seat; using the sound of the pounding rain to drown out his thoughts.

"AABIR!"

"Hmm?" Aabir blinked and turned his focus on Aquilo's frowning face.

"What's wrong with you?" His friend retorted and gestured towards the chardex open in front of him. "If we don't get this done, I'm blaming my disownment on you."

Aabir yawned and straightened in his chair, turning his gaze to the chemistry pages glowing on the lab table in front of him. "One bad grade won't get you disowned."

"Maybe not, but I would rather not fail at something I could easily do myself because my partner is half-asleep."

"Sorry." He tried—and failed—to stifle another yawn. "I didn't get much sleep this weekend." Or the past week for that matter.

Aquilo narrowed his eyes. "Did something happen?"

Oh, how he wished he could tell his friends all the problems he and his family went through for being of Silvanian descent. The excuse he always told himself for not doing so was because they would not understand—least of all Aquilo. Yet, deep down, he knew the true reason was because he did not want them to look at him as being Silvanian. His eyes flicked around to some of his other platoon mates sitting around the chemistry lab. If they did, he knew they would turn away and treat him the way most of his platoon had been doing for the past week.

"Eh. Just normal stuff." He shrugged and moved his chardex closer. "Do you think we could get this done quickly?"

Aquilo stared at him for an awkward moment, then shook his head and turned back to his own chardex. "If you don't fall asleep on me again, we should finish up soon."

Aabir grinned and picked up his stylus. The questions did only take a few minutes to answer, and by the time they finished doing so the bell rang. Once its annoying ringing ceased, Mr. Faull told the class they could leave. Aabir stood and shut his chardex, then picked it up and followed Aquilo out the door before joining those of his platoon as they began moving through the classroom corridors.

They passed by the janitor closet's closed door, and a sliver of dread slid into his stomach. He tightened his hold on his chardex and pushed the stupid emotion away. He had made his decision, and he was *not* going to be a coward about it. No amount of anxious thoughts over the tortures captured spies endured was going to stop him.

I'm not going to be a coward anymore.

More of his platoon mates joined their growing number, and he was able to turn his focus aside from the unwanted thoughts towards the snippets of conversations going on around him. They passed through the entrance hall and into the training hallways in their loud, unruly group that only quieted when Lieutenant Tarson shouted at them to shut up with a sharp glare.

Tetra's escape had left a bad mark on the woman's record and dishonored her greatly, so all the trainees at Norland were staying clear of her for the time being—all except for her own platoon, that is. Aabir was sad for them, but his relief of not being in her platoon outweighed his pity.

Only when she passed down the hall and turned the corner did their noise continue. They made it to their armory, headed inside, then came back out a few minutes later with their armor and respective weapons.

"Hey, Aabir!" Buren stepped up beside him as they trickled back out into the hall filled with more trainees all going to their respective training yards. "Septimus said he'd spar with me today, but then he told me that he forgot he'd done the same for Brutus earlier, so he said I should ask you."

"Why did he say that?" Aabir scrunched his brow. "And why do you want to work with a sword now? I thought you were more of an arbalist."

"I am," Buren nodded, "but ever since the battle, I've realized I need to work on my close-range skills more. So, can you help? Septimus said you're pretty good and that you'd be able to help me more than anyone else."

Septimus said that? Aabir could not help but grin at the thought. His platoon was finally coming back around to not hating him.

"Sure." He glanced over his shoulder where Aquilo and Tycho were talking not far behind them. "Let me just tell Aquilo real quick."

Buren nodded again and continued on while Aabir slowed his pace so he could join his friends. "Hey Aquilo, you weren't expecting to spar with me today, right?"

Aquilo looked over at him with a shrug. "Nope."

"Good."

"Why'd you ask?"

"Because Buren just asked to be my partner."

Tycho's face lit up with a grin. "I told you they'd come back around soon."

Aabir nodded, trying to keep a relieved smile from coming over his face. "Yeah." It was a small relief compared to everything else going on around him, but it was something.

Aquilo quickened his pace a bit as they made it to the double doors leading into their training yard, then pushed one of them open. Aabir and Tycho followed him. Soll's pale light filtered through the thin cloud cover above as they made their way to the center of the empty yard where Lieutenant Denir stood waiting for them, his hands behind his back and a stonelike look on his face.

When all forty trainees were lined up in front of him, he took a step forward and said in a voice that echoed off the stone walls, "Trainees, I was just informed this morning that we will be receiving a new trainee into our platoon. He is transferring from Stelgan Military Academy."

A new trainee? Aabir scrunched his brow in confusion, then immediately fixed his expression back to neutral as Lieutenant Denir's gaze landed on him for a moment.

He had never heard of any trainee transferring to Norland before. You either got in as a first-year or not at all.

"He will be joining your classes and training starting tomorrow." He gave them one last, hard stare. "Now that that's out of the way, get in your sparring circles and begin!"

Aabir looked around for Buren and spotted him. The other teenage boy gestured for him to follow, and he did. Buren stopped in an empty ring and unsheathed his longsword. Aabir came to a stop at the other end and pulled out his own blade. He tightened his grip as he brandished it, energy beginning to buzz through him. This was what he needed—a good release from the mental strain he had been under.

"Alright." He locked eyes with Buren, "Attack me."

The other trainee lunged towards him. Aabir deflected his blade away, then slashed his own across the armor protecting Buren's throat. Buren's eyes widened under his helmet, and he stumbled back. Aabir could have called the fight finished, but instead, he sliced the sword point back toward Buren's throat; stopping only a hairsbreadth from it.

Warm satisfaction filled his chest, but it was immediately washed away by an icy blast as the memory of the Frigian woman being at his mercy blew into his mind. He pushed the thought away with a blink and met Buren's wide eyes.

"If you're not dead, don't stop fighting," he said in a hard voice. "Got it?"

Buren nodded, and Aabir removed his sword. The clash of metal rang around them, bringing back the haunting memories from Trivsau. He shook his head to keep them away and took a step back. He lifted his sword with both hands into a guard position and turned his focus onto the present task.

"Again." He ordered.

Throughout the rest of the session, Aabir released his frustrations and worries against Buren's unsuspecting person. He knew it was unfair, but Buren had chosen the wrong day to spar with him. Aabir won every match, yet he did not feel like he was winning. At the end of each quick fight, they would stop long enough for his memories to come whispering back, which took away every good feeling winning gave him and brought back the tension he had begun to release during the fight.

When training was over and Lieutenant Denir gave them leave, Aabir rushed out of the training yard towards the armory. He removed his armor and cleaned up quicker than he ever had, using the swirl of tense emotions to propel his actions.

As he was heading out the armory door, Tycho came up and asked, "What's the rush, Aabir?"

He stopped and glanced down at the ground as he tried to come up with an excuse. Rasiela's words came to his mind, *"Come up with a cleaning-related excuse to see me..."*

"I...have a few shirts with bloodstains on them." He looked up and met Tycho's questioning gaze with a forced grin. "My matha told me she's getting tired of trying to get them out and that if I don't find a solution then I'll still have bloodstained shirts."

Tycho shook his head. "Man, Aabir—you and your clothes." He grinned. "Why do you even care if your training shirts have some blood on 'em? Y'know the more you have the more of a man it makes you."

"Is that why you don't ever wash yours'?"

"I wash them!" Tycho gave him a mock look of shock. "I just don't get the stains out. Each one is a reminder of how many enemies I've bested."

Aabir pushed the door open. "Or how many times you've been stabbed."

"I haven't been stabbed since—!"

The door closed on his defense, and Aabir started down the hall with a satisfied smirk. It faded as he stepped into the entrance hall and maneuvered through the few people milling about in the natural light streaming in through the windows. He forced himself to keep at a normal pace as he strode through the entryway into the classroom halls. As he did so, Mister Grahan stepped out of his own classroom and headed down the hall in Aabir's direction.

Just act natural, just act natural, just act natural... he chanted to himself as his history teacher moved closer. His muscles stiffened as they passed.

"Trainee," Mister Grahan acknowledged him with a nod.

Aabir nodded back as his teacher moved on in the opposite direction. Only when his footsteps faded did he let out a relieved sigh, his muscles relaxing. He rubbed his hand over his buzzed head as he turned a corner.

Why was he so anxious? He had an excuse—and a good one, if Tycho's reaction meant anything. He sent a wary glance around the hall. No one was here. And even if they were, he had an excuse...

The *"janitorial services"* door came up ahead of him. He took a deep breath to calm himself and to push his focus solely on the task ahead. No worries. No fear. Just the job ahead.

He slowed to a stop at the door and knocked. Only a moment passed before it opened on silent hinges and Rasiela looked up at him.

"Can I help you, trainee?" She asked.

Aabir wondered for a moment if he had only made up their entire meeting in his head, but then he saw the light of recognition in her eyes and mentally slapped himself.

"I—I need some...do you have anything that might remove bloodstains?" He gritted his teeth as the question left his lips. That had sounded better in his head.

Rasiela lifted an arched brow and nodded her head. "I'm sure I have something in here somewhere." She opened the door wider and gestured for him to enter. "You can come in if you want. It might take me a few minutes to find it amidst all this other stuff."

Aabir nodded and stepped into the dim room as Rasiela moved over to the shelves of cleaning supplies. She picked up a bottle and, without turning to face him, asked in a lowered voice, "What did you decide?"

"I accept."

Part of him expected something monumental to happen once the words left his mouth, but nothing did. Rasiela nodded, still not looking at him. "Are you sure?"

He put as much conviction in his voice as he replied, "Yes ma'am."

"Good." She nodded again and bent down to look through one of the lower shelves. "You do realize what the job is, yes?"

"Yes ma'am. It didn't take me long to figure it out."

"Then you know the risks. I promise I will do everything to keep you out of any trouble if I'm ever caught." Aabir's heart skipped a beat right as she sent him a quick, reassuring glance. "But I haven't been caught in over fifteen years; and if I ever thought I was going to be, I have orders to leave the empire as quickly as possible."

At the mention of leaving, Aabir straightened his shoulders and pushed the annoying thoughts of fear to the side with his resolve. "Then what do I need to do?"

"First, I need you to realize that this entire thing is a trust exercise." She picked up a box and set it on the floor beside her before looking up at him with a hard stare. "I will ask you to retrieve information, but I will double—and sometimes triple—check every single scrap you give me. This is not necessarily a "real" version of the job, just a major trust exercise."

A small bit of the invisible weight pressing upon his shoulders lifted at her reply, but it also raised a question. "I want to help people—like you said I would do if I accepted, but how is my getting info that you will end up checking multiple times going to help anyone? Isn't that only giving you more work to do?"

"I didn't say I would always check your information, but I know I will at first." She shrugged. "I may always check it. I don't know what the future holds, Trainee Sorrel, but even if it adds a little more work to my schedule, you're still helping. There's no doubt about that." She paused and turned her head back in the shelf's direction. "You can get to places as a trainee a Silvanian-descended janitor can't. That is a major help."

"Oh." He scratched the back of his neck. "I...didn't see it like that before..."

"So, for your first assignment, I need you to get me any information you can on the 'Silvanian Fire Attacks'."

Aabir's eyes widened. "So, it really was Silvas who did that?"

"No," Rasiela raised her brow, "I'm only calling them what Igrium does because I had a feeling it was what you knew them by."

"Oh. Right." He mentally slapped himself for sounding so Igrian in front of the Silvanian spy. "Of course. I mean—I don't know who actually did them, personally, but no one seems to agree on that, either..."

Rasiela nodded. "And that's what I want you to find." She stood up and continued looking through the shelves. "Get me pages in books, conspiracy threads, videos, anything. Put it all down in your holonode and send it to me."

"Anything?"

"Yes, no matter how far-fetched it is. I want it all." She picked up something off a shelf and turned to face him. Her eyes locked onto his as she continued, "You have one week, Trainee Sorrel. The only way you can mess this up is if you don't find me anything."

"How do I send the information to you?"

"Give me your contact number and I will message you on a secure connection. Whenever you get anything, send it to me there." She stepped towards him and held out a small bottle. "In exactly one week come by here again and I will give you your new assignment. Understand?"

"Yes ma'am." Aabir told her his number and took the bottle from her hand. He looked down and read the label, *"Stain Remover"*.

"Good. Then I will see you in one week." She turned back to the shelves and began rearranging the cleaning supplies. "Good day, Trainee Sorrel."

"Wait." He lifted his head and locked eyes with her again. "Why are you doing this? Why—of all people—would you want to help *me*?"

Without missing a beat, she replied, "Because I can see you and your family are in danger, and your actions have shown you will do anything to keep them safe—even if it's not ideal." She shrugged. "And I have needed someone to help me for a while now, anyway, so it might as well be you."

Aabir nodded slowly as he processed her words. "Then...thank you. For this." He lifted his arms to gesture around them.

"Of course." Rasiela nodded sharply then turned back to the shelves. "You need to go now. If the cameras are watching, security might wonder why you're staying this long."

"Oh! Right." He cleared his throat and turned around to head out the door. "Thank you again."

"And don't lose that stain remover, Trainee! I need it back in one week."

"Yes ma'am."

He half-turned and closed the door before heading back down the hall to get to his dorm, the small bottle clutched tightly in his hand. Now that it was over, his heartbeat began to slow with every step, and he found that he could breathe a little easier. He sent up a silent *"thank you"* to Deleyon that he had not been caught, and that his first assignment seemed to be an easy one.

The conversation played through his head as he walked, planting a small ember of hope in his chest. Now his family had a chance to be safe, and his past mistakes would not be able to hinder it. In fact, his being at Norland would actually help him.

His holonode sent a buzz through his arm. He moved his sleeve back and turned the small watch-like device on. A new message beckoned him. He tapped the holographic screen, taking him to the messages app.

"Aabir, this is your Cousin Ori. I have a new number now and wanted you to know it," the message read, *"I will try to see you and your family in a week."*

Aabir scrunched his nose up in a moment of confusion, then understanding immediately dawned on him like a blow to the head. *Rasiela.*

He rolled his eyes at himself and turned his device off without replying. He walked through the open entryway into the entrance hall and made a beeline towards one of the halls at the back.

Now to get some information on those housefires...

Chapter Twenty-One

"Not bad," a voice said behind Tetra.

She turned her gaze away from the throwing knife handle sticking out of the bullseye and met Finnegar Knightley's guarded look.

"Thank you, sir," she replied.

He dipped his pointy chin and spun on his heel before heading over to two club members sparring on the opposite end of the training grounds. Tetra let out a breath once he was gone and turned her attention back to the line of targets ahead of her. She passed her other throwing knife from her right hand to her left and eyed the blood-red center of her target, gripping the dagger's handle tightly.

After her discussion with Chief Baene, the chief advisor had made a few calls then asked Lady Felicita to take her to Duschel University. When they got there, Tetra was given the mandatory entrance exams, passed them, then she chose two courses to take—general and military history. Lady Felicita gave her a tour of the university, took her to get her schoolbooks and some clothes and other essentials she needed, then dropped her off at her single-person dorm that night.

Tetra lifted the dagger over and behind her head. She had been at Duschel for exactly one week since then—and was beginning to think that a prison cell might have been the better option.

Her classes were enjoyable—but only because she was learning about history she had not been taught in Igrium; while having her own, quiet room and being able to eat as much as she wanted in the dining hall was amazing. Yet despite those things, she was becoming aware of just how much her family name was truly hated in Silvas. She already knew it was, but seeing the sharp hatred and disgust in the expressions of her professors, and the other students when they found out, was a dampener on the whole experience.

She had failed her first quiz in general history, one on Igrium's War of Freedom (a topic she had had pounded into her head ever since she joined Norland), so she thought she had failed because of her pride at thinking she knew practically everything one could on the subject. But she later came to find out it was because her professor didn't agree with her view—her "biased, Igrian view" he had told her—on certain things she had written about in the essay questions.

A spark of fire ignited in her chest at the memory, and she threw the dagger. It thunked into the wood below the bullseye.

The same thing happened with a short paper she had written for military history. Apparently, everything Tetra had been taught about Igrium's military was "biased" or outright "wrong". Even though she had gone to an Igrian military academy her entire life where she was taught practically everything she would need to know to join their army—including their honorable history.

She knew Norland's schooling was designed to brainwash her, but—with Aabir's help—she thought she had done a good job of keeping herself from coming into the "everything Igrium and the Ignis family does is honorable and right" mindset. Her Silvanian professors said otherwise, however, and told her to be "more open-minded in future projects".

She rolled her eyes at the ironic thought and limped down to the target on her crutches.

It was sometimes even worse in weaponship club. Everyone had acted so nice at first, especially Finnegar and the other leader, Ambra Knightley. They helped Tetra find a few throwing knives in their varied arsenal of weapons so she could still do something without having to use her leg much; and the other members had been more than willing to help her if she needed it. All of them even gave her helpful advice and tips about living at the university and the surrounding parts of Urbselva during her first visit to the training grounds.

Then, at the very end, Lady Felicita had ended up coming to get Tetra for their first questionnaire meeting and called her "Miss Cairn" for all those around them to hear. So, at the next club meeting, Tetra immediately felt the tension rise in the air when she walked in. No longer were Finnegar and Ambra the helpful teachers they had originally been. Instead, they—and everyone else—treated her with either cold indifference or showed their feelings for her family outright. It was basically the same way she had been treated at Norland; only no one physically threatened her, and she got to hear a whole new slew of Silvanian curse words she had never heard before.

She stopped in front of the target and yanked the daggers out as her thoughts swirled through her head like a windstorm. A quiet prison cell would have been better than this.

A small sigh escaped her lips as she turned around and headed back to the beginning of the throwing lane. As she did so, she caught the stares of two other club members watching her from their positions at different throwing lanes. When they both caught her eyes on them, they immediately turned away and continued throwing their own knives and axes as if she wasn't there.

Her lips twisted into a frown. She shook her head and tried to ignore them as she made her way back up the marked lane, but she continued flicking her sight in their direction even as she told herself not to let their dislike bother her. She had joined this club to keep growing the skills that she had learned in training, not to make friends.

One of those who had been staring removed her ax from its target then sent a withering glare in Tetra's direction. Tetra flicked her gaze down to the floor as she slowed to a stop at the lane's marked beginning. Maybe her parents' Fire Raids had destroyed the young woman's childhood home and that's why she was angry. Or maybe she just had a hatred for anything that had to do with the Cairn name like it seemed everyone else in Silvas did.

"Miss Cairn."

Tetra jerked her neck up and locked eyes with Lady Felicita. The other woman's smile faded as her eyebrows drew together. "Are you alright?" She asked in her Pon-Yelish accent.

"Sure." Tetra nodded with a shrug.

Lady Felicita didn't look convinced. "If this is about me comin' ta pick you up, I have some good news. Chief Baene had me order you a holonode and I was plannin' on givin' it ta you today. Tha' way I can just call you instead of coming in here—"

"—No ma'am. It's not that," Tetra cut in.

The crinkles in Lady Felicita's forehead smoothed out in recognition. "Ah, so there is somethin' botherin' you."

Tetra mentally slapped herself. "It's nothing, my lady. Can we—um—go now?"

Her muscles tensed as the weight of a few stares hit her. Chill bumps rose along her arms as she fought the urge to lower her head. Maybe if they thought their actions weren't bothering her then they would stop. It never worked at Norland, but it might in this situation.

Lady Felicita's eyes flicked around them as she nodded. "O' course we can."

Sending her a grateful glance, Tetra walked over to Finnegar to give him the throwing knives. Lady Felicita moved to stay beside her. Finnegar stepped over to them, his intimidating stature towering above them both. Tetra wouldn't meet his cold stare as she handed the knives to him.

"Thanks for letting me use these, Finnegar."

He took them and stepped back. "You're welcome."

She nodded and stepped towards the direction of the exit. Once they were out of earshot, and she could no longer feel any stares, Lady Felicita asked in a low voice, "Is the awkwardness due ta my pickin' you up, or is it because o' your family name?"

"My family name," Tetra replied in an equally low voice.

"I'm sorry, Miss Cairn. I should 'ave just called you by your first name..."

"It's fine." She shrugged the apology away. "You didn't know. I probably would've done the same thing."

"Well, I should 'ave..." Lady Felicita's voice died away. "Never mind."

Tetra sent her a questioning look, but then a sharp pain in her palm jerked her focus away. *Oh no.* She gritted her teeth as the pain of pricking needles spread throughout the rest of her right hand and up her arm at an alarming rate. *Not here!*

This was the third time this week the same pain had happened—only the other two times were in the safety of her dorm. And as the needles multiplied throughout the rest of her arm and into her chest, she realized this was also the quickest it had ever happened.

Her breaths grew labored as she silently begged the pain to leave. Lady Felicita's pace seemed to quicken as Tetra tried to get air into her lungs. Daggers tipped with fire plunged into her arm muscles. She dropped her right crutch with a groan and instantly leaned into the left one as the horribly familiar pains raged through her torso and down into her legs with the same fiery, slicing knives that always came later.

She fell to the floor with another sharp groan.

"Tetra!" Lady Felicita's footsteps pounded the ground as she ran to Tetra's side. "What's wrong?"

Invisible knives stabbed at her jaw when she tried to move it to answer. She didn't know what was wrong, only that this might be a punishment from the gods and her dead parents.

She squeezed her eyes shut as hot tears fell down her face in a steady, uncontrollable stream. Above the ringing in her ears, she barely registered more voices and footsteps around her. The pounding in her head melded with the rapid beat of her heart into one agonizing pulse. Then, as if someone flipped a switch on inside her brain, the fiery knives grew into an inferno that burned in every cell of her body.

Tetra couldn't even open her mouth to scream as her bones broke under the weight of the flames, then melded back together with excruciatingly hot irons. Her muscles spasmed as fiery claws squeezed and tore through them. The same claws stretched and juggled her organs around. It was as if an army of invisible gelatscies rubbed their poisonous tentacles over her skin. Exhaustion seeped into her mind, and she begged for it to take her.

Then, the inferno dimmed. Tetra took in a short breath as all the pain seemed to melt away into soreness. Tentatively, she inhaled a longer, deeper breath, then let it out in a sigh of relief. She could breathe again.

"Oh Deleyon..." Tetra blinked her eyes open at Ambra's loud voice.

"Miss Cairn—er, Tetra..." Lady Felicita sounded as if she was speaking close to her ear.

Tetra lifted her head and turned her gaze in the direction of the woman's voice. She narrowed her eyes at the sight of the group of people—Lady Felicita at their head—standing a few meters away from her, their weapons drawn and aimed in her direction.

"What are you all doing?" There was an awkwardness to her words as she spoke, and she could tell something was wrong with her jaw. It felt...different.

"Someone call the guardsmen!" Tetra cringed at the shout and glanced around. It sounded like the person was shouting right next to her, but there was no one.

"Can you not do that, please?" She asked, then smacked her lips as if she had eaten something with a weird taste. Her tongue felt heavier, and it didn't move the way it usually did when she spoke.

"Tetra, can you hear me?" Lady Felicita's strange accent drew Tetra's attention back towards their wary group.

"Yes..." She nodded her head slowly. "Why wouldn't I be able to hear you?"

A sudden jolt of realization hit her. Lady Felicita was standing far enough away that Tetra shouldn't have been able to hear her as well as she did. It sounded like the chief advisor's assistant was talking right next to her, not meters away. *What on Afreean...?*

And now that she had realized that, she noticed her vision was better too. She widened her eyes as her sight hyper-focused on the shades of brown and gold in the woman's eyes.

What had happened to her? Did the pain somehow strengthen her senses? Was this an apology gift from the gods for putting her through all that pain? "*Oh, we'll put you through a* lot *of pain, but in honor of your parents' deeds we'll give you heightened sight and hearing! Enjoy!*"

She rolled her eyes at the stupid thought. There must be some other reason for all of this. She took in another deep breath and scrunched her nose as a pungent odor hit her nostrils. What was that—?

"Tetra, I need you ta listen ta me," Lady Felicita said. "Mister Finnegar is going to give you somethin' tha' will help you. Please don't move."

Something to help her? She didn't need— A sharp prick stabbed Tetra in the side.

"Hey!" She jerked her neck around and focused on Finnegar. The stray thought that he wasn't as tall as she remembered him to be was pushed aside at the sight of the dart blower he was lowering from his lips. His eyes widened in fear as he met her gaze, and he took a step back.

She narrowed her eyes. Why was he acting so strange? And why had he hit her with a dart?

She kept her gaze locked on him and asked, "How is hitting me with a...a darttt..." her tongue grew even heavier with each word, "—supposed tooo...supposed to helpppp...helpppp...meeee...?"

Her vision blurred as fog thickened in her skull. Her head fell to the ground, and she barely registered the strange rattle that followed before her mind was forcibly plunged into darkness.

Chapter Twenty-Two

THE SHARP SMELL OF metal hit Aabir in the face as he stepped into Norland's library. His eyes roved over the metal shelves full of thin, rectangular boxes that held the separate data for each downloadable book, and he sighed wearily. He tried to keep away from this part of Norland as much as he possibly could—reading was not his favorite activity—so hopefully no one would question why he was there.

He blew out another breath and moved down the main aisle, only stopping at the end of a long bookshelf where he remembered a directory of all the library's books was located. He tapped the small button on the gray surface and blinked his eyes as the blue light of a small, holographic screen appeared in front of him. Aabir tapped a tab at the bottom of the screen and pulled up the directory's keyboard.

With a quick glance around, he typed in all the words he could possibly think of that might be related to the Silvanian (well, not actually Silvanian) Fire Attacks. A few books came up. He scrolled through the short list with his finger, found two books that looked promising, and turned the directory off before heading towards the history section of the library.

He mumbled the titles and authors of the books under his breath as he walked through the aisles of shelves, his eyes skimming the titles on each data-holder. He spotted the label "history" on one of the shelves and turned to head down it. He slowed to a stop in the history aisle and began looking for the two books.

He found the first one and lifted his chardex up to the data-box. Three small dots appeared on the box's surface for only a moment before disappearing one-by-one. A low buzz vibrated Aabir's chardex, and he opened it; the opening window where he could see all the "covers" for his schoolbooks he had blinking into existence between its foldable cover. He tapped the newest one and the simple cover appeared; the title "Unsolved Mysteries of our Day" in bold print, and the author's name in a smaller print at the bottom.

Soft footsteps scuffed along the floor. Aabir lifted his head and looked over in the direction of the sound. He blinked in surprise and did a double take at the new face. The guy looked to be around his age and was wearing the dark gray uniform of a trainee, but Aabir had never seen him before.

The new trainee turned his neck in Aabir's direction and their eyes locked. "Um...can I help you?" He asked in a thick eastern Igrian drawl.

"Who are you?" Aabir scrunched his brow. "I've never seen you here before."

"Oh, that's because I just transferred here from Stelgan Military Academy." The other trainee took a few steps towards him and held out his hand. "I'm Ezen Kevler."

Lieutenant Denir's words from training came back to Aabir's mind. He took Ezen's outstretched hand and shook it. "I'm Aabir Sorrel," he said as they let go. "I think my C.O. said you're going to be in my platoon."

Ezen's blond eyebrows lowered. "Are you in Lieutenant Denir's?"

"Mm-hmm."

"Yeah, I guess I am." He took a step back with a glance down at the chardex in Aabir's hand. "Well, I won't keep you from your reading. I'll see you later, then, Aabir."

"Wait!" Aabir held up his hand to stop him. "I have something I need to ask you."

Ezen turned back around and crossed his arms, a questioning look on his face. "Sure..."

"I just wanted to know how you were able to transfer here." He shrugged. "I've never heard of anyone doing that before, let alone from a city on the other side of the old empire."

Understanding dawned on Ezen's pale features. "Oh, well...I guess my grades were good enough for someone to think I should be given the chance to come." He shrugged and lowered his gaze. "I'm a ward of the empire, so I don't have any parents to keep me back in Stelgan. Plus, I really like the study of bioweaponry and Norland is one of the few military schools that has a class dedicated to it, so that also gave me a reason to transfer."

There's a bioweaponry class? Aabir shook the distracting thought away. "That's cool." He managed to give a small smile. "I have a friend who enjoys that sort of stuff, too. You might want to talk to him about the class."

"Is he in it?"

"No, but he might be able to tell you what you need to know about it." Since Aquilo prided himself on knowing everything. "His name is Aquilo Warlin. Actually, he usually comes here around this time."

"Warlin?" Ezen stroked his dimpled chin in thought. "I think I've heard that name before."

"His patre is a general." Aabir folded his arms. "And his matha was Marin Cairn's sister."

Understanding dawned in Ezen's eyes. "Oh—that's probably it."

"Yeah, so if you see him around here just tell him I sent you."

"Thanks." Ezen nodded and turned back to face the shelf.

Aabir did the same on the opposite side and quickly found the other book he was looking for. He downloaded it, glanced at the cover, then walked out of the aisle. He turned and headed towards one of the small study-cubicles in the library.

A couple trainees, who looked to be first or second years, were whispering to each other with their chardexes spread out before them on the table. Accaly Lavrai—a fifth-year who was in Lieutenant Tarson's platoon—sat at another table, fiddling with a loose strand of her short, blonde hair. She turned the glowing page of her chardex. Aabir did not realize he was staring until she jerked her head up and their eyes locked. She sent him a smile and he immediately turned his face away, heat creeping up his neck.

He hoped he had not just given her the wrong impression. Accaly was pretty, but she was one of the biggest gossips at Norland and the few times he had ever talked to her she ended up going on rambles about anything and everything happening at school, in Rubrum, the news...*everything*. On top of all that, any romantic relationships were prohibited at Norland, and if you were caught the punishment was one of the worst. So, if it was with Accaly, then everyone else would eventually find out about it—including all their commanding officers.

Aabir walked towards an empty table near one of the arched windows and sat at the seat facing it. He glanced over his shoulder in Accaly's direction and saw she had returned to reading her book. Breathing a small sigh of relief, he looked back down at his chardex and opened it, going back to the first book he picked out.

His eyes glanced over the chapter and section titles until he found one that sounded like it might have something to do with the Silvanian Fire Attacks. He flipped through the holographic pages of light and stopped at the beginning of the chapter, titled "*The Year Fourteen-Fifty-One*". Aabir skimmed through the different sections until he found the one on the attacks and began to read:

"The 'Silvanian Fire Attacks', as many Igrians say, were a supposed attack by the aforementioned Silvas Kingdom to take out the main sources of Igrium's authority—besides the Emperor Himself. However, the current leaders of Silvas at the time denied all accusations that said their kingdom was the one to do so. Many believe they were lying, but some have questioned why they would not take full credit for the deaths of Advisor Gregorin Hareley, General Illuvia Unival, and—most importantly—Generals' Aries and Marin Cairn. Why would they not take the responsibility of killing the two people responsible for over a million deaths within Silvas' borders? If they had said it was them,

then surely it would have boosted Alliance morale during one of their toughest times in the war thus far.

"Another question arises after this: why would Silvas also burn down the house of Prince Joash Ignis—the highest Igrian authority to stand against Emperor Ignis' war efforts and the Cairns' 'Fire Raids', then the one later executed for treason? There are even rumors of the late prince's wife and daughters fleeing to one of the Alliance nations after his execution. So, if those rumors are actually true, then why would Silvas try to kill Prince Joash and his family with the fire in the first place?

"'Well,' you might be thinking, 'then if it was not them, could it have been Emperor Ignis?' But that also does not make sense. He would have never tried to kill five of his top generals. High General Bravren Paristan, Generals Aries and Marin Cairn, General Illuvia Unival, and General Rashka Fell were, or still are, completely loyal to the Imperial Ignis Family and would give no reason for him to even try harming them. It might be possible he tried setting Joash' house ablaze, but most reports say the two brothers were together when the house burned down—only the prince's two daughters were reportedly at home. Yet if he was not the one to do it, then who would have the resources, and the motive, to coordinate such an organized attack?

"Sources say that right as all seven houses or fortress quarters went up in flames, Emperor Ignis and Prince Joash were having one of their usual arguments. One of the sources said she overheard His Imperial Majesty accuse the prince of treason—and only a few days later the imperial report that he was executed for doing so was released.

"There were also reports of Advisors Gregorin Harolyn and Aquila Tralp both being accused of traitorous actions by receiving messages from a supposed secret organization. The former received messages from the secret group, but he also had his responses to them—a firm 'no'—and was found innocent; while the latter was found guilty of conspiring with them and immediately executed.

"It is also speculated that the other four families had been receiving death threats in many different forms and ways, but the culprit (or culprits) was never found and the threats soon stopped coming almost as quickly as they had come. Then their houses were set on fire.

"So, was it truly Silvas? Was it Emperor Ignis? Or was it another group with a vendetta against the empire? Sadly, no other mentions of this group have been found, and the events are still a mystery to this day."

Aabir put down the chardex and leaned back in his chair. Chill bumps rose along his arms as he tried to process all the information. So according to Rasiela (and this book), Silvas had not been the one to initiate the attacks, and Emperor Ignis would have no logical reason to do it, either…

His gaze drifted to the everpine trees outside the window. It would be easy for any secret group of people to hide in the shadows their great boughs cast, and he thought he saw movement near one of their thick trunks. Cold went down his spine, but he pushed the fearful thought to the side. It was probably a scurrus, not some pyromaniac.

If the book was believable, then whoever set the fires had not done anything else since. So why would they be hiding in some trees around Norland? They obviously had bigger plans than hurting a school of trainees. Yet even with that thought, his fear brought up the words one of the Silvanian soldiers back in Trivsau said in reply to Aabir's pleading, *"we're not stupid enough to let three platoons of perfectly-trained, future soldiers go free."* So, maybe killing them all was not such a bad idea in the grand scheme of things.

He pressed his hand against his forehead with a quiet sigh. Well, *that* thought did nothing to stop the small worry niggling at the back of his mind, nor the questions it brought up. What if there was some secret group of people just waiting to attack? And if they attacked both those who were loyal to Igrium and those who were traitors to the empire, then which side of the war were they fighting on? Were they even fighting on a side at all?

Another shiver went down Aabir's spine. He shook his head at himself and turned his holonode on. He needed to focus. His family's endangerment was the real issue here, not some possible group of secret killers.

Sneaking a glance around to make sure no one was watching, he went to Rasiela's "cousin Ori" message and tapped the microphone icon to speak the passage, but then he remembered where he was and stopped himself. He glanced down at the long paragraphs with a frown. Did he really have to type all of that out? Unless…

With another furtive glance around, he swiped out of the message app to his holonode's camera, took a picture of the dark words highlighted by the glowing pages, then sent that to Rasiela. Satisfied, he exited out of that book and tapped on the next one, titled "*The Beginning of the Ignis War*". He went to the table of contents and scanned them all until he found one that sounded helpful. He flipped through the pages to that chapter then skimmed through the words until his sight landed on the one he wanted.

"The deaths of Generals Illuvia Univel, Aries Cairn, and Marin Cairn led to Igrium losing two major battles over the Republic of Verlim—and the imminent defeat in taking over it. The Calorian nation joined the Alliance soon after…"

Aabir continued reading for a few more sentences but found nothing else relating to the housefires. He shut the chardex with a sigh and put his head in his hands. What a waste of time. He lifted his head and turned his holonode on. At least he had the Net for research.

"What are *you* doing here?"

Aabir's heart jumped at the sudden voice, and he jerked his head up as Aquilo sat in the seat next to his. His friend's brow was creased in confusion as he stared at Aabir with narrowed eyes.

"Oh...um—just reading." He shrugged and tried to keep his countenance nonchalant as he turned his holonode off.

"You?" Aquilo raised an eyebrow. "Reading? Voluntarily?"

"Mm-hmm." Aabir nodded slowly and tapped the cover of his chardex with his fingers.

His friend's eyes narrowed even more. "Then...what book has the honor of bringing your willing presence here?"

Aabir shrugged again as his heart began to beat a worried rhythm. "Just a couple history books." He opened his chardex and gestured towards the two small covers on the screen. "And I wasn't really reading them. Just skimming."

"Uh-huh. And why would you be skimming those two books in particular?"

He was silent for a moment as he tried to think up an answer. "Homework."

"OK..." Aquilo did not look convinced, but the confusion faded from his features.

Wanting to change the subject before he could ask any more probing questions, Aabir said, "I met the new guy joining our platoon."

"You did?" Aquilo straightened in his seat.

"His name is Ezen Kevler. He said he was joining the bioweapons class, and I told him if he had any questions to come ask you. I hope that was OK..."

"Yeah, sure." Aquilo cupped his chin in his hand, a faraway look in his eyes. "I was going to take that class this year, but it happens at the same time as tactics, and I can't afford to skip that."

"I didn't even know we had a bioweapons class..."

Aquilo nodded. "It only has about four people in it."

"Oh."

"Did you find out anything else?"

"He said he transferred here because of his grades..." Aabir lifted his hand and rubbed the back of his neck. "And I think he said he was a ward of the empire."

The corners of Aquilo's lips tilted downwards into a frown. "Well..." His words died off as his eyes moved to focus on something behind where Aabir was seated.

"What?" Aabir turned to look behind his shoulder and understanding dawned on him as he spotted Ezen Kevler's skinny form coming towards their table. "Oh, yeah. That's him."

Ezen slowed to a stop near them with a nod. "Hey."

"Hey, Ezen." Aabir nodded back and gestured to Aquilo. "This is who I was telling you about. Aquilo, this is Ezen. Ezen—Aquilo."

"Hello." Aquilo nodded towards the new trainee, "Aabir told me you were joining the bioweaponry class."

"Yeah." Ezen nodded again. "I actually wanted to ask you a few questions about it, if you're not busy."

"Of course." Aquilo gestured towards the seat next to Aabir's.

Aabir watched as Ezen moved around his chair to sit down, then put the chardex he was holding on the table and folded his arms atop it. His brown eyes flicked over in Aabir's direction before focusing on Aquilo.

"Now I'm not in the class," Aquilo continued, "but I wanted to join this year."

"Really?" Ezen asked, "Is there somethin' wrong with the class?"

"No, I just needed to take tactics and they both happen at the same time."

"Ah." Ezen's gaze lowered to his chardex. "So, what do you know about it?"

All the details Aquilo knew about the class gave Aabir's brain the perfect backdrop to once again whirl with all the worries and questions he had been able to suppress until that moment.

Was Ereliev OK? She and Zeke should be coming back home around this time. Would they come home to a ransacked house?

Was Patre making enough money? The job market was against Silvanians at the moment and if his garage went under, Aabir doubted any of them would be able to get jobs. He certainly could not right now. When he—no, *if* he—joined the army after graduation, then he would make money from that. However, he really wanted to avoid enlisting—and no amount of accusations for being a coward could stop that feeling. He could not fight for the empire that was destroying his family's private life, threatening his siblings' lives, arresting people for "treason", and then putting those same people in the Constantia Tourney to be murdered on live holovision in the most dishonorable ways.

He flicked his gaze between Aquilo and Ezen, a hard knot growing in his stomach. He did not want to leave his friends at Norland, but he also did not have the luxury of living freely in Igrium like they did. If this new Constantia rule came out, then him being the "golden trainee" would not help him out of that fate if someone were to accuse him of being an Alliance supporter, or if they found out he was helping a Silvanian spy. It would probably just boost his chances of getting placed into the Tourney.

Aabir shook his head as worry tightened his stomach. Why did he do this to himself? Worrying never helped him before, so why did his mind always go back to it? He held in a sigh and turned his focus back to the conversation in front of him so that the questions and worries had to fade into the back corners of his mind.

"...research on the Feran plague back at Stelgan." Ezen was saying, "I was tryin' to figure out how they made a lab-grown disease with the characteristics of a naturally-born one."

"I've wondered that, too," Aquilo replied, his eyes bright. "But I never researched it. Never had time."

A smile grew on Ezen's face. "Well, I can send some of what I've collected to you if you want. But like I said, I'm not done yet so it's not complete."

"Sure." Aquilo nodded eagerly.

Despite the dark thoughts he had just been having, Aabir smirked at the exchange. "You two are weird." They both turned to look at him as he spoke, "I've never seen anyone get that excited about diseases."

"It's not just any disease, Aabir." Aquilo gave him a pointed look. "It's the Feran plague. *The* plague that started this whole war in the first place."

Aabir raised his brow. "I thought Emperor Ignis started the war."

"Well, he did, but it was in defense of our empire!" Aquilo rolled his eyes. "You know that."

He did know. He just enjoyed pushing Aquilo's "buttons" from time to time. It was fairly easy to do, but Tycho was the master at it.

"Do you not like science, Aabir?" Ezen asked.

Aabir met his questioning look. "Nope. Never have."

"Wow." The new trainee's lips twisted thoughtfully. "But you like history?"

"Um, no..." He tilted his head in confusion.

"Oh, I just thought because you were in the 'history' section that you did."

Aabir's heart skipped a fearful beat as he looked down at his chardex. "Uh—that was for homework." He smiled to hide any fear showing on his face. "I'm not a fan of history."

He mentally chided himself for the blunder. If he was going to be working with Rasiela, he would need to get better at thinking on his feet.

And speaking of spy work...

"Anyway—" he stood abruptly, grabbing his chardex in the process, "—I'll leave you both to your disease conversation. See you later." He locked eyes with Ezen and sent him a nod. "I hope you enjoy Norland, Ezen."

"Thanks." The new trainee said the same time as Aquilo replied, "See ya."

Aabir turned and headed towards the library's doors. His holonode buzzed and he lifted his wrist to see it. The holographic screen automatically appeared to show a message notification from Rasiela. It read, "*Thank you. I hope to see more from you soon.*"

With a flick of his wrist, the screen disappeared. The worries in the dark corners of his head slithered back to the forefront and wrapped around the memory of Rasiela's message. He gritted his teeth at the tension tightening around his insides, but it helped pound this thought into his head even more so: the faster he found more information, the faster he and his family could leave.

He pulled one of the library doors open and exited into the dim hallway. His rushed footsteps echoed along the stone walls as he headed back in the direction of his dorm. Even if it took up all the free time he had this week, he would search online for any information he needed. He would sacrifice his sleep, too, if he found nothing during that free time.

A sliver of Aabir's familiar shame joined the churning of his thoughts. His family would not suffer any longer because of his mistakes. Deleyon willing, he would make it up to them. He would finally protect them the way he had always tried to—and his parents would finally have the son they could be proud of instead of the cowardly excuse for one they still had now.

With those thoughts spurring him on, he practically ran up the stairs leading to the boys' dorms. He had more research to do.

Chapter Twenty-Three

Beeping jolted Tetra out of the calm darkness encompassing her mind. She opened her eyes with a small gasp and jolted upward. Something, however, stopped her. Straps were clamped around her wrists, but she had to wait a few seconds for the fog in her mind to dissipate before that fact truly registered. Her heart leapt into her throat as it did, and she jerked her neck up.

Sterile white walls surrounded her, drawing her eyes to one of the few spots of color: the tight, brown leather straps around her wrists and ankles. The beeping escalated with her heartbeat. A shiver went through her as the cold of the metal table seeped through her thin clothes, raising chill bumps along her exposed arms. She now wore a pair of white pants and a white t-shirt instead of the pants and long-sleeved shirt she had worn in weaponship club. Her boot was gone, too.

She lowered her head back down, but was forced to turn her head to the side as the fluorescent lights on the ceiling blinded her. She blinked her eyes until the afterimage from them disappeared, and that's when she noticed the dark wall to her left. Another shiver went through her as she locked eyes with her pale reflection in the dark glass. Was there someone behind it watching her?

The incessant beeping of the heart rate monitor spiked again as she stared at her wide-eyed reflection, and she finally moved her gaze off the dark glass onto its holographic interface projecting from the wall near her head. Why was it so loud...?

Her annoyance immediately disappeared as her gaze landed on the blue-armored guardsman standing in the corner. She turned her neck and swept her gaze around the rest of the room. Three more guardsmen stood at each of the corners, while another stood next to the room's single door.

"Um..." she laid her head back down to clear her throat then raised it again. "Hello?" She tried to meet any of their gazes, but they stood at attention, unmoved. "Why—why am I here?"

No answer.

She inhaled a shaky breath and lowered her head back down onto the hard metal surface. Their faces didn't have the blank looks Emperor Ignis' personal guards had, but their presence—and her present circumstance of being strapped to a table—sent her imagination reeling with frightening images of brainwashing and being turned into a personal guard.

"Look—" Tetra lifted her head again and set her frightened gaze on one of the guards to try and break his concentration, "—I know you all aren't like the emperor's brainwashed guards, so could someone please tell me why I'm here?"

Nothing. She kept her gaze on the one guard until her neck muscles began to cramp from holding her head up for so long, and she lay it back down with a quiet sigh through her nose. Maybe these guards were trained to keep all emotions hidden like Igrium's honorguard; and if that was so, then questions would get her nowhere.

Her eyes strayed again to the dark wall of glass, and she met her scarred reflection's fearful gaze. A new slew of questions rose inside her as she stared, all of them coming as quickly as the anxious beeping of the heart rate monitor.

What happened after Finnegar shot her with the blow dart? She remembered everything from before—Lady Felicita coming to take her to their questioning session, the excruciating pains, her heightened senses, and the strange, frightened way everyone was acting— but it all seemed more like a disjointed dream than reality.

She turned her face away from the mirror-glass and looked up at the ceiling tiles. What had happened that made everyone seem so...*scared* of her? Where had her heightened senses gone? And how did that even happen in the first place?

Tetra squeezed her eyes shut and curled her hands into fists. Was this more punishment from the gods? What else would she have to endure before they were finally appeased?

The door opened and Tetra jerked her head up in its direction, the heart rate monitor capturing her pounding heart. A woman wearing a lab coat as white as the walls stepped into the room and shut the door with her free hand; a red chardex clutched in the other. Tetra's gaze stayed locked on the doctor as she slowed to a stop next to her head.

"Hello, Miss Cairn." The woman's dark purple gaze shone behind matching purple glasses as their eyes locked. "I am Doctor Esthra Prin, Head of Biological Studies here in Silvas." She paused and looked away to lower the monitor's volume, then turned her sharp gaze back on Tetra. "How are you feeling?"

Tetra licked her lips as she tried to come up with a response. "I...I've been better."

Dr. Prin pressed her thick lips into a line and opened the small chardex in her hands. Its faint blue light tinged her rounded features as she lifted it close to her face and pulled a stylus from her short ponytail of black hair.

"Are you hurting anywhere?" She asked.

"No ma'am..."

"Hmm. So, you're feeling no side-effects from your...*fall*?"

The way she said the last word sent a chill down Tetra's spine. That and the doctor's calculated expression told her something else really had happened besides her fall. She made sure her expression was neutral before she nodded.

"And what about mentally?" The Silvanian biologist continued as if this was a normal set of questions.

Mentally? The fear-mongering thoughts inside her head came back to the forefront as if the question was personally for them—and in a way, it was.

"What do you mean?" Tetra asked.

She wasn't falling for any mind games. Was this Chief Baene's doing? Did he think she was hiding something because her first session with Lady Felicita hadn't brought up any missing memories? Maybe he thought she had lied to Lady Felicita about not finding anything. The image of his impressive dagger collection came to mind, and another shiver went through her.

Dr. Prin twisted her lips to the side thoughtfully. But after a moment, she blinked and her cool, professional demeanor returned.

"Do your thoughts feel fuzzy?" She tapped her stylus against the chardex. "Are you having any thoughts that...might not have come up before your fall?"

"My thoughts were a little fuzzy when I woke up," Tetra replied haltingly, "but other than that they're normal."

The biologist nodded once and lifted her head in the dark wall's direction. Tetra's anxiety grew as she snuck a glance towards the one-way glass out of the corner of her eye. There really was someone watching them, wasn't there? A sigh drew her gaze back to Dr. Prin, and that was when she noticed the single auric-bud inside one of the woman's ears.

"Alright, Miss Cairn—" She turned her piercing gaze back in Tetra's direction, "—I'm not going to dance around this question any longer: do you know what happened after you fell in the gym?"

Tetra opened her mouth to reply that "yes, she did", but something in the woman's gaze stopped her from doing so.

"Well...I remember it was kind of weird..." she said instead.

"What do you mean by 'weird'?"

"I...I could see better..." She licked her lips as embarrassed heat flushed her face, "and hear better, too." Oh *straudwin*, it sounded worse spoken aloud. "I—I remember everyone acting very strange...and then I was shot with a blow dart and fell asleep."

"And that's all?"

"Yes ma'am.

Dread churned her stomach. What had happened?

Dr. Prin sighed through her nose and shut her chardex with a snap that brought Tetra's heart to pounding erratically. After setting it down at the end of the table, she moved her wrist until her holonode's small, semi-translucent screen floated between their faces and pulled up a video on it.

"This is footage of your fall that the gym's security cameras picked up," she said as she flipped the projection one-hundred and eighty degrees so Tetra could see it better. "Seeing as how you are not lying about your memory, I'm going to show you what everyone else saw."

Tetra gulped but nodded slowly as the churning in her stomach grew. At least she was getting answers...

Dr. Prin reached around, tapped the center of the screen, and the video began to play.

Tetra watched as she and Lady Felicita walked away from Finnegar and the others, then out of the camera's line of sight. The video's angle changed as a different camera showed their continued walk. A few moments went by, and she saw herself stiffening at the moment when, she assumed, the familiar pains came. Her filmed self slowed to a stop as one of her crutches fell with a clatter, and then she fell right after it.

Lady Felicita's voice came from the holonode as she called Tetra's name and ran over to her shaking, collapsed form. More voices and pounding footsteps soon joined hers as everyone in the weaponship club moved in a circle around her. Tetra noticed Miss Ambra calling someone on her holonode, and barely heard her asking for an ambulance amidst the other sounds.

The snap of a bone sounded from the holonode. Tetra's eyes widened, and she gritted her teeth in horrified silence as more cracking noises, and the screams of those around her, came from the small speaker to create the backdrop for the horrible sight of her spasming body flopping on the floor. She lifted her brow and barely leaned her head forward as she watched her flailing limbs *grow*. Blood pounded in her ears as, in the footage, the rest of her body impossibly grew larger with her limbs.

People scrambled back with more screams as her mouth grew longer. Her fingers on each hand melded together as her feet grew—shredding through her boot and cast—and her toes separated. Two auburn, feathery limbs sprouted out of her back. Her pale skin gave way for pale fur.

It took less than a minute for Tetra's crumpled form to be replaced with a huge, sprawled-out peryton's. Darker splotches discolored the peryton's fur and feathers where her birthmarks were, and all its scars stood out where hers did. Its back talon even looked mangled and was missing most of its fur and feathers. She glanced down at the toe of her cast, but immediately lifted her gaze back to the video as the peryton lifted its long head to the sound of Lady Felicita's voice.

The peryton's long ears swiveled in the young woman's direction and it opened its mouth in a rumbling growl. Someone shouted "Call the guardsmen!" and the peryton pinned its ears back as it tilted its head upwards. Another strange growl came from its throat.

Uneasy realization dawned on Tetra as her memories played out in her head along with the video's footage.

Lady Felicita asked if the peryton— if *she*...—could hear them. The peryton nodded with another growl. It—no, *she*—pricked her ears and stared at the group of frightened, weapon-brandishing young adults for a few seconds. In the corner of the camera's footage, Tetra could see Finnegar loading, then aiming, a blow dart gun at her winged backside.

Again, Lady Felicita's voice rang through the speaker right before Finnegar fired the dart into Tetra's back. Her head swiveled around on her long, peryton neck in his direction. She growled in the video, then her head wobbled and fell back down with a clatter as the short, white antlers sprouting from the top of it hit the ground.

The horrible sounds of snapping bones, popping joints, and tearing muscles came through the speaker again as the peryton diminished until it completely disappeared for Tetra's body; the shreds of what had been her clothes covering most of it. She silently thanked any gods who were listening for that small blessing in this otherwise horrifying situation.

Dr. Prin turned the holonode off with a flick of her wrist and met her wide-eyed gaze. "That is what happened after your fall, Miss Cairn," she gestured to the small room around them, "which is why you are here."

Tetra flicked her gaze away from the biologist to stare at the ceiling. Her anxiety gleefully played the horrible images repeatedly as the ugly truth slowly came to her.

She had just watched herself turn into one of Afreean's most dangerous predators as if she was one of the mythical shifter beings in a fantastical movie or fairytale where events like this were common. Invisible legions of bugs crawled along her skin at the thought, and another shiver went through her muscles.

"So that...that was real?"

She met Dr. Prin's eyes again and saw the answer displayed in their firm sympathy before the woman even opened her mouth to reply, "It was."

Tetra swallowed back the bile rising in her throat. "But...how?"

"That's what I was hoping you could tell me."

"I don't know." She squeezed her eyes shut and inhaled slowly, silently begging her stomach not to release its contents. "I didn't—I didn't even realize that was happening when it did."

So, this was the final punishment from the gods, huh? They didn't think to stop with the malscar and the horrible pains—oh no, they just had to go and make her turn into one of Malackin's creatures at the invisible fire's beckoning.

Dr. Prin sighed and picked up her chardex again. Tetra noticed her gaze flicking over to the one-way glass before she straightened and looked back down at her.

"Well. I'll be seeing you soon, Miss Cairn." She nodded once. "Good dein."

With that, she walked out of the room and shut the door behind her.

Tetra scrunched her brow as silence took over the room once again, confusion joining the many thoughts circling in her head. She turned her neck to stare at the one-way glass. Were they just going to leave her in here? Or did they have something else in mind?

Anxiety tightened around her chest at the frightening conclusions her imagination began to come up with, so she closed her eyes to try and turn her focus to her breathing. Breathe in...breathe out. Inhale...and exhale. Inhale—

The door barely squeaked, and her eyes popped open. She lifted her neck to see who it was, and the cords of fear tightened their hold on her as she met Chief Baene's unreadable gaze. He shut the door and strode over to her, stopping in the same spot Dr. Prin had. Tetra turned her head slightly to see his face.

A strange, almost sympathetic look softened his features for a fraction of a second before being replaced by aloofness. It was so quick she wondered if she had only imagined it.

"Miss Cairn," he said simply.

"Ch—Chief Baene, sir." She barely nodded her head towards him.

Oh, how she wished she could read through his hard expression! But it was like trying to discern what Emperor Ignis might be thinking through his stone-like facade.

"I can see the video came as a surprise to you," he added.

She nodded slowly. "Yes sir."

"Which leads me to wonder if that's what Emperor Ignis was trying to hide."

"Sir?"

"In your memories, Miss Cairn." Chief Baene raised his brow, just as understanding dawned on Tetra.

"Oh..."

Could it really be true? Could Emperor Ignis know something about this?

"So how did it happen?" He asked.

Holding back a sigh, she replied, "I don't know, sir."

"Forgive me, I didn't mean it in the context of what Dr. Prin already asked. What I want to know is: what happened before the event that led up to it?" He tilted his head slightly. "Something was obviously not right since you fell, so would you care to explain?"

"Oh. Um...I, uh—I was having these horrible...pains." She gritted her teeth. Why was this so hard to say? "They've always felt like...um—like fiery knives were stabbing me...everywhere. And I...well, I've been having them for a while."

Chief Baene blinked. "All the time?"

"No, sir. Just every once in a while the past month, but they grew worse this past week."

"I see."

He scratched the underside of his chin, his eyes growing distant with thought. "And do you know if it's possible if this peryton-shifting business could have happened when that pain hit before?"

Tetra scrunched her brow as she recalled the other times it had happened since her last night in Xich. "Not that I know of..." she replied slowly, "It—it never ended as quickly as it did this—this last time."

Chief Baene was silent, still with that thoughtful look on his face. "Did you ever mention them to anyone?"

"Only a medbot."

"Good." He nodded again, a new light entering his gaze. "Then that means the emperor most likely doesn't know about this."

Tetra stared at him in confusion. "But, you just said this...*event* might've been the thing he took from my memories."

"He might have been hiding the possibility of it happening, or the way you are able to do it. Him using the C.B.M. on you doesn't mean he knew *when* this would happen; only that he might have tried hiding *how* it did."

Tetra processed his words in silence. As she did so, she found they brought a small bit of relief. Though she couldn't answer why the thought of Emperor Ignis not knowing of this...*ability* made her feel better, it did help to ease the churning in her stomach. Just a little.

Still, the chief advisor's explanation brought another worry. "Will I...uh—can I still try to get my memories back?" She asked.

"Yes." Chief Baene sent her a reassuring look. "If this is what the emperor was hiding, then I want to know how you are able to do it—and I have the rest of the *Buleutcil*'s approval in doing so. The woman you just met—Dr. Prin—has also been given approval to see if she can find out the same."

Her heart began to race again. "What—" her voice hitched on the single word, and she had to clear her throat before adding, "—what does that mean?"

"You need not worry, Miss Cairn." He held up his hands as if trying to calm a wild animal—and as the analogy went through her head, Tetra had a sinking feeling it might be closer to the truth than she wanted it to be. "We're not about to do anything that requires human experimentation. Deleyon would not allow it, nor would I. It will only consist of simple tests as you shift into a peryton again."

Even though the words were supposed to be comforting, the leather straps around Tetra's wrists seemed to grow tighter.

"Why?" Her voice sounded pitiful and small even to her own ears.

Hot tears pricked her eyes, but she tried to blink them away. She didn't want to turn into a peryton again. She didn't want to be able to turn into a monster. Her family name already ostracized her here, but this...this was so much worse.

Chief Baene sighed, and the sound drew her gaze back up to his. A jolt of surprise went through her as she noticed a sincerity that she hadn't seen before.

"Because," he replied, "the Buleutcil wants to see if they can duplicate this ability of yours. They deem you a danger to the public and have decided the best course of action would be to keep you where you won't hurt anyone."

The tears blurred Tetra's vision, and this time she couldn't stop a couple from escaping. Heat rose into her face as she tried to turn her head so he wouldn't be able to see them.

"I'm sorry, Miss Cairn." Chief Baene turned his head away, "This was not what I had in mind when I had you brought here. However, I will continue to talk with my fellow Buleutcil members to figure out a way to make this easier for you. I promise."

Something in his words struck a chord inside Tetra, and, despite the tears still flowing down her face, she turned her head to look up at him sharply. "On your honor?"

A tiny part of her regretted the words, but Emperor Ignis had broken his promises towards her far too many times and never once promised them on his honor. For a moment, she wondered if honor would even have the same weight in Silvas as it did in Igrium, but Chief Baene locked eyes with her and gave her a solemn nod.

"I promise on my honor that I will make sure the Buleutcil does nothing to harm you, that Lady Felicita will continue working with you to try and gauge those lost memories, and that no one will do anything to you just because your family name is Cairn."

His equally-sharp eyes did not leave hers as he spoke, and she finally had to break the contact with a blink. "Thank you."

She didn't know what sort of power the chief advisor had, so she could only hope he had enough to be able to keep his promise.

"Now then, Miss Cairn," he lowered his arms to his sides and sent her a sharp nod, "let me see what I can do about moving you into a better room."

Lady Felicita stood from the couch as Baene entered his office, the small chandelier casting warm light into the room as the shadows of night took over the view outside his window. He met her hope-filled eyes and could not help the small smile that escaped his lips at the sight.

"She is safe, Felicita." His guards closed the doors behind him with a heavy ***thunk*** as he strode towards her. "I had Lord Jachen move her to one of the empty living quarters a few floors above so no one, except a few guardsmen, know where she is."

Felicita smiled with a small sigh. "Thank you, Baene. How...secret is this matter?"

"The Buleutcil has deemed it one of national security and have paid off all those who witnessed it to secrecy." He scratched the side of his jaw. "Thank Deleyon I didn't have to press them about it. The last thing we need is another war on our hands."

"You don't think—"

"—I wouldn't put it past them." He shrugged. "At least it's one less problem we have to deal with."

Felicita nodded; her nose was scrunched in deep thought.

With a quiet sigh, Baene went over to his desk and stepped past Duse Gravlin—head of his personal guards, and one of the few people he could fully trust—who he sent a sharp nod towards. Felicita's soft footsteps followed him. He sat down, thoughts racing like a swarm of buzzgnats through his mind, and put his head in his hands. Felicita stopped and seated herself on one of the chairs in front of his desk.

"Wha' is wrong?" She asked.

"I'm only thinking." He waved her comment away with a sigh and lifted his head to meet her gaze. "How are *you* feeling?"

The same hope he had seen shining on her face the past week came back again with a faint smile. "Though I probably should not be, I'm glad it finally happened. It means my suspicions were true, and tha' she...she's..." Her voice hitched on the last word as she blinked rapidly.

Baene sent her another small smile. "Yes. It is good news." The Buleutcil meeting from earlier that day came back to the forefront of his thoughts, and his smile faded. "However, I cannot see the path being easy for her."

"Wha' did they say?" Felicita's tone rose as it always did when she was worried.

"They...were not happy." It was an understatement, he knew, as the outbursts or deathly-calm of every Buleutcil-member came to his mind, but he did not want Felicita to worry any more than she already was. "I was able to talk some sense into them, however, and kept them from any...*harmful* ideas."

A frown marred Felicita's features. "They were not thinkin' about anythin' inhumane, were they?"

Lord Wenyan and Army General Taoghn had both mentioned human experimentation in more subtle terms, but Baene had shot their suggestions down. Thank Deleyon, Lord Jachen, Dr. Prin, and a few other members had all agreed with him—or he and Felicita might be having a different conversation.

"A couple did," he replied slowly, "but I told them the truth of their words, and Lord Jachen and a few others agreed with me."

"Thank You, Deleyon," Felicita mumbled. Anger sharpened her features as she added, "I can't believe tha' any o' them would even think ta suggest such a thing!"

"Well, they did—but it's over now." He cupped his chin between his fingers, his gaze moving to the wall behind her as he thought. "And we have more important things to discuss."

Felicita managed to perfect her already near perfect posture. "O' course." She blinked. The anger sparking in her almond-shaped eyes abated; although Baene could tell by her clenched jaw she was only hiding it for his benefit.

He pushed the thoughts that sprang forth from that issue to the side and folded his hands atop his desk. "I need you and Tetra to go through the questions every day."

She blinked. "Every day?" Her head tilted to the side, mouth curving downward. "Bu' if we did tha' we would get through all o' them in less than a week."

"Then make up your own," he replied. "We need her to get those memories back as quickly as possible—and I know you will be able to come up with questions that will work much better than the list you already have."

"Yeah, tha' is true..." She peered at him strangely. "But why the sudden rush? You're beginnin' ta sound like me."

"I want to keep as little secrets as I must," his frown deepened and he pressed his fingers against his temples, "and the quicker those memories resurface and the truth comes out, the easier it will be for all of us."

Guilt reddened Felicita's face as he spoke, and his compassion for her situation grew. However, he forced himself not to dwell on it for the sake of their situation's reality. Straightening, he looked her square in the eyes and began, "Felicita..."

"I know, I know." She turned her gaze from his and played with the gold ring on her finger. "I still regret mine and Matha's decision, but it's too late now ta change it. I'll just 'ave ta deal with the consequences when they come."

Baene sighed. "It will be difficult, but I believe if we go on and tell Lord Jachen—"

"—What?" Felicita jerked her head up and stared at him as if he was crazy. "Now?"

"Yes, now." He put his hands up as if to calm her down. "The longer we wait, the worse it will be. If we go on and tell Lord Jachen, we can get his opinions on the matter. We already need to tell Lord Othnel for him to help us, and it will be better to have Lord Jachen's authority backing us up when we do so."

Felicita's surprise dimmed to resignation with the slump of her shoulders. "You're right."

"Lord Jachen already knows something is amiss." The strange looks Silvas' current steward had sent Baene during the meeting proved so. "It will be best this way."

"Alright."

Despite her words, he could see the news was not *alright* with her, but they both knew this day would eventually come. Baene, however, never thought it would come about like this.

"Then it's settled," he said. "I will set up a meeting with him, and we will both tell him everything."

"Me?" Surprise, and a little bit of fear, flashed across Felicita's features. "You want *me* ta come, too?"

Baene stopped himself before he rolled his eyes. "Of course you're coming!" His tone annoyed, "This is—partly—about you anyway, so why would I not have you come?"

She shrugged. "I just...I'm only your assistant, Baene. And these are very important matters—"

"—That involve you."

"Well, yes." Her lips twisted into a frown, and Baene could easily see the fear darkening her eyes. "But I—well, wha' if I say somethin' wrong? How am I supposed ta win anyone's approval when the Buleutcil finds out? I—I don't think I could live with tha' type o' scrutiny for the rest o' my life."

"Felicita." He leaned forward, forcing her gaze to stay locked with his. "You are more than prepared to face this. You knew it would come, and I know you are able to withstand whatever backlash the Buleutcil, the nobility, or anyone else throws at you."

"But—"

"—No." He shook his head. "I will have none of that. Don't question me on this, Felicita. I have been around many leaders throughout my life, and I know a good one when I see one." A small smile broke through his rigid facade as he shrugged. "Especially when you've had one of the best mentors in Silvas."

Felicita's lips lifted into a smile that she immediately pressed into a thin line. "And I'm supposed to trust *your* judgment on this matter?" She raised a brow.

"Yes," his smile widened, "because I'm right when it comes to these things."

"Mm-hmm..." She rolled her eyes, but amusement shone in them.

They both sat in the light moment until Baene let his smile fade and clasped his hands atop his desk again. "But in all seriousness, Felicita, you know I mean every word I said, and I trust that you will be able to handle everything that may or may not come from this situation."

"Thank you, Baene."

Another true, albeit small, smile flitted across Felicita's face—one that reminded him of her patre. A pang of old grief went through him, but he kept himself from dwelling on it by sending a sharp nod towards her.

"So, you understand what needs to be done?" He asked before clearing his throat.

"Yes." She nodded, her long braids bobbing around her shoulders at the movement. "Do I have the Buleutcil's permission ta ask her those questions tomorrow?"

A small bit of pride sparked in Baene's chest. "It has already been taken care of. However, you will have to meet in her new quarters from now on instead of your office."

"Tha' is fine. When do you suppose we will have our meetin' with Lord Jachen?"

"In the next couple days."

Fear flashed across her face again, but it disappeared as she nodded towards him. "Then I will prepare myself for it."

"You will do well," Baene replied. "I have no doubt about that."

"I hope so." She sighed, then abruptly stood from her chair. "I must be goin' now, Baene, but I will see you tomorrow."

"Of course." He also stood. "And remember to tell your matha and Matias about dinner tomorrow night."

Felicita dipped her chin respectfully towards him. "O' course. We wouldn't miss it for the world."

"Thank you."

With that, she turned around and exited his office with quick steps. Only when the doors closed did Baene finally let out a deep sigh.

"Chief?" Duse finally asked in the silence, "Are you alright?"

"I will be, Duse." Baene looked over and met the man's eyes. "Do you ever wish you could go back in time and change it?"

Duse shrugged his armored shoulders. "Sometimes." He raised a questioning brow. "Is this about you or Lady Felicita?"

"Both."

Baene stepped around his desk and moved towards his throwing knife collection. Memories resurfaced as his eyes glanced over the weapons. A mix of pride and guilt flashed through him as he studied the pieces that represented his life. There was the small, crude knife he had made under his father's approving gaze; a long, green-tinged dagger of an unknown metal he received as a parting gift; and a knife with a thick, bejeweled hilt too heavy to throw successfully.

His gaze finally stopped on a small throwing knife with a dark gray, gritanium blade and a hilt made from the carved antler of a peryton. Weight pressed upon his shoulders as he picked up the old blade, the small feeling of sadness from before coming back.

"What are you wishing to change?" Duse asked.

He looked up and met his friend's eyes. "The war."

Duse frowned. "I meant about the past."

"Exactly."

"I...don't understand."

"One day you will, Duse." Baene looked back down at the knife. "One day the whole world will finally know."

And then, hopefully, he could be free of these burdens he carried.

As his thoughts continued down that road, the memory of a woman's tear-streaked face popped into his head, along with the promise he had given her and all of Silvas.

"I have no doubt that you will be able to do this, Baene." Orinna's hands shook as she signed the words, a soft smile on her face; yet it did nothing to mask the pain in her violet eyes.

Baene swallowed back the lump in his throat and gave her a solemn nod. Her bandaged arm shook as she reached with her free hand for the small stack of papers on her bedside table. He let go of her other hand and helped her pick them up, then placed them on the side of her bed.

Their eyes met again, and Baene's heart ripped at the sight of the burns that scarred her once-beautiful features. The emotional pain was immediately followed by a wave of cold hatred that settled into his bones like lead.

Rexcan Ignis would pay for this. The Cairns would pay for this. Igrium and its allies would all regret ever having declared this war upon his home kingdom by the time he was through with them.

"Read the..." She clutched her hands together with a grimace, then opened her eyes and continued, "Read the last paragraph."

He took the last page of the document out from underneath the stack and lifted it up in shaking hands so he could read the small, printed words.

"I, Baene Ruzek..." His voice hitched on his family name and he dropped the paper in frustration.

He glanced back over at Orinna's encouraging smile and, swallowing another lump in his throat, lifted the paper up again. It did not matter what he thought he could or could not do. This was for Orinna; for everyone in Silvas—who were all rallying together to answer the Igrian emperor's declaration of war at that very moment. A war Baene himself would now have to lead them through.

He started over, "I, Baene Ruzek, do hereby take up the position of Silvas' Arbitruer *in the hearing of these witnesses." He paused and glanced over at the*

Buleutcil members watching the exchange in silence. "By the will of Deleyon, I will search for, and crown, a new ruler worthy of the title. If death, or any other circumstances, hinder me from doing so, the Buleutcil will choose a new arbitruer they deem worthy of the title.

"I also do hereby take the position of steward of Silvas—" tears blurred his vision, and he had to blink them away so he could continue, "—as given to me by Queen Orinna Fairlen Dovhust the Third. I will lead in her...in her place until my death, or if I choose another one to take my place. So help me, Deleyon."

He lowered the page and met Orinna's beautiful eyes. She smiled and mouthed "thank you".

Baene wearily shook the memory away and pinched the bridge of his nose for a few moments.

"Chief?" Duse's heavy footsteps moved towards him. "Do you need me to get you something?"

"No, no." He lifted his head and put the throwing knife back on its brackets, then turned and caught Duse's worried gaze. "What I need you cannot get me."

"Oh." Understanding dawned on his friend's features. "You mean a new ruler, yes?"

"Partly."

A questioning look drew Duse's eyebrows together, but he said nothing else.

Baene sent him a grateful nod and turned to stare out at the dark view beyond the curved window. After Orinna's death and his swearing in as Silvas' steward, he promised the Buleutcil that he would see this war ended—and Silvas as its winner. Looking back, he regretted that promise greatly. It was spoken more out of grief and short-sighted naivety than anything else, but he had said it. And now, eleven years later, he had almost lost hope of being able to keep that promise—until Tetra Cairn fell from the other side of the fence and shifted into a peryton, proving Felicita's suspicions to be true.

Since his swearing in, Baene had learned much about planning for the future, and he had come to the realization a few years ago that his plans to only win the war were short-sighted. They did not answer many of the questions he had later come to ask himself; questions such as: "how could they prevent Igrium from trying to take over the world again without completely destroying the empire and its citizens?" or, "was there a way the Alliance nations and Igrium could find an easier way to peace once the war was over?". These, and many other heavy questions, always sat in the back of his mind—and no amount of meetings with the Buleutcil and other Alliance leaders gave him the answers he was looking for.

That is, until this new development happened, and it looked as if Deleyon was finally opening the doors Baene had been praying and offering sacrifices for since he took office. So, the quicker Felicita helped Tetra regain her memories, the closer he would feel to getting some of those answers he—and, eventually, the rest of the world—needed.

A buzz went through his wrist, and he frowned as he lifted it to look at his annoying, but needed, holonode. The holographic screen appeared in the air with a sharp movement of his wrist, and an update from Rasiela appeared. He clicked the notification to read the whole message. As his eyes swept over her findings report, the weight upon his shoulders grew heavier.

He sent a short reply and turned the device off. At least the problem he faced there was not dire...yet.

"Duse," he turned to fully face the man.

The guardsman stood at attention. "Yes, Chief?"

"I believe I'm done for the day. Have the next shift take over."

"Of course." Duse bowed his head with his fist over his heart, and Baene acknowledged it with a quick nod before turning on his heel to exit his office.

It had been a long day, and he needed some time to sift through his thoughts and, most importantly, rest.

Chapter Twenty-Four

Soll's light barely shone through the clouds above Rubrum. Despite the forecast saying it was going to rain, it appeared that half of the city's population was clogging the sidewalks and streets of the fortress' public shopping center. A cold wind blew into Aabir's face and pulled his hood off his head. He reached his arm back and jerked it up again with a frown. He hated the cold, and would definitely not have chosen today to hang out with his friends, but his parents had practically begged him to do so earlier that morning because his constant string of worried questions and chatter were annoying them.

So, he was here, walking in the cold when he should have been researching for Rasiela. Besides schoolwork, it was practically the only other thing consuming his time; and part of the reason for his paranoid chatter came from the fact he had not told his parents about this new job. He battled with telling them all week, but when he came home from Norland and saw Nevaze sobbing about how she had been threatened at school by a couple kids, he decided not to say anything about it. Yet.

He told himself he would soon, but the last thing they needed at that moment was another thing to worry about. And if he told them at the wrong time, then there was no doubt his plan would come crashing down and they would still find themselves stuck in Igrium.

All because of him, of course. Him and his stupid decision to join Norland.

"I never realized how big the fortress was," Ezen said as he craned his neck to look up at the huge, connecting towers lining the walls that surrounded the stores and restaurants. "The pictures I've seen don't do it justice."

"Yeah, and if Aquilo was here, he'd probably give you a history lecture on how it was all made." Tycho rolled his eyes, hands in his pockets.

"Oh, well." Ezen shrugged and turned his face towards them. "Hey, I know you all probably don't want to do this, but is there a public library in the fortress?"

"Yeah," Aabir replied.

"Well, when we get a chance, could you show me where it is?" He shrugged and turned his gaze down to the cobblestone sidewalk. "I'd just like to know for future reference."

Tycho sighed dramatically, but Aabir could hear the grin in his voice as he said, "I guess so."

"Thanks." Ezen lifted his head, the corner of his mouth tilted upwards in a small smile.

Aabir grinned and sent him an affirming nod. Ever since Aquilo and the new trainee spoke in the library, Ezen had somehow become a part of their friend group. Granted, it did help that the empty bunk in their dorm now belonged to him, and that Lieutenant Denir put him in their small team for certain training exercises.

Yet even with those things, Aabir barely knew anything about him since he was so quiet. So, he hoped this socialization outside of campus would help them get to know him better.

"If Aquilo were here he'd take you himself—since you two seem to like books and that sort of stuff," Tycho sent Ezen a strange look as he continued, "but he couldn't escape his parents."

"What were they doing today?" Ezen asked.

"Don't know. I messaged him to come and hang out with us, but he never replied."

"That's because his patre came back from Xich this week," Aabir said. "He told me yesterday."

"Poor guy." Tycho shook his head in mock sympathy.

A thoughtful look came over Ezen's face. "I wonder what it'd be like to have parents so highly honored."

Tycho snorted. "From what I've seen and heard, it's not what it's cracked up to be."

Scattered memories of talks with Aquilo, and others with Tetra, came to Aabir's mind. "There's a lot of pressure to bring honor to the family name," he said as they stopped at a crosswalk, joining the other pedestrians waiting for the 'go' signal. "At least that's what I've heard."

"And some, like Aquilo, make it their life's mission to do absolutely no wrong to keep a good image—not even if it's something fun." Tycho frowned slightly, but then a mischievous smirk came over his features. "And then some do everything in their power to ignore the honor and run away to Silvas in the process."

Aabir's stomach tightened at the obvious jab towards Tetra, so he kept his face forward and neutral as they began to follow the group of other pedestrians crossing the magnetic road. He was not going to give Tycho any satisfaction in a reaction from him—especially since he was also planning on doing the same thing she had done.

They made it to the other side of the street in an almost tense silence, but a whiff of mouth-watering spices soon averted Aabir's attention from it. He glanced around at the restaurants and storefronts lining the wide sidewalk before his eyes landed on a sign boasting the best barbecued corafish.

"How about we eat over there?" He gestured towards the small restaurant. He had not eaten barbecue in quite a while, and it sounded amazing.

Tycho and Ezen both turned their heads in the same direction, both their countenances brightening at the sound of food.

"Sure." Ezen said at the same time Tycho replied, "Fine with me."

He took the lead through the milling crowds of people, and Aabir and Ezen followed right behind him. A few moments later, all three were sitting at a booth ordering their food.

"I'll have the barbecued corafish with fried tomeplant." Aabir snapped his menu shut and lifted it towards the waitress for her to take.

She sent him a strange glance and blew a curly piece of hair away from her face as she took the menu. He nodded towards her, but she turned around so quickly without acknowledging them he thought she was either ignoring him or was so busy she completely forgot to say anything. He glanced around at the full restaurant and silently tried to tell himself it was the latter.

He turned his focus back on Tycho and Ezen, who sat across from him, as a tightening sensation filled his stomach. It had been a couple years since he felt any public scrutiny, but he was beginning to wonder if that was what the waitress' strange look pointed towards.

"—maybe twice." He barely caught Tycho's words as he turned his focus away from the unsettling thoughts.

"I haven't even gotten that far," Ezen replied, his eyes focused on the table's wood surface. "All my siblings learned, but they were older, and my parents never got to teach me. Yet now that I'm here—" his hand gestured weakly to the dim restaurant around them, "—I doubt I'll need to learn since you all have so many taxis."

"What are you talking about?" Aabir cut in.

Tycho and Ezen both looked over at him. "Driving," Tycho replied.

"Oh."

Patre taught Aabir to drive on Mister Falap's farm. However, he never tried to get his license. Like Ezen said, Rubrum was full of taxis, trams, and a subway system. Most people in the city never tried to learn until they had to. The only people he knew who had one were his parents.

"Didn't your parents teach you, Aabir?" Tycho asked.

"Yep."

Ezen tilted his head. "How hard is it?"

"Not too hard. You just have to get used to it." He shrugged, then twisted his lips to the side. "But I only ever drove off-road, not in actual traffic. I wouldn't want to drive in that madhouse out there."

"Same." Tycho nodded, shadows coming over his expression for a moment. "That's why I never learned how. Androids are better drivers than humans."

"Well..." Aabir almost told him about the amount of wrecked hovercars his patre had fixed that were driven by androids, but the look in Tycho's eyes told him to stay silent. So, he shook his head and said, "Never mind."

Though Tycho had never shared details, he remembered the day when his friend had been told that his older and younger brothers died in a car crash. It had happened two years ago, and when Tycho finally came back to Norland a week after the news, the only things Aabir and Aquilo had been able to get out of him were that it was his brothers' fault, and that he had moved out of his patre's house and into his older sister's apartment. Other than that, it was the quietest he had ever been on a subject.

Aabir flicked his gaze over the restaurant again to try and dispel those thoughts, and his eyes landed on one of the holovisions along the walls that showed two sports commentators talking about the Constantia Tourney veterans that were returning in this year's competition. One of them mentioned a veteran utilizing the once-forgotten "Rule One-Hundred and Twelve" as a game highlight, with two competitors fighting in what looked like a frozen tundra, took over the screen.

His stomach turned at the sight, but the waitress came back with their drinks and he was able to shift his focus away. She set them down without saying a word, then turned around and left as quickly as she had come.

A frown took over Tycho's face. "They need better service around here."

Aabir picked up his straw and took it out of its wrapper, glancing out of the corner of his eye at the waitress' retreating form. She stopped at a table not far from theirs' and, smiling, asked the couple sitting there if they needed anything else.

"Hmph." His friend added, "Strange."

Aabir's stomach grew tighter and he glanced down at his bubbling soft drink with a grimace. Its sugary fizz no longer held its usual appeal.

"Hey, Aabir—" Ezen's thick drawl drew his gaze upwards towards the new trainee's confused expression, "—you Ok?"

"Yeah." He shrugged and took a sip of his drink to feign normalcy, then regretted it a moment later as his tight stomach did a flip.

Ezen eyed him for another long moment before blinking and turning his gaze back on Tycho. "Well back to what you were saying—I've heard androids aren't as good of drivers as everyone says they are. In fact, they're banned in Stelgan because two people were killed in a wreck with one driving."

Tycho shrugged and leaned back, arms crossed. "That was *one* time."

"I'm sure it happens a lot here, too." Ezen picked up his cup and took a sip. "You just don't hear about it 'cause you all rely too much on them and no one's been able to get rid of 'em because of it."

"There is some truth to that," Aabir said, hoping the conversation would turn his focus away from the waitress' attitude. "My patre has had to send a few hovercars driven by them to the junkyard because they were too badly damaged for him to fix."

Ezen's eyes widened slightly, and he set his cup down. "Is your patre a mechanic?"

"Yeah..." Aabir scrunched his brow. "Why? Do you need one for something?"

"Well, no—at least, not for a specific vehicle." He cleared his throat and looked back down at the table. "I just have a question."

"Well, you can ask me." He let a small grin escape his lips and hoped the tightness of his stomach didn't show it as pained. "And if I can't answer it, I can always message him."

"Really?" Ezen glanced back up and their eyes locked. "I...OK. Um...well, this may sound stupid, but I don't know a thing about hovercars, so. Um...how likely would it be for the electromagnetic generator to explode?"

Aabir blinked at the question. "Oh! Uh...it's not common..." Memories from Xich slid forward at Ezen's words, but he pushed them aside before he could linger on them. "My patre replaced a few after they exploded, and one almost exploded as he was trying to fix it...but it doesn't happen very often. Why do you ask?"

Ezen shrugged and turned his gaze away again. "I was just curious."

Aabir could not help but stare at him strangely. "I can ask my patre for a clearer answer, if you want."

"No that's fine." The other trainee shook his head and smiled, but Aabir could tell it was forced.

Tycho played with his straw, a faraway look in his eyes. "That's what you said happened to us in Xich, right?"

"Yeah," Aabir nodded. He could still hear the high-pitched squealing in his nightmares. "I think the Alliance used some sort of device to block the electromagnetic pulses the generator sent out."

"You can do that?" Ezen stared at him, wide-eyed.

"Mm-hmm. A few militaries have created machines that will, but I don't think there are any available to the public."

Something akin to horror darkened Ezen's features, but before Aabir could ask anything about it the waitress came back to their table—and a man was with her.

"Excuse me..." He lifted his eyes and met the man's hard stare as he spoke, "but I'm going to have to ask you to leave."

The small sip of soda threatened to come back up as he noticed the suppressed anger in the man's tight-lipped look.

"Sir?" He deepened his voice in hopes of keeping it from breaking.

"What'd we do wrong?" Tycho piped up.

The man turned his head in Tycho and Ezen's direction for a moment before returning the force of his stare back on Aabir. "You two can stay, but we don't serve any like *him* here."

He swallowed back the bile rising in his throat. "I don't know what you mean, sir..." Even he could hear the lie in his voice, and the man's eyes only narrowed dangerously.

"You know exactly what I mean," he replied, "And as the owner, I am ordering you to leave my restaurant. I don't want any business of *your* kind here—"

"—But he's a trainee!" Tycho abruptly stood and gestured to the three of them. "We all are, and we aren't going to take any of this dishonor—!"

"—I don't care what you say you are." The man barked back, and the chatter filling the restaurant ceased. Aabir wished he could shrink into the booth's cushion as the hairs on his neck prickled with the stares of everyone around them. "I'll call the patrolmen if he doesn't leave right this second!"

"Why you—!"

"—Tycho, stop." Aabir stood and looked the owner in the eyes, using every ounce of will to keep his expression neutral. "I'll go."

The man nodded sharply and stepped aside for him to leave.

"But..."

Tycho's voice died away as Aabir, without turning his head, marched out of the restaurant. His face burned with the heat of everyone's stares, but he kept his head held high—as Norland had taught him—until the glass door closed behind him and he was swept away in the sea of pedestrians.

Humiliation and anger fizzled in his stomach, and he clenched his jaw tightly to keep from shouting out his frustrations. He curled his hands into tight fists and stuffed them in his sweatshirt's front pocket. Usually saying he was a trainee protected him from such blatant scrutiny, but obviously the owner had no sense of honor.

Aabir shook his head, fire building in his chest. And this was why he was risking his life with Rasiela—because he should not have to be asked to leave someplace because his eyes were purple. It was stupid. He glanced back over his shoulder at the restaurant's seemingly friendly front and frowned. If he did not have his family to worry about, he would march right back in there and tell the owner how much of an idiotic straudwin he really was.

"Aabir!"

He jerked to a stop and turned around—and immediately spotted Tycho and Ezen elbowing their way towards him.

"Aabir, wait up!" Tycho called again.

He stepped to the side out of the flow of people and waited for his friends to catch up. They finally did, and Tycho's reddened face told Aabir exactly how his friend felt.

Yet all he asked was, "Are you OK?"

"I mean...yeah." Physically, yes. Mentally, no.

Tycho's lips twisted into a frown as his eyes narrowed in a glare. "I can't believe he did that to you!" A few people walking past glanced over at his outburst but continued on their ways. "Of all the straudwins—"

"—Has that ever happened before, Aabir?" Ezen's question broke through Tycho's beginning tirade.

Aabir turned his gaze down to his boots. "Not like that, no."

"Hmm." Ezen paused for a moment, then added, "I'm sorry it did."

"Me too." Tycho lowered his tone back to its normal pitch, "He had no right to do that to you, of all trainees. No one—besides Aquilo—has as clear a record as you. He should be dishonored as the lowliest of cowards for such an act. I'm ashamed he's even Igrian."

Despite his good intentions, his comment caused the knot that was Aabir's stomach to tighten even more. If his friends knew what he was planning, they would be agreeing with the restaurant owner's decision to call the patrolmen after him.

"One day there won't be any more cause for that to happen," Ezen said. And in a lowered voice, he added, "Hopefully soon."

Aabir sent him a questioning look, but then shrugged it off with a "Thanks." Though the comment was supposed to be encouraging, it could not take away from the reality that his plight—and the plight of every other person of Alliance descent—would only grow worse if Igrium won. He looked back down at his boots, again turning his thoughts to the things he could have said to the restaurant owner.

There was a tense pause. Then, "Well...do you still want to eat?" Tycho asked.

"Nah." Aabir lifted his head. "I'm not really hungry anymore."

Ezen shook his head, hands in his pockets. "Me neither."

Tycho nodded slowly. "Then how about we go to the library? That way we can get it over with."

"I'm up for it." The ghost of a grin came over Ezen's features as he glanced over at Aabir. "How about you?"

"Sure." He shrugged, unable to grin back. Maybe he could find something about the fire attacks for Rasiela there.

Tycho sighed dramatically. "Then let's get on with it—because I'd still like to do something fun today."

"Thanks for sacrificing." Ezen rolled his eyes, but his grin was now evident.

Tycho put his hands on both their shoulders, a smirk taking over his glare, and steered them back into the flowing crowds. Aabir met his friend's eyes and forced a smile to keep the moment light—at least for them. Tycho sent him a knowing look but said nothing more about the encounter, instead keeping the conversation going in a light, joking way as they navigated through the streams of pedestrians.

The further they walked away from the restaurant, the easier it became for Aabir to push his broiling thoughts to the back of his mind. He knew they would come back to haunt him later, but for now he tried to press through the gloom and anger so as to keep Tycho and Ezen from worrying. The less they thought about his family's "dishonorable" descendants, the safer his secret would be. Just like he always did when Lieutenant Denir sent a Silvanian jab towards him, he would make it seem as if the whole ordeal did not faze him. Even if it was a lie, at least it would keep him safe—and that was the most important thing at the moment.

Chapter Twenty-Five

"Not bad, kid," Rasiela said as she tightened a screw on a dismantled cleanbot.

"Thanks." Aabir nodded, pressing his lips together to keep from smiling.

He had been hoping to hear those words all week—especially with the mounting tension he could feel rising inside him. The faster he was able to gain Rasiela's trust, the faster he and his family would find themselves in Silvas and away from all the public scrutiny for not looking Igrian.

"I'm still reviewing what you sent me on Sixthdein, but so far everything is looking good." Rasiela placed the screwdriver into the tool chest sitting atop her office's workbench. "You did exactly what I asked, and—from what I can see—you did it efficiently."

Aabir straightened at the praise.

She lifted her head and locked eyes with him. "I have your next assignment. I need you to find me anything you can on the events that happened after the housefires."

"What do you mean?" He furrowed his brow.

"I mean anything political, economic, conspiratorial—anything of that nature—which stemmed from that event."

"OK..." He nodded slowly. "So, you mean stuff like Prince Joash's execution?"

"Exactly."

"Alright." Well, that didn't sound too hard. He had already found a few things related to this topic on his former assignment. All he would have to do is expand on it. Easy as pomen pie. "Meet here next week?"

Rasiela shook her head. "No. Someone may start realizing something is off with you visiting so many times." She paused for a moment, tapping the cleanbot's spherical head with her fingers. "Let's meet in the everpine trees after your last class period next Firstdein."

"Sounds good." Aabir nodded and turned to go. "I'll see you then."

"Hold on."

He turned halfway and met her eyes again. "What?"

Rasiela's face was a hard mask as she spoke, "I've noticed that the new kid spends a lot of time with you and your friend group. Tell me: who is he?"

"Ezen?" Aabir narrowed his eyes and turned to fully face her, arms crossed. "Why does it matter?"

She copied his stance and raised a brow. "Because it's my job," she replied. "I'm not asking for his life story. I just want to know who he is and how he got here since I've never heard of anyone transferring to Norland before."

Aabir thought of not saying anything, but then he wondered if this was a trust test, and he relented, "He told me he came here from Stelgan's military academy, and that he was able to transfer because of his grades and our bioweapons class. He likes it for some reason."

"Bioweapons?" A thoughtful expression came over Rasiela's features but then quickly disappeared with a shrug of her shoulders. "What else?"

Something about this conversation rubbed him the wrong way, but one thought of his family's plight and he said, "I—I think he also said he's a ward of the empire. He says he has siblings, but I don't think they have the greatest relationship—which is why he's a ward."

"Anything else?"

Aabir went through some of the memories he had regarding Ezen, and then shook his head. "Nope. Unless you want to know his favorite movies, or that he's mildly allergic to greenberries, then..."

Rasiela frowned, but he thought he saw a flash of amusement in her eyes as she waved him off. "Thank you, Aabir. That will be all."

The corner of his mouth curled into a smirk, and he sent her a nod. "I'll see you next week."

She nodded and turned her eyes back in the cleanbot's direction. Aabir took that as his cue to leave; so, he spun on his heel and exited the open door of her office, closing it behind him.

As he walked down the hall towards chemistry, giddiness filled his chest. So far, this whole spy thing was working out far better than he would have expected. And Rasiela complimented him on his efficiency! That had to count for something when it came to building trust, right?

"Hey, Aabir."

Aabir jerked his neck around as Ezen walked up beside him. His heart rate slowed back to normal as he sent the other trainee a nod. "Hey."

"Where are you headed?"

"Chemistry."

"Oh." Ezen sent him a questioning look. "So, you do like chemistry...?"

Now it was Aabir's turn to look confused. "No. Why would you think that?"

"You just looked really happy there for a moment." Ezen shrugged, but his eyes never left Aabir's. "So, I just wondered if there might actually be a class you enjoy."

"Ha." Aabir grinned and hoped it hid his mounting worry. "Nope, there are zero classes besides training that make me happy."

Oh Deleyon. Was I grinning like an idiot?

Ezen moved the chardex in his hand to the other. "OK. You just looked *really* happy coming out of the janitor's closet."

"I did?" Maybe feigning surprise could help the subject to change.

"Yeah."

Aabir waited for him to elaborate, but Ezen only stared at him silently. "Well, I only went in there to return this stain-remover." He shrugged and lifted his arm to scratch the back of his neck. "I mean—my matha is going to be happy that I'm not coming home with a bunch of blood-stained clothes this week, so maybe that's why."

Ezen nodded. "Alright then." He quickened his stride. "I gotta go to history but I'll see you in training."

"See ya."

Aabir watched him speed up and turn into another corridor. Only when he left did he let himself breathe. That was too close. He mumbled a quiet "thanks" to Deleyon for the stain-remover excuse as all the giddiness from before was replaced with the weight of what he was doing.

If Ezen was not new and actually knew Aabir as well Tycho or Aquilo did, then that conversation might have gone in a horribly different direction. He needed to be more careful from now on. No matter how easy the spy work seemed, there could be no room for error, he chided himself. His parents and siblings depended on him, and he was not going to make any more mistakes that would burden them.

He settled his facial features into an emotionless mask and turned into the corridor where the chemistry lab was. However, the expression soon dissipated into one of concern as his thoughts moved onto chemistry and the homework assignment he could not remember doing. He immediately opened his chardex and slowed to a stop near the lab's open doorway, wondering if he would have enough time to answer the homework questions before the break ended.

"WATCH YOUR BACK, SORREL!" Lieutenant Denir yelled.

Aabir spun just in time to block Septimus' downward stroke. The taller trainee grinned as Aabir stumbled away from the next swing of his battle ax and hit his shield. A jolt went up his arm, and he gritted his teeth against the dull throb. A maniacal light grew in Septimus' face as he pounded his victory into Aabir's struggling defenses.

Aabir could feel the stares of Lieutenant Denir and a few other trainees fixed on their sparring match. He inhaled a shaky breath and leapt back in a moment's pause between Septimus' swings to get his bearings. Losing this match while others watched was not an option.

Septimus lunged forward with a yell; ax raised. Aabir raised his shield to meet the attack. A jolt went through his bones at the weight of Septimus' downward strike, but he was able to push the bigger trainee back with his shield before swinging his sword in an arc. Septimus grunted and stumbled to the side.

A small grin escaped Aabir's lips at the sight of victory. He lunged forward and pushed Septimus' ax away with his shield, then stabbed his blade forward. A sharp breath sounded from the other trainee as resistance pushed against Aabir's blade.

Satisfaction filled him and he lifted his gaze to lock eyes with Septimus. "I win."

Septimus only glowered in response. Aabir pulled his sword away and glanced down at the blood now trickling from Septimus' side. His satisfaction dissipated and he immediately averted his gaze before anything could show on his face.

He took a few quick steps out of reach of Septimus' ax and inhaled a deep, shaky breath. He lifted his head and locked eyes with Septimus' glowering countenance. "New round?"

Septimus was silent for a few moments, then he replied with a simple "Yeah" and brandished his single-headed ax.

Aabir nodded sharply, although he was beginning to wonder how smart it was to fight with an angry Septimus. It would be difficult, but maybe he could use the trainee's anger issues to his advantage. With that encouraging thought, he barely lifted his sword and moved into his guard stance.

Just as he did, the other trainee raised his ax with a cry and charged towards him. Aabir rushed forward with his own yell, and their weapons clashed together with a resounding clang.

Round and round they went trading strikes, with Lieutenant Denir shouting commands and warnings in their most heated exchanges. Aabir's heart pounded in his chest as the thrill of the fight buzzed through him. He feinted a strike at Septimus' leg, then swiped his sword up at the last moment and hit the other trainee's forearm. Instead of knocking his weapon away like Aabir had hoped, it only seemed to anger the larger trainee.

Aabir's eyes widened as the ax head came for his side. He barely blocked it with his shield. Too late, he realized his mistake as Septimus rammed his own shield into Aabir's stomach, pushing him to the ground. A chill went through him as cold *furrum* metal bit into the skin right below his chin.

"I win," Septimus said.

Aabir lifted his gaze from the ax head towards Septimus' smirk. "Yeah, you did."

The other trainee snorted and moved the blade away from his throat. Aabir held in a sigh of relief and pushed himself back into a standing position.

"Again?" Septimus raised his brow expectantly.

He nodded and stepped back towards the edge of their sparring ring without turning away from the other trainee. "Sure."

Septimus did the same to the opposite edge. Aabir gripped the hilt of the shortsword tightly as their eyes met, wishing for a moment that he had his longsword. It was his most comfortable weapon—especially against Septimus' rage.

He shot a furtive glance out of the corner of his eye at the small crowd still watching, and a jolt of surprise went through him as he noticed Lieutenant Denir was still among them. Usually he went around to the other sparring rings instead of staying near only one.

It sent a strange feeling through Aabir's stomach, but he ignored it as Septimus let out his battle cry and rushed forward. Aabir charged towards him less than a moment later. His sword thunked against Septimus' shield, just as a jolt went through his own shield arm.

Then a scream rang out.

He jerked away from Septimus, eyes wide. The other trainee lowered his ax and looked over in Lieutenant Denir's direction. Aabir did the same and noticed Denir's brow was lowered in confusion as he turned his head to glance around them. *Where had that—?*

Another scream echoed, silencing the rest of the metallic ringing and clashing happening in their training yard.

Aabir tilted his head to the side and tried to listen for anything else through the blood pounding in his ears, but it did not take much for another scream to slice through the erratic beat. Now the horrific screeching soon took over any silence from before.

"Trainees!" Yet somehow Lieutenant Denir's shout sounded above even that. Aabir lowered his gaze back to his commanding officer as he continued to yell, "It sounds like another platoon is having trouble, so ready yourselves and follow me!"

The second lieutenant unsheathed his sword and headed out of their training yard with quick strides. Aabir gripped the hilt of his own blade even tighter and joined the rest of his platoon mates as they followed him into the hallway and down towards the next training yard.

Even from inside Norland's thick walls, it sounded like the screams were growing in number. He ground his teeth as the unsettling caterwaul grew louder with each stride he took. Occasionally, screaming occurred in training, but nothing like this.

A hollow pit yawned open in Aabir's stomach as he came to a stop behind Lieutenant Denir and noticed the first-years pouring into the hall. "What—"

Someone rammed into his back, and he almost fell on his C.O., but stumbled to a stop just in time. He sent an accusing glare over his shoulder at Buren, but immediately looked ahead again at the panicked first-years spilling into the hall.

"What's going on?" A harsh voice called out, and he glanced over to see another platoon—this one second-years—coming down the opposite end of the hall towards them, their commanding officer in the lead.

The scrambling first-years began to huddle in a circle in the middle of the surrounding platoons. Blood splattered their clothes, and a few even had arrows sticking out of them. Horror slithered down Aabir's spine as he noticed one twelve-year-old boy leaning against the wall with an arrow shaft sticking out of his stomach between armor plates. For a moment he pictured Nevaze among the bloodied first-years, but then quickly pushed that thought to the side.

What kind of accident could have caused this much damage?

"What happened, trainees?" Lieutenant Denir's voice was calm as he stepped towards their growing huddle.

One boy, who was cradling his bleeding arm, replied in a shaky voice, "The—the training droids—they just—they started—started shooting at—at us!"

"That's...that makes no sense..." Buren's low words died away as the other commanding officer slowed to a stop near them.

"So, this was a training droid accident?" He looked between the first-years still piling into the hall and Lieutenant Denir.

"Seems so," Denir replied. "We'll take care of the androids if you and your platoon get these trainees to the infirmary."

"Of course." The other C.O. nodded and spun on his heel, barking orders at his platoon.

Lieutenant Denir spun around to face his own, his eyes alight and jaw set. Aabir straightened as their eyes met for a moment. No matter how he disagreed with Igrium and its morals, he agreed with what was evident on Lieutenant Denir's face—whoever would hurt a bunch of twelve and thirteen-year-olds was about to be shown Igrium's wrath. Even if those "someones" were only robots.

"We have a training droid incident on our hands," Lieutenant Denir said. "Break into your teams and be on your guard for flying arrows—shields ready!—and take out those training droids."

"Yes sir!" They all responded with salutes.

Aabir turned around and spotted Aquilo, Tycho, and Ezen coming towards him amidst everyone else splitting up into their teams. Aquilo got to him first.

"You ready?" He asked.

"Yeah." Aabir nodded and squeezed the hilt of his sword. "You?"

"Always."

Just then, Tycho and Ezen appeared. A grim smile hardened Tycho's features, while Ezen looked as if he had swallowed spiced gelatscy. Before either of them could say anything, Aquilo led them forward towards the emptying doorway where Lieutenant Denir stood, ushering the last remaining first-years through. An angry heat burned in Aabir's chest as he watched two of the last trainees dragging their unconscious friend through the doorway into the hall. One arrow protruded from the boy's limp leg, and he spotted a few sprouting from the boy's back like the quills of a needled badger.

Once they were safely indoors, their own C.O. stepped inside and joined Lieutenant Denir near the doorway. Aabir only heard a couple muttered words between them as he and his friends moved into the new training yard behind Septimus and Buren's team—where they were all immediately accosted by a storm of arrows.

He jerked his shield upwards right before two of them clinked against it. Then he peeked below its rounded rim and locked eyes on their targets.

Silver-skinned training droids shot arrows in every direction with zero care for if they hit anything. Some were standing and shooting, some were running, and one was even doing flips. Every time it landed, it would go through the motion of loading its bow—even though its quiver was empty—then would pull back its string and fire in whatever direction it was facing. He even spotted one training droid shooting arrows up into the air, only for them to fall back down around it.

A wave of relief washed over Aabir. At least it was not a coordinated attack.

"Aabir, watch out!" Tycho's voice brought him out of his thoughts in time to lower his shield to block a stray arrow from hitting his face. His heart panged nervously, and he reminded himself that they were still in a dangerous situation—no matter how uncoordinated the androids were.

"Thanks." He glanced over at Tycho.

Tycho nodded and brandished his shortsword. "So, what's the plan?"

"We take 'em down like we would in training," Aquilo replied and waved in the direction of two androids who stood shooting arrows solely at their group. "Come on!"

They all let out battle cries and charged towards their opponents. The androids continued firing arrows with inhuman speed, but they did not move from their standing positions.

As they drew closer, Aabir set his sights on one. He noticed Ezen running closer to him as Tycho and Aquilo split off to attack the other android. They came right up on the android and Aabir stabbed its unprotected stomach from behind the safety of his shield. Ezen sliced one of its metal arms clean off. The droid fell to its knees as it was programmed to do, and its bow fell to the ground with a clatter. Yet its other arm continued moving in the same, continuous motion as if it still had a bowstring to pull.

Aabir scrunched his brow and sent Ezen a questioning look. *What on Afreean?*

"They won't die!"

He spun around at the yell, heart hammering, and noticed Septimus' team chasing the acrobatic android. Despite missing a leg and having multiple holes in its chest, it was somehow still flipping and shooting pretend arrows. He glanced around and realized a few of the other teams were having trouble with their android opponents as well. A metallic screech sounded behind him, and he turned back around as Ezen muttered an "oh no".

The android they took down was standing again, its arm back on and strung bow aimed right at his face. Aabir had no time to think, instead letting his instincts tell him to duck and put his shield up as the arrow whizzed past his head.

Ezen swung his sword at the android's legs and chopped one of them off. The android fell to the ground, stringing its bow with another arrow aimed towards the sky.

"Thanks." Aabir breathed out a sigh of relief and stood.

A strange look plastered itself across Ezen's face as he spoke, "We need to get into its mainframe and shut it down."

"What?" Aabir watched in surprise as the new trainee dropped his sword and shield, even as arrows flew through the air around them, then stooped down to their android's head. "Ezen! What are you doing?"

"Cover me, Aabir." Was all he replied as he turned the android's smooth, metal head around and opened a small hatch on its back.

Now that he could see Ezen was not completely crazy, he did as he was told and covered them both from any random arrows that sailed towards them. Ezen muttered a few words as he worked, but Aabir could not hear exactly what he said over the chaos of malfunctioning androids and war-crying platoonmates.

"Done!" Ezen exclaimed as he rushed to pick up his shield, then his sword.

Aabir glanced over his shoulder at the still android, then back over at Ezen's worn countenance. "What did you do?"

"Destroyed its main circuit board." Ezen lifted his shield above his head as an arrow clinked against its metal surface.

"We need to tell the others." Aabir moved his gaze over the frantic fighting and finally locked it on the one person out of their platoon who would know how to do what Ezen did. "Buren!" He shouted.

The other trainee slowed to a stop from chasing the flipping android and turned in Aabir's direction. "What?" He shouted back.

Aabir dodged an arrow then shouted, "Destroy the main circuit board!" He gestured with his sword to their fallen android. "It's the only way to stop them!"

Even from a distance, he noticed the realization dawning on Buren's features. The other boy sent him a nod and ran to join his team again.

"Aabir!" Ezen called. He spun around and caught sight of Tycho and Aquilo holding down the other android while Ezen waved for him to come. "Over here!"

He jumped over the fallen training droid's body and moved over towards them.

"About time." Aquilo remarked with a strained grimace as he and Tycho each held down one of their android's jerking arms. Ezen was standing next to the android's head, protecting them with his shield.

"Sorry," Aabir replied.

"We can't hold this thing down forever, and we need Ezen—"

"—Right." He nodded and took his position as guard over their huddled group.

Once he did so, Ezen dropped his weapons and bent down next to the android's head. Aabir blocked an arrow from hitting Tycho's back and jumped over the android's jerking limbs to protect Aquilo from a similar attack.

"So, Aquilo, you see those two—" He only caught snippets of Ezen's thick drawl as their newest platoonmate, he assumed, told Aquilo how to destroy the android's circuit board. A couple arrows flew towards their group and he skirted around Aquilo to block them. Their armor would protect them from most of the arrows, but there was too much chance of one slipping between the plates and through their polyanium-shirts to hit something vital for him to just let them go. So, he practically ran circles around his friends, keeping his eyes on incoming arrows and the scene around them.

Buren and his team somehow got the flipping android underneath them, and Aabir caught a glimpse of him digging into its head like Ezen. Three arrows rained down towards Aabir's group and he turned his head to raise his shield to block them. They each ***clinked*** off his shield and fell around them. He lowered it again and noticed Lieutenant Denir on his knees, doing the same thing Buren and Ezen were doing while a group of trainees kept the android he worked on from moving.

"And...done!" Ezen finally said.

Tycho and Aquilo both lifted their arms off the training droid with relieved sighs. "Thank Vatharin," Tycho said as he wiped the sweat off his forehead.

"Yeah," Aquilo added, "and now we need to help everyone else." He grabbed his shield and sword, then stood. "We'll split up. Aabir and Ezen, you both go together. Tycho and I will do the same."

"Sure." Ezen also picked up his weapon and shield, that same indecipherable look from before on his face.

Aabir narrowed his eyes. The trainee's features seemed more pale than normal... Was this whole situation reminding him of a similar one in his past?

"Come on, Aabir." Aquilo's voice took on a bossy tone as he shot him a 'let's go!' look.

He rolled his eyes but said, "Coming."

They split up, with Aabir and Ezen both running towards the closest android and the team trying to chase it down. Its quiver was empty, but it still continued to string its bow and fire as if it still had arrows—while it ran at an inhuman speed. Aabir and Ezen intercepted it and helped to slow it down from its course so the others could catch up. Once they did, they all piled on top of it so Ezen could get into its now-spinning head. He soon dispatched it, and they continued to the next. And the next.

Aabir counted seven training droids they dispatched before he realized he no longer had to shield himself, or anyone else, from flying arrows. His shield arm drooped ever so slightly as he glanced around at the quieter training yard.

"I think we did it," he said between breaths.

Ezen stood with a groan and turned his neck to look around. "Yeah," was all he replied.

Aabir scrunched his brow and looked over at his newest friend. "You OK, Ezen?"

"Sure," Ezen replied quickly with a shrug. "Why wouldn't I be?"

"I don't know..."

The strange look from before had disappeared, but Aabir could see something still darkened Ezen's brown eyes.

"Really, I'm fine," he replied, "Just...thinkin', that's all."

"OK." Aabir took the hint and dropped it. For now.

"Trainees, come here!" He jerked his head at the sound of Lieutenant Denir's order. Their commanding officer stood in the middle of the training yard, seemingly unfazed by the metallic bodies and body parts strewn about the walled space.

Despite the weariness creeping into his muscles, Aabir ran over to where his platoon gathered in their usual formation in front of their C.O. He slowed to a stop and sheathed his sword as Lieutenant Denir slowly paced down their line with his limping gait. He stopped in front of Ezen and said, "Good job figuring out how to take them down, Kevler."

Aabir waited for the demeaning phrase that always followed the man's praise, but instead he took a step back and addressed the rest of them, "You all did well, and I'm honored to lead this platoon."

Aabir clamped his jaw so tightly his teeth hurt so as to keep his mouth from dropping open in shock. Had something like the training droids' circuits happened to his commanding officer's brain? Despite how happy the praise was probably supposed to make him feel, it only made him uneasy. Surely something else was wrong.

"I promise that we will find out what—or who—caused this..." A dangerous glint sparked in Lieutenant Denir's eyes, "and whoever it was that tried to harm our own will pay accordingly."

And he was back.

"You're all free to start your break." He nodded sharply. "Dismissed."

Aabir saluted him—as did the rest of his platoonmates—and they all headed out of the training yard towards their well-deserved break. When he stepped into the hallway, he glanced down for a moment and noticed blood splattered across the stone tiles. The angry flame from before burst into his chest, and he found himself walking quietly while the rest of his friends and platoonmates talked in excited tones around him.

Whoever did this—because all the training droids acting up at once could not be accidental—obviously had some sort of dangerous agenda that involved hurting trainees. Immediately, he remembered what he had read about the housefires and the many conspiracy theories about the pyromaniacal group that supposedly started them. Despite the absurdity of some of the theories, there were a few that sent chills down Aabir's spine at how closely they resembled what just happened.

Part of him knew it was ridiculous and that he was jumping to conclusions, but the other part of him had to wonder: could these two events be related? And if so, what other plans did this supposed secret group of people have? Who all was in danger of their next scheme? And the question that seemed to top all the others in Aabir's brain was: did any of them know he had been looking up information that just so happened to include the conspiracy theories about them?

Another shiver went down his spine and he tried to push the questions to the side, but he could not stop thinking about them. It reminded him of the new assignment Rasiela had given him, and he silently made a promise to himself: if there was a chance of someone from the secret group finding out he was doing research, then it would be best if he no longer looked up anything that had to do with those theories—even if it meant giving less info to Rasiela. He silently prayed that it would not affect the trust exercise and, consequently, his family's safety.

Aabir breathed out a quiet breath through his mouth and tried tuning in to the conversation Tycho, Aquilo, and Buren were having to turn his mind on something else. It helped, and he soon found himself joining in with the worries retreating into the dark corners of his mind where he hoped they would stay. It was a fool's hope, yes, but he held onto it anyway.

"THIS IS A MESS." Vindic Windap, the director of Norland, sighed and rubbed his hand over his face.

"Indeed," Lieutenant Dalmin Denir replied, "but it could've ended up much worse."

They both stood in the middle of the training droid carnage. Another, much taller, uniformed man stood on Denir's other side—the exact opposite of the portly, studious-looking director.

"I can't believe this happened." Lieutenant Aloysuis Trouran shook his head slowly, but Dalmin could hear the sharp edge in the man's voice as he spoke, "Half my platoon is stuck in the infirmary, and the rest are too frightened to leave their dorms!" He lifted his hand to squeeze the hilt of the sheathed segione on his belt. "What is going to be done about it, Vindic?"

"I sent word to His Imperial Majesty, and he promised he would send a few programmers to figure out what truly happened to the training droids," Vindic replied. "We hope that whatever they find will lead us to a suspect."

"And if they're found?"

Vindic sent him a side-eye glance. "You will have your chance to get your revenge, but only *after* they are questioned."

"Good." Aloysuis nodded and crossed his arms.

There was a stretch of silence between them, then Dalmin asked the question burning in his mind, "How long do you believe it will take them to reprogram the androids?"

"I haven't the slightest idea." Vindic raised his brow and locked eyes with him. "Why do you ask?"

"I was hoping to use them for those I choose to fight in the Tourney this year. I wanted to use their...*spontaneity* to help prepare my two."

"Smart move." Aloysuis replied, "I wish I had done that with my boys last year."

"You'll have another chance, Aloysuis." Vindic turned his gaze back on Dalmin, "And I wish I could tell you, Dalmin, but all we can hope for is that they'll be up and running within the next two weeks."

One corner of Dalmin's lips tilted downwards in the beginnings of a frown. That shouldn't disrupt his training plans too much. It would still leave four weeks of training with the androids, but he had hoped to give whoever he chose six weeks to train with them. He decided he could still work with it.

"That sounds good," he finally replied.

"Do you know who you're going to choose?"

Faces flashed through his mind. "I have a few ideas, but nothing set in stone."

"Hmm. Do you think any of them will make it far?"

Dalmin shrugged. "Possibly." A grim smile broke through his weathered features. "But even if they don't, I want them to still bring me honor by not looking like complete fools for as long as they stay in them."

"Good idea." Aloysuis smirked. "Hopefully neither of them will get shot in the back with a crossbow bolt like Hendriss did."

"He did make it to the second day, though," Dalmin replied.

"Yes, but he should've known better than to turn his back on an enemy—even if there was that king scorpion close behind him."

"At least there was no loss of honor on your part."

"True."

"And now, I hear he's become a lieutenant, yes?"

Aloysuis seemed to grow taller with pride. "He has—and I used to think when that bolt hit him that he'd never make it far in the ranks. Praise the gods he proved me wrong."

"It's always honoring to see those you trained going further than you thought they could." This was the second platoon Dalmin had led since joining Norland, and a few from his first were also high-ranking in the army.

"It is."

Another pause came into the conversation, and Vindic used it to clear his throat. "Now that you two are caught up, I will keep you both up to date with whatever results the emperor's programmers send me."

"Thank you." Aloysuis replied, and Dalmin sent the director a sharp nod.

Vindic nodded and clasped his hands behind his back. "Then I believe I'm finished here. Gentlemen."

He, again, nodded towards them both then turned around and left; his receding footsteps echoing off the tall stone walls. Once the door groaned shut, Dalmin turned to face Aloysuis.

"Do you have any ideas who would've done this?" He asked.

Aloysuis shook his head. "I made a few enemies throughout my life, Dalmin, but I doubt any of those that are still living would go to the trouble of doing something like this." He gestured towards the android parts strewn around them.

"Hmm." Dalmin stroked his chin in thought. "Well, whoever it was, they have no idea what they've gotten themselves into."

The dangerous gleam returned in Aloysuis' hardened features. "No, they don't," he agreed.

They both stood there in the still training yard, each with their own vengeful thoughts and plans going through their heads; because such a dishonorable act could only be paid in blood.

Chapter Twenty-Six

"Is there anyone you know tha' was important in your life—other than your parents—tha' you could try to remember?" Lady Felicita asked from the desk chair in Tetra's new room.

Tetra shifted her bandaged leg to a more comfortable position on her bed, then she closed her eyes to help her focus. She remembered the video of her parents' home as it burned down, and the unrecognizable woman—her nanny—who could be seen carrying her out. Apparently, the nanny whom Tetra couldn't even remember the name of was supposedly more a part of her life than her parents were. She tried to conjure up a face, a name, anything that would lead to a memory resurfacing, but it was like reaching out into dark water with her bare hand and hoping she might catch something with it.

After a few minutes of wracking her brain for any lost memories to show themselves, she let out a frustrated sigh and put her head in her hands. "Nope. Nothing." Just like every other question they had gone through the past few days.

A small sigh came from Lady Felicita, but her voice didn't lose its hopeful tone as she replied, "Well, we always have ta'morrow ta try."

Tetra shrugged without moving her head.

There was a pause. Then, "Miss Cairn—Tetra..."

She lifted her gaze, then her neck, at the calm—but serious—look Lady Felicita was sending her. A wave of familiarity went through her as their eyes locked, and she held in another sigh of frustration. What it was about the chief advisor's assistant that felt so familiar she couldn't guess, but this wasn't the first time that feeling had come. It always left her with an uneasiness she couldn't quite place, but she pushed those thoughts to the side for the moment as she replied, "Yes, My Lady?"

Lady Felicita pursed her lips. "You don't 'ave ta call me tha', Tetra. Please, just call me 'Felicita'."

"Oh. Right." It wasn't the first time she had been asked to do so, but she always forgot. "Sorry, My—er, *Felicita*."

A small smile came over Felicita's beautifully soft features. "As I was goin' to say: Chief Baene has told me ta begin askin' you my own questions ta see if their specificity will help at all. So tha' is wha' we will begin tomorrow."

Tetra nodded. "OK."

If Lady Felicita was expecting a complaint, she wasn't going to receive any. Tetra was getting more and more frustrated with herself, and with Emperor Ignis—for stealing her memories away in the first place—in each of these fruitless meetings. The only thing she was able to remember were the memories she already could. Nothing new—well... nothing old, actually.

Felicita stood from the chair and walked across the room towards the door. She stopped as she passed Tetra and their eyes locked again.

"Don't worry, Tetra." Determination laced her accented words as she spoke, "We will get your memories back. Even if it takes a little longer than either of us expected, I promise we will find them." Something flashed across the woman's face as she was speaking, but it was so quick Tetra couldn't decipher it.

"Thank you, My—uh—Felicita." A sheepish smile escaped Tetra's lips before she could stop it.

Amusement lit up Felicita's almond-shaped eyes. "O' course, Tetra." She dipped her chin in her direction. "I will see you tomorrow, then."

Tetra did the same, and the woman stepped out of the room with a flurry of her skirt. Once the door closed behind her, Tetra's new holonode immediately sent a buzz through her wrist. She frowned at the sensation and glanced down at the small screen floating just above it.

She still was not used to the device, nor had she figured out all its features. It seemed like she discovered a few new things on it every day (usually by accident), which made her feel like an idiot at times. Everyone she had ever known had a holonode and knew how to use it, yet here she was—eighteen years old—and had never touched one until the past week. Which was just one more way for her to feel completely different than everyone else.

Her frown deepened at the thought, but she pushed it out of her mind as she tapped the floating screen and a new message appeared. She made the projected screen a little bigger with two of her fingers so she could read the small print from Dr. Prin.

"Miss Cairn, I wanted to give you a heads-up about what we are doing tomorrow. I want to test your flying abilities more, so the Buleutcil has given me permission to take you on a testing mission outside of Urbselva's city limits in the ambulate forest. We will begin at eight in the morning, so be prepared."

When Tetra finished reading the message, she flicked her wrist to turn the holonode off and turned her gaze towards the leafy, nighttime view her single window afforded. She had been wanting to see the forest where the living ambulate trees lived. Perhaps this wouldn't be as horrible as every other testing session had been so far.

A shiver went down her spine, but it wasn't due to the tests themselves. Like Chief Baene promised earlier that week when this whole mess started, none of them could be considered "human experimentation".

Dr. Prin, along with a few other scientists and doctors, had only taken blood and DNA samples while Tetra was human and while she was a peryton. Scans had also been done, and she had even been given muscle regeneration therapy to keep her leg healing at its quickened pace.

The problem wasn't the monotony of testing, it was the looks sent her way by those same scientists and doctors and the whispered words they didn't realize—or they didn't care that—her peryton ears could pick up. *"She's an anomaly"*, *"they should lock her up instead of letting her roam free"*, and *"the Cairns really did birth a monster like themselves"* were only a few of the more minor comments they had made.

And to think that only a few days ago she had thought being at Duschel was the worst situation she could find herself in.

Tetra lowered her gaze to her hands and imagined them turning into large, sharp hooves. A prickling, phantom pain sparked in her palms at the thought, and her heart stopped—until reality struck, and she curled her hands into fists with a shake of her head.

One of the few good things that had come about in the testing sessions was that she had learned how to turn into a peryton and back into a human at will. It had taken a few tries for her to figure out how to access the "switch"—as she liked to call it—in her brain that helped her to do it. But now that she knew how and was forced to do it daily, the action had started to become easier. More natural.

Nothing should be natural about turning into a peryton. She gritted her teeth and pressed her fists against her temples as she had the thought; the tirade of whispers she had overheard during the tests coming back to plague her at its urging. No matter how hard she tried, she could never get away from them—especially the new voice that dominated them all.

"You were always a monster," it whispered, sending another chill through Tetra's muscles, *"born from monsters, raised by them...but now you've reached even beyond their abilities. The only person who can do the impossible, and that impossible just so happens to be turning into a dreaded peryton. Maybe this is just payback from all the dead people your futile rebellion never saved... Or, maybe...just maybe...it's all your past mistakes coming out into the light for all to witness—"*

"—STOP!" Tetra inwardly screamed at the voices. They only continued, completely ignorant to her pleas.

She opened her eyes and looked around frantically for anything to turn her mind off the thoughts. Her gaze landed on the chardex sitting atop the small desk in the room's corner. She scooted over to the side of her bed and set her feet down on the smooth, wooden floor. With careful movements, she lifted herself off the bed and hobbled the few, limping steps it took to get to her desk.

Turning her focus onto something else usually helped, so Tetra had already read through almost the entirety of autobiographies, biographies, and historical fiction books she had requested Lady Felicita to download for her from Urbselva's massive library. She made a mental note to ask for more tomorrow as she picked up the chardex and opened it. Then she pulled up the one she hadn't read yet—a historical fiction novel—and hobbled back over to her bed.

A sigh escaped her lips as she sat down and propped her bandaged leg back up. The only other good thing about all of this was how much more quickly it was healing with the muscle regeneration therapy. She could complain about many things, but she couldn't about that.

Tetra opened the chardex and dimmed the light of its pages before beginning to read. The book was set in Xich a couple hundred years ago during the Raval War, and its descriptions of war-torn Trivsau sounded eerily similar to what was actually happening in the desert capital city. Her focus drifted from the story to her memories of Trivsau, of her and Stellinga's escape, and the kindness Stellinga and Rabetta showed her.

A longing ache filled her chest as she thought of the short, but nice, time spent with them. She hadn't really thought about it, but now that they were on her mind, she realized she missed them. There was something about sharing a life-or-death situation that bonded you to someone—no matter how little you really knew them. Stellinga and Rabetta had been so caring of her, even when they themselves were living in such turmoil and loss. It was unlike anything she had ever experienced.

Tetra glanced down at the holonode on her wrist. If only she knew what their number was. Calling them sounded like it would be a breath of fresh air amidst the turmoil and corrosive thoughts plaguing her.

She sighed with a shake of her head. There was no reason to work herself up over something that wouldn't happen anytime soon. So, she lifted the chardex closer to her face and tried to immerse herself in the story, but her thoughts continued to take over and she found herself zoning out only to realize she had read over two paragraphs and couldn't recall what happened.

Tetra gritted her teeth and tried harder to focus on the words in front of her face. It took a few minutes, but the story finally began to take its hold on her again. She flew through the pages of light, caught up in the mystery plotline and inner conflict of the characters. And before she knew it, she had already gone through half the book and had no intention of stopping. That is, until one of the characters called someone "as ruthless as a peryton," and her thoughts clung to it.

What would Stellinga and Rabetta think if they ever found out about what Tetra could do? Would they regret having helped her? Would they think of her as a ruthless monster that would try to eat them like all the myths and fairytales supposed?

She shivered at the thought and closed the chardex with a yawn. It's not like she wanted to turn into a peryton. In fact, every time she did so the same fiery pain that started the whole mess still came over her whenever she did it and whenever she turned back into herself. The looming thought that she would have to do it again the next day, and possibly multiple times, always filled her with dread. Like it was doing right now.

Another yawn escaped her, and only then did she realize how heavy her eyelids were becoming. So, she picked up the chardex and put it on the nightstand, then brushed her fingers along the light sensor right above it. The warm light dimmed off, encompassing her in a darkness that only magnified every thought. She was able to ignore them for the few moments it took to wiggle herself into a comfortable position underneath the covers, but then they returned to the forefront of her memory.

Dread wormed its slimy way into her stomach, and she turned over to try and get into another comfortable position that would be able to push the thoughts away. More and more she tossed and turned into the lengthening hours of the night until her body's exhaustion caught up to her flowing thoughts and she fell asleep with almost zero answers for the armies of questions she had asked herself.

Chapter Twenty-Seven

WIND STIRRED THE BLUE-GREEN leaves high up in the great boughs of the ambulate trees. Tetra turned in a slow circle, wide-eyed, as she took in the enormous trees towering over their little group. Thunderous creaking echoed from somewhere further away in the huge forest. She wondered if the noises might be one of the trees walking, but her attention was soon taken away from it by Dr. Prin's heavy accent.

"The wind shouldn't give you much trouble, Miss Cairn." She stood a few steps from Tetra, her gaze lowered to her holonode's screen. "Your tracking device has a monitor in it that will tell me if something is wrong." She finally lifted her head, and Tetra met her inscrutable gaze. "So, let's begin."

The dreaded time had arrived. An invisible rope tightened around her chest, but Tetra nodded sullenly and shuffled away from Dr. Prin and the small line of guardsmen standing like statues behind her. Each of them had a loaded crossbow in hand, ready to shoot the peryton if it decided to turn on them.

She frowned and came to a stop with cautious movements. She had almost face-planted a few times already since coming out here because of her weak leg, the extra weight of her metallic jumpsuit that grew with her body when she changed into a peryton, and the coarse dirt that covered the ground of the forest. It was almost like walking on the loose sand of a beach, but worse.

Now that she was steady, Tetra lifted her head and took another quick glance around at the shadows between the building-sized tree trunks; rubbing her hand across the thin pieces of metal that made up her computerized jumpsuit. If only she could run away and go somewhere else...maybe to one of the uninhabited islands of the Chain.

Just as the thought came, she whisked it away. The new tracking device Silvas put in her after she turned into a peryton the first time wouldn't allow for that to happen. Also, she admitted to herself, living on a deserted island sounded like it would get boring rather quickly, and there would be no way for her to fulfill the oath she had sworn back in Xich. Even if nobody except for her knew of its existence, it was still a promise, and she wasn't going to break it.

Though her hopes of being able to fulfill it were deteriorating every day.

She glanced over her shoulder and noticed the impatient frown marring Dr. Prin's features. "We don't have all day, Miss Cairn," her voice echoed in the still forest.

Tetra gritted her teeth to keep from snapping back something that would only take away the tiny bit of freedom she had. "Yes ma'am."

Her heart began to race as the invisible ropes continued tightening around her chest. She inhaled deeply to try and calm some of the anxiety, but with the feeling of Dr. Prin's stare burning into the back of her head, she didn't give herself enough time to exhale before she "flipped" on the mental switch in her head. Immediately, the invisible, fiery daggers began tearing through her insides.

The cacophony of snapping bones reached her ears before a loud ringing took over. She vaguely got the impression of falling, but it was overshadowed by the sensation of phantom claws shredding through her organs and nervous system.

Finally, the excruciating pains dissipated, leaving Tetra panting for air to fill her sore lungs. A wave of new smells accosted her sensitive nose as she blinked her eyes open. The shadowy forest floor looked much brighter to her peryton eyes than it did her human ones, which led her to wonder for a moment if perytons had night vision.

"That was the quickest you have ever changed, Miss Cairn." She swiveled her long ears in Dr. Prin's direction before lifting her head and looking over her winged shoulder at the Silvanian biologist. "It only took thirty-seven seconds this time."

Tetra flicked her ears back. Only thirty-seven seconds? She tilted her head to the side. Maybe if she kept doing it, then it would go down to only a few...but that would mean that she would have turned into a monster more times than she wanted to.

She shook her antlered head at the thought and moved into a stand. Her sharp hooves and talons dug into the loose dirt easily as she turned around to face the wary look Dr. Prin was sending her. Tetra lowered her long neck to get eye-level with her to show she was paying attention and not thinking any "hungry-peryton" thoughts.

"OK, Miss Cairn," Dr. Prin turned to look back down at her holonode as she spoke, "let's see if you can just make it off the ground without falling."

If Tetra had human lips, she would have frowned at the reminder of yesterday's failures in flight, but with her new long, peryton face her lips curled back to show the hint of teeth. A pungent odor came from the small group of people, and she immediately lowered her lips back into a neutral expression.

Throughout the week, she had come to find out that the strong, foul odor she had first smelled back at the weaponship club was fear. It was the strongest the first couple days of tests, but had lessened with each passing day. Now it only came in waves whenever she did something that everyone thought meant she was hinting at attacking them, but most of the time the expressions she made were only showing her displeasure or her own fear.

From her new point of view, she was beginning to wonder if perytons were as evil and ruthless as everyone said they were, or if all the races of intelligent beings were only misinterpreting their actions. She knew they were not prey animals by any means, but even predators could feel threatened by something that didn't smell like it had good intentions and would act accordingly.

Dr. Prin lifted her head, eyes narrowed as she peered up at the lowest ambulate tree boughs high above them—even with Tetra's towering new height.

"See if you can reach the lowest of those branches," she said.

Tetra nodded and lifted her neck to stare up at the blue-green leaves, her heart beginning to race with rising fear as her eyes focused on their details. Her old fear of heights was one of the reasons she had failed so miserably during her first flight yesterday. She had tried to fly to the top of the huge ceiling of the Altelo room they did testing in, but when she had looked down, her heart stopped with her wings. She had crashed to the floor and blacked out, only to find that when she woke up that she had turned back into herself (similar to what happened when Finnegar shot her with the dart and she fell asleep).

So, no matter how many times she told herself she now had wings to catch herself from any height, there was now that added fear of *"what if I faint while in the air and turn back into myself while freefalling?"*, to top off the other problem that she was dealing with.

She turned her neck around to watch herself as she unfurled her auburn-feathered wings. She had never had wings before, and it was like trying to learn how to walk again when she used them. They were so...different, and her brain was still learning the best way to use them that wouldn't lead to death-by-falling.

"Come now, Miss Cairn," Dr. Prin cut through her thoughts, "We don't have all day."

Yeah, I know. Tetra huffed a breath and recalled the videos she had watched in the past that had had perytons flying in them. From what she could remember, it looked like they jumped into the air and then began flapping their wings to lift themselves off the ground.

So, lifting her eyes again to the great boughs above, she raised her wings as she lowered the rest of her body, then she jumped. She flapped them once and rose higher, dust billowing in a cloud below. A buzz of elation went through her but was taken over by a wave of fear as she felt herself falling back down amid the dust cloud.

"Try again," Dr. Prin ordered right after her hooves hit the ground.

Tetra gritted her teeth as she took a few deep breaths to steady her racing heart. There was no reason to be afraid. It wasn't like she was climbing up a tree with guards waiting below for her to fall again, or as if she was going to slip off the rain-soaked walls of Emperor Ignis' fortress.

Determination silenced some of the fear. She had *wings* now, and she *would* learn how to use them so nothing like that could ever happen again.

Without waiting for her fear to talk her out of it, she opened her wings again and jumped. She flapped them once, twice, and continued to beat them in a rhythmic pattern. She kept her gaze upwards, the leaves growing a little closer with each flap. The new, and unused, muscles in her wings began to burn with exertion as she flew higher and higher. She breathed in deep, but quick, draughts of air through her bigger peryton lungs as her heart raced almost as fast as a human's.

"Don't look down, don't look down, don't look down..." became the rhythm she flew to. The thick ambulate tree boughs drew closer and closer. Tetra clenched her jaw as the muscles in her back and neck began to burn along with her wings. She kept her eyes glued to one spot above her—the lowest branch of the tree—and flapped her wings harder.

Satisfaction bloomed in her pounding chest as she finally made it to the bough that looked to be as big as a strip of townhomes in Rubrum. She slowed her wingbeats down, like she had seen perytons do in videos, until she stayed in relatively the same spot near the tree's leafy branch. She tried to angle her wings to fly in a forward direction and was rewarded with the tree coming closer. Again, she angled her wings and flew in the same way until she was hovering above the safety of the branch's middle.

Tetra could only wonder for a moment on how she was supposed to land before her tired wings gave her an answer. Her muscles gave out, and she abruptly fell. Leaves and twigs scratched her as she landed on all fours, wings spread out for balance. Pain ricocheted through her injured leg at the impact, and she lifted it slightly to relieve the pressure.

At least one good thing about being a peryton was she still had three other legs to walk around on. She glanced down at her front hooves. It would've been nice to have hands, though—especially thumbs. She rolled her eyes at herself, but couldn't keep a small grin (or, what she meant as a grin) from escaping.

A small breeze ruffled through her fur and feathers. She lifted her head above the greenish-blue leaves surrounding her. Elation sent her pounding heart into an erratic beat. She had done it. She flew! It might not have been the prettiest display of flight, but she had been successful.

"Yes!" She immediately snapped her jaw shut as the breeze carried her roar away.

Her fur stood on end as a wave of embarrassment washed over her, but it did nothing to impede her excitement. She hadn't meant to do that, but facing her fear of heights—and winning against it—filled her with a buzzing warmth she couldn't contain quietly.

"Miss Cairn?" She flicked her ears in the direction of Dr. Prin's faint voice. "Are you alright?"

She was better than alright. This was the first time she didn't find herself dreading the idea of being a peryton.

She took another sweeping glance of her grand surroundings and inhaled a deep breath to calm her heart's racing. The earthy scents of the leaves and dirt, the clean smell of the wind, and even the sharp smell of an animal climbing along one of the branches above filled her nostrils. It was amazing, and Tetra wanted more—more of whatever this feeling was.

"Miss Cairn, if you are fine then come back down here," Dr. Prin's order broke through her daze.

Tetra shook her head with a long sigh. She should get back down before the head biologist could think to punish her by making them leave early. She lifted her eyes one last time to the leaves and branches above, took another deep inhale—and caught the whiff of a new, fainter smell along with the others—then opened her sore wings and leapt into the air.

Her earlier elation evaporated as she flew back into the open air near the thick branch. She finally looked down, and her heartbeat sped up as her fear rushed back. Even with her enhanced vision, Dr. Prin and the guards looked like large insects as they watched her from far below. She gulped as the memory of when she fell from the everpine tree back at Norland popped into her head.

Her wings faltered in their flapping rhythm and she began to fall. *NO!* She gritted her teeth and opened her wings wide to try and glide down as she had seen in those same peryton videos. It worked—but it was much harder than the videos made it look. She wobbled and shook as she turned to swoop around in a circle. It almost took more concentration to keep her wings in their still position along the faint currents of wind that blew through the huge trees than it did to flap them.

Another, stronger wave of the new scent hit her nose, and her tiring wings faltered for a moment as she almost lost her balance. She turned her head slightly to peer into the shadows under the trees. Was there another animal nearby?

Not seeing anything unusual, she pricked her ears in the direction from where the wind was blowing the scent. Above the whistling breeze and fluttering leaves, she thought she heard wingbeats. Yet before she could dwell on it further, she realized how close she was to the ground and tried to angle her wings for a slow landing. She misjudged it, though, and flew right over Dr. Prin and the guardsmen.

Her back talons hit the dirt first, then the rest of her immediately followed. A surprised roar escaped her lips as she fell and twisted into a roll. Her wings and flailing limbs kicked up dust as she finally came to a stop.

"Miss Cairn!" Alarm laced Dr. Prin's usually uptight voice.

Tetra groaned as she blinked her eyes open. Dust particles floated by lazily. She lifted her head with another groan, then sneezed as dust filled her nose.

"Miss Cairn," she turned her head in Dr. Prin's direction as the group slowed to a stop before they reached the dust cloud, "are you hurt?"

She opened her mouth to reply, but then remembered she couldn't speak Alenguan and shook her head.

Dr. Prin breathed out a quiet sigh her peryton ears barely caught. "Good."

Tetra went to move all her legs underneath her to stand, but when she moved her injured leg another jolt of pain like the one she felt earlier went through it. She gritted her teeth against the throbbing pain and pushed herself into a standing position on her other three legs.

A layer of dirt covered her whole body, turning the silver hue of her jumpsuit into a dull brown, so she tried to shake it off like she had seen some animals do. More dust flew around her, inciting another sneeze from her, but as she folded her aching wings by her side she was glad to feel they were grit-free.

She limped out of the settling dust cloud and lowered her head to meet Dr. Prin's incredulous expression. "You're not hurt?" She asked, brow raised.

Tetra turned her head to look at her injured talon, then back at Dr. Prin. She shrugged her shoulders and kept a neutral expression so she wouldn't cause unneeded panic with any emotions that might flit across it.

Dr. Prin rolled her eyes but stepped towards her. "Let me take a look at it."

The pain had already dimmed, but she turned so the biologist could get a closer look. As she did so, she picked up the weird smell again—though it was heavier this time. Her heart picked up a fearful rhythm as she jerked her neck up, ears pricked, in the direction the loud, flapping wing beats were coming from. How could she be so stupid as to forget that?

"Miss Cairn?" Dr. Prin began, "What's wrong...?"

Her voice died away as all of the guards turned, crossbows at the ready, in the same direction Tetra was looking in. *What could it be...?*

"Hello?" A deep, grumbling voice called out.

Tetra blinked in surprise as she saw a winged shape appear in the distant shadows of the trees. Was that...a peryton?

"Hello?" The strange voice called again, "Is everything all right?"

Right as it did so, she heard one of the guardsmen whisper, "Remember to always aim for a peryton's wings if it's flying. Then once it's down, aim for its head and sides."

Wait a minute. That was a peryton. Tetra's eyes widened. A peryton that had *spoken*. She flicked her eyes between the line of waiting guardsmen and the oncoming peryton. They couldn't kill it! Not if she had heard it speak!

In that split second decision, Tetra called out, "Don't shoot it!"

A fresh wave of fear-scent hit her in the face as all the guards jerked in her direction. One of them accidentally fired their crossbow bolt into the ground in his haste.

"What is wrong with you?" The same guardsman who had whispered the commands barked as Dr. Prin exclaimed, "Miss Cairn! What—"

Tetra leapt over the guards before she could finish speaking. Another strange scent mingled with the one coming from the peryton as she raced towards it. The new peryton was still heading towards them, but she could tell its pace had slowed a bit.

"What's going on?" The roar echoed in the spaces between the trees.

Tetra took a few steps forward and waited, keeping herself between the incoming peryton and the small group of humans. "Um—sorry," she replied in a growling voice that didn't sound like her own, "You—you scared us, is all."

She watched as the peryton tilted its wings and glided down into a soft landing—that put Tetra's earlier crash to shame—then strode towards them. With her night vision, the forest's shadows couldn't hide the golden-brown coloring of his fur, nor the golden-yellow feathers of his wings and tail. His white antlers were huge—like all male perytons had—and reached up towards the sky with many sharp points. Even without them, he still would have towered over Tetra by almost half her height.

She didn't think her heart could take much more activity as it began to pump adrenaline through her veins. If this peryton decided to attack, she was not sure she would be able to do much damage to him.

He came to a stop a few steps away from her, and she flicked her ears at the sounds of the guards moving back into their positions. Hopefully none of them would try to shoot the *talking* peryton—unless he attacked, of course. She would definitely need their help if it came to that.

The peryton's honey-brown eyes widened as he seemed to take in the scene before him. Another wave of the same scent that had come from him before came back, and by the look in his eyes Tetra wondered if it might mean confusion. That thought only made another question pop into her head: could perytons feel confusion?

"What in the world?" He asked. Their eyes locked, and the feathers of his wings ruffled. "Oh! Um..." He lowered his long neck as if to get a closer look at her, "Are you OK?"

Tetra didn't respond, her eyes staying on his. Those weren't the eyes of some curious animal. There was intelligence in that gaze, and it struck her.

The peryton's eyes flicked between her and the guards she was trying to block with her legs. "Have they...hurt you?" His gaze lowered in the direction of her leg.

"Um—no." Was all she said.

"Oh." More waves of the confusion smell came off him as he lifted his gaze back up to meet hers again. "Well, then if I may ask: what—what are you doing with a bunch of no-furs?"

"No-furs?" Tetra tilted her head.

"Yeah..." Another scent came off the peryton, but she couldn't place what it was. "The creatures behind you... They—they haven't killed you with their flying claws... I've never seen one so close before..."

Understanding dawned on Tetra, but she didn't risk moving her head to glance back at Dr. Prin and the guards. "They—they won't hurt you." *I hope*, she thought to herself. "I was just—flying. And I crashed. So...there's nothing to worry about. Nothing's wrong."

Except for the fact that she was talking to a peryton, as a peryton.

"I...see." Yet by his tone, she could detect he didn't. There was a pause, but then he asked, "What...what is your name?"

She narrowed her eyes, but replied, "Tetra..."

He blinked then dipped his head towards her. "Then hello, Tetra." Her name sounded strange in his rumbling voice, as if his tongue wasn't used to the syllables. "My name is Leaves Of Gold. I—I think I heard you roar a few minutes ago, and I came to make sure everything was well."

Oh, *that*. Tetra ruffled her wing feathers as a wave of embarrassed heat shot through her. Leaves Of Gold lifted his head again, and she noticed the new softness in his gaze.

"Well, I'm—I'm fine," she said, "I was just...erm—excited."

"I see." Leaves Of Gold nodded slowly. "Then...you are well? You're not in any trouble?" His eyes flicked back in the direction of the guards. "Because if you are, I could help you get out of it..."

"No!" Tetra growled deep in her throat, then immediately jerked her head back in surprise. She hadn't meant to do that... "I'm fine," she added in a more even tone. "Thank you for asking, but everything's good here."

"OK then..." Leaves Of Gold sent her one more confused look before taking a step back. "I will leave you all be. May the Unrivaled King carry you upon his winds, Tetra."

With that, he took a few backwards steps, unfurled his huge wings, and leapt into the air. He ascended with great flaps of his wings, then turned in a fluid half-circle and disappeared behind the closest tree. Tetra stayed in her position until she could no longer hear his wingbeats or smell his scent. Once she figured they were in the clear, she let her tense muscles relax and turned her head to face Dr. Prin.

The woman was staring at Tetra with wide eyes, her mouth in an "o" shape. The guards shared looks of either surprise or confusion as they, too, stared up at her.

Her heart skipped an excited beat. So, they had heard the peryton talk, too.

After a moment, Dr. Prin seemed to shake herself out of a daze and looked Tetra in the eyes. "Miss Cairn, I need you to turn back into your human form. Now."

She obliged without complaint, her curious excitement taking over her dread of the pain. She "flipped" the mental switch and let the invisible blades slice and burn her back into her normal, human self. When the pains were finally gone, she blinked her eyes open and pushed herself up into a sitting position. Soreness laced through her back muscles, and she reached her hand back to rub them with a frown. Why did all her aches and pains have to transfer over?

"Here—" Tetra lifted her gaze up at the new, deep voice.

One of the guardsmen held his hand out for her to take. She peered at his face with narrowed eyes and tried to discern whether this was some kind of trick. Her plethora of ever-present guards usually acted as if she didn't exist, but maybe this one was new. Tetra didn't recognize him, but that could have been because she tried not to look at any of their faces—she didn't like to see the unhidden emotions in their eyes as they stared at her.

The new guard barely raised his brow as if to ask, "Are you going to take it?" She saw no hostility or anything worrisome in his purplish-blue eyes, so she reached out and took his hand. He helped pull her up then let go.

"Thanks." She nodded towards him.

He only dipped his chin in reply and stepped back, his empty expression having returned to his face. Soft footsteps moved towards Tetra and she turned in their direction, locking eyes with Dr. Prin. Her earlier excitement returned as she saw the surprise still on the woman's face.

"You heard it talking too, didn't you?" She blurted without waiting for the biologist to say anything first.

Understanding dawned in Dr. Prin's eyes before she shook her head. "No, Miss Cairn, I didn't hear it talk—I only heard you two growling and rumbling like perytons do—but it...it did look like there was some sort of structured communication going on..." She paused, then asked, "You...truly heard it speak?"

"Yes ma'am." Tetra lowered her gaze and attempted to wipe away the dirt coating her arms and jumpsuit. "I...I thought you all had heard it, too, by your expressions..."

"No, we were only surprised by the fact it didn't try to attack us, and that it looked like you two were...having a conversation..." Dr. Prin's wistful tone trailed away.

Tetra looked up in surprise and caught the almost dreamlike expression on the biologist's face, the total opposite of its usual calculating sharpness.

"Um...yeah, we—we actually did," she replied slowly, "It was like...well, talking to you or any other human."

"Really?"

"Yes ma'am. He—he asked me if I was OK and if I needed help. So, I told him 'no', he asked me what my name was, I told him, and then he said his name was 'Leaves Of Gold'."

Dr. Prin raised her brow. "Leaves Of...Gold?"

Tetra shrugged and ran her thumb over her segione scars. "That's what he told me."

"Hmm..." There was another pause. Then, "Well, Miss Cairn, let me think more on what just happened before I make a decision on how to move forward." She aimed a hard stare towards the guards, "Word about this does not leave this group unless I give permission. Is that clear?"

All the guards put their fists over their hearts in unified agreement. Dr. Prin nodded sharply and turned her gaze back on Tetra. "The same goes for you, Miss Cairn."

She nodded with her own salute—done more out of habit than anything else.

"Good." The biologist also sent her a firm nod before turning her gaze down to her holonode, all wisps of dreamy softness gone from her tone. "I don't want to waste any more time while we are out here, so let's get you flying again."

Tetra nodded again and turned around to head towards a spot further away to give her space to change. Not even the thought of the incoming pain could keep her buzzing excitement down. She had talked to a peryton *and* flown successfully in the same day. And she was about to fly even more. Maybe she would even get that same exhilarating feeling from before...

Bolstered by that hopeful thought, she "flipped" the switch in her brain without hesitation and changed back into a peryton, ready to fly.

Chapter Twenty-Eight

Aabir shut his chardex with a groan and buried his face between his arms on the library's table. He squeezed his eyes shut to dull the ache behind them. When they had finished fighting the training droids, he thought sitting in the library and reviewing things he had already begun to research the week before would have been a good use of his time. Instead, his head pounded from the couple hours of reading and information overload, and he felt more exhausted than if he had been using all this time in training. That was even with avoiding any and all books or websites that had to do with conspiracies.

The bell rang to signal it was time for dinner. Aabir was not even hungry, but he lifted his aching head and sluggishly got up from the chair. If he did not at least go to the dining hall then he would get in trouble. Best to just sit in there and doze while waiting for the period to end then to be found here asleep.

He yawned and picked up his chardex, then made his way down the center aisle of shelves before exiting Norland's library.

"What on Afreean were you doing in there, Aabir?"

Aabir jerked to a stop in the hallway and turned to face the mock-surprised look Tycho was sending him. His heart began to race as he tried to think of an excuse. "Um—studying."

"Uh-huh. You—Aabir Sorrel—*studying*." Tycho raised a dubious brow. "Y'know, when Aquilo told me you might be here, I thought he was lying. And even though he was obviously right, I still don't believe it."

Oh Deleyon. Aabir racked his brain for any other excuses that would sound more like him. "Uh..."

Just then, the library doors opened behind him. He glanced over his shoulder as Mabel Frauss and Accaly Lavrai stepped through the doorway. They both came to a stop as they caught Aabir and Tycho's gazes on them.

"Do you two need something?" Mabel frowned and crossed her arms as the doors shut behind her.

"No." Aabir replied as Tycho said, "I have a question, actually."

Both girls shared a glance, then Accaly asked, "Yes?"

Tycho sent Aabir a smirk before asking, "Did either of you happen to see what Aabir was doing in there?"

"Uh...I think he was studying." Her brow pinched in confusion. "Why?"

"Just wonderin', is all."

The girls shared another glance with each other, then Mabel rolled her eyes and started down the hall. Accaly sent a strange look towards Aabir and Tycho before following right behind her. When they were far enough down the hall, Aabir looked back over at Tycho, whose eyes were narrowed in thought.

He tried to hide all his relief as he said, "Tycho?"

"Hmm?" His friend's eyes did not lose their unfocused look.

"Are you satisfied now?"

Tycho shrugged. "I'm not sure..."

Now it was Aabir's turn to roll his eyes. "I was in there reading." He gestured towards the library's doors on the opposite side of the room. "Even Accaly and Mabel saw it. So can we please go to dinner now?"

Tycho said nothing, his expression still thoughtful, but he took a few steps down the hall. Aabir joined him, silently thanking Deleyon for Mabel and Accaly (something he never thought he would find himself doing).

He would have to think of a better excuse if he was to continue going to the library for Rasiela. No one who disliked studying as much as he did could keep up *that* charade for long.

"So..." Tycho began as they entered the entrance hall teeming with more trainees all heading in the same direction, "You got Accaly to help with your excuse, didn't you?"

Annoyance warred with Aabir's worry as he looked at Tycho out of the corner of his eye. "No."

"But you hate studying. Unless..." A mischievous grin spread across Tycho's face, "She was only covering up for both of you."

"Excuse me?"

"Wow. Of all the things...and of all the people..." Tycho met Aabir's eyes. "I never thought Accaly was your type, but I guess I've been wrong before—"

"—Tycho!" Aabir hissed, then frantically looked around to make sure no one had heard him.

"So, it *is* true," Tycho said in a lower voice, his grin widening.

"No, it's not!" Far from it. "I just don't want to get in trouble for something I haven't done because of your big mouth." Even though what he was really "studying" would be far worse than some mere rumor of romance.

"Cut the act, Aabir. I know you, and you've never willingly studied a day in your life."

"That's because I wasn't failing in any of my classes." He never thought he would be thankful for a bad grade before but having them was better than

Tycho's alternative. "I need to get my chemistry and history grades back up before Lieutenant Denir confronts me about it."

"Eh. It's not that bad when he does." Tycho waved his comment aside. "I only had to clean the bathrooms for a week. My patre didn't even find out about it."

"Yeah, well mine probably would, and I'd rather not clean any bathrooms." He no longer had that kind of time to waste.

His friend said nothing for a long moment. Then he sent Aabir a side-eye glance. "So...you really were studying?"

"Yes..."

"Alright, then." Tycho shrugged. "I believe you—but even if you two had been hiding out in the library, you know I wouldn't have told anyone about it. You can trust me, Aabir."

"I know, but sometimes you just don't know how loud that mouth of yours is."

"So kind."

"But thanks, anyway."

Tycho slapped him on the shoulder. "No problem. I mean—if you can't trust your friends, then who can you trust?"

Guilt stabbed Aabir's heart, despite his relief that Tycho had dropped the accusation. He tried to combat the constricting feeling by reminding himself his spy work was not doing anything to harm his friends or anyone else at Norland. In fact, if it was going to affect anyone it would be the possible creepy group of pyromaniacs he was trying to avoid. *If* they even existed.

"So, what'd you think about this afternoon?" Tycho's question jabbed through his thoughts. "You didn't say much about it earlier."

Aabir shrugged. "What's there to say?"

"I don't know." They moved through one of the entrances leading into the classroom corridors and had to slow their pace as the other trainees in front of them also slowed. "I could tell something was upsetting you, though."

Aabir did not reply immediately as he tried to come up with an answer. Tycho was his oldest and closest friend besides Aquilo, so despite his multitude of jokes, he was usually the first one to notice things like this. Aabir hated keeping all the secrets about his family's problems—and now Rasiela—from him, but not even one of his most trusted friends could be trusted with any of this.

Even with that reasoning, the guilt he was feeling slimed its way into his stomach.

"I just...I have a lot on my mind right now," he finally replied as the open dining hall doors came into view.

"Does it have anything to do with what happened on Sixthdein?"

"A little, yeah."

Aabir glanced over at Tycho and noticed his glare. "I still can't believe that straudwin idiot did that to you." There was a sharp edge to his tone as he spoke, "No one should ever disrespect a trainee just because he's descended from Silvas. It's dishonoring, is what it is."

Though his comment was not necessarily pouring love onto Silvas or any of the Alliance nations, it did light a tiny spark of hope inside Aabir amidst his shame and tumultuous thoughts. Maybe it would be possible for his friend to one day see past the Igrian brainwashing.

"Thanks, Tycho," he said, "I'm...I'm glad you think that."

"Hey, if I could I'd go back there and give that guy a piece of my mind." Tycho sighed. "But I have a feeling I'd just end up in the back of a patrolman's hovercar if I did that—and my patre would definitely hear about *that*."

"Probably."

They finally entered the dining hall and joined the long line of trainees waiting to get their food at the counter. Aabir replayed Tycho's words over again in his mind as they waited. He never thought he would be happy for someone to get angry, but he was. If that small event upset his friend that much, then there was hope of Emperor Ignis and his advisors playing their hand too far in their mission to destroy anything that had to do with the Alliance. Because if it made a proud, full-blooded Igrian trainee angry, then it must be making other people angry as well; people not only of Alliance-descent, but those who were also fully Igrian.

Tycho said something Aabir did not catch, and he tucked the thoughts aside for a later time. He would need to think about them more deeply when he got the chance. Yet even with them tucked away and his focus turned on what his friend was saying, they left him with a warm—almost peaceful—feeling that settled the waves of guilt and worry churning his insides.

His stomach growled and he inhaled deeply of the delicious smell coming from behind the food counter. Whatever dinner was going to be, he was ready to eat it. His appetite had returned.

"I'M GLAD IT ALL turned out OK," Matha said, her brow pinched in worry, "but I hate that it happened to all those kids. I still can't believe anyone would be sick enough to attack a group of twelve-year-olds."

Aabir nodded, even though he did have an idea of who might be crazy enough to do so. "Yeah."

Buren passed by him in the dorm corridor and Aabir lifted his head to send the other trainee a nod of acknowledgement before returning his focus to his parents' faces on the holonode's screen. It was much quieter, and more private, out here where only a few trainees lingered than it was in his own dorm.

"And you're OK, Aabir?" Patre asked.

"Yes sir," he replied with a small smile, "I had my shield on the whole time, and my armor, too."

"That's not what I meant."

His smile faded. "Yes sir." He never told his parents what happened at the restaurant, but he had a feeling they both had seen it on his face when he came home that night because they had continued to ask him similar questions since.

Patre gave him a hard look. "I just don't want you to be in trouble and not tell us."

Well, Ereliev might be dealing with some kind of trouble, but he remembered his promise to her and remained silent on the subject. Zeke had been questioned at school again, but—thank Deleyon—nothing as bad as the first time. Oh, and Aabir himself was doing spy work for Silvas which could possibly land him in trouble if it were ever discovered...

Suppressing a sigh, he shook his head. "I'm not in trouble, Patre. I promise." At least he could say that was not a lie.

"But there is *something* bothering you," Patre said. "I can see it in your eyes. You can't hide everything from us."

Aabir's heart gave a nervous leap, which was immediately followed by a prick of guilt. He had already lost his parents' trust a couple more times than he had ever wanted to, and if they could already tell he was hiding something, then he might as well give them a hint of what he was dealing with...

He glanced around to make sure no one was close enough to hear him. Buren was the last person in the hall, and he was already at its other end, so Aabir turned his face back down towards his parents.

"There...there's a lot going on right now." He began, "And I'm just...worried, is all. About...about you." Along with his new secret job and crazy, conspiratorial groups, but he did not have the courage to tell them that yet.

Patre sighed. "Well, you don't need to be. The patrolmen have not been by in almost a week, and Nevaze had a good day at school without any incidents." He gave Aabir a pointed look. "Your worrying is not going to be able to protect anyone, so you need to just let it go. Let me and your matha handle...*things*—" he sent Aabir another significant look, "—and we will let you know when we come to a conclusion."

Aabir twisted his lips into a frown. He had a feeling Patre was talking about escaping Igrium, but since he could not say he was already working on a solution for their dilemma, he only replied, "Yes sir. I'll try to let it go."

Not that he could ever see it happening, but at least he could say he would *try* not to worry.

Patre nodded sharply. "Thank you." He paused for a moment, then said, "So, how are you doing about those grades of yours'?"

Aabir looked anywhere but at his holonode's screen. "I...am working on them." He grinned sheepishly and scratched the back of his neck.

Patre snorted. "I hope so. Because the last time I checked, you were failing two classes."

"Aabir!" Matha scolded, "Why are you failing?"

He heaved a heavy sigh and leaned his head back against the wall. One thing he did not like about having parents from Silvas was their push on his academics—the one thing at Norland he could care less about.

"I...I keep falling asleep in chemistry." He dared to look down at their faces; but instead of the disappointment he was expecting, he only saw confusion and worry there. "And I forgot to do my homework a few times..."

Disappointment took over the worry in their eyes.

"How could you *forget* to do your homework?" Patre asked incredulously.

Aabir shrugged with a yawn. He had been so focused on getting information for Rasiela he just...forgot.

"You're better than this, Aabir." Patre continued, "I know how smart you really are. What could be so important during your breaks that you would forget homework?"

Trying to get a Silvanian spy to trust me so we can all escape this empire. "Random stuff."

A frown twisted Patre's lips. "Then I don't want you to do anything during your breaks until you finish your homework. No matter what is happening here, you know you need to keep up with that. Do I make myself clear?"

"Yes sir."

Aabir knew part of his lecture was only to keep up appearances—both for anyone who might be spying on their conversation, and for those who might wonder why they seemed to not care that their son might end up dishonoring them with failing grades—but he knew Patre well enough to detect the hidden truth in his words. Silvas was one of the most academically driven kingdoms in the world, and his parents had grown up with the idea that "you can't succeed in life if you don't do exceedingly well in school" ingrained into them. So, even amid the other chaos around them, having to keep up appearances gave them the perfect excuse to worry about his grades.

"And why have you been falling asleep?" Patre asked.

In a much softer voice than his, Matha added, "Have the supplements I gave you not been working?"

Aabir shook his head with a tired sigh, thankful for the subject change—even if it was this subject. "I mean—I have been sleeping better than I was." He rubbed the side of his face without meeting her eyes. “But no. They don’t seem to be working like I hoped they would.”

The nightmares of Xich still continued, and he had a sinking feeling the training droid attack would only add to them.

“Hmm.” Matha twisted her lips to the side. “You have been remembering to take them, yes?”

“Yes, Matha.”

“Then I will start looking for something else that might be able to help. Until then, if you wake up in the middle of the night, you can take another pill if you need to. Your patre had to do that a few times when he took them.”

“I’ll try that.” He yawned again. All this talk of his lack of sleep was making him even more tired than he already was. “I should probably go now, but I’ll call you tomorrow when I get a chance.”

“Of course, Aabir.” Matha smiled knowingly. “I will be praying you get a full night of sleep tonight.”

He smiled back. “Thanks.”

“Aabir,” Patre’s eyes locked onto his through the screen, “I don’t want you to think I’m being insensitive to what you are dealing with, I just don’t want you to waste your time dealing with things that you shouldn’t have to carry.” A small smile lifted one of the corners of his mouth. “Especially when you have more important things to think about—like homework.”

Aabir snorted and shook his head. “Uh-huh.”

“We love you, Aabir,” Matha said, “Good night.”

“G’night.”

The call ended and he turned his holonode off. Then he stared at the wall across from him for a few moments before finding the energy to push himself from the one he leaned on. He turned and headed back into his dorm, mumbling prayers of protection over his family, and pleas for him to be able to sleep.

Chapter Twenty-Nine

Tetra lifted her head from between her hands. "Nothing," she sighed.

She looked over and saw the pursed-lip look Lady Felicita had on before she, too, also sighed.

"Well, I'm glad ta say tha' was the last o' the official list o' questions, so we can begin with some o' the ones I created." Her voice was light as she spoke, "Hopefully, these will bring out something more."

"Yeah." Tetra nodded slowly and turned her neck to look out the window. The bluish-green leaves outside its view brought back the memories of that morning's events. She still couldn't get over the fact she had heard a peryton speak, or that she had actually held a conversation with it—albeit a short and awkward one. It was like finding out sky-whales or spotted tigers could communicate like any race of the three intelligent beings.

And his eyes... She kept returning to the memory of the depth she had seen in them. There was intelligence behind that gaze, and her curiosity was itching to learn more.

"Alright, then. Here is tha' first one," Tetra brought her focus back to Lady Felicita as the woman's accented voice shook her from her thoughts, "can you recall a time when you did something fun with your parents? Maybe...a trip o' some kind? Or even somethin' simple—like going clothes shoppin' with your matha, or just eatin' a meal together?"

Clothes shopping? With Marin Cairn? Tetra raised a dubious brow but closed her eyes anyway. It couldn't hurt to at least try, even if the question sounded absurd when compared to the Aries and Marin Cairn she had grown up hearing about.

She ran the question over and over again in her mind, hoping the repetition would conjure up a memory from the depths of her brain. When nothing appeared, she gritted her teeth and pressed her hands against her temples.

Come on! She berated herself, *A trip. They must've taken me on some trip before...or even just a meal! Surely we ate supper together at least once.*

A memory—one of a few she could remember of the time before her amnesia—emerged in all its fuzzy, confusing glory. All she could see of it was swirls of color, and...was that *laughter*? Her heart skipped a beat at the new remembrance, and she turned all her focus onto the memory.

Come on... She waited for something else to happen; for her brain to remember another noise or even some sort of feeling associated with the blob of colors. A few moments passed, and so did her hold on the memory.

"Nothing." She opened her eyes and sent a withering glare towards the white bed sheets. "I thought...I thought I remembered something...but when I tried to focus, the memory only disappeared."

"But you did see something different?"

"I don't know." Tetra shrugged and folded her arms. "I thought I remembered...well, laughter—of all things—happening in it, but it's not like I saw or felt anything."

"But, tha' is still good." Hope laced Lady Felicita's words, "It means we're on the right track now..."

Tetra twisted her lips to the side but didn't reply. She had been hoping for an actual memory to come up, not a random snippet of something connected to a swirl of colors.

Chief Baene was probably beginning to regret having his assistant waste all her time with this.

"Here. I'll give you one tha' is similar—then maybe it'll help bring more o' tha' memory back." Lady Felicita cleared her throat. "Can you recall a memory of you playin'? It doesn't even have ta be with your parents, necessarily. Just one memory of you playin' like any child."

Tetra lifted a glare onto the chief advisor's assistant. "How is a memory of me *playing* supposed to help us figure out how I can turn into a peryton?" She snapped. Felicita blinked in surprise, and a worm of guilt pricked Tetra's conscience. She immediately averted her gaze back down to the sheets with a sigh. "Sorry, I'm just...frustrated."

Lady Felicita's chair squeaked as she moved. "I understand, Tetra." She said, "Believe me, I do. I very much want you ta find *all* your memories, but we both need ta' remember tha' they've been locked away for a decade. It will probably take a little while for us ta find anythin' remotely helpful for Chief Baene. So, let's not lose hope when we've barely even begun."

Tetra lifted her head and their eyes locked. The annoyingly unhelpful feeling of familiarity came again, but she ignored it.

"Why are you so hopeful about all of this?" She narrowed her eyes. "Is there something in it for you if I do end up finding these memories?"

Felicita shifted her position on the desk's chair as she lowered her gaze. The gesture only made Tetra more wary. She had never met anyone who seemed to be so patiently-hopeful before, and something about it seemed...unnatural. At least, about as unnatural as a human turning into a peryton.

"Well, there is somethin', yes." Lady Felicita finally replied, her face shadowed. "I truly want ta help you, Tetra. I think it's cruel tha' Emperor Ignis would steal your memories away. No one—not even if they are emperor—should be allowed ta do tha'." A sharp glint entered her eyes, and it shown in her voice as she continued, "An' if he was tryin' ta hide somethin' in regards ta your shifting into a peryton or something completely different, I want ta see his attempts backfire in any way they can."

Tetra found herself leaning back a little at the suppressed anger coming from the last person she would expect it from. "So, you want revenge?"

"Yes, I suppose tha' is it." A rueful expression came over Felicita's face. "I'm usually not tha' kind of person, but...whenever I think o' that man and the pain he caused my matha and I..."

Tetra noticed her hands clenching into fists and could only imagine what was going on inside the woman's head. She straightened back up as her wariness from before dissipated in the light of Felicita's anger.

"I'm sorry that happened to you," she replied, "I know what it's like to be angry with him, yet not being able to do anything about it." A new thought came to her, and she voiced it, "But, y'know, I've never been able to tell anyone before until now." Not without getting a new segione tally for it, that is.

A smile broke through Lady Felicita's rueful look, but it was still tinged with sadness. "Yeah, havin' the freedom ta' speak your mind about anythin' is one o' the best things about Silvas." She paused. "Some would say it's one o' the worst, but I don't think any o' them ever lived without it."

"Yeah..." Tetra licked her lips and moved her gaze from Lady Felicita to her bandaged leg, then back onto the young woman. " Lady—um, sorry." She shook her head and tried again, "*Felicita*, do...do you like living in Silvas?"

Her sad smile lifted into a dreamy one. "I do. There are many things I love about it more than I ever did Igrium." She fiddled with a ring on her finger, a faraway look in her eyes. "In fact, if my patre's work had not been there, they would 'ave moved us here before the war started instead o' stayin'."

"But was it hard for you to live here when you first came?" Tetra frowned as she remembered the idiotic scrutiny she had felt ever since she was brought into the ambulate forest kingdom.

"It was at first." Felita nodded. "But once I made a couple friends at school, it got much easier."

Tetra's frown deepened. That wasn't exactly in the picture for her right now, nor could she see it ever being possible. The peryton-turning, malscarred Cairn was probably not on the top of anyone's "future-friend" list.

"And just like it did me, it will get easier for you too." Lady Felicita sent her a reassuring smile. "But it may take some time. People will just 'ave ta learn ta see past your family name ta see who you really are."

A strange feeling filled Tetra's stomach. She didn't think anyone would want to get that far, but she didn't say it out loud. Instead, she blinked and fixed her facial features into a neutral expression.

"Yeah, well... Um, could you remind me what the question was again?" She rubbed her arms like she was cold, but there wasn't even a slight chill in the room.

Felicita nodded as if Tetra hadn't just awkwardly changed the subject. "O' course. Can you recall a memory o' you playin'?"

Tetra closed her eyes with a quiet sigh. A memory of her playing...

Immediately, the same swirl of colors bobbed up to the surface of her mind again. Her heart quickened its pace as she remembered laughter; and with it, a new burst of joy bloomed inside her.

She gasped at the sudden emotion and opened her eyes. They immediately locked onto Felicita's anticipated gaze.

"Wha' is it?"

The blob of a memory faded away again, but some of the excited joy still lingered. "I—I had a weird feeling of...of joy." Fueled by the lingering emotion, she raised her brow expectantly. "What—what's the next question?"

Felicita's gaze lowered to her holonode's screen. "Um—ah! Were you called by any nicknames as a child?"

Nicknames...nicknames...Tetra squeezed her eyes shut again. As she stared into the darkness of her eyelids, she turned her focus to the mental lake where she knew all her earliest memories were submerged.

Come on, come on, come on... She pressed deeper into its dark, thick waters. *A nickname. Just a simple nickname. Or maybe even just my name! I don't care!* Surely she was called something. This shouldn't be hard to remember!

Ripples bubbled from the swamp's seemingly impenetrable depths. She inhaled a sharp breath as something began to move to the forefront of her mind, so she kept all her focus tuned towards the same place. *Come on...*

"*Anora...*" The unfocused face of a man appeared at the front of her mind's eye. Her heart raced with excitement as her brain figured out the reason for the indescribable, but wonderful, feelings the memory brought with it. That was her *patre*. She remembered her patre...!

Tears pricked her closed eyes as the memory faded, but the feelings stayed. She finally opened them and blinked the blurriness away.

"Tetra?" Felicita stared at her with a questioning expectancy.

"I saw him," Tetra whispered, "I saw my patre."

Felicita's eyes lit up. "You did?"

She nodded. "It was—the memory was fuzzy, but I...I know it's him."

Felicita leaned back in the chair, a strange look Tetra could only guess might mean hopeful excitement covering her face.

She tried to pull the memory back up again and was surprised when she could recall it easily—as if it had never been lost in the first place. A smile tugged at the corners of her lips as all her focus remained on her patre's face.

She couldn't make out any details in the fuzzy image, but she could tell he was smiling. The thought sounded so absurd with all the serious pictures of the stoic General Aries Cairn she had seen, but it's what the memory showed her—and she knew it wasn't a lie. The feelings that rose inside told her that was the case. They were unlike any she had felt before, but they were so, so wonderful.

Along with his smile, she could tell he had short, auburn hair; light skin; dark eyes; and a long nose—like all the photos and videos she had seen of her patre. She remembered him... *And* it was a good memory. It wasn't like the judgmental, disapproving stares she always felt when passing by any of her parents' portraits. This was like... well, the closest thing she could relate it to was her time spent with Stellinga and Rabetta, and when she and Aabir were friends.

The longer she dwelled, the fuzzier the memory became until it slipped away, but not before she remembered her patre saying, "*Anora...*" again.

Tetra scrunched her nose. The word was a popular name in Igrium that meant "honorable". She glanced down at her numerous tally marks. Maybe her parents gave her that nickname to remind her to be honorable—if that's even what was happening in the memory in the first place.

"Felicita—" she locked eyes with the young woman, "—do we have time for some more?"

She prepared herself for Felicita's "no" since it was getting late, but instead the young woman straightened with a bright smile. "O' course we can."

"Are—are you sure?" Tetra turned her head in the direction of the electronic clock sitting on her nightstand. *8:07* it read in bold numbers. "It's getting late..." She tried to keep any hope from spilling out into her tone.

"I don't mind stayin' a little longer," Felicita replied with a shrug. "Especially if something's obviously working."

Tetra couldn't help a small smile from escaping. "Thank you."

"O' course." Felicita nodded with a smile of her own. "Now let's see if we can't help you find more o' those memories."

Chapter Thirty

"…UNCOVERED THE TRAITOROUS actions of Aquila Tralp only two days before Silvas' Fire Attack."

Chillbumps rose along the exposed skin of Aabir's arm as the wind picked up around him, throwing the towering branches of Norland's everpine trees into a frenzy. He pressed his folded arms closer against his chest to ward off the chill, then sent a disapproving frown up at the cloudy sky before turning his attention back to the Net article on his holonode.

"The only thing about the secret group the former advisor said during her week of questioning were the words, 'All will soon be cleansed when the powers of this world are put in their rightful place. My eyes have been opened to the truth of our empire and all the other nations of Afreean, and I will not apologize for it.'

"Emperor Ignis, nor any of his advisors, commented on her remark, but speculations and theories have come up that say she was most likely part of a secret society or cult that had plans to overthrow the emperor and set up a new government in Igrium."

Aabir's heart pounded a frightened beat at the mention of a secret group, and he forwarded the article to Rasiela as quickly as he could before turning off his holonode. He set his elbows on his knees and put his face in his hands.

His earlier promise to keep away from all information regarding the pyromaniacal group did not even last a day as he realized most of the aftermath of the Silvanian Fire Attacks was shrouded in rumors and theories about all sides of the war—including the secret group. He knew he would not be able to give Rasiela enough info unless he broke his promise, so whenever he found anything that sounded like it might have something to do with the secret society he immediately sent it to the Silvanian spy without looking further into it. She might not be getting the best of information since Aabir was not reading half of it, but it gave him a sense of safety knowing he personally was not divulging into any of the facts and theories.

Deep down, he knew it was only a false sense of security, but he tried to reason with himself that the group might not even exist anymore. Nothing else had happened since the training droids attacked two days ago, and Aabir had begun concluding that his paranoia over the secret group being the perpetrators of the attack might have something to do with his lack of sleep.

He rubbed his hands over his face with a weary sigh. Maybe he should take a break from researching for now and go take a nap. He doubted taking a break one day out of the week would hurt his chances of earning her trust, and a nap sounded amazing right now...

"Aabir!"

Aabir jolted upright on the bench at the sound of Ezen's call. He turned his neck and caught sight of the new trainee striding towards him from one of the walking trails underneath the drooping everpine boughs.

"Hey, Ezen." He replied as the other trainee drew nearer. "What are you doing?"

"Just clearing my head." Ezen shrugged and stopped when he neared the stone bench. His eyes flickered from the empty side back to Aabir's face. "Um—could I—"

Aabir nodded with a smile. "Sure."

A ghost of a smile flitted across Ezen's lips as he sat. "So, what're you doing?"

"Just looking up something," he replied, "and keeping away from Aquilo."

Ezen grimaced. "Yeah, I've been doing that, too." He scratched the side of his neck. "I mean—I don't really know how to act around him. I—I wanna be able to go to our dorm without feeling like I'm intruding on something, but I don't know if that's possible."

Aabir nodded in understanding. Aquilo had been brooding ever since that morning after his matha called to complain about his grade in training. Aabir understood why he was upset—he could not stand when his parents got onto him about his grades, too—but his friend never hid his chagrin well.

"I know what you mean, but you can go into our dorm anytime—even if he's in there talking with his parents. Tycho and I just ignore him." He shrugged again and turned his vision onto the tiered fountain standing proudly in front of Norland's grand entrance. "You get used to it."

"Do you?"

"Yeah," Aabir smirked, "but I'll be honest, sometimes it still feels like I've just stepped into a warzone."

Ezen snorted and leaned back against the bench. Aabir kept him in his peripheral. Despite it being a couple days since the training droid attack, there was still something dark in the new trainee's expression that he could not discern.

He twisted his lips to the side before asking the question about it that had been burning in his mind. "Ezen," he began, "Um—I hope you don't mind my asking..."

The other trainee barely turned his head in his direction, his brow scrunched up questioningly.

"But are you OK?"

"Yeah..."

"No, I—I mean about the training droid attack. You've seemed...quieter since it happened." The new trainee turned his face away, and Aabir barreled on, "Of course, you don't have to tell me! I didn't mean to pry. I just...if you are dealing with something, I—I know how that feels..."

He shut his mouth before he could say something he might regret and waited for a reply. Ezen was quiet for a few long moments—they were so long Aabir wondered if he would even speak—until he finally let out a sigh.

"Yeah, I...I've been dealing with some stuff." Ezen kept his gaze on the ground as he spoke, "But I'm working through it, so you don't have to worry. I'm good."

Worry. Aabir held in a snort. That is all he seemed to be able to do nowadays.

"Well, if you ever need to talk, I'm here." He grinned and hoped it did not look forced.

"Thanks." Ezen finally lifted his eyes and gave Aabir a serious nod.

"Anytime."

They both sat in silence for a few moments, with only the wind blowing through the trees and the endless splash of water from the fountain filling the silence between them. Aabir inhaled a deep breath in the calm and let it out slowly. If only his life could be this serene. He let himself imagine what that would be like, and the thoughts of living in Silvas with his family filled him with a warmth inside that rivaled the windy chill in the air.

"How are *you* doing?" Ezen asked.

Aabir blinked out of his daydreams and looked over at him. "With what?"

"I know what happened last Sixthdein wasn't fun," Ezen eyebrows drew together as he frowned, "and I've thought it over a lot the past few days..."

A spark of anger lit in Aabir's chest as he remembered the event. "You have?"

"Mm-hm. And I keep coming back to how you reacted. I mean—you got up and left without a fight or anything." Despite his words, his tone was not condescending. "I could tell it bothered you when Tycho and I finally made it out of there, but you never said anything else about it. I...I've seen that happen before, but I've never been around it personally. So..." He shrugged as his words died away and he looked back down at the ground.

Aabir sighed. "Yeah, I'm doing fine. I...have tried not to think about it, actually." He had too many other things clamoring for his attention at that moment.

"Why didn't you react?"

"Because there would have been no point," he replied with a grimace. "It would've brought too much trouble."

Ezen lifted his gaze again. "For your family?"

Aabir jerked his neck in Ezen's direction and locked eyes with him. "How—how did you know?" He could not hide the surprise in his voice.

Ezen's dark brown eyes revealed an understanding he had never seen in any of his other friends' gazes.

"I don't live in a bubble, Aabir." A small grin lifted the corner of the trainee's lips for a moment, then faded. "I see news reports—although I can't say I trust 'em all—so I know about the house raids and the questionings those of Alliance descent deal with."

Aabir's eyes widened. "You do?"

"Yeah..." Ezen nodded slowly.

"Sorry," he shook his head in shock, "I just...I know that people know about them, but no one has ever actually asked me if my family and I deal with them. I think they just believe that since I'm a trainee they don't apply to me." He curled his hands into fists. "And they would have been right a few weeks ago, but now..."

"Because we're losing Xich?"

"Exactly." Aabir turned his glower onto the stone path. "And now my family and I, and all those of Alliance descent, are paying for it—and some may end up paying with their lives soon." He snapped his mouth shut as the bitter, and possibly treasonous, words left his mouth; then shot a wary glance out of the corner of his eye to see Ezen's reaction, but the boy's serious demeanor had not changed.

"I'm sorry that's happening to you, Aabir." There was a hint of sincerity in Ezen's lowered voice, "I'd like to say—as a full-blooded Igrian—that not all of us agree with the emperor's decisions with what he's been doing to you all since this war started. I know my parents didn't agree with him, and neither do I. I also..." He paused for a moment. "I also know a few others who—who feel the same."

"Back in Stelgan?"

"Yeah," Ezen shrugged. "And some others from a few different places."

"Huh."

Aabir never realized there might be other, full-blooded Igrians who were not completely brainwashed—besides his family's friend, Mister Falap. However, that was probably because he spent most of his time living in the only Igrian military academy inside the emperor's fortress. So, it was safe to assume the people he was around were more brainwashed than in other places inside the empire.

"So, is that why Tycho likes to call you the 'golden trainee'?" Ezen asked, "Because you're just trying to protect your family's image?"

Aabir rolled his eyes at the mention of the nickname. "Eh. Yes and no," he replied. "I used to not feel like I had to be that way, but I...well, I did something stupid a couple years ago that—that marred my record. Badly." The memories of that terrible night came back to him as he spoke, sending a guilty churn into his stomach. "So, I try to do the best I can so we won't be put in a bad light again."

He did not know why he was telling any of this to Ezen, but it felt good to get some of it off his chest. He had never felt so *free* to talk about this to anyone other than his parents before. Not even with Tycho or Aquilo did he ever get this way.

Maybe it was the serious, but understanding, look his newest friend was wearing.

Ezen pressed his lips into a thin line as he nodded slowly. "Is that when you tried to escape Norland?"

"How did you know?" Aabir stared at him, slack-jawed, and Ezen immediately got that look as if he had swallowed spiced gelatscy.

"Uh—sorry." The other trainee closed his eyes with a shake of his head. "I didn't mean to say anything. I—I don't really know what happened. I've just heard...things."

Aabir worked his jaw with a glare. It should not have surprised him to know Ezen had been told something about it, but it still sent a stab of guilt through his insides. Even after two years, he could not get rid of the horrible feelings that came with that night.

"Anyway, I didn't mean to bring back unwanted feelings," Ezen continued, "Just forget I said anything."

"No, *you* are fine, Ezen." Aabir squeezed his eyes shut. "I shouldn't be surprised that you found out, but you would think that after all this time people would have let it go by now."

An uncomfortable silence settled between them, but it was soon broken by Ezen's next question, "Did you do it because of how the emperor sees you and your family?"

"Partly." He did not want to tell the story, but it was better for Ezen to hear it coming from him than anyone else. So, with a deep breath, he began recounting the tale his unwanted memories recalled, "I was friends with Tetra Cairn then—I'm sure you've heard of her, too, huh?"

Ezen only nodded in reply. So, Aabir continued, "Well, she already had a reputation for getting in trouble, but she never dragged me into any of it—and I couldn't be a part of it, anyway." Shame curdled his stomach. "However, one day she told me she was going to try and escape again, and she asked if I wanted to come with her. She...she told me we could figure out a way to get me and my whole family out. We just had to make it out of Norland and the fortress without getting caught, first.

"I...I hated Norland," he cast a quick glance in the direction of the guards standing outside Norland's entrance, "and I wanted nothing more than to leave, so I agreed. It took us a week to come up with a plan that we thought might work, and a few days later...we tried."

He shook his head as he remembered their stupidity. "We left Norland at night and scaled one of these walls." He gestured towards the stone wall surrounding the school grounds that could barely be seen between the thick pine trees. "It was going fine until we made it to the top, and then it started to rain. Lightning gave away our position to some of the guards along the walkway, and we ran for it.

"I've never run so hard in my life." He took in another deep breath, the weight of the past emotions from that night pressing against his lungs. "It did nothing, though. We—we ended up getting caught. The rain made the stones slick, and we both slipped and fell—thankfully not off the wall—but it was enough for the guards to catch up with us. And since Tetra was the emperor's ward, they took us to his office right then to explain ourselves."

A shiver went down Aabir's spine, and he ground his teeth. Everyone always called Tetra a coward for her actions, but as he let all the memories from that night come back, he only remembered what she was willing to sacrifice for him and for his family. She had stood up to the emperor, despite the fear plastered across her wet, ashen face, and begged him to give her Aabir's punishments as well for the act. She had taken full responsibility for goading him into doing it with her, and she made it clear to the emperor that his family did not know about their plans.

While she had been doing all of that, Aabir had knelt on the floor, shivering and silent; too consumed by fear to say or do anything. *And you're still the same coward you were then...* his thoughts whispered, and a part of him agreed with them.

Though her words did nothing to keep them both from being punished in the end, they did help keep his parents and siblings safe from any of the emperor's scrutiny—the very thing Aabir was supposed to do in that situation.

Phantom pains throbbed in his back as he recounted the long-subdued memories, but he pressed on. "We ended up getting punished with fifteen lashes and were given the worst cleaning jobs to fill our free time for a month. So, after that I cut all ties with her. My parents didn't want me associating with her anymore, and I—I didn't want to go through that ever again, so I stayed as far away from her as I could and have tried to be obedient to all the rules ever since."

A deep sigh escaped his lips once he finished. He leaned back against the bench and watched Ezen's still countenance as he waited for a reply.

He had not told anyone that story in a long time, and he forgot how shameful it still was to recount out loud. There were so many things he regretted about those decisions, and this was not the first time he wished he could go back in time and change things. The fact that he couldn't only increased the invisible weight upon his chest.

"Wow," Ezen finally said. "Y'know, I've only ever heard of that happening once, and it was this one kid back at Stelgan who tried to run away as a joke."

"A joke?" Aabir raised his brow in surprise. Who would risk the punishment for the "coward's run" on a joke?

"Yeah, he was an idiot," Ezen shook his head with a disapproving frown, "and he got what we all knew was coming to him. His C.O. was so angry, practically the whole school became 'golden trainees' for the next week just to keep him from pouncing on us."

More guilt twisted Aabir's insides. That sounded a lot like what life had been like with Lieutenant Denir and Lieutenant Tarson the week after the failed escape attempt. "That sounds about like what happened here."

"Again, I'm sorry I even brought it up. I can see you didn't want to talk about it."

"No, it's fine." He waved the apology away and forced a grin. "Better coming from me than someone else."

"True." Ezen stood from the bench with a stretch, and Aabir did the same. "So, what're you going to do tonight?"

"I don't know." Aabir shrugged; glad the subject had changed to shallower matters. "I think Tycho mentioned something about watching the third "*Séar-las Trui*" movie, so I may do that."

"Oh. Cool." Ezen nodded thoughtfully. "I haven't seen that one yet."

"Tycho says it's the best," Aabir said as they began heading back into Nor-land, "but the fourth one is my favorite."

"Well, I've only seen the first two, so I'd say the first is the best so far."

"Yeah, the second one is garbage."

"Yep. They should've never had those flying lizards turn into those shifters. It made no sense."

"Agreed."

As they ascended the white stairs and onto Norland's colonnaded front veranda, Ezen asked, "So, what're you going to do for the rest of the break?"

Now a real grin escaped Aabir's lips as their eyes met. "Take a nap."

Ezen smirked. "Well, enjoy it—because I'd love to do the same, but I have homework. Actually, I'm supposed to meet with Aquilo in the library to do it..." His grin faded for a look of worry. "I wonder how that's gonna go..."

Aabir laughed and slapped him on the shoulder. "Good luck."

"Thanks for the support." Ezen frowned.

"You don't have to worry," Aabir tried to reassure him, "Just remember what I said: you get used to it."

"Such helpful advice..."

Aabir shook his head with another, quieter laugh and pushed one of the tall entry doors open. "I'll see you later, Ezen," he said as they stepped inside.

"See ya—possibly for the last time if this doesn't go well." Ezen dipped his chin towards him and spun on his heel, headed in the direction of the library.

Aabir watched him go for a moment before striding down the hall towards the boys' dorms. The pressure in his chest had decreased slightly since the subject of their conversation changed, and he continued to feel it lessen as he went over what Ezen said at the beginning of it.

He was glad to finally tell someone outside his family a little about what was happening, but another part of him wondered if it was the smartest move. Ezen had not even been at Norland for two weeks and he had already spilled some of his guts to the guy.

He lifted his arm and rubbed the back of his head with a sigh. And yet...he felt lighter with some of his secret worries now out in the open. He was not necessarily worried about quiet Ezen telling anyone about what he said, but there was a niggling doubt in the back of his mind that made him wonder if he should have kept his mouth shut.

No, he told himself, *stop worrying about it.* Ezen had probably already forgotten half of what he said, and even if he didn't, there was something about the sincerity in his facial expressions as they spoke that told Aabir he would not need to worry about his words reaching anyone else's ears.

He pushed the brewing thoughts to the side and turned his focus onto happier matters—namely, the nap he was about to take. With that thought, he picked up his pace and raced up the stairs to his dorm.

Rasiela stood at her workbench, surrounded by the same room she had practically lived in for the last fifteen years. She took in a deep breath of the chemical-laden air as her gaze roved over the latest article Aabir Sorrel had sent her. It was one she had never seen before, but she was familiar with the subject matter. She remembered when Advisor Aquila Tralp was executed for treason during Rasiela's first few years in Igrium, and it was one of the events that led Chief Baene and her to the knowledge that there might be more sides at play in this war than most realized.

"...that she was most likely part of a secret society or cult that had plans to overthrow the emperor and set up a new government in Igrium. Due to this, many conspiracy theorists have come to the conclusion that

there is an underground group of some kind with plans to overthrow Igrium and the Ignis family. However, there have been no similar attacks associated with this group in years, leading some to say they disbanded due to safety reasons; while others say they are only biding their time, waiting for the right opportunity to strike next.

"Among the many questions and concerns these events produce, there is one that stands out among them all: if this secret group does still exist, then who is their next target? And how are they going to try and dispose of them?"

Rasiela copied a portion of the article and sent it to Chief Baene. She flicked her wrist to turn the holonode off and moved her gaze upon the blue paint of her newer tool chest. Her lips tilted into a frown as she looked over all the scratches it had already accumulated in her care. Maybe she should try to paint it soon... It was beginning to remind her of her grandappa's old, rusting hovertruck she and her siblings all learned to drive in; the same one her grandemra continuously ragged on him to get rid of.

A small smile escaped her lips. The older she grew, the more she cherished those memories—and the deeper her longing to see her family became. The loneliness had not bothered her when she was young, but eighteen years can wear down any person—no matter how hard their resolve. When she left to begin working for Chief Baene, her youngest brother, Maphtal, had only been ten, but now he would be twenty-eight. A deep pang of sad loneliness gripped her heart, and she pressed her fists against her temples with a weary sigh.

She did not know how much longer she could do this. Chief Baene had given her the option to retire three years ago, but she declined. It had taken her a few years to get this valuable position at Norland, and she could not give it up when—at the time—they were at a crucial point of finally figuring out the existence of the secret group they still did not even know the name of.

Now with all the new information Rasiela had dug up these last three years, they were both beginning to understand the danger these people could cause if something was not done about them. Though Chief Baene had agreed with her that they were not a major threat yet and that she could still keep her focus spying on Igrium, she had begun to wonder if she should have been working harder to find more information about the group. Yet with all her responsibilities, she could not find a way to juggle that into her busy schedule.

Then she found Aabir Sorrel hiding in her office and the problem was soon solved.

Chief Baene had not been too keen on her decision to trust the trainee with the job, but he had never been around Aabir or overheard the secret conversation the boy had had with his matha like Rasiela had. Despite her calling the whole deal a "trust exercise", she could already tell the boy was not like the rest of his fellow, brainwashed, trainees. The "trust" part was more for Chief Baene's conscience than hers.

Her holonode sent a buzz through her wrist, and she glanced down at the screen as it popped into thin air. The small device continued its buzzing until she swiped her finger across its airy surface, and Chief Baene's serious demeanor filled her screen.

"Chief." She bowed her head respectfully.

"Rasiela." Even though he knew her real name, he always called her by the alias she earned in her training.

She lifted her head and locked eyes with him. "Did you receive my last message?"

"Yes I did." He nodded. "And I read over it as well, but that's not why I called."

"Then why did you?"

His stonelike expression never gave way as he let out a deep sigh, though Rasiela could see a storm of calculations and emotions brewing in his bright bluish purple eyes. "The Buleutcil has given me two tasks to accomplish," he said, "They need to know if any of Joash Ignis' notes still exist, and they want to know how many prisoners there are in the Constantia Tourney."

Rasiela straightened. "And you want me to look into them?"

"Only the Constantia Prisoners. I'm going to give the Joash Ignis portion to Halen. He has a better chance of getting them than you do." He raised an eyebrow. "So do not go looking into them."

"Yes, Chief." She nodded. Her days of going above and beyond the call of duty—and almost getting caught by Igrium for doing so—were long gone, but Chief Baene still liked to give her a hard time for those few instances back when she first started spy work.

"Good." A spark of amusement shone in his eyes; then disappeared as he cleared his throat. "Because I need that information by tonight."

Rasiela blinked in surprise. "Tonight?" That would leave her with only a few hours to do it...

"Yes." Chief Baene nodded, a shadow flickering across his face. "With the Tourney coming up, they want to see if it would even be possible to free the prisoners this year."

Rasiela blinked again. She glanced over at the closed door of her office, then back at Chief Baene's serious countenance. "Truly?" She whispered.

He only gave her a sharp nod in response.

Oh, thank You, Deleyon. She had been praying for this moment to come for years and had pleaded with Chief Baene to get the Buleutcil to do something about it for the same length of time. He always did, but usually not enough of the members voted to move on the action—until now, that is.

"I will get you that information tonight, sir," she said.

He nodded again, a ghost of a smile lightening his features for a moment. "I knew you would."

Living in Rubrum, this time of year always brought her into a depressed state. While the rest of the empire was rejoicing in the beginning of the growing season and the upcoming Constantia Tourney, she was only ever reminded of the many lives that would be lost in that same Tourney for the sake of entertainment and a perverted sense of "honor". Heat washed over her at the thought, and she pulled her facial features into a neutral expression to keep herself from glaring at the Silvanian Chief Advisor.

"But—if I may ask—why Prince Joash's notes?" She asked. There would be time to deal with the Constantia Tourney, and her feelings on them, later. So, what better way to change the subject than by gathering information.

Now a small, knowing smile did pull one corner of Chief Baene's lips upward. "The results of Miss Cairn's tests have only brought more questions than answers, and since she has not been able to remember anything about her childhood yet, they want to see if Igrium's former bioweapons expert would have anything on the matter."

Rasiela could hear the added lilt in his voice—the one she had come to know as his "I believe there is something more to this" tone.

She raised her brow. "And you agree with them?"

He only stared at her for a few silent moments before replying, "Yes."

She could see he was not going to tell her anything more on the matter, so she said, "Then I hope and pray that Halen will be able to find something."

"We all do," he sighed.

"How is Tetra doing?"

Ever since Rasiela told Chief Baene about how the Cairn's rebellious daughter was going to try and escape in Trivsau, she had been trying to keep up with the girl's whereabouts. She was surprised when Chief Baene got her into Duschel, and then even more so when he said she was working on a secret project in Silvas' bioweapons department. He would not tell her specifics, but he continued to assure her that the girl was being treated as well as a Cairn could be in her situation.

Rasiela could not remember Tetra ever enjoying the field of bioweaponry, but maybe leaving the empire awakened her love of the study. Whatever had happened, she was glad the Cairn's daughter seemed to be doing well—much better than she would have been in Igrium.

"I have Felicita working with her to try and retrieve her lost memories, and the tests are getting done, despite their confusing results." His countenance sharpened for a moment as he paused. "But I do believe it's hard for her. I have a hunch it won't always be, but I don't know when things will change."

Rasiela sighed through her nose. "I had a feeling that might be the case." She almost felt guilty for pushing Tetra into the situation, but the feeling fled as soon as she reminded herself of the girl's fate if she had stayed in Igrium. "Thank you for taking care of her, Chief. I...am glad you see the same thing in her as I do."

Something flashed in Chief Baene's eyes, but it was so quick she could not catch what it was. "I'm glad you told me about her." He gave her a sharp nod. "If you hadn't, I might be facing a few more problems than I am right now."

She narrowed her eyes at the strange comment but pushed it aside as he continued, "But now I need to know: how is *your* trainee doing?"

"Fine." She nodded, keeping her face blank of all former emotion. "He's done quite a good job so far."

"Hmm." Chief Baene's eyes narrowed in an almost-frown. "Well, I will need quite a bit more proof of his allegiance than what you have sent me, but if he continues to do as well as you say... We shall see."

"Yes, chief."

"I must go now, Rasiela, but I will be expecting the prisoners' information tonight. Deleyon be with you."

"And with you."

She bowed her head towards him, then lifted it as he ended the call.

Well then... She flicked her holonode off then stepped over to the other side of the workbench where her holoputer's projector sat and tapped the metal disc. The large holographic screen and keyboard flickered on, and she lifted her hands to type in her password.

Taking another deep breath of the cleaning-chemical-tainted air, she began her newest assignment.

Chapter Thirty-One

Tetra angled her wings and swooped in a wide arc along the trunk of an ambulate tree. She breathed in a deep breath of all the forest smells around her, then let it out quickly. Energy coursed through her veins as she kept her wings as still as possible, the air flowing above and below them keeping her aloft.

When she completed her arc, she snapped her wings into motion and pumped them to ascend towards the branches above. More spike-tipped leaves filled the full boughs, signaling the coming end of the planting season. Tetra turned her gaze forward and slightly tilted her wings to keep from hitting an ambulate tree up ahead.

If the planting season was ending, then that meant she had been living in Silvas for almost a month now. She blew out a breath. It felt longer with all that had happened. Could it really have only been three weeks?

The sound of creaking branches broke through her musings.

Tetra swiveled her ears in the direction it was coming from and banked to the right, wobbling a little at the tight turn before righting herself. She definitely wasn't as graceful a flier as Leaves Of Gold, but she was getting better. The past week Dr. Prin had brought her out into the ambulate forest to monitor her flying, and during the process she was able to teach herself the things she had been watching on the Net—videos on perytons, griffins, and anything else that might teach her about this new activity she had been flung into.

She flapped her wings to gain some altitude then kept them open to glide between the towering trees, her ears still pricked in the direction of the creaking. The noises grew louder the further she flew, until she finally saw one of the building-wide tree trunks moving slowly of its own accord. Her heart raced excitedly at the sight, and she flapped her wings at an angle to come to a stop in midair. Despite her whole week of flying in the ambulate forest, she had yet to see one of the infamous walking trees move—until now.

She lowered her gaze and watched in wide-eyed wonder as its roots slithered over the ground like thousands of tentacles, churning the dirt in rhythmic circles to propel itself forward. Its creaks and groans echoed in the vast forest, forcing

Tetra to keep her ears pinned back against her head to help block some of the noise from her sensitive ears.

After a few moments, her curiosity was satisfied, and she turned back around in the direction she had come from. She inhaled and her nose caught the faint scents of Dr. Prin and the five guardsmen that always accompanied them amidst the hundreds of smells surrounding her.

The more she had been a peryton, the more her brain was beginning to understand her new senses and way of travel. In the past two days, she had learned that she could pick out the individual scents of different people. Though they were too far away for her to be able to do that just yet, she kept her heightened senses trained on the area she could tell the group was in so she wouldn't get lost in the ever-changing forest...again.

Tetra shook her head at herself and continued on her course, veering only slightly to practice twisting and turning sharply in the open space. Elation bubbled up inside her as she successfully twisted in a barrel-roll, and she made a strange purring noise in her throat she had come to identify as the peryton version of laughter.

Another deep purr vibrated through her as she did another barrel-roll. The same, warm feeling she had gotten the first time she flew successfully—and every time since—came with it, sending a buzz of adrenaline through her veins. She flapped her wings and enjoyed the feeling of the air rushing around them as her eyes strayed to the ground far below.

A twinge of fear caused her heart to skip a beat at the sight, but she ignored it to focus on the invigorating feeling flight brought her. She had wings now and she wasn't tired enough to faint, so there would be no more falling for her (at least while she was a peryton).

She inhaled deeply of the air again and caught a new, strong scent. Her ears pricked as she slowed and lifted her head. She took another deep breath and caught a whiff of the same smell, but this time she realized she had smelled it before. From where, she couldn't remember, but it was familiar.

Tetra slowed her wingbeats and came to a stop in midair, twisting her neck to peer at all the empty areas between the wide tree trunks. Where was the smell coming from? She took in another deep breath. And why was it so familiar?

A moment passed, and her ears caught the faint sound of wingbeats. Her eyes widened and she spun around—as best she could in midair—in the direction they were coming from. Her mind brought up the memories of the peryton, Leaves Of Gold, from the week before as the great, flapping wingbeats and the familiar, earthy scent came closer.

Finally, between the trees in the shadowy distance, Tetra caught sight of movement. She kept her gaze on the huge peryton as he flew closer. The sharp scent she had come to know of as surprise hit her nostrils.

"It is *you*!" His roar reverberated through the trees as he came to a stop in the air ahead of her. His intelligent eyes shone with wonder as their gazes locked. "I thought I smelled something familiar, but I didn't realize it was you." His eyes lit up with joy. "Hello again, Tetra."

"Hello." She flexed her talons with a curt nod.

Despite the excitement thrumming through her chest at seeing the talking peryton again, her common sense told her to be wary.

Leaves Of Gold tilted his head slightly, his nostrils flaring as he inhaled a deep breath. A jolt of surprise went through Tetra as she noticed the small movement, bringing with it a new question: was she giving off waves of emotional scents, too?

An uncomfortable feeling entered her stomach at the thought, but she didn't know if she could do anything to stop the smells other than becoming an emotionless android, so she tried to not let it worry her.

"Oh, I didn't mean to alarm you again." Without turning, Leaves Of Gold moved a little further away from her. "I apologize."

"Um—no, no. You're..." She huffed a breath. "It's all right."

Leaves Of Gold nodded slowly, something akin to a dubious look in his large eyes. "So...I see you're not with the no-furs right now."

Tetra narrowed her eyes warily, her excitement beginning to wane. Was he thinking of attacking her?

His eyes widened and he added, "I didn't mean anything bad by it!"

"Then what did you mean?" She asked, her tone laced in a growl.

"I was just making a comment," he said. "I have only ever heard that the reason no-furs get close enough to us is so they can enslave us, and yet here you are free without them. I'm just...shocked at everything that I have seen."

And if the strong surprise-scent still coming off him in waves was any indicator, then his words were true. Tetra's excitement began to return. Even if she couldn't read his expressions as well as she could a human's, she at least knew he wouldn't be able to hide any deceitful plans from her.

"Oh. Well..." She unclenched her talons. "I'm sorry for jumping to conclusions, then."

"It's OK." He rumbled, the corner of his lips tilting upward into another peryton smile. "I know we've never truly met before, so you have a right to be wary. You're not the only peryton my direct remarks have thrown off."

"Oh." The corners of Tetra's lips barely lifted into her own small smile. "Well, I'm glad I'm not the only one."

"Definitely not." His eyes lit up as a sweetly sharp smell came from him; one Tetra didn't recognize. "So, Tetra, where do you come from? I've met almost everyone from all the villages around the walking forest, but I've never seen you before."

"Uh..." She glanced down at the ground far below them. What should she say? She couldn't just make something up. She hadn't even realized perytons lived in villages and definitely wouldn't know what any of them were called. Plus, he would be able to smell her deceit.

"I'm not from around here," she finally said.

"Ah." Leaves Of Gold nodded thoughtfully. "Then, may I ask where you are originally from?" He paused, then added quickly, "You don't have to tell me if you don't want to, though! I only ask because there have been many perytons coming to live here from the crumbling desert and some of the islands near it."

The crumbling desert? *Oh, he must mean Xich.* She pictured the desert landscape made entirely of outcroppings for a moment, and silently agreed with him that it did have a crumbling appearance.

"I..." How much should she reveal? "I come from past the islands..."

"Oh wow!" Leaves Of Gold's eyes grew huge as they brightened even more. "I've never traveled that far—the furthest was to the crumbling desert—but I've heard tales from some who moved here about how there are vast fields with no trees, striped mountains, and trees that are black-and-white."

Images of the miles and miles of farmland that made up the majority of Igrium's landscape flew through her mind, along with the red and orange clay mountains of Magnae and the towering birch forests of Paleya she had visited on emperor-sanctioned trips before.

"Yeah, I've visited those," she replied.

"Wow..." His rumbling voice trailed off as his eyes lost focus for a moment, then he shook his head and they locked eyes again. "I've always wanted to visit, but with everything I've heard that is happening with the no-furs right now I haven't tried to just yet."

So even perytons knew about the war and were moving from their homes because of it. Guilt pricked Tetra's heart at the thought, but she didn't want to dwell on it and turned her focus back onto the conversation.

"It can be crazy." She nodded.

He dipped his chin slowly, then tilted his head to the side. "I bet. Is that why you left?"

Tetra thought for a moment. "Partly, yes."

"Then, I hope you'll find a village that suits you here."

"Um—thanks."

"And if there is anything you need, you can come find me in the village of Cherry Valley. We're in the mountains next to the biggest lake in the walking forest, not even half a sun-turn's flight from here." With another soft peryton smile, he added, "Or if you just need a good cup of brew, we have some of the best."

Brew? Perytons drank something other than water? And in cups?

"Oh! Um—thanks for the offer," Tetra could feel the conversation waning along with her strength for flying, "but I need to get going now..."

"Of course! I didn't mean to keep you." Leaves Of Gold dipped his antlered head in her direction. "May the Unrivaled King guide your flight, Tetra."

"Uh—and you, too." She followed his lead and dipped her head towards him.

"Thank you." With a great flap of his golden-feathered wings, he swooped around and headed off in the opposite direction. As he left, she saw him turn his head back over his shoulder. "And remember, you're always welcome in Cherry Valley!"

"Thank you!" She roared back as he disappeared behind a tree.

His scent and the sound of his wingbeats soon faded. Once they did, Tetra breathed in deeply through her nose and located Dr. Prin's scent again. She turned back around and continued gliding on her course.

As she flew, she went back over the conversation with Leaves Of Gold a few times in her mind and tried to recall everything the peryton said that would point to him being intelligent—besides the look in his eyes and the fact she had had an actual conversation with him. Dr. Prin hadn't mentioned the first encounter with Leaves Of Gold since it happened, but Tetra knew the woman hadn't forgotten about it—not with the dreamy, uncharacteristic way she had reacted to Tetra's simple explanation. She said she would think about it more, and hopefully this week had given her enough time to do so.

Even though Tetra didn't really trust Dr. Prin, she knew she would need to tell her about this newest encounter with the talking peryton if she wanted the chance to go to this Cherry Valley place. It sounded much further than the designated area she was allowed to fly in right now, and she didn't want the few freedoms she had to be taken away in case her tracker told them that she was trying to escape when she actually wasn't.

She exhaled a sharp huff out her nose. That stupid tracker... If only Leaves Of Gold's assumption of her freedom was correct. She tilted her tiring wings to begin swooping around a tree trunk, and a small burst of the warm, elated feeling filled her chest for a few rapid heartbeats. It passed, however, at the knowledge that this feeling of freedom was only that: a feeling; a fleeting emotion that wouldn't break her of this new prison she had found herself in.

Her wings drooped a little at the thought and she began to descend. Gritting her teeth, she pumped her wings to keep herself aloft and tried pushing all the self-pitying thoughts away.

At least she had her own room and was fed three meals a day. At least she wasn't in Norland anymore, and that it had been over a month since she felt a segione dig into her skin. She wasn't living under the threat of being turned into one of Emperor Ignis' personal guards anymore, nor had any threats of her platoonmates or Lieutenant Tarson reached her ears in quite some time.

And, with Lady Felicita's help, she had actually been able to recall some of her old memories. Her lips pulled back into a smile as the few fuzzy images of her patre came to mind. She hadn't been able to remember her matha, but—as Felicita continued to remind her—dredging up memories was a process that could take months, even years, to complete. Tetra hoped it wouldn't take that long, but she was content with what she could remember. There had been too many successes the past week for her to get frustrated with herself...for now.

So, even if she technically was a prisoner, she had many good things going for her. Yet even with those thoughts, there was still a part of her that longed for something more. She didn't want to do this whole fake "flight-of-freedom" routine anymore. Her heart ached to live; to have a life where she truly felt alive and was doing something that made a lasting impression.

The oath she had promised herself back in Xich popped into her head, and her smile curled into a frown. She wanted to fulfill it, to help stop the sufferings of those affected by this war, now more than ever. Maybe it was because she was in a situation where she didn't have the freedom to do anything with her promise, or maybe it was the guilt she had felt when Leaves Of Gold said perytons were having to leave their homes because of the war, but either way she knew she needed to do something to help.

No matter if it was humans, griffins, merfolk, or even perytons who were suffering, a longing to fulfill her oath fueled her thoughts. Emperor Ignis and his tyrannical reign needed to end. Maybe she could figure out a way to use this new peryton curse to her advantage in doing so. She mulled over the thought some more as she flew. It was definitely something to think about.

Chapter Thirty-Two

As Tetra neared Dr. Prin and their guards, she was able to make out a few new smells among them. Her excitement over meeting Leaves Of Gold dimmed beneath her growing wariness as she came to recognize the new tangle of scents of another group of people.

She pricked her ears in their direction and slowed her pace to see if she could identify who these new people were. Yet no matter how close she flew or how hard she tuned out the rest of the noise around her, she couldn't make out anything other than a few whispers that sounded more like the breeze blowing by her ears than actual words.

Tetra huffed a frustrated breath but flapped her wings to pick up her pace again. She would end up finding out who it was eventually, so might as well be quick about it. Yet even with that thought, she still found herself focusing in on the group with all her heightened senses. Who else would be invited to these outdoor testing sessions? And why would they want to endure the boringness she knew they were to everyone but her and Dr. Prin?

She slowed her flight again as she swooped around another ambulate tree trunk, and then her gaze landed on the group of ant-sized humans ahead of her. Even from far-away, her peryton eyes were able to pick out details to see exactly who each of them was. Dr. Prin stood in a wide circle made up of more guardsmen than their usual five. Next to her stood a man in a dark green military uniform, his hands behind his back. Even in the shadows of the ambulate forest, she noticed the glint of war medals on his chest.

A shiver went down Tetra's spine as she met his hard, intimidating gaze. What was Army General Taoghn doing here? She could read nothing in his watchful expression as she tilted her wings and descended towards them. If the general of Silvas' army was out here and not leading his men in the war, then he must be planning something important. The thought that came to Tetra's mind sent a wave of uneasiness through her bones.

She flapped her wings to slow her descent. A cloud of dust billowed around her as she came to land a short distance away from the group of humans. Her back talons touched the ground first, then her hooves. When she was steady on her feet, she folded in her wings and walked out of the dust towards the group.

"I wondered if you would return," Dr. Prin remarked as Tetra stopped before them. The woman lifted her head as Tetra lowered hers so their eyes could meet. "But I'm happy to see that your endurance has grown exponentially this past week. If this growth continues, I believe you will be able to fly for as long, and as quickly, as an actual peryton is able to."

Tetra barely dipped her head with a blink to show she was listening. Her gaze flicked over to see the army general's reaction, but nothing in his face changed with the announcement.

"Ah. Yes, Miss Cairn, this is Army General Taoghn." Dr. Prin gestured towards him, "He and I have been talking about your progress and what we have learned so far."

Another uneasy wave churned her stomach, and she kept her face neutral before it could show anything amiss.

"Miss Cairn." Army General Taoghn dipped his chin towards her.

She nodded back.

"If you would turn back into yourself, Miss Cairn, we need to speak with you," Dr. Prin said.

Tetra nodded and took a few steps back to give herself room. As her brain was becoming used to everything being a peryton entailed, it had finally become as natural as walking to change between her human self and a peryton. The thought didn't make her feel better, but it also didn't fill her with dread like it would have only a week ago.

In a rush of consuming flames, she turned back into herself. The pain was as bad as it had always been, but it didn't seem to last as long as it once did. Whether that was true or if she had only gotten used to the pain she couldn't tell, nor did she care. She was relieved either way.

The sharp flames died off, and she lifted herself up into a sitting position on weary muscles. The guard who had helped her up before, Sir Rune Whest, was there with his hand outstretched. She met his eyes, took it, and he helped pull her up without saying a word. She sent him a grateful nod, and he nodded back before returning to his position in the half-arc of guardsmen.

Tetra watched him for a moment, still feeling the confusion she had felt ever since his helpful action the first time. Like all guardsmen, he barely spoke, and she hadn't found a good time to ask him why he showed kindness towards her when none of his fellow guardsmen did so.

"Miss Cairn..." Dr. Prin's voice drew Tetra's attention back to the bigger issue at hand. She turned away from Sir Whest and stepped back over to the biologist and General Taoghn.

At the sight of the army general, she straightened her posture and kept her gaze lowered as if she was standing in front of High General Paristan, the head of Igrium's army. Unlike Paristan, Taoghn didn't have a battle scar running halfway down his face that gave him a permanent sneer, but the cold indifference of his expression didn't make her feel any better, either. His countenance was like Igrium's high general, and it sent another icy shiver down her spine. She had seen what High General Paristan had done for the sake of Igrium and Emperor Ignis' honor, and some of those actions made her parents' fire raids look childish by comparison.

"I'm also happy to report that the speed your body changes is also improving," Dr. Prin said with a dip of her chin.

Tetra only nodded in reply, not sure if the biologist was expecting an answer.

"And I believe your flying maneuvers have improved since we first started last week," she continued, and Tetra realized then that she was only speaking for the army general's benefit. "You look much more graceful than those first couple of days."

Tetra dipped her head in the woman's direction to hide her frown at the mention of those first few attempts. When she lifted her head, she accidentally locked eyes with Taoghn and immediately lowered them.

"It sounds like you have been making quite a bit of progress, Miss Cairn," he said.

"Yes sir." Her heart began to pound an anxious rhythm; she hoped he couldn't see the beginning fear in her eyes.

"And what do you hope to accomplish with all of this?"

She sent a furtive glance up at the cold seriousness on his angular features. That wasn't what she expected to come out of his mouth.

"Sir?"

One of his eyes twitched slightly, but he asked the question again, "What do you hope to accomplish with all of this progress?"

"I'm sorry, sir," she replied, "but I don't quite understand what you're asking."

Now the ghost of a frown flashed across his features. "Dr. Prin has told the Buleutcil and me some of her findings regarding this ability of yours," he said. "However, she has also mentioned they are nowhere near knowing how to duplicate it."

Tetra flicked her gaze over towards Dr. Prin. The Silvanian woman's eyebrows were drawn together as a small frown twisted her lips.

Her attention was drawn back to General Taoghn's commanding presence as he added, "Yet some of us—including myself—are wondering if we are only wasting time and resources on these tests when we could be doing something much more worthwhile."

A strange sensation entered Tetra's unsettled stomach. She had a feeling she knew where this was going, but she didn't let it show in her voice as she asked, "What are you suggesting, sir?"

He stared at her for a long moment. "I've been told—and can plainly see for myself—that you don't agree with all of Igrium's ideologies." The skin around her malscar tingled at its not-so-subtle mention. "And I also know that you went to Norland Military Academy for ten years and would have excelled there had your record not been so...rebellious."

Tetra forced her arms to stay at her sides so she wouldn't touch any of her tallies.

"So, I ask again: what is it that you are hoping to accomplish with all of your progress so far?" His gaze locked hers' in a vice-like grip.

She didn't reply immediately, instead going over his question over again in her mind to better come up with an answer. "I'm not sure, sir," she replied honestly, "I didn't think I was allowed to do anything else other than this."

Taoghn raised his brow. "Well, I have another option for you—one that a majority of the Buleutcil has given their approval of."

Tetra's heart pounded against her ribcage as if it wanted to escape its confines. "Yes sir?"

"On behalf of Silvas' Army, I am asking if you would consider joining our ranks as the first ever war-peryton."

Despite how she knew, deep down, this would be his answer, it still sent a cold shock through her insides. She stared at him, dumbfounded, for a few moments before she was even able to get any words out.

"You—you want *me* to join your...to join the Silvanian Army?" She couldn't hide her incredulous tone, "Me? A Cairn? In *your* army?"

"I don't care what family name you possess," he replied. "Not when it would hinder any advantageous results in this war."

Tetra turned her gaze away as she thought through his words. So, despite the backlash the decision would insight, he was willing to let a Cairn into the Silvanian army if it also gave them the world's first ever war-peryton. Yes, she could see how that would be an advantage; especially if Dr. Prin and her team weren't close to duplicating the ability.

Yet the thought of fighting against those who were of the same empire—the same blood—as her didn't sit well either.

"I understand what you are saying, sir," she lifted her head again and looked at his face, "but what reason can you give me to fight against the empire I was raised in? It's true that I don't agree with them on most things, but I also don't want to fight them without a good reason."

Instead of answering, he instead asked, "Why did you get that malscar, Miss Cairn?"

She blinked and fought the urge to touch her face. "I disobeyed my commanding officer." A shiver went through her at the memory.

"And why did you disobey them?"

"Because..." The image of the fear in Stellinga's face flashed through her mind, "There was this Xichian girl, and she was trying to cross the fence—her parents were on the other side—but she fell and was caught. I was told by my C.O. to give her a warning cut across her forehead for being a possible spy, but I knew she wasn't. So, I...I couldn't do it."

"Even with the threat of a malscar hanging over you?"

"Yes sir." She pressed her lips in a thin line. "Even though it would've been better for her if I'd done it—less painful, that is—but I just couldn't hurt her for doing something I could easily see she hadn't done. It was wrong."

"And that's why I am asking you to join." General Taoghn sent her an almost imperceptible nod. "Whoever wins this war will be able to control the outcome of how all those people and all these different nations operate, and having a peryton could help the Alliance achieve that favorable outcome."

A strange feeling went through her as he spoke. That sounded a lot like her oath...

She didn't know how to answer him yet, so she asked, "But don't I have to be a Silvanian citizen to join?"

"Under normal circumstances, yes. But the Buleutcil has the power to let you join ahead of time without taking the citizenship test. However, you would need to take it eventually." He gave her a knowing look. "I don't expect you to answer right now, Miss Cairn, but I will need to know what you have decided soon."

"Yes sir." She glanced back over at Dr. Prin's frown. "But...if I were to join, will the tests end?" Despite her dislike of them at first, she didn't want to give up these flying sessions—not if having them gave her the opportunity to visit Cherry Valley.

General Taoghn and Dr. Prin both shared a look. "No, they won't." He turned his head back to face Tetra, "But they will be limited to only once or twice a week."

She nodded, a small wave of relief washing through her. "Then, thank you for the offer, sir. I'll give you an answer as soon as possible."

"I'll be waiting." He dipped his chin towards her, then looked over at Dr. Prin. "Thank you for letting me interrupt your time here, doctor."

Dr. Prin nodded towards him. "You're always welcome, sir," she replied. "May Deleyon continue to grant you and your men victory."

"Thank you." He gave her a nod and turned one last look in Tetra's direction. "When you have made a decision, Miss Cairn, you can tell Dr. Prin and she will notify me."

"Yes sir."

"Then I must be off now. Good dein, ladies."

Tetra saluted him out of habit as he turned on his heel and headed towards one of the two hovercars sitting further away from their group. Half of the guardsmen broke from their formation to follow him. His hovercar soon lifted off the ground and sped away into the trees in the direction of the watercourse-lined freeway.

When the muffled sounds of the forest surrounded them once again, Tetra turned and met Dr. Prin's eyes. Yet before she even opened her mouth to speak, the biologist beat her to it.

"I'm sorry for not giving you a heads-up earlier, Miss Cairn," she said. "This matter was spoken of in our last Buleutcil meeting, but I didn't realize he would come today."

Tetra blinked in surprise at the apology but accepted it with a nod. "It's OK."

The softness in Dr. Prin's gaze gave way to her usual calculating expression. "So do you have any idea what you plan to do?"

Tetra bit her lip and lowered her gaze to the ground. Even though she hadn't given the army general an answer, deep down she knew what she would choose in the end.

"I think so," she replied.

Dr. Prin sighed. "I figured that was the case."

Tetra lifted her head again. "I'm sorry." She didn't know why she apologized, but it was the only thing she could think of that sounded right in the moment.

"No, Miss Cairn, none of that now." One corner of the woman's lips barely lifted in a smirk. "I doubt you will miss doing this every day."

"Well..." She shrugged and couldn't help a sheepish grin. "I do enjoy flying here, and I'm glad I'll still have the opportunity to do it, but..."

"That's what I thought." Dr. Prin's smirk faded for a more serious look. "But if you do decide to join the military, be careful. You're the only person who has this ability, and if we lose you then we may lose any hope of figuring out how you do it. I know duplicating it is the result General Taoghn and many in the Buleutcil want us to have—not just for this war, but future ones as well." Her voice took on an almost motherly tone as she added, "So be wise in your decisions, and don't risk your life needlessly."

"Yes ma'am."

"Good. Now that that is settled, I believe we're done for the day." The head biologist turned and motioned for Tetra to follow. "Let's go home."

As they headed back towards the hovercar, with the rest of their guardsmen following, the conversation with Leaves Of Gold popped into Tetra's head. "Oh, Dr. Prin..."

Dr. Prin stopped next to the hovercar and turned her head to look back at her. "Yes, Miss Cairn?"

Tetra slowed to a stop near her. With a quick glance at the approaching guards, she whispered, "I need to tell you what happened while I was flying today."

Dr. Prin narrowed her eyes and glanced in their guards' direction. "Does this have to do with another peryton?"

"Yes ma'am."

"Hmm." She nodded and opened the back door of the vehicle. "Then you can tell me when we get back to Urbselva."

Tetra nodded and stepped into the hovercar's backseat. Dr. Prin and the guardsmen soon joined her, and they began their drive back to the Silvanian capital.

Chapter Thirty-Three

An excited squeal yanked Aabir from his nap. He jerked his head up and blinked his bleary eyes, his gaze landing on Yahel's booster seat.

"Really, Yahel?" He rubbed his hand over his face, his vision clearing.

"We—we're here, Aabir!" She gestured excitedly to the view out the windshield.

Aabir turned his head to look beyond the passenger seat in front of him, and was greeted with the sight of an old, white and blue farmhouse rising above the tilled fields surrounding it. A few trees stood sentinel about the rustic building, providing shade from Soll's brightness.

A mix of nostalgic feelings rushed through him as his gaze fixed upon the house. His family visited Mr. Falap at least once a month, be it on weekends or school breaks, and a lot of good memories had been made here in the Sorrel family's small haven.

As Patre pulled into the fence-lined section that surrounded the house and its small yard, Aabir could feel his body relaxing. Even though being here did nothing to stop what was happening in the rest of Igrium, it did help calm the fears that always lurked in the back of his mind. He blew a quiet sigh of relief and sank a little further into the leather seat.

"Gran-patre!" Yahel exclaimed.

Aabir looked out his window as their hovercar slowed to a stop in front of the house's huge, covered porch. Mister Falap leaned on his cane at the bottom of the porch's steps, watching them. Despite Yahel's exclamation, the man was not actually their grandpatre, only a close family friend. However, he was the closest thing to a grandpatre any of them had had in years, so no one corrected her.

The elderly man waved as Patre turned the hovercar off and it landed softly on the ground. Aabir undid his seatbelt and opened the door to let himself out. He did not even try to help Ereliev get Yahel's bouncing form out of her seat, not wishing to get the same glaring response from his middle sister he had earlier when Yahel needed to be strapped in.

He huffed a frustrated breath but tried to push the unhappy thoughts to the side. This was not the time or place to be thinking about them. This was supposed to be a relaxing weekend for all of them, and he would not ruin it for himself by dwelling on things outside of his control—like his sister's attitude. He turned back around and flipped his seat over so Zeke and Nevaze could get out from the back row.

"I'm glad y'all made it safely," Mister Falap said in his thick eastern-Igrian drawl. Aabir turned to face him and met the elderly man's sharp brown gaze. A grin deepened the wrinkles on his face. "How're you doing, Aabir?"

"Fine." Aabir nodded towards him.

Mister Falap's grin lessened, but he said nothing about his reply as the rest of the family got out of the car. Matha took Yahel from Ereliev and rushed over to smother Mister Falap in a one-armed hug.

"I'm sorry we didn't come last week," she replied as they let go, "but Elnim had work to do, and we couldn't pass it up—"

"—I understand, Zerah." Mister Falap put his hand on her shoulder. "You don't have to explain yourself to me. I'm just glad y'all are here."

Matha let out a relieved sigh as she held out Yahel to hug the older man's neck. "We are, too."

Yahel let go, and Mister Falap greeted the rest of the family before ushering them all under the shade of the porch.

"Well, now..." He let out a sigh as he sat down on the porch swing next to Matha and Yahel, "The feastbots are cooking us up a lunch of fried tomeplants, corafish, rolls, a salad, truemelon, and Luisa's famous greenberry pie."

At the mention of pie, Aabir realized just how hollow his stomach felt. He slept through breakfast that morning, and barely made it out to the hovercar in time for them to leave.

"That sounds wonderful," Matha replied.

"Yeah, I'm so hungry I could eat an *equia* right now," Aabir added with a hand on his stomach.

Mister Falap smiled. "Don't you worry." He said with a chuckle, "There should be enough to feed an army."

"Good, because these three eat enough for one." Patre gestured in the direction where Aabir, Zeke, and Ereliev were all leaning against the porch's railing.

Ereliev scrunched her shoulders and lowered her head as if trying to hide from the comment, while Aabir and Zeke both shrugged.

"What can I say? I like food," Zeke replied with a grin.

Patre snorted and rolled his eyes, the rocking chair he sat in creaking underneath him.

"You three can eat as much as you want," Mister Falap said, "and hopefully soon. My feastbots said they'd be done in the next few minutes or so."

Aabir's mouth watered in anticipation. One of the things he loved about visiting Mister Falap were the huge meals his feastbots created.

"How have you been doing, Mister Falap?" Matha asked, "We saw as we drove in that the fields were tilled. Have you planted the seeds yet?"

"Did that last week." The elderly man nodded with a satisfied smile. "Except not on the back four hundred. I'm letting that portion of land rest this year."

"That's good," Matha replied with a nod. "Are you growing filbeans this year?"

"Yep." Mister Falap tapped his cane against the deck. "But enough about me, Zerah." His probing eyes roved over each of them. "I want to know how y'all are doing."

A heaviness Aabir thought they had escaped settled back over them with those words. He lowered his gaze to his shoes as Mister Falap turned his head over in his direction.

Patre let out a sigh and leaned forward in his chair. "Our house is being raided again."

"And we're being questioned," Matha added in a lowered voice.

Aabir felt Zeke stiffen next to him, but his brother did not say anything. Nor did Ereliev.

Nevaze—who sat on the porch next to Patre's chair—looked up at their adopted-grandpatre with her large eyes. "Why is this happening, Mister Falap?" She asked.

The elderly man sighed and leaned forward to look her in the eyes. "Because Emperor Ignis is afraid of the Alliance. They're winning in the war, so to combat that fear he's trying to control as much as he can in Igrium."

Nevaze nodded, a sad, but thoughtful, look on her round face. Aabir curled his hands into fists and stared daggers at the wooden boards underneath him. Unlike what his sister's expression suggested, Mister Falap's words only reminded him of the hopelessness of their present situation—and it lit an angry fire in his chest.

"It reminds me of when I was young and Emperor Rexcan the Third was ruling." Mister Falap continued, "Except instead of those of Alliance descent being targeted, it was us full-blooded Igrians. I can remember patrolmen coming into my parents' house one day because they thought we might've been hiding the fugitives that tried to assassinate him! They tore up our furniture and broke my matha's dishes—which she wasn't too happy about, let me tell you."

He sighed as if his matha's sadness over losing those dishes had passed onto him. "But I know it's much worse for y'all then it ever was for me. I used to think Emperor Rexcan was the worst ruler we ever had, but I'm seeing that that's just not the case anymore." He sighed again. "The Ignis family used to be one made up of mostly good leaders, but the past three generations haven't lived up to their ancestors' honorable ways. I'm sorry y'all have had to live during these times. It...sometimes it shames me to even call myself an 'Igrian' anymore."

"Oh, Mister Falap," Matha's soothing voice caused Aabir to lift his head. She put her hand on their adopted grandpatre's shoulder and continued, "We know it's not your fault, so there is no shame from us."

Mister Falap smiled and patted her hand. "Thank you, Zerah. I just wish I could help you more."

"Allowing us to visit you is very helpful." She sent him a reassuring smile. "Trust me. We all need the break these visits bring."

A thoughtful look came over the older man's face, and after a pause he asked, "Then why don't y'all just come live here with me?"

"What?" Matha, Aabir, and Zeke all exclaimed at the same time Patre shook his head.

"No, Mister Falap," he said. "We would never burden you with that."

Mister Falap waved his comment away like a tacky buzzgnat. "It's no trouble, and you know it." He argued, "I have three extra bedrooms and a basement that y'all could have. And if it's money you're worried about, Elnim, you don't need to be. I wouldn't ask for rent; and I'm always in need of a mechanic around here, so I can pay you to do that."

"That still wouldn't work," Matha replied with a shake of her head. "The kids are all still in school, and I know the closest one to here is more than a thirty-minute drive. Plus, Aabir can't leave Norland—" Aabir's eyes locked onto her understanding gaze as she spoke,"—and I don't want him spending his weekends at school because we lived so far away. Occasionally is fine, but not every week. He needs to be able to come home."

Guilt stabbed his heart, and, despite her loving gaze, he looked back down at his shoes. So, once again, he was at fault for trying to help his family, only for it to end up not helping them at all.

Not for the first time, he wished he could go back in time and change his decision to join Norland. That would fix so many problems they faced now because of him.

"Well, I won't force y'all into anything, but my offer still stands." The fight left Mister Falap's voice, "And you're always welcome to come visit, even if it's not on the weekends."

Matha's voice sounded resigned as she said, "Thank you."

A heavy silence settled over their little circle. Aabir worked his jaw as his past regrets came back to the forefront of his mind. If only he had never joined, then they might all be living with Mister Falap right now—away from all the troubles they were facing in the best place Aabir could imagine.

Yet, the other part of him argued, if he had never joined then he would never have met Tycho, Aquilo, Ezen, or even Tetra; nor would he have learned to swordfight.

And now that he was thinking about it, even with how nice Mister Falap's offer sounded, there was no guarantee they would still be safe from the raids and secret cameras. In fact, their family might only end up bringing all their problems onto an elderly man. Then, not even he would be safe from it.

The front screen door creaked open, and Aabir turned his head in its direction as a round feastbot floated towards them; its four spindly arms hanging down like the tentacles of a gelatscy.

"Lunch is ready." It spoke in a chippy, robotic voice.

Mister Falap clapped his hands and went to stand. "Perfect." His smile returned as he looked at each of them. "Let's eat."

THEY ATE LUNCH IN the farmhouse's open dining room. Aabir filled his plate with food three times during the meal, then ate two slices of greenberry pie for dessert. The only talk around the table came from Mister Falap and his parents as they swapped stories and reminisced. Their voices were light, and everyone seemed content, but Aabir could sense the heaviness from out on the porch had only come into the house with them.

He traded looks with Zeke a couple times during the meal and could tell his brother recognized it too, but neither said anything. Aabir did not want to take this happy moment away from his parents, and he figured his brother felt the same.

Ereliev kept her focus on Yahel as she tried to get their youngest sister to eat her fried tomeplants, while Nevaze ate quietly in the seat beside her. Neither looked over at Aabir at all during lunch, so he could not read in their eyes if they shared the same feelings as he and Zeke.

He ate the last bit of his second slice of pie and pushed the plate away from him. "Thanks, Mister Falap." He turned his head to look at the head of the table where the old man sat.

Mister Falap smiled. "I'm glad you enjoyed it."

"Yes, it was delicious." Matha wiped her mouth with her napkin.

"I wasn't too keen on having those feastbots at first," he shrugged, "but they do a pretty good job."

"They do."

There was a pause, and the unseen weight became heavier. Aabir caught the significant look Matha sent Patre before she said, "Ereliev, why don't you take Nevaze and Yahel outside to play on the swing?"

"But Matha, I—" Ereliev's complaint was cut off at the sharp look from their mother, and she instead grumbled, "Yes ma'am." Standing from her chair, she picked up Yahel from her's and gestured towards their other sister. "Come on, Nevaze."

Nevaze followed without saying anything, and the three of them exited the dining room.

Matha turned her head and flicked her violet gaze between Aabir and Zeke. "Your patre and I need to speak with Mister Falap alone," she said. "So please go outside and watch over your sisters while we talk."

Aabir opened his mouth to protest, but Patre sent him a look that said, "*Don't argue with her*", so he only gave a begrudging "Yes ma'am" instead of the other complaints he would have rather said. He pushed back his chair and stood, then walked out of the dining room. Zeke's chair squeaked behind him, then footsteps followed.

As Aabir strode through the living room, he could not help but sneak a habitual glance up at the beautiful, silvery-furrum longsword hanging above the fireplace mantle before he lowered his gaze back to the front door.

The air was much warmer as he pushed the squeaky screen door open and stepped out onto the porch. Zeke joined him only a moment later.

"I can't believe we have to stay out here!" Zeke grumbled as they both headed down the porch stairs and walked towards the swing where Ereliev was pushing Yahel and Nevaze. "It's not like I don't know all the trouble going on around us."

Both younger girls were laughing as their legs flailed in the air. Yahel must have spotted them, because she cried out, "Aabir! Zee! Come push us!"

Aabir replied, "We're coming!" as he shared a glance with Zeke, who rolled his eyes.

"How are you not angry about being left out?" His brother asked as they neared the tree swing. "Matha and Patre *always* let you in on their secrets."

Aabir scrunched his nose. "No, they don't."

"Yes, they do." Ereliev said as they came to a stop near her. She looked at them both and stepped away from the swing's path. "Your turn."

"Oh, so now you're speaking to me?" He sent her an incredulous look before taking her place.

The swing came at him. He lifted his hands and pushed it as hard as he could. Another bout of squealing laughs came from Nevaze and Yahel as they flew upwards again.

He kept his eyes on the swing as Ereliev replied, "That's because whenever I look at you, you always look at me as if I'm some lost forest kitten."

He pushed the swing again. "No, I don't."

"Actually, yeah, you do." Zeke added, "I've seen it."

Aabir glanced at them out of the corner of his eye. "Well, I'm sorry if that bothers you, Ereliev." He could not hide the frustrated bite in his tone as he added, "I'm just worried about you."

"And you shouldn't," Ereliev replied. "I'm not some little kid who needs help—especially not from my older brother."

He gritted his teeth and stepped away from the swing's path to face her. Her hands were balled into fists, and her eyes glinted with a sharp anger.

"I didn't mean to offend you, Ereliev." He tried to even his tone, but the bite remained. "If I knew that trying to help you would hurt you so much, I never would've asked in the first place."

"You can't help me, Aabir." Light glistened against unshed tears that appeared in his sister's gaze, though it did nothing to dampen the fire he saw there. "No one can. Not you, not Matha, not Patre—no one." Her last words ended in a shout, "So just forget that anything happened and leave me alone!"

The tears broke through and began streaming down her cheeks as she turned and ran away from them.

"Ereliev!" Aabir called to her retreating back, but he did not try to move. She definitely would not want him following after her.

Nevaze gasped and shouted, "Ereliev!" Her glittery shoes skidded in the dirt to slow the swing down.

"Ne-va!" Yahel complained, "Stop!"

Aabir turned and grabbed the swing to help it slow despite Yahel's protests. He met Nevaze's concerned gaze as she asked, "Why did she run away?"

He glanced over his shoulder at Ereliev's huddled form that now sat underneath a tree on the other side of the yard, then he looked back down at Nevaze. Trying to keep his voice calm despite the storm of emotions brewing inside, he replied, "She's just dealing with stuff at school, and I may have said something that upset her."

"Oh." Nevaze turned her head in Ereliev's direction. "Then I think you should apologize."

Zeke chuckled, and Aabir shot him a glare before looking beyond his brother back towards Ereliev's shadowed form. He sighed. "I don't think she wants to see me right now, Nevaze."

"Yes, she does," she replied matter-of-factly. "She tells me about her friends' drama sometimes, and how she hates it when they fight. So, why would she want you two to do the same?"

Aabir blinked in surprise and turned his neck to meet her insistent gaze. Not even his frustrations could keep a small grin from escaping his lips. "Has anyone ever told you that you're pretty smart for an eleven-year-old?"

Nevaze pursed her lips. "I'm almost twelve, Aabir. I'm not a baby like Yahel."

"Hey!" Yahel jerked her neck in Nevaze's direction and sent her a pouty look. "I'm not a baby! I'm three." She held up three fingers to prove her point.

Aabir shook his head with a chuckle. "Thanks for the help, Nevaze." He dipped his chin towards her. "I'll go talk to her."

"OK." Nevaze nodded once then looked over at Zeke. "It's your turn to push us, Zee!"

Zeke's smirk faded into a disgruntled frown. "But I don't want to..."

"It's your turn, Zee." Aabir mimicked his sister with a grin and patted his brother on the shoulder as he passed.

Zeke grumbled under his breath but stepped over to the swing. Once Aabir knew his brother would stay, he picked up his pace and jogged over to Ereliev. A chill went through him as he stepped under the shadow cast by the tree she sat under, and he slowed his pace until he was standing only a few feet from her.

"Go away, Aabir." She did not lift her head from where her arms cradled it.

He took a step closer. "Nevaze said I should apologize to you for what I said, so I came to do that." He crossed his arms and turned his gaze towards the tree trunk her back leaned against. "I'm sorry for how I've been acting towards you. I didn't mean to offend you. I was only worried about what might've happened when you were questioned." A sigh escaped his lips before he asked, "Will you forgive me?"

Ereliev was silent for a few moments. Then she lifted her head enough for Aabir to meet her teary eyes. "I guess so." She shrugged and wiped her face with one of her hands. "And I—I'm sorry, too, Aabir. I—I haven't been angry at you personally. I just..." Her voice faltered and she sniffed.

She tore her gaze from his and lowered her chin onto her propped arms. "I don't want to be a burden. I want to help as much as I can, and...well, I guess whenever you say it, I get...jealous."

Aabir raised his brow in surprise. "Why are you jealous of *me*?" He asked incredulously, "All my 'helpfulness'—as you say—only seems to bring us more problems."

"Yeah, but even though you being a trainee doesn't seem to be helping us anymore, it still did for a few years." She shrugged again. "While I can't even do anything to keep the authorities from intruding into our home; I can't even protect...I can't even protect my—myself..."

A few more tears slid down her cheeks, but she wiped them away with her arm.

Anger flared in Aabir's chest, but he ignored it as he sat down in the grass across from her. "I know you said that me knowing couldn't help you, Ereliev," he began, "but could you at least tell me what happened?"

Ereliev continued to stare at the grass. Aabir waited for what seemed like a full minute before she finally replied, "I...was questioned at school, as you know."

She breathed out a shaky sigh. "When it happened, I was a little scared at first, but I figured it would go the same way it always did when I was home, so I didn't let the fear bother me. The patrolmen took me to this empty classroom and started asking me some questions. But then I mentioned that you were a trainee, and—and they—"

She stopped abruptly to let out another shaky breath, then continued, "One of—one of them put their dagger to my throat. And I—I screamed. He—he put his hand over my mouth and told me that—that if I did that again, he—he would *hurt* me."

The horror that darkened her big eyes told Aabir she did not mean just some physical wound.

"So, I—I stayed quiet unless they wanted me to answer another question, and then they—they let me go. But now I—I'm scared that if I'm sent to get questioned again, they will...that one of them will—"

A sob broke through her words, and she put her face in her arms again. Aabir could only watch her cry as he imagined all the different ways he would hurt the person who threatened his sister in such a way. If he could get his hands on them, they would wish they had died.

"But he didn't do anything to you, right?" He finally asked.

"No." Her tight curls bounced as she shook her head without lifting her face towards him. "I'm OK," she added.

Aabir rolled his eyes at the lie, but he did not say anything about it since he was guilty of doing the same thing. Instead, he asked, "Why haven't you told Matha and Patre? I know you said they can't help you, but I'm sure they could talk to the principal—"

She shook her head as she lifted it. "Our principal's parents were Pon-Yelish, and the patrolmen don't respect his authority. So, I doubt he would be able to do anything. And if I told Matha and Patre, it would only add an extra load to them."

She breathed out another quivering sigh. "They're so tired, Aabir. I don't know how much you can tell because you're away at Norland and everything, but whenever I get home from school, I—I always want to tell Matha...but then I see how exhausted she is and I—I never say anything..." She pressed her fist against her forehead as another tear slipped down her cheek. "I don't know how much more they can take. I just...I just want everything to be normal again."

Aabir twisted his lips into a frown. Did either one of them even know what "normal" was?

There was a quiet pause, broken only by their youngest sisters' squeals. As Aabir thought back over what was said, it only solidified the fact that he could not tell his parents about his deal with Rasiela. If what Ereliev said was true, and she was home a lot more than he was, then it was best if they did not know he was doing treasonous spy work. It would only add more weight on their shoulders, and they would definitely tell him to stop doing it—even if it meant ruining their one chance at leaving the empire.

"Ereliev," he asked, "have Matha and Patre mentioned anything else about leaving Igrium?"

Ereliev lowered her fist as her brow creased in concentration. "Not to me," she replied, "but I know they've talked about it a few times. Why?"

"Just wondering." He shrugged.

Suspicion came over her tear-stained features. "What are you planning, Aabir?"

He looked anywhere but at her. "What do you mean?"

"I know you. You're up to something, aren't you?" Almost as an afterthought, she added, "You and your *helpful* self."

He breathed out a sharp breath through his nose and glared at her. "Really?"

She shrugged without replying, but her expression was expectant.

Aabir rolled his eyes, but then met hers again. "Fine." If she had confided to him, then he could confide something to her—but only a little. "I...may have found out about something that could help us escape."

Ereliev's eyes widened. "Really?"

"Possibly."

She nodded, a ghost of a smile flashing across her wet face. "When do you think it will work?"

"I'm...not sure." He saw the hope in her expression dim, so he added quickly, "But I hope soon. I'm doing all I can to make it happen as quickly as possible. It—it's just going to take some time."

"Hmm... Can I know what this thing you're doing is?"

"No."

She shrugged. "Fine. I figured you weren't going to tell me anyway."

"I would, Ereliev—believe me, I would love to tell you—but I think it would be best for everyone if I kept it secret for now."

"Alright." Her lips barely lifted into a small smile. "I hope it works, then."

He sighed deeply through his nose and turned his gaze out to the tilled fields surrounding them. "I do too."

Chapter Thirty-Four

AABIR SOON GOT UP from the grass and walked back over to the swing. He and Zeke traded turns pushing Nevaze and Yahel until their youngest sisters grew bored. When that happened, Zeke grabbed his frisbee from the hovercar, and he and Aabir were soon throwing it above Nevaze and Yahel's heads to see if they could catch it.

Ereliev joined them a little later, and Aabir was glad to see that her eyes were brighter than they had been, though a little red from crying. She moved into the middle to help their sisters, and immediately caught Zeke's low throw.

"Hey!" He exclaimed, "No fair!"

Ereliev only laughed and steered Nevaze in his direction, handing their younger sister the flying disc. Aabir met her gaze for a moment and matched her grin as Zeke shuffled into the middle, grumbling even as he came to a stop.

"Come on, Nevaze," Aabir gestured for her to throw. "Show Zeke how much better you are at this."

Zeke shot him a glare but then turned it onto Nevaze. "Throw it to me, Nevaze!" He called.

Aabir rolled his eyes then started running as she threw the frisbee. It shook in the air and curved away from all of them. Out of the corner of his eye, he noticed Zeke running near him. He picked up his speed as the disc landed in the grass and grabbed it.

He threw his hand in the air and whooped victoriously, then turned around and headed back to his sisters; shooting a smirk at his brother as he passed him by. Zeke turned and followed behind him, but Aabir could feel the heat of his glare hitting his back.

When they both made it back to their sisters, all five of them continued to throw the frisbee as the shadows lengthened.

Aabir did not even notice the pink tinge in the otherwise blue sky until the front door squealed open and Matha's voice rang out, "Kids!"

He turned his attention towards the house as she, Patre, and Mister Falap all filed out onto the porch. Yahel started running towards them as Matha continued, "You can come in now! We're done talking."

"Finally!" Zeke exclaimed as he followed Yahel before quickly overtaking her scrambling pace. Aabir jogged over to his youngest sister, picked her up, and sped them both towards the house. Nevaze and Ereliev's steps sounded behind him as they followed.

Zeke made it to the porch first and pounded up the creaking wooden stairs. He rushed past their parents and into the house without a word.

"What in Afreean...?" Matha stared at the screen door as Aabir ascended the porch stairs and set Yahel down. The youngest Sorrel scrambled over to her and hugged her legs. Matha turned to face Aabir, understanding on her face. "You could have come inside for *that*." She put her hands on her hips.

Aabir shrugged and crossed his arms. "We figured none of you wanted us to listen in, so he waited."

She pursed her lips but said nothing else about it as Ereliev and Nevaze's footsteps came up the stairs. Aabir turned his head and watched his sisters as they passed him, both breathing hard from their sudden run. Nevaze continued into the house, while Ereliev stopped near him.

"What did you all talk about?" Ereliev asked.

Matha, Patre, and Mister Falap all shared significant looks before Patre replied, "Quite a few things."

Now it was Aabir's turn to ask, "What sort of things?"

"All right, you two," Matha gave them both a hard stare. "We talked about what has been happening, along with other things that you need not know at the moment."

Aabir could not help but frown at the answer. He glanced out of the corner of his eye and saw a similar expression on Ereliev's face. He figured his parents would not divulge much on the subjects they had discussed, but it was still disappointing not to know at least a little more.

"We will tell you about some of those things in the future," Patre said, "but not right now and not tonight."

"Yes sir," Aabir sighed, and Ereliev copied him.

"Matha, I'm hungry." Yahel piped up.

Matha lowered her head in Yahel's direction and replied, "Then let's get you a snack, Yahel."

She picked her up and headed back into the house. Ereliev shared a side-eyed glance with Aabir before following them. Aabir almost did the same, but when he noticed the silent conversation Patre and Mister Falap were sharing with each other, he decided to stay put.

"What's going on, Patre?" He finally asked.

Patre turned his face towards him, and for a moment, Aabir could see the exhaustion Ereliev had spoken of in his eyes before it was taken over by a neutral expression.

"Mister Falap wanted to speak with you alone, Aabir." Patre put his hand on the elderly man's hunched shoulder.

Mister Falap's eyes locked onto Aabir's. "How 'bout we go for a walk?"

Aabir's stomach churned uneasily, but he knew he couldn't refuse the older man. Nor did his curiosity want him to.

"Sure." He shrugged and stepped to the side as Mister Falap hobbled towards the stairs on his cane.

He sent a questioning look towards Patre but could read nothing on his face. So, with a frown, he turned and joined the elderly man as he descended the few steps, then they both walked towards the wood fence surrounding the yard.

"You're not in trouble, Aabir," Mister Falap shot him a kind grin. "I only wanted to talk with you about some things."

"Yes sir." A small wind of relief calmed some of his uneasiness.

Mister Falap did not say anything else for a few steps. Aabir glanced over at him and saw his grin had disappeared for a hard look of concentration.

"Aabir," the older man lifted his sharp gaze upon him, "like your parents said, they told me about everything that's been happening to y'all these past few weeks, and they also mentioned that—even though you're at Norland most of the time—it's been especially hard on you."

Aabir folded his arms and used all his willpower not to look into the man's eyes. "I guess so."

"That's what I figured," Mister Falap nodded and sighed through his nose. "Y'know, my oldest brother was the same way. He had seven younger siblings—including myself—to help take care of, and I didn't envy him, let me tell you. He made a lot of mistakes in trying to control us...I think you know something about that."

Aabir nodded slowly. "Yeah..."

He could not even count how many mistakes he had made in trying to protect himself and his family.

"Well, I mentioned him because one of those mistakes he made in trying to protect us actually ended up being the reason our house was raided."

Aabir's heart began to race as the words left Mister Falap's mouth, and new fears and dark whispers filtered into his head.

Mister Falap continued, "He warned all of us once not to say anything about Emperor Rexcan at school or anywhere public during the unrest after the emperor's assassination attempt—although our parents already told us not to, anyway. Well, one of my sisters was complaining about his bossiness to her friend as they were walking down the street, and some patrolmen overheard them. They stopped her and forced her to tell them what she'd just said. Apparently, they thought we were hiding something and that's why we couldn't talk about him. So less than an hour later they were at our doorstep."

An icy shiver went down Aabir's spine. It was not hard to imagine patrolmen breaking down the door of his home to take his family to prison after it was found he was working as a Silvanian spy.

"I don't say this to upset you, Aabir," a little of the weightiness left Mister Falap's tone, "but I do say it as a warning. My brother only told my siblings and I that because he was afraid our parents hadn't adequately warned us beforehand."

A physical weight landed on Aabir's shoulder, and he stopped to face Mister Falap. The elderly man gave him a sympathetic look. "Your parents don't need you to be the protector of the family—that's not your job while they're still alive."

"But I may be the only one of us who can do something about our problems," he finally replied. "I know what you're saying, Mister Falap—I understand—but I can't stand by and act as if nothing is going on while my family is suffering at home. Matha and Patre can't do everything, but there are a few things *I* can do as a trainee that they can't."

Mister Falap's gaze was piercing as he barely squeezed Aabir's shoulder. "And *I* understand what you're saying. I just don't want to see you with all these burdens. You're not yourself when you carry them—I can see it in your eyes—and your Matha and Patre especially don't want to see you holding onto them. How do you think it's making them feel as your parents to see you going through this needless suffering?"

Aabir blinked and pulled his gaze away from Mister Falap's. These new fears warred with the usual worries that pressed heavily upon his chest. But despite this new warning, the roots of his normal worries ran too deep, and they began to consume the newly awakened, fearful thoughts.

Mister Falap sighed, and the weight of his hand lifted from Aabir's shoulder. He put both his hands atop his cane and turned towards the fence. Aabir stayed put, not saying anything. What could he say? He could see the truth of the older man's words, but his normal fears and anxieties were so much louder...

"Your parents also mentioned that they were trying to come up with ideas for leaving Igrium," Mister Falap said.

Aabir's heart dropped into his churning stomach. He turned his head and caught the side-eyed stare his adoptive grandpatre gave him.

"So, they've told you about that, yes?" The older man raised his brow knowingly.

Aabir shrugged. "A little."

"Hmm." Mister Falap dipped his pointy chin. "Well, if y'all can find a way to, I think you should take it."

"Really?" His eyes widened in shock. That was not the answer he had expected.

Mister Falap smiled knowingly. "Yes—even if it means y'all leaving me. Your safety is more important to me than any of your visits. Not that I don't love you, but if staying here means you're risking your lives, then I'd rather y'all leave." He paused, his smile lessening. "And if things keep going the way they have, I want to see y'all gone as quickly as possible."

"Yes sir." A small smile escaped Aabir's lips. Then it, too, faded as his thoughts continued on their dreary path. "Does that mean you've heard about the new Constantia rule Emperor Ignis is trying to implement?"

"I have." A shadowed look came over Mister Falap's sun-kissed skin. "And I've started praying to y'all's Deleyon that it wouldn't go through...but I fear there's no stopping it—not if it's the Emperor Himself enacting it. I've prayed to the gods about it being a dishonor, but I believe I'm only one of a few that thinks that way, so I doubt they'll do anything to stop it. It goes against much of their nature, anyway."

Another shiver went down Aabir's spine. He and Tetra had had quite a few talks about Igrium's fourteen deities; and from what he knew of them, Mister Falap's comment rang true.

"And that's why I have to do something," he replied.

Mister Falap looked over at him again. "I know, Aabir, and I bet I'd do the same thing in your boots." He smiled wearily. "No matter how many warnings I was given."

Aabir lifted his hand and rubbed the back of his neck with a sheepish smile he could not contain. "Thank you for understanding."

"I won't tell you to stop whatever you might be planning to do," Mister Falap gave him a hard look, "but remember what I said, and don't go getting into something that's too big for you to handle. Understand?"

"Yes sir."

Becoming a Silvanian spy was probably what the elderly man would consider as "too big for him to handle", but after his talk with Ereliev, Aabir knew he would not—could not—back out of it. And if Mister Falap had heard their conversation, Aabir had a feeling he would agree that there was nothing that could be "too big" to stop him from trying to get them out of the empire.

Mister Falap nodded sharply and turned back around in the direction of the house. "*Are* you planning something?" He asked, giving him another side-eye glance.

Aabir had a feeling his face said it all, so despite everything in him that told him to lie, he instead said, "Yes sir."

"I thought so." Mister Falap nodded again. "You had a look on your face when I mentioned it."

"Will you tell Matha and Patre?" His heart skipped a frightened beat at the thought.

"Nope, not my responsibility." The elderly man gave him a pointed look then headed back towards his house.

Aabir, slack-jawed, watched his retreating back for a moment. He was not going to tell them? With a shake of his head to clear it, he took a few long strides to catch up with the older man's limping pace.

"You...you're not?" He asked.

"I said I wouldn't, so I won't." Mister Falap's gaze stayed on his house as he continued, "But *you* need to tell them. They trust you, Aabir, and you trust them. Why would you want to break that by keeping secrets from them? Especially if they're secrets related to helping them."

"But...but they'll tell me not to do it."

Mister Falap glanced in Aabir's direction, his brow raised. "Will they?"

Aabir rolled his eyes. "Of course they will."

He knew his parents; and if he told them he was doing spy work, they would panic, and he would no longer be able to do it.

Mister Falap turned his face away with a knowing look. "You never know. They might surprise you."

Aabir lowered his gaze to the grass without reply, then raised it up towards the farmhouse. He went over the man's words in his mind and tried to come up with a compelling argument against them.

How would telling his parents help any? Sure, it might lift some of the mental baggage the secret of being a spy pressed upon him, but it would also add a new weight of regret by forcing him away from the one opening for escape he had found. His parents might understand what he was doing, but they would say it was too dangerous and force him to stop.

He breathed a quiet sigh and pressed a hand against his forehead. *Oh Deleyon, what am I supposed to do?*

"Think over what I said, Aabir," Mister Falap's voice was low as they neared the house, "I don't expect you to do anything tonight, but promise me that you'll think about it. OK?"

"Yes sir."

And he would. Probably more so than was healthy.

"Thank you." A smile tinged Mister Falap's words and he patted Aabir's shoulder. His limping pace quickened as they made it to the porch, and the boards creaked under his weight as he ascended the steps.

Aabir stopped before stepping on the first stair. Instead of following, he turned around and faced the fence-lined yard. His gaze traveled beyond to the tilled fields stretching out towards the horizon and a group of gelatscies floating in the pink-tinged sky. The sounds of muffled voices and Yahel's laughter filtered outside as the screen door squeaked open and Mister Falap's footsteps faded indoors.

Despite the peaceful setting around him, the many questions and worries in Aabir's head churned like waves of grass in a windstorm. He let out a deep sigh, sat down on the second step, and rested his elbows on his knees.

Cupping his chin in one of his hands, he silently prayed, *Deleyon, I need help with what I'm supposed to do. We need to escape, and I think this is the best option.* He frowned and shook his head. *No, it's our* ***only*** *option. I want to tell them, but I know they'll stop me from doing it if I do.*

He turned his gaze up to the darkening sky. *Please, help us. I need to know what to do. I hate this secret, but I don't know if telling it would be wise...*

Please, help me.

He sat there silently pleading and struggling over if he should do what Mister Falap suggested or not. He did not know how long he sat there in the mental battle, but by the time he had come to an answer, Matha called him inside for dinner.

One moon and a few stars studded the dark violet sky. With one last look up at them, and another silent plea for wisdom, he stood and headed up the stairs back into the house.

Chapter Thirty-Five

A SOFT KNOCK SOUNDED on the door of Tetra's room.

"Come in." She spun around in her desk's chair as the door opened and Lady Felicita stepped in; a small frown marring her features.

Uneasiness came over Tetra at the unusual sight. Usually, Felicita had a contagious smile on her face, especially since Tetra's stolen memories had begun reemerging, but there was something weighing down her countenance today.

"Tetra." Felicita nodded towards her and shut the door.

"Felicita." She nodded back, her brow furrowed. "Um...are you OK?"

Felicita sat down on the edge of Tetra's bed and turned her head in her direction. Their eyes locked, giving Tetra the perfect view of the battling emotions brewing in their familiar brown depths.

"Army General Taoghn sent a message ta the Buleutcil today, and in it he spoke o' givin' you his proposal ta join the army." Felicita's eyes narrowed questioningly as she asked, "Do you know what you're plannin' ta do?"

Tetra took a furtive glance back at the chardex lying open on her desk. Its pages of light were covered in her angular handwriting; notes upon notes of any information she could find online about Silvas' army—including its history, beliefs, and other random things she wanted to remember. Even with her knowing deep down the answer she had to the proposal, the logical side of her wanted as much information as she could get before flying headfirst into the commitment. So, while waiting for Lady Felicita to come, she had researched—and all that research only pointed her further in the direction her gut was telling her to take.

She lowered her gaze to the wood floor and replied, "I think so." The tallied skin on her arm felt rougher than usual as she rubbed her hand over it.

"So, you're thinkin' o' takin' him up on the offer, yes?"

"Yeah." She nodded slowly, still not meeting Felicita's gaze.

Felicita said nothing for a few moments. In the silence, a similar feeling to the one Tetra had felt when Aabir cut all contact with her bubbled up to the surface. She tried to suppress the constricting hurt, but it seemed it wouldn't be quenched as easily as other emotions she ignored.

"Well, I guess I can't stop you," Felicita finally said with a sigh.

Tetra lifted her head. A slight frown still tilted Felicita's lips downwards, but she could read an understanding in the young woman's eyes that mixed with other nameless emotions she saw there. The tight feeling inside dissipated into relief.

"Thank you." Tetra didn't know why she said it—it's not like she was accepting permission from the chief advisor's assistant—but it sounded like the right thing to say in the moment. "What—what did Chief Baene have to say about it?"

"He already knew." Anger flashed across Felicita's face, but she smoothed it out as quickly as it had come. "And although he doesn't agree with it happenin', he told me tha' until the ability is able ta be duplicated—*if* tha' is even possible—then he knew this would be the course the Buleutcil would take. He, Lord Jachen, Dr. Prin, and Lord Othnel were the only ones who voted against it."

Tetra scrunched her brow. She knew who three of those names belonged to, but not the last one. "Who is Lord Othnel?"

"Silvas' chief archivist."

Tetra was about to ask what a chief archivist was, but another, more pertinent, question grabbed her attention. So she asked, "And if I may be so blunt: why do you care so much? It's not like you won't be able to ask me questions anymore. If Dr. Prin can get a day or two for testing, surely Chief Baene would make sure we're still doing this."

"It's not tha', Tetra." Felicita sighed and lowered her gaze, her fingers fiddling with the ring on her finger. "I just...I don't..."

Tetra thought she was going to pick her words back up, but when Felicita's silence continued, she had to ask, "You don't...what?"

Another small sigh came from Felicita. "I don't want you ta die in battle," she lifted her head, and Tetra was surprised to see unshed tears in her gaze, "and much of Igrium's forces will be aimin' at you—the only war-peryton on the battlefield."

Tetra blinked a few times, stupefied by her reaction. Those were tears; *real* tears reflecting the warm light of the room. It immediately caused her to reevaluate the whole situation of these meetings.

Had something happened during the past few weeks she wasn't aware of? Though the constricting feeling from before was gone, she remembered it—and the deeper implications behind it.

She had begun enjoying these meetings and Felicita's company, but she never expected any sort of *friendship* to come from them. She didn't even know if that was the right word to use. Could they be considered friends? Or was Tetra lonelier than she realized and grasping for things that weren't actually there?

Felicita squeezed her eyes shut and pressed her hands against her forehead. "I'm sorry, Tetra," she said, "Forgive me. I don't want ta make your decision any harder." She opened her eyes and Tetra met her clearer gaze. "I can see tha' this is somethin' you want ta do, and I don't want ta stand in your way. Just...be careful. Please."

"I will," Tetra replied with a sheepish smile. "As much as I can, that is."

Felicita nodded with her own small smile. She rolled her shoulders back, and her perfect posture somehow became even straighter. "Well, I will be prayin' tha' Deleyon helps you make the right decision." She flicked her wrist sharply and her holonode's screen appeared. "Now then, since you seem ta be able ta remember your patre better, I have some questions tha' might help you remember your matha."

A buzz of excitement went through Tetra. "Alright."

She spun back around to face her desk, closed the chardex, then turned back to face Felicita. When it came to finding her memories, most other things dimmed in comparison—including the huge decision before her.

Felicita tapped and scrolled through a few things on her holonode's screen before she finally asked, "Did your matha have a nickname for you as well?"

Tetra's heart raced an excited beat as she closed her eyes. *A nickname...* If her patre had one for her, maybe her matha had called her by it at least once. She recalled the memory of her patre saying "Anora", and focused all her attention on the deep, mental lake where her lost memories were coming from.

She didn't have to wait long. It only took a few seconds after she remembered the nickname for a new memory to appear. It was fuzzy like the others, but in it she could tell that her younger self was standing in a kitchen. In the memory, she looked up at a woman who towered above her child stature. The woman looked down at her, and even with the mental fuzz, Tetra could tell she was smiling.

The same feelings she had whenever she remembered her patre came over her as she focused on the woman, but they were immediately overshadowed by a gale of fearful uncertainty. That woman wasn't Marin Cairn.

"Wha' is it, Anora?" The woman asked in a thick Pon-Yelish accent.

Tetra recalled her own reply, "*When will the cookies be done?"*

"Soon." The woman wiped her hands on a towel and picked Tetra up. "You 'ave ta be patient. Good things sometimes take time before they're fully ready."

Something akin to loneliness, but deeper, came with her words. Tetra's fingernails dug into her arm as the hollow feeling yawned open in her chest, but she let the memory continue,

"Is that why Patre doesn't want to see me?" Young Tetra asked, "Because I'm not ready?"

*The woman's smile faded. "No, Anora. Tha' is not it," she replied, "***You** *are ready. I'tis your patre who thinks he's not."*

"Why?"

"I wish I knew." The woman shrugged, and her full lips turned upwards into a soft smile. "But remember wha' I told you, Anora. Your uncle and I love you very, very much. And until your patre realizes just how special you are, we will continue ta do so in his place. You are loved, Anora, and don't you ever let anyone tell you otherwise."

She kissed the top of Tetra's head, and Tetra wrapped her short arms around the woman's neck. "I love you, Aunt Minda."

"I love you."

The memory ended, leaving a mix of longing and hollowness, the wonderful feelings from the memories of her patre, and the present confusion and doubt this newest memory brought with it. Tetra blinked her eyes open, and that's when she finally felt the wet tear tracks running down her face. Heat crept into her tear-stained cheeks, and she immediately wiped them away, cringing as her fingers brushed against her still-healing malscar.

"Are you all right, Tetra?" Felicita's voice held a note of concern.

Tetra nodded with a "Yeah", knowing she wasn't.

The woman in Tetra's memory said she was her aunt, yet Tetra only had one aunt, Impera Warlin (Aquilo's matha), and she didn't have dark brown skin or a Pon-Yelish accent—nor did Tetra believe the woman could speak such loving words. Perhaps it was a nickname her younger self had called her. Maybe she wasn't really her aunt, but her nanny.

She recalled the video she had seen of her parents' house burning down, and of the woman who had run out of it with Tetra in her arms. More confusion joined the beginning swirl of her thoughts. Despite how far away the camera angle of the video was, she thought she remembered the woman being fair-skinned.

And why did Tetra believe her patre didn't love her? From the memories she could remember, and the feelings they brought with them, she could tell she had had a good relationship with him. So why did she still feel this hollow ache inside her?

"Are you sure?" Felicita's question broke her from descending into a deeper spiral. "Do we need ta stop for the day? We can always continue ta'morrow..."

"No, no." Tetra shook her head. "I'll be fine."

She just needed to think through all the confusing thoughts that memory brought with it later. Preferably when she was alone.

Tetra met Felicita's gaze and saw the concern in her soft expression.

"What's the next question?" She asked in as neutral a tone as she could force.

Felicita sent her an unbelieving look, but she said nothing about it as she lifted her arm with the holonode attached to it and read, "Can you remember a special gift you were given as a child? Like...maybe your first weapon, perhaps?"

A pang of regret joined the windstorm of other emotions brewing in Tetra at the mention of "first weapon". In Igrium, it was a tradition that on a child's eighth birthday, their parents give them their first weapon, which was usually a small dagger or a bow.

Her parents hadn't been home during her eighth birthday, and when they did return, they were trapped in their house as it burned down; so Emperor Ignis had given her the one they were supposed to. It was a small, gritanium-bladed dagger with a hilt made from a peryton's antler. A small gust of uneasiness came over Tetra at the thought of it coming from the talking, personable Leaves Of Gold, but she pushed the feeling aside for the far more important matters demanding her attention.

She ended up getting the dagger taken away from her, however, when she threatened her roommates with it after they hid her few belongings and wouldn't tell her where they had put them. That had happened a few days before her second escape attempt when she fell from the everpine tree, and—now that she thought about it—she realized Tarson taking it away had been the final straw for her decision to do so. It was the only personal thing she had needed to remember her parents by (besides the overwhelming mountain of honor she had been forced to carry). Needless to say, she had never gotten it back; but now that it was on her mind, she began to wonder what Tarson had done with it...

Stop getting distracted. At the personal rebuke, she squeezed her eyes shut and turned her focus back onto the mental lake-prison.

Before she even began to mentally yell her demands at it, a memory came to her mind. It was a still image of the same woman as before—whom she called "Aunt Minda"—only this time she was sitting at a table across from Tetra, laughing.

Immediately, another image followed that one, and then another. Tetra's heart began to race as more and more memories followed the same one: a fuzzy picture of her Aunt Minda sitting on a couch with another little girl—who shared the same brown skin and dark hair as her—cuddling underneath her arm; there was a short memory of Tetra squealing in delight as she ran away from the woman in a sunlit, walled garden; another fuzzy memory of the other girl and Tetra dressing up in gaudy amounts of jewelry; then a still image of Aunt Minda and Tetra's patre talking in the same kitchen from her earlier recollection.

More and more fuzzy memories—some like videos, others like still pictures—came rushing into her head like a monsoon. She pressed her fists against her temples as a headache began to pound behind them.

STOP! Tetra inwardly screamed, and the deluge slowly dwindled. She sucked in a sharp breath as the headache ebbed away. Blood pounded in her ears, in tune with her heart's frantic beating.

She opened her eyes and met Felicita's wide-eyed gaze.

"Wha' happened?" Her Pon-Yelish accent sharpened with worry.

Tetra licked her lips and sucked in a few more deep breaths before getting the words out, "I—I remembered...a lot." She shook her head slowly. "I—I almost didn't think I'd be able to stop it..."

"Wha' did you see?"

"This...this woman." Tetra didn't go into details about her mysterious aunt. "And my patre again, and a—a little girl..."

"And your matha?" There was a hint of something in Felicita's voice Tetra couldn't name. "Did you see her?"

"I...don't know." She looked up at Felicita without moving her head. "Could we do this tomorrow? I—I need to think through everything I just saw."

Felicita looked like she wanted to argue, but she only nodded with a flick of her wrist to turn her holonode off. "If tha' is what you want, then o' course." She stood from the bed; her features neutral but for the mix of questions shining in her eyes. "I'll see you tomorrow, then."

"Mm-hmm." Tetra didn't want to push her out so quickly, but she needed time to sort through the barrage of images and emotions she had just been through.

Felicita's high heels clicked against the floor as she opened the door and stepped outside. When it shut, Tetra got up from her chair and limped over to her bed. She laid down then closed her eyes to focus.

She went through each memory, one by one. Each brought new emotions with it that she could feel as if she were reliving the blurry memories at that moment—which, in a way, she was. Most of the images and feelings were good, but each one watered a seed of fear in Tetra's heart that she couldn't stop from growing.

What she heard, felt, and saw in these new-old memories told a completely different story than the one Emperor Ignis and her profile led her to believe all these years.

Instead of what she thought she would recall, Tetra was shown the memories of a girl who was taken care of by her loving Igrian uncle—whom she couldn't yet remember the name of—and her Pon-Yelish Aunt Minda. She remembered a girl who played with her older cousin in a large, immaculate garden filled with towering trees and bright flowers, and who lived in a luxurious home fit for the most highly honored families in Igrium. This girl had felt more love and heard more laughter than Tetra could ever remember feeling or doing in the last ten years; yet the few memories of her real patre, not her uncle, left this young girl with a deep ache that swallowed up every wonderful feeling.

One such memory came to the forefront of Tetra's mind. It was her patre looking down at her with a frown as she hugged his leg. Despite the blurriness, she could tell that he looked similar to her uncle; but the hollow, yet roiling, emotions his blurred face brought up helped her distinguish between the two.

"No, Anora," he said, "I'm very busy."

Even though it was a memory, hot tears pricked Tetra's eyes as she recalled herself crying at his words. *"But—but I miss you!" She cried, "Can't I—can't I go home with you tonight?"*

He sighed and lowered onto his knees to get eye-level with her. "That's not possible."

Something about his eyes—even when fuzzy—sent a jolt through Tetra, as if her brain was connecting the dots without telling her what it was connecting, similar to Lady Felicita's familiar gaze.

He continued, "You need to stay here with your aunt and uncle. You know I can't take care of you like they can."

"Why not?"

"It's for your protection." Another sigh. "And...because I don't have your matha to help me."

"But I have you!" Tetra wrapped her arms around his neck. "Please, Patre."

There was a moment's hesitation, then her patre shook his head. "I'm sorry, Anora. But it won't work." He peeled her arms off him and stood back up. "I have to go now."

The memory ended at that, and Tetra's heart bruised with longing for someone she didn't know. She wiped away a couple tears that trailed down her face, but she didn't open her eyes.

That wasn't Aries Cairn. Aries and Marin Cairn had been married for years before Tetra was born, and they both died at the same time—something this memory contradicted.

More fear watered the roots growing in her heart.

The memory barely began to replay in her mind again before her brain stopped it as her patre spoke the name "Anora". As if the name was a key, a whole new deluge of memories sprang from the open door of their prison. Tetra squeezed her eyes shut even tighter against the growing headache and curled up into a ball atop her bed as she let the memories continue uninterrupted in the silence of her room.

There were more images of her and her cousin playing, laughing, and sometimes arguing over toys and plastic jewelry. Memories of driving around Rubrum, listening to her aunt or her uncle reading bedtime stories, and eating at a huge dining room table together all went through her head. More joy and childlike excitement filled her with warmth as she recalled them, even pulling a small smile out of her.

Then a hint of anxiety dulled the bright feelings as another, much longer, memory came to the surface: *"I—I made a mistake." Her uncle paced in a circle around their elaborate living room while her Aunt Minda watched from the couch.*

"Wha' do you mean?" She asked.

The memory's blurriness kept Tetra from making out either of their facial expressions, but she knew exactly how her younger self felt as more anxiety took over the happiness of the memories before. From the corner of the wall blocking half her younger self's view, she also got the impression she was eavesdropping. Some of Chief Baene's words from her meeting with him came back to mind, *"Children pick up on a lot more than we give them credit for...overheard a secret plan your parents' were talking about..."*

She kept that in the back of her thoughts as she let the memory continue,

"I—I wish I could say, Minda," her uncle turned his back in Tetra's direction and held out his hands in a hopeless gesture, "but I'm afraid if you know about it, then you and the girls will be in danger, too."

A hint of panic touched Aunt Minda's low voice, "Wha' did you do, Joash?"

His name! Tetra's heart jumped excitedly at this new piece of knowledge despite the second-hand anxiety the memory caused.

"I..." his voice trailed off as he shook his head. "No, I can't say. It's...it would put you all in a lot of danger if you knew." He stepped towards his wife and sat down on the couch next to her. "I need you and the girls to pack some of your things—"

"—Joash—"

"—and we will all leave. Tonight."

"Bu' I just put them ta bed!" Aunt Minda stood from the couch abruptly and faced him, hands on her hips. "Where are we goin'? Why won't you tell me anythin'?"

Uncle Joash turned his head towards the double doors Tetra could now remember led out of the living room. He turned his head back up towards his wife's face. "Silvas."

Tetra's younger self barely caught the low word, and the small gasp that came from Aunt Minda. "Wha'? Really?"

"Yes, really." Uncle Joash nodded. "I finally called in that favor Baene Ruzek owed me, and he's already sent a small hovercraft to come and get us."

"Oh, Joash—"

"—I know. It's awful timing, but I can't tell you anything until we get out of Igrium and into Silvas." He stole another furtive glance at the doors. "Rexcan said he needed to talk to me tonight, so after that I'll get our records from the archives and then get a car."

"No, I'll get the records," Aunt Minda replied with a heavy sigh. "If we are doing this, then I will need ta get some of my infirmary ones, and only I have access ta them."

"Alright." Uncle Joash nodded. "That should save us some time then."

"I'll let the girls sleep while I do tha'—Anora still needs ta rest as much as she can—then when I get back, we'll gather our things."

There was a pause. "Have you noticed anything different about Anora?"

"Only the slight fever she still has." Even without seeing her head, Tetra could hear the bite in her aunt's tone.

"Well, if nothing has happened now, then I doubt it worked. She should be fine—better than any of the others we tested."

"She better be."

"But I still can't believe Selio did that." Her uncle sighed, but there was a sharp edge to his voice that sent Tetra's heart rate rising with more anxiety "You'd think after all the years we've known each other that he would tell me before he tried to do something like that to my niece!"

"I know." Aunt Minda's tone went back to normal as she spoke, "But Rexcan...he took care of it—even if I don't agree with how he did so. I'tis over, Joash."

"You're right." He sighed again and kissed her head. "Still, I should have never told him. I'm sorry about that. From now on, I'm going to make sure no one else knows about her or what happened."

There was a pause. Then Aunt Minda asked, "Do you think it's a good idea ta take her with us?"

"He's always telling me he can't take care of her, so I don't see a problem with it. She's just as much ours as his—if not more so."

"Still. You and I both know how he gets—"

"By the time he finds out, we'll be halfway to Silvas."

"Where is this hovercraft even picking us up at?"

"An old hovercraft plant called 'Fugerio'. It's east of here—in the mountains near the coast." Younger Tetra looked away as they kissed, then lifted her head again as he added, "I need to go now, but I should be back in less than an hour."

"We should be ready by then." Aunt Minda nodded. "Do you want me ta pack for you?"

"Just the essentials." He paused. "Oh—and all of my chardexes."

"Fine. I'll go on and get our records."

Uncle Joash nodded and they both headed out the double doors together. Once the doors shut behind them, Tetra turned around and ran back through the hall where she had come from.

The memory ended, leaving her with more questions than answers. She got the impression she had heard about her uncle knowing Chief Baene before, but she couldn't remember from where. It wasn't from one of her new-old memories—they were all still fresh and bright in her mind's eye.

Pushing that to the side for the moment, she again recalled as much of the same memory as she could. What had her uncle done that was so bad they had to leave Igrium that quickly? Why was Tetra sick? Why did her Aunt Minda seem to think it was Uncle Joash's fault?

And why, even with this memory, did Tetra only just recently escape Igrium? What went wrong that night that might've foiled her aunt and uncle's plans?

Something pricked at the back of her mind. Something she had once remembered...

She focused on the impression, and immediately, a memory of bright orange and yellow flames burst into her head. She sucked in a sharp breath as fear overwhelmed her. Her heart began racing again as the memory played out.

Flames towered all around Tetra. Her younger self cried as she spun around in frantic circles. "Uncle Joash! Aunt Minda!" She screamed.

"Anora!" Someone called.

She spun towards the voice but couldn't make anyone out due to the circle of fire all around her.

"I'm coming!" The voice called out again.

Something creaked and sizzled above her. She lifted her eyes in time to see the chandelier falling towards her—

Tetra's eyes popped open as the memory ended abruptly. She sucked in deep draughts of air to calm her pounding heart as the memory's overwhelming panic lingered.

It's over, she told herself, *I'm not there anymore...*

A few seconds went by, and the remembered feelings subsided. Tetra breathed in another calming breath before lifting her hands to move her short hair to the side. Her fingers shook as they brushed over the bumpy scar tissue left behind by that chandelier.

She scrunched her brow. So, despite all these new memories, her getting hit in the head with a fiery chandelier really had happened. The skin around her scar tingled at the memory, and she lowered her hands into her lap.

Then if that really did happen, *and* if she had woken up with no memory in the fortress' infirmary while her burn wound still throbbed in pain...then that meant her aunt and uncle's house burned down on the same night as the Cairn's.

Tetra's heart dropped into her stomach as the realization hit her like a cudgel to the face. Only seven houses or fortress quarters burned down that night in Rubrum, and only one of them was owned by anyone called "Joash".

She glanced down at her hands as if seeing them for the first time. Prince Joash Ignis was her uncle.

Chapter Thirty-Six

"Sorrel! Boll!" Lieutenant Denir's voice echoed in the training yard.

Aabir gulped and blinked the fear from his features as he turned around to face his commanding officer. Tycho and Aquilo both sent him pitying looks as they moved on with the rest of their platoon to the line of—now fixed—Silvanian and Frigian look-alike training droids they were using for crossbow practice.

"Sir?" Aabir lowered his gaze respectfully away from Denir's with a salute.

Septimus' heavy footsteps stopped beside him as he saluted as well.

"I want you both to spar again," Denir replied.

"Just us?" Septimus asked.

Lieutenant Denir's voice lowered dangerously, "Does it matter?"

"No sir."

"Good. Then begin."

Aabir released a quiet breath and traded a confused look with the other trainee before they both moved a few steps away from each other. Despite the strange circumstance, he was happy to skip crossbow training. His skills as an arbalist were "OK" at most, and he enjoyed sword fighting more than anything in training anyway. So, if his C.O. was giving him an excuse to do it, he was glad to take it.

He unsheathed his longsword—he was required to bring it with him to most training periods, even if he was not going to use it—as Septimus pulled his battle ax from where it hung on his belt. They both eyed each other warily as Aabir raised his sword in a guard stance. He shot a wary glance at the double headed ax Septimus held right as the other trainee let loose a battle cry and charged him.

Aabir lifted his sword and blocked the ax's downward stroke with his cross-guard. He pushed the haft away and feinted a stab at Septimus' chest before swinging at his legs.

Metal hit metal as Septimus grunted and stumbled back. Aabir took his chance. He lunged, and the tip of his blade sank between two metal plates in Septimus' side.

They locked eyes as Aabir pulled his red-tipped sword out with a nod. "I win."

Septimus frowned and opened his mouth to say something, but a single word from Lieutenant Denir cut through his excuse, "Again!"

Aabir glanced over at his commanding officer's hard expression before shuffling backwards away from Septimus. Adrenaline buzzed through his veins as he took in a deep breath to help calm his racing heart.

Septimus lunged forward, but this time Aabir anticipated it. He stepped to the side and swung for the charging trainee's arm. Septimus moved out of the way just in time and faced him. He swung his ax in an arc, and Aabir leapt back before it rammed him in the side.

Septimus swung the ax again and he barely jumped away. Again and again, Aabir dodged the powerful swings. His heart rate increased and sweat beaded his forehead as he waited for an opening. He could see Septimus' attacks were growing a bit slower as he wore out, so he continued moving away until the perfect time—

There. Septimus raised his battle ax in a new, downward stroke. Aabir rushed forward, blade raised, and swiped at his armored stomach before leaping back. Septimus grunted and shot him a glare. Too bad it hadn't been a helpful move.

Aabir's eyes widened as the other trainee lunged forward, ax raised above his head. He held up his sword to protect himself, but instead Septimus swung the ax in a curved stroke towards his side.

The breath rushed from Aabir's shocked lungs as he crumpled to the ground, clutching his pounding side as he tried to breathe. Sollight glinted off the ax head as it stopped a mere inch from his exposed neck. With a gulp, he averted his gaze away from the grim sight and onto the cool expression Septimus wore.

"I win," the trainee said.

Aabir gave a weak nod as he sucked in a painful breath.

"Get up, Sorrel!" Denir ordered.

With gritted teeth, he inhaled sharply as he pushed himself onto his hands and knees. Septimus lowered his ax, and Aabir glanced up to see his gauntleted hand outstretched for him to take.

With a grateful nod, he took it. The bigger trainee helped hoist him back up before moving to the opposite side of their invisible sparring circle. Breathing became easier as Aabir took a few steps back. His side still ached, though, and he wondered how big of a bruise would form from the hit.

"Again!" Denir called.

Aabir tightened his grip on his sword, then he lunged forward. A few moves later, Septimus was on the ground with the tip of Aabir's sword at his throat. An angry light ignited in Septimus' gaze as he stepped back to let him up. Of all the people in their platoon, Septimus was probably the worst loser—and if you were careful, it could lead to more victories in the future. The big trainee was a powerhouse, but when his anger blinded him, his moves usually grew sloppy.

"Again!"

Aabir glanced over at his C.O. at the familiar order, then back towards Septimus as the other trainee got up from the ground. He brandished his sword and took a few steps back. Again, he found himself wondering why Lieutenant Denir was making them do this; but no matter what it was, he would try to keep winning—if only to keep his commanding officer happy with him—and using Septimus' anger issues against him would be the key to doing so.

Once Septimus was up and ready, they both lunged towards each other with battle cries. Again and again, they traded blows until Aabir found an opening and took Septimus down with a thrust to his collarbone.

"Again!"

In the next round, Aabir's cockiness got the better of him. He went in for a similar, winning move as last time, but Septimus saw it coming. Aabir stumbled to a halt as the ax almost hit him in the face; sharp gritanium barely touching the tip of his nose. Blood pounded in his ears as he glanced up at the smug look on Septimus' face.

"Again!"

So again, they fought. And again. And again—until Aabir's arms were so sore they shook when he tried to lift his sword. More sweat beaded down his forehead and he wiped it away, panting. His side where Septimus whacked him earlier throbbed with each breath he took.

He met Septimus' eyes and noticed the other trainee looked to be in the same shape as him. Blood dribbled from a small cut where Aabir's sword had nicked his square jaw. It smeared as he wiped his gauntlet against it.

Lieutenant Denir took a step towards them, a ghost of a smile on his face. "Well, you two have outdone yourselves. Boll—you're through with training today. Go get cleaned up."

Septimus saluted towards him and marched off without looking over in Aabir's direction. Aabir watched his retreating back for a moment before sheathing his sword. He turned his head and his stomach roiled as he caught Lieutenant Denir's gaze fixed upon him.

"And you, Sorrel..." Something akin to excitement shone in his commanding officer's eyes, sending a shiver of uneasiness through Aabir's shaky muscles. "Congratulations on beating Boll ten-to-nine."

Aabir blinked, his tired mind processing the unusual complement. "Sir?"

Lieutenant Denir took a step closer and continued in a low voice, "The Tourney is coming up, and as always some of the fifth-year trainees from every military academy in our empire are given the honor of fighting in them. Norland's been given the opportunity to have two from each fifth-year platoon go this year—and you just won one of those spots, Sorrel. Congratulations."

Aabir blinked again as his brain slowly processed the words. Cold horror washed over him as he fully realized what the second lieutenant said.

"Sir, I—I didn't realize that was why we were sparring..."

"I know, and that's how I wanted it to be." Denir nodded sharply. "I wanted to see what you both could do without having the incentive of the Tourney to urge you on."

Oh Deleyon, no...

"I still have to choose someone else, so don't mention this to anyone until I give the announcement." The light in Denir's eyes faded with his usual sharp countenance. "Understand?"

Aabir tried to keep the contents of his churning stomach down as he replied, "Yes sir."

Lieutenant Denir dipped his chin towards him. "Good. I'm planning on choosing that second person tomorrow. But once I do, you both will be put on a separate training routine then your platoonmates, which will include going to the Constantia stadium to train with the other competitors as well. I want both of you to be as prepared for the Tourney as possible. Norland's honor rests on your shoulders, Sorrel."

He leaned forward and got in Aabir's face. "*My* honor rests on you. I've seen you fight, and I know you can do well in them, if not win the third-level. I expect you to get at least to the end of the second day; but even if you're disqualified then, I will still be honored with your efforts. Do you understand?"

That I'm basically being threatened to do well in the one competition me and my family hate? He thought before replying with a simple, "Yes sir, I do."

"Then you are dismissed." Lieutenant Denir straightened and took a step back, his hands behind his back. "Your new training begins in two days, Sorrel. Go now."

Aabir's arm slightly shook as he saluted his commanding officer. Then he spun on his heel as quickly as he could and rushed out of the training yard before anyone could see the dread on his face.

This can't be happening. He pushed the door open and stepped into the training corridor with a glance up at the tall ceiling. *Why Deleyon?* He ground his teeth together and curled his hands into fists. *Of all the people to go into them—why* ***me****? I hate them! You know I do. And I know* ***You*** *hate them, too—unless everything my parents said about You is wrong.*

He slowed as he came upon the door to his platoon's locker room, his gaze lowering to the hilt of his sword. A prick of guilt as sharp as his blade stabbed through his angry thoughts. If it was not for him joining Norland in the first place, and if he did not like sword fighting so much, then this never would have happened.

The door squeaked as he pushed it open. *Alright, I'm sorry,* he silently prayed. *I guess I brought this all upon myself, but how am I supposed to get out of this? What if I somehow make it to the third day and have to kill a prisoner?* Lieutenant Denir seemed to think he could make it to the end of the second day, but Aabir did not know enough about the Tourney to know if that meant he would make it to the third one...

He frowned. He should probably figure that out soon.

More and more similar thoughts went through his head as he took all his armor off, showered, and put his uniform back on. He walked out of the locker room and headed towards the entrance hall, his brooding, questioning thoughts keeping all his focus away from anyone that might have been around him.

Norland's entrance doors appeared ahead, and he pushed one of them open with more force than was necessary. The movement sent a dull shoot of pain through his bruised side, but his attention did not stay long upon it as it dwindled back to a low throb. His footsteps thudded against the stone of the veranda before clomping down the stairs.

Even with the swirling windstorm in his head, he somehow remembered he needed to meet with Rasiela. So, instead of brooding on one of the benches around the fountain, he headed down one of the cleared paths between the everpine trees.

Pine needles crunched underneath his boots as he veered off of it into the same area that he thought he and Rasiela had met in before. Coming upon an everpine tree with exposed roots, he sat down on one of them and put his head in his hands, sighing in frustration.

Why did his life feel so out of control? Why did everything have to be so complicated? Couldn't he do something without it causing problems like this?

He rubbed a hand across his face. Of all the things...it just had to be the Constantia Tourney, didn't it? If only he had known this would happen, then he could have let go of his pride a bit and let Septimus get a few more wins.

Needles crunched somewhere nearby. Aabir jerked his head up and turned his neck in the direction of the noise. His heart began to race as the crunching footsteps drew closer, but then he recognized Rasiela's form moving towards him from between the thick tree trunks and let out a sigh of relief. He stayed seated, flicking his wary gaze to the rest of the trees around them, as she neared the one he sat on.

"Aabir." She dipped her chin towards him and met his eyes.

"Rasiela." He nodded back.

Her eyes narrowed as they flicked over his face. "You got here early..." she said slowly, "Did your training end already?"

"*Mine* did." He could not contain the angry bite that escaped his tone.

One of Rasiela's arched eyebrows rose. "And what does that mean?"

He blew out a frustrated huff and turned his gaze away. Should he tell her? He almost thought better of it, but then he reasoned she would find out eventually and it would be best to just get it over with now. It would sound better coming from him, anyway; less likely to cause suspicion and possibly break what little trust he might have gained with her already.

"I...just won myself a place in the Constantia Tourney."

He looked back up at her face to gauge her reaction, but her expression was a neutral mask.

"You...what?" The slight hesitancy between her words was the only indicator that she was suppressing some emotion.

"I didn't realize I was doing it!" He lifted his hands towards her in a gesture of surrender. "Lieutenant Denir didn't tell me until after I won. If I had known beforehand, I would've let myself lose a few rounds on purpose—"

"—Kid—"

"—and Lieutenant Denir wants me to get *at least* to the end of the second day." Despite the fact he knew he was rambling, all the words began to spill out, "I don't know how hard that actually is since I don't even watch the Tourney, but he thinks I can do it. But I don't want to! I don't want to have the possibility of fighting on the third day! I don't want to fight in the Tourney at all! I just...I just wanted to get better at sword fighting..."

He put his head in his hands again with another frustrated sigh. "I wish I had never joined this stupid school. My family might've been under more scrutiny, but at least I wouldn't be forced to do this."

"Aabir, calm down," Rasiela said. "I believe you."

He jerked his head up and locked eyes with her. "You do?"

"Yes." She nodded sharply. "From what I have seen, it wouldn't be in your character to join them willingly."

He breathed a sigh of relief, "Oh, thank Deleyon." But when he paused, the quiet of the trees surrounding them helped bring his full awareness back to the looming reality of his situation. "I just—I should've known that this would come up. I didn't realize it would happen this soon, though; or that I would be chosen!"

He thought it was common knowledge among his platoon that he did not watch the Tourney, and he figured that meant Lieutenant Denir knew it, too.

Or, Aabir thought with a frown, *he doesn't care; because his honor is more important to him than my convictions.*

"What will this change for you in the coming weeks?" Rasiela asked.

He shrugged. "Lieutenant Denir mentioned a new training routine...but other than that I'm not sure."

"Hmm..." She paused. "Well, if there is anything significant, please keep me posted."

"OK..." He wanted to ask why but pushed the impulse aside. She would not tell him even if he did.

"Now, back to our original reason for being here: I wanted to tell you that you again did well this week, Aabir, so I have your next assignment for you—if you are ready for it, that is. Since you are not technically a real spy, you can take a break this week if you need to sort these things out with your family."

"No, I need to do this." He hoped his resolve showed in his gaze as he kept it on hers.

Something in her expression flickered for a moment, but it was too quick for him to tell what it was. "Good." She said, "Then I need you to find me as much info as you can on the projects Prince Joash was working on."

He scrunched his brow. "OK..." He had been expecting to spend this next week researching along the lines of the Silvanian Fire Attacks, and the possible secret group behind them, again.

"Thank you for not asking questions." The corner of Rasiela's lips curved in a smile. "I know it's strange, but that is your assignment—whether it confuses you or not."

A small smile escaped his lips. "Yes ma'am."

"Then if that is all, I must be going. But I need to tell you first that instead of meeting next week, I will need to send you your next assignment through messaging."

He scrunched his brow questioningly. "That's fine with me. But why now? Why have we not been doing that already?"

"Because it's too risky." Rasiela shooed his suggestion away with a flick of her hand. "Our connection is secure from Igrium's prying eyes, but...even security can fail from time to time. So, when you receive your assignment, delete it as soon as you have memorized what you are to do, then I will fully erase it later. Does that make sense?"

"I guess." He nodded with a shrug.

"Then I'll see you later, Aabir."

With one last parting nod, Rasiela turned on her heel and left in the same direction she had come from. Aabir watched her go. Once she was gone, he rested his elbows back on his knees and pressed his hands against his forehead.

Now that he knew what to do on that end, he needed to call his parents and give them his Constantia news. He shook his head at himself. *Just one more thing to add...*

He still had not told them about his work with Rasiela. He had planned—was still planning—to do it this coming weekend when they were all home, but despite his conviction to do so, he wondered if he should wait another week. The thought was enticing, and it eased his fear of telling them his risky plan of escape, but Mister Falap's words from their earlier conversation always came back to convict him—and he could not help but listen to it above the anxiety.

Pine needles crunched nearby. Aabir jerked his head up. He narrowed his eyes and looked around. Rasiela would not have come back...would she?

The coming footsteps drew closer. His heart began to race, sending a boost of adrenaline through his tired muscles. Oh, Deleyon, he hoped whoever it was had not overheard him and Rasiela's conversation.

"Aabir?" Ezen's familiar drawl echoed between the trees. "Is that you?"

Aabir hoped he looked inconspicuous as he stood and put his hands in his front pockets. "Yeah, it is." He spotted the other trainee coming towards him from between two tree trunks. "I was just clearing my head."

"Ah." Ezen came to a stop as he neared Aabir. "That's why I'm here too."

"Oh yeah?" He tried to keep his face neutral while his heart pounded a fretful beat.

The other trainee nodded. "Yeah, but I won't bother you." Aabir did not see any suspicion on his relaxed features. "See you at supper."

"See ya."

As quickly as he appeared, he disappeared behind some more trees. Aabir sat back down on the exposed root and released a quiet breath. He breathed in a few deep breaths and felt the racing tempo of his heart slow. At least it did not look like Ezen had seen anything.

Aabir mumbled a prayer to Deleyon that he had not, anyway, before lifting his hand with a flick of his wrist. His holonode's small screen appeared in the air above it, and he tapped on his contacts app. His matha's contact appeared near the top of the list.

He stared at it for a few dreadful moments. Should he even tell them? As Ereliev had said that weekend, he could now see how exhausted they both were; and knowing their son was being forced into the televised bloodbath for millions to watch would only add to their burden. He almost turned his holonode back off, but Mister Falap's convicting words whispered at the back of his thoughts.

Breathing out another deep sigh, Aabir tapped his matha's contact before he could change his mind.

Chapter Thirty-Seven

A FEW MOMENTS LATER, Matha's smiling face appeared on the screen; blue sky and the branches of their pomen tree in the background. Sweat beaded her brow and her camera's angle lowered as she wiped it off with her gloved hand.

"Hello, Aabir." Her smile faded as she met his eyes, and her eyebrows drew together. "What's wrong?"

"Is Patre home?" He asked instead.

"No, he went to the parts store for something, but I can tell him whatever it is when he gets back."

Aabir lifted his arm as he rubbed the back of his neck. "I guess that'll work..."

Her eyes narrowed, but not before he saw the fear darkening her gaze. "What happened?"

Help me, Deleyon... "So, Lieutenant Denir had Septimus and I spar for him." He began, "I had no idea what was going on, so I did it. I won one more round than Septimus, and I...I accidentally won myself a place in the Constantia Tourney this year."

He winced and lowered his gaze away from the screen as the last words left his mouth. There was no telling what emotions were going across his Matha's face right now, and he did not want to see any that would fill him with even more guilt over the whole situation.

"Oh, Aabir..." Matha's tone held a gentle note of compassion, "I understand how hard this must be for you, but—as someone who used to watch them before they turned horrible—the first two days are the most chaotic and the easiest to get out of. I don't think you need to worry. As long as you mess up, you could easily get out of this."

"Not according to Lieutenant Denir." Aabir shook his head and lifted it to meet her eyes. "He thinks I can get to the end of the second day, and basically threatened me to do so."

"Why?"

"*Honor*," he spat. "Having one of his trainees get that far in the Tourney will gain him a lot of it."

"But that's too much pressure!" Sharp anger flashed in Matha's gaze. "The Tourney is already unpredictable on any day, let alone the first two! That's ridiculous! What if you accidentally mess up?"

The memory of the silent threat in Lieutenant Denir's countenance went through Aabir's head. "I...don't think I want to know."

Horror and helpless frustration darkened Matha's countenance. "So...messing up on purpose during the first round is out of the question?"

"Yes ma'am."

She exhaled a sharp breath and turned her eyes to look at another point. "But you could still mess up at the end of the second day, yes?"

"I guess so..." He rubbed his hand across his face. "I just...I don't know what the rounds look like during that time. Are they one-on-one, or the kind with wild animals?"

Matha twisted her lips to the side thoughtfully. "A little of both." She sighed with a shake of her head. "I know the last round is always a one-on-one to see which third-level competitor will go on to become a second-level, but what happens in that round changes each year."

"Of course it does." Aabir put his chin in his free hand with a huff.

"I'm sorry this happened," Matha said, "but there is still hope that one of those last few rounds will disqualify you. I'll pray to Deleyon that they do, and if I could offer sacrifices somewhere for you then I would."

"I know you would, Matha," he replied with a nod. "Thanks, anyway."

"I'm always here if you need to talk." She smiled at him, but it was overshadowed by the dark mix of emotions brewing in her violet eyes. "And I'll make sure to tell your Patre when he gets home."

"Thank you."

"I love you, Aabir. Your Patre and I will call you tonight when we can."

"Love you, too. Bye."

He ended the call and turned his holonode off, the silence of the everpine trees sounding louder than any busy street in Rubrum. Turning his neck, he looked out between the tree trunks while his mind ran elsewhere.

If he knew what some of the second day rounds looked like, then he could try to come up with a plan on how to fail in them without it looking like he was purposefully doing so.

He breathed out another sigh and pressed his fingers against his temples. Despite the unpleasantness of the thought, he decided then that it would be a good idea to research as much as he could about the Tourney so he would not end up getting caught off-guard by anything that might happen. He would need to add that extra research to what he was already doing for Rasiela.

A heavy weight of weariness swept through his already-weary muscles at the thought. He would not be getting much sleep this week...

"HE'S FIGHTING IN THE Constantia Tourney?" Chief Baene raised his brow.

"Yes." Rasiela nodded slowly towards the holonode's screen. "He didn't realize he was fighting for the spot, though."

Chief Baene did not reply immediately. He leaned forward in the silence and rested his arms atop his desk. His piercing gaze stayed locked on hers, and the expression there reminded her of the many times in training when he was about to give her a problem or "assignment" she needed to figure out.

"So, what do you think you should do?" He asked.

Rasiela blinked. "What *I* think I should do?"

"Yes."

What *did* she think she should do? She lifted her gaze to the shelves of supplies around her as she thought.

When Aabir told her, she could easily tell by his body language and rambling that he did not mean to end up in this situation, nor did he want to be in it. And like she had told him, willingly joining the Constantia Tourney did not seem like something he—the trainee who was possibly risking his life to get his Silvanian-descended family out of Igrium—would do. Though his record at Norland was impeccable, Rasiela understood it was all to keep his family safe.

"I believe I will keep our trust exercise going." She finally turned her eyes back to Chief Baene's. "Despite what his commanding officer believes, I doubt he will make it far in the Tourney or be able to do anything that would go against his convictions."

"And I would agree," Chief Baene replied, "except for one thing: his actions working with you say he wants to protect his family, but his record at Norland also tells me he may quiet those convictions if it keeps any scrutiny away from them. It leads me to wonder what he would do if he was faced with a hard choice in the Tourney—and we both know there will be plenty of those."

Rasiela nodded slowly. "I see your point."

"That is not to say you can't continue working with him. In fact, I believe it's been good for you." A small smile flashed across his lips. "You seem...happier."

"It has been nice to have someone helping me."

"I can see that."

"Plus, I have been thinking—" she took in a quick breath before forging on, "—with him now being an official competitor in the Tourney, it might give us an advantage in possibly freeing the prisoners."

Chief Baene blinked, thoughtfulness softening the sharp edges of his face. "I will have to think on that...but it could be a possibility."

A small ember of hope warmed Rasiela. "I will give you more updates about his position when he tells me."

"Then I will be waiting for them." His serious sharpness returned. "You can keep this trust exercise going; however, if he ends up making a terrible decision in the Tourney, I will not let him enter Silvas."

Rasiela's heart pricked at his words, but she nodded in understanding. Aabir would be seen as a criminal—a murderer—in Silvas if he somehow made it to the prisoner rounds. There was no way out of them unless he let himself get wounded enough to where he could not fight, and she did not know if he would be willing to do that.

"And if that does happen," she said, "then I will tell him and finally retire."

Chief Baene nodded sharply, understanding softening his gaze. "You can still retire even if nothing happens regarding him."

"I know, chief, but there is still so much I can do."

"You're not the only person I have working in Rubrum, Rasiela. Not everything is resting upon your shoulders."

"No, but it took me quite a while to get this position, and I don't want to waste it."

"Eighteen years of work is not a waste." He gave her a pointed look. "Your position was only a fifteen-year commitment anyway. You have gone above and beyond what I ever asked of you. You have made your kingdom proud." He paused. "I also know your family wants to see you again, so you may want to think about coming home soon—if not for yourself, then for them, at least."

She swallowed back a lump rising in her throat. "Thank you, Chief." She bowed her head towards him respectfully so he would not see the unshed tears pooling in her eyes. "But I must go now."

He sighed. "Then I will let you. Just think about what I said. I know things can change in eighteen years, but that doesn't mean it's all for the bad." He paused before adding, "The decision is yours, of course. I will call you soon. Good dein, Rasiela. May Deleyon be with you."

Not sure if she could trust her voice, she only nodded in reply. He ended the call, and her holographic screen disappeared as she flicked her wrist. She pressed her fingers against her closed eyelids as the tears she had held back finally came. Quiet sobs shook her shoulders, and through the tears she found her workbench's seat and sat down. Memories of her life back in Silvas—her friends, her family, the apartment she had grown up in—filled her head in a gentle flow, and each one only reminded her of the aching loneliness she tried so hard to suppress.

It had been so long since she had seen any of them...Would anything be the same as it once was? Would she even be able to relate with her family after all the experiences she had lived through as a spy? Or would she return home only to find herself an outcast in her own family?

The unknowns were the real reason she had stayed in Igrium these past three years; because facing the idea of Igrian torture seemed so much easier than facing the thought of going home, only to be ostracized by the ones she loved. She was afraid—and that truth made the ache in her chest only grow worse.

Her wrist buzzed with a new message, and she lifted her blurred gaze to the bright screen. She blinked and focused on the name of who sent it, Aabir, then flicked her wrist to turn it back off and placed her tear-streaked face back in her hands.

One of the reasons she could not help but like the trainee so much was because he reminded her of herself a little bit. He was doing everything he thought was right to protect his family, like she had wanted to do when she was around his age. Then, she had been given an opportunity to protect not only them but the whole kingdom of Silvas and had grabbed ahold of it tightly.

She did not regret her decision—not when she thought about all the information and secret plans that she had uncovered that later helped Silvas and the Alliance in the war—but she wished it had not dug such a deep well of fear in her soul. Her whole job was about seeking out the unknowns, yet when it came to the most personal one of all, she fled.

Rasiela shook her head at herself and straightened, wiping the tears off her face. She stood from her seat and stepped over to the shelves to grab a box of tissues. As she opened it, her wrist buzzed again. She lifted it and caught Aabir's name on the top of the new message. Despite her doubts about him at first, he was proving to be quite resourceful—even with the Constantia Tourney looming before him.

She turned the screen off and grabbed a tissue to blow her nose. *Oh Deleyon*, she thought, *please help him to make the right decisions when the time comes.* She threw the used tissue away and pressed one of her hands against her forehead, putting the other on her hip. *Help us both to do so.*

Chapter Thirty-Eight

"ARE YOU ALL RIGHT, Miss Cairn?" Dr. Prin sent Tetra a worried look from the seat across from her. "You don't look well."

Tetra looked away from her probing gaze. "I'm OK."

"We can schedule this tomorrow if you need to rest."

"No, ma'am. I want to do this—I *need* to do it." She met the woman's eyes to show that she was speaking the truth. "I'm not sick. Just...got a lot on my mind."

What an understatement, but the full truth was too complicated to explain.

"Alright, then." Dr. Prin gave her a sharp look. "But if I find out you're truly sick, then I won't allow you to fly outside for the rest of the week—no matter what new information that deters."

"Yes ma'am."

The biologist nodded sharply and turned her gaze onto the open chardex atop her lap. Tetra breathed a quiet sigh of relief and turned her gaze out the same hovercar window Sir Whest was facing.

The ambulate-tree buildings slowly passed by as her eyelids drooped, until she let them shut completely. She had barely slept last night as the truth of who her uncle actually was settled into her brain as calmly as a violent windstorm. When her mind would settle, more stolen memories reemerged—more blurry pictures, more conversations, more feelings, more impressions—and each one cut down everything she had ever known about herself and her family.

Tetra wasn't a Cairn. She wasn't the daughter of the two generals who had initiated the Fire Raids. She had been forced to carry the honor of two dead people who weren't even related to her for the past ten years, and Emperor Ignis had known all along.

A flash of heat filled her chest; the small flame of anger that had been burning inside her all night growing hot again. He had lied about *everything*. Yes, she knew the emperor was not trustworthy—the amount of times he had broken his "promises" towards her gave her first-hand experience of that—but she would never have thought that her whole life, her whole identity, was a lie constructed by him, her *uncle*.

A cold shiver went through her despite the heat of her anger. Being related to the madman who had started the whole war and killed millions of innocent people in the process filled her with a cold dread she had never known. Not even being chased by guards with her past-best friend or getting a malscar compared to the heart-wilting coldness of knowing Emperor Ignis was her uncle.

Thankfully he wasn't her father. Another icy shiver clawed down her spine at the horrible thought, raising chill bumps along her arms. She had also figured that out last night, amidst the chaos of her thoughts. He and Empress Rillunia didn't get married until a few years after Tetra was born, and neither of them had had any prior relationship with each other, or anyone else, beforehand.

However, there were originally eight Ignis siblings—including the emperor and Prince Joash—and most of them had relationships of some kind long before she was born. She had been able to cut down the list to two of them who might be her father, but she couldn't find anything else that pointed to exactly which one.

The first was General Adler Ignis—who had gained himself an honorable reputation like the Cairns'. His wife died in childbirth years ago, but it was never reported if the baby had lived or not; which led her to believe that baby could've been her.

Then there was Advisor Trenson Ignis. The younger Ignis brother had been married four times (his second wife died, and he divorced the other two before his current one). He said he had no kids, but there were rumors that said otherwise. Many believed he didn't want the responsibility of taking care of them, which gave her the impression that he could be her distant father.

Talons squeezed her heart as the hollow loneliness from her childhood memories yawned open into the present. Despite them both being alive, the distance she knew they would try to keep from her if the truth ever came out would only feel like being the daughter of the two dead Cairns'. The skin around her malscar prickled at the thought.

Tears pricked her closed eyes as the ache in her chest grew worse, and she inhaled a deep breath to try and help hold them back. She wouldn't—couldn't—cry right now. Dr. Prin would surely know something was wrong and would ask questions Tetra didn't want to answer. Then this trip would be canceled, and she wouldn't get the escape she desperately needed.

Besides, crying wouldn't make a difference to her life, anyway. It never helped before, so it wouldn't help now.

As if in apology for the turmoil it had caused her the past fourteen hours, her brain reminded her of a few memories of her Aunt Minda and Uncle Joash. She breathed out a quiet sigh and leaned her head back against the car's seat. The lonely ache ebbed a little as she recalled the two people who seemed to have loved her as their own, and even called her their daughter.

But as she sifted through those good memories, a few disconcerting ones also came along. They all involved her older cousin, whom Tetra had come to find out was named "Felicita". At first, she assumed it was a coincidence that her cousin shared the same name as Lady Felicita, but then the truth smacked her in the face as she remembered the young woman's familiar eyes—the same eyes Tetra had seen in her memories.

It answered a few questions about the chief advisor's assistant that she had had; including the hopeful looks she always sent Tetra, the reason many of the questions she created always seemed to hit the bullseye perfectly, and why she had been so upset about Tetra's decision to possibly join Silvas' army. Plus, the woman's reason on why she and her matha came to Silvas matched perfectly with Tetra's memories and the rumors about Prince Joash's missing family running to the Alliance for aid.

Despite all of that, Tetra still had not quite processed the information. She had a cousin; a living cousin who didn't hate her like Aquilo but who, according to her memories, was more like an older sister. It was...weird, to say the least—but not necessarily a bad weird.

Yet she also wondered why Felicita hadn't told her already. The recognition she had seen in her cousin's eyes during their first meeting told her she knew then but refused to say anything for almost the whole month of questioning sessions they had had. All the hope she had seen shining in Felicita's eyes told her it wasn't because she didn't want Tetra (like some people...), but amidst all the turmoil in her mind she couldn't come up with an answer for the silence.

Her thoughts grew sluggish as exhaustion made it harder to think. Maybe she should confront Felicita during their meeting today. Since the truth had exposed itself, the urge to tell someone had only grown, but she knew she couldn't tell just anyone. Being a Cairn in Silvas was bad, but being an Ignis was worse. Much worse

So even though her gut told her Felicita was her cousin, she wanted to do it in a way that wouldn't reveal the full truth in case the young woman wasn't actually related to her at all. She needed a plan...

But before she could come up with one, her thoughts drifted away as much-needed sleep wrapped itself around her mind like a blanket.

TETRA JOLTED AWAKE, BLINKING in confusion as her thoughts came back to their normal speed. She looked out the window and saw the familiar sights of ambulate trees and the dunes of churned dirt covering the forest floor. Sir Whest opened his door and stepped out, leaving it open as Tetra scooted across the seat row to join him. The female guard who had sat on Tetra's other side opened the opposite door and stepped out, while Dr. Prin and the other guards did the same.

"Come, Miss Cairn," Dr. Prin headed away from the hovercar and the five guardsmen near it, "I need to speak with you alone about today's schedule." Tetra caught the significant look on the woman's round face and followed. Her tumultuous thoughts were still sitting in the back of her mind, but her rising excitement helped to lessen their noise.

She had told Dr. Prin everything about her meeting with Leaves Of Gold yesterday, and instead of saying she was crazy, the biologist told her she wanted to know more. Perytons were already on the official list of what she called "possible intelligent beings." So, if they proved the creatures were clever enough to become an official race of intelligent beings, then it would be one of the greatest discoveries in history.

With others, Tetra would've planned on their being a hidden motive behind the discovery, but—in her blunt way—Dr. Prin also told her she wanted to be the one with her name on the discovery; and Tetra was fine with that. She could have cared less about all the attention that had come from it. The less attention on the freak of nature who could turn into a peryton, the better.

When they were both far enough away from any eavesdropping ears, Dr. Prin turned to face her. Tetra met her eyes and noticed the curious-excitement softening them.

"I'm not going to stay here waiting for you, Miss Cairn," Dr. Prin began. "Instead, I'll be here around six o'clock tonight when Soll is setting. That should give you plenty of time to get to this peryton village and get back. And if you get lost, find a single spot to stay in and we will come find you."

"Yes ma'am." Tetra's stomach churned at the hidden mention of her tracker, but her excitement helped tamp out any feelings of ire that would usually come with it. She gestured towards the direction behind her. "East is that way, yes?"

"Mm-hm." Dr. Prin tapped her holonode. "And if you need a compass, there is one on your holonode."

"Oh." Heat filled Tetra's face and she glanced away. "Right."

Of course there was. What wasn't on a holonode these days?

Thankfully, Dr. Prin didn't seem to care about her blunder. "Alright, then. Off you go."

Tetra nodded, then turned and took a few limping strides away from her before she changed into a peryton. The fiery pains came and went as usual, but once she was able to think clearly, they only reminded her of the frightening images of the house fire she could now remember. She blinked with a shake of her antlered head to try and shake the past feelings of fear away, then pushed herself into a standing position.

"I'll see you at six o'clock, Miss Cairn."

Tetra tilted her long head down and locked eyes with Dr. Prin; her nose catching the faintest whiff of flowers coming from the woman. She sent a sharp nod towards her, then opened her wings and jumped into the air.

Dust flew around her as she flapped her wings to gain altitude. When she was high enough, she turned around in midair and flew off into the towering forest. Dr. Prin had shown her a map of Silvas and where the kingdom's biggest lake was located yesterday, along with showing her pictures of what it looked like to help her find it. She had even mentioned that since there was so much peryton activity on the eastern side, most humans stayed away from it.

It had given Tetra more hope that what Leaves Of Gold told her was true. Not that she didn't think he was lying—she hadn't been able to smell any deceit coming from him—but she was beginning to see that not everything she noticed was really the truth. So, even with it being a small piece of information, it was something to hold onto that wouldn't shatter. Like her identity.

She shook her head with a sharp huff and flapped her wings. These thoughts would not take away from her enjoyment of flying. She wouldn't let them.

She turned her focus onto what was happening around her—the currents of air streaming through her feathers, the huge trees she passed by, all the different smells of the forest. The longer she flew, the more her mind tended to wander back to her recovered memories, and the rhythmic pattern of flight helped her thoughts to center upon the shattering fact that she was actually an Ignis, not a Cairn.

Her name wasn't even Tetra.

Her wingbeats faltered for a moment at the sudden thought, but she steadied them again. Talons squeezed her racing heart. Why Emperor Ignis didn't even let her keep her real name she couldn't figure out, but it only made her even more mad at him. He really had stolen everything from her: her name, her memories. He had even killed her uncle—the one person of the Ignis bloodline who actually seemed to have cared for her, and who had been more like a father to her than anyone else seemed to be.

Tetra curled her talons and growled deep in her throat, wishing the emperor was here right now so she could mark *him* with a malscar for all the dishonorable things he had done to her. Because if anyone was a coward who deserved one, it would be the man that hid her existence in the family and then put the blame of every dishonorable action she had done since on the Cairns'.

She had only known about her real family for less than a day, but the joyful, loving memories she now remembered made it seem as if she had known them for all her life—which only made the knowledge of her uncle's death hurt all the more. She was beginning to understand the shows of anger Lady Felicita always tried to suppress around her when Emperor Ignis was brought up in conversations.

When she thought she was the Cairn's daughter, she never really mourned for her parents. She found herself wishing they were still alive, but there wasn't any emotional connection to them that caused her to truly miss them. Yet now with all these real, wonderful memories coming back, she was beginning to miss her uncle and aunt.

And despite how Felicita kept all this from her, Tetra couldn't help her growing desire to know more about her cousin who seemed to be as close as a sister. She tilted her head slightly and pondered the thought. She had never had siblings before, so the only thing she knew about them was what Aabir had told her about his own. Apparently, they could be really annoying sometimes, but also fun. And even with all his complaints about them, it was obvious he loved them.

The longing to tell Lady Felicita grew even more, and it led Tetra to begin thinking through the best ways to go about getting her cousin to reveal the truth without hinting at the fact that she herself already knew it.

The ambulate trees lessened the further she flew, but so lost in thought was she that she didn't notice anything changing in the shadowy forest until she found herself blinking in the sudden sollight that came upon her. She angled her wings and slowed to a stop as her eyes got used to the brightness.

Sollight glimmered upon the waves of the Entransen Lake. Tetra's eyes widened at the vast view before her. The only reason she even knew this was a lake was because her peryton eyes could barely see the faint outline of mountains on the opposite shore. Other than that, it stretched out like an ocean on either side of her.

She glanced down at the calm waves lapping at the muddy shore, then back up at the mountains rising in the far distance. Her racing heart skipped a nervous beat, and a shiver went through the muscles in her wings as she thought about the long flight it would take to reach the other side.

Perytons were known for their endurance in flight, but Tetra hadn't built up the strength to fly for hours on end yet, so she made a quick decision and tilted her wings to glide down to the lakeshore. Her hooves and talons slid in the mud as she landed, but she was able to get them underneath her before she fell face-first into the water. She folded her wings to her sides and lowered her gaze towards the small waves in front of her.

Mud squelched between her hooves and talons as she took a step forward. She breathed in deeply of the moisture-laden air and was disappointed to find that it blocked some of her sense of smell.

A nervous jolt went through her at the realization, and she turned her long neck to look over her shoulder at the tree line, ears pricked. She waited a few heartbeats and tried to smell for anyone else that might be near, but only mud and wet grass filled her nose as she watched a small scurrus skitter up one of the ginormous trees.

After another long pause of nothing, she finally turned her face back towards the lake and plodded through the gritty mud towards the water, her ears pricked in the direction behind her. If anyone was stupid enough to try and sneak up on a peryton, she hoped she would be able to hear them long before they got a chance to reach her.

The waves lapped at her numb front hooves, then a shiver went through her as she stepped her back talons into the cold water. She shot a frowning glance down at her fingerless appendages and found herself wishing—once again—that perytons had hands. Or at least thumbs.

Shaking the thought away, Tetra lifted her head and stared out at the calming bluish-green waters. There was something familiar about the sight that tugged at the back of her mind. She followed the tug, and a new childhood memory popped into her head. She breathed in sharply at the suddenness of it, but watched it play out with her mind's eye:

Tetra stared at the view of the ocean before her.

"Anora!" She turned her eyes away from the shore. A young Felicita, maybe nine or ten, smiled at her. "I'll race you!"

She shared a smile with her cousin. "OK!"

"One...two...three!"

Tetra squealed as she sprang forward and sped towards the large waves, her feet kicking up sand in her wake.

The memory ended, but the excitement and awe from it didn't. Tetra turned her gaze and looked out over Entransen Lake once again with those lingering, childlike feelings of wonder. She took in another deep breath and exhaled slowly, taking a furtive glance back over her shoulder at the shadowy tree line.

Despite its seeming insignificance, Tetra was glad the newest memory had come back. It built up more of her hope that she would one day be able to remember everything a person could about their childhood, and then she would have taken back at least one thing Emperor Ignis stole from her. If only she could do the same with Uncle Joash's death...

A spark of anger flared up inside her again, and she recalled Army General Taoghn's proposition. She had already been thinking of taking him up on it to fulfill her oath, but now she realized she had another reason as well. Emperor Ignis killed her uncle, stole her original life away, and he had done the same to countless others as well. She might not know how this peryton-changing ability of hers worked, but she was going to use it to make him regret ever having touched her family.

Resolve hardened her stomach, and water splashed her legs as she stamped her front hoof in finality. She was going to join Silvas' army—and she would make the emperor pay for all his crimes.

Chapter Thirty-Nine

THE LAKE BLURRED PAST as Tetra flew above its sparkling surface. Her heart raced with exhilaration and weariness as the freeing feeling of flight pulsed through her veins. She had never flown so fast or so far before, and not even her windstorm of thoughts could extinguish her excited energy at doing so.

A school of small, red fish floated above the water ahead of her like a thick cloud. Before she came upon them, they scattered in all directions; their feathered fins and tails flapping crazily. She glided through where they had just been, breathing in their sweet smell. Pushing the urge to eat them aside, she turned her neck to glance over her wings and watched them converge back into their bright red school since her threatening presence was no longer there.

Despite all the peryton activity Dr. Prin said surrounded this side of Entransen Lake, Tetra had only passed by a couple since her break back on the opposite shore; and both times they were too far away for her to distinguish any details about them. The only way she knew they were even perytons was because of their similar smell to Leaves Of Gold that the wind carried towards her.

She turned her head forward again and eyed the imposing mountains rising ahead. Their steep, gray sides took up the entirety of the view before her, and even as a large peryton she was like a speck of dust compared to their size. She lifted her gaze but couldn't see their peaks through the clouds circling around their base.

Deep valleys cut through their jagged sides, and Tetra's racing heart wilted a little. Would she even be able to find Cherry Valley today? She sighed but pushed her sore wings on. Even if she didn't, she would be able to count off a few of these valleys to make her search easier the next time she came.

With that thought, she angled her wings and flew towards the closest one. It looked more like a small sliver between two of the mountains, but definitely big enough to house a village of perytons.

Long minutes dragged by as her earlier excitement dwindled with each tiring flap of her wings. She would need to find some place to land soon before they decided to give out on her.

The slivered valley loomed ever closer in the shadows of the mountains. A chill went through Tetra as she flew into the shade cast by them, but it didn't last. The hot, Silvanian humidity sucked away all cooler temperatures even in the shade.

Finally, she flew through the craggy opening and slowed to a stop. When her eyes adjusted to the darkness, she was met with only steep cliff-faces on both sides. No plants grew along the bare precipices, nor did she smell or see anything that moved. A frown tilted her lips down as a twinge of disappointment pricked inside her, but it was pushed aside with a wind of relief that she didn't have to go any deeper into that darkness.

She turned and flew back out into the open air before alighting on a rocky headland that rose above the lake. When all four feet were on the ground, she folded her wings and sucked in a few panting breaths. She peered out at the other side of the lake, but not even with her peryton eyes could she see the lofty ambulate trees far in the distance.

Sitting back on her haunches in the sparse grass, she continued quietly taking in the amazing view as her heartbeat slowed and the shakiness of her muscles subsided. As she did so, a couple new childhood memories came to the forefront of her eye's mind. They were both similar to the beach one she had had before—both showing her and Felicita playing in the ocean—and they gave her hope that maybe certain sights could trigger the emergence of her lost memories.

However, before she could dwell on that further, she caught a whiff of something carried by the wind. Silently cursing the moisture in the air, she inhaled deeply and again smelled the scent. It took her a few tries before she was finally able to put a name on the smell: peryton.

Her earlier excitement came back, and she stood as renewed energy coursed through her. She turned her gaze away from the lake and over to the next valley cut between the mountains. It was larger than the first, but not by much. Even so, she opened her wings and climbed into the air.

It took her almost half an hour to fly to the next dale, and she found it uninhabited. So, like the first time, she found another headland, took a small break, then was back into the sky as she headed towards the third gorge. The more she flew, the stronger the peryton scent became until not even the moisture in the air could subdue it.

However, before she made it there, her eyes picked up on a dot of movement in the distance. Her pounding heart leapt in excitement, and she quickly bypassed the thin gorge to head towards that movement.

As she flew further on, she spotted the next valley—and even without the strong smell of perytons, the many moving dots that filled the skies above told her that this was the peryton village. Soll's light shone through the clouds upon the green, sloped sides and sparkled along the surface of a river that cut through the bottom of the dale and flowed into the lake.

The closer she got, the easier it was to see even more perytons moving around than what she had seen at first—and a sinking feeling entered her stomach as she realized this might not be Leaves Of Gold's village. It looked more like a city of perytons than a small village.

Another stab of disappointment jabbed at Tetra the closer she flew, but she tried to ignore it. Maybe she could go and ask if anyone knew where Cherry Valley was. It would save her some time, and she might even be able to find out some information for Dr. Prin. Nodding to herself, she flapped her wings to boost her speed.

Hopefully, Leaves Of Gold wasn't the only friendly peryton in the world, and that humanity's perceptions of the creatures weren't true. Because if everything she had learned about them was correct, then she was about to fly into a deathtrap.

But even with those thoughts lurking in the back of her mind, she pressed her tiring wings on. She had flown all this way already, and she wasn't about to let a little fear stop her. She was a peryton now; surely there would be no trouble.

Only a few moments after Tetra had that thought, an even stronger wave of peryton-scent accosted her nostrils. She jerked to a stop in midair, heart hammering, as she pricked her ears and looked around.

A huge, sandy-brown peryton with short, white antlers—like hers—soared towards her. A sharp, almost spicy scent Tetra didn't recognize came from the new peryton as she flapped her great, darker-feathered wings and slowed to a stop ahead.

"Who are you?" Her growling voice rumbled like Leaves Of Gold's but had a distinctly higher pitch than his.

"Um...I—my name is Tetra." Actually, it wasn't, but she wasn't going to correct herself at that moment.

She locked her gaze on the other peryton's dark eyes. Surprise showed in their depths, and was immediately followed by the sharp, emotional scent. However, it was just as quickly overtaken by a new softer, earthy smell as something akin to understanding filled the peryton's gaze.

"Oh. I'm sorry if I scared you." The new peryton dipped her antlered head towards Tetra, ears pricked. "I don't mean to cause you any harm."

Tetra blinked in surprise, her fear dissipating as she saw the peryton's muscles relax. "It's—it's OK."

Were all perytons apologetic?

"I just need to know what business you have here," the other peryton added.

Their eyes lowered from Tetra's face, and the sharp scent heightened for a moment. Tetra dipped her chin to follow their gaze, and only then realized how strange her metal jumpsuit must look.

"Oh, I'm just—I'm new around here, and I'm looking for a village in Cherry Valley," she replied, mentally slapping herself for not taking the jumpsuit off on her flight there. "Do you know where that would be?"

The other peryton nodded. "It's right here, actually."

Tetra blinked in shock and glanced behind the sandy-furred peryton at all the others in the valley. "Really?"

"Yes, it is." She met the peryton's suspicious gaze again. "But again, I ask: what business do you have here?"

"I was invited by someone I met in the walking forest yesterday." She used the name Leaves Of Gold had called the ambulate forest in hopes of keeping whatever was left of her dwindling chances of seeming like a normal peryton.

"Who?" The peryton asked.

"His name is Leaves Of Gold."

Understanding lit up the other peryton's brown eyes. "Ah. Well then, Tetra, you have my permission to enter." She dipped her head again. "And if anyone asks, tell them Strength Like Stone let you through."

"Oh. Uh—thank you." Tetra nodded her head in appreciation.

Strength Like Stone sent her one last look she couldn't decipher before turning and flying off in the direction Tetra had just come. She watched the other peryton go for a few wingbeats before continuing towards the valley.

Leaves Of Gold, Strength Like Stone...were all peryton names so long?

Wingbeats and growling voices filled the air the closer she descended. A huge, dark-furred peryton flew past her without so much as a look in her direction. Another gave Tetra a funny look, but then continued on without saying anything. The fearful pounding of Tetra's heart calmed as most of the perytons who flew past either didn't pay her any attention, or shot her similarly odd looks. She had expected more to react like Strength Like Stone, but instead a couple actually sent her acknowledging nods as they passed.

And with the fear of being attacked no longer an issue, she was able to turn her focus onto all the sights spread out before her. The valley itself looked like someone had used a massive longsword to slice the mountain range in two, leaving a forested gap big enough to hold a human city. Pairs of perytons flew above and between the green, towering trees. As Tetra looked, she noticed that one peryton of each pair was sliding their back talons along the thin branches of these trees, while the other held a basket underneath with their front hooves to catch the red cherries that fell from the branch.

Another burst of excitement went through her as she watched. They were *farming*. The "deadly", "ruthless" creatures were actually farming, and they were doing so with baskets that had looped, urn-like handles so their thumbless hooves could hold them.

She also noticed a few perytons standing, almost like sentinels, on differing precipices along both sides of the valley that faced the lake. It reminded her of the guards standing on the walls of Emperor Ignis' fortress, or the balconies of the Altelo.

Small perytons with spots on their backs and nubs for antlers splashed and played in the river below Tetra, while a few older ones (whom she assumed were their parents) sat under the shade of the trees lining the bank and watched them. A peryton glided right over her, the handle of a huge cauldron clutched in its back talons. A delicious, earthy aroma she had never smelled before blew from it towards her despite its lid. She sent a curious glance over her shoulder as the peryton flew away. Maybe when she found Leaves Of Gold, he could tell her what was in that cauldron. Then, she could find some and try whatever it was.

The trees soon ended in a perfect line that gave way to a sloped plot of land, before starting again on the other side of the huge space. She slowed to a stop to get a better look at the new sight, pinning her ears back at the cacophony of echoing voices and thundering wingbeats that bounced off the mountain faces. Holes were cut into the mountains on each sloping side, and she saw perytons—both on the ground and in the air—going in and out of them.

However, her attention was caught on the wide, stone bridge spanning over the river. Booths covered in food and wares covered it, the perytons behind them roaring at the throng of others moving along the tightly packed space. More booths spread out off the bridge and covered the flatter, clear space along both sides of it.

These perytons had a marketplace. Tetra stared in wide-eyed wonder at all the bustling activity. It reminded her of the crowded street markets Trivsau had before any of the recent battles destroyed the Xichian capitol.

After a few moments, she finally shook herself from her shocked daze and swooped down towards the marketplace. Taking extra care with all the perytons around, she landed lightly in a clear spot near the trees. Only when all four feet were on the ground did she fold in her wings so she wouldn't trip. The less attention on herself, the better.

She lifted her head and turned her neck to look around at all the new and exciting sights. Three perytons, who looked to be deep in conversation, walked by her. As they did, Tetra noticed one of them had a bag hanging from around their neck. And now that she had seen it, she realized more perytons with similar bags were moving around the marketplace as well.

Part of her wanted to walk around the booths to see what items might be sold by perytons, but the other part wanted to find Leaves Of Gold first. The latter won, and she turned all her attention towards finding someone who might be able to help her.

Her eyes landed on a peryton with mottled, sand-colored fur and wings who was slowly making his way through the vendors, his head turning to look over each booth. Pushing aside any discomfort, she maneuvered through the milling perytons towards him.

"Excuse me—" she said, and he turned his face towards her with pricked ears, "—um, I'm new around here, and I just wanted to know if you might happen to know who Leaves Of Gold is."

The peryton's eyes lit up and he nodded. "Yes, I do, actually." A wave of something sweet-smelling came from him. "In fact, you probably won't find anyone here who doesn't know who he is."

Oh no. Had she stumbled upon some sort of peryton celebrity?

"Oh. Uh—really?" She tilted her head and hoped he couldn't detect any wariness from her.

His large eyes widened and the feathers on his wings ruffled. "You don't have to worry!" Great, he had. "He's one of our village's leaders—and he's a good one."

Well, that didn't sound too bad. "Alright, then," she said. "Do you know where I could find him?"

The peryton nodded again. "He's probably in his shop right now." He stepped away from her and met her eyes. A sharp whiff of surprise reached Tetra's nostrils, only to be magnified for a moment as his eyes lowered to her jumpsuit. "I can show you if you'd like."

She gave a nod, hoping she wasn't giving off any scent of worry. "Thank you."

His sharp surprise dissipated with a shrug of his wings. Then, he turned his head and strode forward through the crowds as if they weren't even there at all. She picked up her pace to follow him.

Besides her jumpsuit, why did everyone seem surprised when they met her? She glanced down at the dark splotches surrounded by pale fur on her legs, then turned her neck and glanced at her auburn wings. She did seem to have an unnatural coat compared to the rest of the perytons around her... so maybe that was it.

Fighting back the growing feelings of self-consciousness, she slowed her trotting pace until she was at the new peryton's side.

"My name is Wings Like Sand, by the way," he said.

"I'm Tetra."

She lifted her gaze and looked up at his smiling features. Apparently, she was a really short peryton, because all the others around her were about the same height as she remembered Leaves Of Gold being.

Just another thing that's different, she thought with a fleeting frown.

He nodded slowly. "I've never heard that name before. Are you from around here?"

"I came here from the land past the islands."

"Really?" His ears perked up, and he turned his head to face her more as they walked. "Wow! What brought you here?"

"Uh—no-furs."

Wings Like Sand nodded in understanding. "There are a few others who have moved here because of the no-furs. I don't really know them very well, but I'm sure Leaves Of Gold does. Are you planning on moving here?"

She shook her head. "No. Just visiting."

"Well, before you leave, you need to try at least one cup of our valley's famous brew." He smiled again. "We've been harvesting the cherries for almost half a moons'-cycle now, so there's plenty of vendors selling the roasted seeds."

Maybe that's what the delicious-smelling stuff in that cauldron was. "Maybe I will."

"Although you won't find our valley's brew if you're visiting Leaves Of Gold," Wings Like Sand added. "He has to drink a special kind that comes from a different cherry tree."

"That's fine." She barely lifted her folded wings in a shrug. "Maybe I can get some later."

Wings Like Sand nodded once and slowed his pace as they came upon the bottommost holes carved into the mountain's side. She did the same as he headed towards one of these openings. Two marble statues—one of a peryton in flight, and the other a flowering tree—were placed on either side of the entryway. Wings Like Sand stepped through the opening, but Tetra came to a stop to peer at the statues.

Her eyes widened as they picked up all the details of each individual leaf and feather etched into the white stone. A peryton had done this? It looked more like a statue she would find in an art museum, not sitting out on the edge of a busy marketplace.

"Are you coming?" Wings Like Sand stood watching her from the entrance.

She nodded. And with one last amazed look at the statues, she stepped inside. Instead of being greeted by a dim cave, she was surprised to see more statues—all made of either different stones or wood—lining the smooth walls of the cave. Two lit fireplaces filled the room with a warm light, and a few cushions sat on the floor near the one opposite the opening, almost like a sitting area.

Wings Like Sand stepped over to another opening carved into the cave's wall. Tetra's gaze roved over the beautiful statues as she slowly moved to join him. Her ears pricked at the sounds of chipping stone coming from the new room, and her jaw went slack once she caught sight of what was making the noise.

Thousands of tiny holes in one of the cave walls poured pinpricks of natural light onto the familiar golden-brown fur and wings of Leaves Of Gold. The orange light from a single fireplace illuminated the rest of the dust-covered room, including the many oddly-shaped chisels and hammers hanging from the wall opposite her.

Leaves of Gold sat on his haunches with his back to them, a block of white stone almost as tall as him situated before him. From her position, Tetra could see he was chipping away at the stone with one of his front hooves, but she couldn't tell what he was carving.

"Leaves Of Gold?" Wings Like Sand called out.

The chipping stopped, and Leaves Of Gold's antlered head swung around to face them. Tetra's eyes widened even more as she met his gaze from behind a goggled mask—that looked like it was made of animal hide. He gave off a hint of surprise scent that was followed by a stronger, sweetly mellow one.

Something fell off his hoof, but she couldn't see what it was. He lowered his head to the floor and let the mask fall off his long snout. He lifted his neck and looked back over at them, the firelight glowing in his shining eyes and on his soft, peryton smile.

"Hello, Wings Like Sand. Tetra." He stood and turned to face them with a dip of his head. "Sorry I didn't hear you come in. This project has taken much of my focus today."

"That's fine." Wings Like Sand nodded towards him. "I only came to show Tetra where your shop was."

"Thank you. I appreciate it," Leaves Of Gold replied. "How are your parents doing? I haven't seen them in a while."

"They're doing well. Just busy with the harvest."

"Of course. Well, tell them I would love to have you all over soon if they can spare the time away from the orchards."

Wings Like Sand's lips barely peeled back in a grin. "I will mention it to them." He dipped his head towards Leaves Of Gold, then met Tetra's eyes. "If you do end up staying here, Tetra, and need a job, my parents and I always need help with our cherry trees—if you're interested, of course."

"Oh! Uh—thanks." She nodded towards him. "And thank you for bringing me here."

"Happy to do so. May the Unrivaled King carry you both upon his winds."

Leaves Of Gold nodded. "And you as well, Wings Like Sand. Thank you again."

With one final nod, the mottled peryton turned with a flourish of his tail feathers and left the shop. Tetra watched him go. So perytons had jobs, and family units. Her eyes strayed to the elegantly detailed statues lining the rounded walls of the first room. And they could be artists, too.

"I'm glad you decided to visit." She turned her head back to Leaves Of Gold's smiling face as he spoke, "I didn't realize you would come so quickly, but I'm glad you did."

"Me too." She pricked her ears and looked behind him at the block of stone. "What are you working on?"

He blinked and turned his neck back. "Oh, some elders wanted me to carve them a statue of a walking tree for their village's center." He looked back over at her, and she met his large eyes. "You can't tell what it is at the moment, but I should finish it in a few moons' cycles."

"Wow." She had no idea what a moons' cycle was, but it sounded like a long time. "Well, I really liked the ones outside your shop."

The feathers on his wings ruffled, and his front hoof pawed the ground. Was he...embarrassed? "Oh—thanks." A strange, earthy scent wafted towards Tetra amidst the other smells of stone and burning logs in the fireplaces. "They're some of my favorites. That's why I keep them out there: to attract business and to give me an excuse not to barter them off."

So, they traded instead of using money. Tetra tucked the piece of information in the back of her head and smiled at him.

"That's a smart idea," she said.

"Thank you..." The smell of what she guessed was his embarrassment disappeared as he straightened his neck and shoulders back to his tall, intimidating height. "Would you like to sit down, Tetra?"

"Sure." She shrugged her wings.

"Then we can sit in there." He gestured with his head in her direction, then stepped forward and moved past her into the first room of his shop.

Tetra turned in the wall's opening and followed him over to the cushions opposite the entryway, her eyes focusing on some of the details of each statue she passed. Individual clumps of fur were carved into the sides of a wooden peryton that stood majestically next to a blue, marble sky-whale in flight. The drooping branches of a marble willow tree were dotted with tiny leaves, while a cloud-studded sky full of fish and gelatscies covered a flat piece of wood. If someone had told her a week ago that a peryton had made these, she wouldn't have believed them.

Leaves Of Gold sat down on one of the giant cushions, and Tetra did the same opposite him. It looked and felt like it was made of an animal pelt.

"Did you have any trouble coming into the village?" Leaves Of Gold asked her.

Strength Like Stone's abrupt encounter popped into Tetra's head. "Well, I thought I did at first, but she let me through."

He tilted his head questioningly. "Who was it?"

"She said her name was 'Strength Like Stone'."

"Ah." The tips of his mouth lifted in a knowing smile. "Of course. I hope she didn't scare you. She's one of our newest guards and can be a little harsh to outsiders."

So those were guards she saw standing on the precipes of the valley. *Peryton* guards. A thrill of excitement went through Tetra at the new information.

"Are you a guard, too?" She asked. The way he spoke almost made it sound like he was.

He nodded once. "I am."

"And a sculptor?"

"Yes."

Tetra tilted her head. "And Wings Like Sand told me something about you also being one of the village's leaders..."

"I sit with the elders, yes," he said, "but only because I lead the village's guards." His wings ruffled as he purred. "I have a couple more centuries before I'm old enough to truly become one of them."

Tetra blinked in surprise. Two centuries? She knew perytons lived for quite a while, but she didn't realize it was for that long.

She pushed the thought to the side to ask the next question brimming on her mind, "So you...organize patrols?" *Like a human would?*

He nodded again. "I also help train new guards, speak in front of the elders during trials, lead against any attacks, and—since I'm the youngest—the elders usually have me represent them if the king ever calls upon them."

"Wow."

Tetra's heart raced in excitement as she processed his words. They had a *king*, which meant they had a government like all the other intelligent beings did. Could that be who they were referring to when they said, "Unrivaled King"?

"It sounds like a lot more than what it actually is." A wave of embarrassment-scent hit Tetra's nostrils as Leaves Of Gold spoke, "I have only been doing it for a few season cycles, and the only reason they even let me do it was because the Unrivaled King told Giver Of Names to ask the elders to put me in the position."

Giver Of Names? Who in Afreean...? Tetra opened her mouth to ask who that was, but then snapped her jaw shut. The way he mentioned the name (or was it a title?) made it sound like every peryton should know who (or what) that was, and she didn't need him thinking there was anything else suspicious about her than what he had already seen in the last week.

"Well," she said instead, "according to Wings Like Sand, you're a good leader."

Leaves Of Gold shook his head with another purr. "He's biased."

"How so?"

"I scared these no-furs away from taking him when he was a fawn, and I think his imagination got a hold of the whole ordeal." He rolled his eyes. "I don't know if he told you, but it was only *three* no-furs that tried to attack him—no more—and all I did was roar at them. I didn't hurt them or anything."

Tetra held in a sigh of relief. At least he hadn't killed them.

He shifted on his haunches. "Some say I should have killed them, but I just...couldn't do it." His eyes locked onto hers'. "I know it sounds crazy, but...there's something about them that makes me wonder if they are really the territorial killers that we think they are."

Tetra's heart leapt in excitement as the rumbling words left his mouth. She hadn't just imagined that, had she?

Leaves Of Gold lowered his head, but their eyes stayed locked. "I know it's stupid to other perytons," he partially opened and closed his wings, "and I usually don't even mention that to them, but I figured since you were with those no-furs before that you might understand what I was saying."

"I do." Tetra nodded and gave him an encouraging smile.

He had absolutely no idea how much she truly did.

He nodded, a mild scent coming from him. "I never asked before, but if I may now: what were you doing with those no-furs?" A spike of alarm went through Tetra, and he lifted his head with wide eyes. "I'm sorry! I figured this might be a touchy subject, but I had to ask. I have never seen anyone act so protective around them before."

She couldn't smell any deceit coming from him, nor did she see anything different in his brown eyes as he spoke, but Tetra didn't know what to say without revealing the truth.

"Um—I'd rather not say." She looked down at the ground and pawed one of her hooves. "It's nothing against you, Leaves Of Gold, but I...can't say."

She cringed as the words left her mouth. That sounded even more suspicious spoken aloud than it had in her head. Something in the mild scent coming from her peryton host changed, but not enough for her to tell what it was.

"I understand." She lifted her antlered head as he spoke. Instead of suspicion, she saw only a soft understanding in his deep gaze. "I shouldn't have asked so many questions. We all have things we struggle with, and it's not my place to pry. I'm sorry."

Her heart still hammered in her chest, but she couldn't see (or smell) anything that would suggest his words were lies, so she nodded. "It's fine."

He dipped his head in a slow nod and turned his neck to stare at the crackling flames next to them. "I have had my own share of problems in the past, and I know what it's like to not want to share them." He huffed a deep breath through his nose. "I usually don't ask so many questions, but I guess my curiosity is bigger than—"

"—Leaves Of Gold!"

Tetra jerked her neck around at the roar, ears pricked in the direction of the entryway; and she noticed Leaves Of Gold do the same. A light-furred peryton bounded towards the shop and scrambled to a stop at the entrance. Blood dripped from a few scratches in her heaving sides.

"Raiders are attacking near the mountain entrance," she said between breaths.

Leaves Of Gold stood. "How many?"

"Fourteen." The peryton growled, and the look on her furry face caused Tetra's heart to skip a nervous beat. "It's Surly's band."

"How many were with you when they attacked?"

"Only eight of us, but Sky Of Fire sent me to warn you, so now there's only seven."

"Then go get Rolling River and his band, and I will be right behind you." Leaves Of Gold stepped up next to Tetra.

The bleeding peryton nodded once, turned, and bounded off again.

"I'm sorry for cutting this short, Tetra—" she turned her head and met his apologetic look, "—but I need to go help them." A sharp glint entered his gaze. "Surly has been terrorizing our village for seasons and even murdered a couple of our guards only a moons' cycle ago. He needs to be stopped—and I need to be there when it happens."

"Of course." She nodded in understanding, her jumble of emotions from earlier rising back to the forefront of her mind like a dark storm cloud. "I should probably go anyway."

It would take her a few hours to get back to Dr. Prin, and she didn't know how much time had already passed.

He dipped his head towards her with a smile. "You are more than welcome to come back anytime."

"Thank you." She matched his smile with her own. "I'll try and come back soon."

She would've tried to come the next day; but now that she had made her decision to join Silvas' army, she didn't know when, or if, she would be able to do this again.

"Then, hopefully I will be a better host next time and have some coffee for you to drink."

Tetra had no idea what this "coffee" drink was, but she nodded her appreciation.

"I must go now." Leaves Of Gold bounded out of the shop, calling behind him, "May the Unrivaled King bless your journey home!"

Once he was out of the shop, he unfurled his wings and leaped into the air. Tetra strode through the entryway and watched as he flew in the direction opposite the lake. Once his form was swallowed up by clouds, she lowered her gaze and took one last look around the market before leaping into the air herself and flying back towards the Entransen Lake.

An excited buzz went through her as she lowered her gaze to get a good, last look at the valley of towering cherry trees full of its working, playing, and talking perytons. She hoped her words to Leaves Of Gold about visiting soon would come true, because now there was no doubt in her mind that perytons were intelligent; and despite everything she had learned, her curiosity only buzzed all the more with the new information.

Angling her wings to catch a current of air, she sped up a little as the lake's sparkling waters filled her view. Her excitement dimmed, however, as she remembered the more pressing thoughts she had had before coming here. After she told Dr. Prin about everything that had just happened, she was going to give her answer to Army General Taoghn's proposal.

Like Leaves Of Gold had said about the raiders, she also wanted to be a part of bringing justice to those whom Emperor Ignis had murdered. A memory of her Uncle Joash popped into her head, and she curled her talons with a growl.

And now she finally had a way to do just that.

Chapter Forty

"...AND UMBREAL TRAW HAS *been disqualified!"* Brutus Halt, the Constantia Tourney's commentator, practically screamed into Aabir's holonode speaker, *"Congratulations, Oena Winley! You are now going to level two!"*

The crowds cheered as Oena Winley raised the bloodied trident in her hand victoriously, the hand she held it with spilling a line of blood down her arm from where she had lost her finger. The other competitor, Umbreal Traw, hung onto the side of the floating raft they just fought on with one hand while she pressed the other into her bleeding side.

Aabir grimaced and turned his holonode off with a sigh. Then he turned to lie on his back atop his bed, his eyes tracing the lines of the metal bunk frame above him.

The small hope he had before of possibly finding a way to fail out of the Tourney without looking like he was doing it on purpose had been crushed with each video he watched of past rounds. He had spent more hours than he wanted to count watching them this week in the time he could spare between his extended training period and his research of Prince Joash's projects. And as Matha told him earlier, they were even more chaotic and bloody than he had ever realized. Each round he had watched was in a different environment (deserts, forests, icy waters, and mazes just to name a few), there were different numbers of competitors in each one, different objectives to win, different weapons, and sometimes wild animals were brought in to add to the painful chaos.

With each video Aabir watched, he continued to wonder how Lieutenant Denir ever thought he could get far in the Tourney. Half of those who won the rounds he saw did so out of sheer luck, not skill or strategy. Yes, there were a few where being a good swordsman or arbalist would help one win, but there was too much up to chance in the rest of them.

Dread slithered down his spine. What if he accidentally failed before the end of the second day? Would Denir punish him for it? Was the only reason he was threatened to do so because of his Silvanian descent? A knot of anger hardened in his stomach, but before he could dwell on it further, the mattress above him squeaked and rocked as Ezen got down from it.

"You sure have been watching those a lot."

Without lifting his head, Aabir turned his neck to look at him. "Well, I need to." He could not hide the small bite in his tone.

Ezen held up his hands in a calming gesture. "I didn't mean to offend," he replied with a frown. "You've just been a bit...obsessed with them."

"He's just trying to catch up with everyone else." Tycho sat up on the top of his bunk and sent a reproachful look down at them both.

Aabir aimed a glare up at him, sensing the unsaid jab. "I didn't know it was going to happen, Tycho." He pushed himself into a sitting position and swung his legs over the side of the bed.

"I know, I know—but still. I think it's unfair that Lieutenant Denir would choose the one person who doesn't even care about them to fight."

Ezen looked between them both. "But I thought he won it..."

"I did," Aabir replied, "and without realizing I was doing so."

"Whatever." Tycho flopped back onto his bunk, his back to them.

Aabir gritted his teeth against saying something he might regret. Ever since he met Tycho, it had always been his friend's dream to be a competitor in the Constantia Tourney. Aabir knew he was only speaking out of jealousy and would come back around eventually. However, until then, he was stuck with a sour roommate—and a sour platoon.

"Would you quit your whining, Tycho?" Aquilo looked over his shoulder from their desk's chair. "Can't you let it go already?"

"Easy for you to say," Tycho snapped back without moving. "You never cared about joining the Tourney, either."

"Only because I knew there would be no honor in me fighting in them. I would be out before the end of the first round I fought in—and so would you."

"No, I wouldn't."

"Yes, you would." Aquilo gestured towards Aabir even though Tycho was still not looking. "At least Lieutenant Denir thinks Aabir has a chance to honor us."

Their eyes locked for a moment as Aquilo sent him a small nod. Aabir dipped his chin towards him gratefully, even if the thought of having Norland's honor on his shoulders made him queasy.

Aquilo was one of only three people in their platoon who did not seem to hold any hard feelings towards him. Buren—who won the other place in their platoon for his skills with a crossbow, and Ezen were the others. So, even if it meant dealing with the nauseating reminders of holding Norland's honor, he was not going to push away any of the friendly help he could get.

Ezen twisted his lips to the side and met Aabir's gaze. "He really thinks you can make it to the third day?" He asked.

Aabir rubbed the back of his neck with a sigh. "The end of the second, actually."

"Huh." Despite his lack of words, Aabir could read the apology in his newest friend's gaze.

Although he could tell Ezen was also disappointed for not being chosen, he had a feeling the only reason the new trainee did not hold any hard feelings towards him was because he knew the situation Aabir and his family faced as Silvanian-descended.

"What happens if you don't make it?" Ezen asked.

Aabir shrugged and turned his gaze away, another shiver of dread slithering down his spine. "I don't know."

"Wait..." He jerked his head up at Tcyho's voice, "So he's going to punish you if you don't do well?" His sour friend had turned back around to face them, some of the hard edges in his face softened.

So, despite how much Aabir wanted to avoid this subject, he replied, "Like I said, I don't know."

"Oh." Tycho nodded slowly, a strange look coming over his face. And unlike in typical Tycho-fashion, he did not say anything else.

Aabir hoped that was a good thing. He hated being at odds with his oldest friend and did not know how much longer he could deal with it.

"I doubt he would," Aquilo said without looking back at them. "He knows the Tourney can be unpredictable, so he probably only said that to keep you on your toes."

If Aabir came from a highly honored family like the Warlin's, he would have agreed. However, that was not the case for him. Lieutenant Denir never had a problem with singling him out because of his lineage before, and he had a feeling it was one of the main reasons his commanding officer threatened him to do well. Denir did not want any dishonor to come to him because his platoon's best swordsman had Silvanian blood, so Aabir making it to the end of the second day with the best of those in his age level would erase any possible dishonor that might come from the situation.

Instead of voicing any of that, he only replied with a "Maybe".

In the silence that followed, he glanced down at his holonode to check the time. *17:23* it read. More dread churned his stomach, and he shot a glance over at the packed bag sitting at the foot of his bunk. Matha might start to worry if he did not come home soon, but staying at Norland for the weekend almost seemed like a better fate than the one he could only imagine waited for him at home once he told his parents about Rasiela.

"Are you leaving soon?" Ezen's eyes moved between him and his bag.

Aabir held in a sigh. "I guess so."

"Are the pomens ripe?" Tycho asked.

Aabir reached over and grabbed his bag with a simple, "Yeah."

"Has your matha made any pies yet?"

"She has." He stood from his bunk and pulled one of his bag's straps over his shoulder, watching Tycho out of the corner of his eye.

His friend's eyes widened as he put his hand over his chest in mock-shock. "And I haven't been invited yet?"

Aabir shrugged and forced a grin. "Maybe one day you will be..." The only reason he had not invited his friends already was because he did not want patrolmen to come raiding his house while they were visiting.

"Aw, come on, Aabir." Tycho sat up, his lips twisted to the side. "You know I've just been disappointed, is all."

"I know," he nodded dramatically. "So, if you're good, maybe Matha will let me bring you back a few crumbs on Firstdein."

A pillow hurtled towards his face, and he caught it with a laugh before throwing it back at Tycho. "Until then, I'll see you all later."

Aquilo turned his neck and shot him a grin. "See ya."

Aabir dodged Tycho's pillow again and hurried out the door before his friend could think of throwing something else.

PATRE LIFTED HIS HEAD up from beneath the hood of a hovercar as Aabir stepped into the garage.

"Aabir." He slammed the hood closed and wiped his oily hands off with a rag. "You're home a little late. Was traffic bad?"

"No, sir." Aabir's heart picked up its pace at the knowledge of what he was about to tell them. "I stayed a little later at school."

A frown marred Patre's countenance. The hairs on the back of Aabir's neck stood on end as his father sent a furtive glance around them before replying, "Are you training more?"

"Yes sir."

The look in his eyes told Aabir everything he was really thinking about that development.

"I guess that's a good thing, then," he replied in a light tone that sounded forced. "At least you won't be caught unawares."

"Yes sir." Aabir glanced around the garage, too, and silently cursed whoever put the secret cameras there. "I...actually need to talk with you and Matha about something."

"We can in a little bit." Patre gestured towards the hovercar he was just working on. "I need to finish up a few more things, but then we can talk at supper." An emotion Aabir could not discern flitted across his weathered face before he added, "We have something we need to tell you all, as well."

Something about the way he said it sent Aabir's heart racing even more. "Yes sir."

Patre nodded, but there must have been a look on Aabir's face because he asked, "Are you OK, Aabir?"

He opened his mouth to say the familiar "I'm fine" lie, but then hesitated.

"I see." Patre reached over to put his hand on his shoulder, but then must have remembered the oil covering it and lowered it back to his side. "You will do well in the Tourney. There's no need to worry about them."

Aabir caught the veiled meaning behind the words and replied only with a simple "yes sir". The less the cameras had to work with, the better.

Patre sent him a knowingly worried look. "How about you go upstairs while I finish up? Your Matha may need your help setting the table."

"Sure."

With that, Aabir turned and walked out of the garage. When he stepped outside, his gaze immediately landed on Matha, Zeke, and Ereliev moving their wooden picnic table along the path between the garden patches full of growing plants. He ran over to help.

"Oh!" Matha sent him a smile as he stepped between her and Ereliev and lifted the weight from them. "Thank you, Aabir."

"Where are we putting it?" He asked as they both let go.

"Under the pomen tree."

He met Zeke's eyes from across the table as they began moving forward. His arms, which were already weak from training, began to shake as he held up the heavy picnic table, but it did not take them long to make it to the spot Matha led them towards under the tree.

"Thank you, boys, for doing that." She stepped over to him as they dropped it and pulled him into a hug. "I wondered when you would get home."

"Sorry it took so long." They let go, and Aabir noticed something different in her countenance. Almost like a nervous anticipation. He scrunched his brow and asked, "Are you all right, Matha?"

"Yes, I am, actually," she nodded and gave him a reassuring smile, but he noticed as she turned back towards the house that she was wringing her hands together, "but I will need your help bringing out the food."

He sent her another questioning look but nodded. "Yes ma'am."

So he, Zeke, and Ereliev followed her into the house; and a few minutes later, the whole family was sitting underneath the blue-tinged leaves of the pomen tree. A feast of roasted boar meat, steamed veggies, potatoes and gravy, sliced pomens, and greenberry pie covered the white tablecloth, but the delicious aromas coming from the food only caused Aabir's nervous stomach to churn all the more.

As the rest of his family filled their plates, he turned his head and met Patre's eyes. "They can't hear us out here, right?"

"That's what we believe, yes." Patre nodded as he put a slice of ham onto his plate.

Aabir breathed out a long breath and clutched his hands together underneath the table. "Then I need to tell you both something."

His heartbeat sped up as he caught the look Matha and Patre shared.

"What is it?" Matha turned her eyes upon him. "Is it something about the Tourney?"

"No ma'am." He shook his head and took in another breath to try and calm his nerves. "I...found a way for us to escape."

The clinking of dishes stopped as everyone turned their faces towards him—except for Yahel, who was too busy eating her pomen slices. Shock covered everyone's faces except for Ereliev, who shot him a hard stare that told him to tread lightly on what he revealed.

He sent her what he hoped was a reassuring look that he was not going to tell her secret before adding, "And I've been in the process of doing it for the past three weeks now."

Matha blinked. "You—you what?"

"And what have you been doing, Aabir?" Patre's shock hardened into an interrogative look scarier than any patrolman's.

Aabir lowered his gaze to his empty plate. *Deleyon, please help me...*

"Um...the cleaning lady at Norland overheard a conversation between me and Matha, and she figured out we were talking about escaping because of—because of it. Thankfully, she—she's also of Silvanian-descent;" his heart raced as quickly as his rambling words, "in fact, she—she's a Silvanian spy, and she made a deal with me that if I help her with gathering information—nothing dangerous, though! —and win her trust, then she can get us all out of Igrium and into—into Silvas. I—I don't know how long it's going to take, but I hope it won't take much longer—"

"—Hold on, Aabir." He lifted his eyes again to Patre's hard look. "Let me get this straight: you became a Silvanian spy to get us out of here?"

"Yes sir..." Aabir nodded slowly.

Tense silence met his words for a long moment.

"How could you do THAT?" Patre stood abruptly and slammed his fist on the table, his dark violet eyes storming. Yahel began to cry at his outburst, and Matha picked her up to console her.

"I—I promise it's not as bad as it sounds!" Aabir leaned away from his angry countenance and held up his hands in surrender, "All I do is send her information I find in books and online! It's all a bunch of stuff anyone could find if they only looked hard enough. She told me I wasn't going to put us in any kind of danger—"

"—*She* told you?" Patre asked incredulously. "*She* could be lying for all you know. What has she shown you that makes you so sure she actually is a Silvanian spy?"

Aabir opened his mouth to defend himself, but then closed it as he processed his patre's words. What *had* Rasiela shown him that made her words to him true? His pounding blood ran cold.

"I...she is Silvanian..."

Patre only continued to glare at him.

"She never gave you any proof of her identity?" Matha asked in a much calmer, although still firm, voice.

"No ma'am..."

She put her face in her free hand. "Oh, Aabir..."

"But I—I know she's a spy..." The excuse died on his tongue as he put his head in his hands, the possibility of what he might have done seeping into his bones like cold sludge.

Patre's voice was even colder as he said, "You have put us in danger, Aabir. I know you wanted to help us, but becoming a spy is not the way to do it. You need to cut all ties with this woman now—if it's not already too late."

He lifted his head from his hands and met his patre's gaze. "But Patre, this—this is our only chance to escape." The words sounded as pitiful to his ears as he assumed they did to everyone else, but he did not let that stop this last effort, "Even if it *is* risky, how—how could I let this chance pass up? I see no other options for escape—especially one that will help us get into Silvas without them thinking I'm loyal to Igrium. This could solve both those problems—"

"—Don't argue with me, Aabir." Patre gestured to everyone seated around them, "We may now be in danger because of this. Whether this woman is a spy or not, if anyone from Igrium hears about this, none of us will be safe."

Nevaze breathed in a sharp breath and started to cry along with Yahel. Matha sent Patre a sharp look. "Elnim! Watch your words."

Patre turned his face in Nevaze's direction. "I'm sorry to have upset you, Nevaze," he said with a side-eye glance towards Aabir, "but Aabir needs to know the seriousness of this situation."

Indignation flared to life in Aabir's chest, burning away some of the cold dread. "I know the seriousness of what I've done, Patre!" He exclaimed, "And I know the seriousness of the danger we will all face—whether I do this trust exercise or not."

Patre's eyes sparked with anger. "Don't backtalk me!" A sharp bite laced his words, "I am the protector of this family, Aabir, and you will do as I say. You will break all contact with this woman, and I don't want to hear another word about it! Do you understand?"

Aabir stared into his fiery gaze until he could no longer withstand the intensity. He lowered his head and sat back down dejectedly.

"Yes sir." He grumbled.

"Can you contact her on your holonode?"

"Yes."

"Do it now."

Aabir almost opened his mouth to make another objection, but with one glance up at his patre's burning countenance he only nodded. He looked back down and lifted his wrist before turning his holonode on. He found Rasiela's "Ori" contact and—with the stares of his entire family upon him—typed out his message,

"I'm sorry, but I felt like I had to tell my family about our deal, and my parents say I can no longer do it with you. They don't believe that you are who you say you are—and I'm beginning to agree with them on it.

"I never told them your name, though, only that you're Norland's janitor. I hope that doesn't ruin anything for you."

He tapped "send", and turned the device off with a flick of his wrist. "There," he sighed, lifting his head back up towards Patre.

"Good." Although the sharpness in Patre's expression didn't abate, he sat back down and looked Aabir square in the eye. "I only do this for our protection, Aabir."

"I know." But knowing did not make it any easier. "I was only trying to help, and since there's no other way—"

"—We may yet find one," Matha cut in.

"That will also help us win someone in the Alliance's trust so that I can actually cross the border?" He almost shouted.

Matha blinked in shock at his outburst before shooting him a glare. He shook his head with another frustrated sigh. "I'm sorry, Matha. I'm just...upset."

"I know, and I forgive you."

A long pause stretched between them. Aabir lowered his eyes back down to his clenched fists. He should have never listened to Mister Falap. Even if his parents' suggestions about Rasiela not being who she said she was were true, they were going to end up in trouble either way—whether from her ratting them all out, or from the new Constantia Rule. Any one of them could accidentally say something in the coming months and be thrown into the Tourney, while Aabir was shipped off somewhere to fight for the empire he wanted to leave.

A wave of hopelessness crashed through him. They would never escape. His Matha might say otherwise, but he knew deep down Rasiela's offer was their last bit of hope of that ever happening—and now it was gone.

"Well, your Matha and I have some other news we wanted to share with you all," Patre finally said.

Aabir lifted his head and noticed the apprehension behind their otherwise smiling faces. Matha's eyes flicked to meet all their gazes. "I'm pregnant."

"What?" Aabir and Zeke both exclaimed the same time as Ereliev, whose voice held a note of excitement, asked, "You are? Really?"

Matha looked over at her, still smiling. "Yes, Ereliev."

"What's that mean, Matha?" Yahel lifted her chin in her direction.

Matha's smile beamed down on her. "You're going to have a new brother or sister, Yahel." She kissed the young girl's curls.

"I am?"

"You are."

Yahel replied with a squeal of delight as she snuggled closer to their Matha. Nevaze jumped from her seat and joined in the hug, a big smile on her tear-streaked face.

Aabir looked between his parents as a wave of excitement took over his hopeless fears in the bright moment, a smile escaping his tight lips.

"When did you find out?" He asked.

"A couple weeks ago," Matha replied. "It came as quite a shock since we always thought Yahel would be the last, but Deleyon obviously had other plans."

"And we are more than happy about it." Patre put his arm around Matha's shoulder, his proud smile erasing the sharp lines in his face.

"So...when will you know if it's a boy or a girl?" Zeke asked.

"Not for a while, Zee." Matha gave him a soft smile. "I wish I could tell you it was going to be a boy, but I'm not Deleyon."

Aabir glanced over in Zeke's direction as his brother shrugged. "Eh, it doesn't matter," he said. "As long as they're not as annoying as Nevaze, I'll be fine."

"Hey!" Nevaze lifted her head from where she sat huddled next to Matha and shot him a glare. "I am not annoying."

"Yes, you are."

"No, I'm not!"

"Yes, you—"

"—Both of you stop it!" Patre raised his voice, his smile replaced with a glare he shot at both of them. They immediately did so and his features relaxed. Clearing his throat, he continued on in a normal tone, "We know this might not seem like the best time for a new baby," he sent a significant look towards Aabir, "but we also know it's a blessing from Deleyon and have been thinking about what needs to change in the future regarding all of this. So, we have some other news."

Aabir's stomach did a somersault as his earlier worries re-emerged. How were his parents going to take care of a baby on top of everything else happening to them?

"Mister Falap has asked that the whole family stay with him during your growing-season break, and we accepted his offer." Patre continued, "Even I'm going. I have decided to close my garage during that time and do any mechanical work he needs me to do on his farm instead."

"But...I thought you said we weren't going to live with him," Ereliev replied.

"Yeah..." Zeke added.

Aabir said nothing as a noose tightened around his churning middle. The beginning of the growing-season break was when he was going to be enlisted into Igrium's military, so none of this had anything to do with him.

"We're not going to live with him permanently," Matha said. "This is just a longer visit."

"But we believe it will be the best thing for us to do, and when the break ends, we will go on from there." Patre looked at each of them. "Do you understand?"

"Yes sir," Ereliev and Nevaze both said at the same time.

Zeke huffed out an "I guess so", while Aabir still said nothing. He wanted to tell his brother he was lucky enough to be going, but he had already caused one uproar during this meal and was not in the mood to cause another.

Patre locked eyes with Aabir again and said, "I know none of this will necessarily apply to you, Aabir, but don't lose hope yet. We may find some way to leave before the growing-season break ever begins."

Aabir nodded and looked away, not trusting his voice to say anything.

After another pause, his family continued eating while discussing living with Mister Falap, but he stayed quiet and hardly touched any food as his thoughts smothered his earlier excitement with a tangle of worries, regret, and helplessness.

If only he had stayed quiet. Then he would still have a chance of escaping Norland before he ever had to join Igrium's military.

Why did he listen to Mister Falap's words? He should have known the smartest thing to do would be to stay quiet. It might not have built any more trust between him and his parents, but at least the trust exercise would still be going instead of them being back in the hopeless situation where they had started.

He stared down at his almost-full plate of food. Why did every choice he thought was right end up actually being the wrong one? Couldn't he make a big decision without it turning on him and his family?

Maybe if we didn't live in an empire that hated us... he thought with a frown.

But now that he had messed up, they might be stuck with all of their choices being just as difficult to make because they were now, undoubtedly, stuck in Igrium. And no matter how many times his parents tried to tell them otherwise, Aabir knew that that was the cruel reality they were going to have to live in for however long this war continued.

Another pang of dread struck his racing heart at those thoughts, but then his wrist buzzed and he was able to turn his focus upon his holonode's screen as it popped into thin air. He tapped the newest message from Rasiela and read it.

A spark of hope that contrasted against the darkness of all his other thoughts lit inside him as his eyes roved over the message. The noose around his insides loosened, and he found the courage to look up and meet his Patre's gaze.

Patre must have seen the change in his countenance, because his smile vanished as his thick brows drew together. "What is it, Aabir?"

"The spy just messaged me back," he replied, "and she said she'll give you proof of her identity if it will make you trust her, along with a call from her boss."

"WELL, IT'S SENT." RASIELA stated as she swiped Chief Baene's holocall back onto her holonode's screen.

"Good." He dipped his chin.

She had already been on a call with him when Aabir sent her the message about telling his parents. At first, she was angry with him for doing so, but then she told Chief Baene and he said he would take care of it—which led to her sending that last message.

"But are you sure?" She asked again.

"I am. We need someone who can enter the prisons and get a map for us, Rasiela." Chief Baene sighed and rubbed his forehead with his fingers. "So even if I don't trust him, he's our only option. None of our spies will be able to bypass security in that place except for him—if he's even able to do it."

A sinking feeling entered Rasiela's stomach. "So, our only hope of freeing those prisoners is him? Truly?"

"I'm afraid so."

She glanced up at her office's ceiling and mumbled a prayer. As she finished, her holonode buzzed again and she swiped Chief Baene's weary countenance away to read the message.

"Did he respond?" His voice came through the holonode's speaker.

"Yes, Chief." The sinking feeling lifted as she read Aabir Sorrel's newest message. "He said his parents agreed to it only if you will call them right now."

Chief Baene grunted. "Then give me his number and I will call you back in a little bit."

"Of course." She did so, and he ended the call.

She turned her holonode off and stared back up at the ceiling. *Deleyon, please let this work...* She imagined the expectant faces of the Constantia prisoners-of-war in her mind's eye; all their hope put into this one Igrian trainee who did not want to be in the Tourney anyway.

Rasiela continued to pray quietly, the memories of past Constantia Tourneys and the deaths she had witnessed in them pushing her mumbled pleas on.

Chapter Forty-One

Aabir's heart raced with excitement as he sent the message. He could not contain the smile that escaped his lips as he looked back up at his matha and patre's faces.

"Thank you again," he said.

Uncertainty shadowed Matha's features as she nodded. Patre only gave him a hard stare. His stomach did a somersault at the look, but his excitement kept any worry it would have normally caused at bay. *Deleyon, please let this work...*

As if in answer, his holonode began to buzz. A thrill of anticipation went through him as he lifted his wrist for his parents to see the strange number.

Without turning his head, Patre said, "Zeke, Ereliev, Nevaze—take your sister and leave us."

Zeke opened his mouth to argue, "But—"

"Go. Now." Patre's voice was as hard as gritanium.

"Yes sir." Ereliev nodded and got up from the picnic table, stepping over to the other side to take Yahel from Matha. Nevaze, and a reluctant Zeke, followed her back along the garden path towards the house.

Matha watched them go before turning her face back in Aabir's direction. "Go on, Aabir."

Without hesitation, he swiped his finger across the screen. He held his breath as the holograph darkened, then a face he had only seen on the news blinked onto it. A small gasp came from Matha, and Patre mumbled something indiscernible.

"Hello, Aabir Sorrel." Chief Advisor Baene Ruzek's bright purplish-blue gaze locked onto Aabir's wide eyes.

"Uh—Chief—Chief Baene." Aabir bowed his head towards the Silvanian chief advisor. "I—I wasn't expecting...um—you..."

"Rasiela told me about your message and your parents' worries, so I am here to tell you that: yes, she works for me." His brow barely lowered. "Are your parents with you?"

Aabir blinked out of his surprised stupor and quickly nodded. "Yes—yes sir."

He shot up from his seat and moved over to the other side of the picnic table, barely registering that Matha and Patre had both moved to the sides so he could sit between them. He kept his holonode's screen small to make it hard for any secret cameras to make out the person they were talking to. Both his parents moved their faces into the frame with him.

"Chief Baene, sir." Patre bowed his head towards the screen, and Matha did the same. "We...were not expecting you to be this spy's boss."

Chief Baene nodded. "It's not information I like to divulge," he replied in his thick accent—much thicker than either of Aabir's parents', "but I must in this instance."

He paused for a moment before continuing, "Mister and Missus Sorrel, I know the thought of having your son gathering information for Rasiela is worrying. However, I can attest that she is very good at her job and has so far kept him safe."

Aabir's racing heart pounded against his chest as Chief Baene's calculating gaze locked back onto him. "If these were different circumstances, I would not have even bothered to call you. I still don't trust you, Trainee Sorrel—not with your spotless record—but I am willing to let you build that trust, possibly a little more quickly, if you accept my offer."

Despite the sharp feelings of regret the chief advisor's words dredged up, Aabir licked his lips and asked, "What offer, sir?"

"I was told you won yourself a spot in the Constantia Tourney this year." Chief Baene's expression held no emotion as he spoke.

Cold dread slithered through Aabir's veins. "Y—yes, sir."

"And she told me you didn't mean to win it; that you hate the Tourney."

"Yes sir."

"Well, if you want to prove those words true, and possibly help get your family out of Igrium quicker, than you will want to accept my offer."

"Excuse me, Chief..." Matha cut in, "but are you saying that you can truly get us out of Igrium?"

Chief Baene did not seem annoyed by the interruption. "Yes, Missus Sorrel, I can," he replied. "Your family would not be the first I have done it for, nor do I suspect you will be the last."

"You've done this before?" Patre asked.

"A few times."

"Successfully?"

"Yes."

Aabir's hope only rose with each answer to counteract his dread—despite the tension prickling on either side of him.

"Sir, what's your offer?" He asked.

Chief Baene's eyes landed on him again. "Since you're now an official competitor in the Tourney, you have access to the Constantia Stadium that no one else does."

Aabir remembered Lieutenant Denir saying something about how he and Buren were allowed to go there anytime to practice with other competitors that might be there, but he had completely forgotten about it until now.

"And I need that access to get me some information regarding the prisoners-of-war trapped there."

"Sir?" Aabir's jaw slackened.

The creases on Chief Baene's face deepened as he let out a small sigh. "I need a full map of the stadium's prison level, but the only ones kept are in the stadium's databases. Not even the emperor has one."

A claw of fear squeezed Aabir's heart. "What—um, how would I do that?"

"Rasiela will give you a copein chip that you would need to put into the stadium's mainframe, along with directions on how to find the map while you're there. We suspect the mainframe is on the prison level or the one above it.

"But you would have to find a way to get down there without raising any suspicions." The shadows deepened on the chief advisor's face, and Aabir noticed a hint of anger in his eyes as he continued, "The Tourney's Planners sometimes let competitors visit the prison to intimidate the prisoners, so that would be the best time for you to get that information."

Fear tightened around Aabir's chest. "I...I don't know if I would be able to do that, sir..."

The hard lines on Chief Baene's face sharpened all the more. "You want to prove yourself, yes?"

"Yes sir..."

"And Rasiela told you that helping her would be helping a lot of people, too, correct?"

His muscles tensed. "Yes sir."

"Then this is the only way to do either of those things," Chief Baene responded sharply. "There are people in that prison who need to be freed, Trainee, and the only way that's going to happen is if you get those prison maps. I'm not asking you to infiltrate the prison all by yourself. The only thing I need from you is that map."

"But what if someone finds out about what he's doing?" Matha's voice held a note of worry.

"Then he can make up an excuse and continue on with the prison tour." Chief Baene finally moved his intimidating gaze off Aabir and flicked it between his parents. "Under normal circumstances, I wouldn't ask anyone but those I trusted to do this, but your son has an advantage here that I don't want to waste.

I don't mean for any of this to sound harsh, but I would be risking much to get you all out of Igrium, and I don't believe that this assignment is much of a risk. He is a trainee *and* a competitor. He should be fine."

The bench shook under Aabir as Patre shifted his position. "We just don't want anything to backfire and endanger him," he said.

"There is little risk, Mister Sorrel. Rasiela already has access to the arena's basic security footage, and would delete any of it that showed him in places he is not supposed to be. He wouldn't even have to do anything on the database's mainframe. The copein chip he will use will connect him with Rasiela, who will be the one digging into all the information in the system."

Patre made a noise in his throat but did not reply immediately. In his silence, Aabir took his chance to ask the question that had been burning on his mind since Chief Baene's rebuke, "So, you're saying that you'll use this map to free the prisoners before the Tourney?"

Chief Baene gave him a sharp nod with a simple, "Yes."

Aabir's gaze drifted over to the pomen tree's trunk as he thought. If he did this and was successful, then he would no longer have to worry about possibly fighting the prisoners in the Tourney.

Hope ignited inside him with the invigorating thought. In fact, if something as big as all the prisoners escaping did happen, then the Tourney might end up being canceled and he could avoid it altogether. This terrible situation he found himself in might not actually end up being as terrible as he thought.

He could do something good by helping free those people before they were dishonored on live holovision for Igrium's bloodthirsty amusement. He could be brave and do something honorable for once—and help his family in the process.

"I'll do it, sir," he said.

"Aabir!" Matha exclaimed as Patre said, "Hold on, now..."

"I have to, Matha." He turned his head and locked eyes with her, "If I can use this bad situation and use it to help those people, then I will." He then looked over at Patre's weathered frown, "Please, Patre. Those prisoners are even worse off than we are right now. I have to do this."

They met his words with a tense, but thoughtful, silence. Aabir looked between them and added in a smaller voice he hoped the chief advisor could not hear, "I can't be a coward anymore."

"Oh, Aabir," he felt the weight of Matha's arm wrap around his shoulders as she also spoke in a lowered voice, "that's not who you are, nor are we saying any of this to make you feel like one. We only have our reservations because we want to protect you, and this seems dangerous—"

"—We're already living in danger, Matha," he whispered back, "and this is our only chance to escape it. There's no other way. I know it, and you know it."

She sighed, her eyes flicking back to the screen floating above his wrist, then over his shoulder. "Elnim?"

Aabir turned towards his Patre again. The lines in his face looked even deeper as a battle brewed in his shadowed gaze.

"I'm afraid he's right, Zerah," he finally sighed.

Aabir glanced back over at his matha and saw a similar war in her large eyes; but after a few moments, she nodded in agreement. His heart nearly burst out of his rib cage with all the emotions flooding him at that small movement.

"Thank you for giving us clarity on who he's working for, Chief Baene." Patre turned his face back in the holonode's direction. "Now that we know, he has our permission to go if he so wishes."

"I do," Aabir said with a firm nod in the chief advisor's direction.

The sharpness of Chief Baene's features softened a little. "Then I thank you for your help," he replied with a small dip of his chin. "I know Rasiela said she would not be able to meet you on Firstdein, so I will have her put the copein chip in your dorm at Norland. She can message you where she'll put it and will tell you all the details you need to know.

"I must go now, but—again—thank you for your service towards our kingdom. I promise you that if you do this, you will have earned a little more of my trust, Aabir Sorrel." He nodded again. "I hope to be told of your success soon. Good dein."

Aabir bowed his head again towards the chief advisor as he ended the holocall. Turning the device off, he lifted his head and looked between his parents again.

For one of the first times in his life, he could think of nothing to say amidst the rush of emotions except for a simple, "Thank you."

Matha nodded, her lips twisted to the side. He glanced over at Patre's hard expression, and their eyes met.

"Even though I'm not happy you have to do this," Patre sighed again, but Aabir was surprised to see the ghost of a tiny smile flitting across his lips, "I can't say that I'm not proud of you for doing so. Seeing those prisoners free would be... It would be a wonderful thing."

Warmth filled his chest, and a small smile escaped his own lips. "Thank you, Patre."

His patre nodded and turned his unfocused gaze towards the pomen tree without saying anything else. Aabir glanced at Matha's teary gaze and wrapped her in a hug. She squeezed him back, sniffling in his ear.

"We love you, Aabir."

"I love you, too."

Chapter Forty-Two

Chief Baene looked up from the report he was reading on his holoputer as Felicita stepped into the office. The worry etched upon her drawn brow told him she had heard the recent news.

"So, I guess you heard the news." He turned his holoputer off and folded his arms, leaning back in his chair.

She nodded and settled lightly on the chair opposite his desk. "She told me yesterday she would probably do it, but I didn't realize she would answer so quickly."

Baene nodded. It had come as a shock when he read the message Dr. Prin sent the Buleutcil about Tetra Cairn's answer to Taoghn's proposition. He had not expected the girl to act so hastily about the decision, which led him to wonder if something was wrong. Felicita had told him about Tetra cutting their meeting short last night. He had a feeling that might have something to do with it.

"I didn't, either." He paused and locked eyes with her. "Are you about to go up there?"

"Yeah, but I don't know wha' it will look like." The warm light from the chandelier shone on her unshed tears. "I know she saw somethin' tha' upset her last night...but I don't know wha' she saw tha' would've done so."

Baene exhaled slowly. "And you're worried it might be you."

"Well, partly." She shrugged and wiped away a tear before it could fall far. "I 'ave missed her so much, Baene, and I don't want ta lose her when she is so close. Yet...there are things I know she might remember tha'...tha' could scare her away."

"Even if they upset her, you have done nothing but show her kindness since she first stepped foot here, and I doubt she will run away from that."

"And tha' also worries me." Felicita lowered her gaze down to her hands. "I...I haven't told her anythin', so what if she decides not ta trust me because of tha'?"

"You tell her the reason why you couldn't."

"But she may see it as only an excuse..."

"It was a very good one." Baene frowned. "We couldn't trust her at first—not even with your intuitive feelings—and you can't rush that sort of information upon someone who wants to recover from C.B.M. treatment. It's not safe."

She gave an almost imperceptible nod. "Tha' might've been wha' happened a little bit last night."

He pressed his lips into a thin line and stroked his chin with his thumb. "Yes, but—thank Deleyon—I doubt she would have gone with Dr. Prin if it had hurt her." He hoped, anyway.

Felicita did not look convinced. "Maybe not physically..." her words ended in a sigh.

"Felicita," he leaned forward, and she lifted her head to meet his eyes, "you're going to worry yourself out of doing what needs to be done. You can't control how she reacts, just like I can't control the way the Buleutcil, the nobility, or any of our citizens react to any of the decisions I make."

She did not reply as a thoughtful look softened her features, but he could see her eyes were still dark with worry, so he added, "And she is your *cousin*, Felicita. You need to be the one to help her through this. Only you can right now—not even your Matha could."

She nodded slowly and, after a quiet moment, stood. "You're right." She lowered her chin and raised her brow, a ghost of a smile on her lips. "Any other words o' Baene-ly wisdom ta impart before I go?"

A small smile escaped his sternness. "Do you have everything Lord Othnel found for you?"

"Yes." The light caught on her holonode as she gestured with her wrist. "I got it all, and Matha also found the box o' photographs and gave it ta me."

"And how is she doing with all of this?"

"Rarely 'ave I ever seen her this excited." A brief smile flashed across Felicita's face. "She can't wait ta see her again."

Baene's smile turned into a grin at the thought. "I bet."

There was a moment's pause, soon broken by a sigh from Felicita. "I won't waste anymore o' your time, Baene." She took a gliding step away from his desk. "I'll come back here and give you a report when I'm through."

"Thank you." He gave her an encouraging nod. "Deleyon be with you, Felicita."

A flash of resolve sparked in her eyes, and she nodded firmly before spinning around and exiting his office. When the doors shut with their resounding thud, he turned around in his chair to the view of fake greenish-blue leaves out his window. A heavy weight settled over his shoulders as he leaned forward, resting his elbows on his knees and putting his chin atop his folded hands.

"Deleyon, go with her. Give her favor," he mumbled quietly, "and open Tetra's eyes to the truth."

Because he needed her to see it fully if this war was going to end well.

TETRA COULDN'T CALM HER racing heart down no matter how many deep breaths she took to try and do so. She paced in a tight circle around her room while she waited for Felicita to come, going through conversation scenarios in her head.

If she took last night into account, then her cousin would either be worried about her or would be wondering why it only took Tetra one day to answer Army General Taoghn's proposition. She finally decided either option could work in her favor of opening up without giving too much away. All she had to do was wait until Felicita came up.

As the long minutes ticked by, her mind wandered back to the things she had seen of Cherry Valley. Before telling Dr. Prin she was going to join Silvas' army, she had told the head biologist everything she heard and saw in the peryton village. At first, she wondered if the woman would think her crazy and tell her to stop, but Dr. Prin's eyes had held that strangely soft look of wonder as she scribbled down everything told to her.

Apparently, some of the things she had seen in the peryton village answered a few questions scientists had been pondering about the giant omnivores—like why the burnt remains of caffeine cherries were always found in the systems of dead perytons they had studied. The piece of information had shocked Tetra, to say the least; and she would've thanked the gods in that moment—if she knew they were listening—that she hadn't ended up drinking the perytons' "brew". She had never seen a poisonous caffeine cherry tree before, so she hadn't realized that those were the cherries found in "Cherry Valley".

Then after all of that, she had told Dr. Prin her decision—and the woman had sent her answer to the entire Buleutcil, not just the army general. Tetra's stomach flipped at the memory. She didn't like that her decision had to be made known to every powerful leader in Silvas right then, but she also knew she couldn't do anything about it and just remained silent on the matter.

She lifted her hand and rubbed it over her segione tallies. This would probably be her life now that she was Silvas' first, and only, war-peryton, so it was best to just try and get used to it—no matter how uncomfortable it made her feel.

A light knock tapped on her door, and Tetra jerked around to face it. "Come in."

Her heart upped its sporadic beat as the door opened and Felicita stepped into the room. Worry clouded the young woman's brown eyes as Tetra met her gaze—just like she figured would be the case.

"Hello, Tetra." Felicita stepped forward but made no move to sit. "How 'ave you been since last night?"

Here goes nothing... Tetra dug her nails into her skin as she maintained eye contact with her cousin.

"I remembered...a lot," she replied slowly.

Felicita breathed in heavily with a nod. "And wha' did you remember, exactly?" Her posture stiffened as if she was bracing herself for a blow.

"I remembered my aunt and my uncle," she said, "and my...my patre." She forced any emotions from showing on her face as she was reminded of the deep hollowness that had settled itself inside her. "I also saw my cousin."

Felicita flinched, and a few of her long braids fell around her shoulders as she turned her face away. "I see..."

The guilt obviously written on her face gave Tetra the courage to finally speak the words bubbling up inside her, "And I know that's you."

Felicita nodded slowly, still not looking at her. "Yes," she said, "I—I am."

Relief flitted through Tetra like a summer breeze, but it was immediately followed by a windstorm of all the other emotions she had harbored the past day. "So...you're Joash Ignis' daughter."

"Yes."

"And I'm..." she swallowed the lump forming in her throat before speaking the truth of her memories aloud, "I'm not a Cairn. My name isn't even Tetra, is it?"

Felicita finally lifted her head to face her, and Tetra noticed the tears shining in her eyes. "No, it's not," her accented voice warbled a little as she spoke, "Your name is Anora Valrua Aerbre Ignis."

The long name lodged itself like a key in Tetra's head, and more childhood memories spewed forth from behind the locked door. She barely registered sitting on her bed as lost images, words, and feelings flooded her mind.

More memories of her spending time with her Aunt Minda, Uncle Joash, and a younger Felicita went by her mind's eye. There were even a couple she remembered of her patre, and one of them sent a jolt of familiarity through her as she "saw" his dark blue eyes through the image's fuzziness. Which one of her possible patres had she seen with those eyes?

Another, more vivid memory took her attention away from the answer to that question. In it, she was staring up at an Igrian man—a doctor, she supposed, because of his white lab coat—as she lay on a hospital bed.

"Anora Valrua Aerbre Ignis..." he looked away from the holographic screen on the wall near her bed and smiled kindly down at her, "Do you like having such a long name?"

She shrugged with a hoarse cough. "No one—really says—all of it," she replied through more coughing. "So, I—I don't care."

His smile faded and she caught him glancing over at the open door leading out of the small hospital room. Then he turned his head and locked eyes with her, a smile back on his face.

"I noticed that your aunt gave you most of your medicine already, but she forgot one thing."

"Oh?"

"Yes—" he added in a whisper, "—so let's just keep this between you and me, alright? No reason to embarrass her. You know how she can get sometimes."

Tetra nodded with a grin, then immediately coughed again.

His smile faded as he gave her a sympathetic look. "I'll warn you that it is a shot, though. So can you be brave for me and take it?"

Her grin faded and her heart began to race at the dreaded word. She tensed her arm muscles, but then gave him a shaky nod. "Yes sir."

She could be brave; just like her patre wanted her to be.

The doctor sent her an encouraging nod and turned towards the table next to her bed. After a few moments, he faced her again and picked up her wrist. Another coughing fit took over Tetra so she turned her face away from him, but she could feel something cold being wiped over the inside of her elbow.

When her sore lungs finally got a chance to breathe again, she looked back in his direction—and her heart dropped into her stomach at the sight of the needle in his hand. A dark red liquid filled its cylinder.

"Are—are you sure I really need that, Dr. Novem?" She lifted her eyes to his kind, but serious, face.

"Yes, Anora," he replied, "you do."

"OK." The memory went dark as she squeezed her eyes shut, then she opened them again and noticed the needle was empty.

"See? That wasn't so bad." Dr. Novem gave her an encouraging smile. "Now, remember what I said—don't mention this to your Aunt Minda, alright?"

"Yes sir."

As if she had heard her name, Tetra's aunt stepped into the room wearing blue scrubs. "Is everythin' alright, Selio?"

He sent Tetra a wink before turning around to face Aunt Minda. "Just checking up on her."

Aunt Minda nodded and stepped over to the side of Tetra's bed with a smile. "And how are you feeling, Anora?"

"Just tired." Another tickle entered her throat, and she coughed to get rid of it. "Tired of coughing."

"I know, and I'm sorry you 'ave to deal with it." Aunt Minda gave her a sympathetic smile. "But I promise it will pass."

Tetra nodded with a sigh and scratched the inside of her birthmarked elbow.

Aunt Minda leaned over and kissed the top of her head. "You need ta get some rest now. I'll check up on you in a few hours. OK?"

"OK."

An annoying sting itched the inside of her elbow again. She scratched at it furiously, but the sting only turned into a pricking needle.

"Wha' is wrong, Anora?" Aunt Minda crouched next to her bed and grabbed her wrist. "Is it itching?"

The needle-like pains Tetra had grown familiar with the past few months stabbed her younger self's elbow.

"It—it hurts!" She continued to scratch at it wildly, but it only made the pains sharpen.

"Hold on, now. Don't freak out—"

A stab of fiery pain shot through Tetra's arm, and she screamed. More of the familiar pains she had come to know the past month tore through her arm and into the rest of her younger self's body.

She opened her eyes as the vivid memory ended and turned her head to set them on Felicita's wide-eyed gaze, her heart thumping wildly in her chest.

"Wha' did you see?" A hint of fear barely heightened Felicita's tone.

"I—I saw this...this doctor." She pressed her hands against her head as she tried to recall the memory. "I think...I think his name was Novem, or something—and I saw him put this...this medicine in me. And then it...it caused the same kind of pain that turning into a peryton does."

As the words left her mouth, their implication hit Tetra. She lowered her hands and straightened up slowly. Was that red liquid what caused her to turn into a peryton? She lifted her gaze towards the knowing, shadowed look Felicita wore.

"You knew," she said, her voice hoarse.

Felicita nodded and wouldn't meet her accusatory gaze. "If you want me ta tell you all I know, I can do tha'."

"How come you never told me before?"

"Because it's not always safe ta do tha' to someone whose mind has been tampered with by the C.B.M." She lifted her hands and played with the end of one of her braids, "We also had ta make sure it was really you before sayin' anythin'."

Tetra remembered her first meeting with Chief Baene, and the recognition she had seen in her cousin's eyes. "But you knew it was me the whole time."

"I know—and I wanted ta tell you, Tetra, I did! But Chief Baene said we needed ta make sure we were not bein' fooled," Felicita's voice warbled again as she met Tetra's eyes. "So, he and I told Lord Jachen and Lord Othnel about what we thought—well, what I *knew*—and then Lord Othnel was able ta dig for the information so we could 'ave proof. He—he found the true match ta your

DNA, your real birth certificate, and a few o' the files o' data my patre collected for his 'Project Peryton' experiment."

"Project Peryton" experiment? A shiver went down Tetra's spine at the title, and she glanced down at her hands. So, she was some type of *experiment*? And one her uncle had created?

"Alright." She couldn't hide the sharpness in her tone as she said, "Tell me what you know, but show me the DNA match first."

She wanted the question of who her patre was to be answered above anything else.

Felicita nodded obligingly, her face still shadowed, and stepped over to Tetra's desk chair before sitting down. Tetra watched in silent anticipation as her cousin tapped her holonode on, swiped through a few things, then widened the holographic screen so Tetra could see it better.

"This is wha' Lord Othnel found first." Felicita's voice almost sounded monotone as she spoke, "It's wha' anyone sees if they're allowed to investigate the medical records on your profile."

Tetra leaned a little closer to read the official-looking words better: "***DNA match:*** *Aries Fralman Cairn*".

"But when he did a little more digging, he continued to stumble upon a lot of security measures tha' made him suspicious. So, he fought through them and finally found your true patre's DNA match."

Tetra's heart tried beating its way out of her ribcage as Felicita hesitated for a moment before swiping her finger to show a new line, "***DNA match:*** *Rexcan Alveus Orland Ignis*".

No, no, no, no, no... Blood pounded in her ears, and she lifted her gaze to Felicita's watery eyes. "This...that isn't possible..."

"I'm sorry, Tetra," Felicita replied in a hoarse voice, "but it's the truth."

Tetra's heart dropped into her tightening stomach as the jolting memories of her patre's familiar eyes re-emerged. So, that's why they had felt so familiar, because she had seen them on the same man who had orchestrated her life the past ten years; the same man who had threatened to turn her into a personal guard, stolen her memories, killed her uncle, and lied to her about her identity—and even his.

Hot tears pricked her eyes as the cold truth settled like a roiling storm in her thoughts, but she curled her hands into fists and pressed them against her closed eyelids before they could spill down her face.

Emperor Ignis was her father.

Chapter Forty-Three

Tetra jerked her head up as a weight rested on her shoulder. Through her blurred vision, she noticed Felicita sitting down next to her on the bed.

"Again, Tetra, I'm sorry for not tellin' you sooner," she said, "but now you can see why we had ta make sure it was really you before springin' this kind o' news on you."

Tetra stiffened under her touch but didn't move away. Instead, she turned her face towards the ground and tried to blink back her annoying tears.

She swallowed down the lump in her throat before saying, "Tell me what you know."

"O' course." Felicita paused for a moment. "But first: let me go get somethin' tha' will help me explain some things."

"Fine."

The weight left her shoulder, and the bed moved underneath her as Felicita stood. Tetra heard her clicking footsteps fade away, the door open, then her accented words as she spoke to one of the guards outside—but she didn't pay attention to what was said under the demand of her circling thoughts.

Emperor Ignis is my father...I'm his daughter...The emperor is my father, and he hid it from me, and everyone else...

Felicita's footsteps drew near again, and the mattress moved underneath Tetra as she sat back down. Out of the corner of her eye, Tetra noticed a small, gilded box in her cousin's hands.

"Alright, then," Felicita breathed out, "I'm ready now."

Tetra's stomach tightened further in anticipation as her cousin began, "You're matha died a few days after you were born, so your patre said he couldn't take care o' you and gave all legal rights ta my parents—your aunt and uncle." Her tone grew wistful, "I was so happy ta have a sister, and even though we both knew we were cousins by blood, we never called each other tha'. We were just sisters, plain 'n simple as tha'.

"Neither of us were bothered by the reality of it, and I used ta think it would always be like tha'—especially after Ryder was born and there was no threat o' you being taken away from us ta become the crown princess." Tetra's skin crawled along her malscar as she thought about that fate in the pause Felicita took to take a breath. "But then your patre started visitin' you more. You began telling me and our parents how much you missed him, and...and I remember you cryin' a lot whenever he would leave. I started ta worry tha' he would finally take you back. I know how selfish tha' all sounds, but I was around thirteen at the time, so..."

Her voice trailed off as she shrugged, then came back with sharpness lacing it, "Anyway, it never happened. Instead, life continued on about the same for a couple more years—until you contracted the Feran Flu and Matha hauled you off to the fortress' infirmary ta get the cure. During tha' visit, one o' my patre's friends and colleagues, Dr. Novem—as you remembered—made you more sick by injecting an experimental shot in you tha' he and my patre had worked on a few years before. My patre stopped the project back then, however, when all o' its results failed, and the war started.

"So, when Uncle Rexcan heard about what had been done, he immediately had Dr. Novem questioned and then executed for doin' it, and tha' is when he found out about my patre's...traitorous actions."

Tetra folded her arms and rubbed her hands against them as if cold. "How?" Her voice sounded hollow even to her own ears.

"Matha and I didn't find out until after we made it ta Silvas and Chief Baene told us, but apparently my patre had held correspondence with a secret group he thought he agreed with—one tha' would be able ta stop the war and Uncle Rexcan. However, he never joined officially because the loyalty test they gave him went against everything he thought they stood for."

Something in Felicita's tone sent a chill down Tetra's spine. "What...what was the test?"

When her cousin didn't reply immediately, she lifted her head and saw the wet tear tracks running down her face. Their eyes locked, and Felicita finally said, "They told him ta kill you."

Her heart nearly stopped as dread froze inside her veins. She pressed her folded arms tighter against her middle.

"Why?" The breath of a word barely made it past her lips.

"Because they wanted ta end the imperial Ignis bloodline—and in his ignorance beforehand, he told them about you." Felicita wiped her hand across her face. "He, o' course, denied their requests and they only responded by tellin' him tha' he would pay for his refusal of their offer. So, a few days later, our quarters in the fortress were set on fire while you and I were asleep."

The sharp memories of the fire resurfaced, sending phantom pains throbbing through her burn scar.

"When I woke up, half o' the walls in my room were burnin'. I heard you scream, and I jumped out o' bed and went out into the hall. There—there were flames everywhere. I…I've never been so scared in my life…" Felicita cleared her throat. "But anyway, I made it ta your room, but the doorway was blocked by fire. I called your name a couple times, but you were screaming and crying so much I don't think you heard me. Then I heard somethin' fall, and you stopped."

Tetra noticed Felicita's knuckles whiten as she clutched the small box still in her hands. "I thought you died, so I—I jumped into the flames tha' blocked me ta get you out. You were…you were lyin' on the floor with a burnin' chandelier next ta you. I saw you were breathin' and there was a blanket on the floor, so I wrapped you in it and—and hauled you back through our burnin' quarters. Thank Deleyon, we made it out, but I don't remember who found us. I had passed out by then and woke up in the infirmary."

"You were the one who saved me?" Tetra stared at her, eyes wide.

A small smile pulled the corners of Felicita's full lips up, despite the hardness of her usually soft features.

"Yes, I did. I wasn't goin' ta lose you when I knew I could do somethin' about it," she said. "I couldn't stop either of us from gettin' burned, though."

"You were, too?"

Felicita nodded and pulled up her sleeves. Tetra's brow rose as her eyes flicked over the rough scar tissue rising in bumpy ridges along both her cousin's brown arms. They looked exactly like her head scar… And now that she was seeing this, she realized she had never seen Felicita wear short sleeves before.

"When I first went ta school here, part o' the reason I didn't make any friends at first was because o' these, and because I was Igrian. So, even though the Fire Raids had recently happened and I wasn't the only person with burn scars, I had come from the enemy empire…" As her voice trailed away, a real, soft smile lit up the shadows of her countenance. "But then I did end up making a couple very good ones."

Tetra turned her gaze back to the floor as she processed everything she had been told. Felicita had saved her. Her cousin-sister had saved her from dying and even risked getting burned to do it. A comforting warmth filled her chest at the thought, and she connected the feeling to similar ones she had felt when she remembered the good memories of her childhood; the ones where she had felt loved and safe.

Encouraged by it, Tetra lifted her hand and pulled her hair away from her own scar so Felicita could see it. "The same thing happened to me at Norland," she said. "No one wanted to be friends with the burned eight-year-old."

Instead of horror or disgust, Felicita's eyes softened with understanding. "I'm so sorry you had ta go through tha', Tetra." Her voice warbled and she turned her face away, but not before Tetra noticed another tear running down her cheek. "Matha and I didn't want ta leave you in Igrium—it broke our hearts ta do so—but it had only been a few days since you were given the shot, so your patre put multiple guards around your infirmary room ta keep you safe after the fire and we couldn't…we couldn't get ta you."

The warm feeling faded, and Tetra let her hair fall back into place. Felicita also pulled her sleeves back down over her scars before she continued with their story, "We…we had ta rush ta get out o' there. Patre…he'd already been taken prisoner by Uncle Rexcan for dealin' with tha' secret group. Matha was told he was goin' ta be executed the very next morning, and tha' Uncle Rexcan was comin' for us next. So, she and I had ta leave…with—without you."

In a broken voice barely above a whisper, she added, "I'm sorry, Tetra."

So that's why she had been left in Igrium. A small spark of anger ignited in her chest, but when she looked over at the guilt marring Felicita's face, it dissipated. If her loving aunt and the cousin who had risked her life to save her from a fire both had to leave her, then the situation must have been really bad.

"Well, I'm here now." She met Felicita's eyes and tried to give her an encouraging smile. "And I'm glad you're telling me all of this. So… I forgive you."

More tears spilled down Felicita's cheeks, and she wiped them away with a sniff. "Thank you, Tetra. You've no idea how much I've wanted ta hear tha' come from you."

She shrugged and looked away for a moment, moving her hand to rub it over her segione tallies.

"Sure." After a quiet moment of gathering her thoughts, she glanced back over at Felicita and asked, "You never got to the answer of my original question: how did Emperor Ignis—" her stomach curled as she said the name, but she was unwilling to call him 'patre' aloud, "—how did he find out about Uncle Joash—I mean, your Patre—betraying him?"

There was another pause. And in it, Felicita breathed in an audible, shaky inhale, then blew it out through her mouth.

"Well, the only two people he mentioned it to were Chief Baene—who needed ta know so he could get us all here ta Silvas, and Dr. Novem—who only knew because he and Patre were both plannin' on joinin' the group together. It was durin' his questionin' tha' Dr. Novem told Uncle Rexcan about his treachery."

Something flashed across Felicita's face, but Tetra didn't catch it in time to see what it was before it disappeared. "And Dr. Novem's involvement with tha' group is the reason he gave you the shot in the first place. They told him the only way he could join them was if he found a way ta make 'Project Peryton' work, because he said he told them he might've found a solution to its problem."

"So, he put it in me…?" Tetra scrunched her brow and gave Felicita a dubious look. "Why would he do that?"

"My patre was actually the one ta figure out the solution, but he only told Dr. Novem because they were best friends. He thought he could trust the man with the answer. Instead, he used it ta gain himself a place in tha' group—" she took another deep breath, "—and my patre told him you were the only possible person it would've worked in."

Tetra's stomach coiled again anxiously, and she didn't think it would be able to take much more of this conversation. Granted, she didn't know if *she* could take much more of it.

Yet her curiosity continued winning against her fears, and she asked, "Why?"

Felicita's expression changed as if she had just swallowed spiced gelatscy. "Because my patre realized the original formula was missin' a key ingredient tha'—tha' could be found in your DNA."

"My DNA?"

Was there some gift from the gods in the imperial Igrian bloodline that could make a person turn into a peryton with the right catalyst? She stopped herself from snorting aloud at the ridiculous thought. It sounded like something a crazy Igrian priest might say to build up the Ignis name.

"Yes..." Felicita wouldn't look at Tetra as she tapped the box in her hands with one of her fingers. "Have—'ave you ever heard o' the myths about shifters?"

Tetra narrowed her eyes. "A little."

What did fantastical creatures have to do with this?

"Well, you see...Empress Rillunia wasn't your patre's first marriage. Your...your matha was the first person he married."

She lowered her brow even more. "Emperor Ignis only ever had one wife, though."

"Only one tha' the public knew about."

"So, you're telling me that Emperor Ignis had a secret marriage?" It sounded crazier spoken out loud.

"He did." Felicita met her eyes, her expression completely serious. "They had to, or else he would've risked open war with a nation he didn't know the full strength of."

"Which nation?"

"The Revagh-Shiy Provinces."

Tetra scrunched her brow dubiously. "I've...never heard of that nation before..."

"Tha' is because they don't want you ta know about them."

The hinges on the small box squeaked as Felicita opened it. Tetra glanced down at the noise, and her eyes widened as she caught sight of the thin, paper squares lined up neatly inside.

Those were paper photographs... A *lot* of paper photographs.

Due to holographic technology and other digital media, the use of paper and canvas had become almost obsolete and could only be afforded by the wealthy. She had seen a few canvas paintings in Emperor Ignis' fortress, but nothing compared to the goldmine sitting on Felicita's lap.

"Your matha began trainin' as one o' this nation's ambassadors when she was still a child, so she and her mentor visited Igrium many times—as it was one o' the human nations she would be assigned to when she was older—and since their nation is so secretive, the only contact she and her mentor had was with the Ignis family."

Tetra began to understand where this was going, but she didn't say anything so Felicita could continue, "She—she and your patre became friends over the years, and eventually... they fell in love."

The thought of the emperor falling in love with anyone was mind-boggling. Still, she held her tongue and didn't interrupt to ask her cousin if she knew how impossible the thing she had just said was.

"They ended up gettin' married, and the only thing your patre could do ta keep her birth-nation from waging war on Igrium because o' their actions was to promise ta keep their marriage a secret and your matha out o' the public eye. So, they did it. Your matha rarely left the imperial sector o' the fortress; and when she did, my matha would take her out in disguise."

Despite her mounting wariness, Tetra's heart jumped in excitement as Felicita pulled a photograph from the box. "This will explain why your matha had ta hide herself."

Her fingers shook slightly as she took the paper photo from Felicita. She held it tenderly in both hands as she turned it over to see the colored photo. Her heart stopped at what she saw.

It was a picture of a younger Emperor Ignis and a young woman both sitting next to each other at a feast-laden table. The first thing Tetra noticed was the emperor's wide smile—it took her by surprise. It was something she had never thought his hardened face could express, yet it was there as he stared at his bride—her matha. However, once her eyes flicked over to the woman, all her attention for anything else in the photo vanished.

She wore a dark red dress and a laurel of red and white flowers in her black hair like most brides in Igrium did, but the colors contrasted greatly against her light green skin. The features of her face and what Tetra could see of her body looked humanoid—unlike the scaled merfolk with their bioluminescent stripes and fins; yet as she peered more closely in disbelief at the photo, she realized there were a few black feathers interspersed in the woman's long, straight hair as if they were also growing from her scalp.

She wanted to ask Felicita if this was a joke, but then she spotted the dark green splotches covering part of the woman's arms and her neck. She tore her eyes from the photo to glance down at the huge, splotchy birthmarks on each of her own arms, and even reached up to touch the one on her neck that looked as if it was crawling up towards her face.

She turned her gaze back to the photo and studied the woman's facial features as an idea came to her. She stood abruptly and strode towards her bathroom's door, leaving Felicita on the bed. She stepped inside, turned the light on, and held up the picture as she stared at herself in the mirror. A worm of shame wriggled inside her when she caught sight of her malscar, but she did her best to ignore it for the present matter.

Her eyes flicked between her scarred reflection and the picture. With each moment that passed, her heartbeat sent blood pounding into her ears. From what she could tell, she had the same mouth and small nose as the strange woman, but the rest of her...

Tetra squeezed her eyes shut and pressed her fingers against her temples. How could she be so stupid as to not see it before? She looked like *him*. She opened her eyes and stared at her dark blue irises—the exact same as Emperor Ignis'.

A knife tore through her heart. How did she miss it? How did everyone else miss it? Unpleasant visits to the emperor's office were common throughout the past ten years of her life, so how could she—and everyone else—have missed the similarities?

Unless they ignored them because they thought she was a Cairn and not an Ignis. She couldn't help but frown at her reflection. Because it was preposterous to think she, the dishonorable disappointment, was the honorable Emperor Ignis' own flesh-and-blood.

She turned the light off and exited the bathroom. Felicita's eyes followed her as she came and sat back down on the edge of her bed.

"What was her name?" Tetra asked without turning her eyes from the photo.

"Aerbre o' the Wilshe family."

Tetra lightly touched the photo with her thumb. Aerbre...her matha. "And is she a...a shifter?"

"Yes."

She finally turned her neck and stared at her cousin. "But I thought they were fictional..."

Felicita shook her head. "Tha' is a lie the shifters created centuries ago ta keep their kingdom safe," she replied, "I don't remember everythin' your matha told me about them—I was very young when she was still alive—but I do recall her sayin' somethin' about a war tha' happened between humans and shifters tha' caused them ta go into hiding."

"Then, where are they?"

"On Silalum."

Tetra raised her brow. "The continent of hallucinations and death?"

Felicita nodded seriously. "They don't let any intelligent beings onto their land, and tha' is how they keep it safe. I think they use poison darts for the hallucinations. And all the wild animal attacks you hear about? Those are not normal animals. Your matha could turn into a corafish, and she talked about how each shifter could turn into a different creature."

Tetra's heart jumped at her words, and she looked back down at the photograph. So, that was why she could turn into a peryton...

"And that's why he gave me the shot?" She asked, "Because Uncle Joash told him about my matha and how she was a...a shifter?"

"Correct."

"So, that means I'm not...I'm not fully human."

"You are," Felicita's voice sounded small, "but you don't always have ta be. You're a shifter, too."

Tetra nodded slowly as she tried to process the revelation, her emotions flying around like leaves in a windstorm. Her patre—*"no,"* she corrected herself, *"he doesn't deserve the title"*—her father was Emperor Ignis, and her matha was part of a race of supposed-mythical creatures. She could turn into a peryton because of her matha and an experiment her uncle had created. And she was sitting next to her cousin she didn't even know she had until yesterday.

It was all so much to process...

More tears pricked her eyes, and this time she couldn't control them as they fell. The hollowness digging deeper into her chest warred with the loving brightness trying to fill its dark pit. She sniffed and glanced up at Felicita's sympathetic, loving gaze.

"Felicita," her voice sounded pitiful even to her own ears as she asked, "why—why doesn't he love me?" A sob wracked through her body as more words spilled out along with her tears, "Why did—why did he erase my—my memories? And why did he—why did he not claim me afterwards? Why—why would he threaten to—to turn me into one of—one of his personal guards?"

Felicita grabbed her free hand that wasn't holding the photograph in both of hers. "I wish I knew," she said, "but wha'ever excuse he may try ta come up with, it's not good enough. Because you're wonderful, Tetra; and wha' he did ta you was not a reflection on your own character, but on his. Don't let his excuses blind you ta the truth. I love you, and my matha does, too."

The claws around her heart loosened their hold. "Thank—thank you for—for telling me all of this."

Felicita's voice also warbled as she replied, "O' course." Her cousin's face brightened in a wide smile as more tears spilled down her heart-shaped face as well. "I love you, Tetra, and I...I hope you won't be disinclined towards the idea o' possibly spendin' more time gettin' ta know each other better again...I've missed you so much, and I—I don't want ta lose this opportunity..."

The warm feelings of belonging won over the lonely hollowness in that moment, and Tetra nodded with her own small smile as another sob shook her shoulders.

"I'd—I'd like that," she said.

Felicita nodded slowly and put the box of photos on the bed beside her. Then she lifted her arms and pulled Tetra's sobbing form into an embrace.

As she sat there crying into her sister's shoulder, for the first time in ten years Tetra enjoyed the hug. She had found her family, and there was so much hope in that discovery.

Chapter Forty-Four

Gleaming metal columns towered along either side of Aabir as he and Buren walked through the Constantia Stadium's entrance for practicing competitors. He turned his neck and stared up at the towering ceilings above them for a moment, before lowering his gaze back to the numerous patrolmen standing at attention along the sides of the cavernous room.

There were more here than he had ever seen in any one spot before, and this was only the entrance! If the show of security here was any indication, then Aabir had no doubt the mainframe would be guarded just as well—if not more so.

A knife of fear slashed through him, sending a cold rush through his veins. The small CP chip Rasiela left for him felt like a piece of weighted lead in his boot as he snuck more glances out of the corner of his eye towards the patrolmen. Another shiver went through him as their sight brought back the recollections of those who had interrogated him and his family, but it came much easier than it normally did for him to push those thoughts to the side in favor of the hidden reason he was there.

Rasiela had messaged him many times the past three days to answer all his questions and to give him instructions, but he had not seen her in Norland's halls since he left for the weekend. Part of him wondered what she was doing, but it was a very small part as most of his attention was spent on the seemingly impossible matter before him.

"I can't believe we're actually here." Aabir blinked out of his stupor and glanced over at the awestruck look on Buren's face.

"Yeah." He tried to keep his voice level so none of his worry or any other dishonorable emotions would show through.

"Ah, lighten up, Aabir!" Buren rolled his eyes and gave him a pointed look. "I know you don't care for the Tourney that much, but you're looking with the wrong perspective."

He sent a wary glance at the guards around them, but none of them moved to confront the possibly-suspicious words the other trainee had said about him, so he turned his head back in Buren's direction with a questioning look he hoped did not come across as anxious. "What do you mean?"

"All I'm saying is: instead of thinking about this whole thing like it's horrible, just think of it as..." A thoughtful look came over Buren's features for a moment, "As another sparring match."

"Another sparring match?"

"Mm-hmm. Only this one is broadcasted on live holovision."

Aabir snorted and shook his head. "Thanks for the *advice*, Buren."

"Just trying to help." The trainee's grin disappeared for a more serious look. "But really, Aabir, just think about it like that. 'Cause if I end up not making it far, I'd much rather see you win past the third-level than anyone else, and you can't do that if the only thing you're focusing on is how much you don't want to be here."

"Hmm." Aabir frowned, but then looked Buren in the face and gave him a nod. "I'll think about it."

And he would. Because unbeknownst to Buren and almost everyone else, he actually did have to make it that far or suffer whatever consequences Lieutenant Denir had planned for him. Another shiver went down his spine, but he pushed all those thoughts to the back of his mind. There was a much more important obstacle for him to get over first.

Buren nodded, his smile returning. "You don't have to worry about that happening, though, because I will make it far." He put his hand on the unstrung crossbow at his belt.

Aabir rolled his eyes but could not help the smile that broke through his frown. "I hope you do." *Just not far enough to get to the prisoner rounds*, he added quietly to himself.

"Thanks." Buren gave him a sharp nod before his attention was pulled towards the wide opening they were approaching.

Aabir turned his gaze in the same direction, and his jaw went slack at the huge sight before them. His heart pounded as they stepped out onto the bare, metallic arena floor where the Tourney's fighting happened. He blinked as his eyes adjusted from the dimness of the entrance hall to the bright stadium lights shining full force down upon them. When they did, he turned his neck in both directions to take in the huge, round space surrounding them.

Four giant, holographic jumbotrons projected from the domed ceiling above the thousands of empty spectator seats. Aquilo had mentioned that the stadium could hold one-hundred thousand people, but Aabir did not realize how big that number actually was until he was surrounded by the levels-high seating. He gulped as he tried to imagine fighting in front of all those people, but then his attention was taken to the arena itself as Buren walked on ahead of him towards a group of people who looked like ants in comparison to the space they were in.

A tall wall circled the empty arena, reminding Aabir of one of his matha's pie pans, but it did not take away from any spectator's view as the rows of seats began at its top. Tall posts—that reminded him of an electrical fence, but on a much bigger scale—lined the edge of the wall. He gripped the pommel of his sheathed sword as his stomach churned. He had already seen some of the wild animals the Tourney's Planners put into them—poisonous eels, leos cats, and trodfish to name a few—but seeing the possible electric fence that would have to contain them only made the reality of his situation all the more real.

As he moved to follow Buren, he glanced down at the large, square, metal tiles under his feet. He had also come to find out from his week of binge-watching the Constantia Tourney that a huge labyrinth of a machine was nestled underneath the arena's seemingly harmless floor. He watched in those recap videos as the tiles he walked upon would give way for brand new environments in each round, so nothing seen in the previous one would be the same as the next.

With his longer stride, he soon caught up with Buren before they both came upon the other practicing competitors spread out in a small part of the wide arena. The hairs on the back of his neck prickled with tension as the atmosphere around them slowly changed the closer they drew near. There were a few pairs sparring on one side, others shooting crossbows and throwing axes at moving targets on the other, and a couple people were throwing spears on the outer edge of the group.

Aabir and Buren slowed to a stop and shared confused looks.

"Do you know what we're supposed to be doing?" Buren asked in a lowered voice.

"No idea," Aabir replied in an equally low tone.

His gaze scanned over all the practicing competitors before them until it landed on the only person he saw who was not wearing armor. The man stood talking to one of the various patrolmen stationed around the group of competitors not too far from he and Buren.

Aabir elbowed the other trainee lightly and gestured towards the man. "Let's go talk to him."

Buren only nodded in response, so Aabir found himself leading the way towards him. They both slowed to a stop as the man's conversation came to an end, and he turned towards them with an easy-going smile.

"I assume you two are some of Norland's competitors?" He took a step towards them.

"Yes sir," Aabir and Buren both said at once.

"I'm Pax Ryehouse—one of the Tourney's Planners." He stuck out his hand, and they both took turns shaking it. "At least one of us has to stay out here to make sure no one tries to cheat."

Buren stared at the man as if he had grown an extra head. "People have tried to do that?"

Pax nodded seriously. "Yes, they have—and they were immediately disqualified and stripped of any honor to their name. So, I wouldn't suggest trying to do that."

Aabir gulped, despite the fact cheating was not even on his mind. "We wouldn't, sir," he said.

"Definitely not," Buren readily agreed.

The man's smile returned as he barked a laugh. "I know you wouldn't. Trainees never cause us problems."

Aabir tried to look relieved as his stomach roiled.

"So, are any of the other trainees coming by today?" Pax asked.

Aabir shared a glance with Buren before shrugging. "We don't know, sir."

"Ah, well." The Tourney's Planner turned to face the other practicing competitors. "We don't usually get many third-level competitors during practice, and I'm afraid you two are the only ones here. So, if you want to spar, it'll have to be with someone in the second-level."

"That's fine," Buren replied. "I'd rather practice at the targets, anyway."

Sparring against someone a few years older than him did not sound appealing to Aabir, but he knew he needed to sell his "loyal trainee" act if he was going to find a way into the prisons. So, he gave a nonchalant shrug and said, "I can do that."

Pax nodded towards Buren. "Then you can head on over there. If you can't find an empty target, then come talk to me and I'll get one for you." Then he turned towards Aabir with a wave of his hand. "And you can follow me. Someone got here only a few minutes before you, and they don't have a partner to spar with yet."

Aabir nodded and sent Buren one last look before following the Tourney's Planner. Pax led him on the outskirts along the sparring rings towards another competitor who was practicing guard positions by himself. His armor looked like the standard-issue dark gray, furrum armor soldiers in the army wore—the same type Aabir himself was wearing.

His racing heart somehow picked up its erratic pace even more so. If this man was old enough to be in the second level and had standard-issue armor, then he had the experience of surviving multiple battles—unlike Aabir, who had only ever been on the outskirts of one and still had nightmares over it. He pushed the horrible images that came with that thought to the side, and silently prayed to Deleyon that he would not get crushed before the Tourney even began.

"Rolav!" Aabir leapt in his skin at Pax's call.

The other competitor—Rolav, he assumed—stopped mid-position and turned in their direction.

"Sir?" His voice had an almost nasally, Tulin lilt to it.

"I found a sparring partner for you if you're interested." Pax put his heavy hand on Aabir's armored shoulder.

Aabir met Rolav's bright green eyes. The older competitor nodded sharply and flourished his curved sword. "That's fine with me."

"Then I'll leave you both to it."

The weight left Aabir's shoulder, and he glanced back as Pax walked off. He then turned to face Rolav and unsheathed his own sword.

Before he could even move into his guard stance, Rolav rushed towards him. Aabir lifted his sword in time to deflect the man's stroke, then swung at his leg. Rolav faded back and lunged again.

Around and around they went, and Aabir began to fully realize how much the Constantia Tourney meant to its competitors. The tip of his sword screeched as it slid across Rolav's armored shoulder, close to his neck. The Tulin man snarled as their eyes locked for a split second.

In that moment of time, Aabir saw an intense hunger in the other competitor's face he himself was not feeling—and it, again, made him question how he was ever going to make it far in the Tourney.

He lifted his sword to block Rolav's next attack and deflected it. But then the man hit him with another he barely had time to block. Teeth gritted, Aabir clutched his sword tighter to block the succession of quick attacks Rolav unleashed upon him. His movements were almost desperate, as if winning against Aabir right now would win him the Tourney itself.

The thought fled as the curved sword arced towards his head. Aabir bent back and lifted his sword to block it—but he was too late. Metal screeched against his helmet, and the sword tip appeared not even a hairsbreadth from his nose.

Heart racing, he lifted his eyes and met the man's fierce gaze.

"Do you yield?" Rolav asked.

"Yes." He fought the urge to nod so as not to get his nose cut off.

Rolav nodded sharply and removed his blade before taking a few steps back. Only when the sword was gone did Aabir let the muscles in his neck relax.

His muscles shook with adrenaline, only adding to the churning of dread in his stomach. He was in over his head. How could he hope to make it far in this competition if he did not even want to win it? He was going up against people who were desperate to win the honor of being the Constantia Champion, and he had learned from multiple experiences that that desperation usually made someone fight harder.

"Again?" Rolav asked.

He let himself think about his family's own desperate predicament, and determination hardened in his chest. He would make it as far as the second day's end—but no more—so that they could all escape Igrium without worrying about anything Lieutenant Denir might do to punish him for not doing so.

Aabir moved into a guard stance before replying, "Yeah."

Without waiting, Rolav lunged forward. This time Aabir met him. Their blades rang as they hit, and Aabir pushed with all his might against his thinner opponent. His blade slid down the other with a metallic screech.

With a final heave, he pushed the man's blade away from him, ducked, and stabbed his sword's point into the man's side with all the force he could muster. Aabir's blade hit resistance, sliding cleanly between the man's armor plates, as the whistle of his opponent's blade sliced the air above where his head had been. A thin line of blood trailed down his sword from the man's new wound. He glanced up at the shock on Rolav's bearded face before pulling his sword out and pressing the edge below the man's chin.

"Do you yield?" He asked.

Rolav's eyes glinted dangerously, but he said, "Yes."

Aabir lowered his blade and went to step back, but Rolav lifted his curved sword in one quick movement and pressed the end of it into the same spot below Aabir's chin. His heart leapt into his throat as he stared into the man's angry, narrowed eyes. What had he done...?

"You better be glad you're a competitor, Silvanian, or else I'd be slitting your throat right now," the man's nasally accent deepened as he spoke.

Blood pounded in Aabir's ears. He swallowed, the sharp furrum biting deeper into his skin at the movement.

"I'm not Silvanian. I was born and raised here in Igrium," he replied without taking his eyes off Rolav's fierce expression.

The man snorted, but he did not remove his blade. "I don't care where you say you're from," he said. "I bet the only blood you have is of the Alliance, which means it should be dealt with the same as any of those same Alliance straudwins fighting this year."

Aabir, again, swallowed nervously and tried to think of something that would diffuse the man's anger. The first thing that popped into his head was something he figured Aquilo might say. So, without letting himself overthink it, he shot a glare towards the man.

"How dare you dishonor me like that?" He raised his voice to try and draw attention towards them. Hopefully if he made enough of a fuss, he could get a new sparring partner who did not have a vendetta against his purple eyes.

Rolav blinked in surprise at the outburst as Aabir continued, "I'm a trainee of Norland. I have one of the cleanest records at that school with less than ten segione tallies in five years, and some of the highest marks of swordsmanship the school has ever seen. And you have the audacity to threaten *me* because I look Silvanian? I should—"

"—What's going on here?" Out of the corner of his eye, he saw Pax stepping towards them.

Aabir had never been so happy to hear someone's voice as Rolav quickly removed his blade and took a scrambling step back. Before the Tulin man could open his mouth to defend himself, Aabir turned to face the Tourney's Planner.

"He threatened to kill me." He noticed the group of competitors who were also watching from behind Pax, and a flash of embarrassment went through him. Yet he continued with his excuse in his 'superior-Aquilo-esque' attitude, "*And* he dishonored me greatly by saying I should be counted as one of the prisoners in the Tourney."

Pax crossed his arms and sent a disapproving glare towards the man. "Threatening a trainee?" He asked.

Rolav said nothing. Pax looked between the two of them for a moment, then let out a sigh.

"I'm sorry that happened, trainee," he met Aabir's eyes, "but I know where Rolav is coming from; and if I'd just come back from Xich like he did, then I might have done the same thing—even if it was dishonorable."

He sent another disapproving glare in Rolav's direction, but it soon morphed into a dark look that sent a chill down Aabir's spine. It almost reminded him of the broodingly superior expression he had seen on artwork of Igrium's god of death, Malackin.

"So please accept my apology for that, trainee—"

"—Sorrel." Aabir's stomach churned fearfully at Pax's look, and he found he could no longer hold the man's gaze. He glanced down and added, "Aabir Sorrel."

"Then I hope you'll accept it, Trainee Sorrel. I know you can't help your similarities to those straudwins in the Alliance," Pax continued cooly, "but you must understand that many of us—including Rolav here—are still upset with how the war has gone in Xich."

Similar dark looks came over a few of the competitors standing behind him, and the hairs on the back of Aabir's neck prickled again as more tension entered the already heavy atmosphere. His heart skipped a fearful beat.

Deleyon, what have I done?

He had not meant for his charade to do...this.

"I understand, sir." Aabir hoped his fear did not show on his face.

"Good." There was a pause, then Pax turned to face the growing crowd behind him. In a louder voice, he said, "I know many of you are upset with our losses in Xich," he glanced back in Aabir's direction, "so I believe it's a good time to show you all the *real* enemies we're fighting to keep this from happening again."

Aabir tilted his head up at the man's words. Wait. Was he talking about the prisoners...? Hope mixed with dread buzzed in his veins, and he again became aware of the CP chip in his boot. Was Deleyon giving him an opportunity to use this situation for something good?

"You don't have to, but you're all welcome to come with me to see the prisoners that many of you will be fighting this year." Aabir tightened his grip on his sword's hilt at the nonchalant way Pax spoke. "The rest of you can continue practicing here."

He turned and walked off towards the wide entryway Aabir and Buren had come through before, and almost everyone followed him. Aabir wiped the blood off his sword, sheathed it, and joined the group. A few moments later, he noticed Buren walking next to him—a look of excitement on his freckled face. He gripped the pommel of his sword and looked away before his platoonmate could see how much it bothered him.

Most of the patrolmen who had been in the arena with them now joined the competitors, and Aabir caught a quick glance out of the corner of his eye at the closest one. *Great.* More patrolmen to try and get past.

Pax led them out through the entryway, down a cavernous corridor lined with even more patrolmen, down an elevator—that they had to take multiple trips in because of how large the group was, and finally through a short hall that ended in two huge, metal doors guarded by four honor-guards.

"Planner Ryehouse, sir." One of the guards acknowledged as they all saluted him.

"I've come to show these competitors some of the rivals they'll be facing in the coming weeks," Pax said.

"Yes sir."

The honorguardsman who had spoken turned around, and the beeps of a keypad sliced through the thick atmosphere. Aabir's neck muscles tensed with each piercing tone until the tall doors slid open with a hydraulic hiss.

The cacophony of their heavy footfalls echoed as they continued through the doorway then down a long corridor lined with more hydraulic doors and honorguards, but the blood pounding in Aabir's ears made the thunderous noise seem distant. Pax slowed to a stop at one of these doors, and one of the two guards by it turned and entered a code onto another keypad. It slid open, and Pax led them through.

Before Aabir even stepped forward to follow, he scrunched his nose up as a foul odor wafted into the corridor. It smelled even worse than the first-years locker room at Norland. He noticed out of the corner of his eye a similar look on Buren's face as they went through the doorway, and his racing heart skipped another tense beat. What was down here that could cause such a stench?

"Here they are, competitors," ahead, Pax Ryehouse gestured to the furrum bars now lining the walls on either side of him, "the captured Alliance straudwins—your future opponents."

Aabir gritted his teeth before barking out a sharp reply. The only thing his words would do was put him behind those same bars.

The CP chip moved a little against his foot as he moved forward with the group. None of his words would make a difference, but his actions still could. As he passed the first cell, that truth only hardened itself into a fiery resolve.

He locked eyes with the dull, purple gaze of a Silvanian woman sitting in the first cell. Fear paled her gaunt features, and she jerked her head down, pressing her bony form into the dim cell's corner.

Aabir's eyes widened as he took in her greasy tangle of dark curls and the dried blood splattered on her dirty clothes. A few deep slashes covered her exposed, dark-brown skin.

His anger burned at the pitiful sight, and he clinched his hands into fists at his sides. She was one of the people they would force to fight in the Tourney? She did not look like she had the strength to stand, let alone pick up a weapon and defend herself!

What had they done to her? A chill went through his taut muscles as his mind came up with a few—torturous—answers to that question. He turned his head away, but his eyes immediately landed on the other person in the cell.

Gray eyes like a storm cloud glared a bolt of lightning in his direction. Aabir took a step back and bumped into the person behind him.

"Hey! Watch it." The person shouldered past him, but he barely recognized the movement as images of the Frigian woman in Xich filled his head and dug sharp claws into his conscience.

"What are you looking at, *show-grat*?" The Frigian woman in the cell spat the words in her heavy accent.

Instead of replying, Aabir lowered his head and picked up his pace to keep up with the group. As he came upon the next cell, he sent a furtive glance out of the corner of his eye and saw the same thing: two malnourished women sitting on the floor with cuts and bruises covering their skin. He turned his head away—more heat building up in his chest—and looked to his other side. The same scene there, as well.

Their group passed more and more cells, each with weak, starving occupants. A few of the competitors ahead of Aabir cursed the prisoners and called them things worse than he had ever heard people call Tetra at Norland. One of the voices he recognized as Rolav's, and it only acted as fuel towards the guilt and anger warring inside him.

He always knew prisoners-of-war were killed in the Constantia Tourney—it was one of the reasons he and his family were so adamant about not watching them—but he had never stopped to think about where they were held beforehand. And now that he knew it was this, it only made the bloodbath of the Tourney that much worse. There was probably more respect for the animals that fought than for these humans.

Pax turned a corner at the end of the hall and led them into another cell corridor filled with more prisoners. Aabir flicked his gaze between the cells on either side of him and the floor. Instead of worry, his blood pounded with an increasing anger.

A woman with long, dark braids in the Pon-Yelish style locked fearful, hopeless eyes with Aabir. His gaze caught on the crushed, cybernetic arm that laid uselessly against her side; her hopelessness seeping into the raging windstorm of his emotions. *Oh Deleyon...how could they make* her *fight?*

Aabir lowered his head as they turned a corner again and were led through another cell corridor that ended up leading them back out into the main one—like a giant "U".

He did not know how much more of this tour he could take, but the tiny weight of the CP chip pressed him not to leave.

They entered one of the opposite doors and were greeted with almost the same awful sight (and smell). The only difference was it was men who sat or paced in the grim cells instead of women.

Again, they went through the "U"-shaped halls; and with each step, a suppressing feeling of darkness pressed upon Aabir's chest. He silently pleaded to Deleyon for mercy for these people, and for a way to get that map today without getting caught. He could not bear the thought of any of those he passed being trapped here any longer, especially when he had the means to do something about it.

He continued to silently pray while keeping his gaze to the floor for the rest of that section of the prison, and the only reason he lifted his head again was because Pax's cool tone beckoned him to, "And this next area is where we keep our most prized prisoners—and a few troublemakers."

Aabir narrowed his eyes and wished he could punch the Tourney's Planner in his pudgy face. They were people! Not exotic animals to be collected.

The next hydraulic door hissed open, and Aabir trudged through the doorway at the back of the group. Instead of furrum bars lining the walls, tinted panels of glass were spread out down the newest corridor. Pax came to a stop and gestured to one of these panels.

"This is Sergeant Glin," he said as the group began to gather around the glass. "She was picked for one of the routine lashings a few days ago, but instead of complying, she attacked the two guards who went to take her and tried to help some of the others get out of their cells. We caught her before she did, though, and now she gets to sit here until the Tourney." A harsh smile came over his face.

"If any of you make it to the fourth day, you can request to fight her. She won a few awards in Frigac for her abilities with an owry and would be an honor to fight."

Aabir craned his neck to look over someone's shoulder to see, and his heart nearly dropped into the waves of his roiling stomach. Through the pane of glass, he saw a shivering skeleton of a woman sitting huddled in the back of the small cell. Wounds—some old, some still bleeding—were lashed across her face, her arms, and her legs. She pressed the end of her blood-soaked shirt to her eye. He almost lost his lunch right there when she lowered the wadded end for a moment, and he noticed the gaping hole where her eye should have been.

He jerked his gaze away and pressed a hand to his nauseous stomach. That was obviously a new wound. Had they done it because she tried to escape this evil pit?

Aabir lifted his head as the group's footsteps moved on down the hall. Despite his nausea, he made sure to keep up with them so no one would suspect anything was wrong.

"And if any of you make it to the fifth day, you can ask to fight Sergeant Whare here," Pax pointed to another panel of glass. "He was one of Silvas' best with an ax—before he was captured in the Battle of Trivsau."

Aabir tried not to look—he did not think his stomach could handle it—but morbid curiosity got the better of him and he lifted his eyes to see a tall, muscular man limping a tight circle in the cell. His face was puffy with bruises, and his nose was bent. Wounds like Sergeant Glin's covered his limbs and his shirtless chest.

Another flash of anger went through Aabir, and he let it simmer as Pax continued, pointing out a few more prisoners that they could fight if they made it far enough. Then, he led them back down the hall and into the original corridor.

"So, there you have it, everyone." Pax's smile made Aabir even more nauseous as the planner addressed them, "These are your real enemies in the Tourney—not any other competitor."

His eyes landed on Aabir's face for a moment, and Aabir immediately dipped his head in a nod he hoped looked grateful, before forcing his face into a neutral expression as he lifted it again.

Pax sent him an almost imperceptible nod before continuing, "If any of you want to go back up and practice, you're more than welcome to. However, if you want to continue this tour, then follow me."

Aabir stayed standing where he was as a few people—including Buren—turned and went back towards the prison's entrance, a couple of patrolmen going with them. His stomach swam as he caught the grim satisfaction on some of the other competitor's faces who stayed.

How could they have seen what he just saw, and come out of it with expressions that bordered on triumphant? He squeezed the pommel of his sword in a death grip, wanting nothing more than to wipe those looks from their faces. Thankfully, Pax led them to one of the last doors in the main corridor before he let his emotions get the better of him. The newest hydraulic door hissed open, and Pax stepped to the side.

"This is our discipline room," he said.

The competitors moved into a semi-circle so they all could see. Aabir's heart jumped at the morbid sight beyond the doorway. It reminded him of Norland's correction room, only with more chains to hold more people. Blood splatters coated the walls and floor. He gulped down the contents of his stomach that tried to rise.

"And if you'll follow me, I can show you where we keep the weapons we use for discipline." Pax stepped over to the next door and turned back to face them as the guard typed in its code. "Then the last thing I can show you is the new prison sector they're building to keep all the alliance spies our newest rule will bring in."

Aabir gritted his teeth, horror and fury warring within him. He did not know how much more of this he could take.

His eyes roved over the rest of the hall, and he realized that there were only two hydraulic doors left—the one Pax was standing at, and, Aabir assumed, the one leading to the new prison section. He glanced down at his boots in thought. That meant the mainframe was not on this level, but the one above him, which also meant once this tour was over he would have lost his chance to get there. Unless...

Aabir lifted his wrist and turned his holonode on to check the time. He glanced back up at Pax Ryehouse and, without turning his holonode off, stepped forward to get the man's attention before he could go on a spiel about the weapons found in the room before them.

"Excuse me, sir," he said.

Pax dipped his chin towards him. "Yes, Trainee Sorrel?"

Aabir gestured to his holonode. "I didn't realize how late it was getting," he flicked his wrist to turn the device off, "and I doubt my C.O. would be happy if I spent any more time down here instead of practicing. Could I go on back up, sir?"

He hoped his raging emotions did not spill into his eyes as he stared at Pax squarely. The older man did not even bat an eye as he gave Aabir an understanding smile.

"Of course you can," he replied. "Did you enjoy the tour?"

The pressure in Aabir's chest increased, but he did his best to give the man a grim smile.

"Yes sir," he said. "It was an honor to be here."

Pax gave him an approving nod. "Good. You can go on back up."

With a parting salute, Aabir spun on his heel and walked out of the Constantia prison.

Chapter Forty-Five

To Aabir's dismay, a patrolman followed him back out of the prison's main corridor, through the hall, and into the elevator. The patrolman said nothing as the elevator doors slid closed, leaving Aabir feeling awkward atop all the tension roiling inside him.

He glanced out of the corner of his eye at the statuesque patrolman. Memories of the times he had been questioned by similar officers popped into his head, but he pushed those thoughts aside. He was a trainee fighting in the "honorable" Constantia Tourney—there would be no reason for the man to harass him. Unless he was like Rolav.

Aabir rolled his eyes at the unhelpful thought and, without moving his head, glanced over at the holographic floor-number pad on the wall. He spotted the level button he needed to get to, but he did not know how that would be possible with the guard.

The elevator beeped with each floor they passed, sending his heart rate higher and higher as his mind raced for ideas. Rasiela never gave him any helpful tips for gathering information with someone watching his every move. Oh Deleyon, what could he do...?

As he had the thought, he immediately remembered how he was even able to get to the prisons in the first place—albeit unknowingly. With a deep, quiet breath to steady himself, he turned his face towards the guard.

"So, what's it like to be an officer here?" He asked.

Because when in doubt: talk.

The patrolman shrugged and gave him an almost bored look. "Not bad," he said, "but it can get boring. Although, I will say, that prison tour was quite entertaining. I've been stationed here around this time for the past five years, and this was the first time I saw it."

Aabir tried to deflect his anger at the comment with another question, "Five years? And you've never seen it?"

"Yeah. I was always stationed somewhere else when they did tours."

"Guess I was lucky, then, huh?"

"In more ways than one, trainee." The patrolman relaxed his stance a little. "I've heard it's even harder for third-level competitors to get into the Tourney than it is for any of the others, and yet you did it." Their eyes met, and the weight upon Aabir's chest grew heavier. "You've gained quite an honor for one so young, so don't try and spoil it for yourself by false visions of grandeur. That's the problem I've seen most third-levels have: they expect too much out of themselves and let their pride get in the way, then they lose and never try to compete again.

"So, if you lose, you lose. Don't beat yourself up and keep practicing. There's always next year, and if you've been in the Tourney once before, it's easier to get in again."

That was the opposite of Aabir's problem, but something about the officer's words still gave him a strange feeling. He pushed it aside, however, as the doors opened, and he sent another glance down to the floor-level screen right in front of him. Swallowing down his pride, he turned his head and looked back over at the officer.

"Thanks for the advice," he said with a nod right as he stepped forward.

His armor clanked as he stumbled into the wall—and the holographic screen. He put his hand out to steady himself and pressed the button he needed in the same movement.

"Are you all right?" The patrolman asked as the doors closed.

Aabir nodded, his heart beating wildly inside his chest. "Yeah." He glared at the closed doors and hoped it looked authentic enough. "Sorry. That was stupid."

"It's fine." The guard stepped over to him as the elevator began to go back down. "I can override it and get us back up there so you don't miss any more practice."

"Thanks." Aabir took a step back with a shake of his head, and the guard took his place by the screen.

A rush of adrenaline buzzed through him as he stared at the guard's half-turned back. "Wait," he said and glanced around at their small surroundings, putting one hand on the wall and the other on the pommel of his sword. "Did you feel something?"

The patrolman stopped pushing the buttons and straightened. He sent Aabir a questioning look. "No..."

"Oh. I thought I felt it shaking."

"Hmm." The man frowned slightly but turned back to the screen. "Well, when we get off, I can call a repairman to come and—"

Before he could finish, Aabir unsheathed his sword and hit him on the side of the head with its pommel. The guard crumpled to the ground, and Aabir sheathed his sword. He reached over and swiped away the new window on the screen, then again tapped the button to the level he needed to go to.

Oh Deleyon, oh Deleyon, oh Deleyon... Never had his heart raced so much in such a short span of time as he moved the patrolman's unconscious form into a position that, Aabir hoped, made it look like he had rammed his head on the wall and blacked out. The elevator's beeps seemed much slower this time around as he stood and waited for it to lower through all the different levels.

"Come on, come on, come on..." he said through gritted teeth, tapping the pommel of his sword nervously.

He glanced back down at the patrolman, still out cold. Hopefully he would be for as long as Aabir had been when Tetra whacked him on the side of the head.

And, please Deleyon, he silently prayed, *make him believe there really was something wrong with the elevator.*

Finally, the feeling of the elevator's movement died, and the doors slid open with a resounding beep. Aabir took in a furtive glance of the empty hall and ran forward. The doors closed behind him with a foreboding sense of finality, but he pressed on—his heart hammering against his rib cage despite the invisible weight that remained there.

A single door lay ahead at the end of the hall, and Aabir slowed as he reached it. He sent another glance around, half-expecting guards to materialize out of thin air to take him to the prisons right below his feet, but none did. A new worry entered his head at the suspicious lack of them. Maybe the mainframe was on another level.

He grimaced at the thought and turned his neck to glance behind him at the elevator. There had been at least forty numbered buttons on the elevator's screen, and he did not have the time, or enough excuses, to go through all of them.

Mumbling more prayers under his breath, he turned his attention to the locked door. His hope slowly wilted at the old-fashioned barcode scanner he saw on the metal wall to its right. Now he knew why no one felt the need to waste any manpower guarding this door: you needed an actual, physical card to open it instead of a code.

Despite these new doubts, he turned his holonode on and called Rasiela like she had told him to do. Her face appeared only a moment later on the screen.

"Are you there?" She asked.

"Yeah," he turned his holonode's camera to the scanner, "but I can't get in."

"Oh. Well, that's unexpected..."

Aabir's hope snuffed out with a hunch of his shoulders. "We can't get in, can we?"

"I didn't say that." Rasiela turned her face away from his screen, the clicking of a holographic keyboard following only a moment later. "Let me try and get you something to help, but if this doesn't work then we'll have to wait until I can get you a card."

Aabir clenched his jaw as the prisoners came to his mind. "We need to do it today," his voice came out harsher than he meant it to, but he made no apology for it.

Rasiela raised her brow, but only made a noise in her throat before turning back to whatever else she was looking at. In the moments that passed, Aabir continuously turned his gaze in the direction of the elevator doors. A knot tightened his stomach as his imagination supplied him with images of those doors opening and guards bursting in to take him down to the prison level.

Oh Deleyon, please, please, please don't let anyone come in.

"Alright, try this." He leapt in his skin at the suddenness of Rasiela's voice and jerked his neck back in the direction of his holonode's screen.

The device buzzed with a new message, and he tapped it, sending Rasiela's face away. It was a picture of a barcode, with little numbers right below it.

"Turn your holonode's density up all the way to make it look as opaque as possible," Rasiela ordered him. "If that doesn't work, then I need you to leave immediately and go back to your normal schedule. I'll erase any footage of your whereabouts, and we can finish this another time."

"Fine."

The thought of failure sent a hard stone splashing into Aabir's stomach, but he did as she said and turned the density of his holonode's screen up. Its usual semi-translucency looked like it was hardening in the air above his wrist. He switched back to the picture Rasiela sent him and noticed the battery icon slowly dwindling away at the added power.

His heart skipped another worried beat as he flipped the holonode screen around and set it in front of the old scanner. *Please let this work...*

A green light blinked on it, and the door in front of him slid open. Aabir immediately turned his holonode's density back down to save its battery power.

"Did it work?" Rasiela asked as he went back to the holocall screen.

He sent her a nod and stepped through the doorway. "It did."

"Thank Deleyon," she whispered, then her voice returned to its normal pitch, "Turn the screen around so I can see what we're up against."

He did as she commanded, his eyes roving over the sight before them. The only thing in the small room was a metal table with a holoputer projector sitting atop it. He stepped over to it, his heavy footsteps bouncing along the claustrophobic walls.

"Get the CP chip and stick it in the projector," Rasiela said.

Keeping his arm with the holonode up, Aabir bent down and unlaced his boot, then pulled the CP chip from it. Clutching it in his shaking hand, he straightened back up and found the single port on the holoputer's round projector, put the CP chip in it, and then turned the projector on. A wide holoscreen flickered into existence, a single password line in the middle of it.

"Thank you, Aabir." Rasiela nodded once and turned back to the holoscreen he assumed she was using. "I'll take it from here."

He breathed a sigh of relief and watched the holoscreen in front of him. It flickered, and he blinked in surprise as a new window appeared in the top corner.

"Is that you?" He asked.

"Yes." Rasiela's face was set in concentration. "Now hush."

Aabir jerked his head back at the sharp order but did as she said. He turned his gaze back to the wide screen and watched as coded numbers and letters began to fill the new window, then a single dot appeared on the password line. A few minutes went by—wherein he spent some of it tying his boot's laces back up—and the password finally appeared.

"Yes!" He shut his mouth and spun around as the word echoed in the room.

"Aabir!" Rasiela hissed and sent him a glare that he could feel even through the screen.

"Sorry."

She gave him another hard look before returning to her own holoscreen. "This shouldn't take me long, but I need you to be quiet."

A moment later, the elevator made a strange noise. Aabir's heart leapt into his throat, and he spun around towards the open entryway. Fear and adrenaline pumped through his veins as he grabbed the hilt of his sword.

"What was that?" He whispered without taking his eyes off the doors.

"That was me," Rasiela replied in a calm tone. "I shut it down so no one will be able to use it until I finish."

"You can do that?"

"I can now."

Then that should help his excuse of getting trapped in a shaking elevator. With that pleasing thought, he took a few deep breaths to calm his racing heart as he turned his attention back towards the screen.

He did not know how long he stood there watching Rasiela do her work—he could not keep up with all the different screens, passwords, and codes that flew across the screen—but she finally pulled up a document that lit the hope inside Aabir once again. It was a detailed, three-dimensional map of the Constantia prisons. He almost said something in his rising excitement, but instead sent a quiet "thank you" up to Deleyon instead.

After a few moments, the map disappeared, and the document page came back up again.

"I have the map, Aabir." Rasiela looked back at him and sent him a small, knowing smile. "However, if you'll give me another couple of minutes, I want to see if I can get anything else that might help—"

Aabir spun around, hand on his sword hilt, as the elevator made a strange groaning noise again.

"That was you, right?" His voice cracked at the last syllable, and he cleared his throat.

"Get the CP chip and hide!" Rasiela snapped.

The door shut behind him, closing him in. Aabir spun back around, turned the holoputer off as he grabbed the CP chip, and pulled his sword from its sheath. His gaze flicked around the empty room. "There is nowhere to hide!" He hissed in panic.

Despite her calm features, Aabir could see the worry in the spy's gaze. "Then you'll have to knock them out like you did that patrolman in the elevator."

"You saw that?" He rushed into the corner as the elevator's chipper ding echoed ominously in the long hall.

"I already had access to the stadium's basic security footage," Rasiela replied, "but I'm going to let you go, Aabir. I can't blow my cover now. Deleyon be with you."

"Wait—!"

The holocall ended, and he flicked his wrist as he heard the elevator doors open. Blood pounded in his ears in step with the footfalls coming towards the small room. He tried to keep his breathing quiet as they came to a stop outside the door.

Seconds passed, though they felt like minutes to Aabir, before the door slid open and an armored patrolman stepped through.

He held his breath as the man moved towards the desk in the dim light without turning to look at his surroundings. He squeezed the leather hilt of his sword tightly and watched the man stop at the desk then turn the holoscreen on. At least he did not seem to be the most observant...

Instead of typing in the password like Aabir thought he would, the patrolman also placed a CP chip into the projector. A few moments passed, then he tapped the button on the projector's side and the holographic keyboard appeared on the desk before him.

Aabir narrowed his eyes as a small window of code, similar to Rasiela's, popped into the holoputer's corner. Suspicion wormed its way into the fear clouding his mind. What was going on?

He loosened the grip on his sword as the man did a similar thing like Rasiela had to get the mainframe's password. Once in, he also began to go through the pages of files and other password screens.

As this unfolded before Aabir, realization began to form in the back of his mind, and it brought up almost every conspiracy theory and news article he had researched for Rasiela regarding the "Silvanian Fire Attacks".

Oh Deleyon. His eyes widened as fear gripped his pounding heart. Could this be someone in the secret pyromaniac group?

He glanced between the back of the man's shaved head, and the CP chip stuck in the port. If his speculation was true, then he needed to do something—and he needed to do it now.

Without letting his thoughts take over his actions, he sprang forward. The guy spun around right as Aabir hit him on the side of the head, his eyes rolling back before he crumpled to the floor in much the same way as the real patrolman had. Aabir stepped over his body, grabbed the newest copein chip, jammed both in his boot, turned the holoscreen off, and rushed out of the room.

He tapped the scanner on the door, and it closed with a beep. He then ran down the hall and frantically tapped the elevator's button. His muscles shook with adrenaline as he cast a frantic glance back at the closed door behind him.

The elevator's ding caused his heart to jump, but he welcomed the security of the small elevator as he stepped inside and tapped the button to get to the main level. Only when the doors closed did he relax, and that was when he noticed the real patrolman he knocked out was no longer in there. His eyes widened. Oh Deleyon, he hoped that did not mean they were looking for him...

As the elevator continued its ascent, Aabir paced as he tried to think up a good excuse that would work with his breaking-down-elevator one. As the elevator came to a stop, he realized he still had his sword unsheathed and immediately put it back in its scabbard.

The doors opened, and he was greeted with the sight of a group of patrolmen surrounding the unconscious one.

"You!" One of them hollered and rushed towards him.

Aabir moved out of the elevator to meet him. "Thank the gods you found him!" He hoped the panic he still felt shown fully on his face as he spoke, "The—the elevator just stopped! And when it did, it—it shook! He—his head slammed against the wall and I—I couldn't do anything to wake him up. But I hit the emergency button and the doors opened, so I tried to find someone to help on that floor, but—but then there was another guardsman on that floor who looked like he was knocked out."

He took a gasping breath before finishing, "I checked to make sure he was still alive, and then ran back to the elevator." He gestured towards the unconscious patrolman, "I noticed he was gone and hoped that meant someone had found him."

The officer who had yelled at him put his hand on his shoulder and said, "Take it easy there, trainee." He looked Aabir in the eyes. "Can you remember what level the other unconscious officer is on? And did you notice anyone else there?"

Aabir shook his head. "I didn't see anyone." He paused, wondering how much he should indulge. He did not think the mysterious guardsman had seen him, so if they did catch the man and he tried to tell them what had happened, Aabir doubted he would be able to give away who knocked him out. "And all I know is that it was a short hallway with a single holoputer room at the end of it."

The officer nodded sharply, then turned his head towards one of the others around them. "Make sure that elevator is still operational, then send a team down to the sixth floor."

One of the other patrolmen nodded with a "yes sir", then pulled up his holonode and began rounding up some of the others around them as well.

Aabir watched them enter the elevator, silently praying that the man had not actually seen his face. Once the elevator door closed behind them, he turned his attention back towards the main patrolman as he asked Aabir, "We wondered what had happened when the elevator locked up, but how did you and Officer Trail end up in it at the same time in the first place?"

"I had to end the tour of the prisons so I could have more time to practice, and Tourney Planner Ryehouse sent him to take me back up here." Aabir turned his gaze to Officer Trail's body. "Is he going to be OK?" He had wondered how much damage his hit might have caused.

"He's going to be fine." The patrolman paused. "The question now is: are you OK?"

"Yes sir." Aabir sent him a firm nod, his breathing coming back to normal as his heart beat calmed. "Just shocked is all."

Shocked that he and Rasiela had been able to get the map without getting caught, and that he now had a new CP chip that might belong to a secret group of pyromaniacs.

The patrolman nodded and patted his shoulder. "Then if nothing is wrong, why don't you go back to the arena with some of the others? Those on the prison tour aren't back yet, but they should be soon."

"Yes sir." Aabir sent him another nod before turning and heading in the direction of the arena.

As he walked, his adrenaline began to wane; leaving him as tired as if he had done a full period of training. But he had been successful. He glanced down at his wrist, wishing he could call Rasiela back to tell her what he had taken, but it would have to wait.

Despite his fatigue overtaking his muscles, he had not felt so light in a long time. The arena's wide entryway came up ahead of him, but not even its dooming presence could ruin his mood.

The map of the prison was theirs! Now there was a chance of those prisoners being set free.

As Aabir stepped back into the arena, he erased any emotions from his face and headed back towards the smaller group of practicing competitors. All he had to do now was get that CP chip to Rasiela, then she—and Chief Baene—would be able to take care of it.

Aabir spotted Buren and headed in his platoonmate's direction. The thought of practicing for the Constantia Tourney did not seem as horrible anymore. Even if he made it to the end of the second day like Lieutenant Denir wanted, if the prisoners were free then there was no point in worrying over having to face the decision of either killing them or letting them wound him so badly he would have to be honorably disqualified.

The weight upon his chest lightened at the thought, and he picked up his pace. He could finally practice without it feeling like a death-sentence.

Chapter Forty-Six

After Tetra's crying episode, she and Felicita had gone through the rest of the paper photographs in the gilded box—with Felicita explaining what she knew about each of them. Hours flew by, and right after her sister left, Tetra immediately fell asleep without another thought of what might lay ahead of her.

However, those thoughts did come when she woke up the next day. As she got out of bed and went through the normal rhythms of getting ready for the day, her mind sent her on a twisting, emotional amusement park ride that was not very amusing.

She glanced over at the gilded box sitting on her desk as she got dressed. The annoying prick of tears pounded the beginnings of a headache through her skull. She sniffed and blinked back the blurriness taking over her vision.

So, it really wasn't a dream. Felicita really was her cousin—her sister. Prince Joash Ignis was her uncle, and Emperor Ignis...

Tetra clenched her jaw and pressed the tips of her fingers against her closed eyelids as another dark wind of loneliness sent an ache through her bones. She couldn't stifle the sobs that shook her shoulders, nor the tears that leaked from her closed eyes.

All those years...and he had never told her. He had never claimed her as his own daughter...

She clenched her hands into fists as the fires of her anger burned within the deep, hollow hole of her soul. Ten years he had lied to her; ten long years of loneliness and almost never feeling like she was wanted—and yet he could have told her and it might have changed things.

Another sob escaped her lips, dousing some of the angry flames licking the inside of her soul.

No, she didn't agree with many of the things he had done—and had shown her disagreement bluntly—but had he hated her so much that he couldn't even bother to tell her even if it might have changed her attitude? Not that she wanted to be like the rest of Igrium's brainwashed masses, but she only wanted to know who she came from. Was it too much to ask for her to at least know the identity of her real father?

She stepped over into the bathroom to get a tissue, and her eyes trailed over to the mirror as she blew her nose. They immediately landed on the splotchy birthmark on her neck, the same kind as her matha's...

As if having the emperor of Igrium as her father wasn't bad enough, but having a matha who could have stepped out of a fairy tale was almost harder to deal with. She had never been one for fantasy stories, but even with her limited knowledge of them it still came as an impossible shock. It was like saying her matha had been a fairy or a flying lizard. The only thing keeping her from believing the paper photos were edited was the fact she herself could turn into a peryton, just like her shifter matha could turn into a small, green corafish—as Felicita and a couple of the photos told.

A soft knock on the door jerked her from that hovertrain of thought. She quickly wiped her face of her emotional breakdown and rushed out of the bathroom. She opened the door to her room and was surprised to find Felicita's smiling countenance on the other side.

Before she could open her mouth to say anything, Felicita said, "Chief Baene contacted the Buleutcil and had them cancel everythin' on your schedule today, so I made plans." She gestured with a wave of her hand. "He gave them an excuse about it involvin' some recent developments he would explain later, and they relented."

Despite Felicita's excited countenance, her accented words sent a worrying churn through Tetra's stomach.

"What does that mean?" She asked, even though she already had a feeling she knew.

Felicita's smile lessened, and she sent a quick glance to the guards on either side of the doorway before stepping past Tetra into the room. Tetra narrowed her eyes and shut the door behind her as their gazes met.

"Well, Chief Baene already knew your true identity," Felicita fooled with the ends of one of her braids, "and we had ta tell Lord Jachen and Lord Othnel my suspicions so tha' we could get the proof o' your DNA and your real birth certificate, so they know as well..."

Tetra's eyes widened. "They do?"

She had already figured out that Chief Baene knew, but the fact that the Steward of Silvas and the kingdom's Head Archivist (whatever that meant) also did tightened her throat.

"Yeah," Felicita lowered her gaze. "I'm sorry, Tetra, but we had to."

She folded her arms and gave her newfound cousin a hard stare. "But why should the rest of the Buleutcil know?"

"Because havin' the child o' Emperor Ignis here in Silvas is a big enough deal ta warrant them knowin' who she is."

So, it was the answer she knew but didn't want to hear.

"No." She shook her head frantically, her stomach doing a barrel-roll. "No, no, no, no. Felicita, you—you can't tell them! I'm already despised as a Cairn here. Can you imagine what they'll think if they hear that I'm an Ignis? And not only that, but the daughter of their greatest enemy?"

"I know, Tetra," Felicita gave her an understanding look. "Trust me, I know. Matha and I changed our family name when we first came here—even if we were related ta the one Ignis sibling who stood against the war... However, now...now I wish we had never done it."

"Why not?"

"Because when you hide somethin' like tha' for so long, it can only explode in your face when the truth is revealed."

Tetra could see the wisdom in her words, but the thought of the entire Buleutcil knowing this made her uneasy. She rubbed her thumb across her segione scars and lowered her gaze to Felicita's flowy, blue dress.

"When will they be told?" She asked.

"Not until Chief Baene figures out the best course o' action ta take."

"And what does that mean?" She had been able to tell by the calculating look in the chief advisor's eyes during their first meeting that he already had plans of some sort for her, and though she didn't know if he knew the truth then, she now got the strangest feeling this new plan of his wasn't going to be something she would like.

Felicita lifted her hand and touched Tetra's scarred forearm. Tetra jerked her head up at the touch but didn't move away.

"I wish I could tell you," her gaze sincere as she spoke, "but as his assistant I can't break my confidence with him. He'll tell you eventually. But for now, you mustn't worry about it."

She wanted to argue that if they were plans involving her, she should be able to know them now. Instead, she only shook her head with a sigh of frustration and said, "Fine."

"Thank you." Felicita squeezed her arm for a moment before letting go. "I don't want ta break your trust, Tetra, but I also can't break his, either. You don't 'ave ta worry about any o' his plans bein' evil, though. He only wants ta see this war end in as peaceful a way as is possible."

Tetra nodded slowly, unable to contain a frown from twisting her lips to the side. "Then...what plans did you have for today?"

Despite her own dreary tone, Felicita's next words came out in an excitable lilt, "Chief Baene has given us permission ta leave the Altelo so you can meet our family."

Their family? Her heart began to thump an excited beat despite the worry still lurking in the corners of her mind. "Our—*our* family?"

"Yes!" Felicita nodded, her smile returning. "Matha cannot wait ta see you."

Tetra's jaw slackened. Her matha? Her Aunt Minda?

Immediately, her mind recalled a few of her childhood memories of the woman who had raised her as her own. Warmth filled her chest at their prompting, and a small smile escaped her lips.

She half-turned back towards the bathroom and replied, "Let me finish getting ready, and we can go."

Felicita's smile widened even more. "O' course."

Tetra sent her a nod and walked back into the small room, then proceeded to stare at her wide-eyed reflection in the mirror for a few shocked moments.

She was going to see her Aunt Minda, *and* the rest of her family she apparently had here in Silvas. A thrill went through her at the thought, pushing all her earlier worries back for the time being. She quickly finished getting ready and joined Felicita back in her room.

"Ready?" Felicita asked.

Tetra gave her a firm nod that looked far more stoic than her warm, twisting insides were feeling. "Let's go."

Her cousin sent her another wide smile as they both walked out of the room.

THE GLASS ELEVATOR DINGED, and Felicita led Tetra—as well as Sir Whest and the other, female guardsman who were both obligated to come—off into a round room that surrounded the cylindrical elevator. Two numbered doors stood on opposing sides of the room, and Felicita walked over to one of them.

"Sir Whest, Madame Quen—" Felicita turned and addressed Tetra's guards, "—if you would both be so kind as ta wait out here, tha' would be appreciated."

Both guardsmen shared a look with each other, then bowed their heads with salutes towards Felicita.

"That will be fine, My Lady," Sir Whest replied.

Felicita sent Tetra a nervous smile before turning back and opening the door. "Come on in, then, Tetra."

Tetra inhaled a deep breath that did nothing to calm her racing heart before following her cousin through the open doorway. Her eyes widened as she glanced around at the huge apartment. Natural light flooded the open space from a curved wall of windows ahead of her. A high-end kitchen took up the space on her right, and a long dining room table took up part of the space to her left. Ahead of them sat a white couch overlooking the window's leaf-filled view, and a couple matching chairs opposite it.

She locked eyes with the older woman who stood from one of these chairs.

"Anora..." The woman's gasp rang with the familiar Pon-Yelish accent Tetra had only heard in her memories.

She took a tentative step forward. "Aunt Minda?"

The woman burst into tears and ran towards her, arms outstretched. Tetra's eyes watered as she took a few more tentative steps forward and met the woman's embrace. Her heart thumped a happy beat as her aunt's arms squeezed her, and the warmth in her chest grew to fill the rest of her.

"Oh, I'm so happy ta see you!" Aunt Minda whispered close to her ear. "I never thought I would get to again."

"I'm glad to be here, too." She couldn't stop her tears from escaping.

Aunt Minda's hold lessened, and she moved to look Tetra in the face. A worm of dread defied the joyful feeling of the moment as an angry glint hardened her aunt's soft features—which looked almost the same as Felicita's. Out of the corner of her eye, she noticed Aunt Minda's hand moving towards her face, then flinched as her aunt's fingers sent a slight sting through her still tender malscar wound. Her aunt immediately removed her hand with her own wince.

"I'm sorry, Anora," she said. "I...who did tha' ta you? Did your patre authorize it?"

"My commanding officer." Tetra lowered her head, heat flushing into her face. "And I don't know if he did or not, but I guess I always had it coming."

Aunt Minda blew out a sharp breath, her hold on Tetra's shoulders tightening. "If I had him here, I'd give him a piece o' my mind! No one should 'ave been allowed ta hurt *my* Anora like that." Her nostrils flared, and Tetra found herself being squeezed in another tight hug. "Oh, I am so, so sorry we didn't take you with us. Can you ever forgive us, Anora?"

"I already have," Tetra replied. "Felicita told me what happened and why you couldn't get me. I'm just...I'm just glad to be here now."

"As am I."

After a few moments, Aunt Minda finally let go again. "Well, how about you come sit down?" She kept one hand on Tetra's arm and gestured with the other towards the living area. "I want ta hear about everythin' tha' has happened ta you."

"Uh..." She wanted to hear *everything*? Tetra herself didn't want to recount all of that.

"Matha—" Felicita stepped up next to Tetra and put her hand on Aunt Minda's shoulder, sending the older woman a pointed look, "—there will be time for tha' later."

Aunt Minda sent her own sharp look, but then her eyes flicked back over towards Tetra. Her trepidation must've shown in her gaze because her aunt's features softened with understanding. "O' course."

Felicita nodded then turned her head and sent Tetra a reassuring smile. "There are still two people here I want you ta meet."

Tetra's racing heart slowed with relief, and she gave a nod of assent. With Felicita on one side and Aunt Minda on the other, she was led over to the couch where, she now realized with a jolt, two people in dark green, Silvanian military uniforms stood watching them. The skin on Tetra's face and tallied arm tingled as her gaze flicked between them before resting on the towering man's familiar face. Except for his wide-set eyes, he looked almost exactly like the pictures she had seen of the retired Silvanian Army General Alistrade Eyrie, only younger.

Felicita had mentioned last night that she was married to one of the retired general's sons; which had finally given Tetra the answer as to how she was connected to that family. However, amidst all the other information she had been given, it hadn't truly clicked in her mind until now.

"Tetra," Felicita's bright smile came out in her voice as they stepped around the couch and faced the two people, "this is my husband, Matias."

"Hello, Tetra." Matias dipped his chin towards her, nearly a smile coming over his squarish features. "Felicita has told me much about you."

Tetra nodded towards him, unsure of what to say in his intimidating presence. "Uh...hi."

A real, but small, smile lifted the corner of his lips. "But you don't have to worry—she's only told me good things."

"O' course I have," Felicita replied, then she gestured to the no-less intimidating woman standing beside Matias, "And this is his sister, Galia."

"I'm happy to finally be able to make your acquaintance, Tetra." Galia nodded towards her. "Like Matias said, I've heard a lot about you, and I'm glad we got the chance to do this before tomorrow."

"Thank you," Tetra dipped her chin towards her, despite the confusion her words brought, "but—uh, forgive me—I don't know what you're talking about..."

Galia's dark violet eyes softened a little in understanding, and she gave Tetra a small, reassuring smile. "Let's sit, and then I'll explain."

More questions pushed themselves into her already-flooded mind as she seated herself on the white couch. Felicita sat in the middle beside her, with Matias at the end next to her. Galia sat in one of the seats in front of them, while Aunt Minda stayed standing.

"I'll make us some tea while you do tha'," she said with a nod and headed towards the kitchen.

Tetra's eyes followed her bustling movements for a moment before she turned her neck and locked them on Galia's.

"The main reason I'm here, Tetra, is because I was one of the few people who Felicita—accidentally—confided your true identity to." She clasped her hands atop her lap, her eyes never straying from Tetra's. "I know you are Joash Ignis' daughter, and that you have the ability to turn into a peryton."

Tetra's heart skipped a beat. She sent a questioning glance in Felicita's direction. Her cousin only gave her another reassuring smile before she turned her face back towards Galia.

"So when you accepted Army General Taoghn's proposition yesterday, he contacted me and asked if I would be willing to head up Silvas' new war-peryton program since I'm one of the few qualified people who know the truth about it," Galia continued, "and I accepted the position."

She paused, and it was enough time for the words to sink into Tetra.

Her eyes widened and she asked, "So, you're my new commanding officer?"

"I will be, yes."

She didn't know how to react to that. She just stared in shock at the woman before her. Her mind brought up unwanted images of Lieutenant Tarson, and she couldn't help the shiver that went through her and caused chill bumps to raise along her arms.

She had known, and considered beforehand, that when she joined Silvas' army that she would have a new C.O., and that was fine with her. She knew she would need one, of course; but now that the reality of her decision was sitting right in front of her, a small seed of fear burrowed itself inside her mind.

Somewhere behind her in the kitchen, a tea kettle began to whistle.

"However," Galia's voice rose above the high-pitched whistling, "since you only recently found out about your past, Chief Baene and I have agreed that if you want to forego joining our military, you can." Instead of judgment, Tetra only saw the same understanding in the woman's expression. "Now that you know your father was the emperor's brother, I can understand if you would rather use your peryton ability doing something else—not that I'm saying you're an Igrian-loyalist, but I can see where this knowledge might cause some issues in the future."

Tetra blinked in surprise. She could do that? She knew she had made the decision a bit hastily, but she had been so mad at Emperor Ignis and wanted nothing more than to bring him what he deserved... Yet now that she knew he was her father, did that change anything?

As she pondered that thought, she recalled the way Galia had just referred to her as Joash Ignis' daughter. She sent a strange glance in Felicita's direction, and her cousin met it with a pointed look she tried to hide from Galia's direction behind a cough.

Tetra stared at her for another long moment, trying to figure out what she was missing. Then it hit her, and she turned to meet Galia's eyes.

"I thank you both for the offer, but knowing this doesn't change the fact that Emperor Ignis has done so many awful things and must be stopped. I can help with that—I want to do it. If my ability can't be duplicated, then at least the Alliance will have one more peryton fighting for them than Igrium will."

She lowered her gaze to her clasped hands. "And it's not like I'll be dishonoring our family name any more than what I already have by doing so. I'm already a coward there, and that's not much worse than being a traitor."

Emperor Ignis had called her a disgrace the last time she saw him, so she was only fulfilling what he already thought of her. Her anger flared, sending hot tears to her eyes, but she blinked them back before anyone could see them.

Galia stood, and Tetra lifted her head to see her approving nod. "Then I will go on and refer your answer to Chief Baene," she said. "I have a meeting with Army General Taoghn in a little while, and I don't want to intrude on your time any longer."

"Can you not stay for some tea?" Tetra looked over her shoulder and noticed Aunt Minda setting different dishes on a tray.

"No, Miss Minda," Galia replied with a smile, "but I thank you for the offer."

Beside Tetra, Felicita stood from the couch and stepped over to Galia. "Thank you for comin'." They embraced, then let go a moment later. "I'll see if I can meet you on Seventhdein, alright?"

"That works for me." Her eyes turned back towards Tetra as she added, "I will see you tomorrow, Tetra."

Tetra bowed her head towards her. "Thank you for telling me."

"Of course."

With one final nod, Galia turned and walked out of the apartment. Felicita spun on her heel and opened her mouth to say something, but Tetra beat her to it with her own question, "Does she know the full truth?"

Felicita's mouth opened and closed a couple times before she shook her head. "No, she doesn't." Something akin to guilt shadowed her features as she fooled with the end of one of her braids. "She knows we're both cousins, but she doesn't know you're Emperor Ignis' daughter. I wanted ta tell her the full truth, but I...I felt it safer if she thought you were only Joash's adopted daughter."

Before Tetra could ask what she meant by that, she changed the subject, "So you do still want ta fight?"

Though she wanted to know more about her cousin's answer, she remembered what she had said about "not breaking Chief Baene's confidence" earlier and didn't want to fight her on the matter, so she replied, "Yes. Like I said, I can't stand by and do nothing while more and more people are hurt or killed because of...because of *his* tyrannical nature. And now that I know how I turn into a peryton, I doubt Dr. Prin and her team will be able to duplicate the ability, so there's no point in using that as an excuse—not that I'd want to, anyway."

Felicita twisted her lips to the side with a nod.

"I agree with you." Tetra jerked her neck and looked over at Matias. He sent her a nod of approval, his neutral expression unchanged, "And I think your decision is a highly honorable one."

She lowered her gaze and grabbed her tallied arm with her hand. "Um—thank you."

"I'm not saying it isn't tha'," Felicita interjected, "I'm only...worried, is all." Tetra lifted her head and noticed the sincerity on her sister's features, "I...I don't want ta lose you when we just found you again."

"She will be fine, Felicita." She glanced back over at Matias as he spoke, "Army General Taoghn will not risk losing our first—and only—war-peryton by putting her into impossible situations there would be no chance of her escaping."

Felicita folded her arms but didn't reply as Aunt Minda came over with the tea tray and set it down on the short table in the middle of the living area.

"We both feel the same," her aunt straightened and gave Tetra a knowing look, "but I believe your uncle would be proud o' your decision, and as long as what Matias said is true—" she sent him a side-eye glance, "—than I guess I'll not try ta persuade you otherwise."

Tetra couldn't help a small smile from escaping. "Thank you."

There was a quiet pause as Aunt Minda poured steaming tea into the four teacups placed on the tray. The first cup and saucer she handed to Tetra, who took it tentatively. She glanced down at the rose-colored liquid as she lifted the cup closer. Steam wafted into her face, carrying a sweet, herbal scent with it. She couldn't remember drinking tea before and didn't know what to expect.

"If you don't like it, you don't 'ave ta drink it." She glanced up at Aunt Minda's knowing grin.

"What is it?" She asked.

"I'tis a greenberry and rose tea."

Well, she did like greenberries... She took a small sip and was greeted with the sweetness of greenberries and a floral aftertaste. She took another sip. It wasn't the best...but it wasn't bad, either.

"Do you like it?" Aunt Minda asked.

Tetra swallowed the hot tea with a nod. "I think so."

Aunt Minda beamed as she handed Felicita and Matias their own cups. Felicita thanked her matha and sat back down on the couch next to Tetra.

"I don't want you ta think tha' I despise your decision, Tetra," she said, "I'm only speaking from my worry for you."

"You don't have to be worried, Felicita." Tetra put her cup down on its saucer and looked her cousin in the eye. "I'll be fine."

Felicita's lips pressed into a thin line, but she sent her a nod. Tetra raised her teacup back to her lips and took another sip as Aunt Minda sat down on the chair where Galia had been sitting.

"I don't think you've ever been this worried about *me* before," Matias said.

Tetra almost choked on her tea but was able to swallow it as she sent a surprised look towards him. Despite his intimidating, still neutral, expression, it only magnified the light of amusement shining in his eyes.

Felicita also turned her head in his direction. And even though Tetra couldn't see her face, she could hear the glare in her sister's voice, "*You* 'ave never been the only peryton on the battlefield tha' every Igrian arbalist will be aimin' at."

Matias shrugged as a small grin escaped the corners of his lips. "Even so..."

Felicita huffed and raised her teacup. "You're impossible." She rolled her eyes, but even as she took a sip from the cup, Tetra could see the smile her sister was trying to hide.

Matias shrugged again and lifted his own cup to his lips.

"How long have you been married?" Tetra put her cup and saucer on the table and sent them a questioning look.

"Almost a year." Felicita replied, her smile now evident as she lowered her cup.

"And how did you meet?"

"Middle school," Matias said.

Tetra blinked in surprise. "Really?"

"Yeah..." Felicita nodded and leaned back on the couch, a distant look glazing her eyes, "I think the first time we ever saw each other, he ran into me in the hall and said I had a weird accent."

Tetra glanced over at Matias. He shrugged again as he took another sip of tea. "It's true," he said.

"But then—I think it was a few days after tha', actually—a few girls were picking on me in the hall when he came up behind us and hollered very loudly." Felicita shook her head slowly, but there was a smile in her voice as she spoke, "It nearly gave me a heart attack, but it also scared them away—which was fine with me. Then he ended up runnin' off before I could say anythin' ta him."

Tetra sent another glance in his direction, trying to picture the stoic, militaristic man before her as a middle school boy. He locked eyes with her and added, "That's also true—but I had no idea they were making fun of her. I was only trying to annoy them."

"And I only ever saw him in certain instances like tha' until I became friends with Lady Vierra Tamir, and then Galia—who was her friend, too," Felicita said. "Once I became closer with her, I realized tha' the weird boy who I had crossed paths with at school was actually her brother, and that's when we started ta get ta know each other and became friends. Then after I graduated from Duschel, we decided ta get married—and here we are now."

"Huh." Tetra tried to imagine what it would be like to marry one of the boys she went to Norland with, but the thought was so absurd she had to stop herself from scoffing aloud.

"Did you have any friends at Norland, Tetra?" Aunt Minda asked.

"Well, I was friends with the janitor, although that's because she was Silvanian and was the only person who would talk to me." A picture of Aabir popped into Tetra's head, and she lowered her gaze to her clasped hands. "And I had another for a couple years who was actually a trainee—his name was Aabir—and his parents were descended from Silvas, too. But then I...I messed up and dragged him into one of my failed escape attempts. So, he stopped talking to me after that." She shrugged. "Which I guess I deserved."

A light weight landed on Tetra's arm, and she lifted her head to see Felicita's hard look. "You didn't deserve tha', Tetra, so don't let his actions dictate how you think o' yourself."

Though it was difficult, Tetra finally peeled her eyes away from Felicita's. She folded her arms and kept her gaze on the short table as she replied, "Well...thanks."

A pause ended her words, but then Aunt Minda broke it with another question Tetra was more than happy to turn her focus on. "Did you always stay at Norland?"

She shook her head. "No ma'am. Since Emperor Ignis was my legal guardian," she curled her hands into fists, "he had me travel during most of my school breaks to the nations under Igrium."

Aunt Minda nodded thoughtfully. "Is there a place you want ta visit again?" She smiled dreamily. "I 'ave always wanted ta go back to Paleya. Your uncle and I went there for one o' our anniversaries, and I loved tourin' all the ruins they 'ave there. Plus, the food was amazin'."

Images of the crumbling pyramids amidst the flowering birch forests popped into Tetra's thoughts. "I've been there a couple times, too, but I didn't get to try much of the food." *Sadly*. "I did get to see the ruins, though." She paused as she recalled more memories of her forced travels, and images of Stellinga and Rabetta came to mind. "However, I'd really like to go back to Xich."

She still found herself wondering often about them, and hoped they were doing better now that the Alliance was pushing Igrium out of the desert nation.

"Well, I don't know what your first orders will be—it all depends on how successful we continue to be there," Matias said, "but you might not have to wait long to go again."

She made a noncommittal noise in her throat as a strange feeling went through her. She might go back to Xich; to help the people she had first thought of when she made her oath. Part of her hoped that would be the case, but the other part truly didn't care where she ended up as long as she was fighting against the man who had stolen her life.

Aunt Minda carried the conversation back to her questions, and Tetra answered as many as she could. Felicita, and even Matias, asked her some as well;

and she soon found herself asking them her own questions she had about their lives in Silvas and some of the things that confused her in her memories.

As answers were given and more stories were told, Tetra felt a sense of light-heartedness permeate the apartment's atmosphere. It filled her with a warmth she was only now becoming accustomed to; and despite how the subject wasn't brought up again, it only made her more determined to see Emperor Ignis fall. If he had been evil enough to take this sense of belonging away from her, she wasn't going to let her revenge go until she saw it through.

And that was a promise.

Chapter Forty-Seven

The euphoric feelings from the day before seemed like but a distant memory as Tetra stood in front of the two elegantly carved, towering doors leading to the Altelo's council hall.

"Are you ready?" Felicita asked from beside her.

"I...I don't know." She had been—until she found out earlier this morning that she would take her oath to join Silvas' army in front of most of the Buleutcil.

"You'll be fine." She glanced over and caught Felicita's reassuring smile. "I'll be right there with you. It's not like you'll have ta give a speech or anythin'. Just say the oath, and you and Galia can go on and do whatever she has planned. It'll be quick and painless."

Tetra pressed her lips into a thin line as she turned her gaze back to the guarded entrance in front of them. The ornate doors themselves flaunted the authority and power she was about to walk into, which only served to remind her of every visit she had had with Emperor Ignis; so even though she agreed with much of Silvas' morals, that comparison didn't leave a good taste in her mouth.

"We should go in now," Felicita said.

"Right."

Her cousin sent her another smile coupled with a nod before stepping forward. "We're ready," she told the guardsmen on either side of the doors.

They nodded towards her, then turned and pulled open the heavy doors. Tetra's heart jumped with rising fright that she made sure wasn't showing on her face before following Felicita into the council hall.

Rows upon rows of seats rose on either side of them as they walked through the center aisle in the round room. Tetra glanced around in awe. The sheer size of the chamber was almost as big as the fortress' biggest ballroom. Massive chandeliers hung from the domed ceiling towering a few stories above their heads, casting a golden light upon the few people milling around a huge table in the middle of the room.

Despite the pleasant atmosphere, Tetra could not do anything to stop the nervousness and anxiety swirling around each other like the beginnings of a windstorm in the back of her mind. As they made it to the center of the room, everyone turned to face them—and the force of all their gazes landed upon her. The hairs along her arms stood on end as she slowed to a stop next to Felicita.

She glanced around and recognized only a few faces she had seen during her time here—Dr. Prin, Army General Taoghn, and Galia. The rest were either those she recognized from pictures online and in the news, or people she had never seen at all.

"Hello, Lady Felicita." A tall man—one of those whom Tetra had seen before—stepped towards them both, his brow pinched in a questioning look. "I assume this means Baene will not be here?"

"No, Lord Jachen." Lady Felicita bowed her head towards Silvas' steward, and Tetra quickly followed in doing the same. "He said he would not be able ta come, so he sent me ta represent him."

"Very well." His weathered features softened as he turned his lavender eyes upon Tetra and gave her an almost imperceptible nod. "Welcome, Miss Cairn. I hope you are doing well."

Tetra recalled what Lady Felicita said about him knowing her true identity as she bowed her head towards him again. "Yes, My Lord."

"I'm glad to hear it."

She lifted her head and caught his knowing gaze still on her. She couldn't help but wonder if he would tell everyone the real news, but then pushed the stupid thought to the side as she remembered what Felicita said about Chief Baene being the one to do it. Yet even with that comforting thought, fear whispered cunning little lies in the back of her head that she tried to ignore for the present situation.

"Then let's begin." He turned and motioned towards Galia, who stood off to the side of the room, away from everyone standing around the "U"-shaped table. "First Lieutenant Eyrie, please come forward."

Tetra tried not to show her surprise as Galia stepped forward. Rarely had she seen someone who looked as young as Galia did with that high of a rank before, but maybe it was because her patre was Silvas' former army general.

"Army General..." Lord Jachen turned his head as he spoke.

Tetra glanced out of the corner of her eye and spotted General Taoghn's hardened countenance as he stepped towards them. Her heart skipped another nervous beat as his eyes met hers for a moment before she averted her gaze.

"Miss Cairn," he acknowledged.

"Army General, sir." She dipped her head towards him with a salute, then did the same towards Galia. "First Lieutenant."

Galia sent her a sharp nod in acknowledgement but said nothing as she turned her head in Lord Jachen's direction.

"Miss Cairn," the Silvanian steward's tenor voice rose slightly as he spoke, "we are all gathered here because you accepted Army General Taoghn's proposition to join our kingdom's military, but even though we have all heard this report, I must ask: is it true?"

"Yes sir," Tetra replied, her throat tightening.

"Then Army General Taoghn will swear you in." He stepped back, and she heard Felicita's footsteps move away at the same time.

General Taoghn stepped in the place Lord Jachen had been standing, and she was met with the full force of his probing gaze before she lowered her own respectfully.

"Tetra Cairn," he began, "step forward."

She did so, hoping her steps didn't look as tentative as she was truly feeling in his intimidating presence. With the soft ring of metal, he pulled out a shortsword that reflected the golden light of the chandeliers. Even in the tense moment, Tetra couldn't help but notice how beautiful the ceremonial blade was. With the small emeralds set in its crossguard to its dark-gray blade that was most likely gritanium, it looked like a weapon one would see placed on the walls of Emperor Ignis' fortress—one with a history of many battles that had been used by a person of high honor.

She held her breath as he raised it towards her, then set the tip lightly on her shoulder with the flat of the blade resting there.

"Lift your hand and touch the flat of Zmraidos," General Taoghn ordered.

Tetra did so, barely touching it with her fingertips. Leaving fingerprints on its shiny surface was something she couldn't bring herself to do.

"Tetra Cairn," he said, "do you solemnly swear on this most sacred blade that you will protect and defend the Kingdom of Silvas through all battles and wars you are assigned to?"

She let his words ring in her ears for a few moments before replying, "Yes sir."

Those two simple words held a weight to them she had never known them to have before, but it was a weight she was now more than willing to carry.

"Do you promise to let go of any former allegiances and to be held under the command of our officers here?"

"Yes sir."

"Then repeat these words," Taoghn paused for a brief moment, "'I, Tetra Cairn...'"

Even though it wasn't her birth name, it was still the name she was comfortable with; so she didn't feel any guilt for repeating the words, "I, Tetra Cairn..." Nor did she feel any for the ones she repeated afterward; because despite her name situation, she meant every word of them.

"...Do solemnly swear on the sacred blade of Zmraidos that I will give my all—even with the threat of pain or death—to serve and protect the citizens of this kingdom from any and all forces that would try to come against them. I will uphold and protect the Old Laws given by Deleyon, and will give my all for the peace and prosperity of Silvas to continue on. I swear, in the hearing of these witnesses, that I will do my part in whatever is asked of me. So help me, Deleyon."

General Taoghn nodded sharply. "You may remove your hand."

She did so, and only then realized how fast her heart was beating.

"Tetra Cairn, as you have sworn, so will you be entrusted to uphold that oath—no matter the consequences." The hard stare his eyes bore into her only punctuated the heaviness of the moment.

She took great care to keep her voice even as she replied, "Yes sir."

He stared at her for another long moment, then something new penetrated through the hardness of his eyes as he nodded—almost as if he finally came to the conclusion that she meant every word of this new oath.

"Then by the authority vested in me as General of the Silvanian Army, I accept your oath and swear you in as Private Tetra Cairn, first in our war-peryton training program."

Then he turned towards Galia, lifted the sword to her shoulder, and had her recite a different oath that Tetra barely heard as her thoughts converged onto what she had done. She was in Silvas' army. And in swearing that oath, she was now a true traitor to Igrium.

Despite the words she had sworn and the rightness she felt saying them in that moment, the healing skin around her malscar began to itch as if in protest of the whole ordeal. She gritted her teeth and forced her hands at her sides to keep from scratching it as General Taoghn and Galia finished. Nothing good could come from drawing attention to the wound any more than its placement already did.

All thoughts of scratching it fled as General Taoghn turned to face her direction again.

"Welcome to the army, Private Cairn," he said as he sheathed his sword.

She dipped her head towards him and pressed her fist against her chest in salute.

"As Army General, I have handed over the command of your training to First Lieutenant Eyrie."

He gestured towards Galia, and Tetra barely turned in her direction with a salute. The still-intimidating woman gave her a slow nod and opened her mouth to say something, but a hardened voice on the opposite side of the table beat her to it.

"Cirus, are you sure she is truly trustworthy?"

Everyone turned in the direction of the voice. Tetra's eyes landed on a portly, older man whose dark suit fit him a bit too tightly around his large middle. Even from the distance, she could feel the contempt coming off him as his small eyes peered in her direction.

"She's not lying," General Taoghn replied in an even harder voice that made Tetra's heart leap in nervous fright.

The man raised his brow incredulously as he lifted his chin. "You didn't answer my question."

"It was evident she meant every word of that oath."

"But that still doesn't answer my question."

Lord Jachen took a step towards the man. All eyes turned on him. "She is sworn in, Wenyan," he said, "Your prejudice will not help you any. We all agreed that this would be the best course of action since duplication of Private Cairn's ability is not possible at the moment."

"And yet there would be a better chance of that happening if you all had taken my suggestion from before," Lord Wenyan replied with a haughty sniff.

Dr. Prin crossed her arms and aimed a glare at the man. "Which was a horrible one from the beginning," she retorted.

Tetra narrowed her eyes. What suggestion were they talking about?

"I think it would fit the Cairns' name well." Lord Wenyan's expression darkened as he turned his dagger-like gaze back on Tetra, "Especially since their spawn is as much a monster as they are."

Tetra jerked her neck back in surprise at the verbal slap the same time as Felicita's words rang out, "Lord Wenyan! How dare you—"

"—That's enough, Wenyan." The authority in Lord Jachen's voice echoed clearly in the towering room. "I would have expected more decency from you not to insult the very person who just joined our military to *help* us, but I will not tolerate such talk in this council chamber anymore. Do *you* understand?"

Tetra could feel hot tears rising as the whispers she hadn't heard in a while came back in full force to pound against her hastily constructed mental defenses.

"Even those in the Buleutcil know you're a monster..." One voice said, before another added on, *"Only they don't realize how awful of one you really are, Anora* Ignis*."*

She lowered her head and blinked back the tears before anyone could see them, then fixed her expression back into a neutral mask before looking up again.

"Yes, My Lord," Lord Wenyan finally replied—albeit begrudgingly.

"Private Cairn," Lord Jachen turned, and their eyes met, "I'm sorry for that. On behalf of the Buleutcil I ask that you would forgive us for this spoken dishonor against you."

"Uh—yes sir." She forced her tone to stay even and bowed her head towards the Silvanian steward. "Thank you."

She lifted her head and saw him nod towards her, before turning his attention to Army General Taoghn. "Cirus, if you would please tell Private Cairn the rules we have set in place for her position..."

The army general turned and sent him a nod before turning back around towards Tetra. "Other than those you see here and a select few others, the knowledge that you, Private, are the peryton fighting for us is to be kept as secret as possible. We don't want that information falling into Igrium's hands, and we would like to keep as much public scrutiny off of you as possible."

"And us" she knew to be the real meaning behind his words. She had already become well acquainted with Silvas' hatred of the Cairn name and could see the reasoning of the Buleutcil not wanting to be associated with her while she carried it. Yet even with that logical reasoning, a sharp talon still pricked at her heart.

Taoghn put his hands behind his back as he continued, "And with that, during any dealings outside your new military training where you will be required to fight as a war-peryton, you will be referred to as such and not as yourself."

The talon dug deeper, but Tetra said nothing in protest. She signed up to fight as a peryton, so she should've known she would probably end up being treated as one.

"We have decided your schedule for the coming weeks will be that every Firstdein—except for today—and Sixthdein, you and Dr. Prin will continue the testing sessions as usual," he continued, "while Secondein through Fifthdein will be used for your military training. You will not be required to do anything on Seventhdein. However, when you are called into battle, this schedule will not be used for as long as your efforts in each one are needed.

"The Buleutcil has also decided that if you continue to prove yourself trustworthy, you may earn yourself more freedoms as the weeks go on." He gave her a look that almost seemed to say '*but if you don't, you can bet you'll pay dearly for it*'. "Do I make myself clear?"

"Yes, Army General, sir," she replied.

"Then that is all I have to say on the matter."

He and Lord Jachen both shared looks with each other before Silvas' Steward turned his attention towards the rest of the Buleutcil to address them, "I agree with Army General Toaghn, and say that this matter is closed." He then turned and flicked his gaze between Tetra and Galia. "First Lieutenant Eyrie, Private Cairn—you are both free to begin your new training."

Both of them saluted him at the same time and bowed their heads towards him—although Tetra's head bow was a bit slower than her commanding officer's. She still wasn't quite used to the respectful Silvanian greeting yet.

"Yes, My Lord," Galia replied, then she lifted her head and stepped over towards Tetra. Tetra lifted her eyes at her approaching footsteps. Their eyes locked for a moment before she lowered hers. "Come, Private."

She nodded and, sharing one last look with Felicita, turned and followed her new commanding officer out of the council chamber's thick atmosphere.

Chapter Forty-Eight

Lines of code flew down the screen of Rasiela's portable holoputer. She had been waiting in tense silence in the middle of her townhome's tight, bricked-in backyard for almost fifteen minutes; the walls feeling more claustrophobic than they ever had before. Most wouldn't even consider it a backyard—more like a patio with grass growing on it—but it was the only place where she knew there were not any "secret" cameras.

During a vicious windstorm years ago, she had destroyed the ones out here in hopes whoever was behind them would blame their destruction on the weather, and so far, no one had put any back. She, of course, had found all the ones in her house, but not wanting to raise any suspicions she kept them going.

She glanced up at the dark clouds overhead, the smell of rain on the wind. She bit her lip and turned her attention back to the holoputer floating right above her lap, a CP chip sticking out of the projector's port.

How many more encryptions would she have to get through for this thing to—

Her holonode buzzed, sending a surprising jolt to her heart. She shook her head at herself for being so jumpy as she answered the incoming call.

"Have you found it?" Chief Baene asked as his face appeared on the screen.

"Not yet," Rasiela sent an impatient look towards the still-flying codes, then looked back over at her holonode's screen, "but I hope to soon."

"If anyone can, it's you." He sent her an affirming nod.

No matter how many years went by, she could not help the tiny bit of warmth at hearing her mentor's praise. "Thank you, chief."

There was a pause, and in it she sent another furtive glance towards the holoscreen.

"Are you ready?"

Chief Baene's question sent a strange mix of feelings through her, and she shot him a pointed look.

"I'm always ready." Even when she did not know if she actually was, she had to be.

"Hmm." He sent her his own pointed look. "Then you will be happy to know that all the arrangements have been made for Team Refuge to come pick you up at Fugerio."

"Good." She nodded sharply and turned her head back in her holoscreen's direction. If Chief Baene wanted a reaction from her, he was not going to get it.

"They're scheduled to be there a couple days before our appointed time in case you get there early."

"Thank you." She could feel his probing stare even if it was only coming from her holonode.

"There's no need to be scared, Rasiela."

"I know, Chief," she replied without turning her head from the holoscreen. "This isn't my first mission."

"I'm sure your family will be excited to see you." A rare smile entered his voice as he added, "I will be glad to see you in person for a change, too."

Despite the reservation she wanted to portray, she could not help the small smile that escaped her lips. "And you as well."

Before he could reply, the codes on her screen stopped. A map popped up in the new window.

"I have it," she said.

"Good." Chief Baene's voice returned to his usual seriousness. "Send me the location."

She nodded as her focus landed on the small, red dot shining in an abandoned warehouse area on Rubrum's northside—far enough away from the emperor's fortress and the busier sectors of town, but close enough to easily get information and not raise Igrium's suspicions. She swiped Chief Baene's face away and sent the location of the CP chip's origin to him.

"There." She tapped her holoscreen off and unplugged the CP chip.

"I have it." Chief Baene returned to her holonode's screen. "You can destroy the CP chip now."

At his words, Rasiela stood from the single chair in her backyard, placed the small object on the ground, and crushed it with the sole of her boot. Then, she dropped her holoscreen's projector (which also housed its hard drive), and jumped on it to do the same. She already sent all of its data to Lord Othnel and was only sad to see it go because of how expensive it had been.

"How long do you plan on staying at Norland?" He asked.

"Only for the rest of this week. I'll begin first thing on the weekend."

Chief Baene raised a brow. "And will you be telling the trainee?"

"Only that he will not be seeing me anymore." A pang of guilt clawed at her heart. "But I can tell him to continue looking for those 'project peryton' notes, if you'd like."

Chief Baene shook his head. "You don't need to. I'm no longer looking for those, and I have already told the Buleutcil that they are lost."

Rasiela raised her brow. "Why would you do that?"

"Because even if they were found, the project itself is practically impossible to perfect—and the last thing the nobility needs is a foothold if one of them were to find out taxes were going towards a project with an almost zero-percent chance of success."

She nodded in understanding and then asked, "So what shall I tell Aabir, then?"

"I will send you something in the next few days to give to him." He exhaled sharply through his nose, a shadow pressing across his features. "I haven't had much time to think about it with everything going on, nor will I for at least a couple more days."

"It's not a big deal, Chief. If I need to figure something out for him to do, then I can."

"You may have to." He gave her a small nod. "However, I will try to come up with something meaningful for him to find if I can. Although I don't fully trust him, he has proven himself to be...resourceful—and I don't want to waste that on paltry things."

Rasiela suppressed a smile. "He has indeed." She paused as another thought came to her. "Is...is Jorfa working now?"

"He is."

"How—" she cleared her throat before continuing, "how is it going?"

"I don't know." The shadows on his face deepened. "He isn't supposed to contact me until they are finished getting them all, or if something happens."

"I understand." Rasiela sent a silent plea up to Deleyon that they would succeed. "Then I will continue to—"

"—Hold on." Chief Baene's voice hardened in urgency, "That's him now. I must go, Rasiela."

And with that, he was gone. Blood pumped in Rasiela's ears as she turned her holonode off and whispered a few quiet prayers under her breath. Jorfa and his team were supposed to be freeing the Constantia prisoners now, so she hoped the call Chief Baene received meant they were successful.

Still praying as worries began to whirl through her head, she walked back into her house for the last time. At the back door, she grabbed the raised handle of her suitcase and walked the length of her small townhome. She could not risk staying here anymore in case the person on the other side of that CP chip had tracked her location as well as she did theirs'.

When she stepped out onto the sidewalk and locked the door, a sense of finality came over her. Despite the heaviness of the possible outcome of the prison-break and her mission ahead, there was also a sense of lightness in the air that caused a lump to form in her throat.

If her coming mission proved successful, it would end up being her last—and then she would be able to go back home to Silvas for the first time in eighteen years.

She swallowed back her rising emotions and set her face into the neutral mask she had been taught to use, then turned and walked down the street to find the nearest available taxi.

RAIN DRIVEN BY WIND pelted the indoor training arena's ceiling. Aabir hefted his spear and ran towards the oncoming armored training droid with a yell. He threw it but did not have time to see where it landed as he unsheathed his sword and spun around.

The other training droid's blade rang against his as they hit. Teeth gritted, he shoved the android back and slashed at its arm. His sword screeched against its armor, and he leapt back as its broadsword came arcing towards him.

"Come on, Sorrel!" Lieutenant Denir helpfully called out from the side, "I've seen my grandmatha do better than that!"

Aabir answered his C.O. by lunging towards the training droid. It blocked his next strike and countered with its own. He deflected the arcing blade. Since he didn't have a shield, he improvised and rammed his whole body into the android. It toppled to the ground. He stumbled but gained his footing before striking the robot in its metal throat.

Knowing it would not get back up, he spun around in time to see the spear he had just thrown hurtling towards him. He jumped out of the way, barely missing it. His heart pounded as he stumbled to the ground with a grunt, noticing the training droid he had thrown it at running towards him with its broadsword raised.

He scrambled up and ran towards it, dodging its slash and thrusting his sword into its side. It doubled over like a human would, and he finished it off with a higher strike to its chest.

Panting heavily, he spun around, sword raised, to make sure Lieutenant Denir had not set off any more surprises. Seeing none, he turned to face Denir's direction and gave him a salute.

"I expect better from you, Sorrel," he said with a hard look. "If you had turned a second too late, that android would have hit you in the chest."

Aabir kept his face neutral as his pride took the verbal blow.

"But you're done for the day." Denir nodded neutrally, hiding what looked like pride, "You can go now."

Aabir suppressed a sigh of relief as he lowered his fist and sheathed his sword. He turned and headed towards the training yard's exit on quick footsteps, covering a yawn as he passed by Denir's line of sight.

Three weeks of training, researching, and waiting in anticipation for any news about the Constantia prisoners was wearing him out; but, thank Deleyon, he had only had a couple nightmares keep him up. For the first time in almost two months, he was finally getting the sleep he so desperately needed practically every single night.

He pushed open the door and stepped out into the training hall. The howling wind and thunderous rain echoed along the arched ceiling, drowning his heavy footsteps in their cacophony. A bulbous cleaning bot with a mop attachment coming out of its side pushed a mop bucket—that was almost as big as it was—past him. It reminded him of Rasiela, and he tapped the pommel of his sword as his thoughts converged on that subject.

Norland's janitor had not been at the school much the past few weeks. He had only seen her a few times since he came back from the Constantia Stadium with the suspicious CP chip, and both times had been when he passed her in the hall. They no longer met up for her to give him his next assignments, so he could not ask her the many questions he had on how the prison-break plans were going. She would not have told him anyway, but that fact did not stop the flow of questions that circled in his brain.

He made it to his platoon's locker room and changed out of his armor into his uniform as quickly as he could. Once he was finished, he walked through Norland to his dorm with half-rushed steps. Lieutenant Denir had let him off a little earlier today from his extended training period; he figured he could get a small nap in before dinner if he made it to his dorm quick enough.

On the way up the stairs, he passed by Septimus and Brutus as they were descending them.

"Only one more week, Aabir," Septimus said ominously as they passed.

Aabir slowed and glanced over his shoulder at their retreating backs. Then he shook his head with an eye roll before continuing on. Almost everyone in his platoon had given up their anger towards him for making it into the Tourney, but Septimus still held a grudge since Aabir had been the one to personally beat him from winning the spot. Thankfully, all his words were just empty threats. If anything happened to keep Aabir or Buren from fighting, Lieutenant Denir already threatened a heaping pile of dishonorable punishments on whoever was the one to cause their fall.

He slowed his pace to a normal walk as he went down the dormitory corridor and came to a stop at his dorm's door. He turned the knob and opened it. When he stepped in, he heard the rustle of fabric and lifted his head to see Ezen—who was sitting on his top bunk above Aabir's—lowering a blanket from his face that was turned towards the wall.

He raised a brow questioningly as he closed the door. "Ezen?"

"Hey, Aabir." Ezen's voice sounded rough—almost as if he had been crying; he did not turn to face him.

"Are...are you OK?"

His friend's shoulders lifted in a shrug, but he did not reply.

Aabir nodded slowly, unsure of what to say next. Obviously, Ezen did not want to talk about what he was doing, so he decided to change the subject.

"Do you know where Aquilo and Tycho are?"

The sound of a heavy exhale came from Ezen. "They're in the library. Have been for a while now."

Aabir raised his brow in surprise. "Tycho's in the library?"

"Yeah. I think he asked for help since he's failing algebra, so—y'know—Aquilo jumped at the chance to get him there."

Aabir snorted with a grin. "I bet."

Ezen did not reply, only shifted uncomfortably on his squeaking bed.

Aabir folded his arms and stepped towards the bunk bed. Despite the air around Ezen that demanded isolation, he ignored it.

"Are you alright, Ezen?" He asked.

"I guess." The other trainee shrugged, still without turning so Aabir could not see his face.

"Are you sure? Because you don't—"

"—I'm fine, Aabir!" Ezen spun around and aimed his red-rimmed glare down upon him.

Aabir blinked and took a step back. So, he had been crying... And now that he could see his friends' much-paler face, he realized the same strange look he had seen there during the training droid incident was once again plastered upon his sharp features.

"I—I'm sorry, Ezen." He held up his hands in surrender. "I didn't mean to pry. I just wanted to see if there was anything I could do to help."

Ereliev's "*helpful self*" barb popped into his head as he spoke, but he pushed its annoying presence aside.

Ezen's sharp glare turned mournful in less than a second, and he turned back around. "I wish you could..." His lowered voice trailed off, leaving Aabir to stand silently in the room's uncomfortable atmosphere.

He sighed quietly and stepped over to his bed. If Ezen did not want to talk about it, then that was fine. It was obviously something bad, but Aabir could see nothing he tried to say would help, so he stayed quiet as he sat down on his bed and laid down—his boots still on. If Ezen wanted to talk about it later, he would be ready to listen. But for now, he would give him space. He really wanted a nap anyway. Sighing again, he closed his eyes and waited for sleep to overtake him.

Aabir did not know how long he dozed off for, but when he awoke to the door bursting open, he knew it had been cut too short.

"Aabir!" Aquilo's tone held a suppressed excitement. "Ezen! You both are never going to believe what just happened!

He opened his eyes and sent a glare in Aquilo and Tycho's direction as they stepped into their room.

"What?" He asked irritably.

"Oh, sorry." Aquilo gave him an apologetic look that did not dull the excitement shining in his small eyes. "I didn't know you were asleep—"

"—But you're gonna want to hear it," Tycho interjected with a grin.

"What is it?" Ezen's drawl sounded clearer as his bed squeaked above Aabir.

"The Constantia prisoners tried to escape!" Aquilo exclaimed.

"What?" Aabir shot up into a sitting position and locked eyes with his friend.

Tycho nodded, still grinning. "Yeah, they did."

By their reactions, it was easy to assume that the escape had failed. Dread slimed its way through his veins and filled the yawning pit in his stomach with its weighted sludge.

Trying to keep any of those feelings from showing, he asked in a cool voice, "What happened? And how do you know?"

"It just popped up on my newsfeed a few minutes ago." Aquilo flicked his wrist, and his holonode's screen appeared just above it. "Here, I'll read it to you." He paused for a moment. "Alright, it says: '*Twenty-four people—all who snuck past Igrian border security by still-unknown means—hacked into the stadium's security systems, either killed or knocked out the guards, and were caught leading the freed prisoners through a previously blocked-off sewage tunnel. The tunnel was built underneath the first Constantia Stadium six-hundred years ago, but was forgotten about after the Stadium's multiple rebuildings.*'"

"If it was as forgotten as that says, then how'd they find it?" Ezen asked.

Aquilo rolled his eyes at the interruption. "I'm getting to that. It says their hideout was found in an abandoned building on the east side of Rubrum—and it had an entrance to the old sewage tunnel system. Most of the tunnels have been filled in since it's so old, so that'd probably make it easier to find when you aren't really trapped in a maze."

"Ah...but how'd they get past all the guards? I thought the stadium was swarming with them."

"They shut off the security, then broke through one of the prison's walls through the tunnel."

In the next few, quiet moments of Aquilo scrolling through the article, a chill settled deep in Aabir's bones as the truth pounded through his skull: the rescue attempt failed. He crossed his arms as if it would ward off the internal cold and asked, "If they turned off all the security systems, then how were they found out?"

"Hmm...let me see..." Aquilo pressed his lips into a thin line as his eyes moved down the screen. "Oh! Apparently, the security systems popped back on while they were still breaking the prisoners out of their cells, and the patrolmen were able to get down there to stop it once they found out about it."

"Oh." He nodded slowly as if his innocent curiosity was settled, but inside his stomach was churning despite the ice that seemed to have encased the rest of him. "Does it say anything else?"

"Just that it happened a few hours ago, and that all the attackers who weren't killed are being questioned right now." Aquilo shrugged and flicked his holonode back off. "It also mentioned something about Emperor Ignis making a public declaration regarding it sometime tonight."

"Oh. OK."

Sharp talons pressed down on Aabir's chest. Igrium was known for its awful torture techniques, and he had a feeling those were being used on those who risked their lives to free those prisoners.

As he had the thought, a spark of alarm shot through him. Was Rasiela one of those people?

He almost got up right then to head down to her office, but the common sense in him told him to wait. It would look suspicious if he were to do it now.

"You can go back to your nap now, Aabir." Aquilo nodded "I just figured you'd both want to know."

"Thanks," Aabir replied at the same time Ezen's monotone "yeah, thanks" sounded above him.

Aquilo nodded again and turned before sitting down on his own bed. Aabir noticed his friend tapping his holonode on again before he himself turned over to act as if he was napping—because after that horrible news he knew falling asleep again was not going to happen.

As he lay there with his eyes closed and only the shufflings of his friends as they moved around penetrating the quiet atmosphere, an angry heat began to burn in Aabir's chest as he thought back to all the tortured Constantia prisoners he had seen. His mind's eye replayed all their faces for him to see again, and again, and again.

He curled his hands into fists as the hope he had held onto the last three weeks shattered into more and more pieces with each image going through his head. If he did somehow make it to the end of the second day, there was now the chance that he would have to fight one of those people.

Thankfully, he tried to reason with himself, there was little chance of that actually happening. He would have to win against all the other third-level competitors for that to happen; and according to Aquilo, there were going to be almost two hundred this year—which did not leave him with the best odds of making it far.

If only Lieutenant Denir's threat had not caused that thought to be less comforting than what it should have been.

He heaved a long sigh through his nose and silently prayed to Deleyon, *"Please, Deleyon, make me fail in the Tourney before I ever make it to the third day. I doubt You would want me to even do that, so I ask that it would not happen.*

"And please be with all those prisoners, and those being tortured right now for trying to save them." An image of Rasiela being tortured popped into his head, and he ground his teeth as he pushed his focus away from it. *"And if one of those was Rasiela, help her get free. Help them all get free."*

For the rest of his "nap", he struggled through his memories of the Constantia prison, brutal imaginings of what the failed rescuers were enduring at that moment, and his worries over Rasiela. By the time the bell rang for dinner, he was glad to be pulled out of his heavy thoughts for a little while at the prospect of a distraction food brought.

Ezen jumped down from his bed with a loud ***thump*** as Aabir got up from his with a stretch. A shadowed look still covered his friend's face, but there was nothing to show that he had been crying. Their eyes met for a moment, but Ezen immediately looked away as he strode out of the room behind Aquilo and Tycho. Aabir scratched the back of his neck and breathed out a quiet sigh of frustration as he followed.

Whatever was bothering Ezen, he hoped the other boy would talk to someone about it. He was too quiet sometimes, and it almost reminded Aabir of Ereliev's resistance to talk about what happened to her at school—which was a comparison that made him worry. Even though he had only known Ezen for just over a month, they had become good friends. He knew he could trust Ezen, but the other boy did not seem to feel the same way towards him.

He shut the door of their dorm and followed Ezen's retreating form, soon catching up to him. His friend said nothing, but Aabir noticed he slowed his pace a tiny bit for him to catch up.

So even if he did not talk now, Aabir felt he would eventually. All he had to do was keep on being there for him. Yet even that thought added another weight to his overburdened shoulders. What if he and his family left Igrium before the school year ended? He did not want to leave on a sour note—he would rather not leave his friends at all—but the problems he and his family were facing were far too big of a problem for him to stay.

Aabir shook his head and rubbed the back of his neck. Ezen slightly turned his head in his direction.

"Tired?" He asked.

"A little."

"Yeah..." There was a pause. Then, "Look, Aabir, I'm sorry for how I reacted earlier. I just...I found something out...and I—well, I have a feeling I'll tell you later in the week about it. OK? Just...give me time to think through it."

"Sure." Aabir glanced over at him and nodded. "I understand."

Ezen breathed out a deep breath. "Yeah, I bet you do."

They both turned to look ahead of them, neither saying anything as they made their way to the dining hall in the less-tense atmosphere.

THE NEXT DAY, ALL Aabir could think about were the prisoners. It was hard to concentrate on anything else with the news of the event traveling through Norland's halls faster than yesterday's windstorm. Everyone seemed to want to talk about it, so Aabir found himself not speaking as much as he did around his friends—nor did Ezen, for that matter.

Worries and questions with no answers filled his head and left him actually pushing himself to concentrate in his classes—if only to try and keep those thoughts at bay. Not even training could keep away the images of the torture Rasiela might be going through. Every lunge he took at the training droids, every spear he threw, and crossbow bolt he shot only reminded him of the looming Tourney and the horrible possibilities that awaited him there.

Needless to say, when Aabir finished training, instead of going to his dorm to do homework or take a nap, he found himself in front of the *"Janitorial Services"* door.

Curiosity and fear swirled in his head as he stood there staring at the sign for a few moments. Would she be in there? What if he knocked and no one answered? Did that mean she really was one of those twenty-four people, or could it be she was just not at Norland at the moment?

His heart tried to beat itself out of his chest with each question until he finally lifted his shaking hand and knocked on the door. He dropped it to his side as if the wood had burned him, then waited in tense silence with only the sound of his heart beating in his ears.

Oh Deleyon, please let her be here, please let her be here...

His heart practically leapt into his throat as the door squeaked open and Rasicla's shadowed face appeared in the doorway. Aabir tilted his head back in surprised relief, then he lowered his gaze to hers. Red rimmed her puffy eyes.

"Can I help you, trainee?" She asked without a hint of any emotion in her monotone voice.

"I—I need some more of that...stain remover. If you have it," he replied.

She gave him a sharp nod and opened the door wider. "Come on in." She gestured for him to follow. "I just reorganized some of this stuff so it may take me a couple minutes to find it again."

"That's fine."

He took a few steps into her office until he felt far enough from her door to safely whisper, "I heard the news yesterday."

Rasiela stopped as she faced the shelves, and instead of going through the charade of picking through their contents, she laid one of her hands on the middle shelf and squeezed her eyes shut with a warbling sigh.

"We were so close, too..." Aabir had to strain his ears to catch her whisper, "They freed all the women and those in solitary confinement, but about halfway through the men's side, the security system went off—even though Lord Othnel was the one who helped disable it!"

"I heard that's what happened—though not the Lord Othnel part," he replied.

Rasiela sighed and opened her eyes, her face still in the direction of the cleaning supplies. "Yes, he helped; and that was why I was so...confident that it would succeed." Even from the side, Aabir could see a sharp glint enter her eyes. "But even with him, none of us were prepared for someone to bypass *his* security encryptions."

Aabir tilted his head to the side and scrunched his brow questioningly. "How did that happen, if I may ask?"

"We don't know," Rasiela still would not look at him; the white, fluorescent light of her office bouncing off her glassy eyes, "but we do have our suspicions on *who* did it."

He narrowed his eyes. "Wait...are you saying it wasn't the patrolmen who did it?"

"No, it wasn't." Now she did turn her head in his direction, and the anger in her eyes made him take a step back. "Think, Aabir. Who would do this? Surely you know."

Immediately, he remembered the fake patrolman who he knocked out and stole the CP chip from. His eyes widened as his heart began to race again, sending a buzz of adrenaline through his body.

"You—you mean...it was them?" He did not mean for his voice to come out as a whisper, but it did anyway, "The secret group who caused the 'Silvanian Fire Attacks'?"

Rasiela dipped her chin towards him.

The icy dread from yesterday sliced through his veins. "But—but I thought they hated Igrium... I mean—that's why they burned down all those houses, right?"

Rasiela shook her head. "They hate both sides of the war, Aabir." She pressed her fingers against her temples. "Although we don't know much about them, what we have been able to uncover is that they have no care for who wins this war because they want both sides to lose."

All the conspiracy theories began to float back into Aabir's mind, and he was now regretting ever having read or watched them as chill bumps rose along his arms.

"But why?" He whispered.

"I wish I knew." Her shoulders slumped for a moment as she sighed. There was a moment where she said nothing, and in it she straightened back up and lowered her hands, locking her pain-filled eyes on him. "However, that actually leads me to what I wanted to talk to you about."

His heart jumped in fearful dread, but he gave her a slow nod. "OK..."

Her lips barely twisted into a small frown before she replied, "I'm leaving Norland this week."

He jerked his neck back as if struck. "What?"

"I gave in my month's notice three weeks ago, and by this weekend I will be...gone." The last word ended in a sigh.

She was leaving? His eyes widened further as he spoke aloud the questions popping into his mind, "What about our deal?" His voice rose slightly from its whisper, but not by much. "You—you promised to help me and my family get out of Igrium! How am I supposed to do that if you're not here, Rasiela? I—I thought I could trust you!"

"And you still can—we will continue communicating through messages." Her calm voice sounded strange coming from her weary, shadowed countenance. "That's one of the reasons I have had you do that. Our deal is still on."

The tiny, angry fire that flared to life was immediately doused with relief. "Oh." He gave her a sheepish look. "Um—thanks."

"I would never break a deal, Aabir," she replied. "Not even when I'm gone."

The use of the word "gone" gave him pause. "What do you mean 'gone'?" He asked, "I know you're leaving Norland, but where are you going?"

Rasiela straightened and turned her head back in the direction of the shelves. "My time here in Igrium is finished." She sighed again.

"Oh...well, that's great, right?" He knew if he could leave Igrium right now, he would—and he would be much more excited than the depressed countenance Rasiela was giving off.

"It might be."

He scrunched his face in confusion. "Is...there something bad in Silvas that you don't want to go back to?"

Rasiela was silent for a long time. Aabir almost opened his mouth to ask if she was OK, but then she finally turned her face back towards him.

"That's the problem, Aabir," she finally said, "I don't know what I'm going back to."

He was still confused. "But I figured you grew up in Silvas..."

"I did. But I have been gone for over eighteen years, and...a lot can change in that time."

He blinked. Eighteen years? She had been a spy for as long as he had been alive?

"Oh." He nodded in understanding. "I see what you mean."

"But I'm going no matter what. So..." Her words trailed off, then she took a few steps towards him. Aabir stared at her in surprise as she put her hand on his shoulder. Seriousness sharpened the edges of her face.

"Don't take what you have for granted, Aabir," she said. "No matter what anyone says, keep doing what you're doing for your family. Even when I'm gone, don't stop. Do you hear me? You don't want to lose them." Some of the serious edge in her tone dissipated as she added, "Because when you all get to Silvas, I would like to meet them."

A small smile escaped his lips as he nodded. "I want that to happen, too."

"Good." She nodded sharply and moved her hand off his shoulder, spun back towards the shelves, pulled a box forward, and picked up something in it. Then she faced him again and held out the familiar small bottle of stain-remover.

"You can have this, trainee." A spark of amusement lit up her glazed eyes. "I will not be needing it anymore."

For some reason, Aabir had trouble swallowing as he took the bottle from her outstretched hand. "Thanks, Rasiela." He cleared his throat to try and stop the warbling of his words. "For—for everything."

"No problem." She bowed her head towards him in the Silvanian fashion, and he copied the movement. "I will see you in Silvas."

"I hope so."

His nose felt runny as he turned and strode out of her office for the last time. He sniffed deeply and glanced over his shoulder as the door clicked shut behind him.

Clutching the tiny bottle in his hand, he turned his gaze forward and walked on down the hall.

Chapter Forty-Nine

Once Tetra and Lieutenant Galia Eyrie left the Buleutcil's council chamber, her new commanding officer led her out of the Altelo and into a government-owned hovercar. One of her personal guardsmen drove them through Urbselva's slow traffic until they finally turned into a seemingly deserted part of the tree-city.

The mountains that surrounded it rose up on their left as their hovercar moved down the empty, magnetic street. Graffiti covered the lower levels of the ambulate tree-buildings to their right. Empty spaces pockmarked the sides of them where there should've been the curved window-walls Tetra had noticed most of the Silvanian buildings having. Trash and other debris littered the cracked sidewalks, and a layer of gray dust seemed to cover almost everything in sight.

"What happened here?" She glanced over at Lieutenant Eyrie, who sat in the backwards seat facing her.

This looked nothing like the bustling, metropolitan sectors of Urbselva she had seen. It looked more like a ghost town than the lively Silvanian capital.

"A mining explosion," Lieutenant Eyrie replied. "It happened when they were trying to carve another warehouse into the mountains."

"Why hasn't anyone moved back?"

"With the war going on, the Buleutcil hasn't been focused on clean-up efforts, but when it ends they most likely will—especially with all the refugees coming into our kingdom. The ambulate forest has always afforded us little space to build, and we need it now more than we ever have before." A thoughtful look came over her face. "I believe this place will fill up quickly once it's restored."

Tetra waited a few moments before asking her next question, "Then, why are we here?"

"When everything shut down in this sector, it left many other warehouses empty." Her C.O. gave her a significant look. "Huge spaces perfect for a secret war-peryton to fly in."

Oh, that makes sense. Tetra nodded in understanding then turned her gaze back out towards the dreary view.

The hovercar soon slowed to a stop, and Lieutenant Eyrie glanced over in her direction. "We're here."

Tetra nodded again and followed her commanding officer out of the hovercar and onto the sidewalk. A chain link fence with barbed wire running along the top stood in front of them. Phantom pains went through Tetra's leg as she blinked and lowered her gaze to what Lieutenant Eyrie was doing. She had pulled out a key and unlocked an old padlock that hung from a thick link of chain looped tightly around the fence. The chains fell with a clatter as she unwound them. Tetra cringed as the gate let out a grating squeak as it swung open.

Lieutenant Eyrie strode through the new opening between the fence, and Tetra picked up her pace to follow. Footfalls trailed behind them, and she glanced over her shoulder to see Sir Whest and Madame Quen joining them, with Rune slowing to close and lock the gate back up behind them.

Tetra returned her gaze forward, and her eyes widened as she caught sight of the huge, stone staircase Lieutenant Eyrie was ascending that led up to two wide doors cut into the mountain's base. It reminded her of Urbselva's hovertrain station—only without opulence or windows. However, the plainness couldn't take away from her awe at how big the entrance was. She would've thought after living in Urbselva for nearly a month that she would be used to how giant the forest kingdom liked to build things, but obviously that still wasn't the case.

Blinking from her moment's stupor, she ascended the stairs behind her commanding officer then stepped onto the short landing in front of the doors before heading inside. Shadows she couldn't see through filled the space, no matter how many times she blinked to try and do so. She took a tentative step forward that echoed into the darkness.

In the light of the door Madame Quen kept open, Lieutenant Eyrie walked over to the wall and waved her hand across a motion sensor. Tetra blinked and squinted her eyes as bright, fluorescent lighting overtook the darkness. Once they grew adjusted to the brightness, her brow rose, and her jaw slackened as she took in the cavernous sight before her.

The empty warehouse looked to be twice as big as the Buleutcil's council chamber. Huge factory lights hung from the ceiling, but their downward luminescence didn't reach the shadows covering the towering dome above them.

She lowered her awestruck gaze as Lieutenant Eyrie's footfalls bounced along the rounded walls, and that was when she noticed the group of armored training droids standing not far from the entrance. Not knowing what to do, she followed her C.O. over to the androids.

"Alright, Private." Lieutenant Eyrie spun on her heel and faced Tetra—whose heartbeat picked up speed at the new weight of authority she felt coming from the woman. Her expression was neutral, and her tone calm but authoritative as she said, "You and I both know that no military on Afreean has ever been able to train a successful war-peryton, so what you and I do these next few weeks is new territory."

"Yes, because this new territory is only possible for a monster like yourself."

Lord Wenyan's earlier accusation popped into Tetra's mind at the whisper's urging. She tried to ignore the thoughts by reminding herself that perytons weren't monsters, and that her being able to turn into one wasn't an indicator of how evil her parents were. It was just something she shared with her matha's people. Instead of helping, that last thought only made the returning whispers more creative in their names for her.

"Private—" Tetra pushed the slimy thoughts to the side and glanced up at the scrunched-brow look Lieutenant Eyrie was sending her, "—is there something on your mind you need to tell me?"

"No ma'am." Tetra did her best to keep her gaze lowered to the shiny buttons on the woman's uniform so she wouldn't be able to see the truth in Tetra's eyes.

"I see." And...she had. "Let me make something clear to you, Private Cairn: Lord Wenyan was speaking out of his hatred for the Cairns'. Their fire raids killed his son, and he has, understandably, been bitter about it ever since. So, when you arrived on the scene—and could turn into a peryton of all things—you became the perfect target of his aggression."

"You must not worry over his words, however, as he is only speaking from his anger and his grief. And I can assure you, he is one of the few—if not the only one—that actually believes the words he spoke today."

Tetra didn't know how true that last statement was, but she nodded anyway. "Yes ma'am."

Lieutenant Eyrie didn't look convinced, but she continued, "As I was saying, since we are exploring new territory here, I want to see what you have already learned in your flights with Dr. Prin. Army General Taoghn and I have done some research on the way wild perytons fight and have come up with a set of moves for the beginning of our training, but I want to see what you already know first."

"Yes ma'am." Tetra nodded with a salute, then turned and moved away from the lieutenant to give herself some space to turn into a peryton.

When she felt she was far enough away, she stopped and took a deep breath. As she did, one of the pictures she had seen of her matha came to her mind. Despite the whispers of *"freak"*, *"monster"*, and *"unnatural"* stirring there, she couldn't help the smile that lifted the corners of her lips at the thought of her matha; her *real* matha.

Fiery blades scraped against her nervous system as her bones were crushed and put back together. The tendons in her muscles stretched and snapped around her new, lengthening skeleton, and flames burned inside her growing organs while they moved.

As the fires died down, one of the first clear thoughts Tetra had was wondering if it had been more painful for her matha to shift into a small corafish than it was for her to turn into a large peryton. She huffed a sharp breath through her nose and opened her eyes.

The white lighting was much brighter than it had been to her human eyes, and she had to blink them a few times while she stood to get used to the lights. When she was able to see without it giving her a stabbing headache, she turned her neck in Lieutenant Eyrie's direction and lowered her head to get eye-level with her.

She couldn't detect any fear-scent coming from her commanding officer as the tall woman sent her a sharp nod and said, "Now show me what you can do."

Tetra offered her own nod, then opened her wings and leapt into the air. Her enlarged heart pounded in anticipation with each flap of her wings as she gained altitude, and once she rose as high as the hanging ceiling lights, she forced herself to slow to a stop. She lowered her head and took in a deep breath (and noticed the slight fear-scent coming off of Madame Quen) before tucking her wings back into her sides to fall into a dive—like she had seen Leaves Of Gold do.

Air rushed through her fur and whistled past her ears as the stone ground sped closer and closer. Right before she smacked into it, she flung her wings open with a snap and glided back upwards. Her heart raced in exhilaration as she ascended again before showing her new commanding officer all the things she had taught herself the past couple of weeks. She spun, turned sharply, twisted in barrel-rolls, and dove a few more times until Lieutenant Eyrie's voice drew her back to the ground.

"Come back down, Private! I've seen enough."

Tetra tucked in her wings and dove back down but almost immediately opened them about halfway through her descent so she could softly glide the rest of the way. She landed—without tripping—a few meters from her C.O. and stepped over towards her. The rush of adrenaline was already beginning to ebb away as she lowered her head and tilted it slightly, ears pricked, to show she was listening.

Lieutenant Eyrie gave her a nod. "Now—again—before I show you what Army General Taoghn and I have created, I'm going to turn these training droids on, and I want to see what you might know."

There was a calculating spark in her eyes Tetra hadn't seen before, but she didn't let it worry her. Instead, she dipped her head in an acknowledging nod.

The first lieutenant lifted her hand and turned her holonode on. After tapping through a few screens, the training droids behind her came to life and began to march as one unit towards the center of the massive warehouse.

"I will not set them to any offensive modes." Lieutenant Eyrie looked her square in the eyes despite the fact she was almost four times shorter than Tetra now. "I only want to see what you can do."

Tetra nodded again, turned, then flew back into the air with a mighty flap of her wings. When she was high enough, she swooped in a long circle around the group of twenty training droids to study them for a moment.

They all wore dark armor similar to Igrium's army, but they didn't have any silicone skin to cover their silvery, humanoid frames like the ones Norland usually used. Each one carried a different weapon, but none of them were hostile as they marched around in a continuous circle.

Tetra recalled some of the videos she had seen of perytons fighting when she had been researching for flight. From what she remembered, they seemed to use their talons and hooves the most when fighting in the air. So, with that information, she tucked her wings into her sides and dove towards them.

She replayed one of those videos in her mind as the marching androids drew closer. Right before she landed on them, she opened her wings and flung her talons downward. She knocked over a few of the training droids as she glided over them, then flapped her wings and soared upwards again.

Adrenaline buzzed through her as she angled her wings and swooped in another circle around the training droids. She watched those she had knocked over get back up again as a dark whisper invaded her thoughts, *"Look at you...fighting like the monster everyone knows you already are."*

She shook her head with a growl. *I'm not a monster*, she told herself. Just because she turned into a peryton didn't mean she was automatically like every storybook version of the creatures.

Tetra swooped down upon the training droids again, and managed to pick one up in her talons. Pumping her wings, she ascended back towards the roof and dropped the robot. It's metal body hit the ground with a clatter, and that's when she caught another whiff of fear-scent coming from Madame Quen's direction.

Immediately, she lowered her gaze to the android's body parts—now strewn in the midst of the marching others. Her heart stopped as the whispers she had overheard during testing, and Lord Wenyan's comments popped back into her head at the sight.

Tetra's wingbeats faltered, but she didn't try to keep herself in the air as she normally would. Instead, she made a sloppy dive and almost smacked into the floor. She opened her wings in time to land, but her hooves slid on the stone, and she tumbled in a heap of flailing limbs and feathers.

Her antlered head hit the stone ground and a bolt of pain shot through her skull. She gritted her teeth and rested on the cold floor for a few moments, panting, as the thoughts in her head laughed at her.

She really *was* everything they said she was: a monster. Dangerous. Evil spawn of Malackin.

Dread filled her hollow bones as a new truth revealed itself. She couldn't even fulfill her oath without bloodshed—just like her father was infamous for...

"Private!"

Tetra swiveled her ears in the direction of the oncoming footsteps that almost matched the adrenaline racing through her veins. The headache had begun to fade so she lifted her neck and blinked her eyes open, her gaze immediately landing on Lieutenant Eyrie. A strange, sharp smell that almost smelled like fear-scent wafted from her C.O...she was worried.

"What happened?" Lieutenant Eyrie demanded.

Tetra locked eyes with her for a moment, then blinked and looked away with a shake of her head. What had she gotten herself into? Fighting against Igrium was one thing, but fighting as a peryton?

"That's what I thought." Tetra glanced out of one of her eyes at the understanding look Lieutenant Eyrie was sending her. "You're still dwelling on Lord Wenyan's comments, yes?"

Tetra lowered her gaze but didn't shake her head to deny the fact. The man's comments were only a small part of the many different things she had been called to her face, or overheard, since coming to Silvas.

Lieutenant Eyrie paused for a moment. "You can't go back on your oath, Private."

Tetra nodded, still not looking at her. She knew she couldn't—nor did she want to.

"Look at me, Tetra."

She jerked her head in her C.O.'s direction at the sound of her name. The corner of Lieutenant Eyrie's mouth tipped downwards in a small frown.

"You told me you wanted to join our army to stop Emperor Ignis, yes?"

Tetra nodded once.

"So, do you want to fight?"

Again, she nodded.

"But now that the reality of how you're fighting is finally hitting you, you don't want to do it?"

She glanced down at her hooves without any indication of a reply. Her long ears twitched at Lieutenant Eyrie's small sigh.

"I knew this decision was too hasty," she began. "I should have used wisdom and told Chief Baene you weren't ready to do this. I'm sorry I didn't."

Claws pressed upon Tetra's chest as she shook her head slowly, but still, she didn't lift her eyes. It wasn't Galia's fault. Tetra shouldn't have made such a hasty, emotional decision in the first place.

She squeezed her eyes shut and sighed heavily through her nose. She had always been a planner. Her whole life at Norland had been scheduled, and she leaned to like it. Making plans out of haste wasn't something she had done since she was a second-year, but now she had done exactly that—and the reality of her mistake was one she hadn't even put into consideration.

"I know you now realize that you don't want to fight as a peryton," Lieutenant Eyrie said, "but you must. There is no getting out of this. However..."

Tetra finally turned her gaze and glanced down at her commanding officer, ears pricked up slightly. Their eyes met.

"As your commanding officer, I know it's very unwise to try and push you through this training with all these thoughts in your head." She sent her a significant look "So let me remind you that what you're going to do could possibly help us win the war—and I don't say that lightly. Having a trained peryton on our side would make a huge difference in many of our battles. There are places you could fly to that we can't reach, obstacles you could remove that would save us manpower... Our army will benefit greatly from having you on our side.

"And what you do will save many people, Tetra. Not just the men and women you'll be fighting alongside, but also those who are bound by Igrium's control. If we win this war, those under Emperor Ignis' tyranny will once again be free of it." Lieutenant Galia's stare bore into her. "Some might call your ability 'monstrous' or even 'unnatural', but it will be the very thing that helps save those same people from the threat of Igrium."

Tetra tilted her head to the side as that last statement rang through her head. She had never really thought about it like that before...

Lieutenant Eyrie took a step forward. "So, when you're fighting—be it in training or in an actual battle—I want you to remember all those people, Tetra. Don't think about yourself fighting 'monstrously' or anything else others might criticize you as. Instead, remember all the innocent people your actions will save. Think of the amazing things we will be able to accomplish with this ability of yours.

"And as your C.O., I am ordering you to do this." Her tone held a sharp warning in it, "I didn't sign up to train a disobedient peryton. Do you understand?"

Tetra gave her a sharp nod. The pressure on her chest eased a little as her commanding officer spoke, and she was able to push the accusations to the back of her mind again.

"Good. Then let's try this again. Show me what you can do."

With the creak of popping joints and the rustling of feathers, Tetra pushed herself into a stand. She lifted her head and set her gaze on the group of still-marching training droids; the ones she had knocked down earlier were back up and moving alongside their comrades again.

Bunching her muscles, she sprang into the air with a mighty flap of her wings and headed towards their group. Memories of Stellinga and her family flashed through her mind, coupled with those of everything Tetra had seen in the Trivsau camp. She even thought of Aabir and his family, and everything they faced in Igrium because they were of Silvanian-descent.

She narrowed her eyes as she swooped above the training droids once again, her heart pumping a growing heat through her veins. As she had told herself before at the Entransen Lake, it was possible for her to use this ability for good—and she would.

With a roar that drowned out the dark mutterings in the back of her mind, she swooped towards the training droids with a fiery resolve burning through her. Extending her talons, she snapped her wings open and plowed them through the group of androids. Those she hit fell with a clatter of metal.

She flapped her wings and rose into the air again. A stab of guilt pierced her like a knife as she lowered her gaze and watched the fallen androids pick themselves back up again, but she shook it aside. They were only training droids. She had "killed" many at Norland, and they were built for this kind of treatment, anyway.

With that thought, she tried to keep her focus on the task at hand instead of her remorse as she swooped back down upon the training droids a few more times to copy the few maneuvers she had watched on those peryton videos. Her stomach churned with mounting guilt all the while, but she ignored it as best she could with her former thoughts of all those under Igrium's oppression. It helped...a little.

When she had done all that she could remember, she glided back down and landed in front of Lieutenant Eyrie. Tetra widened her eyes slightly as she caught the knowing expression on her C.O's face. Was she that bad at hiding her emotions as a peryton? Or was it because her eyes were now so big that anyone could read what was going on inside her head?

Lieutenant Eyrie answered that question immediately. "I know it's hard—I can see it in your eyes. You're obviously not a monster, nor are you brain-washed like the rest of your countrymen," she said. "But, the only way anyone will be free is if we win this war, Private. Igrium will not give up easily, and since they won't, neither should we. You can't stop because our enemies won't until the Alliance is destroyed, and everything is under their power. Understand?"

Tetra did, but it still didn't destroy the awful weight sitting heavy inside her.

"This is the only way Emperor Ignis will be stopped." Eyrie continued, "If what you said to me yesterday is true, then I need you to push all those guilty thoughts to the side and focus on those you're protecting. We can help stop Igrium if you keep your focus on that—it's not your fault Emperor Ignis has brainwashed Igrium into giving up their lives for his tyrannical plans."

Tetra nodded slowly and gave a low rumble of assent as her anger ignited in her chest. It really was her father's fault... But now she had a way to help stop him. Despite the weight still in her churning stomach, she recalled her first oath and the one she had recently sworn. Resolve burned away some of the guilt but didn't erase it completely.

Lieutenant Eyrie peered into her eyes for a few long moments, then gave a sharp nod. "Now that that's settled," she lifted her arm and turned her holonode on, "let me show you what Army General Taoghn and I have been working on."

Chapter Fifty

A BREEZE RIPPLED THROUGH the fields of green spread out in front of Aabir, his family, and Mister Falap. He couldn't enjoy the view or the conversations going on around the picnic meal, though. He glanced down at his barely eaten sandwich, but his twisting stomach rumbled in protest at even the thought of eating it. So, he lifted his head and lowered his hands to the soft grass behind him, leaning back on them as he stared out at the fields, his thoughts miles away.

The Constantia Tourney was only two days away, and all Aabir had been able to do the past week was worry about it. Lieutenant Denir had forced him and Buren to go practice at the arena again; and during those two visits, he had heard more dishonorable things said against the prisoners than he ever heard before—and none of that helped ease the weight of guilt pressing upon his chest.

He closed his eyes with a quiet sigh. He had failed. Despite everything he had done to help try and protect people—be it his family or the Constantia prisoners—he always ended up failing somehow. Which made him not only a coward, but a failure, too.

"You need to eat, Aabir." He opened his eyes and turned his neck in Matha's direction. He caught the concern shining in her eyes but shook his head.

"I'm not hungry."

She opened her mouth to say something, but then turned her head in Patre's direction as he put his hand on her shoulder with a shake of his head.

"If he doesn't want to eat, he doesn't have to," he said.

Aabir met his patre's eyes and gave him a grateful nod. He could barely keep down the couple sandwich bites he had forced himself to eat, and the last thing this day needed was for his stomach to be upset.

"I'll eat it, then," Zeke piped up and grabbed the sandwich off Aabir's plate.

He did not even have the energy to roll his eyes as his brother stuffed his face with the food. Instead, he lowered his chin into his cupped hand and stared off at nothing while his thoughts circled around his impending doom.

A weight fell on Aabir's shoulders. He turned his head and met Mister Falap's guilty gaze.

"I'm sorry you're having to do this, Aabir. Like I've said before, I wish the Tourney was what it used to be, but..." he let out a weary sigh, "this empire isn't what it used to be."

"It's OK, Mister Falap." Aabir shrugged and looked down at the red, checkered quilt they were picnicking on. "I know it's not your fault."

The elderly man had been saying things like that all weekend. Aabir appreciated his sincerity, but guilt only made his own remorse grow for finding himself in the situation—even if it was forced upon him.

Mister Falap shook his head and removed his hand. "My leniency, and every other Igrians', towards the things Emperor Ignis has done since he first became emperor could be considered a fault. And now most of them are brainwashed zealots who don't seem to realize we're now doing the same thing to the rest of the world our empire first fought from to become Igrium."

Aabir breathed out sharply through his nose at the irony. Igrium—the empire whose history and culture were built on their love of freedom from bondage was now trying to enslave and rule over every other nation on the planet. Where had it all gone wrong? When did the emperor's wishes replace the truth?

Crimson and gray shadows danced on the quilt's bright surface as wind whistled through the swaying treetops above them. The thought of the blood about to be spilled in the Tourney popped into his head at the sight, and he squeezed his eyes shut as if it would stop his imagination.

"Hopefully it will turn back to what it once was," said Patre in the silence.

"I hope you're right." Aabir barely heard Mister Falap's creaky reply before it was snatched up by the wind.

The only sounds for a while after were the creaking of tree branches, the furious blowing of the leaves attached to them, and the random noises Yahel made as she ate her food happily, completely oblivious to the heavy atmosphere surrounding them. Then, a shrill ring broke through the quiet and sent a buzz through Aabir's wrist. His heart leapt at the sound, and he turned an annoyed glare to his holonode. The screen flashed on as he lifted his arm, and Ezen's name shone on the holographic screen.

His heart jumped again. Despite it being almost a full week, Ezen still had not told Aabir what was bothering him, so maybe that was why he was calling...

He scrambled up and stood from the quilt. "I'll be right back."

He glanced down at the confused looks his family was sending him, but then Patre nodded for him to go, and he sped off into the woods behind their picnic spot for some privacy. When he thought he was far enough away, he tapped the answer button.

Ezen's face appeared on the screen. "Hey, Aabir."

"Hey," he replied. "Did...you need something?"

"Yeah, I...I need to talk to you—in person—about...some of those things I've been dealing with." Ezen cleared his throat. "I know you said you and your family were gonna be gone this weekend, but I was wondering if you were back yet?"

"We won't be leaving until later tonight." Dread again flipped Aabir's stomach at the thought of Firstdein morning coming tomorrow. "Sorry, Ezen. I don't think I'll have time."

"Eh, that's OK. I can tell you when the Tourney is over." Ezen shrugged and looked away from the screen for a moment. "I guess I'll see you later, then."

Aabir nodded. "See ya."

Ezen hung up, and the holonode screen turned black. Aabir tapped the device off, then crossed his arms and stared out at the shadows of the woods surrounding him. A few beams of bright sollight filtered through the towering treetops above, but not enough to dispel the gloomy atmosphere.

A frown marred his countenance as he stared off into the gloom. With everything else he was a failure at, he could add "failing to be available for his friend to talk to" on that list. He kicked a stone, and it flew into a clump of bracken, causing a scurrus to jump out of the foliage and skitter up a russet tree trunk. He watched the fuzzy animal climb higher and higher until it ran into the tree's leafy foliage and disappeared.

If only he could climb away from his problems that easily.

He curled his hands into fists. Yet all he seemed able to do was dig himself deeper into ever-worsening messes—and others as well. Even with his supposed success of retrieving the map, it had only helped those twenty-four people get captured; and had probably made life worse for the prisoners, too. The weight of the guilt upon his chest tightened as the angry fire that had been burning there grew hotter.

All those people were about to be killed. He had failed them. Blood pounded in his ears. He had failed, and he was too much of a coward to do anything else to help them. Just as Mister Falap attributed complacency to Igrium's citizens becoming the brainwashed masses they were, so too was Aabir guilty of the same thing. Though Tetra's actions never seemed to help, she had stood for the morals he himself had introduced her to. She might have been punished more than anyone in Norland's history had been, but she never wavered. She was never a coward, no matter how Igrium tried to label her as such.

Aabir was the real coward. He had stood by in his own selfish bubble and used the excuse of protecting his family to stay in it—when he was really hiding in it for himself—while people were killed year after year in the Tourney, and those of Alliance-descent were questioned and imprisoned.

With everything he had witnessed in those prisons, he could not be a failing-coward. Staying in that bubble was no longer an option he could afford. He had to do something...

As the fire inside him grew, so did the heavy weight of his reality. The only thing he could do was make sure he lost during the end of the second day. He truly could not lose earlier. He knew Lieutenant Denir had high-ranking friends, and Aabir had no doubt since he was of Silvanian-descent that his C.O. would be able to bring his family into the punishment as well if he lost too soon. So that was what he had to do—and he could say with complete confidence it was not only out of selfishness.

So, once he got out of the Tourney, he would figure out something that might help. Maybe if he messaged Rasiela she would come up with some ideas...

Aabir sighed and pressed his knuckles against his temples. This was too much to think about right now. First, he needed to focus on failing out of the Constantia Tourney safely, then he could worry about how to no longer be a coward.

At the thought of the Tourney, the invisible weight grew heavier again, but this time it caught the attention of his sizzling anger. He lowered his clenched fists and glanced around for the closest tree before stepping towards it. He imagined Lieutenant Denir's face on its trunk, then he lifted his arm back and punched it. Pain stabbed his bare knuckles, but he ignored it in the white-hot rage that began to flood through him. Emperor Ignis' face replaced Denir's, and he punched it with his other fist. More faces of Tourney Planners' he had come to see at the arena practices flashed onto the trunk in his mind's eye, and he beat the immovable tree with each one he saw.

He continued to punch out all his frustrations at his current situation, and at the angry injustice he felt for the prisoners and all those of Alliance-descent until a voice cut through the pounding-buzz in his ears.

"Aabir!"

Immediately, he snapped out of the red haze and was hit with the shocking pain in his knuckles. He hissed and pressed his shaky hands against his shirt. Only then did he realize there was blood bubbling out of them.

"Aabir..." He spun around and locked eyes with Matha. She lifted her hand to her mouth as her wide gaze landed on his bloodied hands. "What are you doing?"

Aabir glanced back at the tree. "I..." His voice came out hoarse. Had he been shouting? "I...I'm punching a—a tree."

"Why?"

He turned his head forward again but would not meet her gaze. "I needed to."

"But—"

"Zerah," Patre, who stood next to Matha, put his hand on her shoulder to steer her away, "let me talk to him.

Fire filled Matha's eyes and she turned out of Patre's grip to protest, but he gave her an unmoving look. "Please," he added.

She looked at him for another long moment, the muscles in her neck tensed, but then she nodded in understanding. With one more worried glance in Aabir's direction, she headed back through the woods towards the picnic area.

When she was gone, Patre turned to face Aabir. He crossed his arms and their eyes locked. Instead of the sternness Aabir thought he would see, his patre's dark purple eyes were soft with understanding.

"You scared us all half to death, Aabir," he said, "yelling and going on the way you did. We thought you were being attacked."

"I'm sorry," Aabir breathed out.

"I know." Patre sighed. "But I'm glad you released all of that on the tree and not us."

The corners of his lips lifted in a soft smile, but Aabir could not match it. After an awkward moment, Patre's smile faded as he sighed again.

"Did you do it because of the Tourney?"

"Yes, sir."

"Do you feel better now?"

The stabbing pains in his knuckles screamed "no", but the fire that had been burning in him all week waiting for a release had dimmed.

"A little," he replied with a small shrug.

"Then is there anything else you need to say that might help?"

Aabir glanced down at his bleeding hands as he replied, "I...I've failed too much, Patre. I've been a coward, and I...I no longer want to be that way. I've—I've seen too much for me to keep on with this false sense of security I've been living with my whole life. So, all I want is to do something right. I want to—to help, but all the helping I've done has only made me fall deeper and deeper into messes like this."

"Getting into the Tourney wasn't your fault." Patre's calm voice challenged him to argue.

Aabir lifted his head and accepted the challenge. "You say that, but I know it's not true. *I'm* the one who joined Norland. *I'm* the one who learned how to swordfight there. *I'm* the one who enjoyed it so much I pushed myself to get better at it. And now here I am: facing the consequences of my 'helpful' actions."

Instead of replying immediately, Patre stepped towards him, then lifted his hand and placed it on Aabir's shoulder. "Yes, you did all those things, but you weren't told you were fighting for that spot in the Tourney, nor would I have ever expected you to do so."

Patre twisted his lips as he thought for a moment. "Although the choices you made have not always been the best, your Matha and I already forgave you for them—and we're not oblivious to the fact that you were always only making those plans to help make our lives easier, even though that was never your job to do. So, if you want to do something to help others, I think that's great, but how about you focus first on getting out of the Tourney before the third day, and then we can handle the rest of your grand plans. Alright?"

Aabir only nodded, unable to match the small smile lifting the corners of his patre's mouth. "OK."

"I love you, Aabir," Patre added, "and no matter what happens in that Tourney, that won't change."

"But what if..." He could barely get the words out past the dread they brought up, "What if I do make it to the third day? What—what am I supposed to do then? I don't have any plans that could help me with that..."

Physical weight rested on his other shoulder, and he met Patre's stern gaze. "If that happens, then we'll figure one out. There are so many rules, I'm sure we could find one that would help you—but you don't need to worry about that now, Aabir. Let's just take this one day at a time, alright?"

Pressure built up behind Aabir's eyes, but he squeezed them shut before anything could come from it. With a deep exhale through his nose, he opened them again. "Yes sir."

Patre dipped his chin in a slow nod, then wrapped his arms around Aabir in an almost suffocating hug. And as quickly as it came, it ended—but it was enough. A small smile finally escaped from Aabir's face as Patre lowered his arms and stepped back.

"Are you ready to go back now?" He asked, a ghost of a grin on his weathered face. "Or do you need to punch a few more trees?"

Aabir glanced down at the blood dripping from his wounded knuckles. "I think I'm good for now." He looked back up with his own grin.

Patre gestured to Aabir's hands. "Your Matha will probably want to take a look at those."

He nodded and they both set off back through the woods. Bright blue sky and green hills soon appeared through the thick trunks ahead of them, and the gloom around Aabir seemed to lessen a little with each step they took. He went over his patre's words as they walked and, in the quiet, sent up a silent prayer to Deleyon, "*Help me to know what to do—no matter what happens.*"

Yahel's squealing laughter broke through the quiet woods, and he rolled his eyes with a grin. With a silent "*thank You*", he picked up his pace and followed Patre out of the woods and into Soll's light.

A CROSSBOW BOLT WHIZZED past Rasiela's ear and went straight through the holographic screen in front of her. She spun around and caught a glimpse of a dark figure as she ducked behind the desk's chair. Another bolt struck the back of her barricade, its tip poking out of the chair only a few inches above her nose.

There was the sound of another bolt being loaded, but Rasiela jumped up from her hiding spot and barreled into her attacker before they could shoot again. She grappled the crossbow out of the woman's grip and hit her in the side of the head with it, knocking her out cold.

Rasiela pulled herself up, grabbed the last bolt in the sheath on the woman's hip, loaded it in her newly acquired weapon, and ran out of the dark room. She fled into the maze of hallways and rooms that made up part of the warehouse base the secret group used in Igrium. Her heart pounded inside her chest as the sounds of rushing footsteps roared like an impending thunderstorm behind her.

She had broken into their databases and begun sifting through old messages and loads of files before that woman had come into the records room and ruined her plans of downloading it all. Thank Deleyon, Rasiela had a fantastic memory; yet even if she did not, the things she had seen were too big—too horrible—for her to ever forget them easily.

Urgency aided Rasiela's adrenaline as she turned a corner and fled down a flight of stairs. Chief Baene needed to know what they were planning, and the possibilities of who was in their group before—

Something hit her in the back of the head, and she crumpled without another thought.

Chapter Fifty-One

The sweet, earthy aromas of Cherry Valley flitted past Tetra's nose. She inhaled deeply as the rows of cherry trees lining the valley's sides came into view, unable to suppress the smile that escaped her lips.

After the past few days of training, she didn't realize how much of a break she needed until now.

Wind whistled past her long ears as she tilted her wings and began descending towards the vast peryton village. She wouldn't have thought becoming a peryton would give her such a break after training to fight as one, but she couldn't help the feeling of freedom flight brought her. The open air that surrounded her, the wind blowing through her feathers, and the hundreds of smells she was learning to recognize and distinguish between gave her an exhilaration training in the mountain could never do.

Not that the mountain's limited space was the reason for her new tangle of conflicting emotions...

She huffed a sharp breath with a flap of her wings. Fighting as a peryton was still just as mentally taxing now as it had been the first day, despite Lieutenant Eyrie's words from then still ringing in her head like Norland's bell.

Whispers that spoke of how much of a monster she was for the way she fought continued to assault her whenever she trained—and not even the thoughts of those whom she was fighting for could fully stop them. Sometimes they helped, but many times they didn't; leaving her wishing she wasn't bound by a public oath, and her own private one, so she could quit.

So maybe it was seeing how un-monstrous perytons truly were that could equate to the day's added excitement. She still had so many questions about them, as did Dr. Prin, and hoped that with the more answers she gleaned today, she would be able to combat her unwanted "monster" labels with the truth of what she witnessed.

She could hope, anyway.

A lake breeze wafted the multitude of individual peryton scents towards Tetra. She closed her eyes for a moment and breathed in deeply to try to distinguish between them. A few rose above the rest, but she had no idea why her nose might pick them out above the multitudes of others. Only when she opened her eyes again did she wonder if the perytons she could see flying above the Entransen Lake's shore near her were the owners of those scents.

It became quite obvious that was the case as one of those perytons—a familiar, sandy-furred one—flapped her great wings and ascended towards Tetra's direction.

"Ah, it's you." Strength Like Stone came to a stop ahead of Tetra and dipped her antlered head in greeting. "We were wondering what that new smell was."

A flash of embarrassment went through Tetra, but she immediately tried to squelch the emotion before Strength Like Stone could smell it.

"Oh, no! It's not a bad thing!" The other peryton added in a rush, "It only reminded us of no-furs, that's all."

Tetra ruffled her feathers as more heat went through them. Even she could now smell the sharp, earthy scent she had come to recognize as embarrassment coming from her.

Having one's emotions displayed for all to know was one peryton thing she would've been fine missing out on.

"Anyway, are you here to see Leaves Of Gold again?" Strength Like Stone asked in a more straightforward tone.

Tetra nodded, grateful she wasn't pointing out the diminishing emotional smell between them. "I am."

"Well, you just missed him—Glistening Lake relieved him of guard duty only a few moments ago." The other peryton dipped her head downwards, in the direction of a grayish brown peryton below them. "But I think he mentioned something about heading to the market, so you should be able to find him there."

"Thank you."

Strength Like Stone dipped her head once before diving back down towards Glistening Lake. Tetra breathed a sigh of relief and continued her descent towards Cherry Valley. As she did, she once again tried to distinguish between the many scents belonging to the perytons bustling about the village below. But this time, she tried to recall the memory of Leaves Of Gold's scent amidst the tangle of others while keeping her eyes peeled for his golden-brown coloring.

Even with the higher humidity, there were just as many perytons out as there were the first time she had come. As her searching gaze roved over the landscape, she caught glances of those who were farming the caffeine cherries; others flying with bags hanging on their necks or in their back talons; fawns playing and splashing in the river while, on the opposite shore, older perytons were stabbing their hooves into the water then throwing the eels they had caught onto the bank. All normal, non-monstrous things that humans also did.

She tilted her wings further to quicken her descent until she was flying right above the river's bluish-green waters. More perytons flew around her, and the wind carried snatches of some of their conversations towards her ears,

"...had the best coffee I've ever tasted..."

"...I cleaned the fireplace last time! Mother wanted you to..."

"...never did I think the City Of Willows would become such a dangerous place..."

"...sure he said that?"

"Positive. Why would Veiled Glimmer be distraught..."

With each snippet, Tetra could feel the invisible weight she had been carrying the past week lightening. Those sounded like normal conversations she would overhear humans saying (except for the oddly long names, of course).

Perytons aren't monsters, she told herself, *which means neither am I.*

"*But none of them are fighting like you...*"

She tried to combat the intrusive thought by recalling the bleeding peryton guard who had ended her and Leaves Of Gold's conversation last time. They obviously had to fight to protect their village from raiders, and she wasn't stupid enough to think they had earned their reputation among humanity for nothing, but there was a difference between fighting to defend oneself and only attacking out of a "beastly" nature—and she had to continually remind herself she wasn't doing the latter. She was fighting to defend something, too.

Determination rose around her mind as she followed that hovertrain of thought. She would help fix the problems her father had caused, and somehow gain back her lost honor while doing so.

A burst of excitement immediately followed the resolute thoughts as the market atop the stone bridge came into her sight—along with the familiar coloring of Leaves Of Gold. She pumped her wings faster to try and catch up with his easy-going glide.

With all the smells coming from the busy marketplace, she couldn't distinguish his scent from all the others, but as she drew nearer to him, she noticed his ears perk up as he came to a stop. He turned around and their eyes locked from across the distance.

"Tetra!" He roared; a soft, peryton smile lighting up his furry features.

She couldn't help but smile back as she continued towards him. He flapped his great wings and helped close the distance between them.

"I'm glad you decided to come back," he said as they both stopped in midair. "I began to wonder if I had scared you off."

"I've just been busy," she replied, forcing herself not to dwell upon any of the rising thoughts that might let off some emotional scent she didn't want broadcast.

Leaves Of Gold flicked his ears, a mild scent coming from him—one Tetra recognized but had no idea what it meant. "I'm glad to hear it." He turned his neck to gesture towards the noisy market behind him. "I was just about to go find something to eat before heading to my shop. Would you care to join me?"

She nodded, her curiosity buzzing. "Sure."

His smile grew and he turned in midair with a flourish of his wings. "I can introduce you to some of the vendors." Tetra followed him as he headed towards the bridge. "And I can show you which ones sell the best coffee seeds—all grown and roasted here, of course!"

A spike of dread doused all her curiosity. She tried to think up an excuse to not sound any different than what she knew she was. "I...I didn't bring anything to trade, though."

Obviously, the poisonous cherries were not dangerous to perytons, but she didn't want to take a chance in eating them even as one.

"That's OK." He turned his head back in her direction and shot her a grin. "I've got plenty of favors I can call in."

Tetra swallowed without reply and glanced down at her reflection in the river below. She didn't want to offend the peryton who was taking the time to show her around, but she also didn't want to die from caffeine poisoning. Maybe she could just accept the seeds then drop them in the lake on her way back...

Leaves Of Gold's form came up beside her reflection, and she jerked her head up to meet the understanding look in his big eyes. "If you don't want any roasted seeds, you can just say so."

Great. She had given off a smell, hadn't she?

"I'm sorry, Leaves Of Gold," she replied with a sigh, "I didn't want to be rude, but I'd rather not have any..."

"That's OK." He barely dipped his chin towards her then turned his head forward. "I understand—I can't have our valley's coffee seeds, either. The kind we grow here is too strong, and I...I can't handle it."

Tetra tilted her head and sent a questioning look towards his darkened countenance. Her heart skipped a frightful beat at the shadows she saw there—they resembled the villainous, storybook peryton pictures she had seen throughout human cultures—yet her fear diminished at the almost-shameful look she could see in his eyes. The musty smell she caught a whiff of also silenced her fears. It was nothing like the almost-spicy smells she now associated with deceit and other bad things.

She turned her head forward and flapped her wings a couple times. Whatever had caused that look, it wasn't anything she needed to worry about. And a glance out of the corner of her eye that showed the noticeable lightening of his furry features only bolstered that fact.

A new string of curiosity unraveled amidst the many peryton-related questions she already had. What could make Leaves Of Gold's seemingly always-cheerful countenance change so much? Despite this probing question, she kept it to herself as he angled his wings and swooped into a landing amid the shopping crowds meandering along the bridge.

He glanced up at Tetra with a smile—any hint of shadows gone. "Come on!" He gestured with his front hoof towards the row of booths on the bridge's left side. "I'll introduce you to Wings Like Sand's parents."

Tetra stayed in the air a few moments longer to wait for a couple of other perytons to pass by him before folding in her wings and diving into a land where they had been. She only stumbled a little as her hooves and talons hit the stone, but she folded in her wings as if she was completely confident in the less-than-impressive landing.

With another smile, Leaves Of Gold led her between the milling crowds to a small, wooden booth where a peryton—who had the same mottled, sandy-colored fur and feathers as Wings Like Sand—had his back turned in their direction. The closer they moved towards it, the heavier the scent of roasted cherry seeds grew. Tetra's mouth began to water as she took in a big whiff of the deadly seeds, and she withheld a sigh of longing as they came to a stop in front of the booth.

"Forest Grower..." said Leaves Of Gold.

The mottled peryton—Forest Grower, Tetra assumed—jerked his neck up and around from the cloth bags he was sorting. A smile came across his wider snout as he dipped his head in their direction.

"It's good to see you again, Leaves Of Gold," he said in a deep, gravelly voice that almost reminded her of the ambulate trees when they walked.

He turned around to fully face them, and his eyes locked onto Tetra's. A wave of surprise-scent came towards her from his direction, and she couldn't help but pin her ears back in embarrassment. She should've expected that to happen—what with it happening every other time she had met a peryton so far—yet she didn't like the way it made her feel even more different than what she already knew she was. Being a freak among humans was already hard, but being a freak among perytons only made her wish all the more for a break from being so.

"And who is this?" No more surprise scent came from Forest Grower, and Tetra could see understanding softening his dark eyes. She tried to breathe in any hint of deceit coming from him, but all she could make out was the dull, mellow scent she had come to acknowledge as the normal smell of perytons.

"This is Tetra." Leaves Of Gold tilted his head in her direction. "She's visiting today, and I thought I would show her around the market."

"Ah!" More understanding lit up Forest Grower's eyes. "You're the one Wings Like Sand was telling us about."

Tetra stiffened. "Um...I hope nothing bad..."

Forest Grower shook his head with a deep, throaty purr. "No, no. He only told us he had met a peryton with a strange name who had come from the land across the islands."

"Oh." Tetra relaxed with a relieved nod. "OK."

"He also said he mentioned if you needed a job that we could use your help—and he was right." The mottled peryton blinked with a small nod. "We're always looking for young perytons to help us during this season—and you don't have to know anything about cherry farming or roasting. My mate, Falling Water, and I can teach you everything."

Tetra processed his words for a moment, letting her imagination run with the idea of learning to farm as a peryton. It would give her a lot of information to take back to Dr. Prin, but...

"Thank you for the offer, Forest Grower," she replied, "but I don't think my schedule would allow for that."

Fighting for the Alliance was much more urgent than cherry farming—no matter how curious she was about the process.

Forest Grower shrugged his wings. "That's all right." He sent her another understanding nod before turning his head to Leaves Of Gold. "I'm sorry I haven't stopped by your shop in a while. We've been so busy with the harvest that I haven't had much time to do anything else."

"I understand." Leaves Of Gold dipped his head. "Wings Like Sand usually comes to visit every once in a while to tell me how you all are doing, anyway."

Another purr rumbled from Forest Grower. "Of course he does." He shook his antlered head with a huff. "But I hope he doesn't bother you when he comes."

"Not at all." Leaves Of Gold purred. "I enjoy his company."

"Well, I'm glad, because sometimes I worry about him. He keeps telling Falling Water and I that he wants to move into his own cave soon, but we don't think he's ready for that. I know he's twenty-eight season-cycles, but I didn't leave my parents' cave until I was thirty-one! And there were even a few times where I regretted it afterward and wanted to go back."

Tetra blinked. Did he mean thirty-one years old?

She caught Leaves Of Gold's side-eye glance, and a worm of worry went through her. Had she given off a scent that told him she thought something was wrong with that statement? Yet instead of saying anything, he only turned his attention back on Forest Grower.

"The next time he visits, I can mention something to him about it." A shadowed look like the one from before flashed across his features for a moment.

"If you think it's all right, I can tell him about how I wish I could've lived with my family for longer than I did."

"We would appreciate it, Leaves Of Gold—but only if you are fine with doing that."

"I am." Leaves Of Gold dipped his head, the serious shadow once again gone with a soft smile. "Well anyway, I just wanted to see how you were doing. I would stay longer, but I'd like to introduce Tetra to a few others before I get lunch."

"Of course," Forest Grower replied, "May the Unrivaled King clear your path."

"And yours'." Leaves Of Gold turned to face Tetra, his smile growing. "Are you OK with looking around more?"

She nodded with her own smile, her curiosity growing with his enthusiasm. "Yes!"

"Then let me introduce you to Flowering Ivy. She's a guard, too, but she also makes the best eel rolls in the valley." He stopped himself mid-step and sent her a strange look she couldn't decipher. "Unless you can't eat eel rolls either..."

Tetra pinned her ears back as a rush of nerves laced through her wings. She didn't know what that look meant, but something about it made her uneasy.

Even so, she wasn't here solely for her own curiosity and didn't want to come back to Dr. Prin with only the things she had already told the Silvanian Head Biologist; so, "I've never had eel before," she lifted her head and met his eyes, "but I'll see if I can try it."

Leaves Of Gold's smile returned and he nodded with a blink. "Then come." He turned and merged into the crowds, calling over his shoulder, "Her booth should be right over here!"

Tetra took one sniff to make sure he wasn't putting anything on and caught only a soft, flowery smell coming from him amidst the hundreds of others surrounding them. So, with that assurance, she followed him to Flowering Ivy's covered booth—then all over the rest of the busy marketplace.

As he introduced her and made small talk with the vendors, she drank in everything she witnessed—from the biggest greetings roared out to the smallest details in the carved tables most of the booths were made of—and hoped she would remember it all when she told Dr. Prin later.

By the time Leaves Of Gold led her to his shop, she had met more perytons with long-winded names—Trailing Clouds, Soll That Rises, and Eyes Of Oak to name a few—and had practically been run over by two fawns whom Leaves Of Gold simply called "Crimson" and "Lightning". She had also eaten a few of Flowering Ivy's eel rolls—which reminded her of the stuffed leaf-wraps she had eaten in Xich—and been enthralled by the woven baskets, sparkling jewelry, wooden toys, and the many other handmade (or, *hoof*-made) items she saw being sold. They even passed by a cave shop with shelves carved into its stone face; the ends of real parchment scrolls sticking out of them.

Tetra almost asked Leaves Of Gold if they could stop there, but he had already made it to another booth and called her over to meet the peryton attending it before she could do so. And by the time they were done with that conversation, she was beginning to feel a bit overwhelmed and wanted to find somewhere quiet to sit for a while. So Leaves Of Gold brought her to his shop's calm atmosphere, where she sat to watch him while he poured water from an urn-like cup—with looping handles for him to hold it with his thumbless hooves—into a cauldron hanging in one of the shop's fireplaces.

"Are you sure you don't want any?" He looked over his shoulder and met her eyes with his own. "It might not give as much energy as other kinds would, but it may give you a little."

"No thanks," she shook her head and lowered her gaze to her hooves. "Sitting in here is already helping."

There was a rustling of feathers as he turned back towards the cauldron. "Alright, then."

An uncomfortable silence settled between them. Tetra lightly tapped the stone floor with her hoof anxiously, then finally lifted her head back up at the sound of Leaves Of Gold setting the cup down. She couldn't stop herself from flinching as one of his elbows popped back into its inward position. She sent a glance back down at her own elbows and winced.

Through their market adventure, she noticed the two opposing directions peryton elbows could face—outwards for walking, and inwards (like a human's elbow) for picking things up. She hadn't realized until then the mobility of her peryton joints, but she didn't want to try moving them in that way until she asked Dr. Prin the specifics about it.

The wonderful aroma of coffee seeds wafted past Tetra's nose as Leaves Of Gold brought out a cloth bag, and then a wooden funnel with a piece of cloth poking out of its top, from behind one of the display counters. He placed the funnel in the top of the cup, poured the ground coffee seeds into that, and picked up the now-steaming cauldron by its looped handles and poured some of the water into the funnel.

As he did all this, his eyes lifted to her face. "Are you sure you don't want to try some...?"

She forced a smile she didn't feel with her growing worry. "I'm good, Leaves Of Gold."

"OK..." Another strange look flashed across his long snout before he turned to put the cauldron back on its hanger; the heavy coffee smell almost masking the musty scent coming off him.

She pressed her ears back against her head and glanced around the shop. What should she do...? She didn't want to leave yet, but she was beginning to wonder if it would be wiser to go. That wasn't the first time her peryton host had sent her that look, nor the first time she had smelled that same scent from him.

Tetra didn't know exactly how many things she had said that day that would give him pause, but she knew there had been a few. It wasn't that she meant to, she just didn't know what normal peryton knowledge was. Some of the things she had overheard Leaves Of Gold and the vendors talking about either made no sense or sounded completely absurd to her human brain, so she had tried to ask him with as veiled questions as possible what their answers might be. Sometimes he answered, but it wasn't the answer she intended to get; while other times he would send her that same strange expression before giving her the response she had wanted.

More worry pressed upon her chest as she heard him move to sit back down and felt his eyes upon her; the mild, emotional smell only growing. What could she say...?

Her gaze landed on a wooden sculpture of two fighting perytons. One stood on its back talons, its jaw opened in a roar in the direction of the other, flying peryton. Even in the dim lighting, her eyes picked up the tiny details of each feather, stroke of fur, and willow leaf carved into the background. Though she shouldn't have been surprised at this point, her worry was momentarily overshadowed as she, once again, marveled at the patience and creativity her peryton host must have to make such a piece.

Still without turning her neck in his direction, she asked, "What is that sculpture called?"

"Which one?" The mild smell was overtaken by a sharper one as he spoke.

"The one with the fighting perytons."

"Oh! It's called 'Fight for Kingship'."

Tetra tilted her head and locked eyes with him, unable to contain the wind of curiosity blowing anew in her mind. "Is it depicting a real fight?"

"It's my depiction of when King Weathered Eyes was challenged by the future King Trails Through Air."

"Ah." Tetra nodded as if she knew exactly what he was talking about.

Despite her attempt, his musty scent came back in full force. His golden-brown eyes stayed locked on hers; and despite how her heart raced with heightened anxiety, she couldn't look away.

"Not that you would even know who those perytons are," he finally said, "or why that challenge was so important."

Oh no.

"I—"

"—No, Tetra," he interrupted with a shake of his head. "You can't lie to me. I know you are not really a peryton."

No, no, no, no... Her heart leapt into her throat as she tried to stand, but his gaze had hers locked as if in a gritanium clamp. As she stared, motionless, in those heart-pounding moments, something in his eyes gave her pause. There were no shadows; nothing sharp. In fact, something akin to *excitement* sparkled in their brown depths.

"You...you do?" She was finally able to say.

He dipped his chin, his eyes never leaving hers. "Yes." A ghost of a smile barely lifted the corners of his lips. "I could smell your surprise when Forest Grower said he left his family's cave at thirty-one season-cycles; you've refused every offer of coffee I've given you—even the weakest brew one can find; you continued asking me questions about things I thought everyone would know; I have never seen anyone wear metal like you do before; your name is...well, strange—I don't mean to be rude, but it's hard to pronounce; and—again, I don't mean to sound rude, but—I've never known a peryton to have *blue* eyes before. Not even over-caffeination can change someone's appearance that much.

"But even before today, I knew you weren't truly a peryton." He paused to take a breath—and in the moment's silence, Tetra again wondered if she should leave, but his next words stopped her from doing so, "After the first time we met, I had many questions about why you would be protecting no-furs, so I...I hid in the leaves of a walking tree and watched as you—as you somehow...*changed* into a no-fur."

Tetra's fur stood on end. "Leaves Of Gold..."

"And it was incredible!" The firelight flashed in his eyes as he smiled. "I've always thought no-furs were more than the territorial fawn-nappers most of our stories say they are—I mean, there are even rumors that King Bringer Of Misery looks the way he does because no-furs did something to him when he was a fawn, so they must be somewhat intelligent to do that—but anyway... After I saw you change, I asked the Unrivaled King if I could somehow meet with you again—and then we did!"

He pawed his hoof and lowered his neck apologetically. "I've been waiting for the right time to tell you all this, and I'm sorry that I've kept my knowledge of what you are for this long, but I couldn't find a good time to reveal it. I...I didn't want you to get scared and run away."

Tetra narrowed her eyes. From what she had learned of Leaves Of Gold so far, it didn't seem to be in his character to turn someone away, but she still felt the need to ask, "Why wouldn't you want that?"

"Well, because I have many questions," his smile dimmed with a sharp scent Tetra didn't recognize. His eyes lowered to the floor as he pawed it with his front hoof. "And I hope you don't take this the wrong way, but I also did it because I needed to know if you were a threat."

Tetra shot a quick glance towards the entryway, but turned her eyes back on Leaves Of Gold as he continued, "It's my responsibility to protect this village, and I...well, like I just mentioned with King Bringer Of Misery and the rumors surrounding him, I needed to make sure that you, or the no-furs with you, weren't planning on harming us."

"So, you invited me to your village to *protect* it?" Worry caused the words to come out sharper than Tetra meant them to be.

"I wanted to see how you would react when I showed you around," Leaves Of Gold shrugged his wings. "During our second meeting, all I could sense when I flew into you was wariness and excitement—which were about the same things I was feeling about meeting a no-fur. So I knew if you had some evil intention, I'd be able to smell it easily—along with every other peryton around you."

Embarrassment ruffled Tetra's feathers, but Leaves Of Gold only lifted his head with a smile. "Which is not a bad thing," he added. "If you had been good at hiding it, I never would have trusted you."

She blinked and stared into his bright eyes, taking a few moments to breathe in his now-flowery scent. He didn't seem like he was lying, and she doubted he would be able to fake that perfume-like smell...

"So...you aren't going to run me out of here?"

He straightened his neck and blinked at her as if she had grown a third antler. "Of course not! Though you've kept what you are secret, I don't fault you for it. I would do the same if I could turn into a no-fur and visited one of your villages."

Tetra turned her face away and stared at the orange and yellow flames as they licked the cauldron's blackened sides. So, he had known all along, yet he hadn't tried to fight, or kill, her. She glanced over at his expectant expression out of the corner of her eye. Instead, he had shown her hospitality, introduced her to some of his friends and fellow villagers, and even bartered for her lunch of eel rolls.

"Well...I guess I should thank you, then." She turned her neck and looked him square in the eyes, "Even if it was all to gauge my trustworthiness, you still showed me around your village and have been more friendly to me than...than most no-furs. So...thank you. Could you forgive me for keeping this a secret?"

"Of course!" He nodded with a smile. "Like I said, I understand why you didn't tell me before, and I don't fault you for it."

She gave him a small smile of her own. "Well, thank you."

He nodded again, and it was followed by a thoughtful silence that settled between them. A tinge of curiosity-smell mingled with the flowering-scent in the pause, and Tetra breathed in deeply of it to settle the pounding of her heart.

She hadn't even realized until that moment how taut her muscles were, so she relaxed them.

If it weren't for her heightened senses, she would've been flying across the Entransen Lake back to Urbselva at that moment; yet she was confident enough to know she would be able to tell if something was off. This didn't feel like any of her experiences with Emperor Ignis. Nor did it resemble her meetings with Felicita—before the truth had been known—when Tetra just knew there was something going on she didn't know about. This seemed as honest as her conversations with Felicita now were.

"So..." Leaves Of Gold's rumbling voice broke through the stillness, "I assume from all the questions you were asking me earlier that you are just as curious about us as I am about no-furs."

She smiled sheepishly. "Yeah..."

He purred. "Then I would be more than happy to answer any other questions you might have. I don't know everything, but I'll try my best." He shifted on his haunches. "And...um—if I have some questions about no-furs, would you...?"

Her smile grew as she dipped her head. "I'd be happy to."

His ears perked up and he straightened. "Great! Thank you, Tetra."

"And since you've answered so many of mine already, how about you go first?"

The bigger peryton brightened all the more at her words. "Alright! Let me think..." A thoughtful look came over his face before he asked, "How long have you been able to change into a peryton?"

"Not long." She shrugged. "Only about two moons'-cycles." She had tried to say 'months', but her brain interpreted the latter words from her growl instead.

"Really?" Leaves Of Gold tilted his head. "And...how are you able to do it?"

Tetra didn't reply immediately as she tried to figure out how to answer. Should she tell him the truth? Would he even understand what she was trying to tell him? She recalled what he just mentioned about humans being in stories, so would they have them about shifters, too?

Yet as she had these thoughts, she came to the realization that she was worrying over this as if she was about to tell another human her matha's identity. Leaves Of Gold wasn't a human, nor could he tell other humans the truth about her. He was probably the safest being to tell out of anyone. And if his knowing ever backfired on her, then she just wouldn't interact with any peryton ever again—no matter how displeasing that thought was.

"Well, I don't know if you'll understand..." she began, "but I'll try to tell you the best I can." She paused to inhale a steadying breath. "Have you ever heard of shifters?"

He sent her a confused look, so she tried to reiterate, "Y'know—these beings who kinda look like no-furs, but they can change into other creatures?"

More confusion swirled with thoughtfulness in Leaves Of Gold's honey gaze. "I'm trying to remember..." He was silent for less than a moment before his eyes brightened. "I think there's a story in our History of Creation about beings who could do that!"

Tetra perked her ears up. "Really?"

Perytons had a history of Afreean's creation? She could only wonder what it consisted of for a moment before Leaves Of Gold's reply.

"Yes, but I wouldn't be able to give you the specifics. Our Chief History-Teller hasn't told that one in a long time, and since all of our History Scrolls are destroyed, I won't be able to read it to you." His countenance fell as his ears drooped. "I'm sorry, Tetra."

She shoved aside her disappointments with a shrug of her wings. "It's OK. As long as you know what I'm talking about, that's all that matters."

Leaves Of Gold nodded slowly, his ears barely perking back up. "So...you're not a no-fur?" He asked, "You're one of those beings?"

Tetra lowered her gaze to the ground. "Well...I'm actually both."

She lifted her head back to his inquisitive countenance, and—pushing aside any lingering feelings of self-consciousness—began to tell him about her parents. That led to him asking about her family, and she gave him the simple explanation of the complicated situation she was still learning to understand. He continued to ask her more and more questions about her life, and about humans in general, and she was soon able to ask her own questions about perytons as well.

As the conversation continued and turned to Leaves Of Gold telling her the story about how he saved Wings Like Sand, all of Tetra's lingering worries melted away in the warmth of the friendly atmosphere. That same feeling reminded her of how she felt when around her newfound family, and even of the time she had spent with Stellinga and Rabetta back in Xich.

It was...great. And completely unexpected. Because as the hours ticked by and the two of them continued to talk and laugh, one single question lodged itself into the back of Tetra's mind: was she becoming friends with a *peryton*?

Chapter Fifty-Two

A CLOUD OF BOLTS flew towards Tetra's gliding form near the warehouse's shadowy ceiling. She spotted the biggest empty space amid them, pinned her exposed wings to her armor-covered sides, and dove towards it. She spun as they sailed around her, with a few clinking off her new set of armor and snapping her wings open again as the floor came rushing towards her. A couple bolts pierced her wings as she ascended, but she pressed herself on despite the spurts of pain they caused with each movement.

Once she was high enough, she folded her wings in again and dove towards the growing ranks of training droids. The robots stopped shooting at her and scattered to escape, but Tetra was quicker—even with her new set of gritanium armor on. Her hooves and talons crushed a few as she landed amidst them, and her tail knocked a couple others down. The rest began firing more bolts at her—until she rammed the points of her antlers into their metal sides.

A bolt pierced her wing. Then another clinked off her armor. Tetra shook her head and an android fell from her antlers.

Before she could dwell on the guilty thoughts pounding against her mental defenses, she turned her long neck to get sight of the few remaining androids left. They all stood in a group together with weapons drawn, facing her.

Despite the bolts sailing around her, Tetra pawed the ground with her hoof and ran into the group. *This is for Stellinga and all of Xich*, she told the accusations. *This is for my family*. Metal screeched as weight dragged her long neck down.

This was for her honor.

She growled and galloped through the robotic ranks, decimating all but one. She turned, locked her eyes on it, then lunged. One of her front hooves smacked it to the ground, finishing it off.

Her chest heaved as she lifted her head and glanced around at the strewn, metal body parts surrounding her. The buzz of battle diminished with each shaky breath. And despite the reasons she was doing this, some of the accusations were able to beat through her defenses into the forefront of her thoughts.

"I'm impressed, Private." She jerked her head, ears pricked, in the direction of the deep voice that boomed in the chamber. "You did quite well—Igrium's forces will be surprised."

Army General Taoghn dipped his head towards her in an approving nod. Then he turned to face Lieutenant Eyrie.

"You've done well, First Lieutenant," he added.

"Thank you, sir." Lieutenant Eyrie saluted him. "I'm glad you're pleased with our progress."

"I am." The army general again turned to face Tetra. "So much so, in fact, that my top generals and I have agreed: if the rest of the Alliance's army generals also agree, then you're to fight in the next battle, Private Cairn. This week."

Tetra's heart skipped a nervous beat. She had only been training for about three weeks—which was not enough time, in her opinion. Had Silvas lost a major battle she didn't know about, and now they needed something to help tip the balances back in their favor?

She took a few loping steps towards them and lowered her head so everyone wouldn't have to look up at her.

Taoghn locked his piercing gaze on hers and said, "I know it's short notice—and in other circumstances I would rather wait until your training is further along, but there won't be time for that." He turned his face between her and Lieutenant Eyrie. "Fourteen Igrian transport-crafts are flying over the Deltide Chain right now to destroy our armies stationed in Xich. There is little chance we will be able to get enough manpower and hovercraft to reach them before the battle begins, so we're planning on sending you.

"But before you're deployed, I want to bring some of my own generals to see a demonstration of what you can do. That way none of them will blindly put you somewhere in the battlefield that might prohibit the fullness of what your abilities and training offer."

Tetra blinked her big, peryton eyes and nodded.

General Taoghn dipped his chin towards her then looked behind his shoulder at Lieutenant Eyrie. "Lieutenant," he began, "I want to remind you that almost everyone believes Private Cairn is an actual peryton, and the Buleutcil wants to keep it that way for as long as possible. So, whenever you and Private Cairn are training with others besides those present here, or when you are leading her on the battlefield—" he gestured towards Tetra with a sweep of his hand, "—make sure to only call her 'the peryton'."

Tetra pressed her ears back against her head. Even with the knowledge she had learned so far about the intelligence of perytons at Cherry Valley, and the growing friendship she now had with Leaves Of Gold, she couldn't stop the flow of accusatory names in her head, *"Unnatural animal...spawn of Malackin..."*

"I know it will take some getting used to—for both of you." Taoghn shot Tetra a significant look, but it immediately disappeared under his stern countenance—leaving her to wonder if she had just imagined it, "but we believe it's the best way to keep the secret safe and out of enemy hands. We still don't know how you're able to do it, Private, but there is a chance someone in the world does, and if that person is on the enemy side, then we don't need to give them confirmation of their success."

Tetra sent a furtive glance over towards Lieutenant Eyrie before turning her eyes back on General Taoghn. Part of her wanted to tell the Army General right then how he didn't need to be concerned with that since the only two people who knew how it worked were dead, but then that would lead to the truth of what family name she actually held—and the thought of letting that information out sent a fearful shiver through her wings; even if Chief Baene was still planning on sharing it in the future.

"Of course, sir." Lieutenant Eyrie replied, "When are we scheduled to leave?"

"In two days."

Tetra flicked her ears in surprise. Two days?

"Tomorrow I will have some of our generals meet here to watch you, Private, and then your hovertrain for Xich leaves the next day."

"We'll be ready, sir." Lieutenant Eyrie nodded sharply.

"Good. Then my time here is done."

The army general spun on his heel and strode off towards the warehouse entrance. Tetra and Lieutenant Eyrie both watched him go for a few seconds; then she felt her C.O.'s gaze on her and turned her head to face her.

"Let's try that dive-spin a few more times," she said. "We need to get you used to that armor before you're called into battle."

Tetra nodded once and lifted her head, though she was still a bit shocked by the news. Her thoughts warred with each other as she opened her wings and jumped into the air, the usual sounds of rustling feathers now accompanied by a metallic clinking.

The first time she had worn the peryton armor was a week ago. The gritanium it was made of was light—for armor, that is—but she and Lieutenant Eyrie both noticed that she was a bit slower in her flight maneuvers than when she wasn't wearing it. So, her C.O. pushed the combat training less, and Tetra's flight maneuvers more.

Her armor was composed of a jumpsuit similar to the one she already wore, only it was made of flexible polyanium fibers like the base for every metal suit of human armor was. Thin, dark gritanium plates attached to it to cover her neck, sides, stomach, and her legs; while a separate helmet covered the sides of her face.

However, since she had no thumbs, Lieutenant Eyrie, Sir Whest, Madame Quen, or any of Tetra's other rotating guardsmen had to assist her in getting the plates and helmet on. It reminded her of the squires she had learned about in history who used to help soldiers put their complicated suits of armor on before someone finally invented an easier, more flexible version that could be put on quickly and by only one person.

Tetra flew high into the shadows of the topmost height of the ceiling where the luminance of the warehouse's hanging, industrial lights didn't reach. She glided in soft circles a few times to get herself used to the extra weight before folding in her wings and diving back down towards the ground.

Lieutenant Eyrie had her practice the same move repeatedly until the muscles in her wings were shaking from exertion, and the fear that she might overwork herself enough to black out pumped through her racing heart. She had already pushed herself to hard a couple times during training and done that—falling to the hard ground and waking up to find herself surrounded by training droids as a human.

Thankfully, she didn't have to fret for long. Lieutenant Eyrie must have seen something in the vital scans her jumpsuit sent because she finally said they were done for the day and Tetra was able to turn back into herself. When the shifter part of her DNA sheathed its searing knives, she found herself underneath a pile of metal that was heavier than she could hope to carry in her human form.

"Private Cairn?" Lieutenant Eyrie asked.

"I'm coming," Tetra lifted herself out of the pile of gritanium plates and waded through them until she was standing in front of her C.O. Their eyes locked.

"Are you prepared to fight?" Her commanding officer sent her a knowingly pointed look.

Resolve hardened her stomach despite the names and the threats her accusing thoughts shouted in the back of her mind. "Yes ma'am."

"Remember what I told you, Private."

She hadn't let herself forget those words even with the weeks that had passed. "Yes ma'am."

Lieutenant Eyrie peered into her eyes for a moment longer, then nodded. "Now then," she said, "Chief Baene messaged me a couple hours ago and told me once we were finished that he wanted you to come to his office."

Tetra's heart leapt nervously. "Do you know what for?"

She hadn't heard from the chief advisor since she joined the army. Not even in all the time she spent with Felicita did her sister rarely ever say anything about him—or the plans he apparently had that involved Tetra.

"No," Eyrie shook her head, "but I doubt you need to fear. Chief Baene is a good man, and—in my opinion, at least—one of the best leaders Silvas ever had."

Tetra kept a frown from marring her neutral expression. Despite the trust she now had for her commanding officer, the chief advisor didn't have any secret plans that involved *her*. Even with Felicita working under him, Tetra still didn't quite know how to feel about him.

"So, let's go." Lieutenant Eyrie spun on her heel towards the warehouse's wide doors, and—with only a moment's hesitation—Tetra followed.

THE SAME SECRETARY AS before gave Tetra clearance into Chief Baene's office. She kept her head lowered as she walked through the small sitting room to hide her malscar from the woman's blatant stare, and only lifted it when the chief advisor's guards closed the heavy doors behind her.

"Private." Chief Baene's accent drew her eyes towards the three people that sat on the couches to her left.

Aunt Minda stood from beside Felicita and bustled over to give her a hug, which Tetra accepted despite her own stiffness at the touch. When her aunt let go, their eyes met. Reservation tightened her aunt's soft features, sending a worm of uneasiness down Tetra's spine.

She narrowed her eyes. "Why am I here?"

Chief Baene stood from the other couch and set his light lavender-blue eyes on her. Shadows dulled their color, and it looked like someone had etched even deeper lines into his face with an awl. Yet despite the almost grieving air about him, it did nothing to diminish his authoritative countenance.

"There are some things I need to discuss with you, Tetra," he replied.

The way he spoke tightened Tetra's stomach. Was this about the plans that involved her?

Aunt Minda must've read something in her expression because she put her hand on Tetra's forearm and gave her a comforting look. "I'tis OK, Anora." Even after all these weeks of everyone calling her 'Tetra', her aunt still called her by her birth name. "Please, come and sit."

Tetra flicked her gaze between her and Chief Baene's stern countenance before slowly nodding and letting her aunt guide her to the couch Felicita sat on. As she sat beside her sister, Aunt Minda moved and took up the spot on her other side. A strange, almost-tense look shadowed Felicita's normally bright features, and more uneasiness tightened around Tetra's insides. What was going on?

Chief Baene sat back down on the couch in front of them, and their eyes locked again. "Tetra," he began, "Felicita told me that you've been recovering more of your childhood memories."

She nodded in acknowledgement but said nothing.

"So now you know—partly—why I had her do those question sessions with you."

Again, she nodded as if she was still a peryton and couldn't speak Alenguan.

Chief Baene exhaled deeply through his nose and leaned forward, resting his elbows on his knees. "Well, now I'm here to tell you the full reason as to why we did so." Tetra couldn't seem to look away from his eyes as he spoke, "When Minda and Felicita finally arrived in Silvas, I was the only one who knew their true identities. They wanted to keep it that way because they felt it was safer. I agreed at the time, but I warned them that if the truth ever came out, it might be more disastrous later than if they went on and made it known."

Tetra felt both women stiffen beside her, but she kept her gaze glued onto the chief advisor's stoic expression.

"As time went on, I believe we all forgot that warning—yes, including myself—and found ourselves hopeful that the truth would never come out. Then you jumped over the fence in Xich, were brought here, and Felicita told me who she believed you were." He steepled his fingers together. "And now that there's evidence of who you really are, we have all come to realize now is the time for the truth to be known."

Tetra knew this would come soon, but her heart began to beat an anxious rhythm anyway.

"When you get back from this battle in Xich, Lord Jachen has called for the Buleutcil to meet so we can tell them the truth about the Cairns' supposed daughter," something in his calculating eyes changed, but she couldn't tell what it was, "and the possible plans we have regarding you."

Finally. Her heart rate increased as wary curiosity bubbled up inside her.

"And what plans would those be, sir?" She asked.

Chief Baene didn't break eye-contact. "As I've gotten older and this war has raged on, I have found myself debating a possible problem the Alliance may have if we win. If we do, who is to say Prince Ryder won't end up like your patre? And if he does, how can I possibly try to prevent another war from breaking out in the future?"

He answered his own questions, "I would need to reverse almost two decades of brainwashing from an entire empire if that were to happen, but I don't want Silvas to occupy Igrium and do what they have been doing to other nations to try and make that succeed. That will just cause another war—which might end up wiping out the entirety of your native empire—and I don't want that to happen, either. Until now, Igrium has been vital to the human nations, and obliterating it is not the course I believe Deleyon would want us to pursue. So here is my answer to both of our questions..."

Tetra almost told him to stop talking as her thoughts converged onto what he was implying, yet she only stared at him in horror as he continued, "You are

Rexcan's daughter. The imperial blood of the Ignis family runs in your veins, and even though Rexcan did not choose you to rule, I believe the citizens of Igrium will not grumble too much if the Alliance won this war and put you on the throne instead of one of our own."

Her heart dropped into her stomach like a heavy stone.

"Then you would be able to lead them back to the former glory it had before Rexcan caused them to soak the soil of so many other nations in innocent blood." A slight hitch deepened his accent on the last word, but it didn't appear again as he ended with, "So that is the basis for the plans regarding you, Tetra Ignis."

She could only stare at him, slack-jawed, in shock. The air of the office grew electric with tension as she tried to come to terms with what he had thrown on her.

"You...you want *me* to—to rule...to rule over Igrium..." She could barely get the absurd thought past her lips.

Igrium wouldn't have her as their ruler! They would much rather have the teenaged Prince Ryder become emperor than her dishonorable, malscarred self.

"It may sound crazy now," Chief Baene replied, "but when we announce this to the Buleutcil, Lord Jachen and I plan to help you begin learning how to lead a nation. We would not leave you to figure it out on your own."

Tetra's heart hammered against her ribcage. She put her head between her hands as she rested her elbows on her knees.

No, no, no. She couldn't do that! That wasn't her! She...she was a dishonorable coward. If she was put on the throne, no matter what Chief Baene thought, Tetra knew her countrymen well enough to know there would be some form of mutiny.

A hand barely touched her arm, but she jerked away from the light touch, and it didn't reach for her again. An angry swirl churned her stomach, and she found she couldn't even muster up a tiny bit of guilt for the action. Felicita and Aunt Minda obviously both knew about this and hadn't told her. Even with all the time she had spent with them in the last month, they hadn't even given her a warning of what the Silvanian chief advisor had planned for her.

She lifted her head from her hands and took extra care not to look at either of her family members as she replied, "But I—I don't want to rule Igrium! I've never had any desire like that before in my life! I can't—I don't think I can do it, sir..."

Chief Baene's gaze hardened, and she couldn't help flinching at the sudden change in his demeanor; yet she didn't look away as he spoke, "You did join the army to help people, did you not?"

"Yes sir..."

"Then let me make this clear: this will help many more people than any war-peryton in this war could. Not only would it help this generation, but it would help future ones as well. This isn't just about you or your doubts, Tetra," his tone took on a sharp edge, "this is about the future of all the nations embroiled in this war. If a good ruler isn't put on the throne of Igrium now, then there can be no doubt that future wars will arise because of that mistake."

She finally averted her gaze and noticed the guilty look Felicita wore as their eyes met. "He's not wrong, Tetra," she said in a small voice.

Tetra ground her teeth and lowered her gaze to her clasped hands. She knew he wasn't wrong, and that's what made this situation so much worse.

"Tetra," Chief Baene said, "let me make something else clear. Despite how it may seem, I can't make you do this."

She lifted her head and met his frosty lavender-blue eyes hopefully. "You can't?"

"No. Having a reluctant ruler would be just as bad as having someone with Igrium's twisted morals on the throne." A small needle stabbed her heart at his comment, but she tried to ignore it. "But I told you all of this because I want you to at least think about it. I don't want an answer made hastily."

He raised his brow in a knowing look, and she sent a side-eye glance towards Felicita before looking back over at him. The only way he could've known about her former regret of joining Silvas' army as a war-peryton was if her sister had told him. She squeezed her hands tighter but pushed the thought to the side.

"Instead," he continued, "the earliest I want to know a decision is when you get back from Xich. If you have come up with one by then, I'll be open to hearing whatever it is; but until then, I'm not accepting any answers right now."

She gave him a sharp nod and looked back down at her white-knuckled hands. "I understand, sir."

"Good."

A long stretch of silence settled between them, allowing Tetra's emotional thoughts to swirl like fallen leaves in a windstorm.

Me...as empress of Igrium... She shook her head and glanced back up at Chief Baene.

"Is that all, sir?" She asked.

He nodded once, the sharpness in his gaze dulling to their former shadowed look. "It is."

"Then, may I be excused?" She paused for a second. "I...I need to think about all of this."

"You may."

Keeping her gaze on the floor, she stood and shuffled out of the heavy atmosphere as fast as she could without another look towards any of them.

Chapter Fifty-Three

THOUSANDS OF CHEERING VOICES pounded against Aabir's skull as he stepped out into the arena with forty-nine other third-level competitors. They all moved in a mass of armor and heavy footfalls towards the center of the desert landscape.

His heart raced as the desert-like heat beat down upon him. It reminded him of his time in Xich, and another wave of fear turned his already-churning stomach. Matha had forced him to eat breakfast earlier that morning so she would not have to watch him faint or get needlessly hurt, but now he wondered if fainting on live holovision would be worse than throwing up for millions to see.

The people around him slowed to a stop, and Aabir did likewise. He looked up at the closest rubber-like suchwriy that dotted the sandy arena and wondered for a moment if they were actual plants or part of the huge machine underneath the layers of sand.

He never would have thought he would think this, but he was glad for all the time he spent watching the Tourney. If he had not, then he would be completely clueless as to what was happening. However, none of those replays could have prepared him for the overload of the roaring crowds to his ears, the dry heat that was already making him sweat underneath his armor, and the fierce tension from all the other competitors that surrounded him—things he wished he could have known beforehand.

Oh Deleyon, help me...

"Welcome to the seven-hundred and thirteenth Constantia Tourney!" A familiar, excitable voice Aabir recognized from the replays came through the stadium's loudspeakers and calmed the roars of the crowd. "As you all know, I'm your host, Brutus Halt, and I'm excited to once again bring you the coverage for this exciting week. The Tourney's Planners have quite a few surprises up their sleeves this year, so I hope you're all ready—because these will be like nothing we've ever seen before!"

The shouting clamor rose again for a few moments as if in answer.

When it died down, Brutus Halt continued, "And now, before we begin, I'm honored to present His Imperial Majesty, Emperor Ignis the Second!"

Aabir turned his head to follow everyone else's gazes to the raised platform in the middle of the stands. His eyes flicked to the jumbotrons that showed closeups of the royal family. His stomach did a flip as Emperor Ignis appeared on the screen. He looked the exact same as he had when Aabir and Tetra were brought before him after trying to escape, only now he was surrounded by a hundred-thousand of his empire's citizens. The small show of authoritative-power only made him all the more frightening.

The camera angled turned and Empress Rillunia, in all her famed, brunette beauty, filled the screen as she sat on the throne next to the emperor. Then the angle changed again, and Crown Prince Ryder was shown. The teenage boy looked small and awkward sitting next to the regal presence of his parents; and when he noticed the jumbotron was showing him, he looked away from the direction of the camera.

The chant "Ignis! Ignis! Ignis!" pounded throughout the stadium like a heartbeat. Aabir could feel it rattling up the soles of his feet and into his bones. He gritted his teeth and fought the urge to cover his ears. That would be a great way to get him thrown in prison for possible treason.

When the chanting finally died and he felt like he could breathe again, Brutus Halt's voice filled the stadium, "Now, it's time for the first round to begin!"

Cheers met his announcement. Aabir cringed underneath his helmet and wondered if he would go deaf from all the noise.

"In this round, the only way any of our first group of third-levels here will be able to continue on to the next one is by surviving the next fifteen minutes without getting attacked by any of their opponents. Competitors—there are a limited number of weapons hidden throughout the arena. If you find one, use it to defeat as many of your opponents as possible, and don't let anyone take your weapon—because that is allowed. Remember: death and dismemberment are against the rules. If you are hit by someone's weapon in a place that would be fatal, then you're immediately disqualified.

"Now that that's out of the way, let the Constantia Tourney begin!"

Brutus Halt's voice was immediately drowned out by a buzzer. The group of young adults around Aabir sprinted in different directions, leaving him as one of the last to move before he headed off in a random direction. He had watched a similar round to this one before, and silently prayed to Deleyon that he would find a sword lying around. If he could, he might have a better chance of making it to the next round. Or he could end up attracting unwanted attention.

The adrenaline racing through his veins seemed to be amplified by the cheers of the crowds, the echoing yells of the first fights beginning, and the quick narrations of these same fights by Brutus Halt. Someone yelled closer to him, and he slowed to a stop, breathing quickly. Two competitors were fighting on the next dune over, the fluorescent lights of the stadium shining against the metal of their weapons. One had a short sword, and the other found a spear that she was using to block the quick attacks with.

With Lieutenant Denir's threat whispering in the back of his mind, he turned his head in the direction of the struggle and headed towards them. His boots slid in the sand as he half-ran, half-climbed down the dune he had been standing on, then he began running and sliding up the next one.

As he got closer to the scuffle, he was able to make out each fighter more clearly, and the moves they used. They both looked like they had had some training in weaponship, but not as much as a fifth-year trainee would have.

Keeping that in mind, Aabir slowed to a stop behind a tall, bluish such-wriy with long, rectangular leaves that poked out of the dune. He watched as the girl with the spear jabbed its point into the guy's chest and knocked him down.

"...Lucras Duneval is out! And it looks like there's another—"

Aabir blocked out Brutus Halt's voice as he stepped out from behind the plant and charged the girl. She spun and looked up at him—both weapons now in hand as Lucras skulked off towards the entrance. Aabir slowed his pace as he got close, and she thrust the spearpoint at him. He leaped to the side, and that's when he noticed the blunt end of the weapon. He flicked his gaze to the blade in her other hand and realized it was blunted, too. Enough to bruise if you were hit by it, but not sharp enough to cut through.

The sword came towards Aabir's head. He sidestepped the stroke, blood pounding in his ears. He noticed the repetition of her moves. So, with that knowledge, he waited for her to thrust the spear at him again. As he had hoped, she did so; then she thrust the sword towards him. He jumped to the side and chopped his arm towards her sword arm. She grunted as the dull blade dropped to the sand.

As quick as a griffin, Aabir picked up the sword and half-slid, half-tripped away from her prodding spearpoint. He spun and let his years of training take over. He lowered into a guard stance and turned all his attention to the light blade in his hands and the angry, jerky moves of his opponent.

She sent him a withering glare before swinging the spear at his feet like a polearm. Aabir jumped out of reach, slid again, but was able to lunge forward. He sliced downwards on her now-open arm and heard the satisfying ring of metal sliding against metal.

The girl leapt back with a stumble, but Aabir only lunged forward again and thrust his blade into her stomach. Her eyes bulged as she looked down at the sword, then back up at Aabir in shock.

"—Rayan Yeal and Feyla Warston are both out!"

As the words boomed through the stadium, the girl's surprise turned immediately to anger. She cursed at Aabir, dropped the spear, and spun on her heels back to the entrance. Aabir took in a shaky breath and wiped sweat beads off his forehead as he watched her go.

His stupor was broken at the sound of approaching footsteps. Sand flew as he spun around in time to stop a sword blade from slicing at his exposed back. The two blades rang as they hit. Aabir sprang back, miraculously keeping his balance as he moved into a guard stance. He eyed his attacker and could tell by the way she held her sword that she knew how to use it well.

He pushed the thought away and lunged towards her. She blocked his stroke and countered with her own. Aabir blocked the blade with his sword's fuller and used his greater body weight to push back. The girl slipped and stumbled back in the sand.

Aabir did not waste his chance. He swung his blade down upon her, but she raised her arms and blocked it. Again and again he pounded at her blade, but she was able to block them all—albeit with failing strength.

Just as he could sense his victory, another buzzer rang through the arena. His heart leapt into his throat at the sudden noise, and he stumbled back from the other competitor.

"Time's up, competitors! The round is over!" Brutus Halt called out.

Relief flashed across the girl's freckled face as her arms, and her sword, flopped onto the sand beside her. Aabir lowered his own, shaking blade as he looked around the circular desert.

"Out of fifty competitors in this round, only thirty-six survived," Brutus Halt continued. "Congratulations to those of you who made it! Now please make your way to the arena's exits so the next round can begin."

Aabir seemed to blink out of a stupor at the words, and he exhaled a deep sigh of relief. *I made it.* Thank You, Deleyon, he had made it through the first round!

Out of the corner of his eye, he noticed the freckled girl was slowly getting up. He stepped back over to her and held his hand out to help. She glanced at him strangely for a moment but then took his outstretched hand. He helped pull her up and their eyes met.

"Thanks." She had a deep, Eastern Igrian drawl like Ezen.

"Sure." Aabir shrugged. He might be forced to fight these people in the rounds, but he was not going to be a jerk when they were not fighting—no matter how much they probably disagreed on certain moral points.

He turned his neck and spotted the open entrance doors not too far from their sand dune. Dropping his short sword on the sand, he began heading in that direction. Soft, shuffling footfalls landed behind him, and he glanced back to see the girl following. She did not acknowledge his presence, so Aabir just shrugged to himself and looked ahead.

They came upon the entryway, and he silently thanked Deleyon for air-conditioning as coolness washed over him. Two more competitors were already in the hall as he and the girl joined them; and as he quietly spent the next minute breathing in the cool air, the rest of the remaining competitors joined them as well.

Hydraulics hissed, and he jerked his head to look over his shoulder as a huge door slowly lowered behind them to block anyone from entering the arena. Then a tall man in a nice, gray suit appeared and led the hot and sweaty competitors down the hall, into an elevator, up multiple levels, and into a huge room complete with tables full of food and couches overlooking a huge wall of glass panels.

"This is where all of you will stay until your next rounds," the man told them. "You are welcome to eat as much of the food as you want while you watch."

Then he entered the elevator again and its glass door slid closed. Aabir shared an awkward glance with a few of the other competitors before it was broken by one guy who silently made his way over to the table of steaming foods. A few others also broke from the awkwardness and followed him, while the rest—including Aabir—moved over to the comfy seating section.

As he passed the table, he caught a whiff of something spicy and his stomach did a flip. He inhaled a deep breath and moved around an empty couch, then sighed as his sore muscles were cradled by the cushioned seat.

As he got comfortable, his eyes turned to the view outside the glass. The room they were in was right above the highest stands in the stadium, giving a full view of the arena and the unhindered view of the two jumbotrons opposite them.

The sand dunes he just ran across and fought on shifted and moved like churning sea waves. The suchwries bobbed atop the golden sea as a huge crack split open across the middle of the desert landscape. Each side of the desert rose and folded inwards like a chardex to pour all the sand into the dark crack. The suchwries remained on both sides of the now-vertical metal floor Aabir remembered from practicing in the arena. Then, the floor moved back to its original position and the plants lowered into the machine underneath the metal panels.

Suddenly, a huge wave of water spilled from one of the doors on the arena's side, filling the rounded space until it resembled a lake. Small, empty islands rose up out of the water in front of the arena's three entryways and scattered about the small lake randomly. Then the entrance doors opened and fifty more third-level trainees crowded together on the three small entrance islands. Brutus Halt's voice could be heard clearly even with the walls separating the room as he explained to the new competitors the exact same rules Aabir and the others of the first group had been given.

As the commentator was speaking, the freckled girl from before came over and sat next to Aabir. He stiffened and turned his head in her direction.

"Are you a trainee?" She asked.

Aabir blinked at the non-hostile question. "Uh—yes."

She nodded. "I thought as much." She pulled her helmet off, and he was able to see the freckles on her pink-tinged face better. "Only a trainee could fight as good as you."

Was that a compliment? "Um...thanks?"

He had been expecting a tense quiet to fill this room for the rest of the day, not...this. Was this normal?

The girl's lips twitched. "What school are you from?"

"Norland." Why did she care?

"Cool." She nodded again and turned her face towards the beginning fights happening on the islands and in the waters below them. "I'm from Stellain Military Academy. I think one of the guys in my year transferred to Norland."

"You mean Ezen?"

"Yeah." Her eyes flicked back towards Aabir's direction. "I assume you know him?"

He nodded, a trickle of worry for his friend joining all the other thoughts in his head. "Yeah, he's in my platoon."

"Huh."

A strange look came over her face and she turned her gaze back to the view outside the window. Aabir scrunched his brow. Was there something about Ezen he needed to know? Something his friend was hiding from his old life back in Stellain? Was that what he wanted to talk to Aabir about?

"Is there something wrong with him?" He finally asked in the lengthening quiet.

The girl blinked and looked back over at him. "Well...not exactly." Her lips twisted into a frown. "He's just...a bit strange, is all. We were all surprised when we heard the news that he transferred to Norland. He was never great in weaponship training or tactics class—which everyone thought was your school's specialty—but he always got the highest grades in science and history."

That did not sound weird to Aabir, but he did not try arguing when she added, "But that wasn't the weird thing."

She glanced around them then locked her brown eyes onto Aabir's again as she leaned closer. He barely leaned his head away, his brow lowering even more in confusion.

"I heard he once said the C.B.M. was being used the wrong way," she whispered in a conspiratorial tone, "that instead of using it to erase bad memories or make the emperor's personal guards, it should be used to plant new ideas into people's heads."

Maybe it was her voice, but Aabir could not help the shiver that went down his spine at the mention of the controversial brain-manipulation machine. He and his parents agreed that even with the supposed good things it did, it was capable of being used for evil purposes—like the emperor's personal guards—and should be completely destroyed. However, he never heard Ezen speak of the machine before, so he figured he should take this girl's words with a grain of salt.

"I also heard rumors that he actually said things against the imperial crown." The girl turned her head back in the direction of the arena, but she continued looking in Aabir's direction out of the corner of her eye. "There were also a few other things I heard he said, but anyway—he's weird, and you should be wary of him. Some of the things he's said could be considered treason, so we were all thanking the gods when he left."

A spark of anger for Ezen flared to life inside Aabir, but he did not voice it. Instead, he only nodded and said, "Thanks for the heads up."

The girl nodded and moved her attention fully onto the arena. Aabir turned his gaze to the jumbotrons showcasing some of the different fights in greater detail as he began to ponder the girl's words about Ezen.

He had never heard his friend say any of those things before, so maybe this girl was just trying to get into his head to get him to mess up in the next round. He shot her a side-eye glance before his eyes trailed back to the crazy struggles happening below.

Amid the animalistic fights, he spotted a girl from Lieutenant Tarson's platoon, Cilla Draven, right as she was "stabbed" in the gut while fighting over an ax on one of the small islands. He watched as three other trainees pushed and shoved against each other in the otherwise calm waters to try and reach a spear that was floating in the middle of the arena. A tall girl with a longsword hit another person in their unsuspecting backside as they grappled for a spear with someone else.

He winced and grimaced as he watched, yet despite how much he did not want to join the ranks of gawking, cheering crowds, he kept his eyes trained on the jumbotrons to study the other competitors in case he had to fight any of them later. The island round ended, and he subjected himself (and his tense stomach) to two more similar rounds that all happened in wildly different landscapes.

At the end of each one, the quieter atmosphere of the competitor's room began to fill with more chatter; and more competitors sat on the same couch as Aabir as the winners of each round joined them.

"Hey, Aabir."

He lifted his head and noticed Buren's grinning face standing next to the couch chair.

"Hey," he replied with a nod.

"Nice job out there," his platoonmate said, "We got to watch the earlier rounds while we waited, and I saw what you did."

Aabir shrugged and lowered his gaze. "It was nothing."

Guilt pressed against his chest as the words left his mouth. Not that they were a lie, but because they were true. Even though he knew he was doing it to keep him and his family safe from the possible wrath of Lieutenant Denir, instead of making him better about how much easier it had been, he had begun to wonder what those who were watching him thought as he was out there.

As he had been watching the other competitors fight, he saw only a bunch of people who were all intent on winning the honor and glory the Tourney gave to those who lasted longer than their first day. His mind went to Rasiela and what her thoughts of his actions might be if she were watching him. She herself had told him on their second meeting that his obedient actions at Norland made him untrustworthy in her sight; so even if she knew his forced position in the Tourney, was she now thinking otherwise?

"Yeah," Buren replied, "but it'll only get harder."

Aabir made a noncommittal noise in his throat and turned his eyes to the jumbotrons back in front of him. The surviving competitors were trudging through the snow back to the entrance tunnel, and he wondered if it was really as cold as it looked.

"If I could have everyone's attention." Aabir twisted around on the couch as the same man who had led him and the others from his round up there stopped in the middle of the room. "Those who fought in the first two rounds, come follow me. It's time for your next chance to win."

A pit yawned open in Aabir's stomach atop the pressing guilt, but he stood and moved towards the man along with the other competitors who were called. Buren sent him an encouraging nod and took his place on the couch.

"May the gods grant you favor, Aabir," he said.

Aabir continued forward without replying as his heart raced with nervous tension. *Oh Deleyon*, he pleaded, *help me to keep my family safe. And maybe, somehow, miraculously help me not to look like any of those who actually want to be in the Tourney... I know it sounds stupid, but I would really like that, so...thank You.*

The constricting guilt lessened slightly as he made the silent prayer, and he was able to take a deep breath as he joined the growing group of competitors all waiting to enter the elevator.

Onto the next round, then.

LEAVES HIT AABIR IN the face as he ran through the dark forest. Quick, rustling footsteps followed him, matching the beat of his pounding heart. He blinked the continuous rain from his eyes as he took another furtive glance over his shoulder, then barely looked forward again in time before he hit another tree.

Unlike the last rounds where competitors were pitted against each other, this time Aabir and the other competitors were thrown into, as Brutus Halt called it, a "forest full of surprising, and dangerous, creatures", with the objective to kill as many of the twenty wild animals as possible. As long as he killed one, he would go on to the next round, but—since it *was* a competition—they were all encouraged to kill as many as possible to keep more of their opponents from continuing on.

When Aabir heard those words, he heard it as an answer from Deleyon to his former plea. After all, how could one look like they were enjoying the Tourney if they only shot a crossbow bolt into one of the animals? And even with Brutus Halt's "dangerous" adjective, how hard could the wild animals in one of the first rounds on the first day actually be? As the crossbow and quiver were given to him before entering the arena, he found himself breathing lighter. He might not have been a great marksman, but he had had experience hunting on Mister Falap's land a few times with his patre, so he figured this round would be about as easy as the former one.

All those thoughts fled as he and the others stepped out into the dense foliage of the mini forest now covering the arena. It was not even fifteen seconds into the round when one of those creatures immediately attacked the small group around Aabir and he found himself running for his life—using the screams and animalistic screeches behind him as a motivator.

The quiver of crossbow bolts bounced and clattered on his back, telling every creature—besides the one chasing him—the vicinity of his position. A screech rang not far behind, and he clutched the crossbow even tighter in his fists. Blood pounded in his ears as he looked around for an escape; a place he could hide and kill whatever was after him. Then he would be able to go on to the next round without worrying over Lieutenant Denir's threat for a little while. Yet despite all the thin trunks of the lofty trees, the tall ferns, and the moss that seemed to cover almost everything, none of it was big enough to hide him.

Thunder rumbled and the arena floor shook slightly. Aabir risked another glance behind his shoulder and noticed the short, furry figure in the shadows not far behind. He picked up the pace despite his aching legs, and wondered for a fleeting moment what animal was chasing him.

The toe of his boot caught on something, and he fell with a startled grunt. The creature behind him screeched in triumph and a heavy weight fell on his back. Even with armor on, small, fiery sparks stabbed at Aabir's backside; going through the polyanium-shirt in between his armor's plates. He howled and rolled over, squashing the creature underneath his weight. It only dug its fiery claws deeper into him. He scrambled up, then immediately fell on his back again to squash it.

With a pitiful cry, the animal let go and Aabir got up again; albeit much more slowly. He grimaced as pinpricks of pain stabbed his back muscles when he went down to pick up his crossbow and the bolts that had fallen in the scramble. He hissed through his teeth but pushed through the pain to pick up his weapons.

As he did so, he recalled some of the advice of the patrolman whom he had knocked out in the elevator, "*...let their pride get in the way, then they fail...*". He glowered down at the mossy rocks underneath his feet as he straightened back up, but then let out a huff as the hurt from his wounded pride lessened with the reality of the warning. He sent a grateful glance skywards and silently thanked Deleyon before turning around to see the animal he had squashed.

A needle badger lay in the dirt, its breaths coming out in tiny spurts as it lay in a daze. Tiny droplets of venom dripped out of the tips of its needlelike claws and fell onto its brown-and-white patchy fur.

Sending another thank you to Deleyon, Aabir stabbed the crossbow bolt into the creature's furry chest. He winced as it squealed but felt no guilt for doing it as the pain it caused began to spread throughout his back muscles.

"And Aabir Sorrel has earned himself a spot in the next round!" Brutus Halt's voice rose above the rain, and the crowds' following cheers thundered above all other noise.

A thin fog seemed to be settling itself in Aabir's head. It took him a few moments to process the clamorous noises. When he did, he squeezed his eyes shut as a small chain of guilt tightened around his chest. Hopefully they were only cheering because something exciting happened and not because they were actually rooting for him.

Human screams and the yowls of what sounded like a big cat broke through the roaring clamor. Aabir opened his eyes and spun around in the direction of the blood-curdling noises. Even with the weighty fog wrapping itself tighter around his thoughts, his instincts told him to run away as fast as he could. He almost did so, but then the eerie screams echoing through the dim forest gave him pause.

Well, you wanted to help people, didn't you? Aabir pressed his fingers against his head as the thought was concealed in the thickening fog. *What is wrong with me?*

More pain sparked in his back, and it sparked an idea in his head amidst his darkening thoughts. Was a foggy brain one of the symptoms of needle badger venom?

Even with the worry that thought caused, he gave himself no more time to listen to it as he ran towards the ongoing noises. He clenched his jaw as the quiver bounced against his screaming back muscles, but he pressed on. As the noises grew louder, he reached over his shoulder, took a thick bolt out of the quiver, and went through the process of trying to load it while he stumbled through the overgrowth; the thoughts in his head growing slower.

As he stumbled towards the roaring, screaming noises of the fight, he noticed ringing began to take over his hearing. He slowed, but then another yell tore through the forest and he picked his pace back up even as anxiety shook through his tiring muscles. Through the dense sludge in his head, he wondered for a moment if needle badger venom was lethal.

Then the forest grew blurrier. Aabir squeezed his eyes shut then immediately opened them again. The blurriness went away for a few quick breaths, then came back. Fear struck his pounding heart, keeping his thoughts away from the worries the danger he was now running into half-blind would normally cause.

The pain in his back, the fog in his head, the ringing in his ears, and the blurriness taking over his vision became so overwhelming that he did not notice the struggle he stumbled upon until a snarling growl shot a new spike of bright fear into his sludge-like thoughts.

Chills spread across his arm as his blurry eyes locked onto the huge, white spotted-tiger that looked like it was trying to eat a huge piece of metal. Aabir blinked his eyes until the scene came into clearer focus for a few moments. The cat's pale fur shimmered in the forest's shadows like a ghost as its jaws shook a competitor's armored shoulder. Its huge front paws kept the struggling person pinned against the mossy ground.

Without thinking, he lifted the crossbow in his shaking arms and shot it in the tiger's general direction. A yowl broke through the ringing in his ears, and through the blurriness he noticed the cat fall back, a streak of bright red flowing down its white coat.

Aabir rushed over to the blurred form lying still on the ground. *Oh Deleyon...* His pounding fear helped lift some of the darkening fog in his brain enough for him to think coherently for a few moments. He fell on his knees next to the person and blinked his eyes until he was able to see the rise and fall of their chest.

A sigh of relief passed his lips, but it came to a stop as he saw all the bright, crimson blood on the person's shoulder. The tiger had somehow pulled off their armor's pauldron and was able to get through the poor competitor's polyanium shirt. He winced at the blurred sight, his own back aching in sympathy with the badger's venom running through it. He needed to get them to safety before something else tried to attack, and possibly kill, them.

Only a few competitors had died in the Constantia Tourney ever since their creation—all by accidents—and he could easily see this becoming one of those accidental scenarios.

Resolve hardened in his churning stomach, and—being careful with the person's injured shoulder—he reached down, put his hands under the guy's arms, and began to move him away from the tiger's body. He was not going to let anyone die on his watch, even if the blurriness in his vision was getting worse.

Aabir's thoughts slowed again as the moment's boost of adrenaline faded away. He did not know where he was going or what he was going to do to protect the guy, he only knew he needed to keep moving away from the tiger—the tiger that moved.

His heart skipped a beat, and he was able to register his growing fear again as, even with his impaired vision, he saw the zig-zag pattern of dots on the cat's side glow in the shadows. It let loose a mewl that would have been pitiful had it not ended in a dangerous growl.

Aabir dropped the guy—who only let out a grunt as his body flopped on the ground again—and fumbled for one of his crossbow bolts. His arm shook terribly as he saw the huge, glowing blob move. Even through the mental fog, he could feel its eyes land on him. It roared and his heart leapt into his throat.

"Oh Deleyon!" He exclaimed as it lunged towards him.

His hand wrapped around the bolt as the tiger rammed into his legs, sending him tumbling to the ground. Claws hooked between the plates of his armor, and he twisted in the grip of the beast as waves of pain went through his back and his legs. In the dark, ringing haze surrounding him, his survival instincts kicked in and he stabbed the bolt into the moving blob.

A roar. Then the cat dropped on Aabir's legs like a deadweight. He blinked slowly and could only stare at it as the weight of the haze in his head pressed down further. He loosened his hold on the weapons in his hands, and they fell to the ground the same time as Aabir's head hit the soft dirt. The overwhelming mental cloud took over completely, and darkness cradled his vision as he blacked out.

LESS THAN AN HOUR later, Aabir woke up in the stadium's infirmary with all his senses restored, no brain fog, and a few new scars on his back and legs.

"—running with a king scorpion's venom in your veins is not a good idea, folks." Brutus Halt's voice spoke through his holonode's speaker as he watched the round's replay, "Desem will be feeling *that* soon... Oh! And it looks like Aabir is trying to help Erastos get away from the wounded tiger! With needle badger venom running through his blood, this should be interesting—"

Dull pains went through his back as he watched the tiger knock him to the ground, before he struck the bolt through its throat.

The crowds cheered as Brutus Halt exclaimed, "And the beast is dead!" Aabir watched the glow of the tiger's bioluminescent spots die out as it fell, dead, upon him. Then he himself fainted next to the guy he tried to pull away. "Rarely have I seen a third-level risk themselves in such a way in these first rounds. But now it looks like—"

The camera angle switched from Aabir's fainted form to another competitor being chased up a tree by a king scorpion as big as the badger. He stopped the video and turned his holonode off, then put his head in his hands.

That...was awful. After binge-watching them for weeks, he thought he would have been prepared for all the fights—including the ones with wild animals. But now all he could see were the images of Erastos' bleeding, still form burned into his brain (that were now clearer thanks to the replay).

He sighed through his fingers. Even with everything he had already seen—from the gruesome replays he had watched the past few weeks to the dehumanizing Constantia prisons—he thought it was impossible to dislike the Tourney any more than he already did; but now that he had heard the crowds screaming bloodlust as he was attacked by the needle badger and Erastos was used as a chew toy, a deep hatred for them burned even more inside him.

Igrium was desensitized beyond anything he formerly realized, and his fighting in the Tourney was only helping build it.

He lifted his head and glanced over at the pillow on his bed, curling his hands into fists. Even with the dull throb that entered his bandaged knuckles at the movement, it did not stop the urge of letting his hopeless anger out on the pillow.

The door to his infirmary room swung open and immediately squelched it. He turned and jumped from his bed with a salute as Lieutenant Denir strode into the room on his limping gait.

"At ease, Sorrel." Lieutenant Denir put his hands behind his back and looked more pleased than Aabir had ever seen him.

"Sir." Aabir put his fist at his side, uneasiness pressing upon his chest.

"Well, I came to congratulate you on making it to the second day. Your successes today have honored Norland and made us *very* proud." His commanding officer's hard features sharpened as he got in Aabir's face. "I know you can keep at it, so don't mess this up. You hear me?"

Aabir swallowed back his anger and replied, "Yes sir."

"Good." Denir straightened and stepped back. "I'll be watching your efforts tomorrow, Sorrel. May the gods grant you success."

With that, the second lieutenant marched back out of the infirmary, his threat lingering in the air. Aabir clenched his aching hands back into fists and sat back down on the bed, his shoulders sagging as the weight upon his chest pressed upon them, too. He let out a long sigh.

Just one more day, he told himself, *and then I will be free.*

Chapter Fifty-Four

Empress of Igrium.

Tetra glared at her reflection in the mirror and tightened her grip on her toothbrush and toothpaste, wishing they were throwing axes. She slammed the drawer that used to house them and walked back into her room where a duffel bag sat atop her bed. She put them in one of the wide side pockets and zipped it shut.

Chief Baene's plans still rang through her head like Norland's annoying bell, even though it had been over a day since the news was given to her. She had paced and grumbled for hours in her room after she left his office, thinking and overthinking what he had told her.

Even earlier that morning when Army General Taoghn brought a few of Silvas' generals to watch her train, the chief advisor's plan stayed fixed in the back of her mind like a foreboding storm cloud. So instead of letting her usual heroic thoughts of stopping Emperor Ignis lead her on, she let the training droids know of her helpless anger at the newest situation being thrown upon her. Some might call it unreasonable to be angry, but Tetra ignored those thoughts.

She turned her glare down to her half-full duffel bag as if it was the one causing all her problems, and more annoying tears sprang to her eyes. She breathed out sharply through her teeth and pressed her fingertips to her forehead.

She had never cried so much in her life; which made her wonder if her body was using the emotional turmoil of the last month to finally release all the tears she had suppressed the past ten years. It was annoying, and only served to remind her of another reason she would be unfit to rule. Igrium couldn't have a weak ruler, and crying was one of the weakest things Tetra figured a human could do.

She zipped the bag closed with a huff. Her eyes locked onto her segione tallies as she did so, and another weight pressed her straight posture down.

Nor could the empire have someone with such a dishonorable reputation as herself ruling. No member of the Ignis family ever had a malscar before, and if they had then that person must have been disowned and their name forgotten in history.

So despite what Chief Baene said, the citizens of Igrium would never be satisfied with her on the throne—even if she did have Ignis blood running through her veins.

And what about her matha? If the hidden nation of shifters found out the new leader of Igrium could turn into a peryton, what would they think? Would they try to attack? She knew next to nothing about her matha's birth country—only the few tidbits her aunt and Felicita had told her—but one thing she did know was her parents' marriage wasn't looked upon highly by its leaders. She assumed Felicita or Aunt Minda told Chief Baene about her matha's real identity even though he didn't mention it yesterday, but that didn't give him the knowledge of how much of a threat the hidden nation might be.

A frustrated sigh escaped her lungs as she turned and sat down on the edge of her bed. No matter how long of a list she came up with of reasons she shouldn't rule, she knew, deep down, that Chief Baene's plan was probably the best option—no matter how much she didn't want it to be. His sharp words and her personal oath both tore down all the fear-born excuses she came up with.

Yes, Chief Baene was willing to let her go, but what would happen if Prince Ryder ascended, and he ended up worse than their father? The things she had overheard Emperor Ignis calling his son didn't necessarily bode well for the strong, just ruler Igrium would need if they lost the war. Plus, he was only fifteen—not that Tetra's eighteen years were much better, but there wasn't exactly a large choice of siblings in this generation of their family to choose from.

If that were to happen, Tetra knew—despite her current feelings on the matter—she would regret not taking the chief advisor's offer. In fact, if she didn't and something horrible *did* happen (like another war, or the complete destruction of Igrium), then, technically, it would be her fault. She was the only person who had a means to keep that from happening, but if she forsook it because of her own selfishness...

A chill went down her spine as guilt knotted in her chest. Her conscience wouldn't be able to handle it.

There was a familiar soft knock at the door. She jerked her head up at the unexpected noise but said nothing; the knot of guilt beginning to melt in the heat of her rising anger. She hadn't spoken to or seen Felicita since yesterday, and part of her wanted to keep that going. She had trusted her cousin and her aunt...and yet during all the time they had spent together the past three weeks, neither one of them told her what Chief Baene was planning.

Another knock, this one a bit harder. "Tetra?" Felicita's muffled accent carried through the door, "May I come in?"

Tetra almost replied "no", but then her gaze wandered to her duffel bag, and she remembered she wouldn't be seeing her cousin for at least a week. So, squashing down her ire for the moment, she called out, "Sure."

The door slowly swung open, and Felicita stepped in tentatively. Their eyes locked, and her cousin gave her a small smile that didn't reach her eyes.

"Hello, Tetra," she said.

Tetra only nodded, unable to keep a frown from pulling her lips downward. Felicita's own smile faded, and she closed the door behind her.

"How..." Her accented voice faltered, "How are you doing?"

"I've been better," Tetra replied flatly.

Felicita nodded slowly. "How are you feeling about this coming battle?"

Better than a certain plan she didn't want to be a part of. "Fine."

Felicita lifted her hands and fooled with the end of one of her braids. "Matha wanted me ta say 'good-bye' for her, and ta apologize for yesterday."

Tetra let the words settle between them before she asked, "Why didn't either of you tell me?" She noticed Felicita's wide eyes flinch at the sharpness of her question, but she didn't try to apologize as her anger overtook the rest of her emotions. "You could've at least told me in advance about what Chief Baene was planning—I know you've known about it for a while—but did you have the decency to do that so I could've had some time to think about it these past few weeks? No! No, you didn't."

"I'm sorry, Tetra," Felicita's eyes grew glassy, "but as Chief Baene's assistant I'm sworn ta secrecy on matters such as this. I would've told you—I truly would 'ave if I could—but my position doesn't allow me ta do tha'."

The look in her watery eyes told Tetra she wasn't lying, and the valid excuse cooled some of her anger—although it didn't stop the small pang in her heart. Withholding a sigh, she crossed her arms and turned her gaze down to the ground.

"I just wish I could've had some more time to...to know about all of this—and I don't only mean this plan, but also my...who *I am*—before the Buleutcil had to be told." Her voice lowered, "I've barely had enough time to think about it all myself."

As the underlying truth left her lips, sharp tears stabbed at her face and she squeezed her eyes shut with a silent curse. Felicita's soft footsteps approached her, then a light weight landed on her shoulder. She didn't jerk away, but instead lifted her head and met her cousin's teary eyes.

"I know." Felicita pressed her lips into a thin line. "And I wish we could give you more time, Tetra, but the longer this stays hidden, the easier it'll be for it ta hurt us in the long run. Matha and I 'ave already hid for far too long, and I know tha' will probably end up hurting us; but you... Well, the truth o' who you are needs ta be told, Tetra. This kind o' secret won't stay idle for long. The quicker it comes, the easier it'll settle."

Tetra discerned the extra meaning in her words: with how heavy the truth was, she might find herself crushed by it if she didn't let it out in the open soon—before someone else found out.

She nodded with a small sigh and pressed her forehead against the palms of her hands. "Why me?" The question sounded pitiful even to her own ears, but she continued, "I've—I've never had ambitions of ruling before... Actually—I've never really had ambitions of any kind before." She breathed out a dry laugh that didn't match the helpless tears blurring her vision. "All I wanted to do was escape Norland...if I survived it. I never thought about what I'd do if I did escape, or if I did somehow graduate..."

And becoming empress was definitely not something she would've planned if she ever had thought that far before.

There was a rustling of fabric, then the mattress moved a little and Tetra turned her head to meet the warring emotions in Felicita's gaze.

"You were born for this." Felicita's accent deepened as her tone took on a more serious edge. "And why it's you? Well, I don't hold the answers ta the universe, but I do believe tha' Deleyon made you for this time. It might not seem like a good thing now, but if you do end up becoming empress, Tetra, then just imagine the changes you could make in Igrium! Imagine the lives tha' could be saved in the future if you were ta lead tha' nation."

Tetra took in a deep breath before the weight pressing upon her shoulders could expand and constrict her lungs. "But it's all so big..." She said slowly, "And the only thing anyone in Igrium thought I was capable of doing was messing up my—no—the *Cairn's* honor. So how can *I* lead when all my dishonor is forever marked on my face?"

"Because tha' scar shows how much you will fight." Felicita's gaze bore into her "It'll show everyone tha' they will 'ave a strong leader who doesn't let the opinions o' others keep her from doin' what's right."

Tetra raised her brow in a dubious look, and her sister continued, "I know the malscar has been around since Igrium's founding, but I believe the reasons it's been given 'ave differed with the circumstances. So once this war is over and your patre is no longer on the throne, then I believe people's perceptions will change. And as they do, they'll see the reason you got tha' malscar not as an act o' cowardice, but as a sign o' strength."

"I don't know..." Tetra shook her head and looked down at her socked feet. Igrium accepting her *malscar* as an act of strength was about as possible as all the ice in Frigac melting.

"Tetra...I know you're scared," Felicita said. "I wish you didn't 'ave ta be put in this situation, but you are the only one who Chief Baene and Lord Jachen believe is able ta do this. They cannot put their trust in Prince Ryder because he has grown up underneath Emperor Ignis' tutelage, but—ta add on ta what we were saying earlier—the evidence of your opinions on Igrium's morals is quite clear. So, they believe they can trust you."

Tetra glanced over at Felicita's small smile but couldn't match it. "They do?"

"Yes. I've heard them both say it."

"Really?"

"Yes."

She twisted her lips to the side and rubbed her thumb over her segione scars. "Well...I haven't made a decision yet, but...thanks for—thanks for coming in here."

Felicita's smile grew a little bigger. "I couldn't just let you leave without saying 'good-bye'; nor could Matha—no matter how angry we both figured you were at us."

At its mention, Tetra realized the earlier heat of her anger had simmered down to a small ember. She still wasn't happy with how her newfound family had handled the situation, but at least she knew they were sorry, and that Felicita did have a valid excuse.

Yet even with that thought, she found herself saying, "Felicita, I want you to make me a promise."

"Wha' kind o' promise?"

Tetra lifted her head and locked her eyes on her sisters'. "I know you're bound to secrecy with your job, but if anything major like this comes up that involves me, then please—just tell me Chief Baene is possibly planning something major that might involve me. I don't have to know what it is, but I do think I have the right to know when something is being planned that I might have to be a part of."

Felicita's gaze lowered for a moment as she bit her lip. "I..."

"You can even tell Chief Baene you made this promise—I don't want you to lose your job because of me. I only want to know if something is up." She dug her nails into her arms as she added, "I'm coming to find how much I hate secrets, and I don't want there to be any between us where there shouldn't be. I know you want your privacy and I also want mine, so I don't want you to think we'll be telling each other everything—but I don't think this promise is asking too much."

Felicita was quiet for a few heart-pounding moments before she replied, "I'll tell Chief Baene tha' I want ta do this, Tetra," she lifted her gaze again, "and then when he gives me the 'all-clear,' I'll be able ta make tha' promise. It's not because I don't want ta make it—I do—but I say tha' because some o' the things I know are considered national security and I would 'ave ta 'ave permission from a higher source ta even mention them vaguely."

Tetra forced her face into a neutral expression to keep from frowning. "That's fine."

It was better than what she should've hoped for, anyway.

A light weight barely touched her forearm, and she noticed Felicita's fingertips were barely touching her birthmark. "I hate secrets, too," she said, "but some are not mine ta tell."

"Sure." Tetra nodded in understanding, even if it wasn't the exact thing she wanted to hear. "Thanks for agreeing, though—if he gives you permission."

"Thank you for understanding." Felicita lowered her hand into her lap with a long sigh. "I know these past few weeks have been hard on you and that I haven't made it any easier withholding things, so thank you for letting me speak ta you now. I didn't..." Her breath hitched before she continued, "I didn't want ta have our last meeting turn into a fight before you leave—and I'm glad it hasn't been."

"Me too."

"Tetra..." Tears again sprang up in Felicita's eyes, "I want you ta know tha' I'll be prayin' and offerin' sacrifices ta Deleyon on your account while you're away. Matias continues ta assure me tha' you won't be put into any mortal danger during the battle, but I know tha' battles are crazy and accidents can happen, so...just be safe."

Her eyes pleaded with Tetra to do so, "Don't do anything rash, follow all o' Galia's orders, and use wisdom in whatever situation you're thrown into. OK?"

Tetra's lips lifted in a small smile. "I'll try my best."

"Thank you." Felicita bit her lip again before asking hesitantly, "Um—I know you don't like them, but—well, since you're about ta leave..."

"Sure."

Before Tetra could brace herself, Felicita flung her arms around her shoulders and squeezed her in a tight hug. She wrapped her arms around her sister in a much less enthusiastic way and patted her back awkwardly as the air was pressed out of her lungs.

"I love you, Tetra," Felicita said close to her ear.

"Yeah...I love you, too..." Tetra barely breathed out under the force of her embrace.

And even with the awkwardness of the hug, coupled with her roiling emotions that couldn't seem to settle these past three weeks, she meant those words.

Chapter Fifty-Five

THE SECOND DAY OF the Constantia Tourney went by in what Aabir could only describe as a slow blur. He and the thirty remaining third-level competitors (none of whom were from Norland except for him) began their day with a short breakfast in the stadium's dining hall specifically for them, then he was rushed off into the flooded arena to fight for his place in the Tourney.

In the first round, he found himself on a small boat surrounded by eel-infested waters with two other competitors. The goal was to use whatever weapon they had chosen before the round started to knock their opponents off the ship. Whoever was left standing got to go to the next round. Aabir, of course, chose a sword similar in weight and design to his own back at Norland.

With many silent pleas to Deleyon, he successfully fought off the other two competitors and made it to the next round. As the last one fell into the dark water with a scream, he pushed all his focus away from the guilt pressing in upon his chest. He only had to make it another round or two before he could "accidentally" fail and be honorably disqualified.

In the next one, he fired crossbow bolts at another competitor while fleeing king scorpions and, by the grace of Deleyon, somehow won. The next time he fought, it was during the middle of the day, and he figured he could finally let himself lose.

So, with that in mind, he faked a fall and let the other competitor he faced grab the only weapon in the rock-strewn arena. Then he let himself get chased—until his opponent pushed him towards a tall cliff and he almost fell a couple stories onto more rocky terrain. The other competitor swung the ax towards him, and Aabir barely dodged the sharp blade before it hit him in the face. Again and again, his opponent swung at him. He almost slipped off the cliffside in his attempts to dodge.

Adrenaline pumping, he ducked under the next swing and moved away from the cliff at the same time. His opponent turned sharply, swinging the ax wildly as they did so. Aabir spun back around to face him, just in time to see the competitor's leg give way under a loose rock. He fell forward, giving Aabir no excuse to not take the ax.

He did so, silently cursing his luck, and tackled his opponent back to the ground. He pressed the ax against the guy's throat until he called for mercy, and Brutus Halt immediately announced him the winner.

Guilt and dread pressed their icy fingers upon him, but he again pushed his focus away from them with the hope that he still had a chance to lose another round. In the next one, he and a few others were forced to find, and attack, each other in a pitch black so dark the only thing Aabir could see were the ghostly bioluminescent spots of more white tigers the Tourney's Planners added to make the round "more fun". His recent wounds from yesterday's round had throbbed with dull pain as he ran for his life from one that chased him and another competitor.

The tiger ended up grabbing the other person and Aabir ran back to help them, even though the only thing he could see were the tiger's flashing spots. Using the dagger he had been given before the round, he went to attack the beast—but instead of stabbing the wild cat, he accidentally stabbed the other competitor in their arm and won himself a spot in the next round.

Still, he tried not to let dread get the better of him as he was forced to fight another competitor underwater, ran through a maze of fire, and won a duel while standing atop a spherical stage. Only when he found himself sitting alone in the same large waiting room from before did he let some of the dreadful, guilt-ridden thoughts trickle into the forefront of his mind, while his wide eyes stayed trained on the arena.

One of the two competitors fighting atop the small, but tall, outcroppings covering the arena floor hefted his spear and hurled it towards his opponent, who stood a few outcroppings away. Aabir flinched in sympathy as the thin spear struck the other competitor's leg. The same thing had happened to him a few times throughout his years at Norland. It was not fun.

The competitor fell with a cry as the crowds roared wildly; yet even with their thunderous clamor, Brutus Halt's amplified voice rose above it all, "—and Galleza goes down with a beautiful throw! I've never seen a third-level use a spear with that much precision before, folks! But it's not over yet! Nassum still has to make it across to finish the fight—if he can..."

As Nassum began leaping from outcropping to outcropping as if he had been doing it his whole life, Aabir was able to tune out the announcer's commentary in his fixation over the approaching fight. He glanced back over at Galleza, who was struggling to make it over to another outcropping in the opposite direction of her approaching opponent.

Although he did not care who won this battle, his heart still raced in anticipation as Nassum closed in on her. Neither had a weapon anymore (except for the spear sticking out of Galleza's leg), but that had never stopped anyone in any earlier round before.

Nassum landed on the outcropping where Galleza kneeled. On the jumbotrons, Aabir saw her reddened face racked with fury as she pressed her hands against the back of her leg. Without missing a beat, Nassum tackled her to the ground, then pulled the spear out of her leg. Aabir widened his eyes in horror and leaned forward as the competitor pressed the bloodied spear against Galleza's exposed neck.

"Do you yield?" He barely caught Nassum's projected words above the noise of the crowds.

Only by the size of the jumbotron was he able to catch the begrudging nod Galleza sent her opponent, her eyes blazing with pained fury.

"—and Nassum Rundi wins!" Brutus Halt exclaimed as the cheers of the crowd rose until the floor underneath Aabir shook with the weight of the noise. "What an amazing show, folks! These last few rounds have been some of the best I've seen in years, and I hope that leaves you as excited as I am for what's coming next—" Aabir's stomach tightened with Brutus' next words, "—because we have finally come to the culmination of Level Three!"

Aabir did not think the crowds could get any louder, but the increased shaking of the floor proved him wrong. His stomach twisted even more, and he pressed his fists against his temples.

"After this break, Nassum Rundi and Aabir Sorrel will fight for the chance to move to Day Three as a Level Two competitor! I hear the Tourney's Planners have a special surprise up their sleeves for this day's final round, so don't leave yet!"

The third day. The small lunch Aabir ate a couple hours ago threatened to come back up as dread dripped into his tense stomach. He never meant to make it this far, yet—with the combination of sheer luck and his own survival instincts—he had. The only good thing about this situation was Lieutenant Denir was probably happy with him right now. That was one less threat he had to worry about, at least.

Even so, it did nothing to stop the worries from bombarding his imagination. Pictures of him winning against Nassum in a duel flitted through his head, followed by the killing blows he would have to deal out when fighting against a Constantia prisoner. The images from Xich also came back to join the attack against his conscience, and he breathed out a sharp breath as blood pounded in his ears.

Deleyon, I have to lose! He pleaded through the roulette of horrible, gory mental images plaguing his mind, *Please, please, please make me lose this round. Show me how to lose without it looking like I'm trying to! Please, Deleyon—the Tourney goes against everything I've heard about you! Don't make me fight in them anymore. I can't kill anyone...*

The only thing that helped him stop the deluge of frightening thoughts was when someone came up to bring him down for the day's—and hopefully his—last round. With more silent prayers, Aabir got up and followed the man out of the waiting room. The horrible mental images tried to come back with each second that passed in the quiet elevator ride, but he was able to push them aside for the time being as he thought back to the fight he just witnessed—namely the things he had watched Nassum doing.

Usually, Aabir would do this to find weaknesses in his opponent's during training duels. However, this time he was going for the opposite strategy. From what he witnessed, Nassum was obviously a skilled spearman and was agile despite his large frame. So, Aabir might be able to lose this fight without even trying to if they were given spears or put in some environment where agility was necessary.

Brutus Halt did say the Tourney's Planners had something special planned, though, and past replays told him it would probably be something unexpected. More dread wriggled its way through his insides, but he tried to not let it show as the elevator stopped at the ground level and he was ushered near one of the arena's entrances. Another attendant handed him a long, thick spear and a sword similar in size and weight to his own back at Norland.

His eyebrows rose and his heart skipped a beat as he stared down at the two weapons. Had the Tourney's Planners done this on purpose to give both final third-level competitors a chance?

Aabir's stomach flipped as he wondered how in Afreean he would be able to fake a mistake sword fighting while knowing Lieutenant Denir was watching. He lifted his eyes to the wide, hydraulic door in front of him as it hissed open; bright lighting and ear-splintering cheers coming through. Hopefully, with it being the last round, the environment would make mistakes easy to make.

He blinked his eyes to get used to the stadium lights as he stepped out into the arena. The roar of the crowds vibrated in his chest, accompanying the worried rhythm his heart thumped as he turned his narrow-eyed gaze around the arena's bare, metal floor. It looked as it had during the times he and Buren had come to practice, and a chill of uneasiness went through him. He tightened his shaking grip on the sword in his right hand. What was going on?

"Welcome to the final round of Level Three!" Aabir blinked in shock as Brutus Halt's voice boomed through the empty arena. The cheers grew for a few moments, then lessened as the Constantia announcer continued, "Nassum Rundi, Aabir Sorrel—you'll both be glad to know that what you see before you will be your environment for this round. No surprise chasms, no water—nothing of the sort."

At the mention of their names, Aabir finally locked eyes on the lone figure he recognized as Nassum coming towards him from the opposite arena entrance.

"In fact, instead of fighting each other for your place in the next level, the Tourney's Planners have decided to add a twist this year," Brutus said in his ever-cheerful voice. "You'll both be joined by a very special guest in a moment, and whoever kills them will be the one to advance."

At the words "special guest", the images of the Constantia prisoners popped into Aabir's head, and he squeezed both his weapons even tighter, fear spreading like ice through his veins. *No, no, no, no, no—it's only the second day!* Were the Tourney's Planners doing this in revenge for the failed prison break? Make some unlucky prisoner fight to the death on the second day?

"And here it is!"

Aabir turned his gaze towards the arena door to his left as it hissed open. His heart tried to escape his ribcage as the taller entry door fully opened like the shadowy maw of an animal. He could not see anything through the darkness, but he heard a heavy pounding coming from it despite the noise of the crowds.

A darker silhouette entered the shadows and a deep, menacing growl echoed into the arena. Aabir bunched his muscles, a different kind of fear rising within him at the noise. His eyes widened as the towering figure emerged into the open, and he found himself wishing he could have fought Nassum instead. The stadium lights illuminated the creature's copper-colored fur as it stepped forward into the arena, the door closing behind it. It lifted its huge, antlered head and turned its long neck around, ears pricked, to gaze around at the gawking crowds. Then it lowered its head—and its eyes landed on Aabir.

A *peryton*? It let loose a roar that rivaled those watching, and another chill of fear went through Aabir's shaking muscles. The Tourney's Planners wanted two young adults to go up against a *peryton*? From the replays he had watched, if perytons were ever in the Tourney, it was only for those in the First Level—the Tourney's veterans and those who won the Second Level.

He took a step back at the look in the peryton's dark eyes. If he did not know any better, he would have thought it was brilliant enough to be furious at him with that look. None of the other predators he had faced looked at him with such...*intelligence* before.

He gulped and averted his gaze—and that was when he noticed a gleaming metal collar wrapped around its neck. He had no other thought about it, however, as his eyes roved over the long, fresh scars slashed along its legs, neck and sides. The weight of the weapons in his hands suddenly grew heavier, and he took another step back as understanding hit him like a battlehammer.

Those scars looked like they were caused by sharp weapons or whips, not another wild animal. It probably thought Aabir was the one to torture it, or at least associated the weapons he held with the terrible experience.

The peryton took a menacing step towards him and lowered its head until the sharp points of its antlers faced in his direction. Its front hoof screeched against the metal floor as it pawed the ground.

The awful noise shattered Aabir out of his fearful stupor, and he ran to the side as the beast charged him. Its heavy steps reverberated through the floor underneath Aabir's feet. He glanced behind his shoulder and saw it had stopped near the arena's curved wall. It lifted its head and watched him with those sharp eyes.

He gulped but slowed to a stop, turning to face it. He lifted the spear over his shoulder and locked his eyes on the peryton's flank. He would not try to throw to kill it, but if he could wound the creature then he would not look like he was trying to get out of winning—

Something rammed into his side and he fell to the floor with a grunt. *What the—?*

Cold furrum touched his neck, and he lifted his gaze to meet Nassum Rundi's. More fear sliced through him at the cold look in the other competitor's hard gaze. He gulped, and the blade barely bit into his skin.

Was there a rule he had missed after he turned his focus away from Brutus Halt's prattling? Were they actually supposed to fight each other?

"I'm winning this thing, Sorrel," Nassum's voice was as sharp as his sword. "Don't get in my way, or else."

Aabir did not think his voice would be strong enough to reply, so he kept his mouth shut. Nassum glared at him a moment longer before getting up off him.

When the other competitor turned to face the peryton, Aabir finally let himself breathe a full breath and got up, picking up his dropped weapons in the process. That was when he realized neither one of them had become the peryton's next meal. He looked over at the creature and noticed it was watching them both, its head tilted slightly. Then it shook itself and the dangerous anger returned to its furry countenance.

Nassum lifted his spear over his shoulder with a battle cry and threw it. The peryton jumped away from the projectile, opened its mottled, copper wings, and flew into the air as the crowds roared for its blood.

Aabir craned his neck to watch the huge predator circling above them. It tried to soar in the air above the crowds, but its flight faltered as it seemed to hit an invisible wall in midair. Aabir's attention moved back to the collar on its neck, and then down to the tall posts lined atop the arena's wall—an electric fence.

His attention was immediately taken by the echo of running footsteps. He spun around in time to see Nassum throw his spear up at the peryton again. The beast roared as the weapon sliced its side. In reply to the attack, it tucked its wings in and dove towards them.

Aabir jumped to the side and fell on the ground as it soared above his head. The attack was followed by an ear-splitting, metallic screech that rang over the cheers and Brutus Halt's commentary. Aabir gritted his teeth and pressed his hands against his ears at the noise. Thankfully, it stopped as suddenly as it had come, and he was able to push himself off the ground before turning to face the peryton.

Thin scratches in the metal led to the peryton's new position in the arena. Nassum wove between its legs, slashing at them with his sword, as it smashed its hooves and talons where the competitor once was. Aabir watched the exchange for a few moments as he tried to breathe evenly, unwilling to move anywhere near the beast or the competitor who would injure him if he did so.

Yet as he stood there doing nothing but watching, Brutus Halt's voice broke through his barrier of focus, "—was a close one! It looks like Nassum's plan is working! But what is Aabir Sorrel doing? Is he planning his own attack, folks? Or is he letting thoughts of cowardice get to him? In this last Third-Level round, it can be difficult to know—"

The old wound inside him that never seemed to heal broke open again at the announcer's jab. He gripped the hilt of his sword tightly and ground his teeth. *I'm not a coward,* he tried to tell himself, *and I don't have to prove that to anyone watching.*

Even as he had those thoughts, Lieutenant Denir's warning came back into his mind—and it made him grind his teeth even more until his jaw hurt. His commanding officer was undoubtedly watching him at that moment, and he would probably still find his threat viable if it looked like Aabir was acting in any sort of cowardly way—even if he had made it to the end of the second day.

He blinked his eyes to turn his focus back onto the fight before him, then hefted the spear over his shoulder again and rushed towards the peryton—that was still trying to crush Nassum with its hooves. His eyes landed on the creature's thigh—a place that would not lead to a killing blow—and he let out a yell before throwing the spear towards its target.

The peryton stopped its pounding and lifted its neck as the spear sailed into its back leg, right below its thigh. It roared and turned its head towards the spear, then pulled it out with its jaws and threw it to the ground.

It turned its head back in Aabir's direction. Their eyes met, and it roared a challenge that caused his leaden heart to fall into his stomach. Then it leapt towards him.

Aabir scrambled back with a yell as its front hooves pounded the ground where he had been. He lifted his sword and slashed it across the beast's front leg before scrambling further back as it lifted one of its hooves to crush him.

As suddenly as it seemed it was about to attack, it stopped—hoof raised in the air. In that half-second, Aabir wondered what it was doing—then something sliced across the armor plate on his back. He grunted in surprise and pivoted on his heel, raising his sword in front of him to block the next attack. His eyes widened in even further surprise as his blade deflected Nassum's next blow.

"What are you doing?" Aabir asked incredulously.

There was a giant peryton right behind them! Did the guy want them to get crushed? Nassum's brow lowered as he pressed his sword blade against Aabir's.

"You won't take this victory from me!" he grunted out.

Aabir slid his blade free and retreated a step, wishing he could come up with some truthful reply about how he did not want to take this win from Nassum, but all of his half-formed excuses died on his tongue.

Nassum's eyes sparked with indignation, as if Aabir's silence was answer enough, and he lunged towards him with a yell. Aabir blocked the downward stroke and advanced with a swipe at Nassum's middle, the familiar movements calming some of his fears. Nassum faded back, then lunged forward again. Aabir warded off the blow and thrusted his sword's point towards his opponent's middle.

Nassum blocked his move. "I will not let you take this moment away from me!"

Then he yelled and raised his sword for a stroke at Aabir's head. Aabir went to duck from the attack but realized Nassum feigned the move as the opposing blade sliced towards his legs.

"Ah!" He grunted and barely blocked the sword as he stumbled out of the way.

Instead of continuing the fight he started, Nassum ran away from Aabir. Aabir scrunched his brow, baffled at the odd behavior, as he turned his neck to watch his fleeing opponent. Then he noticed what he was running towards, and all his confusion faded.

The peryton now stood a few paces away from them. It seemed to shake itself out of a daze as Nassum came running towards it. It lowered its antlers in greeting and pawed the ground with a hoof. Aabir watched with wide eyes as, before the creature ever moved forward, Nassum jumped onto its huge, bough-like antlers and began to climb up them as agilely as a scurrus. The peryton roared in fury and swung his head back and forth, but Nassum clung on.

Despite the other boy's ferocity, Aabir ran towards the now-bucking peryton to help. If Nassum was flung off, he would probably break a few bones in his body and would be unable to compete—no matter how much his Igrian blood might curdle at the thought of surrender—which would leave Aabir as the only person left to kill the peryton. The only third-level left to go to the next day.

The cheers of the crowd grew with Brutus' excited commentary as the peryton leapt into the air with Nassum still hanging onto its antlers. It spun in midair with wild roars, but still Aabir could see the glint of the other competitor's armor amidst the pale antler points.

It suddenly dove, and he fell on his back as the wild creature flew over him and landed with another metallic screech. He scrambled up again and ran towards it. Blood pounded in his ears as his eyes followed Nassum, who had begun to climb again. The creature went back to swinging its head from side to side with angry snorts.

It was so focused on getting Nassum off that Aabir was able to come up and stab his sword into the flesh above its hoof. He jumped back as the peryton roared and leapt into the air again, then silently chided himself for the stupid mistake as he watched the peryton flap its wings wildly while it twisted and spun—yet Nassum continued hanging on.

There was nothing he could do until the peryton landed. However, just as he had the thought, he remembered his spear. He lowered his gaze from the fight of stubborn wills above him back to the empty arena. He spotted one of the spears lying in the middle of the space, while the other lay further away on the side opposite from him.

Inhaling deeply, he ran for the closest one. The peryton roared madly above him, and he picked up his pace until it matched the beat of his heart. Only when he neared the spear did he slow enough to reach down and pick it up before wrapping his hand around its wooden shaft. His eyes lifted towards the flying peryton once again as he ran. He could not aim to kill, but he could aim to injure it again...

Setting his eyes on its massive wings, Aabir skidded to a stop on the metal floor and lifted the spear over his shoulder. His eyes stayed locked on the twisting, circling peryton as he waited for an opportunity. When the animal opened its huge wings to swoop down again, Aabir took a running start and threw the spear.

It sailed through the air and hit a little above where the peryton's wing and shoulder met. Aabir pumped his free fist in the air as the creature roared and tried to use both its wings. It soon crashed to the arena floor opposite him.

He brandished his sword at his side as he watched the peryton slowly get up. His heart leapt into his throat as the beast turned its neck in his direction. He realized Nassum was no longer hanging onto its antlers. *Oh no.* He sent a quick glance around the empty arena but did not see the other competitor. Had he fallen off without Aabir realizing?

Then the peryton mewed like a wounded forest cat and turned its head to look at the place where Aabir's spear hit it. Aabir noticed Nassum clinging to the peryton's antler burr near its head, and his fear abated for the moment. Seeing the other competitor was still alive and awake, he rushed forward to continue his act of fighting the peryton to win. The peryton's legs filled his sights, and he raised his sword with a battle cry.

Then, out of the corner of his eye, he noticed something hurtling towards him. Pain shot through his shoulder. Aabir cried out and stumbled to a stop. He clutched his shoulder with a wince and looked at the wound. The wooden shaft of a spear stuck out of it, the weapon's head barely poking out between the plates of his armor. He tried to move his neck to see how far it had gone through him, but bright pain exploded at the sharp movement, and he sank onto his knee with another cry.

"I warned you!"

He lifted his eyes towards Nassum, who now clung to the peryton's moving neck. Aabir lifted his other hand to the spear's shaft to keep it from moving and shot a glance over at the spot where his spear had struck the peryton. Only a bleeding wound remained there.

"Don't make me do anything worse," Nassum added.

Aabir returned his glare to the other competitor and stood back up. More pain grated against the bones in his shoulder as he did so. He sucked in a sharp breath through his teeth. The peryton began to buck again and he took a few steps back to keep from getting squashed. As he did, he looked back up at Nassum and watched in wide-eyed, shocked silence as the older competitor clung to the peryton's swinging neck with one hand, his sword in the other.

With a yell, Nassum stabbed the peryton's neck. The beast roared and moved its neck to try and bite him. The competitor removed his blade and ducked underneath the snapping jaws, stabbing the peryton's neck again and again.

Aabir's pulse began to spike painfully through his wounded shoulder as he watched. He thought of taking the spear out, but immediately pushed the idea to the side. He wanted as much of his blood to stay in his body as was possible.

The peryton's movements grew sluggish as Nassum continued stabbing its neck, dark crimson blood pouring out of its wounds. Despite the bloody sight and the spear in his shoulder, a wind of relief blew over Aabir. He had not killed the peryton, which meant he was not going to the next day. If there had not been a crowd of over a hundred-thousand people watching him, he would have let out a smile. Nevertheless, he did it on the inside.

Now that the threat of the peryton was slowly dying before his eyes, the buzz of his adrenaline began to ebb away. The weight of the spear grew heavier, but not even that could do anything to stop the joy Aabir felt in that moment.

"Rundi! Rundi! Rundi!" The crowds cheered as Nassum stood triumphantly on the peryton's back.

Even with his relief over his opponent winning, Aabir had to stop from laughing aloud when Nassum almost tumbled off as the peryton finally fell on the ground. However, the other competitor straightened again and raised his bloodied sword in the air as if nothing had happened. The cheering of the crowds only grew. The noise made it hard to breathe as it reverberated in Aabir's chest.

"And the winner of the Third Level is: Nassum Rundi!" Brutus Halt cheered along with the crowd. "Congratulations, competitor! Aabir Sorrel, you put on a good show but your time here is through. If you would please make your way to the exit..."

Aabir nodded to the disembodied voice as he gritted his teeth and turned towards the nearest exit to leave. He passed by the peryton's head, then stumbled to a stop as his eyes locked onto the animal's. It panted heavily as the last of its life drained away, but what made Aabir's blood run cold was the defiant anger he saw in its large, brown eyes.

The peryton sent him one last glare as it heaved a deep breath—then it lifted its long neck and snapped Nassum up in its jaws.

Chapter Fifty-Six

Nassum screamed, and it was followed by more screams and yells from the audience. Aabir's heart nearly stopped as the peryton's neck fell back down. Something akin to satisfaction lit up its eyes right before the light left them for good.

He shook himself from his surprise and ran over to the peryton's head, despite the way his pounding footsteps jostled the spear from his shoulder. He slowed to a stop at the beast's mouth and fell to his knees, his eyes frantically snapping over the sight before him.

Nassum struggled between the peryton's teeth, its jaw almost completely closed around his body. Sweat beads formed on Aabir's forehead underneath his helmet. It was a good thing Nassum was wearing armor or else... He grimaced as the gruesome thought flitted through his head.

"Where are you hurt?" He asked.

Nassum tried pushing the creature's jaws apart with his free arm but gave up with a sharp intake of breath. "It's on my legs," he said through gritted teeth, "I think—I think one of them's broken. And its teeth are breaking through my...my armor."

Aabir nodded once as his brain scrambled for a plan. His gaze lowered to the tip of the beast's mouth, and he noticed a small pool of blood running out from under its chin. He gripped his sword tighter and winced as it sent another stab of pain through his shoulder. That was too bright to be peryton blood...

Nassum let out a pained grunt. Aabir looked up and saw him struggling to free himself again.

"Stop moving, Nassum," he ordered. "You'll lose more blood that way."

Nassum glared at him, but then squeezed his eyes shut as pain sharpened his already-sharp features. "Fine," he breathed out.

Aabir ran his thumb along the hilt of his sword as he looked at the situation before him. He could not pull Nassum out through the top, but he could try to open the peryton's jaws...

Dropping his sword, he shuffled closer to the peryton's mouth, sat down, and wedged himself as much as he could between its partly open jaw. He glanced up at Nassum once to make sure he was still conscious, then turned his attention to the task at hand.

Counting to three under his breath, Aabir pushed with his back and feet on the peryton's top and bottom jaws. He hissed as his shoulder erupted in pain. He had to stop to take a few breaths as his vision blurred for a moment. When it cleared, he again pushed against the stiffening bones, inching them further and further apart.

Aabir's weary muscles shook as he pressed with all his might. The pain in his shoulder screamed at him to stop, but whenever that happened, he only had to look up at Nassum's weakening form to give him the motivation to keep going. No one was going to die on his watch—especially not the guy who had won so Aabir did not have to.

With a final cry, he fell onto his back between the now-open jaws of the stiffening peryton. He heaved an exhausted sigh and turned his head in the direction of a heavy thump.

His eyes widened at Nassum's bloodied, still form. He rolled onto his good side and pushed himself up with his uninjured arm, though a stab of bright, fiery pain tore through his shoulder at the movement. He squeezed his eyes shut with a hiss and sat still for a few moments, lifting his hand to hold the spear's heavy shaft in place while his pulse stabbed through his skull.

Only when he opened his eyes and saw the broken body lying before him did he gain some strength to stumble forward on his knees. The other competitor's armor was pockmarked with bleeding, gaping holes where the peryton's sharp, back teeth had snatched him. Blood covered his mangled legs where the peryton fell on them. Aabir looked away before his weakening stomach threw up the contents of his lunch and turned his focus onto the task at hand.

Using his good arm, he pushed Nassum onto his side, checked to make sure he was still breathing, then hooked his arm around Nassum's shoulder and began to drag him away from the smelly mouth of the beast.

Even though he was on his knees, with the combination of Nassum's weight and the pain his shoulder was giving him, Aabir stumbled and fell. The spear's shaft struck the ground, and bright pain exploded inside his shoulder as his fall pushed it to the side. He could not help the cry that escaped his lips as the spearhead tore from his shoulder. Blood gushed out from the gaping wound as he was plopped on the ground.

Silence enveloped the arena as Aabir's vision grew dim, causing Brutus Halt's calmer voice to ring out louder than his normal, excitable tone, "Aabir Sorrel, on behalf of the Tourney's Planners, we thank you for your honorable actions. Medbots are on their way to help you both, and then you'll be able to leave the Tourney with honor."

Aabir's heart hammered away in his chest as a discordant ringing filled his ears; yet even with the overwhelming pain throbbing through his whole body, he had never felt so relieved in his life. He had lost—and that was worth all the pain he was in.

Thank Deleyon, was the last thought he had before darkness took him from the pain-filled reality and into nothingness.

Aabir awoke to a headache. He slowly opened his eyes and squinted at the harsh lighting that greeted him. As he blinked to adjust his vision to the brightness, his gaze was met with the same infirmary room he had been in yesterday. He drew his eyebrows together as confusion bombarded against his aching head, and he pushed himself into a sitting position—which was when he noticed the bandages wrapped around his shoulders.

All at once, the memories returned: the Constantia rounds he fought in, the peryton battle, and freeing Nassum. Relief washed through him as Brutus Halt's last words about him leaving honorably popped back into his head.

He had done it. He had lost. And not even Lieutenant Denir could be disappointed in the honorable way he was leaving.

Soft footsteps approached outside the room he was in. Aabir jerked his head up as the doorknob turned and the door swung open. A man in a white lab coat stepped into the room with a tray in his hand. His long face broke into a smile as he met Aabir's eyes.

"I'm glad you're awake, Trainee Sorrel." He moved over to the side of Aabir's bed. "You've been out for quite some time. How are you feeling?"

Aabir lowered his gaze with a shrug before the doctor could see how happy he was. "I'm fine."

"How's your shoulder?"

At the mention of it, he turned his eyes back onto the bandages and moved it in a circle. His brow lifted in surprise at only the dull soreness he felt.

"What did you do?" Aabir asked.

"We stopped the blood flow then sped up the muscle regeneration process," the doctor replied. "That's why your shoulder might be sore. The process isn't finished yet, but as long as you don't do anything strenuous, it should be completely healed by morning."

"Oh. OK."

Aabir had heard of muscle regeneration techniques, but Norland's infirmary did not employ those unless the case was serious. So, he never got to experience being almost completely healed only hours after a major wound until now. He moved his shoulder in another circle. It felt...strange, to say the least.

"It's a good thing the spear didn't penetrate any deeper or you would've been honorably disqualified from the Tourney," the doctor added. "Some wounds are so bad it can take weeks for the muscles to grow back even with the best of technology."

Aabir nodded, but then stopped himself as he finally processed what the doctor said. "Wait...I *was* honorably disqualified from them."

The doctor's eyes widened before giving Aabir a sheepish look. "I'm sorry, Trainee, I forgot that you haven't had a chance to be told."

Aabir's heart stopped. "Told what?"

A shadowed frown flitted across the man's face. "Even with everything you did to save Nassum Rundi, he...didn't make it."

Shock and dread jolted through Aabir, leaving him speechless for a moment. "He...he's dead?"

Had Aabir really been too late to save him?

"Yes—he lost too much blood," the doctor answered with a small nod.

He's dead. A twinge of guilt wove into Aabir's thoughts. Even with everything he had tried to do to help get Nassum free from the peryton's mouth, it had not been enough.

"And since he can't compete," the doctor's voice pulled his attention back to the present, "you automatically took his place in the competition as winner of the Third Level."

No... Aabir immediately turned his face away before the man could see the horror plastered there.

He had made it. For all of his efforts to lose, he had actually made it.

A flash of angry heat sparked inside him. *I thought you were listening to me, Deleyon!* He mentally cried out, *Why would you do this to me? Why couldn't Nassum have lived?*

Then there would be one less death in the world, and Aabir would be free to go back to normal life without having to bring another one in the prisoner rounds.

"When can I leave here?" He asked aloud, keeping out any emotion from slipping into it.

The doctor gestured to the tray in his hand. "You can after I put more salve on your wound."

Aabir nodded for him to do so. The quicker he got out of there, the quicker he could go to the privacy of his own room to deal with the beginnings of this mental mess.

The doctor set the tray on a wheeling table next to Aabir's bed and began peeling the bandage off. Aabir kept his eyes on the foot of the bed as the doctor worked, saying nothing as his thoughts swarmed in a flurry of mixed emotions. He did not trust his voice to not betray them.

The doctor finished dressing and wrapping his wound, then gave him leave to go. Once Aabir was free, he headed out of the infirmary and walked through a maze of empty halls and up a flight of stairs towards his room in the stadium. All the competitors who made it through their first day onto the next were given a room to call their own until they lost and were disqualified.

Aabir ascended the last step and trudged down the bustling corridor towards his room. The third-level competitors who filled the hall last night had been replaced with the new, older Level Two competitors that were going to begin tomorrow.

He hunched his shoulders as he maneuvered around a group of chatting people who all looked at least ten years older than him. When he successfully made it past them without making eye-contact, he saw his room number and headed towards it with an extra burst of speed.

"Hey, kid!"

Forcing a neutral expression upon his features, he stopped and turned around. One of the competitors—a tall woman with short, blonde hair and a face made up of hard lines—stepped away from the now-silent group.

"You're the one who tried to save that other kid from the peryton, right?" She asked.

Another sting of guilt at his failure stung Aabir. He did not feel like answering, but he also wanted to avoid being rude—with his luck, it might get him seriously injured before the rounds tomorrow got a chance.

"Um—yeah. I am."

The woman nodded once. "I haven't seen anyone do something like that in the Tourney before—especially not after they've been disqualified. So good job."

He scratched the back of his head and lowered his gaze. "Oh. Uh—well, thanks."

She nodded again and turned back around as the conversation picked back up. Aabir took that as his cue and turned around before heading towards his room, his heart hammering as he tried to push all feelings of pride down.

He never realized going into the Constantia Tourney how honored his actions of trying to help the other competitors would end up being. Amid the battles and bloodlust he had watched and been forced to take part in, he had forgotten how honorable Igrian solidarity was held to be. It was not that his actions were moved by that idea, but the thought of standing by and watching someone get needlessly hurt did not sit well in his conscience.

He opened the door to his room and stepped inside, slamming the door shut behind him. The muffled voices from the hall filtered in from under the door. Other than that, it was quiet. He stepped over to his unmade bed in the middle of the small room and sat down with a sigh, putting his face in his hands.

The little pride he felt dissipated in the room's cold atmosphere, making space for even more hopelessness and anger to fill the void it left behind.

Why would Deleyon let this happen? From the knowledge he gleaned from the hundreds of replays he had watched, he had come to find out the winner of Level Three was always the first to fight a Constantia prisoner out of any of the competitors. It was supposed to be a high honor, but it made Aabir feel more like the prisoner he was supposed to murder rather than the honorable soldier he was trained to be.

He clenched his jaw until it ached, squeezing his stinging eyes shut as memories of the Frigian woman from Xich and the Constantia prisons pressed against his mental defenses. How was he supposed to *kill* someone who had already been enduring a living death for Deleyon-knew-how-long? His stomach twisted abruptly, and he leapt from the bed towards the room's small bathroom as his stomach decided to finally empty its contents.

When it was done, the nausea dissipated for a heavy emptiness that settled into his bones as bright fears and more sickening images filled his head. A buzzing went through his wrist, and he stumbled out of the bathroom to flop back onto his bed before swiping his finger across the floating screen.

Leafy shadows and sollight barely moved across Matha and Patre's faces as they filled the screen, and the strained smile on Matha's face immediately turned into a pale look of wide-eyed surprise.

"Aabir!" She exclaimed, "Are you alright? You look sick..."

The combined weight of Matha's sympathy and the heaviness already suffocating Aabir broke down the last of his mental strength. Despite the odd angle his parents might see on his holonode's camera, he pressed his hands against his face as deep, but quiet, sobs wracked his weary body.

"I'm so sorry this happened, Aabir," Matha's whispered reply came out as a normal pitch near his ear.

He sniffed but did not reply.

"We watched what you did today," Patre said, "and despite how it turned out, I'm proud of your actions, Aabir. I believe you fulfilled your words from the other day about wanting to help others." He paused. "And no matter what happens, you're still our son, and we love you. That will not change with tomorrow's events."

His words only brought another eruption of quiet sobs. His parents stayed silent for the next few minutes while some of his pent-up emotions drained from his leaking eyes, but even through the holonode he could almost feel their comforting presence.

When his body could no longer give up any more tears, he wiped his wet face with his hands and lowered them, settling his red-rimmed gaze on the holonode's screen.

Clearing his throat, he finally gave a simple, "Thanks."

Matha's glassy eyes shone with concern. "And to add to what your patre said: let me remind you that this is also not your fault—"

"—But it is!" He choked back another sob before continuing, "I know what you're trying to tell me, Matha, but all my actions landed me here. I have no one to blame but—but myself..."

He covered his face with his free hand as he took in a deep breath to keep the lump in his throat from rising again.

Matha sighed, but the sharp tone of her next words did not hold any of its pity, "I don't want to hear any more of that, Aabir. Dwelling on whether this all happened because of your past actions is not going to help you."

He lowered his hand and stared at his matha in surprise, but she continued, "Instead, I want you to take a deep breath to calm yourself. Then, instead of sitting in worry, I want you to turn your focus onto something else—like possibly finding a way to get yourself out of fighting tomorrow."

Aabir opened his mouth to argue, but then snapped it shut at the warning look she sent him.

"And no arguments," she added.

He frowned as he thought of the reply he wanted to say—*"But there is no way, Matha! Not unless I let myself get brutally injured—and then Lieutenant Denir would know I did it on purpose, and that will lead to punishment for, possibly, all of us."*—before actually replying with, "Yes, Matha."

"And don't sound so happy about it, either." A tiny smile curled one corner of her lips upward.

Aabir shook his head, unable to smile back. "I don't know where to start, though...I don't know what to do..."

"Aabir, what have you been doing the past couple months?"

He scrunched his brow in confusion. "Uh...training?"

"Besides that."

"Um...worrying?"

Matha rolled her eyes. "What have you been doing for...you-know-what?"

He continued to stare at her questioningly until realization hit him like Septimus' battle ax. "Oh! Research."

"Exactly." She nodded sharply and sent him a knowing smile.

He let her suggestion settle in his mind for a few moments before it began to produce a few ideas—including something Patre had said to him after his fight with the tree. A small smile broke through his weary countenance.

"Thanks, Matha."

"It's why I'm here." She sent him an encouraging smile.

"And if you need us to help you look up anything, we can," Patre added. "It might help you find a solution faster with more of us working on it."

Aabir nodded slowly, one idea shining brighter than the others in his mind. He remembered in all of his binge-watching the Tourney a few mentions about one of the veterans finding a forgotten rule that helped them win a crucial round. So, if official rules had been forgotten before, then maybe there was one he could find that might be able to help him...

"I'll probably start with the official list of rules." He swiped his parents' faces off the holonode's screen to get to the Net. "Could—would you mind starting with the bottom and working up towards the top? I don't think I can make it through all of them on my own..."

"Of course." Patre's voice sounded from the speaker as Aabir typed "*Constantia Rulebook*" into the search bar. "We can go on and do that now."

"Certainly," Matha added.

"Thank you." When he found it, Aabir swiped back to the holocall and gave his parents another small, thankful smile. "If you find anything that might help, send it to me, please."

"We will." Patre nodded. "Until then, we love you, Aabir. Don't lose hope yet."

The dreadful weight upon Aabir grew heavier for a few moments at those words, but he pushed it aside with the new, lighter thoughts emerging in his head. "I'll try not to."

"Good."

"We will message you when we find something, Aabir." Matha's smile faded. "Deleyon be with you."

Aabir nodded and ended the call. His holonode's screen immediately went back to the first page of the list of rules, and he let out a deep sigh at the sight.

A few months ago, he would have scoffed at the thought of him ever voluntarily spending his time researching the Tourney, yet here he was...

He exhaled another shaky sigh, then swiped his finger down to the first rule and began to read. If Rasiela could see him using the skills she taught him for something other than only spy work, she might actually be proud, he mused. Even if it was the Tourney.

He pressed his free hand against his forehead for a moment to try and dispel the thought. *Focus,* he lowered his hand down and set his gaze back on the rules in front of him, *no more distractions.* Almost as an afterthought, he added, *Deleyon, help me.*

With that, he turned his focus back onto the words floating in front of him and began to search for any sliver of hope.

Rasiela squinted her eyes in the light as she stepped over the unconscious body of the arrogant man who had come to interrogate the silent prisoner by himself—without backup. Despite how much the secret group had grown, she was beginning to see that there were still a few places that had trouble communicating.

She hissed as pain shot through her broken fingers when she went to close her dark, cramped prison's door with her dominant hand. Muttering a curse, she closed it with her left hand, locked it, and sent a glance down both directions of the warehouse hallway before turning left to head towards the nearest staircase.

The skin of her bare wrist prickled as she hurried down the hall, but she tried not to let the lack of her holonode get the better of her. She had a sharp mind and remembered much of what she found out on the warehouse's mainframe four days ago. There was no use wasting time trying to find it in this huge place—not with the threat of capture, or possible death, looming over her like a hungry peryton.

Rasiela slowly made her way up the twisting flight of stairs on light feet. Chief Baene needed to be warned of what they were up against, and she was the only one who could do that.

Chapter Fifty-Seven

EVEN WITH THE PROTECTION of the window in front of her, Tetra could still feel some of Soll's furious heat through the thick glass. Her narrowed gaze roved across the desert landscape spread out before her and Lieutenant Eyrie. Though the circumstances that brought her here weren't the best, she was glad to be back in Xich—it had given her more of a break from the onslaught of worries over her future than she thought it would.

The ground of outcroppings created a mosaic of greens, browns, and oranges below. Unlike in Trivsau where dark chasms stretched between them, countless rivers glimmering with sollight broke through the different shapes of the ground. The sand that covered the rest of the desert kingdom was instead taken over by oases of lofty palms and suchwries. And in the midst of them, in the largest bare section of the surrounding land, stood two opposing army encampments: the Alliance's side marked by different flags and banners that represented all the nations in it—including Silvas, while Igrium's red flag could be seen far more than any other in the opposing camp

From this height, the temporary structures and tents of both looked like two giant anthills of activity. Tetra inhaled deeply as her heart gave another nervous jump. She could practically feel the tension coming from both camps as more and more reinforcements poured into each one by the day.

"Are you ready, Private?" Lieutenant Eyrie asked from beside her.

"Yes ma'am." This wasn't the first time her C.O. had asked the question since they began their journey to Xich a couple days ago. And each time, Tetra's answer was the same.

"Then remember that what you see before you will end up being your part of the battlefield. There's a high chance your goal in this battle will be solely to take out Igrium's mounted crossbows and nothing more." Eyrie paused. "But I have also been told that that might change with this next meeting."

Her heart skipped another frantic beat. "Yes ma'am."

Army General Taoghn had told Lieutenant Eyrie that morning that the other Alliance army generals wanted to see what "the peryton" could do before the battle, and he agreed to let them onto the hovercraft Tetra had stayed on for the past couple days to see how "it" fought. To say she was nervous for the confrontation was an understatement. Despite how she had done a similar thing for some of Taoghn's top generals back in Urbselva, doing it for the top Alliance army leaders seemed a much bigger deal–one she didn't want to mess up.

It also didn't help that *if* she agreed to Chief Baene's plans, then these might end up being people she would have to deal with in the future—as their superior.

Her stomach did another nervous flip, so she pushed that thought to the side for the time being. She glanced over at Lieutenant Eyrie out of the corner of her eye and asked, "When will they be coming, ma'am?"

The first lieutenant's stoic face didn't change as she replied, "When we land again."

Tetra glanced back out the window at the oncoming ground, and her stomach continued its acrobatic routine. So soon?

"We should head back to the transport bay now," Eyrie added, "I want to be in there when we land."

"Yes ma'am."

Without complaint, Tetra spun on her heel and followed her commanding officer through the hovercraft's bridge. She followed Lieutenant Eyrie's movements and saluted Captain Fellin as they passed him. He dipped his chin towards them in acknowledgement but said nothing as his attention turned back to the officer who was speaking to him.

He was one of the few people Army General Taoghn had entrusted with Tetra's peryton secret. The transport bay where she trained—where "the peryton" was supposedly held twenty-five/seven—was off-limits to everyone but those with special access. So, most of the crew and soldiers who were tasked with guarding her were oblivious to the fact. Instead, they believed she was being trained by Lieutenant Eyrie to train the peryton.

They exited the bridge and marched down a long, bare passageway; then slowed to a stop at a locked, hydraulic door guarded by two soldiers dressed in the dark, green-tinted armor of Silvas' military. Lieutenant Eyrie tapped in the door's passcode, and it hissed open.

Without thinking, Tetra inhaled a deep breath as she stepped into the huge bay, expecting the hundreds of metallic smells to fill her nostrils, but then she immediately realized what she had done and sent an embarrassed glance out of the corner of her eye towards Eyrie. Thankfully, her C.O. didn't seem to notice as she closed the door behind them. Even so, Tetra couldn't help the heat rising up her neck. She hadn't realized how much of a habit that had become as a peryton.

"Private—" She spun around at the sound of Lieutenant Eyrie's voice and stood at attention, hoping her face wasn't as red as it felt, "—go on and turn into a peryton so you'll be armored up and ready by the time they get here.""Yes ma'am." Tetra saluted and turned around before heading towards the middle of the long bay.

Normally, the mostly empty bay would've been used for the transportation of armored vehicles or troops. This time, it was empty—save for the heap of armor plates lying in the corner near Eyrie, the large shipping container with the barred door that was said to cage "the peryton" in the shadows of that same corner, and a large, empty food bowl and half-full water bowl to keep up "the peryton's" authenticity. As she passed by them, her stomach spun in another churning motion as one of the mental whispers she couldn't seem to fully silence broke through her thoughts like a sharp dagger, *"Animal spawn of Malackin..."* She gritted her teeth and turned her gaze away from their sight.

Her footsteps, though light, bounced off the tall, metal bulkheads as she came to a stop. Her mind's instinctual fear of pain rushed through, but she didn't let it stop her as she turned into a peryton.

The bone crushing, muscle-shredding pain consumed her, but it soon ended as it always did and Tetra found herself heaving deep breaths while lying on the cold floor; hundreds of noises and smells bombarding her enhanced senses. She blinked her eyes open and lifted her long neck, turning her gaze in Lieutenant Eyrie's direction. Her commanding officer nodded once and stepped over to the pile of armor plates.

"Now let's get this on," she said.

Tetra got up and stepped towards her obediently, then lowered back to the ground to help her C.O.'s reach as she stuck the plates on her polyanium jumpsuit. Usually there were three people to do it, but the past couple days Galia had had to make do with only Tetra's thumbless self for help, causing the process to take twice as long as it normally did.

Once Lieutenant Eyrie finished putting Tetra's narrow helmet on, she lifted her gaze and their eyes met.

"Let's begin," her C.O. said.

Tetra blinked in acknowledgement and lifted her head. She took a couple steps back as she opened her wings before jumping into the air. She could only flap them a few times before their tips brushed the top of the transport bay, but the big space gave her enough room to glide in a circle without touching the bulkheads. The ground was far too close for diving to be possible, but there were still maneuvers she could do that didn't require the mountain warehouse's space.

"Charge!"

Tetra flicked her ears as Lieutenant Eyrie's simple order bounced off the bulkheads. She angled her wings and swooped towards the ground. Even before all four legs hit the floor, she began running—head lowered—towards the opposite side of the long bay. They hadn't brought any training droids with them, but it didn't impede Tetra's performance as her commanding officer barked more of the simple commands.

"Jump!"

She opened her wings and leapt back into the air before she hit the opposite bulkhead. She then turned in a tight circle to face Eyrie's direction again.

"Spin!"

She flew as high as she could and pinned her wings to her side with a twist.

"Attack!"

Tetra opened her wings and used the momentum to lower her talons to pick up the imaginary enemies, then flapped her wings and "dropped" them as she ascended again.

Lieutenant Eyrie barked more quick orders, and Tetra obeyed them as best she could in the smaller space. If she wasn't supposed to be a surprise attack for Silvas, then she figured that she would be able to train outside. Be that as it may, she hadn't left this hovercraft since leaving Urbselva's military base and wouldn't be allowed to until the battle began, and she was called into the fight.

As she flew back into the air from another ground attack, she pricked her ears as the familiar hum of the hovercraft's engines came to a stop. A new wave of nervous energy went through her wings, ruffling her feathers, and she pinned her ears back against her head.

There was a sharp knock on the door. She jerked her head in its direction, her body following its lead. Lieutenant Eyrie did the same. A hydraulic hiss followed, then Captain Fellin stepped into the bay through the open doorway.

"Lieutenant Eyrie," he dipped his chin towards her, "we've landed, and Army General Taoghn told me they are ready."

"Thank you, Captain," Lieutenant Eyrie replied with her own respectful nod. "We are ready for them."

"Then I will order the bay door open."

"Of course, sir."

He nodded again and left. Once the heavy door closed and they were alone again, Lieutenant Eyrie turned back around in Tetra's direction. "Come down, Private."

Tetra followed the order and glided down, all four of her feet making it to the ground with barely a stumble as she steadied herself. She folded her wings in and lowered her head to meet Lieutenant Eyrie's unreadable gaze.

"Let me remind you that from now on, you will be called 'the peryton' unless the Buleutcil has decided to let our allies know." Her voice was reserved, though Tetra could see a flash of disdain in her C.O.'s dark violet eyes she never would've noticed without her enhanced peryton vision. "I believe Army General Taoghn would rather have the other army generals know, so he might have persuaded the Buleutcil to let him reveal your identity. But until I know for sure, we must keep up the act."

Tetra blinked in response. She agreed wholeheartedly with her commanding officer's view on the situation and wished she could say so without possibly upsetting the very people in control of her life. There were already too many secrets surrounding her. She was tired of them—even with her uneasiness about the upcoming reveal of a certain, imperial one. Plus, if the truth was known, then it would stop everyone from referring to her as an animal.

"So don't do anything that would seem out of character for a normal peryton to do." Lieutenant Eyrie gave her a significant look. "Understand?"

Tetra gave her a small nod, glad her peryton tongue couldn't disclose the secret intelligence of perytons she was also sworn to keep silent about.

"Good. Then don't nod to me anymore, or even acknowledge that you can understand everything I'm saying. It looks too human."

Tetra almost nodded out of habit but stopped herself and blinked instead. Hopefully that didn't look too suspicious...

A ghost of a smile came over Lieutenant Eyrie's stern countenance, but it vanished as a deep, hydraulic hissing filled the transport bay. Tetra turned and lifted her head in its direction, ears pricked, as bright light flooded into the space. A fourth of the floor lowered into a ramp, and hundreds of new smells immediately accosted her nostrils as she blinked at the brightness. She hadn't realized how dark the bay's fluorescent lights were until that moment.

A few stronger scents rose above the others as she watched a group of shadowy figures ascend the ramp. The hissing sounded again, and the moment of bright sollight ended almost as quickly as it came.

Tetra heard Lieutenant Eyrie's footsteps move towards the new group of people, but she didn't move a muscle in her body as she watched the army generals marching towards them.

"And here she is." General Taoghn's booming voice filled the dense atmosphere as he led the group of armored generals.

Pungent whiffs of fear-scent floated towards Tetra from the group, but she noticed the more neutral smell of caution and the earthy, almost-sharp scent she had come to know as curiosity also dominated the intimidating group standing before her.

"Army General, sir." Lieutenant Eyrie's tone was full of respect as she slowed to a stop near the group with a salute. "And army generals."

"Yes," Taoghn gestured towards her, "everyone, this is First Lieutenant Eyrie. She is Private Cairn's commanding officer."

Tetra blinked in surprise (and caught a whiff of sharp surprise-scent coming from Lieutenant Eyrie) as all six acknowledged her C.O. with either nods or heavily accented curt replies. Then the weight of all their gazes landed upon Tetra, causing her fur to stand on end.

An olive-skinned woman wearing the thick, leather armor of Frigac stepped forward from the group, a calculating look in her slanted eyes. In a thick accent, she asked, "And you are Private Cairn?"

Tetra glanced over at Lieutenant Eyrie before giving the woman a slow nod.

"Then look me in the eyes and tell me."

She lowered her head to get eye-level with the Frigian woman and met her cool, gray gaze. Even though she knew no one would be able to understand, she said, "Yes, I am," in the peryton tongue anyway. It came out as a low rumble in her throat, and a mixture of scents came from the woman the instant after she did it.

Lieutenant Eyrie stepped forward towards them, "She can't speak as a peryton—"

The Frigian woman put her hand up to stop the first lieutenant. "That is fine." Her gaze never left Tetra's as she spoke, "I have confirmation enough of what you say is true—even if it is impossible."

"And she truly is the Cairns' daughter?" A Pon-Yelish accent thicker than even Aunt Minda's reached Tetra's ears, and only when the Frigian woman looked away did she turn her long neck in the same direction.

A tall woman with dark brown skin and the light gray armor of Pon-Yelum stood near General Taoghn as he replied, "She is."

"But how do you know she can be trusted?"

"She swore to protect Silvas—and the Alliance—upon Zmraidos."

A man wearing the same leather armor as the Frigian woman stepped forward. His eyes narrowed to slits as he looked upon Tetra, and she couldn't help but scrunch her nose as the mildewed smell of mistrust wafted from him.

"I know the power an oath can hold upon a person, Cirus," he said in an accent as thick as the woman's, "but she is Igrian and they are not known for being disloyal to their own. What sort of proof do we have that she can be trusted to destroy them instead of attacking our forces?"

Tetra felt General Taoghn's hard stare turn to her, and she barely moved her head to meet it. "Private Cairn, change back," he ordered.

Under the weight of his authoritative gaze, she immediately did so without another thought. The, now familiar, pain came over her like a wildfire full of knives, but it passed and she found herself under the weight of her peryton armor plates.

"Here, Private—"

The weight lifted as Lieutenant Eyrie spoke, then she helped lift Tetra out of the pile.

"Thank you, ma'am." Tetra nodded.

Her C.O. gave her a sharp nod before they both turned to face the direction of the army generals. Tetra forced her expression to remain neutral as she caught the wide-eyed surprise upon their hardened faces.

"*Hil frerywren!*" The Frigian woman gasped.

Instead of standing there awkwardly, Tetra saluted them and lowered her head to bow it in the Silvanian show of respect. "Army Generals," she acknowledged.

"You are truly Tetra Cairn, aren't you?" A masculine voice with an accent that reminded Tetra of Stellinga's—although more fluent in Alenguan than the teenage girl—asked.

"Yes sir." At least, she was for now.

"Lift your head, Private." The Frigian woman's commanding voice rang out, and Tetra did as she was ordered—but not enough to meet any of their eyes. "*Frerywren!*" She said again, surprise sharpening the already-sharp Ivachkuan word.

"And there is your proof, Aleque," Army General Taoghn said.

Understanding dawned upon Tetra, and the muscles in her neck tensed as she forced herself to keep her scarred face up instead of lowering it again. Though all her scars were visible while she was a peryton, the malscar wasn't as noticeable on her long snout as it was when she was herself. Chill bumps rose along her rigid arms, reminding her of the few tally scars her jumpsuit's long sleeves didn't cover. She ignored the impulse to shield them with her hand under the weight of all those gazes.

This isn't Igrium, she tried to tell herself. She knew what General Taoghn was doing, yet her stomach began to hurt like it always did as shame pooled its depths.

"Is it real?" The pon-yelish general asked.

Heat filled Tetra's face as the second-hand humiliation of her memories came back. She forced her tense jaw to slacken somewhat as she replied, "Yes ma'am."

The Frigian generals shared a glance—and thanks to Army General Taoghn and her Norland classes, Tetra now knew them as Army Generals Aleque and Calau Avhinoe: the husband and wife who shared the responsibility of Frigac's army general. After a pause, General Aleque moved towards her. Tetra braced herself as if she was about to get hit as his domineering presence stopped only a few feet from her. Though she kept her gaze lowered, she could feel his eyes boring into her face.

"When did you get it?" He asked.

"A couple months ago, sir."

"Why did you get it?"

She kept her facial features under control as the pain and mocking laughter of her recalled memories flowed through her head. "I disobeyed my commanding officer, sir."

"And why would you do that?"

"Because she wanted me to give a warning mark to someone who I could see was not a spy."

Army General Aleque didn't reply immediately. In the stretch of silence, Tetra found it hard to breathe as the heat of everyone's stares continued upon her.

Finally, the Frigian general asked, "And who was this person that you thought was not a traitor?"

She found her mouth was dry as she opened it in reply, "She was a Xichian girl who was caught trying to climb over the fence into Trivsau."

"And did your disobedience help her?"

Another wave of gross shame slimed its way into her tight stomach, and she pressed her open hands at her sides to keep from making fists. "No sir."

"Did you know it would not help beforehand?"

"Yes sir."

"Then why do it?"

Tetra didn't reply immediately. She swallowed back the rising lump in her throat as the skin around her malscar burned with all the attention it was receiving.

General Aleque's tone held a sharper lilt as he said, "Answer me, Private. Why did you do it?"

"I was a coward." The whispered words barely made it past Tetra's lips. So, she cleared her throat and said in a louder voice, "I was a coward, sir. I couldn't hurt her when I knew she was innocent, and I couldn't mark her when I wasn't willing to be marked, either." A pang of anger lit inside her amid the heavy slime. "Emperor Ignis already planned on me being an obedient, brainwashed soldier by the time I got back from Xich anyway, and I couldn't bear the thought of letting myself become brainwashed willingly, so I took the coward's way out and disobeyed."

"And then you took the true 'coward's way' and left Igrium?"

"Yes sir."

There was another stretch of silence, and each constricted breath she breathed in it only added fuel to the internal flames burning inside her as she recalled her father's threat of turning her into one of his personal guards. It was another horrible thing she had forgotten Ignis threatened to do, and the only thing keeping her anger from growing any more than what it was were all the army generals still staring at her.

"I can see that is the truth," General Aleque's deep voice brought her focus fully back to the present, "and though I believe cowardice is a horrible crime, your actions speak differently. So, I am willing to watch you continue to prove yourself in this battle ."

"Thank you, sir," Tetra replied tentatively.

"And I agree." General Calau's harsh accent slashed through the air.

"Although I can see your words are true," a man with an accent similar to a Silvanian one spoke up, "I would like to see what you can do before I give my consent to the Cairns' daughter fighting for us as a peryton."

The Pon-Yelish woman—whom Tetra now remembered was Army General Talule Rain—also added, "Yes, I would also like ta see wha' sort o' power we will be unleashin' upon the battlefield."

In case I turn loyal to Igrium? Tetra thought as she sent a glance over in General Rain's direction, and she didn't have to have a peryton's sense of smell to see the wariness etched upon the older woman's weathered features.

"Of course." General Taoghn spoke, drawing her attention back towards him, "Private Cairn, change back and show us what you have learned."

Tetra did as she was told. And after she shifted back into a peryton and Lieutenant Eyrie had helped her get all her armor back on, she and her C.O. again went through all the commanded moves the smaller space afforded. Though their faces revealed nothing, Tetra's nose picked up the scent of fear mingled with caution and curiosity that came from them every time she charged through invisible ranks, or when she let out a roar while spinning in midair.

"Jump!" Lieutenant Eyrie barked.

Tetra leapt into the air again and flapped her wings before reaching the overhead. The fear-scent was no longer as heavy as at the beginning, and it was easier for her to discern the other smells in the transport bay—including the new, almost-spicy smell she pinpointed coming from Generals Aleque and Calua.

"Spin!" Eyrie's command made her lose focus for a moment as she folded her wings in a spin.

"Again!"

Tetra huffed a quiet breath of frustration as she did so. She opened her wings again to glide and caught another whiff of the spicy scent. She glanced down at the two army generals and noticed the significant look they both shared with each other; but even with her peryton sight, she couldn't discern what it meant. Her fur stood on end in uneasiness as she lifted her gaze. What could that mean—?

"Land!"

Tetra swooped in a sharp turn before she hit the wall and angled her wings to land before Lieutenant Eyrie. When all four feet touched the ground, she lowered her head to get eye-level with her commanding officer. Eyrie sent her a tiny nod before turning around to face the army generals. She began to speak to them, but a putrid scent of fear mingling with an earthy smell drew Tetra's attention away from the words she spoke.

She in took a deep breath and jerked her head in surprise at the direction of the smell. Instead of coming from the only humans she could see in the large bay, it was coming from the shipping container. She pinned her ears back and turned around to face it, then took a tentative step towards the shadows wrapped around it.

"Private?" Lieutenant Eyrie's questioning tone took a sharp edge. "What are you doing?"

Tetra turned her long neck and sent—what she hoped looked like—a significant look towards her C.O.'s disapproving countenance, then turned her head back in the storage container's direction as she moved towards it. Her hooves and sharp talons clicked against the metal floor rhythmically in the heavy silence her behavior seemed to be causing.

Following the powerful odor's trail and the sounds of shuffling even her peryton ears could barely pick up, she climbed on top of the shipping container and caught sight of a person sitting in the tight space between the box and the wall. If not for her peryton eyes, she would never have been able to see them amidst the shadows filling the claustrophobic crack. Her head was too big to fit in the space, so she took in a deep breath and let loose a loud roar.

A mighty wave of fear-scent punched her in the face, and she staggered off the container as sharp footsteps pounded across the floor. Tetra took in quick breaths to try and clear her nose as she spotted a person running out from behind the container, still concealed in the shadows that would be too dark for human eyes to see through. She roared again and lunged towards the person. They screamed as she shot her head forward and grabbed them in her jaws as gently as she could while they struggled. Metal coated her tongue, and she realized they were wearing armor.

Multiple sets of heavy footfalls drew near as Tetra turned around to face the army generals. Her eyes, and nose, caught their surprise as she stepped towards them and lowered her head.

"What in Afreean are you—?"

Lieutenant Eyrie's question stopped abruptly as Tetra dropped the fearfully smelly, armored person onto the floor. There was a smooth ringing of metal, then the trembling person found himself in a sharp ring of weapons.

"State your business." General Toaghn ordered as he pressed his longsword towards the man's throat.

"I—I just patrolling, sir!" A rancid, spicy smell came from the man as he spoke, and Tetra let out a low growl at the obvious lie.

Taoghn's tone took on a dangerous edge similar to his double-sided blade's. "Your orders state that no one is allowed in here."

"I got lost!"

Despite his dark green-tinged armor, the man had a gruff, halting Xichian accent, and something about it rang of familiarity. As Tetra tried to think where the feeling came from, the Xichian man lifted his chin and glanced up at her face as it towered above him. Another wind of fear-scent accosted her nostrils. This time she couldn't help scrunching her nose at its rancidity.

"Who are you?" Tetra glanced over at the army general who had the Xichian accent. The golden-hued, sickle-shaped blade he pointed towards the intruder matched the golden hue of his armor.

"Just a common soldier who get lost, *Huxk Vai*." The awful smell that gave the impression of spices being burned in trash wafted towards Tetra again.

"Then let us see an ID."

The man stayed still on his knees in reply.

The Xichian army general gave a slow nod. "That is what I thought."

A strong, but also dull, smell came from General Taoghn as he gave the man an even harsher look. "How long have you been here, *spy*?"

Tetra took a step back at the overwhelming smell of fear with a sharp huff. Lieutenant Eyrie sent her a questioning look, and the spy sent a wary glance over his shoulder—his large eyes shadowed in panic.

"Answer me," Taoghn said, "or I'll give you to the peryton as her next meal."

"I know she not a peryton." Despite his sharp retort, the man's fear didn't go away—much to the dismay of Tetra's dying nostrils. "I know she will not eat me."

"Well tha' answers tha' question." Tetra pricked her ears at Army General Rain's mutter. In a louder voice, the Pon-Yelish woman asked, "Who are you working for?"

The man stayed silent.

The fear-scent was still strong, but Tetra found herself getting a little more used to it as the moments passed. As she did, she was able to think more clearly on why the man's voice might be familiar. She thought back to her time in Trivsau and tried to remember all the people she had come across.

One of the army generals asked another question, but Tetra didn't hear it as her thoughts centered around her memories of the Palace of Commons. A jolt went down her spine and ruffled her feathers as she remembered the Tulin and Xichian men talking in one of the Palace's halls. Though she had never seen his face, she realized that's where this man's gruff voice was from.

She almost turned back into herself to tell the army generals he was an Igrian spy, but then she thought to recall as much of the conversation she had overheard in the Palace hallway and stopped herself. They had both seemed like they were trying to hide from the Igrian-run cameras as much as she had been during her escape, which meant he wasn't an Igrian spy. Yet he couldn't be working for Silvas or any of the other Alliance kingdoms, since the awful smell that came from him when he spoke told her he was lying.

So, if he wasn't working for either of them, then who was he working for?

Even with these doubts, Tetra knew she had to say something about what she knew. Taking another deep breath of the putrid air, she forced herself to flip the mental switch in her head. After the long moments of fiery blades tearing through her cells passed, she worked her jaw and moved her tongue to make sure they worked.

"I've heard him before!" She said from underneath the pile of armor.

She lifted herself out from underneath the plates, her eyes catching the surprise on everyone's faces. Disapproval took over General Taoghn's features as he sent her a stern look.

"What are you talking about, Private?" He asked.

Tetra waded through the armor pieces and stepped out from the pile before replying, "Forgive my interruption, sir, but I remember hearing this man in the Palace of Commons when I was escaping."

Despite his beginning scowl, he nodded for her to continue. She didn't look in the spy's direction as she said, "I never saw his face—as he had already turned around when I finally looked out of my hiding place—but I remember hearing his voice as he spoke to a Tulin man in the hall."

"A Tulin man?" General Aleque raised a brow towards her, then pressed the points of his owry into the man's exposed neck. "So, you are an Igrian spy."

"No sir." Tetra's heart stopped for a moment as his sharp eyes again landed on her. "I—I overheard some of their conversation and they sounded as scared of being found out by the Palace's security cameras as I was."

There was a moment of tense silence. Then General Taoghn asked, "What else did you hear?"

She went back over those memories and tried to sort through what she had heard. "I believe they mentioned something about turning the networks off and being free of some sort of powers." She licked her lips and fought the urge to fold her arms as if cold in the transport bay's warm atmosphere. "I figured that meant Igrium or the Alliance...sir."

Even out of the corner of her eye, she could see the man's posture stiffen. Everyone else noticed it too, because those that didn't have the points of their weapon barely pressed against his exposed throat followed General Aleque's example in doing so.

"Now that is interesting..." General Calau's rough voice lowered an octave, "Especially since we thought Igrium was the one to turn our communication networks down in that battle."

Tetra's heart skipped a beat at the unsaid implications in the woman's dangerous tone. Was there another side in this war besides the Alliance and Igrium?

The man continued to say nothing. The tension in the air grew with each moment of silence punctuated only by the pounding of Tetra's heart and the soft hum of machinery in the background. Finally, General Aleque asked, "Cirus, since he does not seem keen on saying anything at the moment, might Calua and I take him with us to see if we can persuade him?"

Tetra's heart skipped another fearful beat as General Taoghn's harsh gaze stayed locked on the spy's face. She had only heard rumors of the torture Igrian spies endured under Frigac's cruel techniques—some that were said to even rival Igrium's. The thought sent an icy shiver down her spine.

"You may." General Taoghn nodded as he moved his longsword away from the man's neck and sheathed it.

Both Frigian army generals nodded grimly and moved their owry's away from the man, then took him by the arms and hauled him to his feet. The rest of the army generals, except for Taoghn, kept their weapons trained on him. Tetra forced her gaze to stay in General Taoghn's direction as the Xichian man shot daggers towards her with his glare.

"Well, since our time here has been cut short—" General Rain sent a disapproving glare towards the spy, "—I say we finish this conversation in the command tent."

"I agree." The other army general who wore the almost-white armor of Quazesig nodded.

"Then have this prisoner taken to a secure location and we will reconvene in an hour," General Taoghn said.

The Frigac army generals nodded and dragged the struggling man towards the closed bay doors, the rest of the Alliance generals circling around them protectively.

"*Ik*!" Taoghn called to their retreating backs.

They all stopped and looked behind their shoulders in his direction. In words that sounded like harsh Ivachku, he said, "*Tiqurtet Laogravock*."

Army General Calua nodded as her husband replied, "*Yashva*."

Then, both Frigac generals continued, with the rest following only a moment later. As they marched away, Tetra noticed Army General Taoghn speaking into his holonode. A few moments later, the doors opened and bright sollight once again filtered into the transport bay.

As the small group descended the lowering ramp, Lieutenant Eyrie sheathed her sword and sent an approving nod towards Tetra. "Well done, Private Cairn," she said.

"Thank you, ma'am." Tetra dipped her head in a respectful nod.

"Yes, you did well." General Taoghn stated, the earlier disapproval on his face having evaporated into stone. "I believe everyone was impressed by what you showed us, Private. Though we will not continue our meeting here, I'll send you word, Lieutenant, on what the final verdict is."

"Yes sir." Lieutenant Eyrie nodded.

"And until you hear from me, I want you both to stay in your cabins here on board until Captain Fellin has everyone's IDs checked." The lines on his face darkened as a dangerous glint entered his eyes. "We don't want this secret to be discovered by any more spies. Understood?"

"Yes sir." Tetra and Lieutenant Eyrie both said in unison.

"Good. Then I must go."

They both saluted him as he spun on his heel and exited the transport bay. Once he left, the ramp lifted with a hiss and the noonday brightness was shut off, leaving only the bay's fluorescent lighting to darken the shadows.

"You heard him, Private." Tetra turned as her C.O. spoke, "Go to your cabin and don't leave until you get the 'OK' from me."

Tetra saluted her. "Yes ma'am."

"Then let's go."

With that, they both left the transport bay and headed down the corridor towards their cabins, the spy's presence causing Tetra's thoughts to wander upon ideas she had never thought of before. Were there only two sides to the war? Did the battle of Trivsau happen the way it did because of a possible third-party? And if so, what was this third party's motive?

And if they ever found out about what Tetra had just done to one of their own, would they come after her for doing so? Had she made herself a target without realizing it?

These questions and more piled into her head as she made it to her cabin, tension tightening around her middle as she closed the door behind her and sat on her bunk in the quiet. Despite the other things she forced herself to try and think upon in the lengthening silence—namely, the imperial decision she had to make—she couldn't stop the seed of worry taking root in the back of her mind that the spy's presence brought. Only when Lieutenant Eyrie entered her room after what felt like hours did the tiny, mental plant stop growing for a few moments.

"Private," Lieutenant Eyrie met her eyes, but Tetra couldn't discern the emotions veiled behind her dark violet gaze, "Captain Fellin has ID'd everyone and they are all who they say they are. So, we're free to go."

She paused for a moment, and Tetra found herself holding her breath as she waited for her to continue. "And General Taoghn also messaged me." The lines in Galia's face hardened ever so slightly. "The rest of the Alliance's army generals have come to a decision: you've been given permission to fight."

All earlier worries faded as Tetra's brain clung to this new update. Instead of the overwhelming fear she had thought would have come once the final barrier keeping her from fighting was gone, she inhaled a deep breath as resolve hardened inside her stomach. There was still some fear, of course, but Lieutenant Eyrie's words rang in her head along with the memories of those she had put herself into this position for.

If the Alliance won this battle, then Xich would be completely free of Igrium's hold—which included Stellinga, Rabetta, and all the Xichians she had seen both in Trivsau and the city's camp. And if they won, then this victory would be the first Tetra would fight in to continue freeing people of Igrium's—of her *father's*—tyrannical rule.

She curled her hands into fists as a vengeful heat washed through her. "Yes ma'am.".

Lieutenant Eyrie blinked. "Then come. I want to get some more training in since you're going to fight soon."

Tetra didn't argue as she filed out of the small cabin behind her commanding officer, stoking the flames of her quiet wrath with each step she took.

Chapter Fifty-Eight

Aabir inhaled deeply before stepping out into the arena. As his foot landed on the bare, metal floor, the crowds cheered. Some even chanted his name, but he could not see any of the stands encircling the arena due to the dense fog surrounding him.

He took a few tentative steps forward, pushing the embarrassing thought of tripping on live holovision out of his mind. There were more important things to worry about; namely, the round he was entering and the plan he had to get out of it. Icy fear shot through his veins at the thought, but he gritted his teeth and pressed forward into the thick fog.

"Welcome back, Aabir Sorrel!" Brutus Halt exclaimed. His declaration was followed by more cheers that shook the floor underneath Aabir's boots. "Sorry about the fog from the last round, but don't worry—the Tourney's Planners promised me it will disappear soon."

Aabir narrowed his eyes as he peered out into his foggy surroundings. It did appear to be clearing, thank Deleyon. The less obstacles he had, the better. He wanted to get this done as quickly—and painlessly—as possible.

"Anyway, as the heroic winner of the third-level, you are now receiving the special honor of facing off in a battle of blades with the first Alliance prisoner of this year!"

A mixture of cheers for the fight and boos at the mention of the Alliance erupted around Aabir. He kept his features steady under the tumult of booming voices that bounced around in the fog. Thank Deleyon for gauntlets, or else the cameras would have picked up the white-knuckled grip he had on the worn hilt of his sword.

Lieutenant Denir had brought him his own weapon from Norland that morning to congratulate him on getting so far—then reminded him of the honor he still upheld and told him he was going to be watching in the stadium that day. Aabir's reply to the concealed threat was just a nod.

Since he and his parents finally came upon the one rule last night that could possibly help him, he had resolved himself to the—most likely—painful fate these proverbial doors of Malackin would lead him to, but it did nothing to stop the fearful pounding of his heart. He closed his eyes as he swallowed back his rising nausea, then exhaled deeply through his nose. He blinked his eyes open and noticed he could now see the blurred outlines of the stadium's lowest stands through the dissipating fog.

"And now here is our honorary competitor's opponent: Private Eklanos Knill of the Twenty-Eighth Silvanian Combat Division." Aabir's heart leapt into his throat as Brutus spoke, "He fought in four battles before being captured in the Battle of Trivsau and was one of the prisoners who helped the perpetrators of the Constantia prison break locate the positions of the guards!"

A dark figure emerged in the disappearing swirls of fog ahead of Aabir. The floor shook as the boos and curses of the crowds thundered through the stadium. Aabir's chest tightened. He cringed at the onslaught of hatred flooding his senses. If it was this bad for him, he knew it was worse for his forced opponent.

And if the crowds' disapproval was horrible now, how much worse would it be when he utilized the unheard-of rule he had found?

"I know, I know." Something akin to bitterness laced Brutus Halt's usually chipper tone, "We're all upset about the dishonor thrown upon us by those who tried to destroy our honorable Tourney."

Aabir ground his teeth until his jaw hurt to keep from rolling his eyes. There was nothing honorable about torturing, then murdering, prisoners-of-war for entertainment.

"However," Brutus Halt continued in his normal tone, "to make up for that, the Tourney's Planners have informed me that tomorrow they will be adding an extra round specifically for all those same perpetrators—who have survived, that is—to be shown the might of our grand empire!"

Aabir's jaw ached as the words rolled through the stadium. Cheers and cries for Silvanian blood pounded against his skull. He glanced upwards and swept his gaze over the hundreds of thousands of fans he could now see through whatever was left of the thinning fog.

A tremor went through his muscles as his eyes landed on the raised platform where Emperor Ignis and his family sat. Though he could not see the emperor's face from this distance, he could feel the daggers coming from that cold, calculating gaze he still saw in his nightmares.

He lowered his gaze back down towards Eklanos' approaching figure; and for the first time since he came up with this plan, he doubted if he could actually do it.

It was not only Lieutenant Denir he might be dishonoring. During his research last night, he read that the rule he found had only been used a few times in the Constantia Tourney's seven-century history, and during times of war it was nicknamed "The Coward's Rule". So even if it was considered an official rule of the Tourney, there was also the chance of the Emperor Himself finding offense at him using it, and then Aabir and his family would only find themselves in a situation none of his "helpfulness" could help them avoid.

Eklanos stopped a short distance away from him. Their eyes met, and Aabir found it easy to shove all the worries he just had in the back of his mind. Even with the short distance, he could see the blade shaking in the man's hand, and his green-tinted armor hung loosely on his skinny frame. Aabir could not have been much older than him, but his brown skin sagging on his bruised face made him look much older. A long scar had been slashed down the right side of his face, and that was when Aabir realized he had no right eye.

Another shiver wracked through his muscles, and he swallowed back another bout of nausea. He remembered the other Constantia prisoner he had seen that happen to, and that memory brought up more of those he had seen in the prison underneath their feet. The outrage he had felt then came back to his mind, and he narrowed his eyes as a fiery anger washed through his muscles.

There was no way he could murder this man; not even with the future pain he would most definitely have to endure because of it.

He lowered down into a guard stance, using the angry heat burning inside his chest to fuel him. Eklanos did the same, albeit with much more shaking.

He would not fail, and he would not be a coward. Not anymore.

"Deleyon, help me," he breathed as he lunged forward.

Eklanos' eye widened with fear as he raised his shield. Aabir feinted the high attack and jabbed the man in the leg instead. The crowds cheered as his blade bounced off the prisoner's armor and he blocked Eklanos' own downward stroke.

Round and round they went trading blows. Anger and adrenaline coursed through Aabir's muscles as he dodged Eklanos' slow attacks and moved in with his own swift ones. Unlike what the bloodthirsty crowds wanted him to do, his only goal was to tire Eklanos out. Then he would make his final strike.

"...looks like Aabir Sorrel's plan is working!" Brutus Halt's commentary buzzed in the background of Aabir's focus, "It seems Eklanos Knill is weakening—which means we might soon see our first Alliance death in the Tourney!"

Aabir's arms shook as Eklanos' blade slammed against his own. *Not on my watch, Brutus.* Eklanos paused with a heavy breath after the major swing, and Aabir took his chance. He rammed into the skinny man and watched as he toppled over with a grunt. Pushing all the guilty thoughts trying to rise, he kicked the man's sword out of his weakened grip and pressed his own blade against the man's exposed neck.

The crowds screamed for blood as Aabir stared into Eklanos' shadowed, single-eyed gaze. He sent a silent plea up to Deleyon before whispering, "You don't have to worry. I'm not going to kill you."

The fearful shadows in the man's features lightened for a moment in confusion. He licked his chapped lips, and his throat bobbed against Aabir's blade as he swallowed. "What—what are you talking about?"

His distinct Silvanian accent reminded Aabir of his parents' own, and it only reaffirmed the reasoning for his next action as he imagined them watching him.

Without replying to Eklanos' question, he lifted his neck and looked up into the crowds of screaming fans roaring for the prisoner's blood.

Heart slamming against his ribcage, Aabir took in a deep breath then shouted, "I, Aabir Sorrel, call upon the mercy rule! I have bested this man—as you all can see—and as the winner, I grant him mercy according to rule number seventy!"

The cheers died down into a stunned silence that was heavier than their oppressive bloodlust. Blood pounded in his ears as he glanced back down at the lines of confusion creasing Eklanos' weathered face, and his fiery anger dimmed somewhat in the lightness of that moment.

He had done it.

"Um—well..." For what might have been the first time ever in his career as the Constantia Tourney commentator, Brutus Halt seemed at a loss for words. It only lasted a few seconds, though. "I—uh... I've just been informed by the Tourney's Planners that the rule Aabir Sorrel called upon is, in fact, real." He cleared his throat. "The prisoner, Private Eklanos Knill, will be allowed to live, but will not be able to join the Tourney anymore this year. Aabir Sorrel—you have given up your position—and your honor—in the Tourney in exchange for this prisoner's life. Exit the arena now."

Aabir removed his sword from Eklanos' neck and sheathed it. Eklanos looked up at him with shock as four Igrian honor guards came running towards them to escort the prisoner out of the arena. As they lifted his skinny frame, their eyes met for a moment. Even though Aabir's action did not save Eklanos fully from the Tourney like he thought it would, the hopeful light now shining in the man's eyes silenced some of those worries.

He offered a nod to the man and turned on his heel before heading back towards the closest arena entrance with light steps. The crowds began to boo and curse his name as he walked.

Even with the relief filling his sore muscles at his victory, he kept his face lowered as a half-eaten sandwich hit the side of his helmet. A bag of popcorn spilled at his feet, and he gritted his teeth as something hit the back of his head and liquid spilled down his back, its icy fingers getting into the cracks of his armor.

Heat crept up his neck at the jeering of the crowds, but he did not back down from his decision—even with the dark whispers in his mind telling him he could turn back around and kill Eklanos. Even with what some might call a dishonorable method, he could still regain *some* of his lost honor…

The entrance door opened before him with a menacing hiss, and he lifted his head as he exited the arena. He would not back down. Even if the rest of Igrium thought he was a coward for imploring a rule that had not been used in decades, he knew the truth.

Lieutenant Denir was the only one who stood in the hall. Aabir lifted his gaze to his commanding officer's face for a moment before immediately lowering it at the dangerous look the man was sending him. His heart pounded against his ribs as the fear he had been able to stop during the fight came back full force at the wrath he could feel coming from Denir's still, dark countenance.

The hydraulic door shut behind him in a sense of finality, and Aabir swallowed back the bile rising in his throat. A muscle ticked in Lieutenant Denir's jaw as the shadowed lines in his face darkened with a scowl.

"Sorrel…" he began, "you and I are going to have a little chat."

RASIELA LIMPED THROUGH THE overcrowded streets of Rubrum. Despite her hatred for the Constantia Tourney, she could not deny the fact that if it weren't for these crowds she never would have lost her pursuers. She gritted her teeth at the jolts of pain each step wracked through her bruised body, but she never stopped to take a break.

Don't stop, she told herself, *keep going*. Chief Baene depended on her. The entire Alliance depended on her making it. A pang of guilt added itself to the bone-wracking pain going through her body. Aabir Sorrel needed her to make it. He had to be warned—and quickly.

Though she doubted Chief Baene would let him into Silvas this quickly, she could at least warn the boy that he needed to hide. They had found out it was him who stole their hard drive—and the only thing keeping them from coming for him was the fact he had been under the protection of the Tourney. Despite that, Rasiela hoped she would be able to find him at Norland since it was the third day, but if he had somehow made it…

Pushing that disheartening thought to the side, Rasiela turned her gaze back to the traffic-clogged street. She needed to find a taxi. Even if the Tourney only multiplied Rubrum's awful traffic, it would be quicker to get to Norland on a hover-taxi than at the limping pace she was keeping.

A delicious whiff of spices went past her nose as she breathed in, and a wave of hunger weakened her already-weak muscles. Rasiela glanced longingly at the sports bar she was approaching, then back over at the street. She had eaten only a few pieces of bread the past four days of her imprisonment, and she was starving...

Nodding to herself, she veered towards the sports bar. Carefully taking her left hand out of her hoodie's single pocket so as not to disturb her broken fingers hiding inside, she slowed to a stop and opened the door. More delicious aromas wafted towards her as it swung open, and she stepped inside. Hopefully, this place was not owned by someone who hated Silvanians.

She blinked her eyes to adjust them to the dimness of the place as a waitress stepped towards her. "How can I help you?" The woman asked.

"Just a table for one, please," Rasiela replied as a raucous cheer broke through the bar's atmosphere.

"Right this way..."

The waitress picked up a menu from a stand holding them and led her to a booth next to the circular bar in the middle of the restaurant. Numerous holoscreens projected their blue light into the dimness above the bar and its seated occupants. As Rasiela sat down on the booth's cushion, she glanced up at one of the screens. A spark of anger lit in her chest, but it was immediately followed by annoyance at herself. Of course she just had to pick a *sports* bar during the biggest sporting event in Igrium. She turned her gaze away from the muddy mess of a round being fought in high definition as the waitress placed the menu in front of her.

"Actually, I know what I want already." Rasiela lifted her eyes and was glad the dim light helped to mask the fading bruises on her face, "Just a glass of water and a grilled-corafish salad, please."

What she really wanted was a colami steak with grilled vegetables, a loaded baked potato, and the biggest slice of pomen pie they would give her; but she knew her stomach would not be able to handle that much food after four days of eating next to nothing. So, a salad it was.

The waitress sent her a strange look but then shrugged it off as she picked the menu back up and left. Rasiela sent a furtive glance around the bar, then turned it towards the tinted glass doors spilling their darkened light at the entrance. She sat there in her own thoughts, fighting the urge to look up at the Tourney she so hated with each rowdy cheer that filled the air.

The waitress came back only a few minutes later with her salad and water. Rasiela thanked her before she left again, then forced herself to take small sips and measured bites so as not to look like the starving prisoner she had recently been.

Only when she almost finished her salad and given the waitress her card's number did her gaze flick over to one of the huge holovisions as one of the bar's louder occupants said, "I can't believe they even let this guy into the Tourney."

"You're only angry because you lost that bet yesterday." The man sitting beside him responded.

"That Nassum guy was the *real* winner—"

Rasiela tuned his voice out as her eyes widened in shock. There, on the holovision before her, was Aabir Sorrel walking into the arena's foggy atmosphere. On the third day.

Her salad threatened to come back up, but she kept her eyes glued to the screen. *Oh Deleyon, no...*

Forgetting the hurry she was supposed to be in, Rasiela sat in the dreary bar and watched in horrified silence as the boy she had hoped to help stopped in front of a Silvanian prisoner. *Help him,* she pleaded silently as he lunged towards the prisoner and the round began.

Chapter Fifty-Nine

"You straudwin coward!"

Lieutenant Denir's fist struck Aabir's eye. A harsh cry escaped Aabir's lips as pain slashed through his skull, and he stumbled to his knees. The lash marks on his legs and back screamed in fiery pain at the movement, but the chains and furrum manacles clamped around his wrists kept him from falling face first onto the ground.

Lieutenant Denir punched the side of his head, causing his neck to jerk awkwardly at the force of the blow. He gritted his teeth at the new wave of pain, then opened his mouth a little to pant in quick, sharp breaths. He had never wanted to blackout so much in all his life, yet every time the feeling came, it decided to disappear before taking him under its still spell.

"How could you be so pathetic, Sorrel?" Aabir forced his good eye open and saw the unrestrained fury reddening his C.O.'s face. "I thought you were above your *Inrelin*-cursed, Silvanian blood—"

Another punch to the head. Tears spilled down Aabir's throbbing face, even though he tried to hold them in.

"—and I thought that last correction session with you and Tetra Cairn put a stop to any of your rebellious attitudes."

A sharp pain rammed into Aabir's stomach, and he doubled over with a grunt.

"I should've known you wouldn't have been able to get past that round."

The same ramming force drove into Aabir's chin. He bit his tongue at the impact, and his head cracked against the wall. His brain swam in the darkness for a few moments, but then a cold hand clamped around his sore jaw and jerked him back into the overwhelming pain.

Through the tears, he met Lieutenant Denir's furious gaze. A shiver wracked through his shaky, lashed muscles at the darkness he saw in their depths.

"You dishonored me, Sorrel—" Spittle flew into Aabir's face at Lieutenant Denir's harsh words, "—and right in front of the emperor! You dishonored Norland. You dishonored this grand empire, and the name of 'Sorrel' will forever be tarnished because of your cowardice!"

Aabir could not help the hissing breath that escaped between his teeth as Denir's clamp-like grip tightened around his jaw.

"And I never thought I would have to do this—especially not to someone with so few tallies..."

Lieutenant Denir's voice trailed off as the horrible sound of a blade being unsheathed whispered in the tense air. Aabir's pounding heart leapt into his throat as his good eye landed on the light glimmering against the serrated edge of his commanding officer's segione dagger.

Not even the pain throbbing through his whole body to the erratic beat of his heart filled him with such dread as the sight of that weapon in the hands of his furious C.O.

"No..."

The whisper barely made it past his lips as Denir slashed the serrated blade down. Sharp teeth grazed his cheekbone for a moment, and he hissed again. Warm blood streamed down the side of his neck as the blade's pressure left his jaw, then another sharp slash bit through part of his nose and streamed towards his ear.

"You're a straudwin disgrace," Lieutenant Denir spat, "and the gods curse you for it, Sorrel."

The cold vise that was his C.O.'s grip lifted, and Aabir's chin fell to his chest. Shame boiled inside him as blood flowed from his stinging malscar.

His lifted arm shook, then flopped to his side as Denir unlocked the manacle. The other followed a moment later. Right as he opened his good eye to a squint, Lieutenant Denir kicked him in the side, and he fell with a groan. His bleeding lashes screamed as he rolled onto his back, and the pain crescendoed into his head like a bunch of fiery knifepoints as a heavy weight pressed upon his chest.

He blinked his eye open to a squint and looked his commanding officer in the eyes. "You are hereby dishonorably expelled from Norland, and your name will no longer be spoken of in these halls." Denir's towering presence lowered as he bent towards Aabir's stinging face. "I'm now known as the commanding officer of a coward—and I pray to the gods that scar brings you more shame than it has to anyone else."

Aabir tried sucking in a panting breath under his commanding officer's boot. *Let me die now, Deleyon. I just want to be done with this agony...*

As if Denir could read his thoughts, the weight upon his chest increased until a starburst of pain cracked his ribs. With a final, hoarse cry, Aabir's mind slipped into unconsciousness.

SHUFFLING WOKE AABIR FROM the numb darkness. He tried to breathe through the pain throbbing through his whole body, but more pain exploded in his chest, and he almost blacked out again.

"Uh...Aabir?"

Aabir gritted his teeth and waited for some of the pain to ease before trying to take another, slower breath. It was still painful, but at least it did not bring his struggling mind back into the shallows of unconsciousness.

"Huh?" He panted out.

He tried opening his eyes but was only able to squint one of them open. Each blink hurt his swollen face, but at least he could see. The familiar, interconnecting wires of the bunk above his own in Norland filled his vision. He was...in his dorm?

"Well, Aabir..." Tycho's tone sounded duller than it usually did, "I—I hate to say it...but I don't think you'll be attracting any girl with those looks anytime soon."

A sharp laugh bubbled up inside Aabir, but it came out as a painful cough instead. "Thanks..." It took effort to speak the simple word through the pain in his ribs.

"Because no one wants to date a dishonorable coward!" Aabir slowly turned his head in the direction of Aquilo's biting tone. He met his friend' glare coming from the bunk across from his own. Aquilo sneered before turning his face away. "I can't even look at you anymore. Now you're more alike to my horrible cousin, and even Straudwin himself, than I ever—"

"—Knock it off, Aquilo." Aabir glanced over to his other friend, who stood staring at him with the most serious expression Aabir had ever seen on his usually grinning face.

Aquilo turned his sharp glare upon Tycho. "Well, he is! And you know it." He turned his head, and Aabir's gaze locked upon his for the briefest of moments before the other trainee turned his face away again. "How many others do you know besides Tetra that have malscars? None!"

Aabir's stomach dropped, the left side of his face beginning to throb at its mention. He had forgotten that...

Roiling shame constricted his painful breathing even further as he lifted his bandaged arm. The few lashes it had received in Denir's fury throbbed at the slow movement, but he did not let that deter him as the tips of his fingers barely brushed the side of his face. He squeezed his eye shut with a painful grimace and lowered his hand as the light touch sent a sharp pain through his pounding skull.

He was marked like Straudwin himself had been.

A tiny spark of anger lit in his chest despite the shame. The reminder only went to show just how far Igrium's morals had degraded. What once began as the punishment for a cowardly lieutenant who ran away from a battle, leaving almost his entire platoon to die in the process, now marked Aabir's own face because he could not give in to the bloodbath the Constantia Tourney now was.

Instead of responding, Tycho asked, "Why...why did you do it, Aabir?" Aabir breathed in a few shame-filled breaths in the silence that stretched between his friend's questions, "What was so hard about killing a Silvanian straudwin?"

"Because he is one." Aquilo remarked sharply.

Aabir waited in tense silence until the pain throbbing through his body lessened enough for him to open his good eye. He met the questioning look drawing Tycho's eyebrows together and realized—now that he was expelled from Norland and forever marked a coward—this was the only opportunity he might have to help his friends see through their desensitized brainwashing. Aquilo obviously thought he was a Silvanian coward, so might as well let the truth be known.

Between breaths, he replied, "It was...unfair."

"I know you've said that before about the prisoner rounds, but I still don't get it..." Tycho's words trailed off.

Aabir was quiet for another few moments as he thought of his answer. "Imagine...imagine if the Alliance had their own Tourney..." he said through broken breaths, "and put Igrian prisoners of war in them to...to be killed." He kept his gaze locked on Tycho's. "What would you think about that?"

His heart thumped against his broken ribcage painfully as he breathed in another breath. Tycho's lips twisted to the side as if he was trying to hold back his answer, but after a moment it finally came.

"It'd be dishonorable."

"The Alliance would never do that," Aquilo butted in. "They're all too soft."

"But just imagine..." Aabir turned a glance over towards him again, "...if they did."

Aquilo only glared down at the floor in reply.

Aabir huffed with a roll of his eyes, and immediately regretted the small movement. He gritted his teeth until the throbbing in his face decreased. When it finally did, he lifted his gaze back towards Tycho's face, but could not read the expression there.

"That is what the prisoner...what the prisoner rounds are, Tycho," he said. "They're dishonoring."

Aquilo's voice rose indignantly, "How dare you—!"

"—Not just to the Alliance, but also to...to Igrium." All the things Mister Falap and his parents had said regarding how much Igrium had changed since Emperor Ignis took power and the war started bubbled up inside Aabir. Coupled with his current pain and brewing shame, the words moved past his lips in an unstoppable torrent of pent-up emotions.

"For an empire that says they value their freedom above...above most other things, we sure have taken it away from a lot of other nations..."

"But that's because they try to stop that very freedom we give." Aquilo butted in again before Aabir could finish taking another breath. "Emperor Ignis started this war to protect us, and those who look down upon us for it are a bunch of Alliance straudwins who'd rather live in a false sense of security with their ideas of 'peace' and weak armies than to be part of our strong empire."

Despite the hint of truth Aabir detected concealed underneath the layers of blatant propaganda his friend spoke of, he ignored it to address his main issue.

"Most of Yuln was destroyed because of the emperor's so-called 'protecting'." Aabir inhaled another breath; images he had seen in history of the ruins that made up what used to be the small kingdom bordering Igrium popping into his mind. "Millions of innocents were killed, Aquilo. And most of them didn't even know about their leaders being the ones to create the Feran Plague. Yet Emperor Ignis had them slaughtered or imprisoned!"

He scrunched the blanket underneath him in both his fists as a fierce heat of boiling anger joined the shame pressing upon his chest. "And because a...a few nations realized how awful that was, they are now seen in the same way. And those who came from them that are now living here are treated in the same way. There is no freedom here...unless you're full-blooded Igrian. Everyone else...we must suffer because we have Alliance blood—even if we've done nothing wrong."

"You said 'we'." Tycho tilted his head questioningly. "But you—well, you *were* one of the best students here. And your family...I know you all wouldn't be suffering. You would've told us that..."

Tendrils of remorse lengthened and reached into his stomach, and he closed his eye so he would not have to look at either of his friends. "I only joined Norland to stop the raids of our house, and to keep my family from being questioned," he said, his words still coming out between breaths. "And it worked for a few years. Only recently did...did they start happening again. And with the new Constantia rule Emperor Ignis is letting pass, then we'll also be affected."

"But that's only for Silvanian spies..."

Fear squeezed his thumping heart with sharp talons, but he tried to ignore it. No one knew he was a spy, and if it had been a secret this long then he doubted anyone would ever figure it out—especially since he was not a part of Norland anymore.

"Or those suspected of it..." he replied. "Anything could be used against us to say we're spies." *Because I am...* "But if someone were to say we were, then we would have no choice. Our legal system isn't kind to those of Alliance descent.

"We're living in danger, Tycho. There's no freedom for us. Every day I'm here, I always worry if—while I'm gone—if my parents have been arrested because of something they might've said on...on the secret cameras. And my matha—she's pregnant again, and now I'm even more worried—"

"—Why haven't you told us any of this?" Tycho's tone held a note of hurt.

Aabir opened his eye and caught the shadowed look on his friend's face. It only caused the growing shame in his stomach to churn.

"Because I didn't think you would understand." He cringed as the words left his mouth.

Tycho shook his head and lowered it. "Is that why we haven't been invited over to your place for so long? Why I haven't eaten pomen pie in months?"

"Yeah..."

Tycho shook his head again with a huff. "I can't believe you, Aabir."

Sharp movement caught Aabir's attention. He barely turned his head to see Aquilo standing, arms crossed. He met Aquilo's hard gaze, and—again—wished he could go back in time to fix this mistake.

"So, all of that's been happening, and you never once thought to tell us?" Aquilo's voice strained as he spoke, "We could have helped you, Aabir! I could've gone to my parents. We could've asked Director Windap if he could help...something."

Aabir flinched at the accusation, sending another sharp pain through his face as if Denir's fist had struck him again. With one last glare, Aquilo spun around and headed out of their dorm. He slowed to a stop as he made it to the door and opened it.

"Even with all the things Tetra did, I think you deserve that malscar more than her."

The door slammed shut behind his words.

The air thickened in the few moments of silence his declaration left behind, but Aabir finally gained the strength to speak through it. "Tycho..." He swallowed. "I'm—I'm sorry..."

Tycho sighed. "I..." he put his face in his hands and shook it slowly, "First, you pull that 'mercy rule' stunt in the Tourney, then you get a malscar, and now...this. It's all just...it's a lot, Aabir."

"I know." The reply barely came out as a whisper.

More silence stretched between them. Aabir closed his eye again, the quiet amplifying his guilt.

He should have told them... It was an attack on their loyalty, is what it was. He could have smacked himself for his stupidity. All these years, his whole life, he had lived in Igrium and thought of himself as a loyal guy; but now that he was lying here in more pain than he had ever experienced, he realized there were a lot of things he never actually told his friends—and yet he expected them to be completely honest with him about all of their problems.

At that thought, he remembered Ezen's holocall to him before the Tourney had begun. Another string of shame tightened around his insides. He had told Ezen—a guy he barely knew at the time—all his family's problems, but not his best friends...

"Well then..." Aabir opened his eyes and met Tycho's guarded gaze with his own as his friend spoke, "Um—I heard Denir say you got expelled... Actually, I think the whole school did..."

Heat crept up Aabir's neck, but he did not say anything so Tycho could continue.

"So, I packed all your stuff into your backpack for you, since I figured you probably wouldn't be able to do it yourself—and, well...the medbots who brought you up here said once you woke up that you had orders to leave. So, we should probably go..."

Exhaustion pulled at Aabir's limbs at the thought of getting up, but he gritted his teeth and went to sit. The wounds in his back and arms screamed in accordance with his broken ribs as he tried to do so. He fell back onto his pillow with a grunt and lay there panting until the pain dissipated.

"I...I don't think I can," he panted out.

"Hmm..."

Aabir opened his good eye and glanced back over at Tycho's masked countenance. He had never seen his friend's features so shadowed before. It only tightened the emotional pressure upon his insides.

Tycho met his eyes before turning to go. "Just wait here. I'll be back." He glanced over his shoulder as he slowed to open the door, and a ghost of a smile flitted across his features. "And don't do anything stupid while I'm gone."

Then he left, leaving Aabir to lay in the quiet room with only the terrible company of his thoughts. He squeezed his eye shut with a sharp exhale through his nose.

Too think he always thought less of his friends for being more brainwashed in their ideas.... Now that he was only coming to know of his stupidity like a warhammer to the face, he realized how stupid his worries had been. The anxiety would have probably been right if he had tried talking to Septimus about what was going on, but he always called Tycho and Aquilo his best friends and trusted them with practically everything else. So why had he been so stupid as to keep them in the dark about it all?

He breathed out another puff of frustration since moving the muscles in his face was out of the question. Why did he have to think his friends would ostracize him because of what was happening to his family? Not even Aquilo, with all his hatred towards Silvas and the Alliance, ever once mentioned Aabir's descent in all the years they had known each other. Until the last five minutes, that is.

His malscar throbbed with every regret, but he did not try to stop them. He let each one drag him deeper and deeper into a miry pond of self-pity he would not let himself get out of. The weight of each wave of shame and guilt was nauseating to endure atop the physical pain he was already living in, but he continued to lay in it because he deserved to.

The door let out a tiny squeak as it opened a few minutes later. Aabir blinked his good eye open and caught sight of Tycho as he closed the door behind him.

Right as his friend opened his mouth, Aabir said, "Before you say anything...Tycho, I want to apologize for..." *for being an awful person and not trusting one of my best friends*, "for not telling you."

"Eh, it's OK." Tycho shrugged it off, but his darkened features told Aabir he was hurt. "But anyway—I got these for you."

He stepped over to the side of Aabir's bunk and held out his hand, palm up. Two purple pills rested atop it. Aabir's eye widened as he flicked his gaze up towards Tycho's face.

"Where did you get those?" He asked, even though he knew exactly where they came from. Norland's infirmary was the only place in the school where you could get such strong painkillers, and they never gave them to those who were dealing with the pain of a punishment.

Tycho's lips twitched into an almost-sly grin. "The less you know, the better, my friend," he said. "And if anyone asks, we'll just tell them Lieutenant Denir said you had to leave right after you woke up, so this was the only way we were going to get you out of that bed. So, take them."

"Thanks."

Even though they were stolen, Aabir did not care at that moment because he was in so much pain. He lifted his arm and took the two pills, then popped them into his mouth. Even with no water to wash them down, he swallowed them.

"Now..." Tycho turned towards their dorm's desk and picked up Aabir's bulging backpack, which sat leaning against one of its legs. "I stuffed everything I found in your drawers here—besides your uniforms..." He unzipped it and began rummaging through its spilling contents, "And I know I put a few shirts in here somewhere...Ah—here we go."

He held up a white t-shirt and flung it towards Aabir. Aabir went to catch it with his hand, but the movement sent a slice of pain through his ribs and back and he hissed, wrapping the same arm around his bandaged torso as if it would help the pain.

"Oh, sorry."

When he could breathe again, Aabir slowly turned his head back in Tycho's direction. "It's fine."

Tycho dipped his chin in acknowledgement, then turned his neck back in the direction of Aabir's backpack. He reached into the large pack and pulled out a pair of socks. He lifted his arm as if to throw them but must have thought better of it because he laid them on the floor next to him.

"And your boots are over there." He nodded his head towards the foot of Aabir's bunk as he stuffed all the contents of Aabir's life at Norland back into the bag. "Even if the painkillers haven't set in yet, we need to go on and get you out of here as fast as we can before Lieutenant Denir finds out you're still here."

Aabir's heart leapt into his throat with a painful throb. He turned his face forward atop his pillow and—sucking in a painful breath—pushed himself into a sitting position. His back muscles screeched at him to stop, and he gave into their demands once he was fully sitting up. Each wheezing breath pressed against his broken ribs with bright pangs.

"Here—" Tycho held out the socks towards him.

Aabir nodded slowly as he tried to catch his breath. His arm shook terribly as he lifted it and took the socks. Oh Deleyon, he needed these painkillers to work faster!

"I would ask Aquilo to help me get you out, but I don't think he wants to be anywhere around you right now, so..." Tycho shrugged again.

The pressure around his aching chest tightened with another chain of guilt, but he did not voice it. "Where is Ezen?" He asked instead.

"I don't know." Tycho's eyebrows drew together thoughtfully. "Our platoon skipped training to watch you fight today and he was there at the beginning but left halfway through. I don't know where he went..."

Well, that did not sound good. Ezen was even better about not missing classes than both Aabir and Aquilo were. Only the end of the world could keep him from missing a training period.

Aabir shook his head as if he could shake the worries out of it and tried pushing them to the side to face his present dilemma. He flicked his one-eyed gaze between the socks in his hand and his bare feet, then—with heavy breathing and throbbing pains—struggled to put on his socks and boots. Tycho sat by quietly, his eyes glazed over as he stared far beyond their dorm.

When his feet were finally covered, Aabir went through the same painful process to put his shirt on. As he pulled it over his face, the fabric brushed against his malscar. He sucked in a sharp breath at the duller pain it caused, then realized with a start that the pain medication was finally beginning to work.

"Thank You, Deleyon." He mumbled before saying in a louder voice, "I'm ready, Tycho."

Tycho blinked out of his daze and turned his face towards Aabir. Their eyes met, and a question rushed out of Aabir before he even thought about it, "Why are you doing this, Tycho?"

Tycho raised his brow and gave him a "really?" look. "Because you're my friend, so why would I leave you now?"

"But I...I'm shamed now." The skin around his malscar burned.

His friend only waved his comment away. "I'm not worried about that," he replied confidently, "Because despite what Aquilo says, I know I *can* beat anyone up who may try to shame me for helping you. So why should I be worried?"

Aabir eyed him dubiously but did not try to argue. "OK, then..." He said with the tiniest of smiles he could do without it stinging his face. "Could you help me up?"

"Oh, Aabir..." Tycho shook his head with a click of his tongue, but he held out his hand. "You really aren't going to get any ladies being that pathetic. You're like an old man now."

Some of his guilt lightened in the wake of his friend's normal-sounding comment. "Thanks."

He took Tycho's outstretched hand and made it off the bed with less effort than he had sitting up. He leaned against the side of his bunk as Tycho picked up his backpack and slung it onto his own shoulders. Then Aabir wrapped his arm around Tycho's neck to lean against him.

They both hobbled to the door and exited the dorm. As the door shut behind them, Aabir was finally struck with the realization he would never set foot in Norland again. However, he had no regrets about it—except for his friends—and was almost glad for the pain he was enduring since it meant he would not have to join Igrium's military.

The happiness and relief dissipated as quickly as they had come as Tycho led him down the uncrowded corridor. The few trainees milling about stopped whatever they were doing and turned to stare in judgmental silence as they passed. Aabir lowered his head to try and dispel the burn of their harsh gazes, but it did nothing. He turned his neck slightly to the left, in Tycho's direction, to try and hide his malscar as much as possible.

Only when they began descending the stairs did the whispers and quiet laughs fill the atmosphere behind them.

Embarrassment crept up his neck and burned within his chest at the silent judgment of every person he and Tycho passed while they hobbled down the rest of the stairs, down another corridor, through the crowded entrance hall, the courtyard, and finally into a hall in the fortress that was—blessedly—empty. With each glare he felt, and each whisper or biting curse he heard, the growing army of whispers in his head joined them in speaking of the regret he should feel for his actions in the Tourney. He gritted his teeth under the onslaught of societal shame and ignored those whisperings as best he could.

He knew he was not a coward no matter what the malscar might say. He knew that his actions had saved him and his family from the rejection of entering Silvas one day. And even with the unknown of Eklanos' fate, he knew what he had done was right.

They moved through the fortress' halls slowly and barely came across any people—but those they did treated Aabir in the same way everyone at Norland had—until they made it to one of the parking garages in the fortress' public sector. Tycho located a parked hover-taxi and they headed towards it.

"Y'know, Aabir..." Aabir looked up at the sudden sound of Tycho's voice, "If what you said about the Tourney is true—not that I'm saying it is—but if it was...how much of a dishonor do you think it would be if I competed in them?"

Aabir turned his neck as much as he could until his good eye could see the thoughtful look on Tycho's face. "I don't know," he replied.

Tycho twisted his lips to the side with a nod. Then with a shrug, the thoughtfulness was erased from his features, and he sent Aabir a side-eye smirk.

"Well, my good sir..." He slowed, and Aabir was forced to follow, as they made it to the hover-taxi. Tycho opened the door and, with a flourishing wave of his hand, presented it to Aabir. "Your carriage awaits you."

Aabir rolled his eyes with only a slight sting of pain. The painkillers had kicked in during his walk of shame. "You're ridiculous."

Tycho lowered his hand, still grinning. "I try."

Aabir could not hold back a smirk as he stepped into the back of the taxi. When he was settled into a comfortable position, Tycho put his backpack into the seat beside him. Aabir turned to face his friend and could feel the change in the air between them as the lightness of the moment was pushed aside.

"Thank you, Tycho," Aabir gave him a grateful nod.

Tycho nodded sharply. "No problem."

Silence stretched between them for a few moments, then Tycho said, "I...should probably go."

Aabir nodded slowly and turned his gaze down to his boots. "Sure."

"Maybe I'll see you later...and then I can finally get some of your Matha's pomen pie."

Aabir shook his head with a quiet laugh that only barely hurt his numbed ribs. He lifted his head and locked his eye on Tycho's. "Bye, Tycho."

"See ya, Aabir."

With that, he closed the door. Aabir gave the android driver his address and the robot started up the vehicle. The slight sensation of movement went through him as the humming generator lifted the hovercar off the ground. The robot backed out of its designated parking space, then they slowly made their way towards the parking garage's exit.

Aabir clenched his jaw as he turned his sore torso to look out the back window where Tycho was still standing. Then the car turned sharply, and his friend was no longer in view. He moved back into the semi-comfortable position from before and breathed in deeply of the still, non-judgmental air.

As the car drove on into traffic, he was able to ruminate upon all the things that had happened—and the weight of the shame he now bore forever on his face. Even with the painkillers, his skin throbbed around his malscar, but he tried to turn his focus away from it by looking out the window at the skyscrapers, townhomes, and storefronts passing by.

His eyelid drooped as each flowing memory of the long day brought on waves of exhaustion, and not even the turmoil of churning emotions inside him could keep sleep from taking over.

TYCHO WATCHED THE BLACK taxi until it turned a corner and was out of sight. He let out a sigh once he could no longer hear its low humming, then turned on his heel and headed back out of the dim garage. He put his hands in his pockets and kept his gaze lowered as he took his time walking back the way he and Aabir just came.

Despite what he had said to Aabir, he was not in the mood to try and fight anyone to keep his honor right then. So, once he made it to Norland, he lifted his chin and ignored all the stares aimed his way. Make them think he was brave and confident enough in his own status to be able to think nothing of what he had just done. It would be stupid for them to know the truth any other time, and that was especially true today.

Only when he was finally alone in his dorm did he let the emotions he had been suppressing escape. He crossed his arms and sat down on the side of Aabir's bunk. He lowered his gaze to the wood floor for the perfect backdrop to the thoughts tumbling through his head.

His best friend had been dishonorably expelled, and not just for some prank. The live footage of that unbelievable round in the Tourney spilled into Tycho's head again, and he could not help the wind of second-hand shame he felt for Aabir that pressed against his insides.

What was he thinking? Of all the times to show someone mercy...

Aabir's reasoning popped back into Tycho's head, and he put his face in his hands with a long sigh. "Oh Aabir," he mumbled, "why did you have to go and make this so hard?"

He had never thought of the Constantia Tourney as dishonoring. All he had ever wanted to do after he served his four years was become a competitor in the Tourney. To fight in them, to win them, and then to keep winning them until he won the honor of becoming one of its veterans. That was it. His life would be set, and there would be no chance of dishonor creeping into it.

Then Aabir had to come and tell him that not only were the prisoner rounds "unfair" (as he had told Tycho many times before), but that they were dishonorable to Igrium. Though he wrestled with himself for the truth, he could see where his friend was coming from. Especially with the new rule Emperor Ignis was implementing into them.

He shook his head slowly. Why did it all have to be so complicated? Why couldn't he just enjoy the Tourney without having to *think* about it? He doubted he would be able to watch them as only entertainment anymore after this, because now he had these new thoughts in his head—and he didn't like them.

Footsteps slowed to a stop outside the door. Tycho lifted his head as it swung open and Aquilo stepped into the room. A frown marred the other trainee's features as he closed the door and gave Tycho a hooded look.

"Is he gone?" He asked.

Tycho nodded. "Yeah."

Aquilo made a noncommittal noise in his throat then stepped over to the desk. Tycho watched him quietly as he placed both his hands on the back of the desk's chair and let out a deep sigh.

"I can't believe he never told us."

"Yeah." Tycho couldn't help but frown at the thought, his gaze returning to the floor. "I thought he could trust us."

"Well, we obviously couldn't trust him." Bitterness laced Aquilo's words. "The coward."

"You don't have to call him that..." The words felt hollow as they left Tycho's lips. "He only did what he thought was right."

Aquilo snorted. "Stop trying to defend him, Tycho."

"Well, someone has to."

"It's not like you agree with him, though." Aquilo paused, and Tycho could hear the questioning accusation in his silence. "Right?"

"Nah." He lifted his head and put on a grin he didn't feel inside. "I can't give up the Tourney that easily."

Aquilo stared at him through narrowed eyes for a few moments, then nodded sharply and turned his face forward again. "Good. Because if my parents find out I'm friends with any more malscarred cowards, I have a feeling they'll disown me."

Tycho's heart thudded in his chest. "You don't have to worry about that from me, my friend." He gestured to his face. "I don't plan on getting these handsome looks destroyed."

Aquilo snorted again, but Tycho caught the small smile pulling at his lips before he suppressed it back into his usual-hard look.

A stretch of silence lengthened between them, and Tycho glanced down at the holonode on his wrist. He turned it on and noticed a couple notifications regarding Constantia Tourney updates. His stomach did an odd flip, and he turned off the small device before tapping either of them. He rested his chin in one of his hands and glanced back over at Aquilo.

"You could've at least helped me get him out of here," he finally said. "You are his friend, too..."

"*Was.*" Aquilo snapped back.

Tycho rolled his eyes. "You can't just let it go that easily, Aquilo. If you could, him not telling us about what he was dealing with wouldn't have upset you so much."

Aquilo opened his mouth, but then shut it with a shake of his head. Tycho could tell by his shadowed look what his snappy words weren't really saying, and he fought the urge to continue speaking of the matter as more silence stretched between them; because he knew Aquilo was only trying to deal with this sudden loss the same as he was.

He stared down at his whitening knuckles. Neither of them ever thought they would lose their best friend because of something considered so dishonorable—and now they would both have to deal with it as quietly as possible, or risk someone thinking their low spirits were an agreement with Aabir's actions.

"Don't be like your brothers, Tycho." He pressed his fists against his temples as his patre's warning intruded his thoughts, *"You don't want to bring your matha's spirit down to Malackin's Domain, do you? Because if you screw up anymore, she may find herself suffering there forever—and it'll be all you and your idiotic brothers' faults."*

He shook his head as a trickle of fear sent a shiver down his spine. An image of his matha being thrown down from the Warrior's Hall into the dark pit ruled by Malackin popped into his head, and he pressed his knuckles harder against his temples.

No, I won't let that happen. He would not be held responsible for his matha's second death, nor would he be found as dishonorable as his brothers—may they rot in Malackin's Pit forever.

Yet he couldn't stop these new thoughts Aabir had placed in his head, nor could he stop the ache he felt every time he thought about having to ignore his best friend as if he no longer existed. He sighed and moved his hands to rest his chin atop them. His gaze strayed to the long sollbeams filtering through the window upon the floor.

As the silence continued, Tycho continued to think and ponder on these things—and he prayed to any of the gods who might be listening to let his matha stay in the Warrior's Hall, and to give him wisdom on what actions he should do to keep her there.

Chapter Sixty

Even from up in the air, Tetra's peryton ears could make out the muffled clashes of battle happening below Captain Fellin's hovercraft. She paced alone in the transport bay, awaiting Lieutenant Eyrie's command to be released. Her C.O. was down in the Alliance's camp in the command tent where most of the generals and other tacticians were located, leaving Tetra with only her buzzing thoughts for the past who-knew-how-long.

Energy coursed through her veins as the chorus of the battle ensued, yet somehow, she found herself more focused on the strange spy she had found snooping around yesterday than the muffled echoes her twitching ears picked up. Though it wasn't her job to worry about such things, she couldn't help doing so. Uneasiness still churned her insides at the question of who the spy was working for, and the fact that—according to the short message Lieutenant Eyrie had been given earlier that morning—they still hadn't given in to Frigian questioning techniques yet.

"Private," Tetra almost jumped out of her fur at the sound of Eyrie's voice in her ear, "it's time."

Her heart leapt nervously at the anticipated words, all thoughts for the spy immediately falling away for the task that lay ahead. She grunted in reply and turned to face the transport bay's closed door. Heart beginning to race, she ruffled her wings' feathers and pawed the ground with one of her front hooves as she waited in the tense moments of silence for it to open.

A loud whirring noise almost made her jump again, then was followed by an even louder hissing sound as the bay door began to open. Tetra closed her eyes and inhaled deeply, bright sollight illuminating the darkness of her eyelids.

This was it. Wind ruffled her fur as it blew into the bay, and she blinked her eyes open at its beckoning. She pressed her ears back against her head as the clamorous noises of battle were magnified ten times with the open bay door. Numerous spherical scout drones zoomed past the hovercraft below.

Adrenaline began to buzz through her veins as her enhanced eyesight roved over the clashes happening far below.

This really was it. She swallowed, but kept her thoughts trained on the reason she was doing this: she was going to help free Xich from Igrium's tyranny.

A low growl rumbled in her throat as her heartbeat quickened with rising anger. And after it was all said and done, she would show Emperor Ignis how much of a mistake it was to steal her childhood, kill her uncle, and abandon her.

"Fly, peryton!" Lieutenant Eyrie commanded through Tetra's single earpiece.

With a roar, she flung her wings open and charged down the ramp. She jumped off with a great flap of her wings and entered chaos.

Scout drones zipped around her, and she had to twist and dive more than she ever had amidst the mazes of ambulate tree branches to not hit any of them. None of them were marked, and she didn't want to risk destroying any of the Alliance's. They were the only reason those in the command tent could see what was going on in the battle, and she didn't want anyone to regret having the war-peryton fight because she took out half the Alliance's scout drones.

"Target is to your left," Lieutenant Eyrie spoke in a low voice.

Tetra angled her wings, her gaze landing on the giant hovercraft now ahead of her. Igrium's red flag was painted on its shadowed hull, and resounding booms reverberated from the fiery-tipped bolts it launched at Alliance ground troops and other hovercraft.

"Destroy its crossbows, peryton," Lieutenant Eyrie's voice lowered again as she added, "and remember to keep yourself hidden until the right time."

Tetra grunted an affirmative, then pumped her wings to ascend. As she did, her gaze landed on the edge of a giant, mounted crossbow sitting atop the hovercraft's deck—her first target. She headed towards the bottom of the hovercraft to keep out of sight of those operating it.

The shadow of the hull soon brought a small respite to the Xichian heat, and she glanced upwards at the gray panels above. Sending up a silent prayer to any gods that might be listening, Tetra flew in a straight line upwards, swooping to a sharp right before hitting the hovercraft's hull, and ascending upwards into the open sky once again.

Shouts reached her ears as she crested the hull and appeared for all on the hovercraft's open deck to finally see. Most of the soldiers manning the crossbows gaped up at her, but she averted her attention from them as her eyes locked onto the first giant crossbow. Two bolts were loaded atop it—both the same length as her peryton body with flames licking their pointed tips.

"Take it down!" Despite the chaos around her, Eyrie's voice was steady.

With a roar, Tetra dove towards the weapon. The Igrians manning it scrambled away with yells and putrid fear-scents as she descended upon the train-car-sized weapon, talons outstretched in front of her. She grabbed the taut, metal cord as she passed. Using the momentum and her strength, she pulled it with all her might.

With a snap of metal, the tension loosened, and she was flung forward. She let go and flapped her wings to steady herself, before swooping upwards to survey the damage. The crossbow's cord now hung loose out of one of its pulleys.

More sounds of confusion flew past her ears as Eyrie spoke a simple command, "Pick up."

With another roar, Tetra descended upon the now-broken crossbow and picked up one of the fiery bolts with her talons. She gritted her teeth as she misjudged the weight of the heavy projectile, dropped it, and had to pick it up again. This was one move she and Lieutenant Eyrie hadn't gone over much, but she swept the brewing worry aside. She couldn't waste any time focusing on those thoughts right then.

"Now take it down."

Getting a better grip on the bolt, Tetra pumped her wings and flew upwards away from the hovercraft. A couple crossbows clicked as they turned to fire in a different direction. "Aim for the peryton!" More clicks sounded as cords were drawn and bolts were locked in place as Tetra slowed in her ascent.

"Aim..." Came a singular shout on the deck. "Fire!"

Tetra had already pulled her wings to her sides in a dive. A bolt flew past her head, but she kept her gaze pinned upon her next target. As she came upon it, she opened her wings and swooped over, the bolt she held ramming into the crossbow's metal side. Her talons screeched against it as she let it go and swooped away again.

Screams split the air behind her, and she gritted her teeth as an invisible arrow of guilt struck her heart. She knew this would happen. She knew what she was getting into, and why she was doing it. But that didn't stop the nausea that entered her stomach as her eyes landed on the wounded people her bolt had fallen on.

"Fly down and hide." Eyrie's sudden command helped shock her thoughts to the present.

She pulled her wings into her sides and dove back down under the shadowed cover of the hovercraft. As she did, she noticed out of the corner of her eye a bolt hurtling towards her side. Her heart leapt into her throat. She twisted awkwardly and barely averted the fiery projectile. It sailed past towards the ground as she swooped into safety back under the hovercraft.

That was too close. She slowed to a stop and turned her long neck to watch it fall towards the battle raging below.

"Again, peryton," Lieutenant Eyrie said. "Only come up on the other side."

Tetra lifted her head and did as she was told. Again, she soared back up to the Igrian hovercraft's deck and decimated more of its mounted weaponry. She dismantled more crossbows, dodged more bolts, and threw her own until all that was left were some soldiers who fired normal-sized projectiles at her from their personal crossbows.

A few of these clinked against her armor as she tucked her wings in and dove back down into the safety of the hovercraft's shadow. She slowed to a stop in midair and took a cursory glance around at the wider air battle happening around her. More Igrian hovercrafts drew nearer to hers, Alliance ones not far behind them. With her peryton eyesight, she could see many of the crossbows on the Igrian airships' flight decks were trained upon her.

"Position: ground. Swoop and claw," ordered Lieutenant Eyrie.

Tetra peeled her gaze away from the incoming hovercraft, tucked her wings into her sides, and fell into a dive. Wind whistled past her ears as the armored waves of soldiers and hovercars below drew closer. She angled her tail feathers and headed towards the biggest grouping of dark gray she could see.

The closer she plummeted towards the ground, the more overwhelming the smells of battle became. She almost stopped in midair when the pungent odors of fear, intermingled with the almost-muted layers of determination, smacked her in the face; but she gritted her teeth, took smaller breaths through her mouth, and continued downward. Interspersed among the heady, emotional scents were the sharp smells of blood, sweat, metal, and churned dirt.

Tetra had no time to focus on any more smells as the fighting figures on the ground suddenly came upon her. She snapped her wings open and glided over the ranks of screaming chaos; knocking dark-armored Igrian soldiers over with her hooves, then picking them up with her dexterous back talons only to drop them back to the ground. Bolts clinked against her armor and a couple pierced her wings, but other than slight twinges of pain, they didn't bother her.

With each move, she kept her thoughts on those she was fighting for. Pictures of Stellinga, Rabetta, those she had seen in Trivsau's refugee camp, and even some of Aunt Minda and Felicita filtered through her head as she charged through Igrium's ranks upon the ground and defended any struggling Alliance soldiers to the beat of Eyrie's rapid commands.

"To your left." Lieutenant Eyrie stated simply.

Tetra flicked her gaze left towards a battalion of Igrian troops who had hemmed in a small group of Silvanian soldiers. She let loose a roar and leapt into the air, those fighting near her stumbling under the wind her flapping wings created. She turned left and dodged a hovercraft bolt as it sped towards her, then spun with a tuck of her wings to dodge a cloud of other smaller ones flying in her direction.

Energy buzzed through her veins as she let loose another roar and swooped down upon the Igrian battalion for a charge. She lowered her antlered head in preparation as her hooves touched the ground. A second before her talons did the same, she folded in her wings and ran.

Screams tore at her eardrums. The muscles in her neck tensed with each passing weight she rammed her head against. Sharp edges nicked her exposed wings. Her thunderous hoofbeats pounded in tempo to her racing heart as she followed the path of dark-armored soldiers.

"You're clear," Lieutenant Eyrie finally said, "Now fly!"

Tetra lifted her head and opened her wings again. In the split second of her jump, she noticed the many still bodies lying around the living Silvanian soldiers fighting back against the few remaining Igrians. Claws squeezed at her heart as she lifted her head towards the buzzing sky, but she shoved those feelings down as a line of bolts headed towards her. She tilted her wings and swooped above them.

Don't get distracted, she chided herself with a tiny shake of her head. This was no time to let distracting thoughts get in the way.

"To your right," Eyrie said.

Tetra glided smoothly to her right, then abruptly stopped before a fiery bolt decapitated her. Her heart dropped into her stomach like a stone as she watched it strike the ground. If she had only been a second faster...

"Private..." Lieutenant Eyrie's whisper somehow cut through the commotion accosting most of Tetra's senses, "You're a big target. Get going, or another of those bolts *will* hit you."

Knowing it was safe by the use of her title "private", Tetra grunted in reply with a nod of her head. She pumped her wings and surged forward again. Her eyes roved over the roiling waves of fighting sides, and she spotted another area where dark gray was taking over the brown, white, and gray-green of the Alliance. The muscles in her wings began to strain as she put on a burst of speed towards them.

When she was right above them, Lieutenant Eyrie yelled, "Charge!"

Tetra dove. Before hitting the ground, she snapped her feathered wings open and bowled over the Igrians she landed on. Without skipping a beat, she lowered her antlered head and charged. The sharp smell of surprise hit her nostrils as she sped through the throngs of soldiers like a war-equis of old—only bigger and with sharp, pointy antlers.

Like in her training, Igrian soldiers fell around and below her. She fortified her mental defenses before any unwanted thoughts could break through and ruin her focus. This would show Emperor Ignis he should have never destroyed her childhood. A bolt struck her wing, but she didn't flinch as she stoked the flames of her anger. She would give Igrium what it deserved for all the innocent people they had killed.

She narrowed her eyes and growled. Her father would know the depths of her fury before this war was over.

Something screeched against her neck armor as she ran. A sharp prick of pain barely sliced above her hoof, but it didn't deter her course. Adrenaline laced with anger pumped through her veins as Lieutenant Eyrie gave her simple directional commands to keep up the act of her being a peryton to anyone who might be listening. "Left. Stop. Turn sharp right."

Her neck muscles strained as a sudden heavy weight lowered her head almost to the rough ground. She lifted her gaze, and her stomach churned at the sight of the struggling person stuck in her short antlers. They cursed and swiped at her head with a sword. She couldn't suppress a growl as they sliced a cut across her exposed long snout. She aimed a sharp glare at him and swung her long neck, dislodging him. He flew and knocked over a couple more Igrian troops.

"Fly right," Eyrie commanded.

Tetra lifted her head, opened her tiring wings, inhaled deeply, and jumped into the air. She beat her wings wildly to gain altitude above the chaos, then angled them to glide right. Before Lieutenant Eyrie even said anything, she saw her next targets: a fleet of Igrian armored hovercars zipping through the battle, firing multiple bolts from manned, mounted crossbows atop their bulky frames—smaller versions of the ones on hovercraft.

"Target hovercars in the center..."

Tetra steadied her course as warm blood dripped down her face. She huffed an irritated breath at the stinging cut, but then her attention was pulled to the muffled argument she barely heard coming from her single earpiece. She spun away from another huge bolt hurtling towards her as it continued. What was her C.O. doing?

She soon got her answer.

"Peryton..." A tinge of emotion coated Lieutenant Eyrie's slightly hoarse tone. A seed of worry planted itself amidst her fortified thoughts. What could that mean...?

"Ram the hovercar." Eyrie finished.

Oh. Tetra's heart picked up its erratic pace as her eyes landed on the first hovercar in the short line. The command "ram" was one of the simplest moves she had learned under Lieutenant Eyrie—and the least practiced. It involved exactly what it said: she turned herself into a living projectile midair and rammed into whatever object she was supposed to. The only problem with it was she had only ever hit a moving target twice—and successfully rammed into the ground every other time.

With the new bout of worrisome thoughts taking her focus, she flew right over the hovercars shooting down the Alliance's forces and gained their attention.

Stupid! She huffed an irritated breath at herself and swooped back around in a wide circle. The click of crossbows reached her pointed ears and she jerked sharply to avoid a bolt before it hit her wing. Her eyes again locked onto the lead car as another bolt flew right underneath her. If she was going to do this, she needed to do it now.

Gulping back her rising fear, Tetra locked onto where the hovercar would be in the next few moments, tucked in her wings, and dove at a sharp angle towards the spot.

The ground hurtled towards her. She squeezed her eyes shut then curled into a ball at the last moment. Gritanium armor hit furrum siding. A pause. Then the sharp smell of something burning hit her nostrils as her body tumbled away.

Ringing drowned out the tumult of battle around her. Soreness covered Tetra from head to talon and smoke burned her nostrils, but she opened her eyes and pushed herself back up on shaking legs. It was a good thing perytons had bones as hard as gritanium.

Even so, her steps were stiff as she blinked her searching eyes in the wafting smoke. A couple of harsh coughs rattled her lungs as her gaze landed on the burning remains of the hovercar. Then she jerked her head in the direction of the other cars as a couple bolts clinked against her neck armor.

Even with the ringing still in her ears, Tetra was able to barely make out Eyrie's yelled order, "Fly!"

More bolts flew towards her, and one pierced her wing as she flung it open to fly away. A roar escaped her throat as she pumped her wings and ascended. She glanced down at the metal haft of the bolt sticking out of her feathery wing's membrane. She gritted her teeth as each flap sent jolts of pain through it and down into her spine. A bolt barely missed her head as she flapped her wings frantically.

"Come back to camp, Private," Lieutenant Eyrie sharply whispered. "You need to get that bolt taken care of."

Tetra dipped her head in a nod towards the few scout droids near her, and turned in the direction of the Alliance's camp. With her injured wing, it took her longer to get there than she thought it should've as she dodged more bolts and drones coming from all directions. She came to a faltering landing on the edge of camp and was soon met by Lieutenant Eyrie and a few field doctors who quickly took the bolt out, bandaged up the wound as best they could, then gave her medicine to help dull the pain.

Once they were finished, she was sent back out into the thick of the battle to aid whomever she was ordered to. She dove into the frays, charged into battalions, rammed into more hovercars, clawed and sliced as she glided over the enemy forces, and lost count of the hovercraft crossbows she took out. When too much attention was put on her, she was ordered to retreat towards another part of the battlefield where her presence would be more of a surprise. Or, if

Eyrie could read through her vitals that she was exhausted, then she was ordered to return back to the Alliance's camp for short breaks.

As Soll began to set along the horizon, the battle shifted in the Alliance's favor. So much so that Tetra could almost feel victory buzzing in the air. A bolt flew towards her face and her sore wings barely carried her away from it in time. It had been almost three hours since her last break, and she had finally reached the end of her endurance.

She glided above the Alliance-occupied portion of the battlefield with only little flaps of her wings to try and conserve her waning energy as she waited for her next orders. Lieutenant Eyrie had gone silent for the past few minutes; leaving Tetra's stomach to do acrobatics in the looming quiet. A long, muffled argument had reached her ear from her earpiece in that time, but she had heard no specific orders.

She roared in surprise as a huge bolt hurtled through the air in front of her. Heart pounding, she sent a seething glare up towards one of the last remaining Igrian hovercraft floating above the shrinking, Igrium-occupied piece of the battlefield. She spun in a tight loop and headed in the opposite direction of the enemy airship.

Tetra dodged another fiery projectile and faltered in her flight pattern for a moment. She gritted her teeth and regained the lost height. Exhaustion pulled against her mental defenses, letting in a few fearful whispers that said she wouldn't make it past this battle—and she was beginning to believe them, which was why she needed something to do. It would keep her focus fixed onto something else other than those tired thoughts.

"Private, I'm sorry for not giving you any orders recently," Lieutenant Eyrie whispered into her earpiece, "but there was an argument. I made an excuse to step out for a minute, but they will be expecting me to give you orders in there again soon."

Tetra did her usual grunt of affirmation that she heard her C. O's words and swooped under a couple flying bolts.

Lieutenant Eyrie continued in her sharp whisper, "I know you're getting tired—I can read it in your vital signs, and I have watched your close calls—but there is one more thing our commanders are ordering you to do." She paused for a moment. "Do you see those three Igrian hovercraft flying together?"

Tetra lifted her head to look in the emptying sky around her. Then she spotted the three huge airships floating away from the dwindling battle in a triangle formation. Bolts shot out in all directions from them as they slowly moved towards the Vridi ocean, where islands in the Deltide Chain dotted its bluish-green waters.

Tetra dipped her head towards the closest scout droids with a grunt.

"They are retreating to grab more reinforcements from their island outpost of '*Scatiun*', and none of our hovercraft will be able to reach them at this time."

Tetra turned her lifted head and noticed a couple Frigian hovercraft slowly breaking away from the Alliance's occupied air forces to follow them, but she could see the few remaining Igrian ones would block them from pursuing. Her heart skipped an erratic beat as the knowledge of what she was about to be asked to do dawned in her thoughts.

As if in answer, Lieutenant Eyrie drew a deep breath and spoke that thought aloud, "That's why General Taoghn has ordered you to take down at least one of those ships." She breathed out deeply. "He wants you to take all three of them out, but I told him that would not be possible. So, focus on taking one out, and he will have to be satisfied with it or risk losing you."

Despite Tetra's exhaustion, a new rush of energy filled her as she set her gaze back on the three retreating hovercrafts. It wasn't strong, but it would be enough to carry her through the order. It would have to be. The Xichians needed it to be.

Using that burst of adrenaline, she pumped her weary wings and ascended in the direction of the hovercraft, keeping herself low enough to bypass the remaining Igrian airships as they attacked the Frigian ones. A few stray bolts flew towards her from the ground, but she easily evaded them as she rose higher and higher towards her next targets.

The closer she drew, she began to wonder how she was supposed to take down the giant aircraft. The humans on its flight deck looked like small buzz gnats crawling atop it, and Tetra was only one peryton—and a smaller one at that.

As if reading her mind, Lieutenant Eyrie's voice sounded in her ear, "You're going to take out the magnetic-propulsion generators, but you'll need to take a bolt from one of the hovercrafts. I'll give you the simple orders once I return to the tent, but I wanted to tell you the specifics beforehand. May Deleyon help you, Private."

Tetra grunted in reply as her gaze landed upon the vent-like slits on the bottom of each airship; blue light glowing in the interiors of each one. Those were the entrances to the magnetic-propulsion generators—the machine that used the world's magnetic field to make the airships hover.

She swallowed and lifted her gaze back up to its mounted crossbows. Her heart leapt in anticipation.

"Alright, peryton." A nervous shiver went through her insides as her C.O. spoke, "Target up."

At the order, she pushed her wings to move faster. As she drew nearer, some of the hovercrafts' crossbows clicked and started firing at her. She spun and dodged the bolts, panting air into her tiring lungs.

I can do this. She tightened her jaw and rose towards the closest hovercraft's flight deck.

"Take down."

Tetra twisted as the closest crossbow shot a bolt towards her, narrowly missing her neck. She growled, flapped her wings for a burst of speed, and sailed up past the crossbow's range. Angry shouts touched her ears. She circled back around, extended her talons, and grabbed the crossbow's cord like she had already done many times that day. It soon came out of its pulley, and she was able to let go.

"Pick up."

Tetra turned and eyed the now-free bolt for a moment. Her movements were getting sloppy as her stamina wore. Could she even pick up the heavy, metal bolt?

"Peryton, pick up."

Pushing aside her doubts, Tetra dodged a huge bolt that hurtled towards her, then flew over to the broken crossbow and picked up her own bolt. The muscles in her wings strained with each beat as she lifted it, but she couldn't stop. She wouldn't allow herself to if it meant the Alliance would lose more of its army, or if it would prolong Xich's suffering.

"Fly below target."

Tetra swooped down—barely dodging another bolt—and flew into the shadows underneath the aircraft. She soon reached the huge slits, their soft blue light illuminating the shadows.

"Go into the dark one."

She immediately spotted the one Lieutenant Eyrie was talking about and headed towards it. Darkness overwhelmed her, and she blinked her eyes until they adjusted to it. She pressed her ears back against her head as much as they could to protect against the thunderous hum of the generators that grew the deeper she flew into the bowels of the hovercraft.

It didn't take long before she saw the generators. Her eyes widened at what looked like a maze of oversized wires, circuit boxes, and other pieces of all shapes and sizes she didn't know the names of. How in Afreean was she supposed to do this?

"Target all yellow wires," Eyrie commanded. "Take down."

Tetra flapped her tiring wings and moved closer to the huge machine that spread out before her. It was harder to discern colors with her night vision, but she took a few moments to peer closely at the first individual wires ahead of her and was able to make out—what she hoped were—the yellow ones.

She hefted the long bolt in her talons, then rammed its tip towards one of the snaking wires. It lodged into the machine, cutting the thick wire in two. The rumbling hum around her faltered for a moment, then continued at its normal roll. Taking that as a good sign, she continued cutting all the yellow wires she saw with her bolt.

As she worked across the board, a curious thought entered her head: why was she wasting energy carrying this heavy crossbow bolt when she had sharp talons? She hefted the bolt in her talons again then grabbed it with just one as she came upon the next yellow wire. Then, she reached out with her free talon to cut it. It barely made a scratch.

So that's why. Shaking her head, she wrapped her back leg's free digits around the bolt again and rammed it into the wire, cutting it.

She continued with the monotonous task—the generators' humming cutting out for longer periods of time with each wire she cut. Finally, she made it to the last one and rammed the bolt into it with shaking talons. The generator's rumbling stuttered to a stop. Tetra waited a few moments in the heavy silence, ears pricked, but the overwhelming hums didn't turn back on.

"Get out, peryton!" Tetra's wings faltered in surprise at Lieutenant Eyrie's urgent order.

Dropping the heavy bolt with a relieved sigh, she turned around and headed back towards the light outside. She burst forth into a sensory overload as foul waves of fear and burning metal filled her nose to a chorus of loud groans coming from the hovercraft that were accompanied by shouts and screams. She lifted her gaze and realized the bottom of its hull was falling towards her.

A roar of surprise escaped her throat, and she flapped her aching wings as quickly as she could until she was no longer underneath its shadow. Only when the waves of fear scent weren't so heavy did she finally look behind her shoulder to see what damage had been done. Heaviness pressed against her lungs as she watched the huge airship fall from the sky faster than she would have thought possible for something so big.

It hit the ground in an enormous cloud of dust and sand. There was a pause—then an explosion of white fire burst from its underside. Tetra squeezed her eyes shut against the blinding light; then a gust of air hit her as she flew, throwing her off balance. She opened her eyes to right herself; and as she did so, they landed on the bright fire burning amidst the forest of palm trees and suchwries.

She scrunched her nose as putrid waves of horrible, burning scents wafted towards her, begging her weary thoughts to think upon how many people might have been on that hovercraft. The weight tightened upon her chest, causing her wingbeats to falter. There must've been hundreds of people on that ship...and now they were all dead.

"Private—" Eyrie's whisper pulled Tetra from those dragging thoughts, "—you've done well. Now come back to camp and I'll tell Army General

Taoghn you're through. I'm sure he will understand since we now have a higher chance of winning this battle even if those other ships do get reinforcements."

The two remaining hovercrafts continued their retreat without slowing as she spoke. Tetra flicked her gaze between them and the downed hovercraft, then down to the battle below. If more reinforcements did come, the battle would continue on, and even more lives would be lost. Plus, there was also the chance that the Alliance's palpable victory might be lost, too.

Tetra closed her eyes and inhaled deeply into her aching lungs. Images of Trivsau flashed through her head, along with sweet Stellinga and kind Rabetta who had taken care of her despite the "Cairn" name. She let out the exhale in a huff and opened her eyes, setting them on the retreating hovercraft. Lieutenant Eyrie's words from her first day of training rang through her head as she flapped her shaky wings and ascended back towards the two Igrian airships.

"What are you doing, Private?" Eyrie's voice held a tone of warning. "Your flight is growing sloppier, and your vitals are dwindling. General Taoghn will understand if you can't do anything else. Come back to camp."

Tetra continued on her flightpath without stopping.

"Tetra Cairn..."

Her heart leapt nervously at her C.O.'s sharp tone, but still she continued. She didn't want to disobey Lieutenant Eyrie, nor did she want to possibly fall out of the sky because of exhaustion, but she couldn't leave this chance when there was still some strength left in her—albeit less and less with each movement of her wings. Her one life was not as important as the thousands of others that would be put at risk if those hovercraft escaped—not even if her last name was "Ignis".

"As your commanding officer I order you back to camp!" Tetra cringed as Eyrie's voice sliced against her eardrums, but she didn't deter from her path. "It doesn't matter what your original orders are! You and I both know you can't go on much longer. This is foolishness."

Her stomach churned with nausea, but she kept her eyes on the two hovercrafts as they loomed closer. The skin around her malscar and tally scars tingled, and she blinked back the blurriness stinging her eyes. She had to do this. She wouldn't let Emperor Ignis get another chance to win this battle.

"Tetra, you can't save everyone."

Talons squeezed her heart. No, she couldn't—but she wasn't going to leave these people like a coward. Nor was she going to give Igrium any more reasons to call her one.

Tetra let loose a roar and swooped upward towards the deck as Lieutenant Eyrie went silent. Just like before, she dodged fiery projectiles as she disabled a crossbow and took its bolt, then swooped down underneath the hovercraft and found the magnetic-propulsion generator. The bolt slipped and almost fell from her weakening talons multiple times as she cut all the yellow wires.

Lieutenant Eyrie's voice came back to give her simple commands. Tetra figured it was to keep up the act, but she couldn't discern any emotion in her C.O.'s monotone voice. Guilt churned her stomach with each wire she cut, but she pushed herself to continue—even as the thunderous humming of the generator was soon drowned out by the blood pounding in her ears.

Only a short time passed before all the yellow wires were cut, and Tetra—bolt still in her talons—flew out of the darkness back into the awaiting daylight as the second hovercraft went down like the first. She forced herself to keep her gaze upon the third one, even as the rest of her senses were overloaded with the explosion far below.

As she drew near to her last target, she found every crossbow atop it aimed towards her—and they all released a line of fiery bolts only a moment later. Her heart skipped frantically in fear as a couple barely glanced off her armored sides while she sloppily maneuvered around them before moving under the cover of the hovercraft. The only thing keeping her in the air was pure determination—and its dregs were emptying fast—yet she continued on.

Her wingbeats slowed as she went through the process of finding all the yellow wires for the last time. Once the final wire was cut, she dropped the heavy load she carried and headed out of the quiet generator with jerky movements.

"Target camp," Lieutenant Eyrie stated simply.

Though images of falling from the sky popped into her head at the overwhelming exhaustion filling her hollow bones, they quickly gave way to the thought of the incoming encounter with her C.O. Shivers of fear went through her wings. Even so, she turned her face towards the Alliance camp in the distance and slowly glided back in the cloudless air—empty of everything but the scout drones still buzzing around, the distant remaining hovercrafts still battling each other, and the plummeting one behind her she could hear and smell.

As Tetra tucked her wings into a dive to gain some speed, something rammed into her leg. Pain exploded in her thigh, and she began to plummet in shock. It immediately faded as some part of her brain screamed at her that she was at least a mile high in the air and couldn't give in to the shock. When she realized she was hurtling towards the ground, she sucked in a sharp breath and snapped her wings open to keep her aloft.

Spots danced in her vision; each movement igniting a fire of pain in her back leg. She sent a furtive glance behind her shoulder and saw one of the giant crossbow bolts had pierced through her armor and lodged itself into her thigh. Dark peryton blood spilled out in a steady stream from the wound with each jerky movement she made, staining her talon.

Fog filled her head, but she somehow continued pushing her wings to fly harder, pouring every ounce of strength she had left into them. She wouldn't fall... She couldn't fall.

Her vision darkened. The earlier screams her mind threw at her to stay awake were muffled in the darkness smothering her thoughts. With each stab of pain, Tetra could feel her last reserves of energy fading as quickly as the blood flowing down her leg.

Finally, she could do nothing more. She blinked once and saw she was on the outskirts of the camp before her vision dimmed. Exhaustion dragged her wings down one last time as the pain-filled darkness finally won the battle for her mind, and her thoughts were no more.

Chapter Sixty-One

Aabir jerked awake as the hum of the hovercar's generator stopped. He blinked his bleary eye open. Relief washed through him as his single-eyed gaze landed on the familiar sight of his home. He lifted his bandaged arm with cautious movements but was only met with a dull throb instead of the stinging from before. He opened the hovercar's door and sent another silent "thanks" up to Deleyon for painkillers as he stepped onto the concrete driveway with only slight twinges of pain.

"Aabir!"

He spun in the direction of Matha's cry and noticed his entire family rushing towards him—Matha in the lead. Her footfalls slowed as she neared him.

"Oh, Aabir..." He opened his arms for her incoming hug, and she fell into them. He could not help the grunt that escaped his lips as his broken ribs screamed as she squeezed him, even above the painkillers' effects.

"Oh!" Matha immediately let go and lifted her worry-lined face towards him. "I'm so sorry! I—" Her words stopped abruptly as their eyes met. Nauseating shame churned Aabir's stomach as she lifted her hand towards his face, stopping just before she touched his malscar. "What happened?"

Before he could open his mouth to answer, the rest of his family came to a huddled stop around them. Patre stepped forward next to Matha, and Aabir lifted his head to meet his eyes.

"We watched the round you were in today, Aabir." Patre's tone was steady as he spoke, but—to Aabir's surprise—his dark violet eyes were glassy with unshed tears. "And no patre could have been prouder than I as we watched you walking out of that arena without having killed that prisoner."

Pressure built up in Aabir's throat at the combination of his patre's visible emotion and words. He cleared it and opened his mouth to reply, but was again stopped as Zeke said, "But I can say for all of us that we didn't expect you to come home looking like a beat-up punching bag with a malscar."

Aabir turned his one-eyed glare onto his brother's grinning face and opened his mouth to make a snappy comment, but it died away as he caught the shadows in Zeke's eyes that mirrored their parents' looks. He had no time to think of something to say about it before Patre said, "And I know I'm the only patre in this empire who sees it as an honorable mark."

Aabir turned his good eye back on his patre. "Really?"

Patre's weathered features lifted in a small smile. "Really."

A little of the shame lifted off his chest. Not much, but it made breathing a bit easier.

"But we weren't told what happened after," Matha said.

He turned his neck and looked down at her pinched features. "It was Denir."

An angry light sparked in her eyes as she narrowed them. "I ought to give him a piece of my mind!" She snapped, "How dare he hurt my—"

"—And he dishonorably expelled me from Norland."

Matha raised her brow in shock. "He—he did what now?"

"I'm free, Matha." Aabir cleared his throat again, unable to keep the small smile from lifting the corners of his mouth. "I won't be fighting for Igrium when I graduate, so I can go with all of you to Mister Falap's this summer."

"Oh, Aabir!" Matha smiled and went to hug him again—albeit much more gently this time. "That's wonderful news."

"But how will this affect us?" Ereliev asked.

Aabir and Matha both let go and turned towards her. She raised her brow as their gazes landed on her, then her eyes locked with Aabir's. She put Yahel—who was sitting on her hip—down on the ground before crossing her arms.

"No one can just live a normal life here with a malscar," she continued, "so how in Afreean are we supposed to when we're related to you? Don't get me wrong—I'm glad you didn't have to kill that prisoner—but everyone knows our family name now, Aabir, and it's not in a good light."

"You raise a good point, Ereliev," Patre turned to face her as well, "but we'll figure out a way." He turned his head and locked eyes with Aabir again. "We're just glad this has turned out better than any of us could have hoped."

Despite his patre's words, more guilt oozed into Aabir at Ereliev's comment. "I'm sorry for dragging all of you into this, too." He hung his head and stared at the concrete below his boots. "I didn't mean for that to happen."

"We know," Matha replied, "and we don't hold it against you, Aabir. Like your patre said, we're very happy you didn't have to do the unthinkable in that round; and even if we have to carry this supposed "dishonor" as long as we stay in Igrium, we'll make it work."

Aabir glanced up over his brow and caught her soft smile. "Thanks."

Footsteps drew his attention to Nevaze's short form as she stopped next to him. She lifted her head and their eyes locked.

"So, you don't have to go back to Norland anymore?" She asked.

"Nope." Another wave of relief washed through him despite the other, slimy emotions pressing down upon him. "Not anymore."

Aabir looked over his shoulder at the hum of a hovercar and noticed another hovertaxi turning onto their quiet street. His malscar itched with his shame as he turned his face back in the direction of their house.

"Could someone get my bag?" He asked.

Patre nodded, understanding lightening his eyes, and turned his face in Zeke's direction. "Zee, get your brother's bag out of the car."

Zeke nodded without complaint and walked to the hovertaxi. As he did so, the other taxi slowed and turned into their driveway. Aabir shot a questioning look towards his parents.

"Did you invite someone?" He asked.

Matha wrapped her arms more around Nevaze as Patre stepped over next to Aabir, his hardened expression set on the vehicle. "No," he replied.

The muscles in Aabir's neck tensed and he also turned to face the new vehicle as one of its doors opened. Who in Afreean—?

Ezen stepped out of the second taxi and slammed the door shut. Aabir blinked in surprise, then immediately remembered their holocall from only a few days before.

Their gazes locked, and Ezen's eyes widened. More itching stings arose in the skin around Aabir's malscar, and he gritted his teeth to try and fight the impulse to scratch it.

Ezen blinked and his surprise faded for a shadowed look. "Um—hey, Aabir." He turned his face away and kicked the toe of his boot against the ground. "I—uh—I need to talk to you."

"Aabir, who is this?" Patre asked, his questioning tone edged with distrust.

"This is Ezen," Aabir replied. "He's a friend from Norland."

Patre sent him a side-eyed look. "Then why is he here?"

"Because I need to speak with all of you." Ezen stepped towards them, a pleading look entering his eyes. "Please. I know this—that this is a horrible time, but I need to..." His voice faltered for a moment. "I need to explain some things to Aabir, and I...I think you all will want to hear about them, too."

Aabir almost wanted to tell his friend it was not a good time, but the look on his face gave him pause. "What's the matter?"

"I..." Ezen sent a wary glance around them, and Aabir's heart jumped a fearful beat. Before he could dwell on the strange action further, their eyes locked again. "Do you know of any place here that isn't watched?"

Another spike of fear drove itself into Aabir's heart. "Um...yeah..."

"Hold on." His attention was drawn to Patre's firm voice. "Aabir—do you know what this is about?"

He glanced out of the corner of his eye at Ezen's still form, then shook his head. "No sir."

Patre frowned and asked in a lowered voice that only Aabir could hear, "Then why did you just mention the garden's safety?"

"He..." Aabir sent another glance in Ezen's direction. "He's not like everyone else at Norland, Patre. I—I already told him about our house getting raided, and he told me he didn't agree with them either."

Patre raised a dubious brow. "Really? He said that?"

"Yes sir," Aabir forced as much conviction into his voice as possible, "and I believe him." The memories of Ezen's outburst last week popped back into his head. "Patre, please let him talk. I think...I think he's been dealing with something for a little while now, and I did tell him to come to me if he ever wanted to talk about it..."

Patre continued giving him the same dubious look for a few long moments, then he finally asked, "Do you trust him?"

"Yes sir."

More than your other best friends, apparently. He ground his teeth at the thought and shoved it away as Patre nodded slowly.

"Then he can come."

Aabir breathed out a sigh of relief. "Thank you."

Patre nodded again and turned to face the full force of his hardened countenance upon Ezen. He did this without saying anything until even Aabir began to feel uncomfortable. Then he spun on his heel abruptly and put his hands on Matha's and Ereliev's shoulders to steer them back to the house. Zeke joined them; Aabir's backpack slung on his shoulder.

Aabir waved his hand for Ezen to follow. "You can come, Ezen."

His friend nodded once without saying anything and stepped forward. Aabir turned, finally shut the door of the hovertaxi he came in, and followed his family towards the house. Ezen's heavy footfalls followed him as they moved through Patre's garage and into Matha's flowering garden. Patre, Zeke, and Ereliev were all heading towards the picnic table in the corner of the garden, and Aabir followed to help them move it.

"Aabir! You are in no condition to help," Matha called out.

He turned his head in her direction. "But I feel fine—"

"—I don't want to hear it." She put her hands on her hips and gave him a hard stare, "Your friend can help, but not you."

A weight landed on Aabir's shoulder, and he jerked his head to meet Ezen's eyes. "You better listen to her, Aabir," he said, a hint of a smile playing on the corner of his lips. "No one as bandaged as you should be lifting anything for a while."

Aabir twisted his lips into a frown. Did he really look that bad? But then rolled his eyes with a defeated sigh. "Fine."

Ezen patted his shoulder then went over to help. Aabir watched them lift the table and carry it along one of the garden's paths to the center of the enclosed area, before finally placing it underneath the pomen tree.

He soon found himself sitting on the bench, surrounded by his family, as they all stared at Ezen—who stood near the pomen tree's trunk looking uncomfortable underneath their combined scrutiny.

"Alright, Ezen," Aabir said, "What did you want to talk about?"

"Well, first—I'd like to say that...well, I watched what you did today, Aabir—why you got that malscar." Ezen kept his eyes lowered as he spoke, "And I—well, I'm glad you did it."

Aabir scrunched his brow and tilted his head slightly. "You...are?"

He knew Ezen had sympathized with him about his family's struggles, but he never thought his newest friend would end up agreeing with what he had done in the Constantia Tourney.

"Yeah," Ezen nodded slowly. "I think it's something that's needed to happen in the Tourney for a long time now, but no one's wanted to risk their honor in doing it—until you."

"Uh—thanks."

Ezen nodded again as he folded his arms. "But anyway—that's not why I came here." He paused, the shadowed look on his face darkening as he frowned. "I—I came to warn you, Aabir."

"Warn me?"

His heart began to pound against his numbed rib cage as Ezen finally lifted his gaze and their eyes locked. "The Emaipur knows you took their CP chip in the Constantia Stadium," his friend said. "They know that you're working as a Silvanian spy, and...and they're coming for you."

The world around Aabir seemed to stop at Ezen's words. He could only stare in wide-eyed, slack-jawed silence as he processed his friend's words. As his brain put together the pieces, all his anxieties over the secret group of pyromaniacs tightened around his chest like heavy chains.

"The—the Emaipur...?" He stuttered, as Patre asked in a hard tone next to him, "Who is coming for him? And how do *you* know all of this?"

Ezen flinched and lowered his head. "The...the Emaipur is a group of people who I used—who I used to be a...a spy for," he said. "That's how I know they're coming for you, Aabir; because I—I caught you and the cleaning lady talking a—a few times, I overheard what you both were saying, and then I...then I told them."

"What?" Patre shouted.

Ezen jerked his head up, eyes wide, as Patre stood and took a threatening step towards him.

"But—but I'm not a part of them anymore!" He cried, "In fact, they're—they're after me, too!"

It was hard for Aabir to breathe under the tension in the air.

"You...you what?" He finally asked. He stared at Ezen as if seeing him for the first time.

His friend was a spy, too? And for a bunch of pyromaniacs?

"And you came here?" Patre roared, his hands clenched into fists at his side as he took another threatening step forward

"I had to warn you!" Ezen put his hands up as if to shield himself from Patre's rising rage. "They're already after him, anyway! My being here isn't going to make matters worse, sir!"

Silence met his words. In it, Aabir was finally able to break his gaze away from Ezen to Patre's tense countenance.

"Who are the Emaipur?" Ereliev asked from behind Aabir.

He blinked and turned his gaze back onto Ezen as he processed his sister's question. "Yeah, Ezen..." His words died off and he had to clear his throat to continue, "You never answered my question. Who—who are they?"

Ezen's eyes flicked between Aabir and Patre, his arms still raised in surrender. "They're a—a secret group of people who have a vision for all the human nations of this world to become a single one," his voice took on a monotone lilt as if he was reciting something he had read, "where—where everyone is equal, and no one is labeled for where they've come from. No one is abandoned, and there are no orphans. Everyone is taken care of and valued."

"Well, that doesn't sound so bad..." Zeke said.

"But it's all a lie." Bitterness edged Ezen's tone as he lowered his fisted hands to his sides. "They say that's what they want, but—but then they go and—and kill anyone who doesn't agree with their vision, or the way they try to make it happen."

Immediately, Aabir was reminded of all the conspiracy theories he had found for Rasiela. His heart dropped into his stomach like a hard stone.

"Were...were they the ones who caused the Silvanian Fire Attacks?" He asked.

"They are." Ezen nodded, a dark glower coming over his face. "And they killed my parents."

Cold fear sent a shock through Aabir. "But I thought you said you worked for them..."

"I was told the hovercar accident they died in was caused by a faulty generator, and I believed that—until I asked you what the chances of one exploding were, and you said it wasn't common." Ezen's eyes grew glassy as his knuckles whitened. "Even then, I didn't think much of it—like you said, accidents could happen—but after they...after they got me into Norland, I was soon ordered to do something that I'd never done before. And once I did it, I started questioning if everything my superiors were telling me was true."

Ice coated Aabir's veins as Ezen's confession settled over him. A question popped into his head, and he almost did not want to ask it, but he pushed the fear of what the answer might be aside and did so anyway.

"What did you do?"

Ezen pressed his lips into a thin line. "I...was the one who programmed those training droids to...to freak out."

The images of the bloodied, wounded first-years the training droids had attacked popped into his head. Horror slithered through his icy veins, and he could not help the mirroring expression that plastered itself across his face.

"You—you did that?"

"I didn't realize that was what my superiors wanted to happen!" Ezen replied, "They—they told me the code I was given would only shut the androids down. They never told me it would make them go berserk! They didn't tell me that it'd—that it'd hurt a bunch of twelve-year-olds..."

His brown eyes locked onto Aabir's with a silent plea. "I promise I didn't want them to get hurt, Aabir. Like I said, that's when I began questioning if the...if the vision I was following was what it said it was. So, I began to dig. They'd taught me a few basic principles on how to hack, so I started searching through their files to see what they'd actually done since their conception.

"And..." Ezen's voice shook, fear darkening his gaze, "so many horrible things that've happened throughout the years were because of this group. They—they say they care about equality and everyone belonging, but the only way they'll make it happen is by killing people who they consider 'problems' and destroying entire cities in the process."

Nausea flipped Aabir's stomach. "What do you mean?"

"They're the ones who caused the Silvanian Fire Attacks, like you figured out," Ezen replied, "but they've done so much more. The second battle in Trivsau that happened? They were the ones that caused it to happen when it did."

A few memories of that horrible day—both real, and from his nightmares—flashed through Aabir's mind, but he shoved them aside as Ezen continued.

"They were also the ones who sabotaged the Constantia Prison escape attempt."

A flash of heat melted some of the icy fear in Aabir's veins. He curled his hands into fists as the wounds covering his body began to throb.

"They were?" He asked through gritted teeth.

Ezen lowered his gaze. "Yeah."

"What else?"

"A—a lot more." Ezen shook his head. "But I don't have time to explain them all. The point is..." He sighed. "I realized they weren't the utopian group I thought they were the whole time I worked for them. They came to me a few weeks after my...after my parents died and my older brother said he wouldn't take care of me. And—and they lied to me.

"My parents followed them for a while, too, but then they also ended up finding out how—how evil they were. Then someone in the Emaipur found out that my parents were going to tell the authorities everything they knew, so that's...that's why they were murdered." Ezen blew out another shaky sigh. "The Emaipur have lied to me for two years, leading me on to think I was following in my parents' footsteps—honoring them with every scrap of info I found—but now I know the truth, and I want to make up for it.

"That's why I'm telling you all of this." He lifted his gaze and looked at them all. "You're in danger. You need to leave quickly while you still can. They know about you, Aabir, and the other Silvanian spy; and they don't want you spilling any of their secrets."

"But I don't really know any of their secrets!" Aabir replied.

"After I...after I told them about seeing you meeting up with the other Silvanian spy, they didn't see you as a threat at all; but then you attacked one of their other spies in the stadium and stole his CP chip, and a target was put on your back."

Another cold shiver went down Aabir's spine, and he sent a wary glance over his shoulder at the quiet garden.

"Do you think they're coming right now?" Matha asked, her voice lilting with suppressed panic.

"...Yes." Ezen scratched the side of his neck. "I was able to hack into a string of messages that centered around you, Aabir, and I read in them how they were going to kill you once you were back home from the Tourney."

"*Kill* me?" It felt as if icy claws were squeezing Aabir's sore chest.

"That's why you need to go." Ezen stepped away from them. "I've already wasted enough time. I'll only put you in more danger if I'm here anyway, so I should be going—"

The side door leading into Patre's garage burst open, and Aabir's heart almost gave out on him as he jumped from his seat and spun to face the direction. Instead of the pyromaniacs he expected to see storming in, his eyes widened in surprise as Rasiela limped into the garden.

"Aabir!" She exclaimed as she hobbled towards them, "You all need to leave now!"

Everyone at the table stood and turned to face her at the sound of her cry. As she drew nearer, Aabir could make out the bruises puffing up her face. Their eyes locked, and he wondered for a moment if he looked as bad as she did. His itching malscar and swollen eye told him he probably looked worse.

"What happened to you?" He asked as she limped along the garden's gravel path.

"That doesn't matter right now," Rasiela came to a stop near their table. "But what does is your safety. You all need to leave—"

Her words cut off abruptly as her eyes landed in Ezen's direction. A frightening glower darkened her bruised features as she took a threatening step towards the former-Emaipur spy. "You!" She snarled, "What are you—?"

"—He came to warn us, Rasiela!" Aabir stepped between them and into the force of her glare. "He doesn't work for the Ema...Emi..."

"Emaipur," Rasiela spat.

"Right." Aabir gave her a wary nod. "He—he just told us that they're after me, and that we needed to leave."

"Y—yeah," Ezen added from behind Aabir. "So, if this is all settled, I should also go and hide, too..."

"Hold on." Patre stepped forward and sent his own glare towards Rasiela, "Are you the spy Aabir has been working for?"

"Yes." Rasiela nodded sharply.

"And this group...they're after you, too?"

"Yes, they are." Her lips pulled down into a grimace. "I actually just escaped from their base of operations here in Rubrum."

"Then if they're after us, do you know where we could hide?"

"I do—and that's why I must go with you. I went to Norland to find you before this, Aabir, and to contact the Chief. Though I didn't have much time to talk to him about what I found, he told me he watched you in the Tourney—and because of your actions he'll allow you all into Silvas."

A breath of hope lifted some of the tension in Aabir's lungs. "Really?" He could not help the small smile that lifted the corners of his lips despite the death threat he was facing.

"Yes." Rasiela's grimace turned into a smile as well. "You proved yourself more trustworthy in that moment than you would have with weeks of spy missions." Her smile faded as she turned her face towards Patre's direction. "I know this is short notice, but we need to leave now. If you must bring anything, pack only essentials. I don't know how much time we have—"

"—Wait—" Ereliev interrupted, "—we're leaving?"

"If you want to live," Rasiela replied.

Aabir turned to face the differing emotions plastered across each of his family members' faces. "I'm sorry," he said.

Patre put his hand on Aabir's shoulder and gave him a look he could not discern. "I know, Aabir, and I don't blame you for this." He turned a glare on

Ezen's hunched form, then met Aabir's eyes again. "We knew we would leave Igrium eventually, but obviously Deleyon's plans are much quicker than ours."

"But Patre..." Ereliev began.

He turned and gave her a knowing look. "We must, Ereliev." He turned in Matha's direction. "Everyone, grab only what you need so we can leave."

Matha nodded in reply and turned around to head towards the house; Yahel in her arms, and everyone—except for Aabir, Patre, and their guests—following her.

"Then, if you all are leaving, I'll get out of here, too—" Ezen began before Aabir interrupted him, "—Hold on, Ezen." He turned and looked his friend in the eye. "Come with us."

"What?" Patre and Rasiela both exclaimed.

Ezen sent him a bewildered look. "I think I should just go..."

"If you do," Aabir replied, "you may end up like your parents, and I can't let that happen."

Patre stared at him as if he was crazy. "Aabir, he just told us he's been a spy and betrayed you. We're not taking him with us."

"But if we leave him, then we'll be no worse than them." He met his patre's hard gaze. "I know what he did, but I can't leave him to be killed."

"Even if he came with us, the cause he has helped would not get him past Silvas' borders." Rasiela stated.

Aabir turned to face her flinty countenance. "But what if he told you and Chief Baene everything he found out?" He glanced over at Ezen out of the corner of his eye but could not discern what the other boy was feeling by his shadowed look. "Would that help him?"

Thoughtfulness softened Rasiela's features for a moment, then it was taken back over by her usual unreadable mask. "Will you do that?" She turned to face Ezen.

Ezen did not reply immediately, his gaze growing distant with thought. "Yes ma'am." He blinked and turned his face towards her direction with a nod. "If it helps stop them, then I'm all for it." In a lower voice, he added, "And maybe I'll finally be able to honor my parents' memory in doing so."

Rasiela stared at him for a few more moments before nodding and turning to face Patre. "If that's alright with you, Mister Sorrel," she said, "I believe it would be wise to take him."

Aabir also turned to look at him as well. Patre worked his jaw as a deep thoughtfulness glazed his eyes. Finally, he let out a deep sigh and turned a hard glare upon Rasiela, then Aabir.

"I don't like this," he said, "But since you know more about this than me, I'll trust you both. He can come with us—but if he causes any more problems, I have no qualms with throwing him out of the hovercar."

Aabir nodded gratefully. "Thank you, Patre."

Patre sighed again as he turned and moved to step around the bench. "I should go help your Matha to make sure she's not packing the entire kitchen."

"I can come help." Rasiela moved to follow him.

Patre did not argue with her, and they both soon disappeared into the house. Once they were gone, Aabir faced Ezen again and stepped towards him.

"Are you OK with leaving?" He asked.

Ezen shrugged and played with the hem of his sleeve. "It doesn't really matter. I don't have much of a choice. And this looks like the best option, so I'll go with it..." He lifted his gaze and their eyes locked. "But—why would you even want me to come along, Aabir? After everything I've done and kept from you?"

He was silent for a few moments as Tycho's words, and actions, from earlier popped into his head. "You—well, you were my friend, Ezen," Aabir finally replied with his own shrug. "How could I leave you to die if I knew I could do something to keep it from happening?"

Ezen stared at him without reply, the wind in the pomen tree's leafy branches the only sound in the garden.

Finally, he said, "Well...I don't deserve it."

Aabir sighed and folded his bandaged arms. "Neither do I," he replied quietly.

Silence followed, and in it he took one last look at his matha's garden, soaking in the bright colors and flowery smells surrounding him. Then his gaze turned to their house, and to Zeke—who was walking down the stairs with his and Aabir's backpacks slung on both his shoulders.

We're leaving Igrium. The thought had seemed impossible for so long that now that it was finally happening, he could not quite believe it. They were actually headed to Silvas; the kingdom they would be able to live in free of raids, of questionings, and of the threat of the new Tourney rule.

Yahel and Ereliev stepped out the front door and descended the stairs behind Zeke, a bag on Ereliev's shoulders and a stuffed forest cat in Yahel's arms. Nevaze was next, her pink backpack bouncing on her shoulders as she practically skipped down the stairs after them.

They would be free. He and his siblings would finally get to live in a freedom he had only ever heard his parents and Mister Falap reminisce about.

Matha, Patre, and Rasiela exited the front door, too. Matha descended the stairs with a laundry basket full of heirlooms and pictures in her hands, while Rasiela followed with a duffel bag in one of hers. Patre closed the front door and locked it before following them, a full backpack slung on his shoulder.

"Come, Aabir," Matha called to him as she stepped off the last step. "We're ready."

"Coming!" Aabir glanced over his shoulder at Ezen, who sent him a nod, before jogging through the garden one last time.

Chapter Sixty-Two

An annoyingly familiar beeping broke through the heavy fog enshrouding Tetra's brain. She let out a groan as her mind became aware of a painful throb cutting through her right side like a dull knife. With each rhythmic beep, more of the fog dissipated, and more and more of Tetra's thoughts were freed from their cloudy prison.

What happened...?

With more effort than it should have taken, she blinked her heavy eyelids open and was greeted with the bare tiles of the ceiling. She blinked some more as her brow scrunched in confusion. That didn't look like the overhead of the hovercraft...

"Private."

Tetra's heart leapt into her throat at the sudden noise, the beeps racing in tune with its rising beat. She went to sit up, but the dull knife stabbing her side turned sharp at the movement. She gritted her teeth with a hiss as her head fell back onto the pillow.

What had happened? She let out a quick exhale as the pain began to dissipate. Why did it feel like a dagger was lodged in her hip? She tried to remember, but the disappearing fog still covering some of her thoughts made it difficult.

As she lay in the tense stillness, the pain soon went back to its normal throb—and that's when she realized just how sore the rest of her body was.

"I'm sorry. I didn't mean to scare you."

Tetra opened her eyes again and turned her neck in the direction of the voice. Lieutenant Eyrie sat on a chair in the corner of the room, her features as hard as if they were set in stone.

At the sight of her C.O., Tetra began to remember the battle—and her outright disobedience to Lieutenant Eyrie's warnings. The heart rate monitor's beeping didn't slow as their eyes met.

"You've been out for quite some time." Eyrie commented with zero emotion.

Tetra swallowed and dared to ask, "Um...I—I have?" Her voice cracked from disuse, and she cleared her throat with another swallow.

"Yes. Two days."

Tetra's eyes widened, her side beginning to throb again. What could have happened that would take her out for two days? The last time she had done the same was when her leg had been caught in barbed wire during her escape in Trivsau; and judging by the pain arcing through her side, she had a feeling something else similar had happened...

"Ma'am—uh...if I may ask: why?"

Something about Lieutenant Eyrie's features sharpened, and it sent the heart rate monitor into another beeping frenzy. "A hovercraft bolt hit your leg." Her tone grew sharper with each word she spoke, "An eight-meter-long, metal bolt struck the side of your peryton leg and stayed there as you flew back to camp then plummeted from the air."

She paused, and the memories of those last few moments came back to Tetra's mind. Her side throbbed sharply as if to help her relive the worst pain she had felt then.

Anger glimmered in Lieutenant Eyrie's eyes as she continued, "And part of it was still found sticking out of you even after you crashed outside the camp and were found—not as a peryton—but as *you*."

Oh. Tetra shivered as dread sent a chill through her muscles. *Oh no.*

It must've shown on her face because Lieutenant Eyrie nodded slowly, a muscle in her jaw ticking. "Exactly," she said. "Silvas' 'secret' peryton project is no longer a secret, Private. Now everyone knows."

Tetra could no longer handle her commanding officer's piercing glare, so she turned her neck to look back up at the ceiling. Invisible chains tightened around her middle like a noose as the implications of Eyrie's words hit her like another bolt. Everyone knew—and it was all her fault.

"Lieutenant Eyrie—ma'am...I'm—I'm sorry..."

"You should have obeyed me, Tetra!" Eyrie's voice rose from its contained volume, "You and I both knew it would be risky to take out one hovercraft with your failing strength—yet you willfully went against my suggestion and did all three! We may have won the battle, yes, but we almost lost our peryton in the process! And you are far too valuable to lose.

"Yet because of your foolish choice, you ended up losing so much blood you almost *died*! And even after you were miraculously brought back from death's door, General Taoghn ordered you to be brought back here to Urbselva because our field doctors didn't have the equipment to fix your leg." She gestured to the hospital room around them, "And even with you here, you almost lost it anyway."

Tetra flinched at the verbal blow but kept quiet as Lieutenant Eyrie continued.

"I thought you left your days of disobedience behind at Norland...so why did you decide to disregard my proposal?"

She barely turned her head and met Eyrie's cold, questioning glare. "I...I didn't want to disobey you, ma'am." The oppressive guilt she was feeling now for doing so almost didn't seem worth it... "But I had too."

Eyrie's expression didn't change. "Why?"

"Because I...well, it's like you told me before: I joined the army to—to help protect people from Igrium, and to help free those who are under its oppression." She licked her lips. "And I—I knew that...well, I swore to give my all to protect Silvas, and I knew that if I didn't take out those other two hovercraft, I wouldn't be fulfilling that. I'm just one person, and...and I know I'm the only peryton any army has ever had, but I figured that even if I did die I would be saving thousands of others. And that...that seemed like a better trade than having one peryton."

"One peryton who could turn the tide of this war and save billions."

The noose tightened, and Tetra found it hard to inhale another breath. "I—I didn't think about it like that at the time..."

"That's because you went with what *you* thought was best instead of listening to me—your commanding officer." Lieutenant Eyrie shook her head with a sigh. "I've been doing this for years, Private, and though I'm not perfect at it, I do know when those under my command are in danger—and you were already lagging even before that order was given."

Their eyes met again. "I know how appealing the thought of saving thousands of lives is, but you must remember that—as your C.O.—I'm not only thinking about this one battle. I have to account for the countless others you will fight in, and the changes you could possibly bring into them. And because of that, I'm the one who decides if the risk is worth it or not—and I still don't believe it was at that moment.

"What you did was foolish. You're the only person who has this ability, Tetra, and the only one who could possibly remember how you have it. This war is not the only one riding on your shoulders—the possibility of more being won in the future might only be able to happen because you may remember how your patre was able to create it in the first place!"

Tetra averted her gaze so her C.O. wouldn't see that she actually *did* remember how she could. "Yes ma'am.".

Even so, something must've shown in her tone because her C.O. added, "Even if it's not what you want, this is the fate you've been given. And with it, you at least have the chance to help change warfare in the future—or to even stop wars like this one from ever starting in the first place."

The weight upon Tetra's chest grew heavier as she related those words with the truth of her identity. With imperial Ignis blood running through her veins, she truly would have power to stop wars—to keep the possible deaths of hundreds of thousands of people from happening—but even that nice thought didn't make the weight of her future decision any easier to hold.

"So, with that in mind, I want you to remember all of this the next time you think of making a decision that goes against your orders," Lieutenant Eyrie commanded. "Understood?"

"Yes ma'am." Tetra flicked her gaze to the ceiling then back onto Lieutenant Eyrie. "What—what's my punishment going to be, ma'am?"

"I believe the wound that bolt shard gave you will be a good reminder of what happens when you don't take my professional advice, so I'm not going to punish you—this time." She frowned. "The doctors did the best they could in fixing it without having to use cybernetics, but they said you may limp the rest of your life because of the damage done to your hip."

Tetra couldn't stand her commanding officer's piercing gaze anymore and averted her eyes again, shame roiling through her insides.

"Yes ma'am," she replied. "Thank you."

Lieutenant Eyrie nodded sharply. "Then I'll leave you to rest, Private." She stood from her chair, and as she did so she added, "Oh, yes—I also was to tell you that once you're given the clear to leave, the nobility and our allies have called for a meeting regarding you, the 'Igrian girl that can turn into a peryton'."

Tetra's heart leapt anxiously. "Why do they want me there?"

"I assume it's to answer any questions they may have for you."

Tetra nodded slowly, her imagination beginning to weave images of her standing in front of hundreds of powerful people as they all questioned her in a similar manner to Lord Wenyan's comments.

"But there is nothing about it that needs to worry you." Lieutenant Eyrie gave her an understanding look. "The Buleutcil will not let anything happen to you, and—from what I have heard—many in the nobility are only curious about your ability. No harm will come to you through this, Private."

"Yes ma'am."

She grabbed hold of that promise and tried to use it to help dispel her anxious imaginings. It helped—a little.

"Now then, I've said all I must and will leave you." Eyrie dipped her chin in a small nod. "Good diem, Private."

Even lying down, Tetra lifted her fist and put it to her chest in salute. "First Lieutenant, ma'am."

With that, her commanding officer spun on her heel and left the room. Once the door clicked shut and she was alone, Tetra gritted her teeth against the pain in her side and pushed herself into a sitting position.

When the sharp knife in her hip dulled again, she went to lift her blanket, but her attention was drawn to the bruises covering her arms. She stared at all the sore splotches in confusion, until she remembered what Lieutenant Eyrie had said about her plummeting to the ground. She couldn't help but wince at the thought and was again glad that peryton bones were so strong.

Tetra blinked and turned her attention back to the blanket she clutched in her hands. With a deep, steadying breath, she lifted it off her legs as gently as possible and put it to the side. Her eyes locked onto the bandage cocooning her right thigh...again. She frowned and lightly touched the bandages, but there was no pain at the touch like there would've been with her wound back in Xich.

So, either this time wasn't that bad, or she was on more pain medication than had been given her there. And if Lieutenant Eyrie's words were true, then it was probably the latter. She moved her hand and touched her hip—and was greeted with a sharp pain as if she had stabbed a knife to it instead of placing her fingers atop it. She jerked her hand away with a wince.

The pain dissipated again, and she slowly laid back down now that her curiosity was satisfied. Once her head hit the pillow and her eyes closed, she began to recall the flashes of memory from the battle. The sights, the sounds, the smells...

She ground her teeth as her mind replayed the first hovercraft's explosion, and an arrow of guilt stabbed her heart. So many people were now dead because of her...

Emperor Ignis now knew of her hatred towards him, but at what cost? Tetra squeezed her closed eyes tighter and lifted her sore arms to press her fingertips against the sides of her forehead—as if it would stop the bloody memories and the accusations.

An image of her charging through Igrium's ranks flashed in her mind. It was followed by the memory of the awful, burning smell of the downed hovercraft, the pungent fear-scent as she destroyed that first crossbow, and the images of the fear she had seen in some of the Igrian soldiers' eyes right before she attacked them...

A piercing pain stabbed through her side as she tried curling her legs up. She held her breath as she moved them back into their uncomfortably-straight position, and only let herself breathe when the pain dissipated for its low throb. Why did the world seem to have a grudge against her leg?

Her self-pity didn't last, however, as chains of guilt once again tightened their hold on her lungs and racing heart with the shameful truth. If she had just obeyed, than she might be in a far better place right now—with no limp, and no one else knowing the truth of her peryton-shifting ability.

He was right... she thought, her throat tightening as she remembered her last meeting with Emperor Ignis, *I really am a disgrace...*

The walls of her mental stronghold finally fell as childhood memories she could now recall came rushing in with the recollections of the battle.

The memory of Emperor Ignis telling Tetra he couldn't take care of her reopened the ache in her pounding heart. It was followed by an image of a flaming crossbow bolt hurtling towards her. Then she remembered one of the burning hovercars she had rammed into, and a shiver went through her muscles as she recalled the burning odor coming from its remains.

"No wonder your patre gave you up. Not even he *could stand to be related to a monster like you..."*

A sob rose up inside her, and she let it out. More memories and feelings flew through her head like leaves in an unstoppable windstorm; battering her with guilt and shame that sliced through her like segione blades.

"Tetra?"

Tetra's heart leapt in surprise at the familiar accent. She blinked her blurry eyes open to clear them of her tears with a sniff. Felicita's worried face came into focus, and she immediately felt the wet tear tracks on her face as she noticed Aunt Minda and Matias also standing near the room's door.

"Is your hip hurting?" Felicita continued, "Do we need ta call a doctor...?"

"Um—no, no." Tetra cleared her throat and swallowed back the lump lodged in it. "I'm—it's nothing."

"...Liar, liar..."

Tetra exhaled sharply through her nose. "My hip hurts, but I'll be fine," she added. "You don't need to call anyone."

Felicita's large eyes narrowed slightly, but she nodded. "If you say so."

"Oh, Anora..." Aunt Minda stepped over next to Felicita and bent down to give Tetra a hug. Tetra received it without complaint, though she couldn't help wincing as the movement caused more pain in her hip. Her aunt didn't notice, however, as she straightened back up. "I'm so glad tha' you're safe."

"Yes, praise Deleyon," Felicita added. "We watched some o' the live footage on the news and saw some o' what you did."

Tetra's stomach flipped. "You did?"

A shiver of fear went through her, and the heart rate monitors' annoying beeping heightened in that moment. What did they think of her actions?

"We did," Aunt Minda met her eyes, and Tetra noticed unshed tears in her glassy gaze, "and then we saw how tha' bolt struck you, and I thought..." her voice warbled, "well I thought..."

"We're just happy ta 'ave you back with us." Felicita finished with a soft smile.

Aunt Minda nodded, pressing her fingers against her eyes. "Very much so."

Matias stepped up next to Felicita, and Tetra turned her gaze over to meet his. The harsh lines in his face softened a little as he sent her an understanding nod.

"You did well, Tetra," he said. "Xich is free now because of our victory—and part of that can be attributed to your actions. So, thank you for all you did."

Tetra blinked as a soft wave of warmth filled her aching chest. "Uh—you're welcome..."

Well, that hadn't been something she thought would've come up in this conversation, but she was happier for it than her simple response said.

Matias only nodded again in reply.

"And though I didn't readily agree with you joinin' the army at first," Felicita said, "with the videos o' the celebrations I've seen happenin' in Xich since we won, I'm now beginnin' ta realize tha' my original opinion was much more selfish than I thought. So I want ta apologize ta you, Tetra, for anythin' I might've said ta try ta guilt-trip you out o' doing it."

More warmth loosened some of the tightness around her chest. "It's fine, Felicita," she replied with a small smile. "I understood where you were coming from, and I never held it against you."

"Thank you." Felicita's smile widened as tears filled her brown gaze. "I—I truly am proud o' you, and I want you ta know tha'..." She paused for a moment, her brow creasing in thoughtfulness, "Well, tha' if anyone tries ta say anythin' against you in this upcomin' meetin', you only need ta remind them tha' your actions helped seal our victory in Xich. But even if you don't, then I will."

"You'll be there, too?"

"Yeah—as Chief Baene's assistant, o' course."

The thought of having her cousin at the meeting helped ease a little more of her anxieties over it. "Well, I'm glad you'll be there," she said.

Felicita's smile brightened as she nodded. "Me too. Although even if I wasn't goin', you would 'ave nothin' ta worry about. Chief Baene told me tha' since we won the battle—and now tha' everyone knows you're the peryton who fought for us in it—many o' the nobility 'ave decided ta let go o' some o' their prejudice against the Cairn name long enough ta hear your comments at this meetin'."

Tetra gave her a dubious look. "They have?"

"Not all o' them, o' course." Shadows stole the brightness of Felicita's smile for a moment, but then it returned as she added, "But I'd say around half o' them, yeah."

Well, around half seemed better than none—especially if she was about to face them all.

"Thanks for telling me."

"O' course."

There was a pause. And in it, Aunt Minda sent Felicita a significant look. Then her aunt turned her eyes back upon Tetra with a soft smile.

"We were told not ta keep you long," she said, "so we'll leave you ta rest—but I promise we'll visit you again tomorrow."

She bent down and gave Tetra another hug, albeit much more gently this time. When she straightened, Tetra almost asked them to stay longer, but a slight fog had settled into her brain again without her noticing until that moment. So, she nodded.

"Thanks for coming."

Felicita smiled and their eyes met one last time before Matias steered her away towards the door. Aunt Minda sent Tetra a loving look, and then she, too, turned and followed them. The door shut behind them, and Tetra closed her eyes with a sigh in the silence they left.

Relief swept through her as the fact she wasn't going to be facing this meeting alone settled over her clouding mind. She quietly thanked the gods who had listened to her earlier pleas that she now had a cousin who happened to be Chief Baene's assistant.

Yet even with the growing brain-fog, a new doubt tore through it like a spear: would having Felicita there actually help? How much could Chief Baene's assistant really do against the hatred of powerful people like Lord Wenyan or the other half of the nobility that weren't willing to give up their prejudice against the Cairns'?

Tetra shook her head to try and shake those rising fears out of her foggy mind. Felicita had seemed hopeful about the situation; and Lieutenant Eyrie did, too. They were two of the few people Tetra had come to trust in her life, and she knew neither of them would lie to her about something like this.

Yet even as she had that thought, she was reminded of when her cousin had kept Chief Baene's imperial plans a secret from her—for over a month. A small bit of hurt pricked Tetra, but it didn't last long as she remembered her cousin's promise to give her warnings if anything else of utmost importance was to come up—which she had just done.

Her thought process slowed as the fog thickened, but it didn't stop a few more doubtful questions from arising. Even with all the answers she might give in this Alliance meeting, would they be enough to satisfy those listening? Or would they all continue to see her as only the supposed monstrous-peryton-child of the Cairns? Could her actions in the battle be used against her by someone like Lord Wenyan to tell everyone she was too dangerous to keep around?

Tetra clutched the blanket in her fists, forcing herself to try and see as logically as possible through the fog and doubt. Despite her own conflicting feelings on the way she fought as a peryton, Matias had said she did well in the battle—and he was a first lieutenant in Silvas' army, just like his sister!

And she couldn't deny the fact that Xich was now celebrating because the battle had been won. A tired smile lifted the corners of her lips as she imagined Stellinga dancing and feasting with her parents. They were finally free from Igrium's tyranny after having lived under the threat of it for over a year. And Tetra had helped to bring that about.

Plus, her fighting for the Alliance seemed to have helped open the minds of some of those in the nobility—even though she still publicly carried the name "Cairn". She might never walk without a limp again, but if what she had done could help her controversial image in Silvas' eyes, then it might be worth it.

However, now that she knew what Chief Baene wanted to do regarding Igrium's future, it might not matter how the populace of Silvas saw her. If she did agree to his plans, and they did end up succeeding in this war, then she would be leaving to live in Rubrum again and none of their hateful opinions would be able to change that fact.

If she agreed...

Tetra couldn't pull up the brainpower to think on that heavy subject any longer. A soothing darkness blanketed all her warring thoughts as she was pulled back into a dreamless sleep once again.

Chapter Sixty-Three

Rubrum's skyline of towering skyscrapers and protective walls grew smaller and smaller until it completely disappeared behind the Sorrel's packed hovercar. Only miles of lofty forests and tilled fields surrounded the freeway Patre was speeding on, and a strange pang stabbed Aabir's heart as he realized this would be the last time he would see them.

He had no time to dwell on that, however, as Ezen's elbow hit his side, and a starburst of pain exploded from his cracked ribs. He hissed sharply through his teeth and held his breath.

"I'm so sorry, Aabir!" Ezen exclaimed, "I didn't mean to do that."

Aabir didn't reply immediately as he waited for the painkillers to once again numb the pain back into a dull ache.

When he could finally pull air back into his lungs, he replied, "It's OK."

He turned his neck and noticed Ezen had pressed himself against Rasiela's rigid form, his eyes staring at Aabir as if he would break right in front of him. Had his outburst really been that pitiful?

"Really, Ezen, it's OK," he added. "I'm fine."

Ezen stared at him for another moment, then nodded slowly and moved back into his original position on the car's bench. Aabir caught the relief that flashed across Rasiela's features as he did so, and he choked back a laugh before it could escape. She sent a side-eye glance towards Ezen, then turned her head back in the direction of Yahel's car seat that sat next to her on the bench.

"The...cat...sat...in...the...tree," Yahel sounded out from the open chardex on her lap.

"Very good." Rasiela nodded, a smile in her voice.

Yahel beamed up at their guest, then immediately returned her attention back to the simple words. "The...fish...flew...in...the..."

Aabir turned his head in the other direction to stare out the window as his youngest sister continued. More trees and fields blurred past, giving his mind the perfect opportunity to wander.

We're leaving. Of all the impossible things... They were really leaving! When he had stepped into the arena that morning, he never even thought this would come from it. Maybe more trust would have been built, yes—but not something as miraculous as this.

He lifted his hand to touch the wounded side of his face, but then stopped himself before actually doing it. His earlier shame for the dishonorable scar had slowly been taken over by an excitable anticipation with each minute they rode towards the destination Rasiela told Patre to drive to (an abandoned mining town Aabir had never heard of before called "Fugerio").

They were heading to Silvas! To freedom.

He glanced down at his wrist to check the time and was immediately reminded that his holonode was gone as he stared at his bare skin. He twisted his lips into a frown and lifted his head back towards the tinted window. Rasiela forced them to leave all their holonodes and any other devices, besides Yahel's chardex, they had back at their house to keep them safe from the possibility of someone tracking them.

It had bothered Aabir at first—the small device was practically part of him since he had worn it for so many years—but Rasiela had promised them all that Chief Baene would provide new holonodes for them once they reached Urbselva, so he quickly forgot about not having it. Until now, that is.

He rolled his eyes at himself and turned his focus back on the blurred view outside. Hopefully, they would be provided with everything else they had lost. Rasiela never mentioned a house being given with the new holonodes, but Aabir tried to ignore the worry that his actions might have only thrown his family into homelessness once they made it to Silvas. He did not know much about Chief Baene, but if the man was willing to risk helping Aabir's family get out of Igrium, then he doubted the chief advisor would just leave them to live out on the streets.

As his thoughts spiraled from that, Aabir found himself glancing back down at his bare wrist with the intention of sending a message to Tycho and Aquilo about what was going on. The nauseating shame from before rose back up into his stomach at the thought, and it was immediately followed by the same pang in his heart from earlier—only this time it was sharper.

They were leaving and entering freedom, yes, but he would never see his friends again. And since he was forever considered a dishonor in Igrium—who would now be living in the enemy kingdom—he doubted they would try to message or call him. Even if there was the possibility that they themselves did not think of him as a straudwin coward, he doubted they would risk their reputations to contact him. He breathed out a quiet sigh through his nose and tried to turn his mind onto other things, but each beat of his heart only reminded him of the ache inside it.

His frown deepened and he turned his gaze away from the window, glancing out of the corner of his eye at Ezen. The expressionless mask Ezen wore as he looked out the front windshield told Aabir nothing about what he was feeling. Was his newest friend sharing the same feelings as him? Aabir knew his parents had died, but he still had at least one brother who lived here, so did he miss him? Was what they were doing hitting him the same way it was now beginning to hit Aabir?

Should he even consider Ezen his friend anymore?

Aabir lowered his gaze to the bandages wrapped around his arms. He still had not processed the fact that the guy who he called his friend—whom he had shared a dorm with, and whom he had trusted enough to share the knowledge of his family's predicaments with even before he ever did with Aquilo and Tycho—had been a spy for the same group of pyromaniacs Aabir had been researching, and worrying, about.

If Aabir had not been involved with spywork himself, he knew he would have been furious at Ezen—enough to possibly leave him in Rubrum to die. But from what Ezen had said, the Emaipur preyed on him when his parents died, and his brother rejected him. Aabir knew what it was like to be that desperate. The Emaipur's false vision of grandeur would have attracted him, too, if he had been in Ezen's boots—just like Rasiela's offer of help did.

He lifted his elbow and placed it on the handle of the door before leaning his forehead against his hand. It was all so confusing...

He barely turned his neck and sent another side-eye glance in Ezen's direction. Though he could find some ways to sympathize with Ezen, how could he ever trust him again? Was anything he knew about his former friend real?

"Uh, Patre..." Ereliev piped up from the back row, "Where are we going?"

Aabir blinked and turned his head to stare at her in confusion, then looked back out the window to see what she was talking about. Patre had turned off onto the exit they always used when going to Mister Falap's.

"This isn't the right way." Aabir looked over at the guarded look Rasiela wore. "We need to stay on the freeway if we intend to get there by tomorrow..."

"I know, Miss Rasiela," Patre replied, "but we need to make one stop before continuing on. It's a very important one."

"Are—are we goin' to see—to see gran-patre?" Yahel asked.

Matha turned around in the passenger's seat to face her. "We are." She smiled.

Ezen's eyes widened, fear darkening the few lines in his face. Both he and Rasiela looked like they wanted to argue, but only Rasiela opened her mouth to do so, "This isn't wise." Aabir's heart skipped a fearful beat as her guarded gaze met his matha's eyes. "We don't know how far behind us the Emaipur is, and each stop we make exposes us more to the possibility of attack."

Matha stared at her with an equally hard gaze. "I will not be leaving Igrium until I say good-bye to Mister Falap. This won't take long," she replied in what

Aabir recognized as her 'do not argue with me tone'. "Plus, we can get more food and other necessities from him that we didn't grab back at the house."

Aabir flicked his gaze between their cool expressions, tension rising with each quiet moment that passed between them. He wondered if a fight was about to break out between the two women—and part of him wanted to see it happen—but then Rasiela's lips dipped into a small frown.

"Fine," she finally said, "but we can't stay there long."

Matha nodded sharply and turned back around to face the front again. Aabir let out a quiet breath as some of the tension in the hovercar's atmosphere eased slightly, but he noticed it did not completely fade away as Patre continued down the familiar roads towards Mister Falap's house.

The next hour passed in a silence punctuated only by Yahel as she showed off her newfound reading skills to Rasiela. During that time, Aabir went from focusing on the familiar sights outside, to overthinking his former friendship with Ezen, and then to worrying over the pyromaniacs who might possibly be following them.

He curled his hand into a fist, wishing for the worn feel of his sword's leather hilt to fill his empty grasp. All this talk about him wanting to protect his family, but he no longer had the tools to actually do so now that their lives were truly in danger.

Oh Deleyon, help us, he pleaded silently.

"Gran-patre!"

Yahel's squeal broke through Aabir's hovertrain of thought. He blinked and turned his gaze out the window. Thousands of green plants were growing in rows behind the old fence lining Mister Falap's long driveway. He turned his neck and caught sight of the elderly man's farmhouse up ahead.

As Aabir stared at it, Matha's earlier comment about saying good-bye to their adoptive grandpatre slammed into his heart like a warhammer, bringing with it a mixture of nostalgic memories and sorrow. There would be no more weekend visits to look forward to anymore, nor would his parents' plans to stay here during the growing season happen. They were leaving Igrium, and only now did he realize that meant leaving Mister Falap, too.

They finally came upon the old farmhouse, and Patre slowed the hovercar to a stop. Matha turned around in her seat to face the back two rows.

"We only have a few minutes to spare," she met Aabir's gaze, then moved it to land on the rest of his siblings, "so we'll get everything we need before saying our goodbyes. Understand?"

A chorus of "yes ma'am"'s answered her, then Aabir opened his door and stepped out. He flipped his seat up so the rest of his siblings could follow. As he did so, he met Ezen's eyes for a moment and noticed something akin to longing had softened the shadows in them. Then the sound of a screen door being closed drew Aabir's attention behind him.

Mister Falap stepped out of the porch's shadows and onto the top stair in the sollight. Their eyes met, and the elderly man's grin faded for a look of horror. Aabir scrunched his brow in confusion for a moment, then he remembered his malscar and jerked his head down.

Sorrow and shame warred within his constricted chest as he turned his body to face the hovercar again. He gritted his teeth as a lump formed in his throat. Stupid malscar. He loved Mister Falap, but the elderly man *was* a full-blooded Igrian and might not think highly of the dishonorable symbol—no matter what he formerly thought of Aabir.

The porch stairs creaked behind him as his siblings began filing out of the back of the car. Matha shut the passenger-side door and her footsteps moved towards the stairs.

"We...we're leaving, Mister Falap," she said in a warbling voice. "Something has happened, and—and if we don't go now then our lives might be at stake. But we have a way of getting out of Igrium, so you don't need to be worried about us. I know—"

"—You don't have to explain, Zerah," Mister Falap replied. "I knew this day would come."

Matha's low sobs sounded behind Aabir as he watched Nevaze get out of the car. When she did, he put his seat back down so Ezen could slide out. The other boy did so with a nod before looking away, his hands in the pockets of the Norland uniform he still wore.

Aabir slammed the door shut and turned around without lifting his face towards the hugging, farewelling group only a few steps away from him. He wanted to join them, but the look on Mister Falap's face stayed firmly fixed in his mind's eye, so he let the weight of his shame keep him rooted to the spot.

Less than a minute passed, then he heard Patre and Matha giving orders to everyone on what they needed to get in Mister Falap's house as a pair of soft footsteps came towards him. Everyone, including Ezen and Rasiela, headed inside right after. He was about to follow when a light weight landed on his shoulder. He jerked his head up in surprise and met Mister Falap's apologetic gaze.

"I'm sorry, Aabir," the elderly man said, "I didn't mean to make you feel ashamed. I've just...I've never seen a malscar in real life before, and I never thought I'd see one on you."

Aabir shrugged and looked away. "It's OK."

"No, it's not." Mister Falap paused with a heavy sigh before continuing, "I watched the Tourney this week for the first time in years because I knew you were competing, and in all the years of my life I've never seen anyone do anything like what you did in them. Trying to free that other boy from the peryton? Calling for that mercy rule? It was different—but I believe it was also needed." He paused again. "Aabir, look at me."

Aabir lifted his chin and blinked in surprise at the unshed tears in Mister Falap's blue eyes. "You did what so many of us full-blooded Igrians have kept silent about for too long: you stood up against the dishonoring bloodshed happening in the Tourney—and I doubt I was the only one who was stirred." The corner of his grandpatre's lips lifted in a small smile. "I never thought I'd say this, but you should be proud of that scar, Aabir. It shows there are still people in this empire who will actually stand up for what's right."

A tear slipped down his wrinkled face as he added, "I'm proud of you."

Aabir blinked in dumbfounded silence for a moment as he processed the words, then he reached over and grabbed the elderly man in a hug. Mister Falap wrapped his thin arms around him as well and patted his back gently. Aabir's broken ribs cried in annoyance, but he ignored their pleas as the worry and shame he felt only moments before was burnt up in a soothing warmth that blanketed his beaten insides.

They soon let go, but Mister Falap kept his free hand on one of Aabir's shoulders and looked him square in the eye again. "You're a good man, Aabir," he said, "and Silvas should be honored to have you as one of their citizens."

Aabir sniffed with a smile that hurt his sore, wounded face. "Thanks, Mister Falap."

Mister Falap nodded with his own bright smile. "If you keep doing what you did in that arena, then nothing this world throws at you will be able to stop you. Courage like yours has the chance to spread quite easily, so don't stop once you get to Silvas. Keep standing up for what's right—but don't let the weight of all the world's problems unbalance you."

"Yes sir." Aabir dipped his chin.

The screen door burst open, and Mister Falap turned around as Nevaze came clomping down the steps with a large, and full, paper bag in her arms. Aabir stepped around Mister Falap and headed towards her.

"Need help?" He asked.

Her large eyes met his. "Matha wanted me to tell you that if you want any pain medicine then you need to go get it."

Aabir rubbed his hand against his bandaged arm and glanced back at Mister Falap. Before he could open his mouth to ask, the elderly man gave him an understanding nod.

"The medicine can be found in the corner cabinet in the kitchen," he said. "You can take whatever you need. I can always get more at the store."

Aabir smiled in relief. "Thank you." Then he turned and headed towards the house.

It did not take him long to find the cabinet in the kitchen—Rasiela was already there wrapping her fingers in a homemade splint. He could not help but stare at their puffy, bruised condition; and a shiver snaked down his spine as he wondered what all the Silvanian spy had been through in the Emaipur base. She lifted her head and their eyes locked.

He could tell by the tightness of her features that she was in a lot of pain, but she said nothing about it as she dipped her head towards the open cabinet next to her.

"We need to take everything we can. We should reach Fugerio sometime tomorrow, but I want to be prepared in case anything happens."

Another cold shiver raised chill bumps along Aabir's arms at the thought of anything delaying their escape, but he did not voice his worries as he nodded in reply. Rasiela went back to wrapping her hand as he stepped over and rummaged through the sparse medicine cabinet, putting everything he thought they might need into a plastic bag he found.

When he finished, he closed the cabinet and walked back out of the farmhouse. Ezen and Rasiela were both packing the extra supplies they had taken into the very back of the car while Matha, Patre, and all his siblings were saying their final goodbyes to Mister Falap. Aabir descended the porch stairs one last time and headed towards them.

Matha turned her tear-streaked face towards him. "Did you find everything?" She sniffed and rubbed her reddened eyes.

"Yes ma'am." Aabir lifted the full bag in his hand then lowered it as he came to a stop near the small group.

"Good-bye, Ereliev." The elderly man hugged Ereliev, and she squeezed him back.

"Bye, Mister Falap," she replied, her voice hitching on the last syllable.

They let go, and then he lowered to hug Nevaze and Yahel both. "I'll miss you two," he told them with a smile that deepened the wrinkles on his face.

Nevaze only cried in response as Yahel said, "I miss you, gran-patre, but maybe—but maybe we'll see you again."

Mister Falap let them go and mussed Yahel's curly hair. "Maybe so, Yahel." Then he straightened and looked over towards Patre. "Where's the gift I asked you to get, Elnim?"

"I put it on the swing." Patre nodded and headed back up towards the porch. "I'll get it."

"Thank you." Mister Falap nodded, then stepped over towards Aabir. Their eyes met, and Aabir had to swallow back the lump rising in his throat before he could speak.

"Bye, Mister Falap," he said. "Thank you for...well, thanks for everything."

"Of course." Mister Falap leaned on his cane with a sad smile. "But I have one more thing to give to you, Aabir. It's nothing fancy, but I know you'll find more use out of it than I ever did."

A rush of excitement buzzed through Aabir as he heard Patre's footsteps coming up behind him. He turned around, and the feeling doubled as his eyes landed on the longsword that was always hanging above Mister Falap's fireplace mantle—now sheathed in Patre's hands.

"That was my patre's sword." Aabir halfway turned back in Mister Falap's direction as the elderly man spoke, "He bought it back when I was around Nevaze's age, then gave it to me before he died. And now I want you to have it."

Aabir's heart leapt as he glanced back over at the sheathed sword Patre held out towards him. "But Mister Falap," he met his grandpatre's eyes, "I—I can't take this..."

"I want you to, Aabir." Mister Falap gave him a firm nod. "It's never been used before, and I doubt it ever will if you don't take it. You're the only person I know who can use it—and who will do so for the right reasons. So please take it. If you don't, it'll only gather dust."

"Take it." Patre lifted it towards him.

Aabir did not have to be told twice. He picked up the sheathed sword in both his hands, then grabbed the leather-wrapped hilt and pulled it out. His heart gave another happy leap at the sweet sound of ringing metal.

Sollight glinted off its beautiful, silvery-furrum blade as he turned it around to inspect both sides. It was of a similar size and weight to the one he had left back at Norland, and he could not help the smile that lifted the corners of his lips.

"Thank you, Mister Falap." He sheathed the blade and looked the elderly man in the eyes. "I'll try to use it only as Deleyon wills."

"I'm sure you will." Mister Falap matched his smile, then turned around to gaze at them all. "Now y'all best be going," his drawl thickened with suppressed emotion. "You have a long trip ahead, and I don't want to keep you any longer."

Aabir tightened his grip on the sword as he met Mister Falap's blue gaze one last time.

"I love y'all." Their adoptive grandpatre's smile turned watery.

"We love you." Matha sniffed with her own teary smile, then she spun around and headed towards the hovercar with Yahel and Nevaze trailing along behind her.

Aabir blinked his stinging eyes as he turned and followed them. Rasiela and Ezen were already waiting in the car as the Sorrel family filed back into it. Aabir placed his new sword upright between his knees, then turned his neck and took in the sight of Mister Falap and the old, blue farmhouse one last time.

The hovercar started up and Mister Falap raised his arm in a wave as they drove off. Aabir's chest tightened as Patre turned the car back onto the driveway and the view disappeared from his window. He sniffed and turned his blurry gaze onto the sword in front of him.

"I'm sorry, Aabir," Ezen said quietly beside him.

Aabir did not turn his gaze from the sheath. "I know."

As Mister Falap's fields passed them by for the final time, the weight of everything they were losing finally hit Aabir. He turned his face towards the window and let the silent tears fall as the memories of his friends and Mister Falap flowed through his thoughts.

Chapter Sixty-Four

A MULTITUDE OF MUFFLED voices drifted into the hallway outside the Altelo's council chamber. Lieutenant Eyrie walked a couple feet ahead of Tetra as they came to a stop in front of the hall's lofty doors. Thin, golden lines embellished the carved scenes depicted in the dark wood of the door, and Tetra let her gaze rove over the many pictures as guardsmen opened them.

Her eyes landed on a scene of a warrior mounted on a six-legged equia, their spear planted in the heart of a peryton. Foreboding slithered down her spine despite all the assurances her family and Lieutenant Eyrie had given her concerning this meeting the past week. She tightened her grip on the handles of her crutches as the doors groaned to a stop before following Lieutenant Eyrie's calm countenance into the chamber.

Immediately, her ears were accosted with the many voices that bounced around the hall's high, domed ceiling. She lifted her neck and stared, wide-eyed, at the rows upon rows of finely dressed people who filled the seats that had been empty the first time she visited. Her heart rate increased with each limping step that drew her closer to the center of the room—and to the center of all these people's attentions.

A spike of fear stabbed her racing heart. How was she going to speak to them all? Would they really listen to her? Or would she end up in as bad a predicament as that peryton on the door?

Tetra shook her head at herself and tried to ignore the thoughts, but she couldn't stop the shivers coursing through her veins they set off. Lieutenant Eyrie stepped into the center of the round room and came to a stand. The Buleutcil members conversing around their u-shaped table stopped and turned to face her—then the force of their gazes landed on Tetra. She picked up her limping pace under their scrutiny, wincing as invisible needles stabbed her hip bone, and came to a stop next to her C.O.

"Lieutenant Eyrie." Chief Baene stepped forward from the table and nodded towards them both. "Private Cairn."

Tetra bowed her head towards him in Silvas' customary fashion, her thoughts converging for a moment onto the decision she had finally made he had yet to ask her about. She lifted her head and met his eyes for a moment. There was a question in their bright purplish-blue depths, but he blinked and turned as Lord Jachen's tall stature stepped up beside him.

"I'm glad to see you doing better, Private," Lord Jachen barely dipped his pointy chin towards her. "Many of us were worried when we watched you get hit by that crossbow bolt."

Tetra became more aware of Lieutenant Eyrie's presence beside her as she dipped her head towards the Silvanian Steward.

"Thank you, Lord Jachen," she replied simply before lifting her head again.

"Ah, Tetra." She turned as Dr. Prin stepped forward; a white, flowy jumpsuit replacing the woman's usual lab coat and khakis. The Silvanian biologist stopped only a few steps from Tetra and said in a low voice, "I wrote down all of the data you gave me during your meetings with Leaves Of Gold the past month, and have sent it to a few of my colleagues for them to review. Once I receive their thoughts on the matter, I'll have a few of the other Buleutcil members read over it, and then we'll be able to move on from there."

"Really?" Tetra raised her brow in surprise. "I didn't think it would happen so quickly..."

The corner of Dr. Prin's lips lifted in a small smile. "When something this big is possible, I make it a top priority to have it done in a timely fashion."

"Welcome everyone," Lord Jachen's accented voice boomed along the high ceilings, causing Tetra to jerk her neck in his direction. "If you will all return to your seats, the meeting can begin."

He stood on a small dais near the middle of the room situated in front of the u-shaped table. Once the echo of his voice died off, he sat down on a chair next to an empty, gilded throne.

"I'll see you for our next flying session in a few days, Miss Cairn." Dr. Prin nodded towards Tetra before heading to her seat.

A weight landed on Tetra's shoulder, and she stiffened under the touch before turning around to meet Lieutenant Eyrie's gaze. Confusion filled Galia's eyes, but she blinked, and it disappeared.

"This way, Private." Her commanding officer gestured towards a row of front seats that created the circumference around the room's middle, then headed in that direction.

Tetra followed as quickly as she could, chill bumps rising along her arms as the weight of hundreds of gazes followed her movements. Felicita and a couple other younger people—whom Tetra assumed were more Buleutcil assistants—sat in the same row of seats she and her C.O. were heading towards. Her cousin gave them a small smile as they both sat down—Tetra situated in the middle of them. She leaned her crutches against her knees and fixed her facial features into a collected mask before lifting her gaze in Lord Jachen's elevated direction.

"Now that we are here, let's begin," he said, "I know you all have questions—and we will try to answer as many of them as possible by this meeting's end—but first, I want to give Doctor Esthra Prin a chance to explain a few things. Doctor..."

Dr. Prin stood from her seat, open chardex in hand. "Thank you, Lord Jachen." She nodded her head respectfully in his direction, then turned to address the other hundreds of people surrounding them. "I have been heading up the study of Private Cairn's ability to turn into a peryton, and I want you all to know that we have not yet figured out how she does it."

Murmurs and sharp whispers met her words. Tetra glanced over at Felicita out of the corner of her eye, guilt pricking her conscience. They both knew how she was able to do it...

"You don't know?" A singsong, Pon-Yelish voice spoke up above the murmurings.

Tetra turned her neck and noticed the row of Pon-Yelish officials sitting almost opposite her on the middle's circumference. One woman with braids as long as Felicita's stared directly at Dr. Prin, and even from a distance Tetra could see her eyebrow was raised incredulously.

Dr. Prin turned to face the woman and replied, "No, we don't."

"Then how come it was decided that she be put into battle—where she almost died—before the chances of duplication were found?" The Pon-Yelish woman asked.

"I was not in favor of that decision," Dr. Prin's tone stayed even as she responded, "but many of my fellow Buleutcil members were not happy with my team's slow progress, so they decided to go on and offer Private Cairn the choice to join our army." She paused. "However, with all the data we've already collected, I want to assure you that my team and I are still studying how Private Cairn can do this even when she isn't here—there is no time being lost with this decision. So even if something were to happen to her, we have collected enough data that there would still be the possibility of duplication in the future."

Tetra glanced over in Felicita's direction again, but her cousin—once again—didn't return the look.

She turned her head forward as the same Pon-Yelish woman asked, "And when you do find out, you will let us know how i'tis done, yes?"

"We will in accordance with what is stated in our treaties," Lord Jachen replied, the serious expression on his face daring her to argue.

"Then my superiors and I will be waitin' for the announcement." The Pon-Yelish woman nodded sharply in his direction and sat down.

"But how do we know Silvas won't try to make up an excuse to hide this finding?"

Tetra, along with everyone else in the room, looked over in the direction the Frigian accent came from. Empress Veruska Linyk's austere countenance stared coldly at Lord Jachen from a huge holovision screen hovering on one of the front rows in her empire's designated section. Army General's Aleque and Calua Avhinoe, and a couple other dignitaries—who both had the dark hair and olive skin common among Frigians—shared the row of seats with her.

The army generals' presence reminded Tetra of the strange spy she had yet to hear anything about, but that thought flitted away as the wrinkles on the Frigian empress' face deepened with her small frown as she spoke.

"This would not be the first time you have done so," the empress continued, "and it does not seem out of the question for it to happen again with something as important as this."

"Silvas follows its treaties to the letter and has not broken one of them since this war began." Chief Baene stood from his seat and sent a challenging stare in the direction of the empress' screen. "We cannot help that the production rates of our mines have been slower than normal."

Empress Veruska's frown darkened, but she did not reply immediately. Instead, she turned that same cold look upon Tetra. Even with her presence only accounting to a screen, a shiver went through her muscles as she met the woman's gray eyes. They reminded her a little too much of Emperor Ignis' dark, probing gaze.

"Then I have a question for *you*, Private Cairn," the empress said. "If you are the one who has this ability, then how come you have not told anyone the reason you have it?"

Tetra's heart leapt into her throat as her mind scrambled to come up with an excuse that wasn't the truth. But as she did, she was immediately reminded of a few of her failed attempts at lying in front of Emperor Ignis and stopped that hovertrain of thought. She couldn't tell them the truth, but she couldn't stand there and say nothing, either—then they really would know she was hiding something.

The weight of everyone's attention upon her grew heavier and heavier with each heartbeat. She almost looked over in Felicita's direction for help, but then stopped herself before doing so. That would look as suspicious as staying silent would. But what was she supposed to say—

"Private Cairn suffers from amnesia due to an old head injury that happened during the burning of her parents' house," Dr. Prin's voice had never sounded so wonderful to Tetra's ears as at that moment, "so she isn't able to remember many things from before—including this matter. But she has been going through a series of tests that—I have been told—have helped her to engage some of those forgotten memories."

Empress Veruska's icy gaze landed back on Tetra as Dr. Prin's words died away in the thick silence that had settled over the rest of the room.

"And is that the truth, Private Cairn?" Her heavy accent deepened as she spoke, "Were you truly hit on the head—or are we just to believe Dr. Prin's words are true?"

Tetra stiffened as everyone's eyes landed on her, but she replied in as calm of a voice as she could, "Yes ma'am, I was."

"What proof can you give us?"

"We have her medical records on file." Dr. Prin replied, "I can send them to you—"

"—Medical records, especially Igrian ones, can be changed," Empress Veruska remarked. "I want to see evidence that cannot be made up—like footage of when it happened, or something else in that same vein."

Tetra was taken aback at the question, unsure of how to answer. In that tense moment of silence, Chief Baene sent her a meaningful look that she couldn't decipher, so she glanced over at Felicita to see if she knew what it meant. Their eyes met, and Felicita barely gestured to the long, flowy sleeves that covered her own arms.

Realization hit Tetra like a crossbow bolt, and her heart began to drum a sporadic beat as the humiliating memories from her first years at Norland sprang forward from their usually locked prison. The skin around her burn scar tingled at the attention of her thoughts.

I can't do this...

"Go on," Felicita whispered and gave her a reassuring nod. "It's nothing ta be ashamed of."

Tetra wanted to make a snide remark about the sleeves her sister was wearing, but she held her tongue as she turned her gaze to look Empress Veruska in the eyes. Squaring her shoulders, she lifted her hands and flipped her hair over to the side so everyone could see her second-most embarrassing scar.

"This is real." She gestured to the bumpy scar that started at the edge of her forehead and ran along the top of her skull. Murmurs began to fill the room, and she raised her voice to try and drown them out, "As my parents' house was burning, a chandelier fell from the ceiling and hit me right here. But thankfully, I was brought out before the rest of the place came crashing down."

She kept her gaze lowered to the floor as the nobility's jumbled voices and the memories of the things she had been called at Norland melded together.

After a few moments, Empress Veruska finally said, "I see that you are telling the truth."

Tetra flipped her hair back over as quickly as she could and clasped her shaking hands on her lap. She lifted her eyes and noticed a slight difference in the Frigian empress' expression. The many lines in her wrinkled face were still there, but they didn't seem to be as deep as before. Nor was her frown as severe.

"I have a question."

Tetra turned around to see the rows of seats behind her, and her brow rose in uncontained surprise at the tall noblewoman who stood three rows back. An air of superiority that couldn't be mistaken exuded from her set posture. The long, green dress she wore matched her bright green eyes—which glared poison-tipped daggers toward Tetra amidst the otherwise calm facade her scarred, melted facial features exuded.

"Yes, Lady Vierra?" A feminine voice Tetra didn't recognize asked from the direction of the Buleutcil's table.

The noblewoman kept her gaze upon Tetra as she spoke, "I'm surprised that no one has bothered to ask how we could even trust a Cairn in the first place."

"Lady Vierra," Felicita's voice rose beside Tetra, "you know she was sworn inta the army with the same oath as everyone else, and you saw wha' she did ta Igrium's forces in Xich. If she hasn't proven herself already, then—"

"—Forgive me, Lady Felicita, if I have a few trust issues regarding anyone with that surname." Lady Vierra's arched eyebrow on the unmelted side of her face rose incredulously.

Tetra blinked as understanding dawned on her—Lady Vierra's burns were because of the Fire Raids. As guilt began to bubble up, she had to remind herself that the Cairns weren't actually her parents to combat the sinking feeling in her chest. But as she did so, she was also reminded that the Fire Raids were authorized by Emperor Ignis—which meant she was still eligible to carry that guilt.

Felicita's tone held a note of understanding as she replied, "And you 'ave the right to. But Tetra here is nothin' like her parents', nor do I believe tha' she is an Igrian spy."

Tetra was finally able to turn her gaze away from Lady Vierra's as she noticed her cousin stand from her seat. "Do any o' you honestly believe tha' someone with a malscar would agree with Igrium and its ways?" Felicita's raised voice came out clear and smooth as she addressed everyone, "Or tha' an Igrian spy would even consider havin' one for the sake o' 'authenticity'? No one who agrees with Igrium would willingly fight against them, and then go above the call o' duty ta take out three o' their hovercraft.

"Private Cairn has proven herself trustworthy ta Silvas and ta the Alliance more than we deserve for all the slander and mistrust we shame her with for bearing the Cairns' name." Tetra stared, slack-jawed, at the authoritative demeanor that seemed to come over Felicita. "You are all here because many o' you decided ta let your prejudice towards tha' name go long enough ta listen—and I thank you for tha'. The fact tha' any o' you are here goes ta show tha' you're truly fulfilling your virtuous nobility roles in the way Deleyon first called your forebears into."

Felicita took a deep breath. "And for those o' you, like Lady Vierra, who are still wary o' Private Cairn: think on my words and let her actions speak for themselves. She isn't on Igrium's side—and let us all be thankful tha' she isn't, or else *we* would be dealing with the war-peryton problem Igrium most certainly is dealin' with right now."

If she knew it wasn't completely out of decorum, Tetra would've applauded Felicita for her courage in standing up in front of all these people on behalf of someone many didn't seem to like. So instead, she suppressed a smile in the silence that followed her cousin's words as Felicita sat back down.

She glanced around at the closest faces and noticed many of them wore thoughtful looks—except for Lord Wenyan, whose scowl deepened as he locked eyes with her for barely a moment before she immediately averted her gaze and set it on Chief Baene instead. Though his sharp features were settled in their usual seriousness, she noticed his eyes were sparkling with pride.

"Well, Lady Felicita—" Tetra turned her head in the direction of the new, accented voice, and her gaze landed on a man who wore a long, yellow-gold robe in the style she remembered from Xich, "—I must say I agree with you. If it was not for Private Cairn, then our nation might still be struggling to keep Igrium out."

He turned his head and met Tetra's eyes even from across the distance between them. "So, thank you, Private Cairn," he dipped his head towards her with a flourish of his arm. "Your efforts were not forgotten, and Xich is honored to have you on our side."

A soothing warmth filled Tetra's insides as he spoke, and when he finished, she dipped her head towards him. "Thank you," she replied before lifting it again.

He nodded in acknowledgement towards her then sat down.

She replayed his words again in her head as he did so, and the warmth grew enough to push some of her earlier guilt aside. Xich was *honored* to have her on the Alliance's side. She had fulfilled her oath in a way she hadn't thought would even be possible only a little over a month ago—and her actions in doing so had been counted as "honorable".

She lifted her hand and barely touched the lowest tip of her malscar. She had done something honorable that hadn't required following her father's role to achieve.

"Does anyone have any more questions?" The same feminine voice who had let Lady Vierra speak before asked the question, and then its owner stood. She turned her long neck to look about the room; her soft, lined features attentive.

"I do."

Tetra looked over in the direction of the new speaker. A man stood in the row of seats next to hers (in what she figured to be the Quazesig section of seats—due to all the white clothing they each wore) and turned in her direction. His pristine, white suit matched the white ring he wore on his left hand. Light reflected off two golden rings he wore on the other—which, Tetra noticed, matched the golden, glowing iris of his cybernetic left eye.

"Yes, Ambassador Terulin?" The Buleutcil woman asked.

The Quazig ambassador crossed his arms and looked Tetra in the eyes. "I've listened to what everyone else says about you, Private Cairn," he said in a smooth accent, "but I want to hear *your* answer to this: what led you to choose to fight against your birth empire? You are the daughter of the Cairns', yet you have a malscar and are now a traitor to Igrium. I doubt I'm the only person here who finds that odd."

Tetra kept both her hands clasped in her lap to fight the urge to rub one of them across her tally-covered arm as she thought through her answer.

"I know that—that most of you don't trust me..." she began slowly, "and I understand why. I know the Cairns' Fire Raids were devastating to Silvas, and that their battle plans caused the deaths of thousands of Alliance soldiers—and I'd like to apologize for everything they did. Despite my carrying their family name, I think their attacks upon all those innocent people was wrong and dishonorable. I wish I wasn't associated with that name, but I didn't choose it, so..."

Her knuckles turned white as her words died off, but she immediately picked them back up before she could dwell too long on that thought. "Anyway, when I—when I woke up in the infirmary after my parents' house burned down, I was soon put into Norland Military Academy as its youngest student—and I hated it." She paused to breathe and gather more of her thoughts before continuing, "Many of you probably think the Cairns' daughter would be honored in such a place, but that wasn't the case. All the other students hated me, and the teachers didn't seem to care what they did to me—they only cared if I was upholding the Cairn name well. So, I grew rebellious and tried to escape a couple times—unsuccessfully, of course.

"Then I finally made a friend." A twinge of guilt and sadness pricked her heart. "His parents were from here, and he told me a lot about what they believed and how he was only at Norland because it protected his family's house from being raided by patrolmen. As he told me all those things, I began to see how—how wrong some of the things they were teaching me at Norland were. So, I began to stand up against my commanding officer and earned myself more segione tallies than I can count. Then I—I got this—" she gestured to her malscar, "—when she finally had had enough."

Ambassador Terulin nodded, so Tetra continued, "And you want to know why I'm fighting for the Alliance? Because I hate Emperor Ignis and...and I wanted to help all the people who've been hurt by his murderous actions." She could feel Felicita and Chief Baene's gazes boring into her, but she kept her eyes on the Quazig ambassador. "I've seen firsthand the destruction his tyranny has caused, and I...I made an oath not too long ago that I would find a way to help those he'd hurt. Then this ability appeared, and I ended up with the chance to fulfill it."

She inhaled deeply before finishing with, "So that's why I chose to fight. I lived under Igrium's power-hungry ruler for too long, and I couldn't—in good conscience—let him and the rest of Igrium keep doing what they have been when I have a chance to help stop them."

A strange silence took over the room once her echoing words died off. Only as it settled did she realize how fast her heart was beating. She finally shot a glance over in Felicita's direction and noticed the small smile lifting the corner of her cousin's lips. A breeze of relief swept through her. Hopefully that meant she had said the right thing.

"Thank you for that answer, Private Cairn." Ambassador Terulin finally replied with a nod. He turned his head in Lord Jachen's position and added, "I will send that to my superiors to make sure they have no further doubts about this situation, Lord Jachen, but I believe they will be satisfied like I am. So, Quazesig stands with Silvas in this decision and will await future updates regarding its duplication."

"So will Xich." The same Xichian man who had complimented Tetra called out.

The Pon-Yelish woman who had spoken at the beginning raised her voice, "As does Pon-Yelum."

Tetra's eyes moved between the rest of the Alliance sections as each one declared their agreement with Quazesig. With each nation that did so, more winds of relief swept through her—blowing away the weight she had been carrying since first hearing about this meeting—until only the Frigac Empire was left to respond.

It seemed everyone's attention finally turned away from Tetra to face Empress Veruska's holoscreen. An emotionless mask covered the woman's face as she said nothing for a few pounding heartbeats.

Finally, she spoke, "Frigac stands with Silvas and its decision to have Private Cairn as a war-peryton—we will be awaiting updates as well."

Tetra breathed out a quiet sigh of relief through her nose. Now that the possibility of Silvas losing its strongest ally over her was no more, the rest of the weight lifted from her shoulders, and she straightened back to her full height.

Lord Jachen nodded and said in his clear, authoritative voice, "Then let it be known that Private Cairn will continue to fight for the Alliance, and that when we find the reason for how she can do this, all of our allies will hear of it." He stopped and looked down in Tetra's direction. "Let it also be known in all your hearing that Private Cairn will now be allowed the freedoms available to every Silvanian citizen as she begins her journey to becoming one."

Tetra's heart leapt excitedly as he dipped his chin in a knowing nod towards her. She shared a subtle smile with Felicita and read the knowing look in her cousin's bright eyes.

She had wondered when she would be allowed to begin studying for her citizenship test. It hadn't meant much to her a month ago, but now with everything she had learned, the chance to legally become Silvanian gave her the impression she was leaving part of her past behind—even if it didn't change the fact that she was still a full-blooded member of the Ignis family.

As she had that thought, she couldn't help but look over in Chief Baene's direction—and caught his probing gaze upon her. Some of her excitement dimmed as Lord Jachen's announcement lost a little of its luster.

Being a Silvanian citizen wouldn't save her from the answer she now had for the Chief Advisor.

Lord Jachen's reverberating voice broke her from those thoughts for the moment, "Though we are now in agreement, we still have time for more questions if anyone has any."

Around the room, multiple Silvanian nobles stood from their seats. Tetra's shoulders barely fell into a slouch as a few began naming off their vastly different questions at the same time.

Withholding a sigh, she opened her mouth to answer them. The quicker she did so, the quicker she could leave to go back to the peaceful quiet of her room, where she could begin studying for her future citizenship test.

A COUPLE MORE HOURS of answering questions went by before Lord Jachen—finally—adjourned the meeting. As the sounds of exiting footfalls and light chatter filled the room, Tetra let out a weary sigh and pressed her fingertips against her temples.

If that was what a normal political meeting was like, she almost didn't know if she would be able to do them for the rest of her life... But the resolve she had built over the past week for her final, imperial, decision kept her from giving in to such a petty thing.

If it meant keeping any more wars from happening on account of Igrium, then she would suffer through as many meetings as she could.

"Good job," Felicita said beside her, "I believe many o' them were satisfied with your answers."

She lowered her hands and matched Felicita's smile with a tired one of her own. "Thanks," she replied. "I'm just glad it's over."

"Hopefully you will not 'ave ta worry about bein' in another one anytime soon."

"Private Cairn."

Her heart dropped, along with her hopes, as she lifted her head and locked eyes with Chief Baene.

"Chief Baene." She barely dipped her chin towards him.

"You spoke well today," he replied with his own small nod. "The Alliance is satisfied, and—by a miracle of Deleyon—it seems many in the nobility are as well."

Tetra could feel the unsaid question thickening the air between them. "Thank you, sir."

"Lieutenant Eyrie," he barely turned to face Tetra's C.O., "would you please excuse us for a few moments?"

Without pause, Lieutenant Eyrie nodded towards him with a salute. "Of course, Chief." She spun on her heel and stepped away from their group.

Once she was gone, Chief Baene turned back towards Tetra. A pointed look sharpened his already-sharp features, and the question she had seen in his eyes before appeared again. "Have you thought about my proposition?"

"I have." She clutched her hands together atop her lap and fought the urge to lower her gaze. "And I made a decision."

"When?"

"Just a couple days ago."

Though she had ultimately known—deep down—her answer to his proposition, she had done as he had asked and spent the majority of her week-long infirmary stay thinking through all the pros and cons associated with the role of Igrium's imperial leader.

He raised his brow expectantly. "And what did you come up with?"

She inhaled deeply—the weight of his and Felicita's gazes becoming heavier upon her shoulders. Despite that, she straightened them and kept her eyes squarely on Chief Baene's.

"I agree with you." She could practically feel the weight of the words as they flew off her tongue.

Chief Baene stared at her for a long, unblinking moment. Then he finally nodded slowly and said, "Good. I'm glad to hear it."

"Are you sure, Tetra?" Felicita asked.

Tetra broke her gaze from Chief Baene's to give Felicita an affirming nod. "I've thought a lot about it, and I wouldn't be able to live with myself if Prince

Ryder ascended the throne and Igrium became worse off than it is now." She rubbed her sleeved arm with her hand as if cold. "And just like I told everyone here: I've been given a chance to do something that could help others, and I don't want to waste it."

No matter how much the idea frightened her.

Felicita gave her an encouraging nod, but a hint of worry still shone in her large eyes. She reached her hand over and barely touched Tetra's arm.

"Then I'm proud of you," she said.

A small bit of warmth wrapped around Tetra's heart at the words, and she couldn't suppress the small smile that escaped her lips. Chief Baene cleared his throat, and she lifted her gaze back in his direction. She noticed there was something softer about his gaze, but she couldn't discern what it meant.

"I believe Igrium will soon become proud of you as well." The softness faded for his usual seriousness. "But now that we have your answer, Lord Jachen and I want to announce it as quickly as possible."

A stone of dread plopped into Tetra's stomach, but she nodded. She had never let fear stop her before, and she most certainly wouldn't do it now.

"So, I'll schedule the meeting with the Buleutcil for tomorrow."

Her heart skipped a nervous beat, and she raised her brow in surprise. So soon?

"Tomorrow?" Felicita's voice shook slightly as the question left her lips.

Chief Baene's eyes moved in her direction. "The quicker we get it done, the easier it will be." His voice took on a more understanding tone as he added, "It will only be the Buleutcil, Felicita—not the nobility or our allies."

"Not yet, you mean."

Tetra scrunched her brow and glanced over at her cousin questioningly. "Are you OK, Felicita?" She asked.

Felicita frowned as their eyes met. "I just...I've been dreadin' this meetin' for a while now..."

"Really? Why?"

"Because I'm goin' ta have ta tell everyone who my patre truly was, and it's been a secret so long..."

"Which is why it must come out in the open now," Chief Baene added. "Especially since you've been allowing them to actually think you're a Malstrum."

Tetra nodded in understanding, her gaze lowering to her crutches that still leaned against her knees. Though Emperor Ignis was far worse than her Uncle Joash, having kept the Ignis name hidden for so long would make it a hard thing to finally reveal—especially in front of the most powerful people in Silvas.

"You won't be alone." Chief Baene continued, "I'll be there to help, and Tetra will be there as well. It's not only you who will be dealing with this."

Felicita didn't reply. Silence stretched between them again, and in it Chief Baene cleared his throat. Tetra lifted her eyes and met his gaze again as he spoke, "I'll go talk to Lord Jachen now to figure out a time, then I'll let you know what we decide."

"Yes sir," she replied.

He nodded sharply and spun on his heel before heading in the Silvanian Steward's direction. As Tetra watched him go, she pressed a hand to her stomach; resolve warring with her dread. She squeezed her eyes shut and lowered her head before putting it in her hands with a quiet sigh.

Well, she had known once she told Chief Baene that this announcement would occur, she just hadn't realized how soon it would happen. She breathed out another sigh and glanced over at Felicita out of the corner of her eye.

At least she wouldn't be alone. No matter how much Felicita obviously didn't want to be there either, she was glad they had each other to stand with.

Warmth wrapped around her heart again at the thought, and she breathed in an easier breath. She would never be alone again. No matter what happened at that meeting tomorrow because of her newfound identity, she couldn't deny the fact she now had a family because of it; and—no matter what figurative gates to Malackin's Domain they opened tomorrow—that was something she knew she would never take for granted again.

Chapter Sixty-Five

After Aabir and his family left Mister Falap's, Patre and Matha drove all the rest of the day, throughout the night, and into the next day with as few stops as possible. At first, it was the quietest, most somber car ride Aabir had ever been on with his family—but it did not bother him like it normally would have. He took advantage of the unusual silence and used it as a backdrop for his mournful thoughts, letting his memories of everything good they were leaving drift through his head like the passing scenery outside the window until sleep overtook him.

Then as Soll rose above the horizon on the next day, Aabir woke up in the same, horrible pain he had woken to after Lieutenant Denir's beating the day before. His broken ribs cried out with his attempt at an inhale, and he grimaced—then immediately regretted the movement as his swollen face throbbed with stings. The wounded muscles in his back joined the symphony of pain as he reached down and grabbed the bag of medicine and bandages from between his feet.

A hiss escaped his lips as he straightened back up and leaned against the car door for a few moments so he would not press his throbbing wounds against the back of the car's seat.

"Aabir?" Matha asked from the driver's seat, "Are you alright?"

"Mm-hmm," he replied unconvincingly.

"Do you need help?" But before he could answer, she said, "Ezen!"

Ezen jerked awake with a low, "Huh?"

"Help Aabir however he needs it."

Aabir looked out of the corner of his open eye and watched as the drowsiness upon Ezen's face drifted off with his rapid blinks. He yawned and turned a questioning look towards Aabir.

"What do you need me to do?"

Aabir looked down at the bag and dug into its contents without answering. He pulled out a bottle of pain relievers and took two of them, then put them back and grabbed a roll of white bandages.

"Here—"

Ezen took the offered roll without saying anything. When his hand was free, Aabir glanced down at the old bandages around his arms. Some of the lash wounds had broken open and bled through, so he began the process of peeling all the old coverings around his arms and torso off before replacing them with Ezen's help.

By the time they were done, the pain had dulled to a low throb and everyone else in the car had finally woken up. Aabir pulled the bottle of pain medicine out, put the old bandages in the plastic bag, then dropped it back at his feet. He placed the medicine in his door's empty cup holder and slowly leaned back in his seat with a relieved sigh. The pain medicine from Mister Falap was not as strong as the kind Tycho had stolen, but at least he could breathe. He silently thanked Deleyon and promised he would not take painless breathing for granted again.

In the back row, Nevaze yawned and asked, "How much longer?"

Matha glanced at the rearview mirror. "I'm not sure..."

"Where are we?" Rasiela asked as she lifted her arms to stretch.

"We just passed Buelva's exit," Matha replied.

Rasiela scrunched her brows in thought as she lowered her arms. "Then we should be there in about an hour," she said. "Actually, there should be an unnamed exit coming up soon—exit thirty-five, I believe—and you'll need to pull out on that."

"Do you know which roads to take after that?" Patre turned in her direction from the passenger seat.

Rasiela paused. "I believe we'll stay on the same road, and it will lead us straight into Fugerio."

"It won't," Ezen interrupted.

Aabir turned and looked at him, as did everyone else, and the former trainee hunched his shoulders as if trying to disappear into the bench underneath him.

"How do you know?" Rasiela's features smoothed into her expressionless mask.

"I—I used to live around here." Ezen flicked his gaze between her, Aabir, and Patre. "And I grew up hearing a lot of stories—mostly ghost stories—about the explosion that happened there."

Aabir raised his brow.

"So it's haunted?" Zeke asked.

"Nope." Ezen shook his head. "I've been there before—we had to pass through it to get to the town my grandparents used to live in—and there's no ghosts. Only a bunch of broken-down buildings."

"Is it exit thirty-five, then?" Matha turned the rearview mirror in his direction.

"Yes ma'am."

She nodded once and pulled the hovercar into the right lane.

The shadowed look Ezen had worn the past week fell over his face in the silence that followed. Though Aabir still blamed him for the Emaipur possibly following them, he knew his friend was also being forced to leave everything and everyone he knew in Igrium, too. So he asked, "Do your grandparents still live around here?"

"They live in Buelva—where we just passed—but I haven't seen them since my parents died."

"Oh." Aabir turned his gaze down to his hands, unsure of what to say.

Thankfully, Zeke's voice broke through his awkwardness, "Hey Matha, I'm going to need us to stop soon..."

"We will at this next exit," she replied.

"Thanks."

Less than a minute went by before she pulled off onto the newest exit and pulled into the empty parking lot of a small rest stop. During the few minutes they spent there, Aabir felt a heightened sense of urgency to be back on the road. Rasiela's comment about them getting there rang through his head, and he could not help the hopefulness that lightened his spirits a little. They were so close...

Soon, they were all finished and Patre was again driving the hovercar back onto the freeway to finish the last stretch of their journey. As they passed through the forested mountains of Igrium, Aabir began to wonder if the painkillers he had taken from Mister Falap had gone bad—because his face was beginning to sting again where his malscar was. He checked the bottle but could not find a date on it anywhere.

"So, Rasiela," Matha's sudden words helped distract him a little, and he put the bottle back in its cup holder before lifting his head to see her turned in the Silvanian spy's direction, "how long did you work in Igrium?"

"Eighteen years," Rasiela replied.

"And were you always in Rubrum?"

"Yes, I was," Rasiela nodded, a distant look growing in her eyes, "but I wasn't working in Norland that whole time. I worked at a tea shop for the first couple months, then in a robot repair shop—"

"What tea shop?"

Aabir suppressed a smile at the lilt that entered his matha's voice. She loved tea almost as much as she did them and gardening and would have had her own tea garden if all her attempts at doing so had not failed in some way or another.

"'*The Herbal Tiger*'," Rasiela replied.

Matha's face lit up. "I loved their tea!" She exclaimed, "It was the only kind that tasted as good as what I remember having in Silvas."

A small smile broke through Rasiela's expressionless facade. "That was the main reason I chose to work there. I had to find a job in that sector of Rubrum anyway, and when I tried their blue passion drink, I knew it was the place I wanted to be."

Zeke leaned forward until his chin was resting on the back of their bench. "Did you say you worked with robots?"

"I repaired them, yes." Rasiela nodded and turned her neck to look at him. "Why do you ask?"

"No reason." He shrugged. "I just think they're cool. I thought about taking a robotics class next year, but now that we're leaving, I don't know if that will happen..."

"If you're worried about Silvas' schools not having robotics classes, you don't need to be. Almost every one of them does—I took them all throughout high school."

A thoughtful look came over Zeke's face. "Huh..."

"Where did you grow up in Silvas?" Ereliev asked from the seat behind Rasiela.

Rasiela twisted her torso to look at her. "A city called Aravarm, and then I moved to Urbselva."

"Do you know where Greenway is?"

"I've heard of it, but I've never been there," Raisela said. "Why?"

"That's where Matha and Patre grew up." Ereliev gestured with her hand towards the front seat.

Rasiela nodded thoughtfully and turned to look back in Matha's direction. "And how did you both find yourselves in Igrium, if I may ask?"

"We both moved here when we were teenagers because of our families," Matha replied. "The company my appa worked for gave him a higher position here, so we moved. And Elnim's parents loved to travel, so when they visited Igrium they fell in love with it enough to move him and his brothers all out here."

"And I wasn't happy about it," Patre added as he pulled onto exit thirty-five, "but then I met Zerah and made some new friends, got my first job as a mechanic, and realized it wasn't as bad as I had made it out to be." Aabir could see the smile spreading across his patre's face. "I sure will be glad to be in Silvas again, though."

"Me too." Matha sighed longingly.

Aabir glanced over in Rasiela's direction, and though she said nothing, he noticed the wistful look on her weathered features.

"Do you have family in Silvas, Rasiela?" He asked.

The wistfulness faded away as she met his eyes, and he blinked in surprise at the pain he saw in their violet depths. "I do," she replied simply.

He stared at her strangely. "Then you'll get to see them again, won't you?"

"Yes."

"And that—that's a good thing...right?"

Rasiela blinked and looked away. "I hope so..." Her faint words drifted off in a sigh that only made Aabir more confused.

"Do you have siblings, too?" Nevaze asked.

Rasiela blinked again and glanced over her shoulder in Nevaze's direction. "I do."

"How many?"

A sad smile barely lifted Rasiela's lips. "Six," she replied. "Three brothers and three sisters—and I'm the oldest."

"And did they ever get on your nerves like Aabir says we do?"

Aabir jerked his head in Nevaze's direction and sent her a glare. "Really?"

Rasiela's sad smile turned into a grin. "They did, Nevaze."

"Oh." Nevaze tilted her head to the side. "Is that why you became a spy and left Silvas?"

Rasiela's grin faded. A strange look came over her face. "No, it's not." She paused. "I never thought of becoming one when I was growing up, but when I joined Urbselva's guardsmen academy the offer to become one practically fell into my lap. So even though I loved my family—I still do, of course, but—at the time my growing need to travel and my ambitions to do something for the greater good made it easy for me to accept the offer."

"Did you ever regret that decision?" Aabir asked.

She turned her neck and locked eyes with him. "Sometimes—but the amount of information I uncovered made it all worthwhile."

Though her voice was steady, something about the shadowed look of her face made him wonder if she fully believed those words.

"Um...Matha..."

He jerked his head in the direction of Ereliev's worried tone, but then squeezed his eyes shut with a hiss as the sharp movement bothered the lash wound on the back of his neck.

"What is it?" Matha asked.

Aabir blinked his eyes open and noticed the fear darkening Ereliev's expression. "This car has been following us for a while, and I think I remember seeing it following us on the freeway, too."

As the words left her mouth, Aabir flicked his gaze to the back window and spotted a red hovercar with tinted windows trailing behind them. Everyone twisted around to do the same.

"All of you turn back around!" Rasiela ordered in a hard voice.

They all did as she said. After another heart-pounding moment, she did likewise. Aabir met her eyes and gave her a questioning look as a mixture of adrenaline and fear began to pump through his veins.

"Do you think it's—?"

"—I don't know." Rasiela cut off his question. "It could just be a random hovercar. However, if it is the Emaipur, then we don't need to give them any clues that we believe it is them." She turned her head in Patre's direction. "Elnim, continue on our route as if we suspect nothing. The rest of you: don't look behind us, and don't worry. We will be in Fugerio soon, and I know the team that will be taking us to Silvas is armed and quite capable of protecting us from anyone that could be a threat."

Aabir ignored the impulse to look behind them as he settled back into his seat. Ezen had stiffened beside him, and he glanced out of the corner of his eye and saw the subtle horror shadowing his former friend's face. He tried to think of something to say, but when nothing came to mind, he only turned to look out the window as apprehension thickened the hovercar's cramped atmosphere.

Silence again settled over them—broken only by Ezen's few directions to Patre—as the roads began to twist and turn through the forested mountains. Despite Rasiela's warning, Aabir snuck a few quick glances behind him and noticed two more hovercars had joined the red one. Fear filled his stomach with nausea as he again turned his gaze to his new longsword.

Oh Deleyon, help us...

More quiet prayers joined that one as the long minutes ticked by; the dull pain throbbing throughout his body increasing with each beat of his heart. He finally gave in and took some more pain medicine despite the warnings on the label that said to wait a longer period before doing so.

"—turn left up ahead and that'll lead us straight into Fugerio's downtown," Ezen was saying as Aabir closed the bottle of pills and put it back in the cupholder.

Patre nodded, his knuckles white as he gripped the steering wheel. As they came upon an old stop sign, he began to slow down. Aabir sent another wary glance over his shoulder and saw the other cars slowing too. He wanted to tell his patre not to do so—that there was no one out there to see them run the sign—but then he caught the set look on Rasiela's face, remembered her warning, and kept quiet. Patre came to a full stop for only a moment before turning, and Aabir found himself breathing a little easier, despite the pain in his ribs, as he picked up speed again.

We're going to be fine. Ezen said it would only take them a few more minutes to get to Fugerio, then they would be safe. They would make it to Silvas without anything else happening—

Glass shattered and screams rent the air. Aabir's heart leapt into his throat. He grabbed the hilt of his sheathed sword, though there was no room to swing it in the confined space.

"Everyone down!" Rasiela yelled.

Despite the pain in his back, he did as she ordered. The hovercar jerked to the side, and he slammed into Ezen with a grunt

"What was that?" Ezen asked above Yahel's cries.

Aabir moved off Ezen, and as he did so his eyes caught on a crossbow bolt sticking out of the back of Patre's chair. Blood pounded in his ears, and he lifted his head to look behind them. A person leaned out the passenger side of the red hovercar, a loaded crossbow in their hands.

"Swerve, Patre!" He called before ducking back down.

In response, the car veered sharply to the right. Aabir slammed into the side of his door with a strangled grunt as a starburst of pain burst through his chest. He gritted his teeth and held onto the side of the door to steady himself as he swayed with Patre's driving.

"Zerah—" Patre said in a voice as hard as gritanium, "—get the crossbow."

Aabir lifted his gaze in surprise as he heard Matha shuffling around in the seat in front of him. He almost lifted his head to see what she was doing, but then stifled his curiosity with a look at the crossbow bolt still sticking out of the seat.

A few moments later, Matha's seat belt clicked, and she turned around to face the back—a crossbow in her hands, and the fiercest expression Aabir had ever seen her wear plastered on her lined features. She pulled the crossbow bolt out of the back of Patre's chair, loaded it into her own, and set it against her shoulder to aim it.

Was this really his matha? He never knew she could shoot a crossbow...

"Everyone, stay down!" She commanded, a dangerous glint shining through the fear in her eyes.

Aabir watched in wide-eyed silence as his sweet, kind matha aimed the crossbow. She pulled back the trigger and the bolt flew off. A moment later, he heard glass shattering further away.

"Their windshield is broken," Matha twisted back around in her seat, "but I don't think it stopped them."

"It doesn't matter." Rasiela's tone held a hint of urgency that dropped another bout of nauseating fear into Aabir's stomach. "Keep doing that, Zerah. It'll keep them more distracted than if we all sit here like open targets."

The click of a crossbow being loaded sounded, then Matha turned back around.

"We just entered the city's limits," Patre said. "Do you think—"

The car rumbled underneath them. Then its low hum turned into a high-pitched screech. Memories of Xich flashed through Aabir's mind at the sound.

"No, no, no!" Aabir lifted his head at Patre's shout and noticed him leaning over the steering wheel anxiously. "Everyone, hold on!"

The hovercar's flat nose tilted downward until it hit the magnetic road with a screech. Aabir gritted his teeth as he fell into the back of matha's seat, metallic squeals accosting his eardrums as it skidded down the road. Their vehicle finally came to a stop, and Aabir fell back with a grunt as its rear fell to the ground.

"Get out!" Rasiela ordered as she began unbuckling Yahel's crying form.

Aabir opened the door and burst out with a hiss as the movements upset his wounds. He ground his teeth and pushed through the pain, however, as he let Ezen scramble out then pulled the lever to lift his seat up.

"Go!" He said as Zeke scrambled out.

"Run to the trees!" Rasiela called from the hovercar's other side.

Aabir glanced over in her direction as Nevaze and Ereliev were getting out. Rasiela handed Yahel off to Patre, who sent her a firm nod before following everyone else towards the thick forest beside the road. A crossbow bolt whizzed past Aabir's vision, and he jerked around—every damaged muscle in his body screaming.

Fear squeezed his heart at the sight of the people clothed in dark colors getting out of the other three hovercars, crossbows and swords in their hands.

"Go, Aabir!" Rasiela screamed before ducking back into their hovercar.

He almost did what she said, then a scream rang out behind him, and he turned around to see Matha had fallen on the edge of the metal road, a crossbow bolt sticking out of her calf. Patre—Yahel still in his arms—ran towards her. Anger lit up like a bonfire inside Aabir's chest, and he turned back around to face their oncoming pursuers.

"Go, now!" Rasiela ordered again.

He ducked as another bolt passed over him and grabbed his sword from where it lay on the car's floor. He unsheathed it and stood back up, his body throbbing with stinging pain that only the burning fury inside him helped dull.

They would not get near his family. Not today. Not ever.

With a cry, he lunged towards the closest person. They held a crossbow that did nothing to stop his sword from plunging into their chest. He met their eyes for a moment as the life died in them, then pulled out his sword as a wave of guilt crashed into his storming emotions.

Oh Deleyon... He stumbled back, eyes wide.

"Don't make me tell you again!" He turned his head in Rasiela's direction and watched as she threw one of Matha's kitchen knives into one of their pursuer's chests. "Get out of here!"

He used her voice to help pull him out of his numbness, and immediately became aware of Yahel's frightened cries coming from behind him. Ignoring Rasiela's order, he lifted his longsword again and ran towards the next person who dared to attack his family.

His next opponent held a longsword as well and swung it towards Aabir. He blocked the swing, then pushed back against their blade. She jumped back and he jabbed his sword towards her. She went to block the move, but he feinted and swung upwards.

She cried out as his sword cut through her sword arm. He gave himself no time to think as he stabbed her in the chest. She went down like his first opponent; the only thing keeping him from falling into a numb spell of guilt and horror were Yahel's ongoing cries and the knowledge that he was only doing this to defend his family.

His eyes landed on another arbalist standing near him, their crossbow aimed towards him. He jumped to the side as a bolt flew past where he had just been standing. He stumbled before catching himself, his lash wounds throbbing painfully as blood seeped through his bandages. Weariness began to creep into his bones at the sight, but he pushed himself into a sprint and took out the arbalist with a quick slice.

Two more swordsmen came towards him, but he struck them down as easily as the training droids at Norland. A crossbow bolt barely cut his shoulder, and he jerked around—thoughts growing fuzzy—right as a flying knife cut the arbalist in the arm. They hissed and dropped their crossbow, giving Aabir the perfect opportunity to take them out.

The smell of blood hit his nostrils as a man carrying a shortsword and shield lunged towards him. Aabir blocked the incoming jab with his own blade and pushed against the man before leaping back then forward again with a wide slice. The man only gave a low grunt as Aabir's sword barely nicked his side.

Aabir leapt away from another thrust and stumbled as a wave of lightheadedness came over him. Nausea rose into his throat, and he barely blocked the man's next stab. Pain stung his side as he moved out of the shortsword's way and swung his longsword wildly. The man screamed and fell as blood oozed out of his side.

At the overwhelming sight and smell of blood, Aabir could no longer hold in his stomach's contents. The whistle of another bolt flew past him, but he could do nothing as his stomach heaved up all of breakfast while his head swam.

There was a cry near him, then a presence came up beside him. His heart nearly stopped until Patre's familiar voice calmed it a little.

"Come on, Aabir!" His tone was urgent, "You're going to get yourself killed if you don't move now!"

Aabir nodded as the last of breakfast came up, then he leaned against Patre as they headed towards the trees. Another cry rose behind them, and he glanced over his shoulder. Through the sharp clouds covering his mind and prodding his vision, he made out multiple people surrounding Rasiela's ferocious, stabbing, knife-throwing form.

Fear chilled his screaming muscles as he made a sloppy attempt to get out of Patre's hold. "I have to...help Rasiela..." The words died on his thick tongue.

"She's buying us time." Patre's reply was hard, and he basically kept Aabir up as they made their way into the first of the trees.

His vision went in and out, and his arms and back seemed to be soaked in a sticky warmth that grew with each stumbling movement. He caught sight of Ezen with Matha's crossbow and barely heard Patre calling his name above the ringing in his ears. He turned his gaze ahead and saw his family as they ran through the trees and foliage—and then it landed on a new group of green-armored people heading towards them.

Aabir's heart jumped hopefully at the sight, but he could do nothing more as darkness dragged him out of the reaches of his pain and fear, and into a numb stillness.

Chapter Sixty-Six

"Thank you all for coming on such short notice—especially after yesterday's meeting." Lord Jachen stood in front of the Buleutcil's table where the open top of the "U" was; close to where Tetra and Felicita sat. "But Chief Baene and I have something to discuss with you all."

"What else is there to know about the Cairn girl?" Lord Wenyan grumbled.

Tetra's racing heart quickened its sporadic pace at the sound of his complaint. She flicked her gaze in the direction of his pudgy frown, but immediately removed it as his eyes met hers.

"You'll be as dead as that peryton on the door once this is through..." She tightened her grip on the small box of photos sitting atop her lap as the dark thought sang through her mind.

Chief Baene stood from his seat and turned his neck to look at all fifteen Buleutcil members. "I know you all have important things to do, but Lord Jachen and I felt it pertinent to have this meeting now," he said. "We believe we found a solution to the problem of how to keep Igrium from waging another war like this in the future."

"And it has something to do with her?" A tall man in a dark greenish-blue uniform, whom Tetra recognized from photos as Admiral Elmir Windstrod, gestured towards her.

"It does," Chief Baene nodded and turned to face the two cousins, "but I'll have Lady Felicita explain."

Just like Felicita had done towards her yesterday, Tetra sent her cousin an encouraging nod. A nervous smile lifted the corners of Felicita's full lips before disappearing as she stood.

"Before I tell you all wha' Chief Baene is referring to, I must first give a little background," she began. "When he had Tetra brought here from Xich, he did so because he thought Emperor Ignis might've been hidin' somethin' she knew underneath the guise of 'amnesia'—and he was correct. When I first saw Tetra sittin' in his office, I...I immediately knew she wasn't the Cairns' daughter."

"And how would you have known that?" Lord Wenyan's tone was thick with disbelief.

Tetra barely heard the small inhale Felicita took. "Because the Cairns' never had children, Lord Wenyan. It was all a ruse to keep Tetra's true identity a secret."

"The Cairns' were not very social people, so most of their private life was unknown," the same woman who had directed the course of the questions in yesterday's meetings said. "I know you grew up in Rubrum, Lady Felicita, but that gives you no reason to know that as a fact."

"That's not the only reason I have for knowin' she is not their daughter." Felicita took another small inhale. "The other one is because...when I first saw her, I immediately recognized her as my...as my younger sister whom my matha and I had ta leave when we were fleeing Rubrum."

Tetra held her breath in heart-thumping anticipation as Felicita continued, "I know many o' you know this already, but for those tha' don't: my patre was killed by Emperor Ignis for treason, and that's why my matha and I escaped with Chief Baene's help. But we weren't like the other Alliance-descended families he sometimes helps free from Igrium. We...my patre was...he was Prince Joash Ignis."

Dumbfounded silence met Felicita's words, and Tetra finally let herself breathe as the first proverbial bolt was fired.

"How can you prove this?" Dr. Prin's question was the first to break through the silent atmosphere.

"I can." A pudgy man with wisps of white hair atop his head stood from his seat. He pressed his rounded glasses up the bridge of his nose before turning his holonode on. "Chief Baene and Lady Felicita asked me to begin searching through Private Cairn's profile to see if I could find any discrepancies in its history—and after some digging, I found many."

He tapped a few things on his holonode's small, floating screen before turning it off. "I just sent you all the matching proof between Prince Joash's DNA and Lady Felicita's."

Every one of the Buleutcil members—except for the man who had just sent it, Chief Baene, and Lord Jachen—lifted their wrists and pulled up the new message. After a few moments of silence, Dr. Prin lifted her astonished gaze in Tetra and Felicita's direction.

"It's true..." she said.

Tetra couldn't help but flinch as General Taoghn's fierce countenance turned towards them as well. "So, you kept this a secret the entire time you've been here?" He barked.

"Yes sir, I have." Felicita stood stoically amidst their disbelieving and scrutinizing gazes, but Tetra noticed her hand shook slightly at her side. "My matha and I thought it would be the safest thing ta do at the time, but over the years we've come ta realize tha' wasn't the case."

Taoghn crossed his arms and turned his head in Chief Baene's direction. "Why did you keep this from us, Baene?"

"It wasn't my secret to tell," Chief Baene replied. "I promised Prince Joash I would keep his family safe. Though I didn't agree with them in keeping this a secret, I let both of them do what they thought was best."

"But how will this help us with Igrium in the future?" A bearded man in a blue suit asked.

Dr. Prin glanced over in Tetra's direction. "And you mentioned Private Cairn's identity earlier... Does that mean you both are the daughters of Prince Joash?"

Felicita looked over her shoulder and met Tetra's eyes for a moment. Though Tetra's heart was trying to beat itself out of her chest, she gave her sister a tiny nod to continue.

"You're going to regret this..." A shiver of fear went down her spine, and she folded her arms as if it would ward off the internal chill.

"We are," Felicita turned her neck to face the Buleutcil's direction again, "but she is by adoption—not birth. Her biological matha died a few days after she was born, and her patre said he couldn't take care of her; so my parents stepped in and raised her."

The bearded man frowned. "Again, I ask: how does this help with Igrium's future?" He leaned back in his chair and folded his arms with a look towards Chief Baene. "I've heard your ideas, Baene, on the best ways to keep Igrium a nation without having this whole war happen again. So, I assume you want to put someone else other than Crown Prince Ryder on the throne."

Chief Baene dipped his chin, and the bearded man turned his small eyes back upon Felicita. "But how will this work in the long run? I know *you* are of Ignis blood, Lady Felicita, but you're not of the ruling part of that bloodline. Igrium's history tells us how quickly those who are not chosen by their current ruler are ousted from the throne." He raised his brow dubiously. "So, unless your parents adopted Private Cairn from Emperor Ignis himself, then there is no point to this plan."

Tetra dug her nails into her arms as a weightiness immediately filled the atmosphere.

"They did, Lord Yardom," Felicita replied simply.

Tetra forced her facial features to remain neutral as almost everyone's gazes landed on her in the thick moment of silence.

"What?" Lord Wenyan roared the simple question in a way similar to that of a peryton's.

She kept herself from flinching at the noise, but she couldn't help digging her nails deeper into her skin until it stung.

"Prince Ryder is the only child Emperor Ignis has ever had." A woman with long, brown hair and the bluest eyes Tetra had ever seen stared at her in wide-eyed disbelief. "Nor has he ever had any relations to anyone other than Empress Rillunia."

"How long have you known, Private?" General Taoghn's narrow stare was impossible to read.

"Only about a month, sir." Her throat felt dry as she swallowed. "Emperor Ignis, he...he used the C.B.M. on me after Prince Joash's house was burned during the Silvanian Fire Attacks and used my head wound to cast the blame on 'amnesia'. Then he used the Cairns' house fire as a foundation for my new identity and shoved me into Norland so he wouldn't have to take care of me."

She snapped her jaw shut as the bitter words left her mouth and lowered her gaze to her lap. She hadn't meant for those last ones to come out, but the small flame of anger that had become her companion whenever she thought about her father flared back to life as she had spoken.

"But you remember now?"

Tetra lifted her head again and looked in the army general's direction. "I doubt I remember everything—but yes sir. I do."

Taoghn nodded slowly. "Then does that mean you remember how you're able to turn into a peryton?"

Tetra glanced down at the gilded box on her lap, her stomach beginning to churn.

"Yes sir," she replied in a low voice.

Only a moment of stunned silence passed before most of the Buleutcil rose from their seats with angry shouts. She pressed herself against the back of her chair, wishing she had the ability to disappear at that moment instead of turning into a peryton.

But even with the accusations, she heard Dr. Prin's surprised tone above them all, "You do?"

Tetra lifted her gaze and looked the woman in the eyes, ignoring the questions and glares the others sent her. She blinked in surprise as, even from the distance, she could see what looked almost like hurt shining in the depths of the woman's purple gaze.

"Quiet!" Lord Jachen commanded.

They did so, though Tetra lowered her gaze again as their dagger-like glares continued to accuse her quietly.

"There is a reason she didn't," Silvas' steward continued in a normal tone, "and it corresponds with her matha's identity, too—but I'll let them explain."

Tetra snuck a glance over in his direction and noticed the sharp nod he sent towards them. She glanced up at Felicita and could see the same anxious worry shining in her cousin's brown eyes that was most likely in hers, too. Without saying anything, she lifted the box of photos towards Felicita and handed it to her.

Felicita's painted nails barely dug into its sides as she turned to face the Buleutcil. "Tetra's matha and Emperor Ignis were secretly married more than twenty years ago—"

"—That's not possible." Lord Wenyan sneered.

"Her name was Ambassador Aerbre o' the Wilshe family," Felicita continued as if he had never interrupted. "Their marriage was a secret because the nation she comes from—the Revagh-Shiy Provinces—have kept themselves hidden from most human contact for centuries, and they didn't want their secret ta be exposed." She paused. "And I would tell you why, but since I know none o' you will believe me, I'll show you."

Tetra clutched her hands together and stared down at them as Felicita's heels clicked over towards the Buleutcil's table. She held her breath as the tiny squeak of the box's lid being opened resounded in the suffocating quiet. Then she stiffened with each gasp and disbelieving comment she heard as the paper photo was passed around.

"For the past nine centuries, the shifters have kept to themselves on Silalum," Chief Baene explained. "The only people of their race allowed to leave the continent are their ambassadors—whose main job is to remind the current rulers of each human nation that if their identity as a race is ever exposed to the public as being real, then they have no qualms in waging war against them."

"This...this is preposterous, Baene!" A feminine voice Tetra didn't recognize spoke up, but not even her curiosity over who it might be could cause her to lift her head. "Lord Othnel, surely this must be edited!"

"I would agree with you, Lady Sola," the voice Tetra recognized as belonging to the man with glasses answered, "but her DNA suggests otherwise—and we also have the proof that she can do as all the myths say shifters can."

Tetra's knuckles turned white as her grip tightened. Names she had been called in the past, and new ones that had only recently sprung into her head since the truth was revealed to her, flitted through her mind like arrows.

"Wait—" Lord Yardom said, "—did Lady Felicita tell you that information, Baene?"

"No." Tetra barely lifted her head enough to see Chief Baene's stoic countenance as he spoke, "One of their ambassadors visited many times when Orinna was queen—all secret visits, of course. Only a select few guardsmen were even allowed to know."

A jolt of surprise went through Tetra. Chief Baene had *met* a shifter before?

"And even though you knew all of this," Dr. Prin's voice was dangerously low, "you never once thought to mention it to me as my team and I were trying to figure out how she could do this in the first place?"

Chief Baene crossed his arms and turned to face the Silvanian head biologist. "I've only done so to keep our kingdom from being involved in another war," he replied firmly. "However, I knew questions would arise concerning who Tetra's matha might be, and since the last thing I want to do is pile on more deceit to try and keep that piece of information a secret, I gave Felicita and Tetra permission to speak of it openly here—but only because you're all now strictly charged to keep this to yourselves."

"What—!"

"—I'm not risking open war with the shifters, Dr. Prin." Chief Baene cut in. "You can't mention this to anyone—none of you can."

"But what about the possibility of duplicating the ability?" General Taoghn asked. "We can't give that up!"

"I agree," Admiral Windstrod added. "We are always in need of another advantage over Igrium."

"And is a declaration of war from this...*hidden* nation even a threat?" Lady Sola's accented voice held a deep note of disbelief. "I would think that having an army of perytons at our disposal would keep your worries of that happening at bay, Baene."

"An entire nation full of Deleyon-only-knows-how-many-people who can all turn into different creatures, and who have weapons of warfare we don't know the full extent of is what I would consider a threat, Lady Sola." Though Chief Baene's words were not towards her, Tetra's heart still skipped a frightful beat at the sharp warning in his tone, "One we don't need to add to our list of existing problems."

"And there's no possibility of duplication," Felicita added. "It came from an experiment my patre created—one that's only successful when there is already shifter DNA in the person it's given to."

"Explain, Lady Felicita." Dr. Prin ordered.

So, she did. She told them almost everything she had told Tetra the night after her memories returned in full force, along with showing them a few more pictures and the matching DNA tests Lord Othnel had found. As the long minutes ticked by, Tetra continued to stare at her hands as her whispering thoughts wore down her mental defenses even more with their fear-arrows and monstrous titles she didn't want to claim, but that made too much sense to only be lies...

Her hands shook as sharp tears blurred her vision. There went the small bit of freedom she had felt after yesterday's meeting. No longer would the Buleutcil see her as the Cairn's weird, peryton-turning daughter. Now all they would see would be the half-human, peryton-shifting spawn of Emperor Ignis and a woman from a race of fantastical creatures.

When Felicita finally finished the short version of Tetra's childhood, a silence that reminded Tetra of the calm before a windstorm settled over the hall. In it, she found the courage to blink back her forming tears before finally lifting her aching neck. She was met with the disbelief, anger, contemplation, and outright shock on most of the Buleutcil member's faces, causing her stomach to knot anxiously.

Why had she agreed to do this? It was bad enough being known as Emperor Ignis' daughter; yet now that the full truth was out, she realized she hadn't put much thought into how horrible her matha's identity would end up sounding, too—and it sounded almost worse than her father's. Almost.

"And now that you all know her identity," Chief Baene's calm voice drew everyone's attention towards him—including hers', "you can see what my plan is."

"You want to put her on Igrium's throne," Lord Yardom answered.

Chief Baene nodded towards the man. "Yes."

"But she has no training."

"I know." Chief Baene's eyes flicked over in Tetra's direction as he spoke, "Which is why Lord Jachen and I are going to help teach her—along with all of you."

Tetra's shoulders drooped slightly under the amount of less-than-enthusiastic looks his words were met with.

General Taoghn cleared his throat, and everyone turned to look in his direction. His squarish features were stonelike as he stared across the table in Chief Baene's direction, arms folded.

"That's all fine and well, Baene," he said in an even tone, "but what about the war-peryton our allies only now agreed to keep? Are you going to stop her from fighting against those you plan to place her over because of this?"

Tetra's heart leapt nervously as a tendril of a new kind of worry wormed its way into her head amidst the rest of those plaguing her. Despite her earlier qualms about fighting as a peryton, and the guilt and nightmares she was now dealing with because of what she had done, she realized she didn't want to stop fighting. The Xichian man's reaction yesterday had calmed some of those heavy feelings. It didn't make them all disappear, but it reminded her of why she had made her oath—to help those suffering because of the war—and she couldn't deny the feeling of purpose that came from the fact she could gain honor fighting for those same people.

She flicked her gaze back in Chief Baene's direction as he spoke, "Lord Jachen and I want to keep Tetra's true identity a secret for as long as possible, so she will continue to fight—as was stated yesterday—until we decide it's time to make the announcement." A slight frown pulled his lips downwards. "Though I don't want her to fight those who will one day be her future subjects—especially since they all now know the peryton is her—" A twinge of guilt-driven pain entered Tetra's hip as he spoke, "—we must for the sake of protection."

"So, you're going to protect her by throwing her into a life-and-death situation?" The woman with the straight hair raised her arched eyebrows in a dubious look.

"I'll make sure she's only put in positions where her victory is apparent." General Taoghn sent Tetra a hard, knowing look.

Her hip twinged again as the skin around her malscar began to itch.

"Then it's settled." Lord Jachen's voice took on an even more authoritative tone as he said, "Private Cairn—now also known as Princess Anora Ignis among us—will begin learning how to lead under us, in hopes that she will one day rule Igrium. Private—" she straightened in her seat as he turned to face her, "I want to thank you for taking the time to think through this decision, and for giving us your answer."

His eyes shone with a knowing-kindness as he gave her a gentle nod. "I know it's not an easy thing to step into, but Chief Baene and I believe future generations in Igrium—and the rest of the world—will come to thank you for your sacrifice in doing so. The weight of imperial leadership is not a light one, but you will not be left alone in learning how to carry it—nor once you do begin to rule."

Tetra bowed her head respectfully towards him. "Thank you, Lord Jachen." She lifted it and forced herself to look at each of the Buleutcil members' faces. "And I want to thank you all for the help you may give in the future."

She paused to think through her next words carefully before speaking, "I know most of you probably hate me right now, or at least don't trust me, but I hope that someday you'll all see it was worth it. I've never had any desire to rule anyone before, but I know I've been given a position that could help many people—both now and in the future—and I can't squander that in good conscience."

She took a deep breath. "So, I promise I'll learn all that I can to one day help lead Igrium back to the honorable position it once held among the nations, and I ask that you be patient with me in that process. I'm not perfect—nor do I pretend to know a thing about leading an empire—but I promise I'll try my hardest to do what's asked of me, and to do it in good conscience. I don't agree with the choices my fa—Emperor Ignis has made as Igrium's ruler, nor do I want to follow in his footsteps when I take the throne. Thank you all for your acceptance and help in this situation, and I promise that you won't regret it."

As she finished, Tetra glanced over where Felicita was still standing near one of the table's ends. Her sister's eyes sparkled, and she could tell by the way she pressed her lips together she was trying to contain a smile. A breath of warmth filled her chest for a moment at the look, and she had to suppress her own smile from escaping under the weight of everyone's attention.

"I doubt we will," Chief Baene said with a nod in her direction; and though his sharp features were neutral, she noticed his light bluish-purple eyes were brighter than normal.

She bowed her head towards him, then looked out over the Buleutcil again—but this time with the knowledge that they would be teaching her how to lead as the future empress of Igrium. Though her stomach still churned with fear at the thought, it was too late to back down now—and, funnily enough, she realized she didn't want to.

Like she had just said, becoming a leader—especially the ruler of an entire empire—had never been a dream of hers before; but as had happened with the Xichian man's words, she couldn't deny the purposeful resolve the thought filled her with. Yes, it scared her almost more than Emperor Ignis' threat to turn her into one of his personal guards had, but she wouldn't have to face it alone.

She met Felicita's shining gaze again as images of her newfound cousin and Aunt Minda popped into her head like beams of light amidst her emotional, swirling thoughts. She would be able to keep people like Stellinga, Rabetta, and even Aabir and his family safe; and she could stop future wars from even beginning.

A twinge of sadness pricked her heart as a memory of her Uncle Joash joined the bright, hopeful images flowing through her mind.

She could keep people like her uncle from being killed. She would have the power to bring justice to those who had never had it because of her father's tyrannical rule.

No longer would she be known as the Cairns' rebellious, dishonorable daughter in Igrium's eyes. She would be known as Empress Anora Valrua Aerbre Ignis, honorable ruler of Igrium. And though it was a title she had never imagined carrying, it was part of the destiny she had been given—and she vowed to herself in that moment that nothing would deter her from its course.

Chapter Sixty-Seven

"Aabir?"

The voice pierced through the darkness covering Aabir's mind like a heavy quilt. He barely moved his head as the pinprick of wakefulness stirred his dormant thoughts.

"If you sleep anymore, you're not going to be able to do so for the next two days." His thoughts quickened at the voice's prompting, pushing through the mental sludge filling his head. "You need to get up now."

Flashes of memory of being chased, fighting off their pursuers, Matha getting shot, Rasiela being surrounded, and stumbling through the forest consecutively hit him like a battlehammer. A weighted touch shook his shoulder, and the physical contact hurtled him the last of the way into full consciousness.

He shot up out of bed—heart-pounding and good eye wide open—and reached for the sword on his belt. His hand grabbed empty air as strong arms reached out and gripped his shoulders.

"You're safe, Aabir." He blinked and turned his neck in the direction Patre's calm voice came from. Their eyes met, and his patre smiled. "We all are."

Aabir stared at him for a few moments as his mind caught up with the words. "We made it?" He asked in disbelief.

"We did."

"We're heading to Silvas?"

"We are." Patre gestured to the gray and white cabin around them. "We boarded this hovercraft in Fugerio and have been traveling for over a day now. Captain Shiler—he's the man who runs it—and his team came and found us after you passed out. They helped keep those...whoever it was that was following us—I can't remember their name—away while we escaped."

"We made it..." Aabir turned his head and stared at the bare wall in front of him as the impossible words made it past his lips. "We really made it..."

A peace he could not remember ever knowing before filled him like Soll's light breaking through the clouds after a dark windstorm. They were *safe*. No longer would he have to live with fears over his family's safety, nor would they have to deal with a morally perverted culture surrounding them constantly.

The hopes and dreams he had clung to for so long were no longer being chipped away with each brutal blow circumstances struck them with. He could practically feel them being built up again as his thoughts settled in the new peace.

"By the grace of Deleyon we did." There was something different in Patre's voice as the soft words left his mouth that caused Aabir to look back over at him. Surprise jolted through him as he noticed a tear spilling down his patre's weathered cheek, and more unshed ones in his glassy eyes.

Patre squeezed his eyes shut and lowered his head, pressing his fingers against his eyelids. "I thought..." His voice warbled and he cleared his throat. "As I was helping your matha and I—and I watched you fighting, Aabir, I thought...I thought we were going to lose you."

A sobering heaviness filled Aabir's chest at the sight of his patre's unrestrained emotion, but the peace from before continued to stay.

"I knew you could fight—" Patre lifted his head again and his red-rimmed gaze met Aabir's, "—but then I looked back and saw the amount of people coming after us, the blood seeping through your bandages, how slow your movements were becoming...and I asked Deleyon if I was about to watch you get killed right before my eyes."

A small talon pricked Aabir's heart with guilt. "I'm sorry, Patre," he swallowed back the rising lump in his throat, "but I couldn't leave Rasiela to defend us by herself."

"I know." Patre nodded slowly as he wiped his hand over his face. "And now that we're finally free from Igrium, I pray I will never have to witness that again. Even so," his eyes narrowed in a pointed look, "I don't want to ever see you do that again, Aabir. I don't...no parent should ever lose their children. So, the next time you decide to go off and do something like that, just think about how it may affect your matha and I before you actually do it, alright?"

Aabir nodded. "Yes sir."

"Thank you." Patre's seriousness morphed back into a small smile. "Now on that note—your matha sent me in here to make sure you were doing well. So how are you feeling?"

Now that his attention was drawn to it, Aabir realized he was not in any pain. "Um—fine, I think." He glanced down at the clean, white bandages wrapped around his arms and his torso. "Am I on pain medication?"

"Yes—that's why you've been out so long."

He nodded again. "That makes sense."

"The doctor on board said you have two fractured ribs, and that the reason your eye is swollen shut is because it's fractured, too." The lines in Patre's face darkened as he turned a glare onto the white sheet covering Aabir's legs. "Denir should be glad we left so soon, or else I might have ended up doing something drastic."

The look on his face made Aabir believe those words—even though he would not have at almost any other time. He lifted his hand and lightly touched the swollen area under his shut eye, his fingers brushing against the topmost stitch in his malscar, as memories of Denir's pounding popped into his head.

A chill went down his spine despite the fact he was now safe from any and all threats his old commanding officer had ever thought up, and he forced his focus to turn onto the present to keep those thoughts from eventually going downhill.

"How is matha?" He asked.

"She's much better." Patre lifted his head and met Aabir's eyes, his still sparking with anger. "She was also given the same pain medicine and woke up less than an hour ago."

Aabir let out a relieved breath. The image of the crossbow bolt sticking out of Matha's calf popped into his head, but he was able to push it aside as another memory from their escape followed.

"And what about Rasiela?"

The last he saw of her, she had been surrounded by their pursuers. And he had been unable to help...

"She's—surprisingly—doing well, too. The crew were able to get to her just in time. They even captured a couple of our pursuers." Patre's frown deepened. "They've been questioned a couple times since we left, but only Ezen has said anything."

Aabir straightened up in alarm. "They questioned him, too?"

"Of course they did, Aabir." Patre shot him an incredulous look. "He did admit to being a spy for them. Though, I will say, even Captain Shiler mentioned how agreeable he's been through the whole process."

"But..." The word turned into a sigh as he hunched his shoulders.

Of course they did. He should have known this would happen, but he had been so consumed with him, his family, and Rasiela's safety he had not even thought about what the fate of the Igrian, Emaipur spy might be.

Patre sighed. "I know he was your friend, but he was also a spy for that group."

"I know." Aabir put his head between his hands as he shook it. He let out a deep sigh before asking, "He's OK, though, right?"

He lifted his head and noticed Patre's nod. "Since he also admitted to not being a part of that group anymore, and his reasons why, he's been taken care of like the rest of us—although he's not allowed to leave his cabin."

Aabir pressed his lips into a thin frown, but he nodded. "Can I see everyone?"

Patre's features softened as his smile returned. "You can if you're up for it."

In reply, Aabir pulled the sheet away and swung his legs over the side of the bed. A shock of cold went through him as his bare feet touched the metal floor.

"Let me get you a shirt and some shoes first." Patre pushed himself up from the chair he had been sitting in.

Aabir glanced down at the athletic shorts he was wearing then lifted his head back up to Patre's face. "Thanks."

Patre nodded and exited the small cabin. As the door closed and his footsteps faded away, Aabir turned his neck and glanced around his current quarters. Wisps of cloud floated past in a blue sky outside the thin, rectangular port on the wall opposite to the door Patre just left from. Another door faced the foot of his bed.

Aabir got up and headed towards it. As he did so, his eyes landed on Mister Falap's sword propped up in the corner of the cabin in a different leather sheath than the one he had left behind. Images of the fight popped into his head at the sight of it, and the relief he felt for not losing it was overshadowed by his horror at what he had done.

He took a staggering step towards the door before opening it. The bathroom's light turned on automatically as he stepped inside, drawing his attention immediately to the small mirror on the wall. Shame and embarrassment joined the windstorm of roiling emotions as he took in the sight of his bruised, puffy, and scarred face; but it was all overshadowed by the memories pounding inside his skull.

He had *killed* people. He met his reflection's good eye and could easily see his own horror in its wide, purple gaze.

Yes, it had all been out of self-defense, but there were now more dead people in the world because of his actions. What if they had family, or friends, who were waiting for their return—only to be met with the cruel realization that they were never coming back? That they had been killed? By *him*?

Nausea bubbled in his empty stomach. His gaze lowered to his malscar as an alarming thought popped into his head: he had done the very thing he was supposed to do in the Tourney.

"Aabir?"

Aabir jerked his face in the direction of the open doorway and stepped back out into the cabin. Patre stood with a shirt and a pair of socks in one hand, and a pair of boots in the other.

"Here." He held them up towards Aabir, his eyebrows drawing together in a questioning look.

Aabir said nothing as he took the articles of clothing, then dropped the boots and socks on the floor beside him. Patre folded his arms and stood in watchful silence as Aabir put the shirt on, then picked the socks and boots back up, stepped over to the bed, and sat back down to put them on.

"What are you thinking about?" He finally asked.

Aabir forced his foot down into the first boot, then could only stare at it for a few long moments as he built up the courage to reply, "I...I killed people, Patre."

The words sounded a lot worse spoken aloud.

"But it was out of self-defense." Patre's tone held no condemnation, only a factual firmness. "I know you, Aabir, and you wouldn't have done it out of your own pleasure."

Even so, he could not shake the guilt clawing at his insides.

"But I chose to stay and do it."

"Because you felt the need to protect us and Rasiela—which you did. It might not have been my first choice for you, but I believe the only reason we're all alive and safe now is because of your actions."

Aabir felt Patre's presence draw near, then a weight gripped his hunched shoulder. He finally lifted his head and met the sincerity in his patre's expression.

"What you did was brave, Aabir, and no one thinks of you differently because of what happened," he said with an understanding nod. "And if they did, your actions in the Tourney would show your true character and prove that to not be the case."

He tried to grasp the truth of his patre's words, but the guilt still had a claw hold on his conscience. "But...but I did end up doing what everyone wanted me to do in them..."

The lines in Patre's face hardened, and he put his other hand on Aabir's other shoulder. "The Tourney is an excuse Emperor Ignis uses to make himself feel more powerful over his enemies." A firm look entered Patre's eyes. "They're a bloodbath, a killing spree, a method of torture he uses to try and make Alliance soldiers afraid. Your act of self-defense was none of those things. You weren't doing it out of bloodlust or an act of perverted 'honor'. You did it because we were in danger, and you had the means to help get us out of it. Aabir, listen to me..."

The look in Patre's eyes softened in understanding, but his voice stayed firm as he continued, "You're not a killer. No one thinks of you that way. There's no reason for you to feel guilt for what happened." His grip on Aabir's shoulders tightened. "You need to let all of this go, or you won't be able to function. We love and still need you, Aabir, and we won't ever have you if you let yourself live in these thoughts."

Aabir finally averted his gaze. "It's a lot harder than you make it sound..."

"Yes, but when you come to your Matha and I with these issues instead of letting them take root in your head to grow even worse, we can help you see the truth. You don't need to live in all of this—and we don't want you to."

The wounded skin around Aabir's malscar itched as he began to ruminate over Patre's words, and he lifted his hand to scratch it as lightly as he could.

"I guess I *do* have this malscar for not giving in to the Tourney's bloodthirstiness..."

He glanced back up and caught the small smile lifting Patre's lips. "And no Patre could be prouder to have a son with it than me."

Aabir shook his head but could feel a tiny bit of the heavy guilt lifting at the irony of the situation. He never realized having a *malscar* would prove to be such a good thing.

"Thanks, Patre."

Patre nodded and clapped him on the shoulder. "And I meant it." His smile faded for a serious look. "So, if you ever start to feel that way again, you come talk to me or your Matha about it, alright?"

"Yes sir."

And he would. The past few days had shown him the destruction caused by keeping things hidden, and he was getting tired of seeing that—both in him and those around him.

The mental claws loosened their grip some more as he put on his other boot and laced them both up. When he was finished, he stood and, again, met Patre's gaze with his own.

"I love you, Aabir, and I'm proud of you."

Aabir nodded, clinging to the conviction he heard in his patre's tone like a lifeline. "I love you, too."

They embraced for a moment, then Patre led him out of the cabin. Right as they stepped into a long, metallic passageway, Aabir's eyes immediately landed on Rasiela and the claws of guilt were loosened by a wave of relief.

"Rasiela!" He called and headed over towards her.

She turned her attention from the armored woman she was speaking to in the hall and met his eyes. Surprise caused his pace to slow for a moment as he saw the same relief he felt reflected in her gaze.

"Aabir," she stepped towards him, the rest of her face an expressionless mask. "I'm glad to see that you're up."

He came to a stop in front of her—and finally noticed the cast on her right hand and the bandages wrapped around her arms that looked identical to his.

"I can say the same about you." He lifted his gaze back to hers. "I thought for a moment there that you might...well..."

"And I thought the same would happen to you." A tiny frown barely pulled a corner of her lips down. "Even after I told you to leave—multiple times."

Guilt pricked his conscience again. "I...I couldn't leave you to fight them all by yourself."

"You were wounded, Aabir."

"So were you!"

Rasiela shook her head as she folded her arms. "I still had one good hand..." Her words died off as a ghost of a smile softened her features. "But I guess that just means we're both stubborn."

The prick dissipated at the lightness of her countenance. "Maybe so." He shrugged with his own smile.

As silence began to stretch between them, the woman who Rasiela had been talking to stepped forward and lifted her chin to meet Aabir's eyes.

"So does that make you Aabir Sorrel?" Her thick Silvanian accent curled around the long vowels of each word.

"Yes ma'am," he replied, now aware of how Igrian his own voice sounded compared to hers.

"Mister Kevler has asked about you a few times today." She gestured towards the door she had just been standing in front of. "So, if you would like to step in and tell him how you are yourself, you may."

Aabir glanced over her shoulder at the door. "Sure."

He had no idea what he would say to his former friend, but since he was practically the one responsible for bringing Ezen with them in the first place, he knew he needed to at least check in on him.

The Silvanian woman nodded sharply and turned around to face the door. She typed in a code on the holographic keypad next to it and a hiss followed as the hydraulic door opened.

She glanced back over at Aabir with a nod. "You may go in."

"Thank you." He nodded and stepped towards the doorway.

"Your matha and I will be waiting for you." He turned his head back in Patre's direction as he gestured towards one of the doors lining the passageway. "We're in that cabin over there."

Aabir nodded again. Then, taking a steadying breath, he stepped inside Ezen's cabin. His eyes immediately fell on the bed in the middle of the small space where his former friend lay.

"Ezen?" He asked as he took a step forward.

Ezen lifted his head, brow scrunched, and their eyes met. He blinked in recognition and sat up, the beginnings of a smile showing on his thin face.

"Thank the gods you're alive!" He said, "I thought for sure you had died."

Despite the conflicting emotions Aabir felt as he looked at Ezen, he could not help the smile that escaped his lips. "Yeah, well," he nodded slowly and tried to flex his arms, but the bandages were too tight and constrained his muscles, "it'll take a lot more than that to kill me."

Ezen shook his head, his smile disappearing for a more serious look. "I'm sorry about all of this, Aabir." He turned his face towards the cabin's single port. "I almost got you and your family killed, and..." He sighed and barely turned his head back in Aabir's direction. "I'm sorry."

"Well, we're all alive, so...it's OK." Aabir lifted his hand and rubbed the back of his neck. "And I'm sorry, too."

Ezen looked genuinely confused as he asked, "For what?"

"For...well—this." Aabir gestured to the small cabin around them. "It never even came into my mind that this would happen to you. I was so focused on the Emaipur being after us that I didn't even think bringing you would lead to your being questioned, or kept as...well, a prisoner."

"It's OK." Ezen sighed with a shrug. "Even if you didn't know, I did."

Now it was Aabir's turn to look confused. "Then why did you come?"

"Well, first: I didn't want to die. And second, I knew my coming would help stop the Emaipur—so even if that led to me being imprisoned for working with them, I knew it would be for the best." Ezen turned his head back towards the porthole. "I've now regained some of the honor I lost in working with my parents' killers by doing this, so there's nothing to forgive, Aabir. I chose this, and whatever happens, happens. Don't hold the blame for it, alright?"

Aabir almost opened his mouth to argue, but he could see from Ezen's set posture there would be no deterring his friends' outlook on the situation, so he kept his arguments to himself. "Well, if you want me to do anything for you, I can."

"I'm good." Ezen shook his head then met Aabir's eyes. "But thanks."

"Mm-hmm." An uncomfortable silence began to stretch between them. Aabir opened his mouth to try and say something else, but nothing came to mind; so he shut it with a glance down to his boots.

What was there to say to the person he had considered a friend, someone who he had even trusted above his best friends at times, only to find out Ezen had actually been lying to him the entire time? Aabir was glad they had not left Ezen behind, but that did not mean he was done trying to process everything that had happened. There were too many emotions to try and sort into words.

So, after a few more moments of the quiet, he finally just said, "Well, I should probably go now, Ezen. But—again—if you need anything, just...get someone to come get me, or something."

Ezen dipped his chin. "Thanks."

"Sure."

Ezen turned back towards the wisps of clouds outside the port as Aabir spun on his heel and exited the cabin with quick steps. The Silvanian woman nodded towards him as he passed, and he heard the door hiss shut behind him as he headed down the passageway. When he was a few steps away, he breathed out a quiet sigh of relief.

That went better than he had expected it to. Some of the other guilt he had held onto for putting Ezen into this mess had lifted with the conversation, though some remained in the corners of his mind like a sticky goop.

However, it was easy to ignore it for the time being as another thought came to him. They were headed to Silvas—to a kingdom of safety and freedom. So even if Ezen's past actions might not get him that same freedom and security as everyone else, maybe there might be a way for his former friend to somehow gain it by proving himself to Silvas' authorities.

Aabir twisted his lips to the side in thought. If that could become a reality for the former trainee, then he doubted it would be as hard as when he himself did everything to prove he was loyal (on the outside) to Igrium, only for his efforts to do nothing in the long run.

So, when they got to Silvas, maybe he could put a good word in for Ezen. He doubted it would be hard to do, and it might help relieve him of the rest of his guilt for the whole situation.

With that settled in his mind for the moment, he slowed to a stop in front of his parents' door and knocked.

"Come in, Aabir," Matha's muffled voice replied.

He did so. The first thing his eyes landed on was Matha's smiling face as the door hissed shut behind him.

"Thank Deleyon you're alright!" She stretched both her arms out towards him.

She sat in a bed bigger than either his or Ezen's, with Patre sitting next to her. Aabir stepped around Ereliev—who sat on the edge of the bed—and leaned into his matha's hug. She squeezed him so tightly a spark of pain entered his ribs despite the heavy pain medication he was on.

"I'm good," he replied as he let go and investigated her face. "How are you?"

"Oh, I'm fine." Matha waved her hand as if to wave his concern away. "I just have to stay off this leg for a while, but the doctor on board said when we land, he'll get me some crutches to help with that."

He glanced down at the cast wrapped around her leg, then he let his gaze move up towards Ereliev's violet eyes. "Hey, Ereliev."

Only a moment passed before Aabir found his middle sister's arms wrapped around him. His heart leapt in surprise, and he stared down at the top of her head in shock.

"I thought you were going to die out there, Aabir," Ereliev's voice warbled, wetness going through his shirt where she pressed her face against it. "And it—it scared me. Sometimes you—you do get on my nerves, but I realized in that moment that I—I'd rather have your annoying-self alive than dead. So please don't do that again."

Aabir blinked out of his surprised stupor and wrapped his arms awkwardly around her for a moment. "I'll try not to."

"Good." Ereliev removed her arms then stepped back as she wiped her hands across her tear-stricken face.

Another arm wrapped around Aabir's back, and another jolt of surprise went through him as he met Zeke's grinning face.

"Do I get a hug, too?" He asked mockingly.

Aabir frowned and slapped his brother's arm away as Zeke laughed.

"Really, Zeke?" Matha sighed.

Zeke only continued to grin in response. Aabir rolled his eyes and turned back to face Matha, though he quietly told Deleyon he would not take his brother's stupid jokes for granted again, either.

"Your patre told me what happened while I was...busy," Matha frowned down at her leg then turned her shadowed look back up at Aabir, "and I'm also thankful to see you're alive." She lifted her hand and touched Aabir's bandaged arm, her eyes shining as she smiled. "You've done so well, Aabir, and I'm proud of what you did—even if I may not have seen it all."

Aabir's throat tightened as a comforting warmth filled his chest, loosening the rest of his former guilt from the forefront of his thoughts. He had to swallow before replying, "Thanks, Matha."

A tear fell down her cheek as she nodded and pulled him into another hug. He accepted it gladly and squeezed her as tightly as he knew he could without hurting her.

When they let go, he met her eyes again, and could not suppress his grin. "Y'know, Matha," he began, "I'm proud of you, too."

Her eyebrows drew together questioningly. "What?"

"I never knew you could shoot a crossbow like that," he said, his grin widening. "You actually scared me there for a moment—I've never seen you look so angry before."

"Well, your patre and I have gone to the arbalist range many times these past few years to keep ourselves sharp." Matha shrugged nonchalantly, but the fierce look in her eyes came back into their violet depths. "And those people were trying to hurt *my* babies, and I wasn't going to just stand by and let them do it."

"And it was beautiful," Patre said with a knowing smirk. Then he leaned over and kissed her.

"Ew, stop!" Zeke gagged behind Aabir.

Aabir looked away with a roll of his eyes and noticed Ereliev doing the same.

When he could look at his parents again, he decided to divert the conversation with: "Where are Nezave and Yahel?"

"They're both napping in the cabin next door," Matha replied. "Your Patre said Nevaze barely slept last night because she was so worried about the both of us and the baby, but he finally assured her that we were all fine this morning. So, she's been asleep ever since."

Aabir nodded slowly, thankful they were both OK, and then asked the next burning question on his mind, "Does anyone know how long it will take us to reach Silvas?"

"Two more days." A wistful look came over Patre's weathered features. "Two more days and we'll be able to live our lives peacefully and in freedom."

A thoughtful silence settled over them, and hope sparked in Aabir's chest as he thought about their new lives they would soon be living. Yes, he had a malscar, an Igrian accent, and only the knowledge his parents had told him about Silvas—but none of those things could deter the hope that the thought of living in freedom brought him.

"I can't wait to find out what that's like..." Ereliev said with a sigh as she sat back on the edge of the bed near Matha's cast.

"Me too," Aabir added.

Matha looked between them both, a soft smile on her face. "You will all love it," she said. "You'll finally get to meet your aunt, your uncles, and your cousins; I'll get to have the best tea again; we'll never have to worry about our house being raided..." She turned her head back over towards Patre's direction. "We'll be able to have a home again—and all of us will be there."

Home. The simple word fanned the hopeful flame in Aabir's chest. He looked around at the thoughtful and longing looks covering his family members' faces (even Zeke's), and sent up a silent "thank You" to Deleyon.

Because he and his family were finally safe, and they were headed to a new home.

Epilogue

FELICITA LET OUT A sigh as she stepped into her and Matias' apartment.

"How did it go?"

She turned her neck and looked Matias in the eyes, her heart skipping a beat as their gazes locked. "Very well," she replied with a smile.

His lips lifted in his own soft smile as he strode through the kitchen towards her. She stepped towards him and wrapped her arms around him as they kissed.

After a few moments, Matias lifted his head, and she met his dark violet eyes. "So, is she going to begin learning how to lead?" He asked.

"Yeah." Felicita nodded and leaned her head against his chest.

"So, the whole truth is known?"

"Everything. Our family name, how Tetra can shift—everything."

And for the first time in over ten years, Felicita felt free from the chains that secret had wrought.

"Hmm..."

She lifted her head and stared back up at Matias questioningly. "Wha' is it?"

A pensive look sharpened her husband's squarish features. "I'm just thinking..."

"About?"

"About what the Buleutcil might do knowing the shifters exist."

Felicita's heart leapt nervously, but she pushed the feeling down. "I doubt they'll do anythin'. Baene and I both told them multiple times tha' the knowledge o' their existence can't be known by anyone."

"Yes, but that's still quite a few people..."

"Baene knew wha' he was doin' when he gave us permission ta tell them," Felicita said—as much to him as to her beginning doubts. "If he thought there was a problem with it, he would've had us come up with an excuse so as not to."

"That's also true." He leaned down and kissed her forehead. "I'm sorry for saying anything, Felicita. Please, don't worry about it. It was just an observation."

"And yet your observations are usually good ones..." she mumbled as she leaned her head back on his chest.

He snorted. "Not always," he kissed her head, "but I'm glad you think so."

A comfortable silence settled between them; and in it, Felicita's thoughts converged on what her husband had said. What would happen if someone in the Buleutcil *did* accidently say something about shifters being real to the public? Would the shifters even be able to find out since they had zero contact with Silvas? If one of their ambassadors was in an Alliance nation right now, would that ambassador somehow find out and tell their leaders?

She had no idea how many shifters there actually were, but it was probably more than enough to make their threats true. She bit her lip. And it would be an entire army of people who could shift into Deleyon-only-knew how many different creatures.

Those thoughts continued to flow through her brain, and as they did, each one only built a foundation for the most important one of all: had she, Tetra, and Baene—in their plans for peace from future wars—accidentally dropped Silvas into another one?

"SHE KNOWS OUR SECRETS," the woman's sing-song voice came out rougher than usual, "and I have no doubt that she's already told Chief Baene some of them."

"I doubt she knows as many as you think," the short man sitting next to her at the round table replied. "You're worrying too much about this—"

"—I'm worried because I seem to be the only one who realizes the danger this may put us in!" The woman turned to face him, her scarred features accentuating the savage light in her eyes. "She was found looking at the list of our members, you *Vireeg*, and you best believe she committed *our* codenames to memory first. We're the ones Chief Baene would be worried about the most, and she would look at it with that in mind."

An unsettled quiet fell around the six people in the small room. One of the other men twisted his thin lips into a frown, his gray eyes moving over the dark looks of his fellow leaders. "Then that means we need to continue our plans with more haste." He leaned forward and folded his hands atop the metal table. "When Chief Baene retaliates—and we all know he will—then we must be ready to defend ourselves."

"We need to be on the offensive when it happens," The woman next to him said in her slow, Paleyan accent. "We'll never win the people's respect if we only retaliate to any attacks he makes. We always made the first move before, and it's the only way the 'high-and-mighty' rulers of this world will ever fear us."

The scarred woman crossed her arms and sent a harsh look towards the oldest person among them—a tall man whose round, wrinkled features only made the acute sharpness in his brown eyes stand out. "And I would agree with you on that, except for the fact that we *still* have no weapon to use offensively, let alone for our own defense!"

"Our team is in the process of perfecting it." The older man sent a harsh look back towards her. "We could release it now, but that would leave us vulnerable to it, as well. I'm sorry that I'm only trying to keep us all from dying along with our enemies..."

The woman rolled her eyes, but some of the fiery anger in her gaze had dimmed. "Then what about the other project? Have you made any advancements in your research?"

"No."

The Paleyan woman shook her head. "I still think we should be putting more effort into figuring out how *that* is possible. If what Dr. Novem said was true, then Igrium could do it before—and I've no doubt Emperor Ignis is making plans to outfit his army with more of them now that he knows it was successful."

"And Silvas has been doing research for *months* now," the scarred woman added. "Though they don't know how to duplicate it yet, they are closer to finding out than we are."

"Because *someone* didn't get the information until it was too late..." The Paleyan woman added with a snarl.

Poison-tipped daggers flew from the scarred woman's eyes. "I can't help it that Felicita is sworn to secrecy in those kinds of matters!"

"Ah yes, the one job you have—and you can't even fulfill it."

"Need I remind you that almost half our funding comes from *my* wealth?"

"Both of you stop it," the sixth person among them—a shorter woman with small features and a rough accent—ordered. "We have bigger issues to deal with than your petty arguments."

"Yes—like the deaths and imprisonment of our fellow members," the shorter man added as a scowl darkened his pale features. "We need to get Malluir out of Frigac's hands before he breaks, and when Ruckos and Ballern finally arrive in Silvas we'll need to send a team to retrieve them."

The gray-eyed man across from him nodded. "And—if possible—we need to get Ezen Kevler as well." He cracked his knuckles. "It's been a while since we've had any traitors. We can use him as another example to show everyone what will happen if they try to back out."

A grim smile took over the Paleyan woman's face. "Good idea." The look immediately turned thoughtful as she added, "Maybe we should do something to that Silvanian spy as well—the younger one, I mean—for the problems he caused us, too."

The Magnian woman waved her hand as if to dismiss the comment. "Waste of resources. He was a pest, yes, but now that he's gotten what he wants, he won't be a bother to us anymore."

"Unless Chief Baene offers to make him a permanent spy for Silvas, then we might have a problem," the older man remarked.

She waved her hand dismissively again. "He would have to accept the offer, and I doubt he would do that."

A dark grin came over the gray-eyed man's long features. "I would usually agree with you on it being a waste of resources, but I just had a thought: Ezen became his friend, yes? Then I say we capture them both, and then kill the spy in front of Ezen as part of the boy's punishment." He shrugged his shoulders. "It would be a win-win for us all: kill the spy that killed our people, and the traitor that helped him—while giving them both the punishments they deserve in the process."

The Magnian woman nodded slowly in quiet thought for a few moments, then she straightened in her chair and turned her unwavering gaze upon each of them in turn. "Then all those in favor of this plan, say 'I'."

A chorus of "I"'s sounded from the rest of the members at the table.

"Then it's settled." She nodded firmly. "When we send for Ezen Kevler, we will send for the Silvanian spy as well—and will once again show the world that no one messes with the Emaipur and gets away with it unscathed."

Emperor Rexcan Ignis watched the footage of his daughter as she took down his army's hovercraft—as a peryton.

"Why do you keep watching that, Patre?"

He removed his gaze from his desk's holoscreen and turned a disapproving glare upon his son. Ryder's wide, blue eyes flinched before he lowered his head.

"To study what we are up against," Rexcan replied; though he was actually thinking through a few seemingly impossible plans of his and using the video as a motivator to try and see them through.

He curled his hand into a fist atop his desk and turned his sharp gaze back on the holographic screen. Too many of his plans regarding Tetra had failed in the past, and he was tired of that happening—which was why he continued to watch the video of his traitorous, malscarred daughter as she did what he and Joash thought would never work.

"She was the one who came in here a lot, right?" Ryder asked.

Rexcan kept his gaze on the screen. "She was."

"Then does that mean you know how she can do that?"

Yes. "Possibly."

"Then why'd you never have her do it for you?"

"Because she couldn't when she was here."

If he had only kept her from going to Xich, then she would have ended up doing it here and all of this could have been prevented from happening. He ground his teeth at his own misjudgment and switched the video to the other one his selfish daughter was in—the newest Alliance meeting regarding Silvas' "war-peryton". He had already seen it a couple times, but the hovertrain of thought he had been on since they lost Xich warranted him to watch it more than once.

"Do you...do you think there might be a way to make more soldiers like her?" Ryder asked as the muted video began to play.

"There is always the possibility," he said without turning his gaze from the video's subtitles. "It was done before, so it can be done again."

But he would first need to find a way to make it so... To find *someone* who could make it so...

Ryder's eyes lit up. "Does that mean I'd be able to turn into a peryton, too?"

"Absolutely not." Rexcan frowned and sent a sharp glare towards his son's awkward frame. "You're a crown prince, not a soldier—there would be no point in wasting the ability on you."

Ryder lowered his head again and sat down with a huff on the chair he had pulled up to Rexcan's desk. "I don't get to do anything fun..." He whined.

The flame of anger that had burned as he watched the battle's newsfeed finally escaped, "I don't want to hear any more of your complaints, Ryder!" Ryder jumped in his seat, fear slashing across his features as he hunched down against Rexcan's order. "I already have enough problems to deal with without adding 'my lazy, whiny son' to the list. If you can't keep quiet, then leave."

"Yes sir," Ryder replied in a small voice. "I promise I won't say anything else."

"Good."

Silence began to stretch between them, and Rexcan breathed out a quiet sigh of relief as he pressed his fingertips against his temples. Oh, why couldn't the gods have given him quiet, obedient children?

A pang of years-old guilt stabbed his heart at the thought, and he let out another sigh. His own patre had probably requested it of the gods when he and Matha first entered the Warrior's Hall—give his peccant, disappointing son the same children he felt he had had to deal with when it came to Rexcan.

He pushed the unwelcome thought to the side and turned back to face the holoscreen, where the subtitles told him Silvas' head biologist was saying they did not know how Tetra could shift. The camera angle changed to show his malscarred daughter's stoic expression—which did nothing to hide the fear he could plainly see in her eyes—and the young woman sitting beside her.

It had been years since Rexcan last saw his niece, but he had recognized her the first time he watched the video. Seeing Felicita as Baene's assistant answered many of the theories he had had about her and Minda's escape from Igrium. And, though he didn't like to admit it, it planted a seed of worry inside him as to what Silvas' Chief Advisor might be planning. The way Tetra answered questions and looked towards Felicita throughout the meeting told Rexcan they knew each other personally. And if that was the case, then Baene undoubtedly knew the truth as well.

He leaned his elbows atop his desk and rested his chin on his knuckles as he watched. It wasn't hard to come up with a few good guesses as to what plans Baene had made now that he had someone of the ruling imperial Ignis bloodline in his power—even if she *was* a malscarred disgrace; nor did he doubt the reasons she could shift were unknown to him, either. Aerbre had said all the human nations were visited by the Revagh-Shiy ambassadors, and the annoying former-guardsman had been on the road to marrying Orinna before her death...

A heavy weight of grief and guilt pressed upon Rexcan's chest, but Empress Veruska's appearance in the video helped him shove it aside. He could practically feel the veiled tension between her and Baene. It was one instance out of quite a few Rexcan had noticed between Silvas and Frigac the past few years, and it made him wonder...

He shook his head and pushed that beginning hovertrain of thought to the side for later. His enemies' tense relationship could wait for the moment. Right now, there were bigger things to worry about: like his daughter's position in Silvas, and her ability to shift into a peryton.

If Felicita, or even Tetra, had told Baene the truth, then there was no doubt in Rexcan's mind his daughter was already being groomed to take his place if Silvas ever won the war—which would destroy everything he had done to build this empire back into its honorable glory.

He ground his jaw and stared daggers at the screen, wishing he could stab his sword through its holographic surface to kill Baene on the spot. Sadly, the gods had not granted him that ability—but they *had* given Tetra an impossible one that even the shifters themselves would deem as such...

If Baene knew the truth, what was to stop him from keeping how she was able to do it a secret? Silvas might begin duplicating "Project Peryton" now that its success was evident; and if they did so, Rexcan could see his beautiful empire being crushed underneath the Alliance, and then his dishonorable daughter destroying whatever was left of it.

He turned the holoscreen off with a sharp movement and stood from his desk. He would not lose this war, nor would he enter the Warrior's Hall as the emperor who failed Igrium even more than his namesake had.

"Ryder, you need to leave."

He strode around his desk and walked towards his office's doors as Ryder asked, "Where are you going, Patre?"

"To the dungeons."

If Silvas did end up broadening their weaponry, he needed to make "Project Peryton" a reality again—and there was only one person on Afreean who would be able to do it. So even if Rexcan had to torture him to get that wish, he would do so.

Weightiness once again pressed upon his chest and claws squeezed his heart as he had that thought.

No. He straightened as two of his personal guards pulled open the office's doors and he stepped through into an opulent corridor. This weakness would not get the better of him. He would do what he must for the sake of his empire, no matter what.

"There can be no more weakness in you, Rexcan! The gods will not have it—and neither will I. If you don't get your act together, then this empire will fall, and you'll go down as the weakest ruler to have ever led her." The memory of his patre's harsh words struck him like a warhammer; but instead of crushing him, he grabbed its proverbial handle in resolve.

He would go to the dungeons and begin "Project Peryton" again. Then, when he had that plan started, he would figure out a way to get his daughter back—whether she wanted to or not. Because in the end, it wouldn't matter. When he had her again, he would get rid of all the dishonorable, Silvanian brainwashing in her, then he would make sure she never had the thought to leave—even if he had to take it from her mind to do so.

Glossary:

Afreean: (Ah-fray-on) The name of the world where the story takes place

Alenguan: (Ah-leen-gwen) The most common language on Afreean

Ambulate tree: (am-bue [rhymes with "blue"]-lat [as in "lat-eral']): the largest trees on the planet, and the only ones that use their huge roots to move around with. Have blue-green leaves and dark brown bark.

Arbitruer: (arr-bi [as in "bit"]-trour [rhymes with "tour"]) A person selected by the dying, heirless ruler of Silvas to choose the next ruling bloodline.

Buleutcil: (Bue-lit-sull) Silvas' highest governing body in Silvas (underneath the king or queen when there is a ruling royal family); made up of a differing number of people that changes with the kingdom's needs (i.e. in times of war, an army general is chosen to join)

C.B.M: (Cerbral Block Machine) A machine that can block selective memories from a person's mind (but cannot fully erase them). Illegal in most nations other than those under Igrium's imperial rule

Corafish: (Core-ah fish) A small fish found in the skies above Magrum

Deleyon: (Dell-ee-yon) The sole diety of Silvas

Equia: (ee-kweye): A six-legged mammal used for centuries as a mode of transportation

Forest Cat: Long-furred, domesticated cats that are a popular pet in most human kingdoms. Grow up to three feet in height; have tufted ears, and have many different colored/patterned pelts.

Furrum: (fur-rum): A soft, versatile metal used mostly in the production of weapons and other metal alloys. It is one of the most common metals found on Afreean.

Gelatscy: (Gel-lot-see): A brainless creature that floats in the skies of Afreean. It has a bell-shaped head and stinging tentacles (lengths vary from each species). The jelly-like body is eaten as a delicacy in many nations. (plural: gelatscies)

Griffin: (Gri-fin) One of the three intelligent beings on Afreean. Have the head, wings, and front talons of a bird; and the back legs and tail of a cat. Live in large family clans on every continent except for Silalum.

Gritanium: (Grih-tay-knee-um): the strongest known metal alloy on Afreean

Inrelin: (in-reh-lin) The Igrian deity that is emperor of all the others; is closely associated with the Ignis Imperial family.

Ivachku: (Ih-vah-cue) The national language of Frigac

Malackin: (Mal [as in "malice"]-ah-kin) The Igrian diety of death; usually depicted as a blood-red peryton, or as a man with the head, hooves, and wings of one.

Malscar: (Mal [as in "malice"-scar]) A criss-crossing scar given below the eye; one of the worst punishments in Igrium's military, used to brand someone as a coward and/or traitor.

Medbot: Robots that hold the role of nurses. They have a small, boxlike head with a single eye lens atop a larger, boxlike body that is full of hidden compartments for its multiple spindly arms and any equipment it might need. They have hover-rings built into their base for movement. Some have specially designed bodies with built-in medical equipment (i.e. heart rate monitors, defibrillators, etc.)

Needle Badger: A large mammal with brown and white fur and needlelike claws. Its claws are full of venom that it uses for hunting and defense. Known for hunting and attacking creatures larger than itself.

Owry: (ow-ree) A native Frigian weapon used for warfare and hunting. Has a long staff with a pointed, metal tip. Most have two long, thin blades attached to the sides of the pointed end of the weapon (like stretched ax heads).

Peryton: (Pear-ah-ten) A huge, omnivorous mammal found on every continent except Silalum. They have the head, body, and front legs of an elk; and the wings, back talons, and tail feathers of a bird. Grow upwards of about thirty to thirty-five feet from antlers to hooves.

Pomen: (Poe-men) A round, green fruit covered in purple spots. It has a soft, juicy flesh on the inside and a cluster of seeds in the very middle. It grows on one of the smallest trees on Afreean.

Scurrus: (Skur-riss) A small, tree-climbing rodent found on every continent. Every species has a long, bushy tail; tufted, pointy ears; and a "mask" of darker fur-coloring on its face.

Segione: (seh-jee-on) An Igrian ceremonial dagger with a serrated edge. Used in the administration of dishonorable tally scars, or a malscar, when a soldier disobeys military conduct. Also used to mark those who have committed a crime.

Shifter: A popular, mythical creature found in many myths, stories, and movies. Most commonly depicted as a race of humanoid beings that can turn into different creatures.

Spotted Tiger: Huge cats that live in rainforests. They have white, gray, or orange fur, and patterns of zig-zag spots covering their sides and faces. Their spots are bioluminescent and are used to attract prey at night and in the deep shadows of the forests they inhabit.

Suchwriy: (suke [rhymes with "duke"]-ree) Giant, rubber-like plants that grow in desert climates (plural: suchwries)

Tomeplants: (toe-mah-plants) A small, round fruit that grows in clusters along a vine. It can be green, yellow, or purple; and has a tart flavor.

Training droid: Robotic androids created for the sole purpose of being an opponent towards students of any form of weaponship or fighting styles. Their robotic bodies are made of millions of tiny pieces that can be torn and destroyed to simulate real-life fighting, and then they easily come back together like magnets that are attracted to each other. Some are made to look like humans, while others only look like the metallic robots they really are.

Vatharin: (Vah-the-rin) the Igrian goddess of victory and harvest

Xinxan: (zeen-zan) The national language of Xich

Name Pronunciation Guide:

Aabir Sorrel: Ah-beer Sore-ral [as in the end of "ru-ral"]

Accaly Lavrai: Ah-cah-lee Lah-vray

Adler Ignis: Add-ler Ig-niss

Aerbre Wilshe: Are-bruh Wilsh

Aleque Avhinoe: Ah-leek Ah-vih-no

Aloysius Trouran: Ah-loy-shoe-ish Trow-ren

Anora: Honor-ah

Aquilo Warlin: Uh-kwi-low War-lin

Aries: Air-ree-iss

Baene Ruzek: Bane Rue-zick

Buren Rodrich: Byur-in Rod-rich

Caloi: Cah-loy

Calua: Cah-lough [as in "loud"]

Cirus Taoghn: Sigh-riss Tay-on

Constantia: Con-stan-tee-ah

Dalmin Denir: Dahl-men Dih-ner

Emaipur: Ih-mah-purr

Ereliev: Eh-ruh-leave

Esthra Prin: Es-th-ruh Prin

Felicita Eyrie Fuh-li-si-tah Eye-ree

Frigac: Frih-jick

Galia: Gah-lee-uh

Igrium: Ih-gree-um

Jachen Summatra: Jah-ken Soo-mah-trah

Joash: Joe-ah-sh

Mabel Frauss: May-bull Frahss

Marin: Mare-in

Matias: Mah-tie–iss

Minda Malstrum: Men-dah Mal-strum

Mister Falap: Fah-lup

Nassum Rundi: Nay-sum Run-dee

Nevaze: Neh-vaz

Othnel Yenla: Oth-null Yin-la

Paleya: Pay-lee-ah

Pon-Yelum: Pon Yell-um

Quazesig: Qwah-zeh-sig

Rabetta Rah-beh-tah

Rasiela Reese: Rah-zee-el-la

Rexcan: Rex-sin

Rillunia: Rih-loo-nee-uh

Rubrum: Rue-brum

Ryder: Rye-der

Septimus Boll: Sep-ti-miss Boll

Silalum: Sih-la-loom

Silvas: Sill-vis

Stellinga: Stuh-leen-gwah

Tetra Cairn: Teh-truh Carn

Trenson: Trin-sin

Trivsau: Triv-saw

Talule: Tah-loo-la

Tulphire: Toll-fire

Tycho Rissis: Tie-koe Rye-sis

Urbselva: Herb-sell-vah

Verlim: Vurr-lim

Veruska Linyk: Veh-rue-skah Li-nick

Vierra Tamir: Vee-air-ruh Tah-murr

Vindic Windap: Vin-dihk Win-dap

Xich: Zitch

Yahel: Ya-heel

Zmraidos: Zim-rah-dose

Acknowledgements

Jesus—It's here, Lord! It's finally here. Thank You for being the Best Co-Writer anyone could ever ask for. I'm so glad I've gotten to take this writing journey with You (even though it hasn't been easy), and I can't wait to see what else You have in store for this series and all the other books we plan to write in the future! I love You. May this book be all that You want it to be.

Momma—Thank you for all of your prayers, your support, and for listening when I needed to talk about God-stuff and all that those kinds of conversations entail (especially with this book-publishing season). I love you!

Daddy—You can finally read it! Thank you for being patient. And thank you for your prayers, support, and especially for trusting the Lord with my life in this book-publishing season (and all the others, too). I know it hasn't always been easy, so thank you for all that you've done. I love you!

Paw-Paw—Thank you, Paw-Paw, for all of your prayers, encouragement, and the blessings that you gave for this book to become what it is. I love you, and I'm so thankful that the Lord would give me a grandfather in you.

Maw-Maw—One of the biggest reasons this book even exists is because of your prayers for me. So, thank you, Ma-Maw. I love you.

Nana and Papa—Thank you both for all of your prayers and encouragement! I love you, and I'm so glad to have you both as grandparents!

Elise—Thank you for all of your encouragement, *darling*. I'm so blessed to have a sister like you. I hope you enjoy this book (even if it doesn't have romance in it).

Adalyn—It's finally in print, so now you can read it. Enjoy. (Even if you're not a character in it. *Yet...)* (Also, thanks for all of the art and the late-night book/writerly talks. I enjoyed them a lot more than I put on.)

Cole—I know you don't read books, but maybe one day you will get into it. And if you do, and if you *just* so happen to pick up this book, then I hope you enjoy it. (But even if you don't, I still love ya.)

Logan—Thank you so much, Logan, for all of your editing help, publishing advice, and encouragement! I never imagined an editor giving as much encouragement as you did amidst the red marks of editing, but I'm truly grateful for all of it. So, thank you.

Andrea—You were, and still are, the true #1 fan of this book. Thank you for being the first person to read this massive manuscript all the way through (*and* you get extra points for doing so with a glitchy document). And thank you for all of your encouraging words, support, and for connecting me with Logan (even if it was accidental).

Wes—Talking your ear off about this story on that beach in Albania was the first time I ever spoke to anyone about what this book actually consisted of, so thank you for letting me do so. And thank you for all the other book talks since then! I truly enjoy discussing plot points and magic systems with you, so I can't wait for our next meeting!

Mr. Brad and Mrs. Charity—Thank you both for all of your help, encouragement, and prayers in regards to this publishing journey. I'm so grateful for all of it.

Leanna—All those stories we created throughout the years are one of the main reasons I love to write now. So, thank you for all those fun times and memories. I'm so grateful to have you as a cousin. I love ya!

A big "Thank you!" to everyone else who prayed, encouraged me, who listened to me ramble on about books, writing, and all the fictional things, and to all those who have been waiting for this story to be printed so that you could finally read it. I hope you all enjoy.

And to you, reader—whether you enjoyed this story or not, thank you for taking the time to read it. I'm grateful for each and every one of you.

About the author

Lilly Grace Nichols is a writing, reading, drawing, painting, and beginner violin-playing daughter of the King. She can usually be found pursuing one of these creative outlets, taking walks in nature, or spending time (and drinking coffee) with her Best Friend.

If you would like to connect, just email: **@lillygnicholsauthor@gmail.com**